MR. BRITLING
SEES IT THROUGH

&

IN THE DAYS
OF THE COMET

MR. BRITLING
SEES IT THROUGH

and

IN THE DAYS OF THE COMET

by

H. G. WELLS

ODHAMS PRESS LIMITED
LONDON, W.C. 2

Printed in Great Britain

MR. BRITLING
SEES IT THROUGH

CONTENTS

Book One
Matching's Easy at Ease

Book Two
Matching's Easy at War

Book Three
The Testament of Matching's Easy

CHAPTER ONE

MR. DIRECK VISITS MR. BRITLING

§ 1

IT was the sixth day of Mr. Direck's first visit to England, and he was at his acutest perception of differences. He found England in every way gratifying and satisfactory, and more of a contrast with things American than he had ever dared to hope.

He had promised himself this visit for many years, but being of a sunny rather than energetic temperament—though he firmly believed himself to be a reservoir of clear-sighted American energy—he had allowed all sorts of things, and more particularly the uncertainties of Miss Mamie Nelson, to keep him back. But now there were no more uncertainties about Miss Mamie Nelson, and Mr. Direck had come over to England just to convince himself and everybody else that there were other interests in life for him than Mamie. . . .

And also, he wanted to see the old country from which his maternal grandmother had sprung. Wasn't there even now in his bedroom in New York a water-colour of Market Saffron church, where the dear old lady had been confirmed ? And generally he wanted to see Europe. As an interesting side-show to the excursion he hoped, in his capacity of the rather underworked and rather oversalaried secretary of the Massachusetts Society for the Study of Contemporary Thought, to discuss certain agreeable possibilities with Mr. Britling, who lived at Matching's Easy.

Mr. Direck was a type of man not uncommon in America. He was very much after the fashion of that clean and pleasant-looking person one sees in the advertisements in American magazines, that agreeable person who smiles and says, " Good, it's the Fizgig Brand," or " Yes, it's a Wilkins, and that's the Best," or " My shirt-front never rucks ; it's a Chesson." But now he was saying, still with the same firm smile, " Good. It's English." He was pleased by every unlikeness to things American, by every item he could hail as characteristic ; in the train to London he had laughed aloud with pleasure at the checker-board of little fields upon the hills of Cheshire, he had chuckled to find himself in a compartment without a corridor ; he had tipped the polite yet kindly guard magnificently, after doubting for a moment whether he ought to tip him at all, and he had gone about his hotel in London saying " Lordy ! Lordy ! My *word* ! " in a kind of ecstasy, verifying the delightful absence of telephone, of steam-heat, of any dependent bathroom. At breakfast the waiter (out of Dickens, it seemed) had refused to know what " cereals "

were, and had given him his egg in a china egg-cup such as
you see in the pictures in *Punch*. The Thames, when he sallied
out to see it, had been too good to be true, the smallest thing
in rivers he had ever seen, and he had had to restrain himself
from affecting a marked accent and accosting some passer-by
with the question, " Say ! But is this little wet ditch here the
Historical River Thames ? "

In America, it must be explained, Mr. Direck spoke a very
good and careful English indeed, but he now found the utmost
difficulty in controlling his impulse to use a high-pitched nasal
drone and indulge in dry " Americanisms " and poker meta-
phors upon all occasions. When people asked him questions
he wanted to say " Yep " or " Sure," words he would no
more have used in America than he could have used a bowie-
knife. But he had a sense of rôle. He wanted to be visibly
and audibly America eye-witnessing. He wanted to be just
exactly what he supposed an Englishman would expect him
to be. At any rate, his clothes had been made by a strongly
American New York tailor, and upon the strength of them a
taxi-man had assumed politely but firmly that the shillings on
his taximeter were dollars, an incident that helped greatly
to sustain the effect of Mr. Direck, in Mr. Direck's mind, as
something standing out with an almost representative clearness against the English scene. . . . So much so that the
taxi-man got the dollars. . . .

Because all the time he had been coming over he had dreaded
that it wasn't true, that England was a legend, that London
would turn out to be just another thundering great New
York, and the English exactly like New Englanders. . . .

§ 2

And now here he was on the branch line of the little old
Great Eastern Railway, on his way to Matching's Easy in
Essex, and he was suddenly in the heart of Washington Irving's
England.

Washington Irving's England ! Indeed it was. He couldn't
sit still and just peep at it, he had to stand up in the little
compartment and stick his large, firm-featured, kindly coun-
tenance out of the window as if he greeted it. The country
under the June sunshine was neat and bright as an old-world
garden, with little fields of corn surrounded by dog-rose hedges,
and woods and small rushy pastures of an infinite tidiness.
He had seen a real deer park, it had rather tumble-down iron
gates between its shield-surmounted pillars, and in the distance,
beyond all question, was Bracebridge Hall nestling among
great trees. He had seen thatched and timbered cottages, and
half-a-dozen inns with creaking signs. He had seen a fat vicar
driving himself along a grassy lane in a governess cart drawn
by a fat grey pony. It wasn't like any reality he had ever
seen. It was like travelling in literature.

Mr. Britling's address was the Dower House, and it was, Mr. Britling's note had explained, on the farther edge of the park at Claverings. Claverings! The very name for some stately home of England. . . .

And yet this was only forty-two miles from London. Surely it brought things within the suburban range. If Matching's Easy were in America, commuters would live there. But in supposing that, Mr. Direck displayed his ignorance of a fact of the greatest importance to all who would understand England. There is a gap in the suburbs of London. The suburbs of London stretch west and south and even west by north, but to the northeastward there are no suburbs; instead there is Essex. Essex is not a suburban county; it is a characteristic and individualised county which wins the heart. Between dear Essex and the centre of things lie two great barriers, The East End of London and Epping Forest. Before a train could get to any villadom with a cargo of season-ticket holders it would have to circle about this rescued woodland and travel for twenty unprofitable miles, and so once you are away from the main Great Eastern lines Essex still lives in the peace of the eighteenth century, and London, the modern Babylon, is, like the stars, just a light in the noctural sky. In Matching's Easy, as Mr. Britling presently explained to Mr. Direck, there are half-a-dozen old people who have never set eyes on London in their lives—and do not want to.

" Aye-ya ! "

" Fussin' about thea."

" Mr. Robinson, 'e went to Lon', 'e did. That's 'ow 'e 'urt 'is fut."

Mr. Direck had learned at the main-line junction that he had to tell the guard to stop the train for Matching's Easy; it stopped only " by request "; the thing was getting better and better; and when Mr. Direck seized his grip and got out of the train there was just one little old Essex station-master and porter and signalman and everything, holding a red flag in his hand and talking to Mr. Britling about the cultivation of the sweet peas which glorified the station. And there was the Mr. Britling who was the only item of business and the greatest expectation in Mr. Direck's European journey, and he was quite unlike the portraits Mr. Direck had seen and quite unmistakably Mr. Britling all the same, since there was nobody else upon the platform, and he was advancing with a gesture of welcome.

" Did you ever see such peas, Mr. Dick ? " said Mr. Britling by way of introduction.

" My *word* ! " said Mr. Direck in a good old Farmer Hayseed kind of voice.

" Aye-ya ! " said the station-master in singularly strident tones. " It be a rare year for sweet peas," and then he slammed the door of the carriage in a leisurely manner and did dismissive things with his flag, while the two gentlemen took stock, as people say, of one another.

§ 3

Except in the doubtful instance of Miss Mamie Nelson, Mr. Direck's habit was good fortune. Pleasant things came to him. Such was his position as the salaried secretary of this society of thoughtful Massachusetts business men to which allusion has been made. Its purpose was to bring itself expeditiously into touch with the best thought of the age.

Too busily occupied with practical realities to follow the thought of the age through all its divagations and into all its recesses, these Massachusetts business men had had to consider methods of access more quintessential and nuclear. And they had decided not to hunt out the best thought in its merely germinating stages, but to wait until it had emerged and flowered to some trustworthy recognition, and then, rather than toil through recondite and possibly already reconsidered books and writings generally, to offer an impressive fee to the emerged new thinker, and to invite him to come to them and to lecture to them and to have a conference with them, and to tell them simply, competently and completely at first-hand just all that he was about. To come, in fact, and be himself—in a highly concentrated form. In this way a number of interesting Europeans had been given very pleasant excursions to America, and the society had been able to form very definite opinions upon their teaching. And Mr. Britling was one of the representative thinkers upon which this society had decided to inform itself. It was to broach this invitation and to offer him the impressive honorarium by which the society honoured not only its guests but itself, that Mr. Direck had now come to Matching's Easy. He had already sent Mr. Britling a letter of introduction, not indeed intimating his precise purpose, but mentioning merely a desire to know him, and the letter had been so happily phrased and its writer had left such a memory of pleasant hospitality on Mr. Britling's mind during Mr. Britling's former visit to New York, that it had immediately produced for Mr. Direck an invitation not merely to come and see him but to come and stay over the week-end.

And here they were shaking hands.

Mr. Britling did not look at all as Mr. Direck had expected him to look. He had expected an Englishman in a country costume of golfing tweeds, like the Englishman in country costume one sees in American illustrated stories. Drooping out of the country costume of golfing tweeds, he had expected to see the mildly unhappy face, pensive even to its downcast moustache, with which Mr. Britling's publisher had for some faulty and unfortunate reason familiarised the American public. Instead of this, Mr. Britling was in a miscellaneous costume, and mildness was the last quality one could attribute

to him. His moustache, his hair, his eyebrows, bristled ; his
flaming freckled face seemed about to bristle too. His little
hazel eyes came out with a " ping " and looked at Mr. Direck.
Mr. Britling was one of a large but still remarkable class of
people who seem at the mere approach of photography to
change their hair, their clothes, their moral natures.   No
photographer had ever caught a hint of his essential Britling-
ness and bristlingness.   Only the camera could ever induce
Mr. Britling to brush his hair, and for the camera alone did
he reserve that expression of submissive martyrdom Mr. Direck
knew.   And Mr. Direck was altogether unprepared for a certain
casualness of costume that sometimes overtook Mr. Britling.
He was wearing now a very old blue flannel blazer, no hat, and
a pair of knickerbockers, not tweed breeches but tweed knickerbockers of a remarkable bagginess, and made of one of those
virtuous socialistic homespun tweeds that drag out into woolly
knots and strings wherever there is attrition.   His stockings
were worsted and wrinkled, and on his feet were those extraordinary slippers of bright-coloured bastlike interwoven
material one buys in the north of France.   These were purple
with a touch of green. He had, in fact, thought of the necessity
of meeting Mr. Direck at the station at the very last moment,
and had come away from his study in the clothes that had
happened to him when he got up.   His face wore the amiable
expression of a wire-haired terrier disposed to be friendly,
and it struck Mr. Direck that for a man of his real intellectual
distinction Mr. Britling was unusually short.

For there can be no denying that Mr. Britling was, in a
sense, distinguished.   The hero and subject of this novel was
at its very beginning a distinguished man.   He was in the
Who's Who of two continents.   In the last few years he had
grown with some rapidity into a writer recognised and welcomed by the more cultivated sections of the American public
and even known to a select circle of British readers.   To his
American discoverers he had first appeared as an essayist, a
serious essayist who wrote about æsthetics and Oriental
thought and national character and poets and painting.   He
had come through America some years ago as one of those
Kahn scholars, those promising writers and intelligent men
endowed by Albert Kahn of Paris, who go about the world
nowadays in comfort and consideration as the travelling guests
of that original philanthropist—to acquire the international
spirit.   Previously he had been a critic of art and literature
and a writer of thoughtful third leaders in the London *Times*.
He had begun with a Pembroke fellowship and a prize poem.
He had returned from his world tour to his reflective yet
original corner of *The Times*, and to the production of books
about national relationships and social psychology that had
brought him rapidly into prominence.

His was a naturally irritable mind ; this gave him point

and passion ; and moreover he had a certain obstinate originality and a generous disposition. So that he was always lively,
sometimes spacious, and never vile. He loved to write and
talk. He talked about everything, he had ideas about everything ; he could no more help having ideas about everything
than a dog can resist smelling at your heels. He sniffed at the
heels of reality. Lots of people found him interesting and
stimulating, a few found him seriously exasperating. He had
ideas in the utmost profusion about races and empires and
social order and political institutions and gardens and automobiles and the future of India and China and æsthetics and
America and the education of mankind in general. . . . And
all that sort of thing. . . .

Mr. Direck had read a very great deal of all this expressed
opinionativeness of Mr. Britling : he found it entertaining and
stimulating stuff, and it was with genuine enthusiasm that he
had come over to encounter the man himself. On his way
across the Atlantic and during the intervening days, he had
rehearsed this meeting in varying keys, but always on the
supposition that Mr. Britling was a large, quiet, thoughtful
sort of man, a man who would, as it were, sit in attentive rows
like a public meeting and listen. So Mr. Direck had prepared
quite a number of pleasant and attractive openings, and now
he felt was the moment for some one of these various simple,
memorable utterances. But in none of these forecasts had he
reckoned with either the spontaneous activities of Mr. Britling
or with the station-master of Matching's Easy. Oblivious of
any conversational necessities between Mr. Direck and Mr.
Britling, this official now took charge of Mr. Direck's gripsack, and, falling into line with the two gentlemen as they
walked towards the exit gate, resumed what was evidently an
interrupted discourse upon sweet peas, originally addressed to
Mr. Britling.

He was a small, elderly man with a determined-looking face
and a sea voice, and it was clear he over-estimated the distance
of his hearers.

" Mr. Darling what's head gardener up at Claverings, '*e*
can't get sweet peas like that, try '*ow* 'e will. Tried everything
'e 'as. Sand ballast, 'e's tried. Seeds same as me. 'E came
along 'ere only the other day, 'e did, and 'e says to me, 'e
says, ' darned 'f I can see why a station-master should beat
a professional gardener at 'is own game,' 'e says, ' but you do.
And in your orf time, too, so's to speak,' 'e says. ' I've tried
sile,' 'e says——"

" Your first visit to England ? " asked Mr. Britling of his
guest.

" Absolutely," said Mr. Direck.

" I says to 'im, ' there's one thing you 'aven't tried,' I says,"
the station-master continued, raising his voice by a Herculean
feat still higher.

" I've got a little car outside here," said **Mr. Britling.** " I'm a couple of miles from the station."

" I says to 'im, I says, ' 'ave you tried the vibration of the trains ? ' I says. ' That's what you 'aven't tried, Mr. Darling. That's what you *can't* try,' I says. ' But you rest assured that that's the secret of my sweet peas,' I says, ' nothing less and nothing more than the vibration of the trains.' "

Mr. Direck's mind was a little confused by the double nature of the conversation and by the fact that Mr. Britling spoke of a car when he meant an automobile. He handed his ticket mechanically to the station-master, who continued to repeat and endorse his anecdote at the top of his voice as Mr. Britling disposed himself and his guest in the automobile.

" You know you 'aven't 'urt that mud-guard, sir, not the slightest bit that matters," shouted the station-master. " I've been a looking at it—er. It's my fence that's suffered most. And that's only strained the post a lil' bit. Shall I put your bag in behind, sir ? "

Mr. Direck assented, and then, after a momentary hesitation, rewarded the station-master's services.

" Ready ? " asked Mr. Britling.

" That's all right, sir," the station-master reverberated.

With a rather wide curve Mr. Britling steered his way out of the station into the highroad.

§ 4

And now it seemed was the time for Mr. Direck to make his meditated speeches. But an unexpected complication was to defeat this intention. Mr. Direck perceived almost at once that Mr. Britling was probably driving an automobile for the first or second or at the extremest the third time in his life.

The thing became evident when he struggled to get into the high gear—an attempt that stopped the engine, and it was even more startlingly so when Mr. Britling narrowly missed a collision with a baker's cart at a corner. " I pressed the accelerator," he explained afterwards, " instead of the brake. One does at first. I missed him by less than a foot." The estimate was a generous one. And after that Mr. Direck became too anxious not to distract his host's thoughts to persist with his conversational openings. An attentive silence came upon both gentlemen that was broken presently by a sudden outcry from Mr. Britling and a great noise of tormented gears. " Damn ! " cried Mr. Britling, and " How the *devil* ? "

Mr. Direck perceived that his host was trying to turn the car into a very beautiful gateway, with gate-houses on either side. Then it was manifest that Mr. Britling had abandoned this idea, and then they came to a stop a dozen yards or so along the main road. " Missed it," said Mr. Britling, and took his hands off the steering-wheel and blew stormily, and then whispered some bars of a fretful air and became still.

" Do we go through those ancient gates ? " asked Mr. Direck after a little pause.

Mr. Britling looked over his right shoulder and considered problems of curvature and distance.   " I think," he said, " I will go round outside the park. It will take us a little longer, but it will be simpler than backing and manœuvring here now. . . . These electric starters are remarkably convenient things. Otherwise now I should have to get down and wind up the engine."

After that came a corner, the rounding of which seemed to present few difficulties until suddenly Mr. Britling cried out, " Eh ! *eh* ! ᴇʜ ! Oh, *damn* ! "

Then the two gentlemen were sitting side by side in a rather sloping car that had ascended the bank and buried its nose in a hedge of dog-rose and honeysuckle, from which two missel-thrushes, a blackbird and a number of sparrows had made a hurried escape. . . .

§ 5

" Perhaps," said Mr. Britling without assurance, and after a little peaceful pause, " I can reverse out of this."

He seemed to feel some explanation was due to Mr. Direck. " You see, at first—it's perfectly simple—one steers *round* a corner and then one doesn't put the wheels straight again, and so one keeps on going round—more than one meant to. It's the bicycle habit ; the bicycle rights itself. One expects a car to do the same thing. It was my fault. The book explains all this question clearly, but just at the moment I forgot."

He reflected and experimented in a way that made the engine scold and fuss. . . .

" You see, she won't budge for the reverse. . . . She's—embedded. . . . Do you mind getting out and turning the wheel back ?   Then if I reverse, perhaps we'll get a move on. . . . "

Mr. Direck descended, and there were considerable efforts.

" If you'd just grip the spokes. Yes, so. . . . One, Two, Three ! . . . No ! Well, let's just sit here until somebody comes along to help us. Oh ! Somebody will come all right. Won't you get up again ? "

And after a reflective moment Mr. Direck resumed his seat beside Mr. Britling. . . .

§ 6

The two gentlemen smiled at each other to dispel any suspicion of discontent.

" My driving leaves something to be desired," said Mr. Britling with an air of frank impartiality.   " But I have only just got this car for myself—after some years of hired cars—the sort of lazy arrangement where people supply car, driver, petrol, tires, insurance and everything at so much a month. It bored me abominably. I can't imagine now how I stood it for so long. They sent me down a succession of compact, scornful boys who used to go fast when I wanted to go slow, and slow when I wanted to go fast, and who used to take every corner on the wrong side at top speed, and charge dogs and hens for the sport of it, and all sorts of things like that. They would not even let me choose my roads. I should have got myself a car long ago, and driven it, if it wasn't for that infernal business with a handle one had to do when the engine stopped. But here, you see, is a reasonably cheap car with an electric starter—American, I need scarcely say. And here I am—going at my own pace.''

Mr. Direck glanced for a moment at the pretty disorder of the hedge in which they were embedded, and smiled and admitted that it was certainly much more agreeable.

Before he had finished saying as much, Mr. Britling was talking again.

He had a quick and rather jerky way of speaking ; he seemed to fire out a thought directly it came into his mind, and he seemed to have a loaded magazine of thoughts in his head. He spoke almost exactly twice as fast as Mr. Direck, clipping his words much more, using much compacter sentences, and generally cutting his corners, and this put Mr. Direck off his game.

That rapid attack while the transatlantic interlocutor is deploying is indeed a not infrequent defect of conversations between Englishmen and Americans. It is a source of many misunderstandings. The two conceptions of conversation differ fundamentally. The English are much less disposed to listen than the Americans ; they have not quite the same sense of conversational give and take, and at first they are apt to reduce their visitors to the rôle of auditors wondering when their turn will begin. Their turn never does begin. Mr. Direck, realising this only very gradually, sat deeply in his slanting seat with a half face to his celebrated host and said " Yep " and " Sure " and " That *is* so," in the dry grave tones that he believed an Englishman would naturally expect him to use.

Mr. Britling, from his praise of the enterprise that had at last brought a car he could drive within his reach, went on to that favourite topic of all intelligent Englishmen, the adverse criticism of things British. He pointed out that the central position of the brake and gear levers in his automobile made it extremely easy for the American manufacturer to turn it out either as a left-handed or a right-handed car, and so adapt it either to the Continental or to the British rule of the road. No English cars were so adaptable. We British suffered much from our insular rule of the road, just as we suffered much from our insular weights and measures. But we took a perverse pride in such disadvantages. The irruption of American cars into England was a recent phenomenon, it was another triumph for the tremendous organising ability of the American mind. They were doing with the automobiles what they had done with clocks and watches and rifles, they had standardised and machined wholesale, while the British were still making the things one by one. It was an extraordinary thing that England, which was the originator of the industrial system and the original developer of the division of labour, should have so fallen away from systematised manufacturing. He believed this was largely due to the influence of Oxford and the Established Church. . . .

At this point Mr. Direck was moved by an anecdote. " It will help to illustrate what you are saying, Mr. Britling, about systematic organisation if I tell you a little incident that happened to a friend of mine in Toledo, where they are setting up a big plant with a view to capturing the entire American and European market in the class of the thousand-dollar car—— "

" There's no end of such little incidents," said Mr. Britling, cutting in without apparent effort. " You see, we get it on both sides. Our manufacturer class was, of course, originally an insurgent class. It was a class of distended craftsmen. It had the craftsman's natural enterprise and natural radicalism. As soon as it prospered and sent its boys to Oxford it was lost. Our manufacturing class was assimilated in no time to the conservative classes, whose education has always had a mandarin quality—very, very little of it, and very old and choice. In America you have so far had no real conservative class at all. Fortunate continent ! You cast out your Tories, and you were left with nothing but Whigs and Radicals. But our peculiar bad luck has been to get a sort of revolutionary who is a Tory mandarin too. Ruskin and Morris, for example, were as reactionary and antiscientific as the dukes and the bishops. Machine haters. Science haters. Rule of Thumbites to the bone. So are our current Socialists. They've filled this country with the idea that the ideal automobile ought to be made entirely by the hand labour of traditional craftsmen, quite individually, out of beaten copper, wrought iron and seasoned oak. All this electric-starter business and this electric lighting outfit I have here is perfectly hateful to the English mind. . . . It isn't that we are simply backward in these things, we are antagonistic. The British mind has never really tolerated electricity ; at least, not that sort of electricity that runs through wires. Too slippery and glib for it. Associates it with Italians and fluency generally, with Volta, Galvani, Marconi and so on. The proper British electricity is that high-grade useless long-sparking stuff you get by turning round a glass machine ; stuff we used to call frictional electricity. Keep it in Leyden jars. . . . At Claverings here they still refuse to have electric bells. There was a row when the Solomonsons, who were tenants here for a time, tried to put them in. . . ."

Mr. Direck had followed this cascade of remarks with a patient smile and a slowly nodding head. "What you say," he said, "forms a very marked contrast indeed with the sort of thing that goes on in America. This friend of mine I was speaking of, the one who is connected with an automobile factory in Toledo——"

"Of course," Mr. Britling burst out again, "even conservatism isn't an ultimate thing. After all, we and your enterprising friend at Toledo are very much the same blood. The conservatism, I mean, isn't racial. And our earlier energy shows it isn't in the air or in the soil. England has become unenterprising and sluggish because England has been so prosperous and comfortable. . ."

"Exactly," said Mr. Direck. "My friend of whom I was telling you was a man named Robinson, which indicates pretty clearly that he was of genuine English stock, and, if I may say so, quite of your build and complexion ; racially, I should say, he was, well—very much what you are. . . ."

§ 7

This rally of Mr. Direck's mind was suddenly interrupted.

Mr. Britling stood up, and putting both hands to the sides of his mouth, shouted "Yi-ah! Aye-ya! Thea!" at unseen hearers.

After shouting again several times, it became manifest that he had attracted the attention of two willing but deliberate labouring men. They emerged slowly, first as attentive heads, from the landscape. With their assistance the car was restored to the road again. Mr. Direck assisted manfully, and noted the respect that was given to Mr. Britling, and the shillings that fell to the men, with an intelligent detachment. They touched their hats, they called Mr. Britling "Sir." They examined the car distantly but kindly. "Aint 'urt 'e, not a bit 'e ain't, not reely," said one encouragingly. And indeed except for a slight crumpling of the mud-guard and the detachment of the wire of one of the headlights the automobile was uninjured. Mr. Britling resumed his seat ; Mr. Direck gravely and in silence got up beside him. They started with the usual convulsion, as though something had pricked the vehicle unexpectedly and shamefully behind. And from this point Mr. Britling, driving with meticulous care, got home without further mishap, excepting only that he scraped off some of the metal edge of his foot-board against the gate-post of his very agreeable garden.

His family welcomed his safe return, visitor and all, with undisguised relief and admiration. A small boy appeared at the corner of the house, and then disappeared hastily again.

"Daddy's got back all right at last," they heard him shouting to unseen hearers.

§ 8

Mr. Direck, though he was a little incommoded by the suppression of his story about Robinson—for when he had begun a thing he liked to finish it—found Mr. Britling's household at once thoroughly British, quite un-American and a little difficult to follow. It had a quality that at first he could not define at all. Compared with anything he had ever seen in his life before it struck him as being—he found the word at last—sketchy. For instance, he was introduced to nobody except his hostess, and she was indicated to him by a mere wave of Mr. Britling's hand. "That's Edith," he said, and returned at once to his car to put it away. Mrs. Britling was a tall, freckled woman with pretty bright brown hair and preoccupied brown eyes. She welcomed him with a handshake, and then a wonderful English parlour-maid—she at least was according to expectations—took his gripsack and guided him to his room. "Lunch, sir," she said, "is outside," and closed the door and left him to that and a towel-covered can of hot water.

It was a square-looking old red-brick house he had come to, very handsome in a simple Georgian fashion, with a broad lawn before it and great blue cedar-trees, and a drive that came frankly up to the front door and then went off with Mr. Britling and the car round to unknown regions at the back. The centre of the house was a big airy hall, oak-panelled, warmed in winter only by one large fireplace and abounding in doors which he knew opened into the square separate rooms that England favours. Book-shelves and stuffed birds comforted the landing outside his bedroom. He descended to find the hall occupied by a small bright bristling boy in white flannel shirt and knickerbockers and bare legs and feet. He stood before the vacant open fireplace in an attitude that Mr. Direck knew instantly was also Mr. Britling's. "Lunch is in the garden," the Britling scion proclaimed, "and I've got to fetch you. And, I say! is it true? Are you American?"

"Why surely," said Mr. Direck.

"Well, I know some American," said the boy. "I learned it."

"Tell me some," said Mr. Direck, smiling still more amiably.

"Oh! Well—Gol darn you! Ouch. Gee-whizz! Soak him Maud! It's up to you, Duke. . . ."

"Now where did you learn all that?" asked Mr. Direck recovering.

"Out of the Sunday Supplement," said the youthful Britling.

"Why! Then you know all about Buster Brown," said Mr. Direck. "He's Fine—eh?"

The Britling child hated Buster Brown. He regarded Buster

Brown as a totally unnecessary infant. He detested the way
he wore his hair and the peculiar cut of his knickerbockers
and—him. He thought Buster Brown the one drop of paraffin
in the otherwise delicious feast of the Sunday Supplement.
But he was a diplomatic child.

" I think I like Happy Hooligan better," he said. " And
dat ole Maud."

He reflected with joyful eyes, Buster clean forgotten.
" Every week," he said, " she kicks some one."

It came to Mr. Direck as a very pleasant discovery that a
British infant could find a common ground with the small
people at home in these characteristically American jests.
He had never dreamt that the fine wine of Maud and Buster
could travel.

" Maud's a treat," said the youthful Britling, relapsing
into his native tongue.

Mr. Britling appeared coming to meet them. He was now
in a grey flannel suit—he must have jumped into it—and
altogether very much tidier. . . .

§ 9

The long narrow table under the big sycamores between the
house and the adapted barn that Mr. Direck learned was used
for " dancing and all that sort of thing " was covered with
a blue linen diaper cloth, and that too surprised him. This
was his first meal in a private household, and for obscure
reasons he had expected something very stiff and formal with
" spotless napery." He had also expected a very stiff and
capable service by implacable parlour-maids, and the whole
thing indeed highly genteel. But two cheerful women servants
appeared from what was presumably the kitchen direction,
wheeling a curious wicker erection, which his small guide
informed him was called Aunt Clatter—manifestly deservedly
—and which bore on its shelves the substance of the meal.
And while the maids at this migratory sideboard carved and
opened bottles and so forth, the small boy and a slightly
larger brother, assisted a little by two young men of no very
defined position and relationship, served the company. Mrs.
Britling sat at the head of the table, and conversed with Mr.
Direck by means of hostess questions and imperfectly accepted
answers while she kept a watchful eye on the proceedings.

The composition of the company was a matter for some
perplexity to Mr. Direck. Mr. and Mrs. Britling were at either
end of the table, that was plain enough. It was also fairly plain
that the two bare-footed boys were little Britlings. But beyond
this was a cloud of uncertainty. There was a youth of perhaps
seventeen, much darker than Britling, but with nose and
freckles rather like his, who might be an early son or a stepson ;
he was shock-headed and with that look about his arms and
legs that suggests overnight growth ; and there was an un-

mistakable young German, very pink, with close-cropped fair
hair, glasses and a panama hat, who was probably the tutor
of the younger boys. (Mr. Direck also was wearing his hat,
his mind had been filled with an exaggerated idea of the
treacheries of the English climate before he left New York.
Every one else was hatless.) Finally, before one reached the
limits of the explicable there was a pleasant young man with
a lot of dark hair and very fine dark blue eyes, whom everybody called "Teddy." For him, Mr. Direck hazarded
" secretary."

But in addition to these normal and understandable presences, there was an entirely mysterious pretty young woman
in blue linen who sat and smiled next to Mr. Britling, and
there was a rather kindred-looking girl with darker hair on
the right of Mr. Direck who impressed him at the very outset
as being still prettier, and—he didn't quite place her at first—
somehow familiar to him ; there was a large irrelevant middle-
aged lady in black with a gold chain and a tall middle-aged
man with an intelligent face, who might be a casual guest ;
there was an Indian young gentleman faultlessly dressed up
to his brown soft linen collar and cuffs, and thereafter an un-
controlled outbreak of fine bronze modelling and abundant
fuzzy hair ; and there was a very erect and attentive baby of
a year or less, sitting up in a perambulator and gesticulating
cheerfully to everybody. This baby it was that most troubled
the orderly mind of Mr. Direck. The research for its paternity
made his conversation with Mrs. Britling almost as disconnected
and absent-minded as her conversation with him. It almost
certainly wasn't Mrs. Britling's. The girl next to him or the
girl next to Mr. Britling or the lady in black might any of
them be married, but if so where was the spouse ? It seemed
improbable that they would wheel out a foundling to lunch. . . .

Realising at last that the problem of relationship must be
left to solve itself if he did not want to dissipate and consume
his mind entirely, Mr. Direck turned to his hostess, who was
enjoying a brief lull in her administrative duties, and told her
what a memorable thing the meeting of Mr. Britling in his own
home would be in his life, and how very highly America was
coming to esteem Mr. Britling and his essays. He found that
with a slight change of person, one of his premeditated openings was entirely serviceable here. And he went on to observe
that it was novel and entertaining to find Mr. Britling driving
his own automobile and to note that it was an automobile of
American manufacture. In America they had standarised and
systematised the making of such things as automobiles to an
extent that would, he thought, be almost starling to Europeans.
It was certainly startling to the European manufacturers. In
illustration of that he might tell a little story of a friend of
his called Robinson—a man who curiously enough in general
build and appearance was very reminiscent indeed of Mr.

Britling. He had been telling Mr. Britling as much on his way here from the station. His friend was concerned with several others in one of the biggest attacks that had ever been made upon what one might describe in general terms as the thousand-dollar light automobile market. What they said practically was this : This market is a jig-saw puzzle waiting to be put together and made one. We are going to do it. But that was easier to figure out than to do. At the very outset of this attack he and his associates found themselves up against an expected and very difficult proposition. . . .

At first Mrs. Britling had listened to Mr. Direck with an almost undivided attention, but as he had developed his opening the feast upon the blue linen table had passed on to a fresh phase that demanded more and more of her directive intelligence. The two little boys appeared suddenly at her elbows. " Shall we take the plates and get the strawberries, Mummy ? " they asked simultaneously. Then one of the neat maids in the background had to be called up and instructed in undertones, and Mr. Direck saw that for the present Robinson's illuminating experience was not for her ears. A little baffled, but quite understanding how things were, he turned to his neighbour on his left.

The girl really had an extraordinary pretty smile, and there was something in her soft bright brown eye—like the movement of some quick little bird. And—she was like somebody he knew ! Indeed she was. She was quite ready to be spoken to.

" I was telling Mrs. Britling," said Mr. Direck, " what a very great privilege I esteem it to meet Mr. Britling in this highly familiar way."

" You've not met him before ? "

" I missed him by twenty-four hours when he came through Boston on the last occasion. Just twenty-four hours. It was a matter of very great regret to me."

" I wish I'd been paid to travel round the world."

" You must write things like Mr. Britling and then Mr. Kahn will send you."

" Don't you think if I promised well ? "

" You'd have to write some promissory notes, I think—just to convince him it was all right."

The young lady reflected on Mr. Britling's good fortune.

" He saw India. He saw Japan. He had weeks in Egypt. And he went right across America."

Mr. Direck had already begun on the liner to adapt himself to the hopping inconsecutiveness of English conversation. He made now what he felt was quite a good hop, and he dropped his voice to a confidential undertone. (It was probably Adam in his first conversation with Eve who discovered the pleasantness of dropping into a confidential undertone beside a pretty ear with a pretty wave of hair above it.)

" It was in India, I presume," murmured Mr. Direck, " that Mr. Britling made the acquaintance of the coloured gentleman?"

" Coloured gentleman ! " She gave a swift glance down the table as though she expected to see something purple with yellow spots. " Oh, that is one of Mr. Lawrence Carmine's young men ! " she explained even more confidentially and with an air of discussing the silver bowl of roses before him. " He's a great authority on Indian literature, he belongs to a society for making things pleasant for Indian students in London, and he has them down."

" And Mr. Lawrence Carmine ? " he pursued.

Even more intimately and confidentially she indicated Mr. Carmine, as it seemed by a motion of her eyelash.

Mr. Direck prepared to be even more *sotto voce* and to plumb a much profounder mystery. His eye rested on the perambulator ; he leaned a little nearer to the ear. . . . But the strawberries interrupted him.

" Strawberries ! " said the young lady, and directed his regard to his left shoulder by a movement of her head.

He found one of the boys with a high-piled plate ready to serve him.

And then Mrs. Britling resumed her conversation with him. She was so ignorant, she said, of things American that she did not even know if they had strawberries there. At any rate, here they were at the crest of the season, and in a very good year. And in the rose season too. It was one of the dearest vanities of English people to think their apples and their roses and their strawberries the best in the world.

" And their complexions," said Mr. Direck, over the pyramid of fruit, quite manifestly intending a compliment. So that was all right. . . . But the girl on the left of him was speaking across the table to the German tutor, and did not hear what he had said. So that even if it wasn't very neat it didn't matter. . . .

Then he remembered that she was like that old daguerrotype of a cousin of his grandmother's that he had fallen in love with when he was a boy. It was her smile. Of course ! Of course ! . . . And he'd sort of adored that portrait. . . . He felt a curious disposition to tell her as much. . . .

" What makes this visit even more interesting if possible to me," he said to Mrs. Britling, " than it would otherwise be is that this Essex country is the country in which my maternal grandmother was raised, and also long way back my mother's father's people. My mother's father's people were very early New England people indeed. . . . Well, no. If I said *Mayflower* it wouldn't be true. But it would approximate. They were Essex Hinkinsons. That's what they were. I must be a good third of me at least Essex. My grandmother was an Essex Corner. I must confess I've had some thought——"

" Corner ? " said the young lady at his elbow sharply.

" I was telling Mrs. Britling I had some thought——"

" But about those Essex relatives of yours ? "

" Well, of finding if they were still about in these parts. . . .
Say ! I haven't dropped a brick, have I ? "

He looked from one face to another.

" *She's* a Corner," said Mrs. Britling.

" Well," said Mr. Direck, and hesitated for a moment. It
was so delightful that one couldn't go on being just discreet.
The atmosphere was free and friendly. His intonation disarmed offence. And he gave the young lady the full benefit
of a quite expressive eye. " I'm very pleased to meet you,
Cousin Corner. How are the old folks at home ? "

§ 10

The bright interest of this cousinship helped Mr. Direck
more than anything to get the better of his Robinson-anecdote
crave, and when presently he found his dialogue with Mr.
Britling resumed, he turned at once to this remarkable discovery of his long-lost and indeed hitherto unsuspected relative. " It's an American sort of thing to do, I suppose," he
said apologetically, " but I almost thought of going on, on
Monday, to Market Saffron, which was the locality of the
Hinkinsons, and just looking about at the tombstones in the
churchyard for a day or so."

" Very probably," said Mr. Britling, " you'd find something
about them in the parish registers. Lots of our registers go
back three hundred years or more. I'll drive you over in my
lil' old car."

" Oh ! I wouldn't put you to that trouble," said Mr. Direck
hastily.

" It's no trouble. I like the driving. What I have had of it.
And while we're at it, we'll come back by Harborough High
Oak and look up the Corner pedigree. They're all over that
district still. And the road's not really difficult ; it's only a
bit up and down and roundabout."

" I couldn't think, Mr. Britling, of putting you to that
much trouble."

" It's no trouble. I want a day off, and I'm dying to take
Gladys——"

" Gladys ? " said Mr. Direck with sudden hope.

" That's my name for the lil' car. I'm dying to take her
for something like a decent run. I've only had her out four
times altogether, and I've not got her up yet to forty miles.
Which I'm told she ought to do easily. We'll consider that
settled."

For the moment Mr. Direck couldn't think of any further
excuse. But it was very clear in his mind that something must
happen ; he wished he knew of somebody who could send a
recall telegram from London, to prevent him committing himself to the casual destinies of Mr. Britling's car again. And
then another interest became uppermost in his mind.

" You'd hardly believe me," he said, " if I told you that that Miss Corner of yours has a quite extraordinary resemblance to a miniature I've got away there in America of a cousin of my maternal grandmother's.   She seems a very pleasant young lady."

But Mr. Britling supplied no further information about Miss Corner.

" It must be very interesting," he said, " to come over here and pick up these American families of yours on the monuments and tombstones.   You know, of course, that district south of Evesham where every church monument bears the stars and stripes, the arms of departed Washingtons. I doubt though if you'll still find the name about there. Nor will you find many Hinkinsons in Market Saffron. But lots of this country here has five or six hundred-year-old families still flourishing.   That's why Essex is so much more genuinely Old England than Surrey, say, or Kent. Round here you'll find Corners and Fairlies, and then you get Capels, and then away down towards Dunmow and Braintree Maynards and Byngs. And there are oaks and hornbeams in the park about Claverings that have echoed to the howling of wolves and the clank of men in armour. All the old farms here are moated—because of the wolves. Claverings itself is Tudor, and rather fine too. And the cottages still wear thatch. . . ."

He reflected. " Now if you went south of London instead of northward it's all different. You're in a different period, a different society. You're in London suburbs right down to the sea. You'll find no genuine estates left, not of our deep-rooted familiar sort. You'll find millionaires and that sort of people, sitting in the old places. Surrey is full of rich stock-brokers, company-promoters, bookies, judges, newspaper proprietors. Sort of people who fence the paths across their parks. They do something to the old places—I don't know what they do—but instantly the countryside becomes a villa-dom.   And little sub-estates and red-brick villas and art cottages spring up. And a kind of new, hard neatness. And pneumatic tire and automobile spirit advertisements, great glaring boards by the roadside. And all the poor people are inspected and rushed about until they forget who their grandfathers were. They become villa parasites and odd-job men, and grow basely rich and buy gramophones. This Essex and yonder Surrey are as different as Russia and Germany. But for one American who comes to look at Essex, twenty go to Godalming and Guildford and Dorking and Lewes and Canterbury. Those Surrey people are not properly English at all. They are strenuous. You have to get on or get out. They drill their gardeners, lecture very fast on agricultural efficiency, and have minature rifle-ranges in every village. It's a county of new notice-boards and barbed-wire fences ; there's always a policeman round the corner. They dress for dinner. They

dress for everything. If a man gets up in the night to look for
a burglar he puts on the correct costume—or doesn't go.
They've got a special scientific system for urging on their
tramps.   And they lock up their churches on a week-day.
Half their soil is hard chalk or a rationalistic sand, only suitable
for bunkers and villa foundations.   And they play golf in a
large, expensive, thorough way because it's the thing to do. . . .
Now here in Essex we're as lax as the eighteenth century.   We
hunt in any old clothes.   Our soil is a rich succulent clay ; it
becomes semifluid in winter—when we go about in waders
shooting duck.   All our finger-posts have been twisted round
by facetious men years ago.   And we pool our breeds of hens
and pigs.   Our roses and oaks are wonderful ; that alone shows
that this is the real England.   If I wanted to play golf—which
I don't, being a decent Essex man—I should have to motor
ten miles into Hertfordshire.   And for rheumatics and longe-
vity Surrey can't touch us.   I want you to be clear on these
points, because they really will affect your impressions of this
place. . . .   This country is a part of the real England—England outside London and outside manufactures.   It's one with
Wessex and Mercia or old Yorkshire—or for the matter of
that with Meath or Lothian.   And it's the essential England
still. . . . "

§ II

It detracted a little from Mr. Direck's appreciation of this
flow of information that it was taking them away from the
rest of the company.   He wanted to see more of his new-found
cousin, and what the baby and the Bengali gentleman—whom
manifestly one mustn't call " coloured "—and the large-nosed
lady and all the other inexplicables would get up to.   Instead
of which Mr. Britling was leading him off alone with an air of
showing him round the premises, and talking too rapidly and
variously for a question to be got in edgeways, much less any
broaching of the matter that Mr. Direck had come over to
settle.

There was quite a lot of rose-garden, it made the air delicious, and it was full of great tumbling bushes of roses and of
neglected standards, and it had a long pergola of creepers and
trailers and a great arbour, and underneath over the beds
everywhere, contrary to all the rules, the blossom of a multitude of pansies and stocks and little trailing plants swarmed
and crowded and scrimmaged and drilled and fought great
massed attacks.   And then Mr. Britling talked their way round
a red-walled vegetable-garden with an abundance of fruit-
trees, and through a door into a terraced square that had once
been a farmyard, outside the converted barn.   The barn doors
had been replaced by a door-pierced window of glass, and in
the middle of the square space a deep tank had been made,
full of rain-water, in which Mr. Britling remarked casually

that " everybody " bathed when the weather was hot. Thyme and rosemary and such-like sweet-scented things grew on the terrace about the tank, and ten trimmed little trees of *arbor vitae* stood sentinel. Mr. Direck was tantalisingly aware that beyond some lilac-bushes were his new-found cousin and the kindred young woman in blue playing tennis with the Indian and another young man, while whenever it was necessary the large-nosed lady crossed the stage and brooded soothingly over the perambulator. And Mr. Britling, choosing a seat from which Mr. Direck just couldn't look comfortably through the green branches at the flying glimpses of pink and blue and white and brown, continued to talk about England and America in relation to each other and everything else under the sun.

Presently through a distant gate the two small boys were momentarily visible wheeling small but serviceable bicycles, followed after a little interval by the German tutor. Then an enormous grey cat came slowly across the garden court, and sat down to listen respectfully to Mr. Britling. The afternoon sky was an intense blue, with little puff-balls of cloud lined out across it.

Occasionally, from chance remarks of Mr. Britling's, Mr. Direck was led to infer that his first impressions as an American visitor were being related to his host, but as a matter of fact he was permitted to relate nothing ; Mr. Britling did all the talking. He sat beside his guest and spirted and played ideas and reflections like a happy fountain in the sunshine.

Mr. Direck sat comfortably, and smoked with quiet appreciation the one after-lunch cigar he allowed himself. At any rate, if he himself felt rather word-bound, the fountain was nimble and entertaining. He listened in a general sort of way to the talk, it was quite impossible to follow it thoughtfully throughout all its chinks and turnings, while his eyes wandered about the garden and went ever and again to the flitting tennis-players beyond the green. It was all very gay and comfortable and complete ; it was various and delightful without being in the least *opulent* ; that was one of the little secrets America had to learn. It didn't look as though it had been made or bought or cost anything, it looked as though it had happened rather luckily. . . .

Mr. Britling's talk became like a wide stream flowing through Mr. Direck's mind, bearing along momentary impressions and observations, drifting memories of all the crowded English sights and sounds of the last five days, filmy imaginations about ancestral names and pretty cousins, scraps of those prepared conversational openings on Mr. Britling's standing in America, the explanation about the lecture club, the still incompletely forgotten purport of the Robinson anecdote. . . .

" Nobody planned the British estate system, nobody planned the British aristocratic system, nobody planned the confounded constitution, it came about, it was like layer after layer wrapping round an agate, but you see it came about so happily in a way, it so suited the climate and the temperament of our people and our island, it was on the whole so cosy, that our people settled down into it, you can't help settling down into it, they had already settled down by the days of Queen Anne, and Heaven knows if we shall ever really get away again. We're like that little shell the *Lingula*, that is found in the oldest rocks and lives to-day : it fitted its easy conditions, and it has never modified since. Why should it ? It excretes all its disturbing forces. Our younger sons go away and found colonial empires. Our surplus cottage children emigrate to Australia and Canada or migrate into the towns. It doesn't alter *this. . . .*"

§ 12

Mr. Direck's eye had come to rest upon the barn, and its expression changed slowly from lazy appreciation to a brightening intelligence. Suddenly he resolved to say something. He resolved to say it so firmly that he determined to say it even if Mr. Britling went on talking all the time.

" I suppose, Mr. Britling," he said, " this barn here dates from the days of Queen Anne."

" The walls of the yard here are probably earlier : probably monastic. That grey patch in the corner, for example. The barn itself is Georgian."

" And here it is still. And this farmyard, here it is still."

Mr. Britling was for flying off again, but Mr. Direck would not listen ; he held on like a man who keeps his grip on a lasso.

" There's one thing I would like to remark about your barn, Mr. Britling, and I might, while I am at it, say the same thing about your farmyard."

Mr. Britling was held. " What's that ? " he asked.

" Well," said Mr. Direck, " the point that strikes me most about all this is that that barn isn't a barn any longer, and that this farmyard isn't a farmyard. There isn't any wheat or chaff or anything of that sort in the barn, and there never will be again : there's just a pianola and a dancing floor, and if a cow came into this farmyard everybody in the place would be shooing it out again. They'd regard it as a most unnatural object."

He had a pleasant sense of talking at last. He kept right on. He was moved to a sweeping generalisation.

" You were so good as to ask me, Mr. Britling, a little while ago, what my first impression of England was. Well, Mr. Britling, my first impression of England that seems to me to matter in the least is this : that it looks and feels more like the traditional Old England than any one could possibly have believed, and that in reality it is less like the traditional Old England than any one would ever possibly have imagined."

He was carried on even further. He made a tremendous literary epigram. " I thought," he said, " when I looked out of the train this morning that I had come to the England of Washington Irving. I find it is not even the England of Mrs. Humphry Ward."

CHAPTER TWO

MR. BRITLING CONTINUES HIS EXPOSITION

§ 1

MR. DIRECK found little reason to revise his dictum in the subsequent experiences of the afternoon. Indeed the afternoon and the next day were steadily consistent in confirming what a very good dictum it had been. The scenery was the traditional scenery of England, and all the people seemed quicker, more irresponsible, more chaotic, than any one could have anticipated, and entirely inexplicable by any recognised code of English relationships. . . .

" You think that John Bull is dead and a strange generation is wearing his clothes," said Mr. Britling. " I think you'll find very soon it's the old John Bull. Perhaps not Mrs. Humphry Ward's John Bull, or Mrs. Henry Wood's John Bull, but true essentially to Shakespeare, Fielding, Dickens, Meredith. . . .

" I suppose," he added, " there are changes. There's a new generation grown up. . . . "

He looked at his barn and the swimming-pool. " It's a good point of yours about the barn," he said. " What you say reminds me of that very jolly thing of Kipling's about the old mill-wheel that began by grinding corn and ended by driving dynamos. . . .

" Only I admit that barn doesn't exactly drive a dynamo. . . .

" To be frank, it's just a pleasure barn. . . .

" The country can afford it. . . . "

§ 2

He left it at that for the time, but throughout the afternoon Mr. Direck had the gratification of seeing his thought floating round and round in the back-waters of Mr. Britling's mental current. If it didn't itself get into the stream again its reflection at any rate appeared and reappeared. He was taken about with great assiduity throughout the afternoon, and he got no more than occasional glimpses of the rest of the Dower House circle until six o'clock in the evening.

Meanwhile the fountains of Mr. Britling's active and encyclopædic mind played steadily.

He was inordinately proud of England, and had abused

her incessantly. He wanted to state England to Mr. Direck
as the amiable summation of a grotesque assembly of faults.
That was the view into which the comforts and prosperities of
his middle age had brought him from a radicalism that had
in its earlier stages been angry and bitter. And for Mr. Britling
England was "here." Essex was the county he knew. He
took Mr. Direck out from his walled garden by a little door
into a trim paddock with two white goals. "We play hockey
here on Sundays," he said, in a way that gave Mr. Direck
no hint of the practically compulsory participation of every
visitor to Matching's Easy in this violent and dangerous
exercise, and thence they passed by a rich deep lane into a
highroad that ran along the edge of the deer park of Claverings.
"We will call in on Claverings later," said Mr. Britling.
"Lady Homartyn has some people there for the week-end,
and you ought to see the sort of thing it is and the sort of
people they are. She wanted us to lunch there to-morrow,
but I didn't accept that because of our afternoon hockey."

Mr. Direck received this reason uncritically.

The village reminded him of Abbey's pictures. There was
an inn with a sign standing out in the road, a painted sign
of the Clavering Arms ; it had a water-trough (such as Mr.
Weller senior ducked the dissenter in) and a green painted
table outside its inviting door. There were also a general
shop and a number of very pleasant cottages, each marked
with the Mainstay crest. All this was grouped about a green
with real geese drilling thereon. Mr. Britling conducted his
visitor (through a lych-gate) into the churchyard, and there
they found mossy, tumbledown tombstones, one with a
skull and cross-bones upon it, that went back to the later
seventeenth century. In the aisle of the church were three
huge hatchments, and there was a side chapel devoted to the
Mainstay family and the Barons Homartyn, with a series
of monuments that began with painted Tudor effigies and came
down to a vast stained-glass window of the vilest commercial
Victorian. There were also mediæval brasses of parish priests,
and a marble crusader and his lady of some extinguished
family which had ruled Matching's Easy before the Main-
stays came. And as the two gentlemen emerged from the
church they ran against the perfect vicar, Mr. Dimple, ample
and genial, with an embracing laugh and an enveloping voice.
"Come to see the old country," he said to Mr. Direck. "So
Good of you Americans to do that ! So Good of you. . . ."

There was some amiable sparring between the worthy man
and Mr. Britling about bringing Mr. Direck to church on Sunday
morning. "He's terribly Lax," said Mr. Dimple to Mr. Direck,
smiling radiantly. "Terribly Lax. But then nowadays
Everybody *is* so Lax. And he's very Good to my Coal Club ;
I don't know what we should do without him. So I just ad-
monish him. And if he doesn't go to church, well, anyhow

he doesn't go anywhere else. He may be a poor churchman, but anyhow he's not a dissenter. . . ."

"In England, you see," Mr. Britling remarked, after they had parted from the reverend gentleman, "we have domesticated everything. We have even domesticated God."

For a while Mr. Britling showed Mr. Direck English lanes and then came back along narrow white paths across small fields of rising wheat, to the village and a little gate that led into the park.

"Well," said Mr. Direck, "what you say about domestication does seem to me to be very true indeed. Why! even those clouds up there look as though they had a shepherd and were grazing."

"Ready for shearing almost," said Mr. Britling.

"Indeed," said Mr. Direck, raising his voice a little. "I've seen scarcely anything in England that wasn't domesticated, unless it was some of your back streets in London."

Mr. Britling seemed to reflect for a moment. "They're an excrescence," he said. . . .

§ 3

The park had a trim wildness like nature in an old Italian picture ; dappled fallow deer grouped close at hand and looked at the two men fearlessly ; the path dropped through oak-trees and some stunted bracken to a little loitering stream, that paused ever and again to play at ponds and waterfalls and bear a fleet of water-lily leaves, and then their way curved round in an indolent sweep towards the cedars and shrubberies of the great house. The house looked low and extensive to an American eye, and its red-brick chimneys rose like infantry in open order along its extended line. There was a glimpse of flower-bright garden and terraces to the right as they came round the corner to the front of the house through a path cut in the laurel bushes.

Mr. Britling had a moment of exposition as they approached the entrance.

"I expect we shall find Philbert from the Home Office—or is it the Local Government Board ?—and Sir Thomas Loot, the Treasury man. There may be some other people of that sort, the people we call the Governing Class. Wives also. And I rather fancy the Countess of Frensham is coming, she's strong on the Irish question, and Lady Venetia Trumpington, who they say is a beauty—I've never seen her. It's Lady Homartyn's way to expect me to come in—not that I'm an important item at these week-end social feasts—but she likes to see me on the table—to be nibbled at if any one wants to do so—like the olives and the salted almonds. And she always asks me to lunch on Sunday and I always refuse —because of the hockey. So you see I put in an appearance on the Saturday afternoon. . . ."

They had reached the big doorway.

It opened into a large cool hall adorned with the heads of hippopotami and rhinoceroses and a stuffed lion, and furnished chiefly with a vast table on which hats and sticks and newspapers were littered. A man servant with a subdued, semiconfidential manner conveyed to Mr. Britling that her ladyship was on the terrace, and took the hats and sticks that were handed to him and led the way through the house. They emerged upon a broad terrace looking out under great cedar trees upon flower-beds and stone urns and tennis lawns and yew hedges that dipped to give a view of distant hills. On the terrace were grouped perhaps a dozen people for the most part holding teacups, they sat in deck chairs and folding seats about a little table that bore the tea-things. Lady Homartyn came forward to welcome the newcomers.

Mr. Direck was introduced as a travelling American gratified to see a typical English country house, and Lady Homartyn in an habituated way ran over the points of her Tudor specimen. Mr. Direck was not accustomed to titled people, and was suddenly in doubt whether you called a baroness " My Lady " or " Your Ladyship," so he wisely avoided any form of address until he had a lead from Mr. Britling. Mr. Britling presently called her " Lady Homartyn." She took Mr. Direck and sat him down beside a lady whose name he didn't catch, but who had had a lot to do with the British Embassy at Washington, and then she handed Mr. Britling over to the Right Honourable George Philbert, who was anxious to discuss certain points in the latest book of essays. The conversation of the lady from Washington was intelligent but not exacting, and Mr. Direck was able to give some of his attention to the general effect of the scene.

He was a little disappointed to find that the servants didn't wear livery. In American magazine pictures and in American cinematograph films of English stories and in the houses of very rich Americans living in England, they do so. And the Mansion House is misleading ; he had met a compatriot who had recently dined at the Mansion House, and who had described " flunkies " in hair-powder and cloth of gold—like Thackeray's Jeames Yellowplush. But here the only servants were two slim, discreet and attentive young gentlemen in black coats and with a gentle piety of manner instead of pride. And he was a little disappointed too by a notable lack of splendour in the company. The ladies affected him as being ill-dressed ; there was none of the hard snap, the " There ! and what do you say to it ? " about them of the well-dressed American woman, and the men too were not so much tailored as unobtrusively and yet grammatically clothed.

§ 4

He was still only in the fragmentary stage of conversation when everything was thrown into commotion by the important arrival of Lady Frensham, and there was a general reshuffling of places. Lady Frensham had arrived from London by automobile ; she appeared in veils and swathings and a tremendous dust-cloak, with a sort of nephew in her train who had driven the car. She was manifestly a constitutionally triumphant woman. A certain afternoon lassitude vanished in the swirl of her arrival. Mr. Philbert removed wrappings and handed them to the man servant.

" I launched with Sir Edward Carson to-day, my dear," she told Lady Homartyn, and rolled a belligerent eye at Philbert.

" And is he as obdurate as ever ? " asked Sir Thomas.

" Obdurate ! It's Redmond who's obdurate," cried Lady Frensham. " What do you say, Mr. Britling ? "

" A plague on both your parties," said Mr. Britling.

" You can't keep out of things like that," said Lady Frensham with the utmost gusto, " when the country's on the very verge of civil war. . . . You people who try to pretend there isn't a grave crisis when there is one, will be more accountable than any one—when the civil war does come. It won't spare you. Mark my words ! "

The party became a circle.

Mr. Direck found himself the interested auditor of a real English country-house week-end political conversation. This at any rate was like the England of which Mrs. Humphry Ward's novels had informed him, but yet not exactly like it. Perhaps that was due to the fact that for the most part these novels dealt with the England of the nineties, and things had lost a little in dignity since those days. But at any rate here were political figures and titled people, and they were talking about the " country." . . .

Was it possible that people of this sort did " run " the country, after all ? . . . When he had read Mrs. Humphry Ward in America he had always accepted this theory of the story quite easily, but now that he saw and heard them——!

But all governments and rulers and ruling classes when you look at them closely are incredible. . . .

" I don't believe the country is on the verge of civil war," cried Mr. Britling.

" Facts ! " cried Lady Frensham, and seemed to wipe away delusions with a rapid gesture of her hands.

" You're interested in Ireland, Mr. Dirks ? " asked Lady Homartyn.

" We see it first when we come over," said Mr. Direck rather neatly, and after that he was free to attend to the general discussion.

Lady Frensham, it was manifest, was one of that energetic body of aristocratic ladies who were at that time taking up an irreconcilable attitude against Home Rule " in any shape or form." They were rapidly turning British politics into a system of bitter personal feuds in which all sense of imperial welfare was lost. A wild ambition to emulate the extremest suffragettes seemed to have seized upon them. They insulted, they denounced, they refused every invitation lest they should meet that " traitor " the Prime Minister, they imitated the party hatreds of a fiercer age, and even now the moderate and politic Philbert found himself treated as an invisible object. They were supported by the extremer section of the Tory press, and the most extraordinary writers were set up to froth like lunatics against the government as " traitors," as men who " insulted the King " ; *The Morning Post* and the lighter-witted side of the Unionist press generally poured out a torrent of partisan nonsense it is now almost incredible to recall. Lady Frensham, bridling over Lady Homartyn's party, and for a time leaving Mr. Britling, hurried on to tell of the newest developments of the great feud. She had a wonderful description of Lady Londonderry sitting opposite " that old rascal," the Prime Minister, at a performance of Mozart's " Zauber-flöte."

" If looks could kill ! " cried Lady Frensham with tremendous gusto.

" Sir Edward is quite firm that Ulster means to fight. They have machine-guns—ammunition. And I am sure the army is with us. . . ."

" Where did they get those machine-guns and ammunition ? " asked Mr. Britling suddenly.

" Ah ! that's a secret," cried Lady Frensham.

" Um," said Mr. Britling.

" You see," said Lady Frensham ; " it *will* be civil war ! And yet you writing people who have influence do nothing to prevent it ! "

" What are we to do, Lady Frensham ? "

" Tell people how serious it is."

" You mean, tell the Irish Nationalists to lie down and be walked over. They won't be. . . ."

" We'll see about that," cried Lady Frensham, " we'll see about that ! "

She was a large and dignified person with a kind of figure-head nobility of carriage, but Mr. Direck was suddenly reminded of a girl cousin of his who had been expelled from college for some particularly elaborate and aimless rioting. . . .

" May I say something to you, Lady Frensham," said Mr. Britling, " that you have just said to me ? Do you realise that this Carsonite campaign is dragging these islands within a measurable distance of civil war ? "

" It's the fault of your Lloyd George and his government.

It's the fault of your Socialists and sentimentalists. You've made the mischief and you have to deal with it."

"Yes. But do you really figure to yourself what a civil war may mean for the empire? Surely there are other things in the world besides this quarrel between the "loyalists" of Ulster and the Liberal government; there are other interests in this big empire than party advantages? You think you are going to frighten this Home Rule government into some ridiculous sort of collapse that will bring in the Tories at the next election. Well, suppose you don't manage that. Suppose instead that you do really contrive to bring about a civil war. Very few people here or in Ireland want it—I was over there not a month ago—but when men have loaded guns in their hands they sometimes go off. And then people see red. Few people realise what an incurable sore opens when fighting begins. Suppose part of the army revolts and we get some extraordinary and demoralising fighting over there. India watches these things. Bengal may imitate Ireland. At that distance rebellion and treason are rebellion and treason whether they are coloured orange or green. And then suppose the Germans see fit to attack us!"

Lady Frensham had a woman's elusiveness. "Your Redmondites would welcome them with open arms."

"It isn't the Redmondites who invite them now, anyhow," said Mr. Britling, springing his mine. "The other day one of your 'loyalists,' Andrews, was talking in *The Morning Post* of preferring conquest by Germany to Home Rule; Craig has been at the same game; Major Crawford, the man who ran the German Mausers last April, boasted that he would transfer his allegiance to the German Emperor rather than see Redmond in power."

"Rhetoric!" said Lady Frensham. "Rhetoric!"

"But one of your Ulster papers has openly boasted that arrangements have been made for a 'powerful Continental monarch' to help an Ulster rebellion."

"Which paper?" snatched Lady Frensham.

Mr. Britling hesitated.

Mr. Philbert supplied the name. "I saw it. It was *The Irish Churchman.*"

"You two have got your case up very well," said Lady Frensham. "I didn't know Mr. Britling was a party man."

"The Nationalists have been circulating copies," said Philbert. "Naturally."

They make it look worse than mere newspaper talk and speeches," Mr. Britling pressed. "Carson, it seems, was lunching with the German Emperor last autumn. A fine fuss you'd make if Redmond did that. All this gun-running, too, is German gun-running."

"What does it matter if it is?" said Lady Frensham, allowing a belligerent eye to rest for the first time on Philbert.

" You drove us to it. One thing we are resolved upon at any cost. Johnny Redmond may rule England if he likes ; he shan't rule Ireland. . . ."

Mr. Britling shrugged his shoulders, and his face betrayed despair.

" My one consolation," he said, " in this storm is a talk I had last month with a young Irishwoman in Meath. She was a young person of twelve, and she took a fancy to me—I think because I went with her in an alleged dangerous canoe she was forbidden to navigate alone. All day the eternal Irish Question had banged over her observant head. When we were out on the water she suddenly decided to set me right upon a disregarded essential. ' You English,' she said, ' are just a bit disposed to take all this trouble seriously. Don't you fret yourself about it. . . . Half the time we're just laffing at you. You'd best leave us all alone. . . .' "

And then he went off at a tangent from his own anecdote.

" But look at this miserable spectacle ! " he cried. " Here is a chance of getting something like a reconciliation of the old feud of English and Irish, and something like a settlement of these ancient distresses, and there seems no power, no conscience, no sanity in any of us, sufficient to save it from this cantankerous bitterness, this sheer wicked mischief of mutual exasperation. . . . Just when Ireland is getting a gleam of prosperity. . . . A murrain on both your parties ! "

" I see, Mr. Britling, you'd hand us all over to Jim Larkin!"

" I'd hand you all over to Sir Horace Plunkett——"

" That doctrinaire dairyman ! " cried Lady Frensham, with an air of quite conclusive repartee. " You're hopeless, Mr. Britling. You're hopeless."

And Lady Homartyn, seeing that the phase of mere personal verdicts drew near, created a diversion by giving Lady Frensham a second cup of tea, and fluttering like a cooling fan about the heated brows of the disputants. She suggested tennis. . . .

§ 5

Mr. Britling was still flushed and ruffled as he and his guest returned towards the Dower House. He criticised England himself unmercifully, but he hated to think that in any respect she fell short of perfection ; even her defects he liked to imagine were just a subtler kind of power and wisdom. And Lady Frensham had stuck her voice and her gestures through all these amiable illusions. He was like a lover who calls his lady a foolish rogue, and is startled to find that facts and strangers do literally agree with him.

But it was so difficult to resolve Lady Frensham and the Irish squabble generally into anything better than idiotic mischief, that for a time he was unusually silent—wrestling with the problem, and Mr. Direck got the conversational initiative.

"To an American mind it's a little—startling," said Mr. Direck, "to hear ladies expressing such vigorous political opinions."

"I don't mind that," said Mr. Britling. "Women over here go into politics and into public houses—I don't see why they shouldn't. If such things are good enough for men they are good enough for women ; we haven't your sort of chivalry. But it's the peculiar malignant silliness of this sort of Toryism that's so discreditable. It's discreditable. There's no good in denying it. Those people you have heard and seen are a not unfair sample of our governing class—of a certain section of our governing class—as it is to-day. Not at all unfair. And you see how amazingly they haven't got hold of anything. There was a time when they could be politic. . . . Hidden away they have politic instincts even now. . . . But it makes me sick to think of this Irish business. Because, you know, it's true—we *are* drifting towards civil war there."

"You are of that opinion ? " said Mr. Direck.

"Well, isn't it so ? Here's all this Ulster gun-running— you heard how she talked of it ? Isn't it enough to drive the south into open revolt ? . . . "

"Is there very much, do you think, in the suggestion that some of this Ulster trouble is a German intrigue ? You and Mr. Philbert were saying things——"

"I don't know," said Mr. Britling shortly.

"I don't know," he repeated. "But it isn't because I don't think our Unionists and their opponents aren't foolish enough for anything of the sort. It's only because I don't believe that the Germans are so stupid as to do such things. . . . Why should they ? . . .

"It makes me—expressionless with anger," said Mr. Britling after a pause, reverting to his main annoyance. "They won't consider any compromise. It's sheer love of quarrelling. . . . Those people there think that nothing can possibly happen. They are like children in a nursery playing at rebellion. Un-scathed and heedless. Until there is death at their feet they will never realise they are playing with loaded guns. . . . "

For a time he said no more ; and listened perfunctorily while Mr. Direck tried to indicate the feeling in New England towards the Irish Question and the many difficult propositions an American politician has to face in that respect. And when Mr. Britling took up the thread of speech again it had little or no relation to Mr. Direck's observations.

"The psychology of all this recent insubordination and violence is—curious. Exasperating too. . . . I don't quite grasp it. . . . It's the same thing whether you look at the suffrage business or the labour people or at this Irish muddle. People may be too safe. You see we live at the end of a series of secure generations in which none of the great things of life have changed materially. We've grown up with no sense of danger—that is to say, with no sense of responsibility. None of us, none of us—for though I talk my actions belie me—really believe that life can change very fundamentally any more for ever. All this "—Mr. Britling waved his arm comprehensively—" looks as though it was bound to go on steadily for ever. It seems incredible that the system could be smashed. It seems incredible that anything we can do will ever smash the system. Lady Homartyn, for example, is incapable of believing that she won't always be able to have week-end parties at Claverings, and that the letters and the tea won't come to her bedside in the morning. Or if her imagination goes to the point of supposing that some day *she* won't be there to receive the tea, it means merely that she supposes somebody else will be. Her pleasant butler may fear to lose his ' situation,' but nothing on earth could make him imagine a time when there will not be a ' situation ' for him to lose. Old Asquith thinks that we always have got along, and that we always shall get along by being quietly artful and saying, ' Wait and see.' And it's just because we are all convinced that we are so safe against a general break-down that we are able to be so recklessly violent in our special cases. Why shouldn't women have the vote ? they argue. What does it matter ? And bang goes a bomb in Westminster Abbey. Why shouldn't Ulster create an impossible position ? And off trots some demented Carsonite to Germany to play at treason on some half word of the German Emperor's and buy half a million rifles. . . .

" Exactly like children being very, very naughty. . . .

" And," said Mr. Britling with a gesture to round off his discourse, " we do go on. We shall go on—until there is a spark right into the magazine. We have lost any belief we ever had that fundamental things happen. We English are everlasting children in an everlasting nursery. . . ."

And immediately he broke out again.

" The truth of the matter is that hardly any one has ever yet mastered the fact that the world is round. The world is round—like an orange. The thing is told us—like any old scandal—at school. For all practical purposes we forget it.—Practically we all live in a world as flat as a pancake. Where time never ends and nothing changes. Who really believes in any world outside the circle of the horizon ? Here we are and visibly nothing is changing. And so we go on to—nothing will ever change. It just goes on—in space, in time. If we could realise that round world beyond, then indeed we should go circumspectly. . . . If the world were like a whispering gallery, what whispers might we not hear now—from India, from Africa, from Germany, warnings from the past, intimations of the future. . . .

" We shouldn't heed them. . . ."

§ 6

And indeed at the very moment when Mr. Britling was saying these words, in Sarajevo in Bosnia, where the hour was somewhat later, men whispered together, and one held nervously to a black parcel that had been given him and nodded as they repeated his instructions, a black parcel with certain unstable chemicals and a curious arrangement of detonators therein, a black parcel destined ultimately to shatter nearly every landmark of Mr. Britling's and Lady Frensham's cosmogony. . . .

§ 7

When Mr. Direck and Mr. Britling returned to the Dower House the guest was handed over to Mrs. Britling and Mr. Britling vanished, to reappear at supper-time, for the Britlings had a supper in the evening instead of dinner. When Mr. Britling did reappear every trace of his vexation with the levities of British politics and the British ruling class had vanished altogether, and he was no longer thinking of all that might be happening in Germany or India. . . .

While he was out of the way Mr. Direck extended his acquaintance with the Britling household. He was taken round the garden and shown the roses by Mrs. Britling, and beyond the rose-garden in a little arbour they came upon Miss Corner reading a book. She looked very grave and pretty reading a book. Mr. Direck came to a pause in front of her, and Mrs. Britling stopped beside him. The young lady looked up and smiled.

" The last new novel ? " asked Mr. Direck pleasantly.

" Campanella's ' City of the Sun.' "

" My word ! but isn't that stiff reading ? "

" You haven't read it," said Miss Corner.

" It's a dry old book anyhow."

" It's no good pretending you have," she said, and there Mr. Direck felt the conversation had to end.

" That's a very pleasant young lady to have around," he said to Mrs. Britling as they went on towards the barn court.

" She's all at loose ends," said Mrs. Britling. " And she reads like a—— Whatever does read ? One drinks like a fish. One eats like a wolf."

They found the German tutor in a little court playing Badminton with the two younger boys. He was a plump young man with glasses and compact gestures ; the game progressed chiefly by misses and the score was counted in German. He won thoughtfully and chiefly through the ardour of the younger brother, whose enthusiastic returns invariably went out. Instantly the boys attacked Mrs. Britling with a concerted enthusiasm. " Mummy ! Is it to be dressing-up supper ? "

Mrs. Britling considered, and it was manifest that Mr. Direck was material to her answer.

"We wrap ourselves up in curtains and bright things instead of dressing," she explained. "We have a sort of wardrobe of fancy dresses. Do you mind?"

Mr. Direck was delighted.

And this being settled, the two small boys went off with their mother upon some special decorative project they had conceived and Mr. Direck was left for a time to Herr Heinrich.

Herr Heinrich suggested a stroll in the rose-garden, and as Mr. Direck had not hitherto been shown the rose-garden by Herr Heinrich, he agreed. Sooner or later everybody, it was evident, had got to show him that rose-garden.

"And how do you like living in an English household?" said Mr. Direck, getting to business at once. "It's interesting to an American to see this English establishment; and it must be still more interesting to a German."

"I find it very different from Pomerania," said Herr Heinrich. "In some respects it is more agreeable, in others less so. It is a pleasant life, but it is not a serious life.

"At any time," continued Herr Heinrich, "some one may say, 'Let us do this thing,' or 'Let us do that thing,' and then everything is disarranged.

"People walk into the house without ceremony. There is much kindness but no politeness. Mr. Britling will go away for three or four days, and when he returns and I come forward to greet him and bow, he will walk right past me, or he will say just like this, 'How do, Heinrich?'"

"Are you interested in Mr. Britling's writings?" Mr. Direck asked.

"There again I am puzzled. His work is known even in Germany. His articles are reprinted in German and Austrian reviews. You would expect him to have a certain authority of manner. You would expect there to be discussion at the table upon questions of philosophy and æsthetics. . . . It is not so. When I ask him questions it is often that they are not seriously answered. Sometimes it is as if he did not like the questions I asked of him. Yesterday I asked of him did he agree or did he not agree with Mr. Bernard Shaw. He just said—I wrote it down in my memoranda—he said: 'Oh! Mixed Pickles.' What can one understand of that?—Mixed Pickles!" . . .

The young man's sedulous blue eyes looked out of his pink face through his glasses at Mr. Direck, anxious for any light he could offer upon the atmospheric vagueness of this England.

He was, he explained, a student of philology preparing for his doctorate. He had not yet done his year of military service. He was studying the dialects of East Anglia——

"You go about among the people?" Mr. Direck inquired.

"No, I do not do that. But I ask Mr. Carmine and Mrs.

Britling and the boys many questions.   And sometimes I
talk to the gardener."

He explained how he would prepare his thesis and how
it would be accepted, and the nature of his army service and
the various stages by which he would subsequently ascend
in the orderly professorial life to which he was destined.   He
confessed a certain lack of interest in philology, but, he said,
" it is what I have to do."   And so he was going to do it all
his life through.   For his own part he was interested in ideas
of universal citizenship, in Esperanto and Ido and universal
languages and suchlike attacks upon the barriers between
man and man.   But the authorities at home did not favour
cosmopolitan ideas, and so he was relinquishing them.   " Here,
it is as if there were no authorities," he said with a touch
of envy.

Mr. Direck induced him to expand that idea.

Herr Heinrich made Mr. Britling his instance.   If Mr. Britling
were a German he would certainly have some sort of title, a
definite position, responsibility.   Here he was not even called
Herr Doktor. He said what he liked. Nobody rewarded him ;
nobody reprimanded him.   When Herr Heinrich asked him
of his position, whether he was above or below Mr. Bernard
Shaw or Mr. Arnold White or Mr. Garvin or any other publicist,
he made jokes.   Nobody here seemed to have a title and nobody
seemed to have a definite place.   There was Mr. Lawrence
Carmine ; he was a student of Oriental questions ; he had
to do with some public institution in London that welcomed
Indian students ; he was a Geheimrath——

" Eh ? " said Mr. Direck.

" It is—what do you call it ?—the Essex County Council."
But nobody took any notice of that.   And when Mr. Philbert,
who was a minister in the government, came to lunch he
was just like any one else.   It was only after he had gone
that Herr Heinrich had learned by chance that he was a
minister and " Right Honourable." . . .

" In Germany everything is definite.   Every man knows
his place, has his papers, is instructed what to do. . . ."

" Yet," said Mr. Direck, with his eyes on the glowing roses,
the neat arbour, the long line of the red wall of the vegetable-
garden and a distant gleam of corn-field, " it all looks orderly
enough."

" It is as if it had been put in order ages ago," said Herr
Heinrich.

" And was just going on by habit," said Mr. Direck, taking
up the idea.

Their comparisons were interrupted by the appearance of
" Teddy," the secretary, and the Indian young gentleman,
damp, and genial, as they explained, " from the boats."   It
seemed that " down below " somewhere was a pond with a
punt and an island and a toy dinghy.   And while they dis-

cussed swimming and boating, Mr. Carmine appeared from the direction of the park conversing gravely with the elder son. They had been for a walk and a talk together. There were proposals for a Badminton foursome. Mr. Direck emerged from the general interchange with Mr. Lawrence Carmine, and then strolled through the rose-garden to see the sunset from the end. Mr. Direck took the opportunity to verify his impression that the elder son was the present Mrs. Britling's stepson, and he also contrived by a sudden admiration for a distant row of evening primroses to deflect their path past the arbour in which the evening light must now be getting a little too soft for Miss Corner's book.

Miss Corner was drawn into the sunset party. She talked to Mr. Carmine and displayed, Mr. Direck thought, great originality of mind. She said " The City of the Sun " was like the cities the boys sometimes made on the playroom floor. She said it was the dearest little city, and gave some amusing particulars. She described the painted walls that made the tour of the Civitas Solis a liberal education. She asked Mr. Carmine, who was an authority on Oriental literature, why there were no Indian nor Chinese Utopias.

Now it had never occurred to Mr. Direck to ask why there were no Indian nor Chinese Utopias, and even Mr. Carmine seemed surprised to discover this deficiency.

" The primitive patriarchal village *is* Utopia to India and China," said Mr. Carmine, when they had a little digested the inquiry. " Or at any rate is their social ideal. They want no Utopias.

" Utopias came with cities," he said, considering the question. " And the first cities, as distinguished from courts and autocratic capitals, came with ships. India and China belong to an earlier age. Ships, trade, disorder, strange relationships, unofficial literature, criticism—and then this idea of some novel remaking of society. . . ."

§ 8

Then Mr. Direck fell into the hands of Hugh, the eldest son, and anticipating the inevitable, said that he liked to walk in the rose-garden. So they walked in the rose-garden.

" Do you read Utopias ? " said Mr. Direck, cutting any preface, in the English manner.

" Oh, *rather !* " said Hugh, and became at once friendly and confidential.

" We all do," he explained. " In England everybody talks of change and nothing ever changes."

" I found Miss Corner reading—what was it ?   the Sun People ?—some old classical Italian work."

" Campanella," said Hugh, without betraying the slightest interest in Miss Corner. " Nothing changes in England, because the people who want to change things change their minds before they change anything else. I've been in London talking for the last half-year. Studying art they call it. Before that I was a science student, and I want to be one again. Don't you think, sir, there's something about science—it's steadier than anything else in the world ? "

Mr. Direck thought that the moral truths of human nature were steadier than science, and they had one of those little discussions of real life that begin about a difference inadequately apprehended, and do not so much end as are abandoned. Hugh struck him as being more speculative and detached than any American college youth of his age that he knew—but that might not be a national difference but only the Britling strain. He seemed to have read more, and more independently, and to be doing less. And he was rather more restrained and self-possessed.

Before Mr. Direck could begin a proper inquiry into the young man's work and outlook, he had got the conversation upon America. He wanted tremendously to see America. " The dad says in one of his books that over here we are being and that over there you are beginning. It must be tremendously stimulating to think that your country is still being made. . . ."

Mr. Direck thought that an interesting point of view.

" Unless something tumbles down here, we never think of altering it," the young man remarked. " And even then we just shore it up."

His remarks had the effect of floating off from some busy mill of thought within him. Hitherto Mr. Direck had been inclined to think this silent observant youth with his hands in his pockets and his shoulders a little humped, as probably shy and adolescently ineffective. But the head was manifestly quite busy. . .

" Miss Corner," he began, taking the first thing that came into his head, and then he remembered that he had already made the remark he was going to make not five minutes ago.

" What form of art," he asked, " are you contemplating in your studies at the present time in London ? . . ."

Before this question could be dealt with at all adequately, the two small boys became active in the garden beating in everybody to " dress up " before supper. The secretary, Teddy, came in a fatherly way to look after Mr. Direck and see to his draperies.

§ 9

Mr. Direck gave his very best attention to this business of draping himself, for he had not the slightest intention of appearing ridiculous in the eyes of Miss Corner. Teddy came with an armful of stuff that he thought " might do."

" What'll I come as ? " asked Mr. Direck.

" We don't wear costumes," said Teddy. " We just put

on all the brightest things we fancy. If it's any costume at all, its Futurist."

"And surely why shouldn't one?" asked Mr. Direck, greatly struck by this idea. "Why should we always be tied by the fashions and periods of the past?"

He rejected a rather Mephistopheles-like costume of crimson and a scheme for a brigand-like ensemble based upon what was evidently an old bolero of Mrs. Britling's, and after some reflection he accepted some black silk tights. His legs were not legs to be ashamed of. Over this he tried various brilliant wrappings from the Dower House *armoire*, and chose at last, after some hesitation in the direction of a piece of gold and purple brocade, a big square of green silk curtain stuff adorned with golden pheasants and other large and dignified ornaments ; this he wore toga fashion over his light silken undervest—Teddy had insisted on the abandonment of his shirt "if you want to dance at all"—and fastened with a large green glass-jewelled brooch. From this his head and neck projected, he felt, with a tolerable dignity. Teddy suggested a fillet of green ribbon, and this Mr. Direck tried, but a ter prolonged reflection before the glass rejected. He was still weighing the effect of this fillet upon the mind of Miss Corner when Teddy left him to make his own modest preparations. Teddy's departure gave him a chance for profile studies by means of an arrangement of the long mirror and the table looking-glass that he had been too shy to attempt in the presence of the secretary. The general effect was quite satisfactory.

"Wa-a-a-l," he said with a quiver of laughter, "now who'd have thought it?" and smiled a consciously American smile at himself before going down.

The company was assembling in the panelled hall, and made a brilliant show in the light of the acetylene candles against a dark background. Mr. Britling in a black velvet cloak and black silk tights was a deeper shade among the shadows ; the high lights were Miss Corner and her sister, in glittering garments of peacock green and silver that gave a snakelike quality to their lithe bodies. They were talking to the German tutor, who had become a sort of cotton Cossack, a spectacled Cossack in buff and bright green. Mrs. Britling was dignified and beautiful in a purple djibbêh, and her stepson had become a handsome still figure of black and crimson. Teddy had contrived something elaborate and effective in the Egyptian style, with a fish-basket and a cuirass of that thin matting one finds behind wash-stands ; the small boys were brigands, with immensely baggy breeches and cummerbunds in which they had stuck a selection of paper-knives and toy pistols and similar weapons. Mr. Carmine and his young man had come provided with real Indian costumes ; the feeling of the company was that Mr. Carmine was a mullah.

The aunt-like lady with the noble nose stood out amidst
these levities in a black silk costume with a gold chain. She
refused, it seemed, to make herself absurd, though she encouraged the others to extravagance by nods and enigmatical
smiles.   Nevertheless she had put pink ribbons in her cap.
A family of father, golden-haired mother, and two young
daughters, sympathetically attired, had just arrived, and were
discarding their outer wrappings with the assistance of host
and hostess.

It was all just exactly what Mr. Direck had never expected
in England, and equally unexpected was the supper on a
long candle-lit table without a cloth. No servants were present,
but on a sideboard stood a cold salmon and cold joints and
kalter aufschnitt and kartoffel salat, and a variety of other
comestibles, and many bottles of beer and wine and whisky.
One helped oneself and anybody else one could, and Mr. Direck
did his best to be very attentive to Mrs. Britling and Miss
Corner, and was greatly assisted by the latter.

Everybody seemed extremely gay and bright-eyed.   Mr.
Direck found something exhilarating and oddly exciting in
all this unusual bright costume and in this easy mutual service ;
it made everybody seem franker and simpler. Even Mr. Britling had revealed a sturdy handsomeness that had not been
apparent to Mr. Direck before, and young Britling left no
doubts now about his good looks.   Mr. Direck forgot his
mission and his position and indeed things generally, in an
irrational satisfaction that his golden pheasants harmonised
with the glitter of the warm and smiling girl beside him.
And he sat down beside her—" You sit anywhere," said
Mrs. Britling—with far less compunction than in his ordinary
costume he would have felt for so direct a confession of preference.   And there was something in her eyes, it was quite
indefinable and yet very satisfying, that told him that now
he had escaped from the stern square imperatives of his
patriotic tailor in New York she had made a discovery of him.

Everybody chattered gaily, though Mr. Direck would have
found it difficult to recall afterwards what it was they chattered
about, except that somehow he acquired the valuable knowledge that Miss Corner was called Cecily and her sister Letty,
and then—so far old Essex custom held—the masculine
section was left for a few minutes for some imaginary drinking
and a lighting of cigars and cigarettes, after which everybody
went through interwoven moonlight and afterglow to the
barn. Mr. Britling sat down to a pianola in the corner and
began the familiar cadences of " Whistling Rufus."

" You dance ? " said Miss Cecily Corner.

" I've never been much of a dancing man," said Mr. Direck.
" What sort of dance is this ? "

" Just anything. A two-step."

Mr. Direck hesitated and regretted a well-spent youth,

and then Hugh came prancing forward with outstretched hands and swept her away.

Just for an instant Mr. Direck felt that this young man was a trifle superfluous. . . .

But it was very amusing dancing.

It wasn't any sort of taught formal dancing. It was a spontaneous retort to the leaping American music that Mr. Britling footed out. You kept time, and for the rest you did as your nature prompted. If you had a partner you joined hands, you fluttered to and from one another, you paced down the long floor together, you involved yourselves in romantic pursuits and repulsions with other couples. There was no objection to your dancing alone. Teddy, for example, danced alone in order to develop certain Egyptian gestures that were germinating in his brain. There was no objection to your joining hands in a cheerful serpent. . . .

Mr. Direck's gaze hung on to Cissie and her partner. They danced very well together ; they seemed to like and understand each other. It was natural of course for two young people like that, thrown very much together, to develop an affection for one another. . . . Still, she was older by three or four years.

It seemed unreasonable that the boy anyhow shouldn't be in love with her. . . .

It seemed unreasonable that any one shouldn't be in love with her. . . .

Then Mr. Direck remarked that Cissie was watching Teddy's manœuvres over her partner's shoulder. With real affection and admiration. . . .

But then most refreshingly she picked up Mr. Direck's gaze and gave him the slightest of smiles. She hadn't forgotten him.

The music stopped with an effect of shock, and all the bobbing, whirling figures became walking glories.

" Now that's not difficult, is it ? " said Miss Corner, glowing happily.

" Not when you do it," said Mr. Direck.

" I can't imagine an American not dancing a two-step. You must do the next with me. Listen ! It's ' 'Way Down Indiana ' . . . ah ! I knew you could."

Mr. Direck, too, understood now that he could, and they went off holding hands rather after the fashion of two skaters.

" My word ! " said Mr. Direck. " To think I'd be dancing."

But he said no more because he needed his breath.

He liked it, and he had another attempt with one of the visitor daughters, who danced rather more formally, and then Teddy took the pianola and Mr. Direck was astonished by the spectacle of an eminent British thinker in a whirl of black velvet and extremely active black legs engaged in a kind of Apache dance in pursuit of the visitor wife. In which Mr. Lawrence Carmine suddenly mingled.

" In Germany," said Herr Heinrich, " we do not dance like this. It could not be considered seemly. But it is very pleasant."

And then there was a waltz, and Herr Heinrich bowed to and took the visitor wife round three times, and returned her very punctually and exactly to the point whence he had taken her, and the Indian young gentleman (who must not be called " coloured ") waltzed very well with Cicely. Mr. Direck tried to take a tolerant European view of this brown and white combination. But he secured her as soon as possible from this Asiatic entanglement, and danced with her again, and then he danced with her again.

" Come and look at the moonlight," cried Mrs. Britling.

And presently Mr. Direck found himself strolling through the rose-garden with Cicely. She had the sweetest moonlight face, her white shining robe made her altogether a thing of moonlight. If Mr. Direck had not been in love with her before he was now altogether in love. Mamie Nelson, whose freakish unkindness had been rankling like a poisoned thorn in his heart all the way from Massachusetts, suddenly became Ancient History.

A tremendous desire for eloquence arose in Mr. Direck's soul, a desire so tremendous that no conceivable phrase he could imagine satisfied it. So he remained tongue-tied. And Cicely was tongue-tied, too. The scent of the roses just tinted the clear sweetness of the air they breathed.

Mr. Direck's mood was an immense solemnity, like a dark ocean beneath the vast dome of the sky, and something quivered in every fibre of his being, like moonlit ripples on the sea. He felt at the same time a portentous stillness and an immense enterprise. . . .

Then suddenly the pianola, pounding a cake-walk, burst out into ribald invitation. . . .

" Come back to dance ! " cried Cicely, like one from whom a spell has just been broken. And Mr. Direck, snatching at a vanishing scrap of everything he had not said, remarked, " I shall never forget this evening."

She did not seem to hear that.

They danced together again. And then Mr. Direck danced with the visitor lady, whose name he had never heard. And then he danced with Mrs. Britling, and then he danced with Letty. And then it seemed time for him to look for Miss Cecily again.

And so the cheerful evening passed until they were within a quarter of an hour of Sunday morning. Mrs. Britling went to exert a restraining influence upon the pianola.

" Oh ! one dance more ! " cried Cissie Corner.

" Oh ! one dance more ! " cried Letty.

" One dance more," Mr. Direck supported, and then things really *had* to end.

There was a rapid putting out of candles, and a stowing away of things by Teddy and the sons, two chauffeurs appeared from the region of the kitchen and brought Mr. Lawrence Carmine's car and the visitor family's car to the front door, and everybody drifted gaily through the moonlight and the big trees to the front of the house. And Mr. Direck saw the perambulator waiting—the mysterious perambulator—a little in the dark beyond the front door.

The visitor family and Mr. Carmine and his young Indian departed. " Come to hockey ! " shouted Mr. Britling to each departing car-load, and Mr. Carmine receding answered : " I'll bring three ! "

Then Mr. Direck, in accordance with a habit that had been growing on him throughout the evening, looked round for Miss Cissie Corner and failed to find her. And then behold she was descending the staircase with the mysterious baby in her arms. She held up a warning finger, and then glanced at her sleeping burden. She looked like a silvery Madonna. And Mr. Direck remembered that he was still in doubt about that baby. . . .

Teddy, who was back in his flannels, seized upon the per-ambulator. There was much careful baby stowing on the part of Cecily ; she displayed an infinitely maternal solicitude. Letty was away changing ; she reappeared jauntily taking leave, disregarding the baby absolutely, and Teddy departed bigamously, wheeling the perambulator between the two sisters into the hazes of the moonlight. There was much crying of good nights. Mr. Direck's curiosities narrowed down to a point of great intensity. . . .

Of course, Mr. Britling's circle must be a very " Advanced " circle. . . .

§ 10

Mr. Direck found he had taken leave of the rest of the company, and drifted into a little parlour with Mr. Britling and certain glasses and siphons and a whisky decanter on a tray. . . .

" It is a very curious thing," said Mr. Direck, " that in England I find myself more disposed to take stimulants and that I no longer have the need for iced water that one feels at home. I ascribe it to a greater humidity in the air. One is less dried and one is less braced. One is no longer pursued by a thirst, but one needs something to buck one up a little. Thank you. That is enough."

Mr. Direck took his glass of whisky and soda from Mr. Britling's hand.

Mr. Britling seated himself in an arm-chair by the fireplace and threw one leg carelessly over the arm. In his black velvet cloak and cap, and his black silk tights, he was very like a minor character, a court chamberlain, for example, in some

cloak and rapier drama. " I find this week-end dancing and
kicking about wonderfully wholesome," he said. "That
and our Sunday hockey. One starts the new week clear and
bright about the mind. Friday is always my worst working
day."

Mr. Direck leaned against the table, wrapped in his golden
pheasants, and appreciated the point.

" Your young people dance very cheerfully," he said.

" We all dance very cheerfully," said Mr. Britling.

" Then this Miss Corner," said Mr. Direck, " she is the sister,
I presume, is she ? of that pleasant young lady who is married—
she is married, isn't she ?—to the young man you call Teddy."

" I should have explained these young people. They're the
sort of young people we are producing over here now in quite
enormous quantity. They are the sort of equivalent of the
Russian Intelligentsia, an irresponsible middle-class with
ideas. Teddy, you know, is my secretary. He's the son, I
believe, of a Kilburn solicitor. He was recommended to me by
Datcher of *The Times*. He came down here and lived in
lodgings for a time. Then suddenly appeared the young lady."

" Miss Corner's sister ? "

" Exactly. The village was a little startled. The cottager
who had let the rooms came to me privately. Teddy is rather
touchy on the point of his personal independence, he considers
any demand for explanations as an insult, and probably all he
had said to the old lady was, ' This is Letty—come to share my
rooms.' I put the matter to him very gently. ' Oh, yes,' he
said, rather in the manner of some one who has overlooked a
trifle. ' I got married to her in the Christmas holidays. May
I bring her along to see Mrs. Britling ? ' We induced him to
go into a little cottage I rent. The wife was the daughter of a
Colchester journalist and printer. I don't know if you talked to
her."

" I've talked to the sister rather."

" Well, they're both idea'd. They're highly educated in the
sense that they do really think for themselves. Almost fiercely.
So does Teddy. If he thinks he hasn't thought anything he
thinks for himself, he goes off and thinks it different. The sister
is a teacher who wants to take the B.A. degree in London
University. Meanwhile she pays the penalty of her sex."

" Meaning—— ? " asked Mr. Direck startled.

" Oh ! that she puts in a great deal too much of her time
upon housework and minding her sister's baby."

" She's a very interesting and charming young lady indeed,"
said Mr. Direck. " With a sort of Western college freedom of
mind — and something about her that isn't American at
all."

Mr. Britling was following the train of his own thoughts.

" My household has some amusing contrasts," he said.
" I don't know if you have talked to that German ?

" He's always asking questions. And you tell him any old thing and he goes and writes it down in his room upstairs, and afterwards asks you another like it in order to perplex himself by the variety of your answers. He regards the whole world with a methodical distrust. He wants to document it and pin it down. He suspects it only too justly of disorderly impulses, and a capacity for self-contradiction. He is the most extraordinary contrast to Teddy, whose confidence in the universe amounts almost to effrontery. Teddy carries our national laxness to a foolhardy extent. He is capable of leaving his watch in the middle of Claverings Park and expecting to find it a month later—being carefully taken care of by a squirrel, I suppose—when he happens to want it. He's rather like a squirrel himself—without the habit of hoarding. He is in-capable of asking a question about anything ; he would be quite sure it was all right anyhow. He would feel that asking questions betrayed a want of confidence—was a sort of in-civility. But my German, if you notice—his normal expression is one of grave solicitude. He is like a conscientious ticket-collector among his impressions. And did you notice how beautifully my pianola rolls are all numbered and catalogued ? He did that. He set to work and did it as soon as he got here, just as a good cat when you bring it into a house sets to work and catches mice. Previously the pianola music was chaos. You took what God sent you."

" And he *looks* like a German," said Mr. Britling.

" He certainly does that," said Mr. Direck.

" He has the fair type of complexion, the rather full habit of body, the temperamental disposition, but in addition that close-cropped head—it is almost as if it were shaved—the plumpness, the glasses—those are things that are made. And the way he carries himself. And the way he thinks. His meticulousness. When he arrived he was delightful, he was wearing a student's corps cap and a rücksack, he carried a violin ; he seemed to have come out of a book. No one would ever dare to invent so German a German for a book. Now a young Frenchman or a young Italian or a young Russian coming here might look like a foreigner, but he wouldn't have the distinctive national stamp a German has. He wouldn't be plainly French or Italian or Russian. Other peoples are not made ; they are neither made nor created but proceeding— out of a thousand indefinable causes. The Germans are a triumph of directive will. I had to remark the other day that when my boys talked German they shouted. ' But when one talks German one *must* shout,' said Herr Heinrich. ' It is taught so in the schools.' And it is. They teach them to shout and to throw out their chests. Just as they teach them to read notice-boards and not think about politics. Their very ribs are not their own. My Herr Heinrich is comparatively a liberal thinker. He asked me the other day, ' But why should I give myself up to philology ?   But then,' he considered, ' it is what I have to do.' "

Mr. Britling seemed to have finished, and then just as Mr. Direck was planning a way of getting the talk back by way of Teddy to Miss Corner, he snuggled more deeply into his chair, reflected and broke out again.

" This contrast between Heinrich's carefulness and Teddy's easy-goingness, come to look at it, is I suppose one of the most fundamental in the world.   It reaches to everything.   It mixes up with education, statecraft, morals.   Will you make or will you take ?   Those are the two extreme courses in all such things.   I suppose the answer of wisdom to that is, like all wise answers, a compromise.   I suppose one must accept and then make all one can of it. .   . Have you talked at all to my eldest son ? "

" He's a very interesting young man indeed," said Mr. Direck.   " I should venture to say there's a very great deal in him.   I was most impressed by the few words I had with him."

" There, for example, is one of my perplexities," said Mr. Britling.

Mr. Direck waited for some further light on this sudden transition.

" Ah ! your troubles in life haven't begun yet.   Wait till you're a father.   That cuts to the bone.   You have the most delicate thing in the world in hand, a young kindred mind. You feel responsible for it, you know you are responsible for it ; and you lose touch with it.   You can't get at it.   Nowadays we've lost the old tradition of fatherhood by divine right— and we haven't got a new one.   I've tried not to be a cramping ruler, a director, a domestic tyrant to that lad—and in effect it's meant his going his own way. . . . I don't dominate.   I hoped to advise.   But you see he loves my respect and good opinion.   Too much.   When things go well I know of them. When the world goes dark for him, then he keeps his trouble from me.   Just when I would so eagerly go into it with him. . . . There's something the matter now, something—it may be grave.   I feel he wants to tell me.   And there it is !—it seems I am the last person to whom he can humiliate himself by a confession of blundering, or weakness. . . . Something I should just laugh at and say, ' That's in the blood of all of us, dear Spit of myself.   Let's see what's to be done.' . . ."

He paused and then went on, finding in the unfamiliarity and transitoriness of his visitor a freedom he might have failed to find with a close friend.

" I am frightened at times at all I don't know about in that boy's mind.   I know nothing of his religiosities.   He's my son and he must have religiosities.   I know nothing of his ideas or of his knowledge about sex and all that side of life.   I do not know of the things he finds beautiful.   I can guess at times, that's all ; when he betrays himself. . . . You see, you don't

know really what love is until you have children. One doesn't
love women. Indeed you don't ! One gives and gets ; it's a
trade. One may have tremendous excitements and expectations and overwhelming desires. That's all very well in its
way. But the love of children is an exquisite tenderness :
it rends the heart. It's a thing of God. And I lie awake at
nights and stretch out my hands in the darkness to this lad—
who will never know—until his sons come in their time. . . ."

He made one of his quick turns again.

"And that's where our English way makes for distresses.
Mr. Prussian respects and fears his father ; respects authorities,
attends, obeys and—*his father has a hold upon him*. But I
said to myself at the outset, ' No, whatever happens, I will
not usurp the place of God. I will not be the Priest-Patriarch of
my children. They shall grow and I will grow beside them,
helping but not cramping or overshadowing.' They grow
more. But they blunder more. Life ceases to be a discipline
and becomes an experiment. . . ."

"That's very true," said Mr. Direck, to whom it seemed the
time was ripe to say something. "This is the problem of
America perhaps even more than of England. Though I have
not had the parental experience you have undergone. . . . I
can see very clearly that a son is a very serious proposition."

"The old system of life was organisation. That is where
Germany is still the most ancient of European states. It's a
reversion to a tribal cult. It's atavistic. . . . To organise or
discipline, or mould characters or press authority, is to assume
that you have reached finality in your general philosophy.
It implies an assured end. Heinrich has his assured end, his
philological professorship or thereabouts as a part of the
Germanic machine. And that too has its assured end in German
national assertion. Here, we have none of those convictions.
We know we haven't finality, and so we are open and apologetic
and receptive, rather than wilful. . . . You see all organisation,
with its implication of finality, is death. We feel that. The
Germans don't. What you organise you kill. Organised morals
or organised religion or organised thought are dead morals and
dead religion and dead thought. Yet some organisation you
must have. Organisation is like killing cattle. If you do not
kill some the herd is just waste. But you mustn't kill all or
you kill the herd. The unkilled cattle are the herd, the continuation ; the unorganised side of life is the real life. The
reality of life is adventure, not performance. What isn't
adventure isn't life. What can be ruled about can be machined.
But priests and schoolmasters and bureaucrats get hold of
life and try to make it *all* rules, *all* etiquette and regulation and
correctitude. . . . And parents and the love of parents make
for the same thing. It is all very well to experiment for oneself,
but when one sees these dear things of one's own, so young and
inexperienced and so capable of every sort of gallant foolishness,

walking along the narrow plank, going down into dark jungles, ah ! then it makes one want to wrap them in laws and foresight and fence them about with ' Verboten ' boards in all the conceivable aspects. . . ."

" In America of course we do set a certain store upon youthful self-reliance," said Mr. Direck.

" As we do here. It's in your blood and our blood. It's the instinct of the English and the Irish anyhow to suspect government, and take the risks of the chancy way. . . . And manifestly the Russians, if you read their novelists, have the same twist in them. . . . When we get this young Prussian here, he's a marvel to us. He really believes in Law. He *likes* to obey. That seems a sort of joke to us. It's curious how foreign these Germans are to all the rest of the world. Because of their docility. Scratch the Russian and you get the Tartar. Educate the Russian or the American or the Englishman or the Irishman or Frenchman or any real northern European except the German, and you get the Anarchist, that is to say the man who dreams of order without organisation—of something beyond organisation. . . .

" It's one o'clock," said Mr. Britling abruptly, perceiving a shade of fatigue upon the face of his hearer and realising that his thoughts had taken him too far, " and Sunday. Let's go to bed."

§ 11

For a time Mr. Direck could not sleep. His mind had been too excited by this incessant day with all its novelties and all its provocations to comparison. The whole complicated spectacle grouped itself, with a naturalness and a complete want of logic that all who have been young will understand, about Cecily Corner.

She had to be in the picture, and so she came in as though she were the central figure, as though she were the quintessential England. There she was, the type, the blood, the likeness, of no end of Massachusetts families, the very same stuff indeed, and yet she was different. . . .

For a time his thoughts hovered ineffectively about certain details of her ear and cheek, and one may doubt this interest in these things was entirely international.

Then he found himself under way with an exposition of certain points to Mr. Britling. In the security of his bed he could imagine that he was talking very slowly and carefully while Mr. Britling listened ; already he was more than half-way to dreamland or he could not have supposed anything so incredible.

" There's a curious sort of difference," he was saying. " It is difficult to define, but on the whole I might express it by saying that such a gathering as this if it was in America would be drawn with harder lines, would show its bones more and have everything more emphatic. And just to take one illustrative point : in America in such a gathering as this there would be bound to be several jokes going on as it were, running jokes and running criticisms, from day to day and from week to week. . . . There would be jokes about your writing and your influence and jokes about Miss Corner's advanced reading. . . . You see, in America we pay much more attention to personal character. Here people, I notice, are not talked to about their personal characters at all, and many of them do not seem to be aware and do not seem to mind what personal characters they have. . . .

" And another thing I find noteworthy is the way in which what I might call mature people seem to go on having a good time instead of standing by and applauding the young people having a good time. . . . And the young people do not seem to have set out to have a good time at all. . . . Now in America, a charming girl like Miss Corner would be distinctly more aware of herself and her vitality than she is here, distinctly more. Her peculiarly charming side-long look, if I might make so free with her—would have been called attention to. It's a perfectly beautiful look, the sort of look some great artist would have loved to make immortal. It's a look I shall find it hard to forget. . . . But she doesn't seem to be aware in the least of it. In America she would be aware of it. She would be distinctly aware of it. She would have been *made* aware of it. She would have been advised of it. It would be looked for and she would know it was looked for. She would *give* it as a singer gives her most popular song. Mamie Nelson, for example, used to give a peculiar little throw back of the chin and a laugh. . . . It was talked about. People came to see it. . . .

" Of course Mamie Nelson was a very brilliant girl indeed. I suppose in England you would say we spoiled her. I suppose we did spoil her. . . ."

It came into Mr. Direck's head that for a whole day he had scarcely given a thought to Mamie Nelson. And now he was thinking of her—calmly. Why shouldn't one think of Mamie Nelson calmly ?

She was a proud imperious thing. There was something Southern in her. Very dark blue eyes she had, much darker than Miss Corner's. . . .

But how tortuous she had been behind that outward pride of hers ! For four years she had let him think he was the only man who really mattered in the world, and all the time quite clearly and definitely she had deceived him. She had made a fool of him and she had made a fool of the others perhaps— just to have her retinue and play the queen in her world. And at last humiliation, bitter humiliation, and Mamie with her chin in the air and her bright triumphant smile looking down on him.

Hadn't he, she asked, had the privilege of loving her?
She took herself at the value they had set upon her.
Well—somehow—that wasn't right. . . .

All the way across the Atlantic Mr. Direck had been trying
to forget her downward glance with the chin up, during that
last encounter—and other aspects of the same humiliation.
The years he had spent upon her! The time! Always relying
upon her assurance of a special preference for him. He tried
to think he was suffering from the pangs of unrequited love,
and to conceal from himself just how bitterly his pride and
vanity had been rent by her ultimate rejection. There had
been a time when she had given him reason to laugh in his
sleeve at Booth Wilmington.

Perhaps Booth Wilmington had also had reason for laughing
in his sleeve. . . .

Had she even loved Booth Wilmington? Or had she just
snatched at him? . . .

Wasn't he, Direck, as good a man as Booth Wilmington
anyhow? . . .

For some moments the old sting of jealousy rankled again.
He recalled the flaring rivalry that had ended in his defeat,
the competition of gifts and treats. . . . A thing so open
that all Carrierville knew of it, discussed it, took sides. . . .
And over it all Mamie with her flashing smile had sailed like
a processional goddess. . . .

Why, they had made jokes about him in the newspapers!

One couldn't imagine such a contest in Matching's Easy.
Yet surely even in Matching's Easy there are lovers.

Is it something in the air, something in the climate that
makes things harder and clearer in America? . . .

Cissie—why shouldn't one call her Cissie in one's private
thoughts anyhow?—would never be as hard and clear as
Mamie. She had English eyes—merciful eyes. . . .

That was the word—*merciful!*

The English light, the English air, are merciful. . . .

Merciful. . . .

They tolerate old things and slow things and imperfect
apprehensions. They aren't always getting at you. . . .

They don't laugh at you. . . . At least—they laugh differently. . . .

Was England the tolerant country? With its kind eyes
and its wary sidelong look. Toleration. In which everything
mellowed and nothing was destroyed. A soft country. A
country with a passion for imperfection. A padded country. . . .

England—all stuffed with soft feathers . . . under one's
ear. A pillow—with soft, kind Corners. . . . Beautiful rounded
Corners. . . . Dear, dear Corners. Cissie Corners. Corners.
Could there be a better family?

Massachusetts—but in heaven. . . .

Harps playing two-steps, and kind angels wrapped in moonlight.

> Very softly I and you,
> One tum, two tum, three tum, too,
> Off—we—go ! . . .

CHAPTER THREE

THE ENTERTAINMENT OF MR. DIRECK REACHES A CLIMAX

§ 1

BREAKFAST was in the open air, and a sunny, easy-going feast. Then the small boys laid hands on Mr. Direck and showed him the pond and the boats, while Mr. Britling strolled about the lawn with Hugh, talking rather intently. And when Mr. Direck returned from the boats in a state of greatly enhanced popularity he found Mr. Britling conversing over his garden railings with what was altogether a new type of Britisher in Mr. Direck's experience. It was a tall, lean sun-bitten youngish man of forty perhaps, in brown tweeds, looking more like the Englishman of the American illustrations than anything Mr. Direck had met hitherto. Indeed he came very near to a complete realisation of that ideal except that there was a sort of intensity about him, and that his clipped moustache had the restrained stiffness of a wiry-haired terrier. This gentleman Mr. Direck learned was Colonel Rendezvous. He spoke in clear short sentences, they had an effect of being punched out, and he was refusing to come into the garden and talk.

" Have to do my fourteen miles before lunch," he said. " You haven't seen Manning about, have you ? "

" He isn't here," said Mr. Britling, and it seemed to Mr. Direck that there was the faintest ambiguity in this reply.

" Have to go alone, then," said Colonel Rendezvous. " They told me that he had started to come here."

" I shall motor over to Bramley High Oak for your Boy Scout festival," said Mr. Britling.

" Going to have three thousand of 'em," said the Colonel. " Good show."

His steely eyes seemed to search the cover of Mr. Britling's garden for the missing Manning, and then he decided to give him up. " I must be going," he said. " So long. Come up ! "

A well-disciplined dog came to heel, and the lean figure had given Mr. Direck a semi-military salutation and gone upon its way. It marched with a long elastic stride ; it never looked back.

" Manning," said Mr. Britling, " is probably hiding up in my rose-garden."

" Curiously enough, I guessed from your manner that that might be the case," said Mr. Direck.

" Yes. Manning is a London journalist. He has a little cottage about a mile over there "—Mr. Britling pointed vaguely—" and he comes down for the week-ends. And Rendezvous has found out he isn't fit. And everybody ought to be fit. That is the beginning and end of life for Rendezvous. Fitness. An almost mineral quality, an insatiable activity of body, great mental simplicity. So he takes possession of poor old Manning and trots him for that fourteen miles—at four miles an hour. Manning goes through all the agonies of death and damnation, he half dissolves, he pants and drags for the first eight or ten miles, and then I must admit he rather justifies Rendezvous' theory. He is to be found in the afternoon in a hammock suffering from blistered feet, but otherwise unusually well. But if he can escape it, he does. He hides."

" But if he doesn't want to go with Colonel Rendezvous, why does he ? " said Mr. Direck.

" Well, Rendezvous is accustomed to the command of men. And Manning's only way of refusing things is on printed forms. Which he doesn't bring down to Matching's Easy. Ah ! behold ! "

Far away across the lawn between two blue cedars there appeared a leisurely form in grey flannels and a loose tie, advancing with manifest circumspection.

" He's gone," cried Britling.

The leisurely form, obviously amiable, obviously a little out of condition, became more confident, drew nearer.

" I'm sorry to have missed him," he said cheerfully. " I thought he might come this way. It's going to be a very warm day indeed. Let us sit about somewhere and talk."

" Of course," he said, turning to Direck, " Rendezvous is the life and soul of the country."

They strolled towards a place of seats and hammocks between the big trees and the rose-garden and the talk turned for a time upon Rendezvous. " They have the tidiest garden in Essex," said Manning. " It's not Mrs. Rendezvous' fault that it is so. Mrs. Rendezvous, as a matter of fact, has a taste for the picturesque. She just puts the things about in groups in the beds. She wants them, she says, to grow anyhow. She desires a romantic disorder. But she never gets it. When he walks down the path all the plants dress instinctively. . . . And there's a tree near their gate ; it used to a be willow. You can ask any old man in the village. But ever since Rendezvous took the place it's been trying to present arms. With the most extraordinary results. I was passing the other day with old Windershin. ' You see that there old poplar,' he said. ' It's a willow,' said I. ' No, he said, ' it did used to be a willow before Colonel Rendezvous he came. But now it's a poplar.' . . . And by Jove, it *is* a poplar ! "

The conversation thus opened by Manning centred for a time upon Colonel Rendezvous. He was presented as a monster of energy and self-discipline ; as the determined foe of every form of looseness, slackness, and easy-goingness.

" He's done wonderful work for the local Boy Scout movement," said Manning.

" It's Kitchenerism," said Britling.

" It's the army side of the efficiency stunt," said Manning.

There followed a digression upon the Boy Scout movement, and Mr. Direck made comparisons with the propaganda of Seton Thompson in America. " Teddy Rooseveltism," said Manning. " It's a sort of reaction against everything being too easy and too safe."

" It's got its anti-decadent side," said Mr. Direck.

" If there is such a thing as decadence," said Mr. Britling.

" If there wasn't such a thing as decadence," said Manning, " we journalists would have had to invent it." . . .

" There is something tragic in all this—what shall I call it ?—Kitchenerism," Mr. Britling reflected. " Here you have it rushing about and keeping itself—screwed up, and trying desperately to keep the country screwed up. And all because there may be a war some day somehow with Germany. Provided Germany *is* insane. It's that war, like some sort of bee in Rendezvous' brains, that is driving him along the road now to Market Saffron—he always keeps to the roads because they are severer—through all the dust and sunshine. When he might be here gossiping. . . .

" And you know, I don't see that war coming," said Mr. Britling. " I believe Rendezvous sweats in vain. I can't believe in that war. It has held off for forty years. It may hold off for ever."

He nodded his head towards the German tutor, who had come into view across the lawn, talking profoundly with Mr. Britling's eldest son.

" Look at that pleasant person. There he is—*echt Deutsch*—if anything ever was. Look at my son there ! Do you see the two of them engaged in mortal combat ? The thing's too ridiculous. The world grows sane. They may fight in the Balkans still ; in many ways the Balkan States are in the very rear of civilisation ; but to imagine decent countries like this or Germany going back to bloodshed ! No. . . . When I see Rendezvous keeping it up and keeping it up, I begin to see just how poor Germany must be keeping it up. I begin to realise how sick Germany must be getting of the highroad and the dust and heat and the everlasting drill and restraint. . . . My heart goes out to the South Germans. Old Manning here always reminds me of Austria. Think of Germany coming like Rendezvous on a Sunday morning, and looking stiffly over Austria's fence. ' Come for a good hard walk, man. Keep fit.' . . ."

" But suppose this Balkan trouble becomes acute," said Manning.

" It hasn't ; it won't. Even if it did we should keep out of it."

" But suppose Russia grappled Austria, and Germany flung herself suddenly upon France—perhaps taking Belgium on the way."

" Oh !—we should fight. Of course we should fight. Could anyone but a congenital idiot suppose we shouldn't fight ? They know we should fight. They aren't altogether idiots in Germany. But the thing's absurd. Why *should* Germany attack France ? It's as if Manning here took a hatchet suddenly and assailed Edith. . . It's just the dream of their military journalists. It's such schoolboy nonsense. Isn't that a beautiful pillar rose ? Edith only put it in last year. . . . I hate all this talk of wars and rumours of wars. . . . It's worried all my life. And it gets worse and it gets emptier every year. . . ."

§ 2

Now just at that moment there was a loud report. . . .

But neither Mr. Britling nor Mr. Manning nor Mr. Direck was interrupted or incommoded in the slightest degree by that report. Because it was too far off over the curve of this round world to be either heard or seen at Matching's Easy. Nevertheless it was a very loud report. It occurred at an open space by a river that ran through a cramped Oriental city, a city spiked with white minarets and girt about by bare hills under a blazing afternoon sky. It came from a black parcel that the Archduke Francis Ferdinand of Austria, with great presence of mind, had just flung out from the open hood of his automobile, where, tossed from the side of the quay, it had descended a few seconds before. It exploded as it touched the cobbled road just under the front of the second vehicle in the procession, and it blew to pieces the front of the automobile and injured the aide-de-camp who was in it and several of the spectators. Its thrower was immediately gripped by the bystanders. The procession stopped. There was a tremendous commotion amongst that brightly costumed crowd, a hot excitement in vivid contrast to the Sabbath calm of Matching's Easy. . . .

Mr. Britling, to whom the explosion was altogether inaudible, continued his dissertation upon the common sense of the world and the practical security of our Western peace.

§ 3

Lunch was an open-air feast again. Three visitors had dropped in ; they had motored down from London piled up on a motor-cycle and a side-car ; a brother and two sisters they seemed to be, and they had apparently reduced hilariousness to a principle. The rumours of coming hockey that had been floating on the outskirts of Mr. Direck's consciousness ever since his arrival thickened and multiplied. . . . It crept into his mind that he was expected to play. . . .

He decided he would not play. He took various people into his confidence. He told Mr. Britling, and Mr. Britling said, " We'll make you full-back, where you'll get a hit now and then and not have very much to do. All you have to remember is to hit with the flat side of your stick and not raise it above your shoulders." He told Teddy, and Teddy said, " I strongly advise you to dress as thinly as you can consistently with decency, and put your collar and tie in your pocket before the game begins. Hockey is properly a winter game." He told the maiden aunt-like lady with the prominent nose, and she said almost enviously, " Every one here is asked to play except me. I assuage the perambulator. I suppose one mustn't be envious. I don't see why I shouldn't play. I'm not so old as all that." He told Hugh, and Hugh warned him to be careful not to get hold of one of the sprung sticks. He considered whether it wouldn't be wiser to go to his own room and lock himself in, or stroll off for a walk through Claverings Park. But then he would miss Miss Corner, who was certain, it seemed, to come up for hockey. On the other hand, if he did not miss her he might make himself ridiculous in her eyes, and efface the effect of the green silk stuff with the golden pheasants.

He determined to stay behind until she arrived, and explain to her that he was not going to play. He didn't somehow want her to think he wasn't perfectly fit to play.

Mr. Carmine arrived in an automobile with two Indians and a gentleman who had been a prospector in Alaska, the family who had danced overnight at the Dower House reappeared, and then Mrs. Teddy, very detached with a special hockey-stick, and Miss Corner wheeling the perambulator. Then came further arrivals. At the earliest opportunity Mr. Direck secured the attention of Miss Corner, and lost his interest in any one else.

" I can't play this hockey," said Mr. Direck. " I feel strange about it. It isn't an American game. Now if it were baseball—— ! "

He left her to suppose him uncommonly hot stuff at baseball.

" If you're on my side," said Cecily, " mind you pass to me."

It became evident to Mr. Direck that he was going to play this hockey after all.

" Well," he said, " if I've got to play hockey, I guess I've got to play hockey. But can't I just get a bit of practice somewhere before the game begins ? "

So Miss Corner went off to get two sticks and a ball and
came back to instruct Mr. Direck. She said he had a good
eye. The two small boys scenting play in the air got sticks
and joined them. The overnight visitor's wife appeared from
the house in abbreviated skirts, and wearing formidable shin-
guards. With her abundant fair hair, which was already breaking loose, so to speak, to join the fray, she looked like a short
stout dismounted Valkyr. Her gaze was clear and firm.

§ 4

Hockey as it was played at the Dower House at Matching's
Easy before the war was a game combining danger, physical
exercise and kindliness in a very high degree. Except for
the infant in the perambulator and the outwardly calm but
inwardly resentful aunt, who wheeled the child up and down
in a position of maximum danger just behind the unnetted
goal, every one was involved. Quite able-bodied people
acquainted with the game played forward, the less well-
informed played a defensive game behind the forward line,
elderly, infirm, and bulky persons were used chiefly as obstacles
in goal. Several players wore padded leg-guards, and all
players were assumed to have them and expected to behave
accordingly.

Proceedings began with an invidious ceremony called
picking up. This was heralded by Mr. Britling, clad in the
diaphanous flannels and bearing a hockey-stick, advancing
with loud shouts to the centre of the hockey-field. " Pick
up ! Pick up ! " echoed the young Britlings.

Mr. Direck became aware of a tall, drooping man with
long hair and long digressive legs in still longer white flannel
trousers, and a face that was somehow familiar. He was
talking with affectionate intimacy to Manning, and suddenly
Mr. Direck remembered that it was in Manning's weekly
paper, *The Sectarian*, in which a bitter caricaturist enlivened
a biting text, that he had become familiar with the features
of Manning's companion. It was Raeburn, Raeburn the
insidious, Raeburn the completest product of the party
system. . . . Well, that was the English way. " Come for
the pick up ! " cried the youngest Britling, seizing upon Mr.
Direck's elbow. It appeared that Mr. Britling and the overnight dinner-guest—Mr. Direck never learned his name—were
picking up.

Names were shouted. " I'll take Cecily ! " Mr. Direck
heard Mr. Britling say quite early. The opposing sides as they
were picked fell into two groups. There seemed to be difficulties
about some of the names. Mr. Britling, pointing to the more
powerful-looking of the Indian gentlemen, said, " You, sir."

" I'm going to speculate on Mr. Dinks," said Mr. Britling's
opponent.

Mr. Direck gathered that Mr. Dinks was to be his hockey name.

" You're on *our* side," said Mrs. Teddy. " I think you'll have to play forward, outer right, and keep a sharp eye on Cissie."

" I'll do what I can," said Mr. Direck.

His captain presently confirmed this appointment.

His stick was really a sort of club and the ball was a firm hard cricket-ball. . . . He resolved to be very gentle with Cecily, and see that she didn't get hurt.

The sides took their places for the game, and a kind of order became apparent to Mr. Direck. In the centre stood Mr. Britling and the opposing captain, and the ball lay between them. They were preparing to " bully-off " and start the game. In a line with each of them were four other forwards. They all looked spirited and intent young people, and Mr. Direck wished he had had more exercise to justify his own alert appearance. Behind each centre forward hovered one of the Britling boys. Then on each side came a vaguer row of three backs, persons of gentler disposition or maturer years. They included Mr. Raeburn, who was considered to have great natural abilities for hockey but little experience. Mr. Raeburn was behind Mr. Direck. Mrs. Britling was the centre back. Then in a corner of Mr. Direck's side was a small girl of six or seven, and in the half-circle about the goal a lady in a motoring dust-coat and a very short little man whom Mr. Direck had not previously remarked. Mr. Lawrence Carmine, stripped to the braces, which were richly ornamented with Oriental embroidery, kept goal for our team.

The centre forwards went through a rapid little ceremony. They smote their sticks on the ground, and then hit the sticks together. " One," said Mr. Britling. The operation was repeated. " Two," . . . " Three."

Smack, Mr. Britling had got it and the ball had gone to the shorter and sturdier of the younger Britlings, who had been standing behind Mr. Direck's captain. Crack, and it was away to Teddy ; smack, and it was coming right at Direck.

" Lordy ! " he said and prepared to smite it.

Then something swift and blue had flashed before him, intercepted the ball and shot it past him. This was Cecily Corner, and she and Teddy were running abreast like the wind towards Mr. Raeburn.

" Hey ! " cried Mr. Raeburn, " stop ! " and advanced, as it seemed to Mr. Direck, with unseemly and threatening gestures towards Cissie.

But before Mr. Direck could adjust his mind to this new phase of affairs, Cecily had passed the right honourable gentleman with the same mysterious ease with which she had flashed by Mr. Direck, and was bearing down upon the miscellaneous Landwehr which formed the " backs " of Mr. Direck's side.

" *You* rabbit ! " cried Mr. Raeburn, and became extraordinarily active in pursuit, administering great lengths of arm and leg with a centralised efficiency he had not hitherto displayed.

Running hard to the help of Mr. Raeburn was the youngest Britling boy, a beautiful contrast. It was like a puffball supporting and assisting a conger-eel. In front of Mr. Direck the little stout man was being alert. Teddy was supporting the attack near the middle of the field, crying " Centre ! " while Mr. Britling, very round and resolute, was bouncing straight towards the threatened goal. But Mrs. Teddy, running as swiftly as her sister, was between Teddy and the ball. Whack ! the little short man's stick had clashed with Cecily's. Confused things happened with sticks and feet, and the little short man appeared to be trying to cut down Cecily as one cuts down a tree, she tried to pass the ball to her centre forward—too late, and then Mrs. Teddy had intercepted it, and was flickering back towards Mr. Britling's goal in a rush in which Mr. Direck perceived it was his duty to join.

Yes, he had to follow up Mrs. Teddy and pick up the ball if he had a chance and send it in to her or the captain or across to the left forwards, as circumstances might decide. It was perfectly clear.

Then came his moment. The little formidably padded lady who had dined at the Dower House overnight made a gallant attack upon Mrs. Teddy. Out of the confusion of this clash the ball spun into Mr. Direck's radius. Where should he smite and how ? A moment of reflection was natural.

But now the easy-fitting discipline of the Dower House style of hockey became apparent. Mr. Direck had last observed the tall young Indian gentleman, full of vitality and anxious for destruction, far away in the distance on the opposing right wing. Regardless of the more formal methods of the game, this young man had resolved, without further delay and at any cost, to hit the ball hard, and he was travelling like some Asiatic typhoon with an extreme velocity across the remonstrances of Mr. Britling and the general order of his side. Mr. Direck became aware of him just before his impact. There was a sort of collision from which Mr. Direck emerged with a feeling that one side of his face was permanently flattened, but still gallantly resolved to hit the comparatively lethargic ball. He and the staggered but resolute Indian clashed sticks again. And Mr. Direck had the best of it. Years of experience couldn't have produced a better pass to the captain. . . .

" Good pass ! "

Apparently from one of the London visitors.

But this was *some* game !

The ball executed some rapid movements to and fro across the field. Our side was pressing hard. There was a violent convergence of miscellaneous backs and such-like irregulars

upon the threatened goal. Mr. Britling's dozen was rapidly
losing its disciplined order. One of the side-car ladies and the
gallant Indian had shifted their activities to the defensive
back, and with them was a spectacled gentleman waving his
stick, high above all recognised rules. Mr. Direck's captain and
both Britling boys hurried to join the fray. Mr. Britling, who
seemed to Mr. Direck to be for a captain rather too demagogic,
also ran back to rally his forces by loud cries. " Pass outwardly ! " was the burthen of his contribution.

The struggle about the Britling goal ceased to be a game
and became something between a fight and a social gathering.
Mr. Britling's goal-keeper could be heard shouting, " I can't
see the ball ! *Lift your feet !* " The crowded conflict lurched
towards the goal-posts. " My shin ! " cried Mr. Manning.
" No, you *don't !* "

Whack, but again whack !

Whack ! " Ah ! *would* you ? " Whack.

" Goal ! " cried the side-car gentleman.

" Goal ! " cried the Britling boys. . . .

Mr. Manning, as goal-keeper, went to recover the ball,
but one of the Britling boys politely anticipated him.

The crowd became inactive, and then began to drift back to
loosely conceived positions.

" It's no good swarming into goal like that," Mr. Britling,
with a faint asperity in his voice, explained to his followers.
" We've got to keep open and not *crowd* each other."

Then he went confidentially to the energetic young Indian to
make some restrictive explanation of his activities.

Mr. Direck strolled back towards Cecily. He was very warm
and a little blown, but not, he felt, disgraced. He was winning.

" You'll have to take your coat off," she said.

It was a good idea.

It had occurred to several people, and the boundary-line
was already dotted with hastily discarded jackets and wraps
and so forth. But the lady in the motoring dust-coat was
buttoning it to the chin.

" One goal love," said the minor Britling boy.

" We haven't begun yet, Sunny," said Cecily.

" Sonny ! That's American," said Mr. Direck.

" No. We call him Sunny Jim," said Cecily. " They're
bullying off again."

" Sunny Jim's American too," said Mr. Direck, returning to
his place. . . .

The struggle was resumed. And soon it became clear that the
first goal was no earnest of the quality of the struggle. Teddy
and Cecily formed a terribly efficient combination. Against
their brilliant rushes, supported in a vehement but effective
manner by the Indian to their right and guided by loud shout-
ings from Mr. Britling (centre), Mr. Direck and the side-car
lady and Mr. Raeburn struggled in vain. One swift advance

was only checked by the dust-coat, its folds held the ball until help arrived ; another was countered by a tremendous swipe of Mr. Raeburn's that sent the ball within an inch of the youngest Britling's head and right across the field ; the third resulted in a swift pass from Cecily to the elder Britling son away on her right, and he shot the goal neatly through the lattice of Mr. Lawrence Carmine's defensive movements. And after that very rapidly came another goal for Mr. Britling's side and then another.

Then Mr. Britling cried out that it was " Half Time," and explained to Mr. Direck that whenever one side got to three goals they considered it was half time and had five minutes' rest and changed sides. Everybody was very hot and happy, except the lady in the dust-coat, who was perfectly cool. In everybody's eyes shone the light of battle, and not a shadow disturbed the brightness of the afternoon for Mr. Direck except a certain unspoken anxiety about Mr. Raeburn's trousers.

You see Mr. Direck had never seen Mr. Raeburn before, and knew nothing about his trousers.

They appeared to be coming down.

To begin with they had been rather loose over the feet and turned up, and as the game progressed fold after fold of concertina-ed flannel gathered about his ankles. Every now and then Mr. Raeburn would seize the opportunity of some respite from the game to turn up a fresh six inches or so of this accumulation. Naturally Mr. Direck expected this policy to end unhappily. He did not know that the flannel trousers of Mr. Raeburn were like a river, that they could come down for ever and still remain inexhaustible. . . .

He had visions of this scene of happy innocence being suddenly blasted by a monstrous disaster. . . .

Apart from this worry Mr. Direck was as happy as any one there !

Perhaps these apprehensions affected his game. At any rate he did nothing that pleased him in the second half, Cecily danced all over him and round and about him, and in the course of ten minutes her side had won the two remaining goals with a score of Five-One ; and five goals is " game " by the standards of Matching's Easy.

And then with the very slightest of delays these insatiable people picked up again. Mr. Direck slipped away and returned in a white silk shirt, tennis trousers and a belt. This time he and Cecily were on the same side, the Cecily-Teddy combination was broken, and he it seemed was to take the place of the redoubtable Teddy on the left wing with her.

This time the sides were better chosen and played a long, obstinate, even game. One-One. One-Two. One-Three. (Half Time.) Two-Three. Three all. Four-Three. Four all. . . .

By this time Mr. Direck was beginning to master the simple strategy of the sport. He was also beginning to master the fact that Cecily was the quickest, nimblest, most indefatigable player on the field. He scouted for her and passed to her. He developed tacit understandings with her. Ideas of protecting her had gone to the four winds of heaven. Against them Teddy and a side-car girl with Raeburn in support made a memorable struggle. Teddy was as quick as a cat. " Four-Three " looked like winning, but then Teddy and the tall Indian and Mrs. Teddy pulled square. They almost repeated this feat and won, but Mr. Manning saved the situation with an immense oblique hit that sent the ball to Mr. Direck. He ran with the ball up to Raeburn and then dodged and passed to Cecily. There was a lively struggle to the left ; the ball was hit out by Mr. Raeburn and thrown in by a young Britling ; lost by the forwards and rescued by the padded lady. Forward again ! This time will do it !

Cecily away to the left had worked round Mr. Raeburn once more. Teddy, realising that things were serious, was tearing back to attack her.

Mr. Direck supported with silent intentness. " Centre ! " cried Mr. Britling. " Cen-tre ! "

" Mr. Direck ! " came her voice, full of confidence. (Of such moments is the heroic life.) The ball shot behind the hurtling Teddy. Mr. Direck stopped it with his foot, a trick he had just learned from the eldest Britling son. He was neither slow nor hasty. He was in the half-circle, and the way to the goal was barred only by the dust-coat lady and Mr. Lawrence Carmine. He made as if to shoot to Mr. Carmine's left and then smacked the ball, with the swiftness of a serpent's stroke, to his right.

He'd done it ! Mr. Carmine's stick and feet were a yard away.

Then hard on this wild triumph came a flash of horror. One can't see everything. His eye followed the ball's trajectory. . . .

Directly in its line of flight was a perambulator.

The ball missed the legs of the lady with the noble nose by a kind of miracle, hit and glanced off the wheel of the perambulator, and went spinning into a border of antirrhinums.

" Good ! " cried Cecily. " Splendid shot ! "

He'd shot a goal. He'd done it well. The perambulator it seemed didn't matter. Though apparently the impact had awakened the baby. In the margin of his consciousness was the figure of Mr. Britling remarking : " Aunty. You really mustn't wheel the perambulator *just* there."

" I thought," said the aunt, indicating the goal-posts by a facial movement, " that those two sticks would be a sort of protection. . . . Aah ! *Did* they then ? "

Never mind that.

" That's *game* ! " said one of the junior Britlings to Mr. Direck with a note of high appreciation, and the whole party, relaxing and crumpling like a lowered flag, moved towards the house and tea.

§ 5

" We'll play some more after tea," said Cecily. " It will be cooler then."

" My word, I'm beginning to like it," said Mr. Direck.

" You're going to play very well," she said.

And such is the magic of a game that Mr. Direck was humbly proud and grateful for her praise, and trotted along by the side of this creature who had revealed herself so swift and resolute and decisive, full to overflowing of the mere pleasure of just trotting along by her side. And after tea, which was a large confused affair, enlivened by wonderful and entirely untruthful reminiscences of the afternoon by Mr. Raeburn, they played again, with fewer inefficients and greater skill and swiftness, and Mr. Direck did such quick and intelligent things that everybody declared that he was a hockey-player straight from heaven. The dusk, which at last made the position of the ball too speculative for play, came all too soon for him. He had played in six games, and he knew he would be as stiff as a Dutch doll in the morning. But he was very, very happy.

The rest of the Sunday evening was essentially a sequel to the hockey.

Mr. Direck changed again, and after using some embrocation, that Mrs. Britling recommended very strongly, came down in a black jacket and a cheerfully ample black tie. He had a sense of physical well-being such as he had not experienced since he came aboard the liner at New York. The curious thing was that it was not quite the same sense of physical well-being that one had in America. That is bright and clear and a little dry, this was—humid. His mind quivered contentedly, like sunset midges over a lake—it had no hard bright flashes—and his body wanted to sit about. His sense of intimacy with Cecily increased each time he looked at her. When she met his eyes she smiled. He'd caught her style now, he felt ; he attempted no more compliments, and was frankly her pupil at hockey and Badminton. After supper Mr. Britling renewed his suggestion of an automobile excursion on the Monday.

" There's nothing to take you back to London," said Mr. Britling, " and we could just hunt about the district with the little old car and see everything you want to see. . . ."

Mr. Direck did not hesitate three seconds. He thought of Gladys ; he thought of Miss Cecily Corner.

" Well, indeed," he said, " if it isn't burthening you, if I'm not being any sort of inconvenience here for another night, I'd be really very glad indeed of the opportunity of going around and seeing all these ancient places. . . ."

§ 6

The newspapers came next morning at nine, and were full of the Sarajevo Murders. Mr. Direck got *The Daily Chronicle* and found headlines quite animated for a British paper.

"Who's this Archduke," he asked, "anyhow? And where is this Bosnia? I thought it was a part of Turkey."

"It's in Austria," said Teddy.

"It's in the middle ages," said Mr. Britling. "What an odd, pertinacious business it seems to have been. First one bomb, then another; then finally the man with the pistol. While we were strolling about the rose-garden. It's like something out of ' The Prisoner of Zenda.' "

"Please," said Herr Heinrich.

Mr. Britling assumed an attentive expression.

"Will not this generally affect European politics? "

"I don't know. Perhaps it will."

"It says in the paper that Serbia has sent those bombs to Sarajevo."

"It's like another world," said Mr. Britling, over his paper. "Assassination as a political method. Can you imagine anything of the sort happening nowadays west of the Adriatic? Imagine some one assassinating the American Vice-President, and the bombs being at once ascribed to the arsenal at Toronto ! . . . We take our politics more sadly in the West. . . . Won't you have another egg, Direck? "

"Please ! Might this not lead to a war ? "

"I don't think so. Austria may threaten Serbia, but she doesn't want to provoke a conflict with Russia. It would be going too near the powder-magazine. But it's all an extraordinary business."

"But if she did ? " Herr Heinrich persisted.

"She won't. . . . Some years ago I used to believe in the inevitable European war," Mr. Britling explained to Mr. Direck, " but it's been threatened so long that at last I've lost all belief in it. The Powers wrangle and threaten. They're far too cautious and civilised to let the guns go off. If there was going to be a war it would have happened two years ago when the Balkan League fell upon Turkey. Or when Bulgaria attacked Serbia. . . ."

Herr Heinrich reflected, and received these conclusions with an expression of respectful edification.

"I am naturally anxious," he said, " because I am taking tickets for my holidays at an Esperanto Conference at Boulogne."

§ 7

"There is only one way to master such a thing as driving an automobile," said Mr. Britling outside his front door, as he took his place in the driver's seat, " and that is to resolve that from the first you will take no risks. Be slow if you like. Stop and think when you are in doubt. But do nothing rashly, permit no mistakes."

It seemed to Mr. Direck as he took his seat beside his host that this was admirable doctrine.

They started out of the gates with an extreme deliberation. Indeed twice they stopped dead in the act of turning into the road, and the engine had to be restarted.

" You will laugh at me," said Mr. Britling : " but I'm resolved to have no blunders this time."

" I don't laugh at you. It's excellent," said Mr. Direck.

" It's the right way," said Mr. Britling. " Care—oh, damn ! I've stopped the engine again. Ugh !—ah ! *so l*—Care, I was saying—and calm."

" Don't think I want to hurry you," said Mr. Direck. " I don't."

They passed through the village at a slow, agreeable pace, tooting loudly at every corner, and whenever a pedestrian was approached. Mr. Direck was reminded that he had still to broach the lecture project to Mr. Britling. So much had happened——

The car halted abruptly and the engine stopped.

" I thought that confounded hen was thinking of crossing the road," said Mr. Britling. " Instead of which she's gone through the hedge. She certainly *looked* this way. . . . Perhaps I'm a little fussy this morning. . . . I'll warm up to the work presently."

" I'm convinced you can't be too careful," said Mr. Direck. " And this sort of thing enables one to see the country better. . . ."

Beyond the village Mr. Britling seemed to gather confidence. The pace quickened. But whenever other traffic or any indication of a side way appeared discretion returned. Mr. Britling stalked his sign-posts, crawling towards them on the belly of the lowest gear ; he drove all the morning like a man who is flushing ambuscades. And yet accident overtook him. For God demands more from us than mere righteousness.

He cut through the hills to Market Saffron along a lane-road with which he was unfamiliar. It began to go uphill. He explained to Mr. Direck how admirably his engine would climb hills on the top gear.

They took a curve and the hill grew steeper, and Mr. Direck opened the throttle.

They rounded another corner, and still more steeply the hill rose before them.

The engine began to make a chinking sound, and the car lost pace. And then Mr. Britling saw a pleading little white board with the inscription " Concealed Turning." For the moment he thought a turning might be concealed anywhere. He threw out his clutch and clapped on his brake. Then he repented of what he had done. But the engine, after three Herculean throbs, ceased to work. Mr. Britling with a convulsive clutch at his steering-wheel set the electric hooter snarling, while one foot released the clutch again and the other, on the accelerator, sought in vain for help. Mr. Direck felt they were going back, back, in spite of all this vocalisation. He clutched at the emergency brake. But he was too late to avoid misfortune. With a feeling like sitting gently in butter, the car sank down sideways and stopped with two wheels in the ditch. Mr. Britling said they were in the ditch—said it with quite unnecessary violence. . . .

This time two cart-horses and a retinue of five men were necessary to restore Gladys to her self-respect. . . .

After that they drove on to Market Saffron, and got there in time for lunch, and after lunch Mr. Direck explored the church and the churchyard and the parish register. . . .

After lunch Mr. Britling became more cheerful about his driving. The road from Market Saffron to Blandish, whence one turns off to Matching's Easy, is the London and Norwich highroad ; it is an old Roman Stane Street and very straightforward and honest in its stretches. You can see the crossroads half a mile away, and the low hedges give you no chance of a surprise. Everybody is cheered by such a road, and everybody drives more confidently and quickly, and Mr. Britling particularly was heartened by it and gradually let out Gladys from the almost excessive restriction that had hitherto marked the day. "On a road like this nothing can happen," said Mr. Britling.

"Unless you broke an axle or burst a tire," said Mr. Direck.

"My man at Matching's Easy is most careful in his inspection," said Mr. Britling, putting the accelerator well down and watching the speed indicator creep from forty to fortyfive. "He went over the car not a week ago. And it's not one month old—in use that is."

Yet something did happen.

It was as they swept by the picturesque walls under the big old trees that encircle Brandismead Park. It was nothing but a slight miscalculation of distances. Ahead of them and well to the left rode a postman on a bicycle ; towards them, with that curious effect of implacable fury peculiar to motorcycles, came a motor-cyclist. First Mr. Britling thought that he would not pass between these two, then he decided that he would hurry up and do so, then he reverted to his former decision, and then it seemed to him that he was going so fast that he must inevitably run down the postman. His instinct not to do that pulled the car sharply across the path of the motor-cyclist. "Oh, my God ! " cried Mr. Britling ; "My

God ! " twisted his wheel over and distributed his feet among
his levers dementedly.

He had an imperfectly formed idea of getting across right
in front of the motor-cyclist, and then they were going down
the brief grassy slope between the road and the wall, straight
at the wall, and still at a good speed. The motor-cyclist
smacked against something and vanished from the problem.
The wall seemed to rush up at them and then—collapse. There
was a tremendous concussion. Mr. Direck gripped at his friend
the emergency brake, but had only time to touch it before
his head hit against the frame of the glass wind-screen, and a
curtain fell upon everything. . . .

He opened his eyes upon a broken wall, a crumpled motor-
car, and an undamaged motor-cyclist in the aviator's cap
and thin oilskin overalls dear to motor-cyclists. Mr. Direck
stared and then, still stunned and puzzled, tried to raise
himself. He became aware of acute pain.

" Don't move for a bit," said the motor-cyclist. " Your
arm and side are rather hurt, I think. . . ."

§ 8

In the course of the next twelve hours Mr. Direck was
to make a discovery that was less common in the days before
the war than it has been since. He discovered that even
pain and injury may be vividly interesting and gratifying.

If any one had told him he was going to be stunned for
five or six minutes, cut about the brow and face and have
a bone in his wrist put out, and that as a consequence he
would find himself pleased and exhilarated, he would have
treated the prophecy with ridicule ; but here he was lying
stiffly on his back with his wrist bandaged to his side and
smiling into the darkness even more brightly than he had
smiled at the Essex landscape two days before. The fact is
pain hurts or irritates, but in itself it does not make a healthily
constituted man miserable. The expectation of pain, the
certainty of injury may make one hopeless enough, the reality
rouses our resistance. Nobody wants a broken bone or a
delicate wrist, but very few people are very much depressed
by getting one. People can be much more depressed by smoking
a hundred cigarettes in three days or losing one per cent. of
their capital.

And everybody had been most delightful to Mr. Direck.

He had had the monopoly of damage. Mr. Britling, holding
on to the steering-wheel, had not even been thrown out.
" Unless I'm internally injured," he said, " I'm not hurt
at all. My liver perhaps—bruised a little. . . ."

Gladys had been abandoned in the ditch, and they had
been very kindly brought home by a passing automobile.
Cecily had been at the Dower House at the moment of the
rueful arrival. She had seen how an American can carry

injuries. She had made sympathy and helpfulness more delightful by expressed admiration.

"She's a natural born nurse," said Mr. Direck, and then rather in the tone of one who addressed a public meeting: "But this sort of thing brings out all the good there is in a woman."

He had been quite explicit to them and more particularly to her, when they told him he must stay at the Dower House until his arm was cured. He had looked the application straight into her pretty eyes.

"If I'm to stay right here just as a consequence of that little shake up, maybe for a couple of weeks, maybe three, and if you're coming to do a bit of a talk to me ever and again, then I tell you I don't call this a misfortune. It isn't a misfortune. It's right down sheer good luck. . . ."

And now he lay as straight as a mummy, with his soul filled with radiance of complete mental peace. After months of distress and confusion, he'd got straight again. He was in the middle of a real good story, bright and clean. He knew just exactly what he wanted.

"After all," he said, "it's true. There's ideals. *She's* an ideal. Why, I loved her before ever I set eyes on Mamie. I loved her before I was put into pants. That old portrait, there it was pointing my destiny. . . . It's affinity. . . . It's natural selection. . . .

"Well, I don't know what she thinks of me yet, but I do know very well what she's *got* to think of me. She's got to think all the world of me—if I break every limb of my body making her do it.

"I'd a sort of feeling it was right to go in that old automobile.

"Say what you like, there's a Guidance. . . ."

He smiled confidentially at the darkness as if they shared a secret.

CHAPTER FOUR

MR. BRITLING IN SOLILOQUY

§ 1

VERY different from the painful contentment of the bruised and broken Mr. Direck was the state of mind of his unwounded host. He too was sleepless, but sleepless without exaltation. The day had been too much for him altogether; his head, to borrow an admirable American expression, was "busy."

How busy it was, a whole chapter will be needed to describe. . . .

The impression Mr. Britling had made upon Mr. Direck

was one of indefatigable happiness. But there were times when Mr. Britling was called upon to pay for his general cheerful activity in lump sums of bitter sorrow. There were nights—and especially after seasons of exceptional excitement and nervous activity—when the reckoning would be presented and Mr. Britling would welter prostrate and groaning under a stormy sky of unhappiness—active insatiable unhappiness—a beating with rods.

The sorrows of the sanguine temperament are brief but furious; the world knows little of them. The world has no need to reckon with them. They cause no suicides and few crimes. They hurry past, smiting at their victim as they go. None the less they are misery. Mr. Britling in these moods did not perhaps experience the grey and hopeless desolations of the melancholic nor the red damnation of the choleric, but he saw a world that bristled with misfortune and error, with poisonous thorns and traps and swampy places and incurable blunderings. An almost insupportable remorse for being Mr. Britling would pursue him—justifying itself upon a hundred counts. . . .

And for being such a Britling ! . . .

Why—he revived again that bitter question of a thousand and one unhappy nights—why was he such a fool ? Such a hasty fool ? Why couldn't he look before he leaped ? Why did he take risks ? Why was he always so ready to act upon the supposition that all was bound to go well ? (He might as well have asked why he had quick brown eyes.)

Why, for instance, hadn't he adhered to the resolution of the early morning ? He had begun with an extremity of caution. . . .

It was a characteristic of these moods of Mr. Britling that they produced a physical restlessness. He kept on turning over and then turning over again, and sitting up and lying back, like a martyr on a gridiron. . . .

This was just the latest instance of a lifelong trouble. Will there ever be a sort of man whose thoughts are quick and his acts slow ? Then indeed we shall have a formidable being. Mr. Britling's thoughts were quick and sanguine and his actions even more eager than his thoughts. Already while he was a young man Mr. Britling had found his acts elbow their way through the hurry of his ideas and precipitate humiliations. Long before his reasons were marshalled, his resolutions were formed. He had attempted a thousand remonstrances with himself; he had sought to remedy the defects in his own character by written inscriptions in his bedroom and memoranda inside his watch-case. "Keep steady ! " was one of them. " Keep the End in View." And, " Go steadfastly, coherently, continuously ; only so can you go where you will." In distrusting all impulse, scrutinising all imagination, he was persuaded lay his one prospect of escape from the surprise of countless miseries.   Otherwise he danced among glass bombs and barbed wire.

There had been a time when he could exhort himself to such fundamental charge and go through phases of the severest discipline.   Always at last to be taken by surprise from some unexpected quarter.   At last he had ceased to hope for any triumph so radical.   He had been content to believe that in recent years age and a gathering habit of wisdom had somewhat slowed his leaping purpose.   That if he hadn't overcome he had at least to a certain extent minimised it.   But this last folly was surely the worst.   To hurl through this patient world with—how much did the car weigh ?   A ton certainly and perhaps more—reckless of every risk.   Not only to himself but others.   At this thought, he clutched the steering-wheel again.   Once more he saw the bent back of the endangered cyclist, once more he felt rather than saw the seething approach of the motor-bicycle, and then through a long instant he drove helplessly at the wall. . . .

Hell perhaps is only one such incident, indefinitely prolonged. . . .

Anything might have been there in front of him.   And indeed now, out of the dreamland to which he could not escape something had come, something that screamed sharply. . . .

" Good God ! " he cried, " if I had hit a child !   I might have hit a child ! "   The hypothesis flashed into being with the thought, tried to escape and was caught.   It was characteristic of Mr. Britling's nocturnal imagination that he should individualise this child quite clearly as rather plain and slender, with reddish hair, staring eyes, and its ribs crushed in a vivid and dreadful manner, pinned against the wall, mixed up with some bricks, only to be extracted, oh ! *horribly*.

But this was not fair!   He had hurt no child !   He had merely pitched out Mr. Direck and damaged his wrist. . . .

It wasn't his merit that the child hadn't been there !

The child might have been there!

Mere luck.

He lay staring in despair—as an involuntary God might stare at many a thing in this amazing universe—staring at the little victim his imagination had called into being only to destroy. . . .

§ 2

If he had not crushed a child other people had.   Such things happened.   Vicariously at any rate he had crushed many children. . . .

Why are children ever crushed ?

And suddenly all the pain and destruction and remorse of all the accidents in the world descended upon Mr. Britling.

No longer did he ask why am I such a fool, but why are we all such fools ?   He became Man on the automobile of

civilisation, crushing his thousands daily in his headlong and
yet aimless career. . . .

That was a trick of Mr. Britling's mind. It had this tendency
to spread outward from himself to generalised issues. Many
minds are like that nowadays. He was not so completely
individualised as people are supposed to be individualised—
in our law, in our stories, in our moral judgments. He had
a vicarious factor. He could slip from concentrated reproaches
to the liveliest remorse for himself as The Automobilist in
General, or for himself as England, or for himself as Man.
From remorse for smashing his guest and his automobile he
could pass by what was for him the most imperceptible of
transitions to remorse for every accident that has ever happened through the error of an automobilist since automobiles
began. All that long succession of blunderers became Mr.
Britling. Or rather Mr. Britling became all that vast succession
of blunderers.

These fluctuating lapses from individuation made Mr.
Britling a perplexity to many who judged only by the old
personal standards. At times he seemed a monster of cantankerous self-righteousness, whom nobody could please or
satisfy, but indeed when he was most pitiless about the faults
of his race or nation he was really reproaching himself, and
when he seemed more egotistical and introspective and self-
centred he was really ransacking himself for a clue to that
same confusion of purposes that waste the hope and strength
of humanity. And now through the busy distresses of the
night it would have perplexed a watching angel to have drawn
the line and shown when Mr. Britling was grieving for his
own loss and humiliation and when he was grieving for these
common human weaknesses of which he had so large a share.

And this double refraction of his mind by which a concentrated and individualised Britling did not present a larger
impersonal Britling beneath, carried with it a duplication of
his conscience and sense of responsibility. To his personal
conscience he was answerable for his private honour and his
debts and the Dower House he had made and so on, but to
his impersonal conscience he was answerable for the whole
world. The world from the latter point of view was his egg.
He had a subconscious delusion that he had laid it. He had
a subconscious suspicion that he had let it cool and that it
was addled. He had an urgency to incubate it. The variety
and interest of his talk was largely due to that persuasion,
it was a perpetual attempt to spread his mental feathers over
the task before him. . . .

§ 3

After this much of explanation it is possible to go on to
the task which originally brought Mr. Direck to Matching's
Easy, the task that Massachusetts society had sent him upon,

the task of organising the mental unveiling of Mr. Britling.
Mr. Direck saw Mr. Britling only in the daylight, and with
an increasing distraction of the attention towards Miss Cecily
Corner. We may see him rather more clearly in the darkness,
without any distraction except his own.

Now the smashing of Gladys was not only the source of
a series of reproaches and remorses directly arising out of
the disaster ; it had also a wide system of collateral consequences, which were also banging and blundering their way
through the Britling mind. It was extraordinarily inconvenient in quite another respect that the automobile should
be destroyed. It upset certain plans of Mr. Britling's in a
direction growing right out from all the Dower House world
in which Mr. Direck supposed him to be completely set and
rooted. There were certain matters from which Mr. Britling
had been averting his mind most strenuously throughout
the week-end. Now, there was no averting his mind any more.

Mr. Britling was entangled in a love-affair. It was, to be
exact, and disregarding minor affinities, his eighth love-affair.
And the new automobile, so soon as he could drive it efficiently,
was to have played quite a solvent and conclusive part in
certain entangled complications of this relationship.

A man of lively imagination and quick impulses naturally
has love-affairs as he drives himself through life, just as he
naturally has accidents if he drives an automobile.

And the peculiar relations that existed between Mr. Britling
and Mrs. Britling tended inevitably to make these love-affairs
troublesome, undignified and futile. Especially when they were
viewed from the point of view of insomnia.

Mr. Britling's first marriage had been a passionately happy
one. His second was by comparison a marriage in neutral tint.
There is much to be said for that extreme Catholic theory
which would make marriage not merely lifelong but eternal.
Certainly Mr. Britling would have been a finer if not a happier
creature if his sentimental existence could have died with his
first wife or continued only in his love for their son. He had
married in the glow of youth, he had had two years of clean
and simple loving, helping, quarrelling and the happy ending
of quarrels. Something went out of him into all that which
could not be renewed again. In his first extremity of grief he
knew this perfectly well—and then afterwards he forgot it.
While there is life there is imagination, which makes and
forgets and goes on.

He met Edith under circumstances that did not in any way
recall his lost Mary. He met her, as people say, " socially " ;
Mary, on the other hand, had been a girl at Newnham while he
was a fellow of Pembroke, and there had been something of
accident and something of furtiveness in their lucky discovery
of each other. There had been a flush in it ; there was dash
in it. But Edith he saw and chose and had to woo. There

was no rushing together ; there was solicitation and assent.
Edith was a Bachelor of Science of London University and
several things like that, and she looked upon the universe
under her broad forehead and broad-waving brown hair with
quiet watchful eyes that had nothing whatever to hide, a thing
so incredible to Mr. Britling that he had loved and married her
very largely for the serenity of her mystery. And for a time
after their marriage he sailed over those brown depths plumbing
furiously.

Of course he did not make his former passion for Mary at all
clear to her. Indeed, while he was winning Edith it was by
no means clear to himself. He was making a new emotional
drama, and consciously and subconsciously he dismissed a
hundred reminiscences which sought to invade the new
experience, and would have been out of key with it. And
without any deliberate intention to that effect he created an
atmosphere between himself and Edith in which any discussion
of Mary was reduced to a minimum, and in which Hugh was
accepted rather than explained. He contrived to believe that
she understood all sorts of unsayable things ; he invented
miracles of quite uncongenial mute mutuality. . . .

It was over the chess-board that they first began to discover
their extensive difficulties of sympathy. Mr. Britling's play
was characterised by a superficial brilliance, much generosity
and extreme unsoundness ; he always moved directly his
opponent had done so—and then reflected on the situation.
His reflection was commonly much wiser than his moves.
Mrs. Britling was, as it were, a natural antagonist to her
husband ; she was as calm as he was irritable. She was never
in a hurry to move, and never disposed to make a concession.
Quietly, steadfastly, by caution and deliberation, without
splendour, without error, she had beaten him at chess until
it led to such dreadful fits of anger that he had to renounce
the game altogether. After every such occasion he would be
at great pains to explain that he had merely been angry with
himself. Nevertheless he felt, and would not let himself think
(what she concluded from incidental heated phrases), that
that was not the complete truth about the outbreak.

Slowly they got through the concealments of that specious
explanation. Temperamentally they were incompatible.
They were profoundly incompatible. In all things she was
defensive. She never came out ; never once had she surprised
him half-way upon the road to her. He had to go all the way
to her and knock and ring, and then she answered faithfully.
She never surprised him even by unkindness. If he had a cut
finger she would bind it up very skilfully and healingly, but
unless he told her she never discovered he had a cut finger.
He was amazed she did not know of it before it happened.
He piped and she did not dance. That became the formula
of his grievance. For several unhappy years she thwarted

him and disappointed him, while he filled her with dumb inexplicable distresses. He had been at first so gay an activity, and then he was shattered ; fragments of him were still as gay and attractive as ever, but between were outbreaks of anger, of hostility, of something very like malignity. Only very slowly did they realise the truth of their relationship and admit to themselves that the fine bud of love between them had failed to flower, and only after long years were they able to delimit boundaries where they had imagined union, and to become— allies. If it had been reasonably possible for them to part without mutual injury and recrimination they would have done so, but two children presently held them, and gradually they had to work out the broad mutual toleration of their later relations. If there was no love and delight between them there was a real habitual affection and much mutual help. She was proud of his steady progress to distinction, proud of each intimation of respect he won ; she admired and respected his work ; she recognised that he had some magic of liveliness and unexpectedness that was precious and enviable. So far as she could help him she did. And even when he knew that there was nothing behind it, that it was indeed little more than an imaginative inertness, he could still admire and respect her steady dignity and her consistent honourableness. Her practical capacity was for him a matter for continual self-congratulation. He marked the bright order of her household, her flowering borders, the prosperous high-born roses of her garden with a wondering appreciation. He had never been able to keep anything in order. He relied more and more upon her. He showed his respect for her by a scrupulous attention to her dignity, and his confidence by a franker and franker emotional neglect. Because she expressed so little he succeeded in supposing she felt little, and since nothing had come out of the brown depths of her eyes he saw fit at last to suppose no plumb-line would ever find anything there. He pursued his interests ; he reached out to this and that ; he travelled ; she made it a matter of conscience to let him go unhampered ; she felt, she thought— unrecorded ; he did, and he expressed and re-expressed and over-expressed, and started this and that with quick irrepressible activity, and so there had accumulated about them the various items of the life to whose more ostensible accidents Mr. Direck was now for an indefinite period joined.

It was in the nature of Mr. Britling to incur things ; it was in the nature of Mrs. Britling to establish them. Mr. Britling had taken the Dower House on impulse, and she had made it a delightful home. He had discovered the disorderly delights of mixed Sunday hockey one week-end at Pontings that had promised to be dull, and she had made it an institution. . . . He had come to her with his orphan boy and a memory of a passionate first loss that sometimes, and more particularly at first, he seemed to have forgotten altogether, and at other times

was only too evidently lamenting with every fibre of his being.
She had taken the utmost care of the relics of her duskily pretty
predecessor that she found in unexpected abundance in Mr.
Britling's possession, and she had done her duty by her sometimes rather incomprehensible stepson.   She never allowed
herself to examine the state of her heart towards this youngster ;
it is possible that she did not perceive the necessity for any such
examination. . . .

So she went through life, outwardly serene and dignified,
one of a great company of rather fastidious, rather unenterprising women who have turned for their happiness to secondary
things, to those fair inanimate things of household and garden
which do not turn again and rend one, to æstheticisms and
delicacies, to order and seemliness.   Moreover she found great
satisfaction in the health and welfare, the growth and animation
of her own two little boys.   And no one knew, and perhaps
even she had contrived to forget, the phases of astonishment
and disillusionment, of doubt and bitterness and secret tears,
that spread out through the years in which she had slowly
realised that this strange, fitful, animated man who had come
to her, vowing himself hers, asking for her so urgently and
persuasively, was ceasing, had ceased, to love her, that his
heart had escaped her, that she had missed it ; she never
dreamt that she had hurt it, and that after its first urgent,
tumultuous, incomprehensible search for her it had hidden
itself bitterly away. . . .

§ 4

The mysterious processes of nature that had produced Mr.
Britling had implanted in him an obstinate persuasion that
somewhere in the world, from some human being, it was still
possible to find the utmost satisfaction for every need and
craving.   He could imagine as existing, as waiting for him, he
knew not where, a completeness of understanding, a perfection
of response, that would reach all the gamut of his feelings and
sensations from the most poetical to the most entirely physical,
a beauty of relationship so transfiguring that not only would
she—it went without saying that this completion was a woman—
be perfectly beautiful in its light but, what was manifestly
more incredible, that he too would be perfectly beautiful and
quite at his ease. . . . In her presence there could be no self-
reproaches, no lapses, no limitations, nothing but happiness
and the happiest activities. . . . To such a persuasion half
the imaginative people in the world succumb as readily and
naturally as ducklings take to water.   They do not doubt its
truth any more than a thirsty camel doubts that presently
it will come to a spring.

This persuasion is as foolish as though a camel hoped that
some day it would drink from such a spring that it would
never thirst again.   For the most part Mr. Britling ignored its

presence in his mind, and resisted the impulses it started. But at odd times, and more particularly in the afternoon and while travelling and in between books, Mr. Britling so far succumbed to this strange expectation of a wonder round the corner that he slipped the anchors of his humour and self-contempt and joined the great cruising brotherhood of the Pilgrims of Love. . . .

In fact—though he himself had never made a reckoning of it—he had been upon eight separate cruises. He was now upon the eighth. . . .

Between these various excursions—they took him round and about the world, so to speak, they cast him away on tropical beaches, they left him dismasted on desolate seas, they involved the most startling interventions and the most inconvenient consequences—there were interludes of penetrating philosophy. For some years the suspicion had been growing up in Mr. Britling's mind that in planting this persuasion in his being, the mysterious processes of Nature had been, perhaps for some purely biological purpose, pulling, as people say, his leg, that there were not these perfect responses, that loving a woman is a thing one does thoroughly once for all—or so—and afterwards recalls regrettably in a series of vain repetitions, and that the career of the Pilgrim of Love, so soon as you strip off its credulous glamour, is either the most pitiful or the most vulgar and vile of perversions from the proper conduct of life. But this suspicion had not as yet grown to prohibitive dimensions with him, it was not sufficient to resist the seasons of high tide, the sudden promise of the salt-edged breeze, the invitation of the hovering sea-bird ; and he was now concealing beneath the lively surface of activities with which Mr. Direck had grown familiar a very extensive system of distresses arising out of the latest, the eighth of these digressional adventures. . . .

Mr. Britling had got into it very much as he had got into the ditch on the morning before his smash. He hadn't thought the affair out and he hadn't looked carefully enough. And it kept on developing in just the ways he would rather that it didn't.

The seventh affair had been very disconcerting. He had made a fool of himself with quite a young girl ; he blushed to think how young ; it hadn't gone very far, but it had made his nocturnal reflections so disagreeable that he had—by no means for the first time—definitely and for ever given up these foolish dreams of love. And when Mrs. Harrowdean swam into his circle, she seemed just exactly what was wanted to keep his imagination out of mischief. She came bearing flattery to the pitch of adoration. She was the brightest and cleverest of young widows. She wrote quite admirable criticism in *The Scrutator* and *The Sectarian,* and occasional poetry in *The Right Review*—when she felt disposed to do so. She had an intermittent vein of high spirits that was almost better than humour and made her quickly popular with most of the people she met, and she was only twenty miles away in her pretty house and her absurd little jolly park.

There was something, she said, in his thought and work that was like walking in mountains. She came to him because she wanted to clamber about the peaks and glens of his mind.

It was natural to reply that he wasn't by any means the serene mountain elevation she thought him, except perhaps for a kind of loneliness. . . .

She was a great reader of eighteenth-century memoirs, and some she conveyed to him. Her mental quality was all in the vein of the friendships of Rousseau and Voltaire, and pleasantly and trippingly she led him along the primrose path of an intellectual liaison. She came first to Matching's Easy, where she was sweet and bright and vividly interested and a great contrast to Mrs. Britling, and then he and she met in London, and went off together with a fine sense of adventure for a day at Richmond, and then he took some work with him to her house and stayed there. . . .

Then she went away into Scotland for a time and he wanted her again tremendously and clamoured for her eloquently, and then it was apparent and admitted between them that they were admirably in love, oh ! immensely in love.

The transitions from emotional mountaineering to ardent intimacies were so rapid and impulsive that each phase obliterated its predecessor, and it was only with a vague perplexity that Mr. Britling found himself transferred from the rôle of a mountainous objective for pretty little pilgrims to that of a sedulous lover in pursuit of the happiness of one of the most uncertain, intricate, and entrancing of feminine personalities. This was not at all his idea of the proper relations between men and women, but Mrs. Harrowdean had a way of challenging his gallantry. She made him run about for her ; she did not demand but she commanded presents and treats and surprises ; she even developed a certain jealousy in him. His work began to suffer from interruptions. Yet they had glowing and entertaining moments together that could temper his rebellious thoughts with the threat of irreparable loss. " One must love, and all things in life are imperfect," was how Mr. Britling expressed his reasons for submission. And she had a hold upon him too in a certain facile pitifulness. She was little ; she could be stung sometimes by the slightest touch and then her blue eyes would be bright with tears.

Those possible tears could weigh at times even more than those possible lost embraces.

And there was Oliver.

Oliver was a person Mr. Britling had never seen. He grew into the scheme of things by insensible gradations. He was a government official in London ; he was, she said, extraordin-

arily dull, he was lacking altogether in Mr. Britling's charm
and interest, but he was faithful and tender and true. And
considerably younger than Mr. Britling. He asked nothing
but to love. He offered honourable marriage. And when one's
heart was swelling unendurably one could weep in safety on his
patient shoulder. This patient shoulder of Oliver's ultimately
became Mr. Britling's most exasperating rival.

She liked to vex him with Oliver. She liked to vex him
generally. Indeed in this by no means abnormal love-affair
there was a very strong antagonism. She seemed to resent the
attraction Mr. Britling had for her and the emotions and
pleasure she had with him. She seemed under the sway of an
instinctive desire to make him pay heavily for her, in time, in
emotion, in self-respect. It was intolerable to her that he
could take her easily and happily. That would be taking her
cheaply. She valued his gifts by the bother they cost him, and
was determined that the path of true love should not, if she
could help it, run smooth. Mr. Britling on the other hand was
of the school of polite and happy lovers. He thought it outrageous to dispute and contradict, and he thought that making
love was a cheerful comfortable thing to be done in a state of
high good humour and intense mutual appreciation.   This
levity offended the lady's pride. She drew unfavourable contrasts with Oliver. If Oliver lacked charm he certainly did not
lack emotion. He desired sacrifice, it seemed, almost more
than satisfactions. Oliver was a person of the most exemplary
miserableness ; he would weep copiously and frequently.
She could always make him weep when she wanted to do so. By
holding out hopes and then dashing them, if by no other
expedient. Why did Mr. Britling never weep ? She wept.

Some base streak of competitiveness in Mr. Britling's nature
made it seem impossible that he should relinquish the lady to
Oliver. Besides, then, what would he do with his dull days,
his afternoons, his need for a properly demonstrated affection ?

So Mr. Britling trod the path of his eighth digression, rather
overworked in the matter of flowers and the selection of small
jewellery, stalked by the invisible and indefatigable Oliver,
haunted into an unwilling industry of attentions—attentions
on the model of the professional lover of the French novels—
by the memory and expectation of tearful scenes.   " Then
you don't love me ! And it's all spoiled. I've risked talk and
my reputation. . . . I was a fool ever to dream of making
love beautifully. . . ."

Exactly like running your car into a soft wet ditch when you
cannot get out and you cannot get on. And your work and
your interests waiting and waiting for you ! . . .

The car itself was an outcome of the affair. It was Mrs.
Harrowdean's idea ; she thought chiefly of agreeable expeditions to friendly inns in remote parts of the country, inns
with a flavour of tacit complicity, but it fell in very pleasantly

with Mr. Britling's private resentment at the extraordinary inconvenience of the railway communications between Matching's Easy and her station at Pyecrafts, which involved a journey to Liverpool Street and a long wait at a junction. And now the car was smashed up—just when he had acquired skill enough to take it over to Pyecrafts without shame, and on Tuesday or Wednesday at latest he would have to depart in the old way by the London train. . . .

Only the most superficial mind would assert nowadays that man is a reasonable creature. Man is an unreasonable creature, and it was entirely unreasonable and human for Mr. Britling during his nocturnal self-reproaches to mix up his secret resentment at his infatuation for Mrs. Harrowdean with his ill-advised attack upon the wall of Brandismead Park. He ought never to have bought that car ; he ought never to have been so ready to meet Mrs. Harrowdean more than half-way.

What exacerbated his feeling about Mrs. Harrowdean was a new line she had recently taken with regard to Mrs. Britling. From her first rash assumption that Mr. Britling was indifferent to his wife, she had come to realise that on the contrary he was in some ways extremely tender about his wife. This struck her as an outrageous disloyalty. Instead of appreciating a paradox she resented an infidelity. She smouldered with perplexed resentment for some days, and then astonished her lover by a series of dissertations of a hostile and devastating nature upon the lady of the Dower House.

He tried to imagine he hadn't heard all that he had heard, but Mrs. Harrowdean had a nimble pen and nimbler after-thoughts, and once her mind had got to work upon the topic she developed her offensive in half-a-dozen brilliant letters. . . . On the other hand, she professed a steadily increasing passion for Mr. Britling. And to profess passion for Mr. Britling was to put him under a sense of profound obligation —because indeed he was a modest man. He found himself in an emotional quandary.

You see, if Mrs. Harrowdean had left Mrs. Britling alone everything would have been quite tolerable. He considered Mrs. Harrowdean a charming human being, and altogether better than he deserved. Ever so much better. She was all initiative and response and that sort of thing. And she was so discreet. She had her own reputation to think about, and one or two of her predecessors—God rest the ashes of those fires !—had not been so discreet. Yet one could not have this sort of thing going on behind Edith's back. All sorts of things one might have going on behind Edith's back, but not this writing and saying of perfectly beastly things about Edith. Nothing could alter the fact that Edith was his honour. . . .

§ 5

Throughout the week-end Mr. Britling had kept this trouble well battened down. He had written to Mrs. Harrowdean a brief ambiguous note saying, " I am thinking over all that you have said," and after that he had scarcely thought about her at all. Or at least he had always contrived to be much more vividly thinking about something else. But now in these night silences the suppressed trouble burst hatches and rose about him.

What a mess he had made of the whole scheme of his emotional life ! There had been a time when he had started out as gaily with his passions and his honour as he had started out with Gladys to go to Market Saffron. He had as little taste for complications as he had for ditches. And now his passions and his honour were in a worse case even than poor muddy smashed-up Gladys as the cart-horses towed her off, for she at any rate might be repaired. But he—he was a terribly patched fabric of explanations now. Not indeed that he had ever stooped to explanations. But there he was ! Far away, like a star seen down the length of a tunnel, was that first sad story of a love as clean as starlight. It had been all over by eight-and-twenty and he could find it in his heart to grieve that he had ever given a thought to love again. He should have lived a decent widower. . . . Then Edith had come into his life, Edith that honest and unconscious defaulter. And there again he should have stuck to his disappointment. He had stuck to it—nine days out of every ten. It's the tenth day, it's the odd seductive moment, it's the instant of confident pride—and there is your sanguine temperament in the ditch.

He began to recapitulate items in the catalogue of his escapades, and the details of his automobile misadventures mixed themselves up with the story of his heart-steering. For example there was that tremendous Siddons affair. He had been taking the corner of a girlish friendship and he had taken it altogether too far. What a frightful mess that had been ! When once one is off the road anything may happen, from a crumpled mud-guard to the car on the top of you. And there was his forty miles an hour spurt with the great and gifted Delphine Marquise—for whom he was to have written a play and been a perfect d'Annunzio. Until Willersley appeared—very like the motor-cyclist—buzzing in the opposite direction. And then had ensued angers, humiliations. . . .

Had every man this sort of crowded catalogue ? Was every forty-five-year-old memory a dark tunnel receding from the star of youth ? It is surely a pity that life cannot end at thirty. It comes to one clean and in perfect order. . . .

Is experience worth having ?

What a clean, straight thing the spirit of youth is ! It is like a bright new spear. It is like a finely tempered sword. The figure of his boy took possession of his mind, his boy who looked out on the world with his mother's dark eyes, the slender son of that whole-hearted first love. He was a being at once fine and simple, an intimate mystery. Must he in his turn get dented and wrinkled and tarnished ?

The boy was in trouble.—What was the trouble ?

Was it some form of the same trouble that had so tangled and tainted and scarred the private pride of his father ? And how was it possible for Mr. Britling, disfigured by heedless misadventures, embarrassed by complications and conceal- ments, to help this honest youngster out of his perplexities ? He imagined possible forms of these perplexities. Graceless forms. Ugly forms. Such forms as only the nocturnal imagina- tion would have dared present. . . .

Oh, why had he been such a Britling ? Why was he still such a Britling ?

Mr. Britling sat up in his bed and beat at the bed-clothes with his fists. He uttered uncompleted vows. " From this hour forth . . . from this hour forth. . . ."

He must do something, he felt. At any rate he had his experiences. He could warn. He could explain away. Perhaps he might help to extricate, if things had got to that pitch.

Should he write to his son ? For a time he revolved a long tactful letter in his mind. But that was impossible. Suppose the trouble was something quite different ? It would have to be a letter in the most general terms. . . .

§ 6

It was in the doubly refracting nature of Mr. Britling's mind that while he was deploring his inefficiency in regard to his son, he was also deploring the ineffectiveness of all his generation of parents. Quite insensibly his mind passed over to the generalised point of view.

In his talks with Mr. Direck, Mr. Britling could present England as a great and amiable spectacle of carelessness and relaxation, but was it indeed an amiable spectacle ? The point that Mr. Direck had made about the barn rankled in his thoughts. His barn was a barn no longer, his farmyard held no cattle ; he was just living laxly in the buildings that ancient needs had made, he was living on the accumulated prosperity of former times, the spendthrift heir of toiling generations. Not only was he a pampered, undisciplined sort of human being ; he was living in a pampered, undisciplined sort of community. The two things went together. . . . This confounded Irish business, one could laugh at it in the day- light, but was it indeed a thing to laugh at ? We were drifting lazily towards a real disaster. We had a government that

seemed guided by the principles of Mr. Micawber, and adopted
for its watchword " Wait and See." For months now this
trouble had grown more threatening. Suppose presently that
civil war broke out in Ireland ! Suppose presently that these
irritated, mishandled suffragettes did some desperate irreconcilable thing, assassinated for example ! That bomb in Westminster Abbey the other day might have killed a dozen people.
. . . Suppose the smouldering criticism of British rule in India
and Egypt were fanned by administrative indiscretions into
a flame. . . .

And then suppose Germany made trouble. . . .

Usually Mr. Britling kept his mind off Germany. In the
daytime he pretended Germany meant nothing to England.
He hated alarmists. He hated disagreeable possibilities. He
declared the idea of a whole vast nation waiting to strike at
us incredible. Why should they ? You cannot have seventy
million lunatics. . . . But in the darkness of the night one
cannot dismiss things in this way. Suppose, after all, their
army was more than a parade, their navy more than a protest ?

We might be caught—— It was only in the vast melancholia of such occasions that Mr. Britling would admit such
possibilities, but we might be caught by some sudden declaration of war. . . . And how should we face it ?

He recalled the afternoon's talk at Claverings and such
samples of our governmental machinery as he chanced to
number among his personal acquaintance. Suppose suddenly
the enemy struck ! With Raeburn and his friends to defend
us ! Or if the shock tumbled them out of power, then with
these vituperative Tories, these spiteful advocates of weak
tyrannies and privileged pretences, in the place of them.
There was no leadership in England. In the lucid darkness he
knew that with a terrible certitude. He had a horrible vision of
things disastrously muffed; of Lady Frensham and her *Morning
Post* friends first garrulously and maliciously " patriotic,"
screaming her way with incalculable mischiefs through the
storm and finally discovering that the Germans were the real
aristocrats and organising our national capitulation on that
understanding. He knew from talk he had heard that the
navy was weak in mines and torpedoes, unprovided with the
great monitors obviously needed for a war with Germany ;
torn by doctrinaire feuds ; nevertheless the sea power was our
only defence. In the whole country we might muster a military
miscellany of perhaps three hundred thousand men. And he
had no faith in their equipment, in their direction. General
French, the one man who had his entire confidence, had been
forced to resign through some lawyer's misunderstanding about
the Irish difficulty. He did not believe any plans existed for
such a war as Germany might force upon us, any calculation,
any foresight of the thing at all.

Why had we no foresight ? Why had we this wilful blindness to disagreeable possibilities ? Why did we lie so open to the unexpected crisis ? Just what he said of himself he said also of his country. It was curious to remember that. To realise how closely Dower House could play the microcosm to the whole Empire. . . .

It became relevant to the trend of his thoughts that his son had through his mother a strong strain of the dark Irish in his composition.

How we had wasted Ireland ! The rich values that lay in Ireland, the gallantry and gifts, the possible friendliness, all these things were being left to the Ulster politicians and the Tory women to poison and spoil, just as we left India to the traditions of the chattering army women and the repressive instincts of our mandarins. We were too lazy, we were too negligent. We passed our indolent days leaving everything to somebody else. Was this the incurable British, just as it was the incurable Britling, quality ?

Was the whole prosperity of the British, the far-flung empire, the securities, the busy order, just their good luck ? It was a question he had asked a hundred times of his national as of his personal self. No doubt luck had favoured him. He was prosperous, and he was still only at the livelier end of middle age. But was there not also a personal factor, a meritorious factor ? Luck had favoured the British with a well-placed island, a hardening climate, accessible minerals, but then too was there not also a national virtue ? Once he had believed in that, in a certain gallantry, a noble levity, an underlying sound sense. The last ten years of politics had made him doubt that profoundly. He clung to it still but without confidence. In the night that dear persuasion left him altogether. . . . As for himself he had a certain brightness and liveliness of mind, but the year of his fellowship had been a soft year, he had got on to *The Times* through something very like a misapprehension, and it was the chances of a dinner and a duchess that had given him the opportunity of the Kahn show. He'd dropped into good things that suited him. That at any rate was the essence of it. And these lucky chances had been no incentive to further effort. Because things had gone easily and rapidly with him he had developed indolence into a philosophy. Here he was just over forty, and explaining to the world, explaining all through the week-end to this American —until even God could endure it no longer and the smash stopped him—how excellent was the backwardness of Essex and English go-as-you-please, and how through good temper it made in some mysterious way for all that was desirable. A fat English doctrine. *Punch* has preached it for forty years.

But this wasn't what he had always been. He thought of the strenuous intentions of his youth, before he had got into this turmoil of amorous experiences, while he was still out there with the clean star of youth. As Hugh was. . . .

In those days he had had no amiable doctrine of compromise·
He had truckled to no " domesticated God," but talked of the
" pitiless truth " ; he had tolerated no easy-going pseudo-
aristocratic social system, but dreamt of such a democracy
" mewing its mighty youth " as the world had never seen. He
had thought that his brains were to do their share in building
up this great national *imago*, winged, divine, out of the clumsy,
crawling, snobbish, comfort-loving caterpillar of Victorian
England. With such dreams his life had started, and the light
of them, perhaps, had helped him to his rapid success. And
then his wife had died, and he had married again and become
somehow more interested in his income, and then the rather
expensive first of the eight experiences had drained off so
much of his imaginative energy, and the second had drained
off so much, and there had been quarrels and feuds, and the
way had been lost, and the days had passed. He hadn't failed.
Indeed he counted as a success among his generation. He alone,
in the night-watches, could gauge the quality of that success.
He was widely known, reputably known ; he prospered. Much
had come, oh ! by a mysterious luck, but everything was
doomed by his invincible defects. Beneath that hollow, enviable show there ached waste. Waste, waste, waste—his
heart, his imagination, his wife, his son, his country—his
automobile. . . .

Then there flashed into his mind a last straw of disagreeable
realisation.

He hadn't as yet insured his automobile ! He had meant
to do so. The papers were on his writing-desk.

§ 7

On these black nights, when the personal Mr. Britling would
lie awake thinking how unsatisfactorily Mr. Britling was
going on, and when the impersonal Mr. Britling would be
thinking how unsatisfactorily his universe was going on, the
whole mental process had a likeness to some complex piece
of orchestral music wherein the organ deplored the melancholy
destinies of the race while the piccolo lamented the secret
trouble of Mrs. Harrowdean ; the big drum thundered at the
Irish politicians, and all the violins bewailed the intellectual
laxity of the university system. Meanwhile the trumpets pro-
phesied wars and disasters, the cymbals ever and again
inserted a clashing jar about the fatal delay in the automobile
insurance, while the triangle broke into a plangent solo on the
topic of a certain rotten gate-post he always forgot in the daytime, and how in consequence the cows from the glebe-farm
got into the garden and ate Mrs. Britling's carnations.

Time after time he had promised to see to that gate-post. . . .

The organ *motif* battled its way to complete predominance.
The lesser themes were drowned or absorbed. Mr. Britling
returned from the rôle of an incompetent automobilist to the

rôle of a soul naked in space and time wrestling with giant questions. These cosmic solicitudes, it may be, are the last penalty of irreligion. Was Huxley right, and was all humanity, even as Mr. Britling, a careless, fitful thing, playing a tragically hopeless game, thinking too slightly, moving too quickly, against a relentless antagonist ?

Or is the whole thing just witless, accidentally cruel perhaps, but not malignant ? Or is it wise, and merely refusing to pamper us ? Is there somewhere in the immensities some responsive kindliness, some faint hope of toleration and assistance, some-thing sensibly on our side against death and mechanical cruelty? If so, it certainly refuses to pamper us. . . . But if the whole thing is cruel, perhaps also it is witless and will-less ?   One cannot imagine the ruler of everything a devil—that would be silly. So if at the worst it is inanimate then anyhow we have our poor wills and our poor wits to pit against it. And mani-festly then, the good of life, the significance of any life that is not mere receptivity, lies in the disciplined and clarified will and the sharpened and tempered mind. And what for the last twenty years—for all his lectures and writings—had he been doing to marshal the will and harden the mind which were his weapons against the Dark ? He was ready enough to blame others—dons, politicians, public apathy, what was he himself doing ?

What was he doing now ?

Lying in bed !

His son was drifting to ruin, his country was going to the devil, the house was a hospital of people wounded by his care-lessness, the country roads choked with his smashed (and uninsured) automobiles, the cows were probably lined up along the borders and munching Edith's carnations at this very moment, his pocketbook and bureau were stuffed with veno-mous insults about her—and he was just lying in bed !

Suddenly Mr. Britling threw back his bedclothes and felt for the matches on his bedside table.

Indeed this was by no means the first time that his brain had become a whirring torment in his skull. Previous experi-ences had led to the most careful provision for exactly such states. Over the end of the bed hung a light, warm pyjama suit of llama-wool, and at the feet of it were two tall boots of the same material that buckled to the middle of his calf. So protected, Mr. Britling proceeded to make himself tea.   A Primus stove stood ready inside the fender of his fireplace, and on it was a brightly polished brass kettle filled with water ; a little table carried a tea-caddy, a teapot, a lemon and a glass. Mr. Britling lit the stove and then strolled to his desk.   He was going to write certain " Plain Words about Ireland."   He lit his study lamp and meditated beside it until a sound of water boiling called him to his tea-making.

He returned to his desk stirring the lemon in his glass of

tea. He would write the plain common sense of this Irish situation. He would put things so plainly that this squabbling folly would *have* to cease. It should be done austerely, with a sort of ironical directness. There should be no abuse, no bitterness, only a deep passion of sanity.

What is the good of grieving over a smashed automobile?

He sipped his tea and made a few notes on his writing-pad. His face in the light of his shaded reading-lamp had lost its distraught expression, his hand fingered his familiar fountain-pen. . . .

§ 8

The next morning Mr. Britling came into Mr. Direck's room. He was pink from his morning bath, he was wearing a cheerful green-and-blue silk dressing-gown, he had shaved already, he showed no trace of his nocturnal vigil. In the bathroom he had whistled like a bird. " Had a good night ? " he said. " That's famous. So did I. And the wrist and arm even didn't ache enough to keep you awake ? "

" I thought I heard you talking and walking about," said Mr. Direck.

" I got up for a little bit and worked. I often do that. I hope I didn't disturb you. Just for an hour or so. It's so delightfully quiet in the night. . . ."

He went to the window and blinked at the garden outside. His two younger sons appeared on their bicycles returning from some early expedition. He waved a hand of greeting. It was one of those summer mornings when attenuated mist seems to fill the very air with sunshine dust.

" This is the sunniest morning bedroom in the house," he said. " It's south-east."

The sunlight slashed into the masses of the blue cedar outside with a score of golden spears.

" The Dayspring from on High," he said. . . " I thought of rather a useful pamphlet in the night.

" I've been thinking about your luggage at that hotel," he went on, turning to his guest again. " You'll have to write and get it packed up and sent down here——

" No," he said, " we won't let you go until you can hit out with that arm and fell a man. Listen ! "

Mr. Direck could not distinguish any definite sound.

" The smell of frying rashers, I mean," said Mr. Britling. " It's the clarion of the morn in every proper English home. . . .

" You'd like a rasher, coffee ?

" It's good to work in the night, and it's good to wake in the morning," said Mr. Britling, rubbing his hands together. " I suppose I wrote nearly two thousand words. So quiet one is, so concentrated. And as soon as I have had my breakfast I shall go on with it again."

CHAPTER FIVE

THE COMING OF THE DAY

§ 1

IT was quite characteristic of the state of mind of England in the summer of 1914 that Mr. Britling should be mightily concerned about the conflict in Ireland, and almost deliberately negligent of the possibility of a war with Germany.

The armament of Germany, the hostility of Germany, the consistent assertion of Germany, the world-wide clash of British and German interests, had been facts in the consciousness of Englishmen for more than a quarter of a century. A whole generation had been born and brought up in the threat of this German war. A threat that goes on for too long ceases to have the effect of a threat, and this overhanging possibility had become a fixed and scarcely disturbing feature of the British situation. It kept the navy sedulous and Colonel Rendezvous uneasy ; it stimulated a small and not very influential section of the press to a series of reminders that bored Mr. Britling acutely, it was the excuse for an agitation that made national service ridiculous, and quite subconsciously it affected his attitude to a hundred things. For example, it was a factor in his very keen indignation at the Tory levity in Ireland, in his disgust with many things that irritated or estranged Indian feeling. It bored him ; there it was, a danger, and there was no denying it, and yet he believed firmly that it was a mine that would never be fired, an avalanche that would never fall. It was a nuisance, a stupidity, that kept Europe drilling and wasted enormous sums on unavoidable preparations ; it hung up everything like a noisy argument in a drawing-room, but that human weakness and folly would ever let the mine actually explode he did not believe. He had been in France in 1911, he had seen how close things had come then to a conflict, and the fact that they had not come to a conflict had enormously strengthened his natural disposition to believe that at bottom Germany was sane and her militarism a bluff.

But the Irish difficulty was a different thing. There, he felt, was need for the liveliest exertions. A few obstinate people in influential positions were manifestly pushing things to an outrageous point. . . .

He wrote through the morning—and as the morning progressed the judicial calm of his opening intentions warmed to a certain regrettable vigour of phrasing about our politicians, about our political ladies, and our hand-to-mouth press. . . .

He came down to lunch in a frayed, exhausted condition,

and was much afflicted by a series of questions from Herr
Heinrich. For it was an incurable characteristic of Herr Heinrich that he asked questions ; the greater part of his conversation took the form of question and answer, and his thirst for
information was as marked as his belief that German should
not simply be spoken but spoken " out loud." He invariably
prefaced his inquiries with the word " Please," and he insisted
upon ascribing an omniscience to his employer which was
extremely irksome to justify after a strenuous morning of
enthusiastic literary effort. He now took the opportunity of a
lull in the solicitudes and congratulations that had followed Mr.
Direck's appearance—and Mr. Direck was so little shattered
by his misadventure that with the assistance of the kindly
Teddy he had got up and dressed and come down to lunch—
to put the matter that had been occupying his mind all the
morning, even to the detriment of the lessons of the Masters
Britling.

" Please ! " he said, going a deeper shade of pink and partly
turning to Mr. Britling.

A look of resignation came into Mr. Britling's eyes. " Yes ? "
he said.

" I do not think it will be wise to take my ticket for the
Esperanto Conference at Boulogne. Because I think it is
probable to be war between Austria and Serbia, and that
Russia may make war on Austria."

" That may happen. But I think it improbable."

" If Russia makes war on Austria, Germany will make war
on Russia, will she not ? "

" Not if she is wise," said Mr. Britling, " because that would
bring in France."

" That is why I ask. If Germany goes to war with France I
should have to go to Germany to do my service. It will be a
great inconvenience to me."

" I don't imagine Germany will do anything so frantic as
to attack Russia. That would not only bring in France but
ourselves."

" England ? "

" Of course. We can't afford to see France go under. The
thing is as plain as daylight. So plain that it cannot possibly
happen. . . . Cannot. . . . Unless Germany wants a universal
war."

" Thank you," said Herr Heinrich, looking obedient rather
than reassured.

" I suppose now," said Mr. Direck after a pause, " that there
isn't any strong party in Germany that wants a war. That
young Crown Prince, for example."

" They keep him in order," said Mr. Britling a little irritably.
" They keep him in order. . . .

" I used to be an alarmist about Germany," said Mr. Britling,
" but I have come to feel more and more confidence in the

sound common sense of the mass of the German population, and in the Emperor too if it comes to that. He is—if Herr Heinrich will permit me to agree with his own German comic papers—sometimes a little theatrical, sometimes a little egotistical, but in his operatic, boldly coloured way he means peace. I am convinced he means peace. . . ."

§ 2

After lunch Mr. Britling had a brilliant idea for the ease and comfort of Mr. Direck.

It seemed as though Mr. Direck would be unable to write any letters until his wrist had mended. Teddy tried him with a typewriter, but Mr. Direck was very awkward with his left hand, and then Mr. Britling suddenly remembered a little peculiarity he had which it was possible that Mr. Direck might share unconsciously, and that was his gift of looking-glass writing with his left hand. Mr. Britling had found out quite by chance in his schoolboy days that while his right hand had been laboriously learning to write, his left hand, all unsuspected, had been picking up the same lesson, and that by taking a pencil in his left hand and writing from right to left, without watching what he was writing, and then examining the scrawl in a mirror, he could reproduce his own handwriting in exact reverse. About three people out of five have this often quite unsuspected ability. He demonstrated his gift, and then Miss Cecily Corner, who had dropped in in a casual sort of way to ask about Mr. Direck, tried it, and then Mr. Direck tried it. And they could all do it. And then Teddy brought a sheet of copying carbon, and so Mr. Direck, by using the carbon reversed under his paper, was restored to the world of correspondence again.

They sat round a little table under the cedar-trees amusing themselves with these experiments, and after that Cecily and Mr. Britling and the two small boys entertained themselves by drawing pigs with their eyes shut, and then Mr. Britling and Teddy played hard at Badminton until it was time for tea. And Cecily sat by Mr. Direck and took an interest in his accident, and he told her about summer holidays in the Adirondacks and how he loved to travel. She said she would love to travel. He said that so soon as he was better he would go on to Paris and then into Germany. He was extraordinarily curious about this Germany and its tremendous militarism. He'd far rather see it than Italy, which was, he thought, just all art and ancient history. His turn was for modern problems. Though of course he didn't intend to leave out Italy while he was at it. And then their talk was scattered, and there was great excitement because Herr Heinrich had lost his squirrel.

He appeared coming out of the house into the sunshine, and so distraught that he had forgotten the protection of his hat. He was very pink and deeply moved.

" But what shall I do without him ? " he cried. " He has gone ! "

The squirrel, Mr. Direck gathered, had been bought by Mrs. Britling for the boys some month or so ago ; it had been christened " Bill " and adored and then neglected until Herr Heinrich took it over. It had filled a place in his ample heart that the none too demonstrative affection of the Britling household had left empty. He abandoned his pursuit of philology almost entirely for the cherishing and adoration of this busy, nimble little creature. He carried it off to his own room, where it ran loose and took the greatest liberties with him and his apartment. It was an extraordinarily bold and savage little beast even for a squirrel, but Herr Heinrich had set his heart and his very large and patient will upon the establishment of sentimental relations. He believed that ultimately Bill would let himself be stroked, that he would make Bill love him and understand him, and that his would be the only hand that Bill would ever suffer to touch him. In the meanwhile even the untamed Bill was wonderful to watch. One could watch him for ever. His front paws were like hands, like a musician's hands, very long and narrow. " He would be a musician if he could only make his fingers go apart, because when I play my violin he listens. He is attentive."

The entire household became interested in Herr Heinrich's attacks upon Bill's affection. They watched his fingers with particular interest because it was upon those that Bill vented his failures to respond to the stroking advances.

" To-day I have stroked him once and he has bitten me three times," Herr Heinrich reported. " Soon I will stroke him three times and he shall not bite me at all. . . . Also yesterday he climbed up me and sat on my shoulder, and suddenly bit my ear. It was not hard he bit, but sudden.

" He does not mean to bite," said Herr Heinrich. " Because when he has bit me he is sorry. He is ashamed.

" You can see he is ashamed."

Assisted by the two small boys, Herr Heinrich presently got a huge bough of oak and brought it into his room, converting the entire apartment into the likeness of an aviary. " For this," said Herr Heinrich, looking grave and diplomatic through his glasses, " Billy will be very grateful. And it will give him confidence with me. It will make him feel we are in the forest together."

Mrs. Britling came to consult her husband in the matter.

" It is not right that the bedroom should be filled with trees. All sorts of dust and litter came in with it."

" If it amuses him," said Mr. Britling.

" But it makes work for the servants."

" Do they complain ? "

" No."

" Things will adjust themselves. And it is amusing that he should do such a thing. . . ."

And now Billy had disappeared, and Herr Heinrich was on the verge of tears. It was so ungrateful of Billy. Without a word.

" They leave my window open," he complained to Mr. Direck. " Often I have askit them not to. And of course he did not understand. He has out climbit by the ivy. Anything may have happened to him. Anything. He is not used to going out alone. He is too young.

" Perhaps if I call——"

And suddenly he had gone off round the house crying : " Beelee ! Beelee ! Here is an almond for you ! An almond, Beelee ! "

" Makes me want to get up and help," said Mr. Direck. " It's a tragedy."

Everybody else was helping. Even the gardener and his boy knocked off work and explored the upper recesses of various possible trees.

" He is too young," said Herr Heinrich, drifting back. . . . And then presently : " If he heard my voice I am sure he would show himself. But he does not show himself."

It was clear he feared the worst. . . .

At supper Billy was the sole topic of conversation, and condolence was in the air. The impression that on the whole he had displayed rather a brutal character was combated by Herr Heinrich, who held that a certain brusqueness was Billy's only fault, and told anecdotes, almost sacred anecdotes, of the little creature's tenderer, nobler side. " When I feed him always he says, ' Thank you,' " said Herr Heinrich. " He never fails." He betrayed darker thoughts. " When I went round by the barn there was a cat that sat and looked at me out of a laurel bush," he said. " I do not like cats."

Mr. Lawrence Carmine, who had dropped in, was suddenly reminded of that lugubrious old ballad, " The Mistletoe Bough," and recited large worn fragments of it impressively. It tells how a beautiful girl hid away in a chest during a Christmas game of hide-and-seek, and how she was found, a dried vestige, years afterwards. It took a very powerful hold upon Herr Heinrich's imagination. " Let us now," he said, " make an examination of every box and cupboard and drawer. Marking each as we go. . . ."

When Mr. Britling went to bed that night, after a long gossip with Carmine about the Brahma Samaj and modern developments of Indian thought generally, the squirrel was still undiscovered.

The worthy modern thinker undressed slowly, blew out his candle and got into bed. Still meditating deeply upon the God of the Tagores, he thrust his right hand under his pillow according to his usual practice, and encountered something soft and warm and active. He shot out of bed convulsively, lit his candle, and lifted his pillow discreetly.

He discovered the missing Billy looking crumpled and annoyed.

For some moments there was a lively struggle before Billy was gripped. He chattered furiously and bit Mr. Britling twice. Then Mr. Britling was out in the passage with the wriggling lump of warm fur in his hand, and paddling along in the darkness to the door of Herr Heinrich. He opened it softly.

A startled white figure sat up in bed sharply.

" Billy," said Mr. Britling by way of explanation, dropped his capture on the carpet, and shut the door on the touching reunion.

§ 3

A day was to come when Mr. Britling was to go over the history of that sunny July with incredulous minuteness, trying to trace the real succession of events that led from the startling crime at Sarajevo to Europe's last swift rush into war. In a sense it was untraceable ; in a sense it was so obvious that he was amazed the whole world had not watched the coming of disaster. The plain fact of the case was that there was no direct connection ; the Sarajevo murders were dropped for two whole weeks out of the general consciousness, they went out of the papers, they ceased to be discussed ; then they were picked up again and used as an excuse for war. Germany, armed so as to be a threat to all the world, weary at last of her mighty vigil, watching the course of events, decided that her moment had come, and snatched the dead archduke out of his grave again to serve her tremendous ambition.

It may well have seemed to the belligerent German patriot that all her possible foes were confused, divided within themselves, at an extremity of distraction and impotence. The British Isles seemed slipping steadily into civil war. Threat was met by counter-threat, violent fool competed with violent fool for the admiration of the world, the National Volunteers armed against the Ulster men ; everything moved on with a kind of mechanical precision from parade and meeting towards the fatal gun-running of Howth and the first bloodshed in Dublin streets. That wretched affray, far more than any other single thing, must have stiffened Germany in the course she had chosen. There can be no doubt of it ; the mischief-makers of Ireland set the final confirmation upon the European war. In England itself there was a summer fever of strikes ; Liverpool was choked by a dockers' strike, the East Anglian agricultural labourers were in revolt, and the building trade throughout the country was on the verge of a lock-out. Russia seemed to be in the crisis of a social revolution. From Baku to St. Petersburg there were insurrectionary movements in the towns, and on the 23rd—the very day of the Austrian ultimatum—Cossacks were storming barbed-wire entanglements in the streets of the capital. The London Stock Exchange was in a state of panic disorganisation because of a vast mysterious selling of securities from abroad.   And France, France it seemed was lost to all other consideration in the enthralling confrontations and denunciations of the Caillaux murder trial, the trial of the wife of her ex-Prime Minister for the murder of a blackmailing journalist.   It was a case full of the vulgarest sexual violence.   Before so piquant a spectacle France it seemed could have no time nor attention for the revelation of M. Humbert, the Reporter of the Army Committee, proclaiming that the artillery was short of ammunition, that her infantry had boots " thirty years old " and not enough of those. . . .

Such were the appearances of things. Can it be wondered if it seemed to the German mind that the moment for the triumphant assertion of the German predominance in the world had come ?   A day or so before the Dublin shooting, the murder of Sarajevo had been dragged again into the foreground of the world's affairs by an ultimatum from Austria to Serbia of the extremest violence.   From the hour when the ultimatum was discharged the way to Armageddon lay wide and unavoidable before the feet of Europe. After the Dublin conflict there was no turning back.   For a week Europe was occupied by proceedings that were little more than the recital of a formula.   Austria could not withdraw her unqualified threats without admitting error and defeat, Russia could not desert Serbia without disgrace, Germany stood behind Austria, France was bound to Russia by a long confederacy of mutual support, and it was impossible for England to witness the destruction of France or the further strengthening of a loud and threatening rival. It may be that Germany counted on Russia giving way to her, it may be she counted on the indecisions and feeble perplexities of England, both these possibilities were in the reckoning, but chiefly she counted on war.   She counted on war, and since no other nation in all the world had ever been so fully prepared in every way for war, she also counted on victory.

One writes " Germany."   That is how one writes of nations, as though they had single brains and single purposes.   But indeed while Mr. Britling lay awake and thought of his son and Lady Frensham and his smashed automobile and Mrs. Harrowdean's trick of abusive letter-writing and of God and evil and a thousand perplexities, a multitude of other brains must also have been busy, lying also in beds or sitting in studies or watching in guard-rooms or chatting belatedly in cafés or smoking-rooms or pacing the bridges of battleships or walking along in city or country, upon this huge possibility the crime of Sarajevo had just opened, and of the state of the world in relation to such possibilities. Few women, one guesses, heeded what was happening, and of the men, the men whose decision to launch that implacable threat turned the destinies of the world to war, there is no reason to believe that a single one of them had anything approaching the imaginative power needed to understand fully what it was they were doing. We have looked for an hour or so into the seething pot of Mr. Britling's brain and marked its multiple strands, its inconsistencies, its irrational transitions. It was but a specimen. Nearly every brain of the select few that counted in this cardinal determination of the world's destinies had its streak of personal motive, its absurd and petty impulses and deflections. One man decided to say *this*, because if he said *that* he would contradict something he had said and printed four or five days ago ; another took a certain line because so he saw his best opportunity of putting a rival into a perplexity. It would be strange if one could reach out now and recover the states of mind of two such beings as the German Kaiser and his eldest son as Europe stumbled towards her fate through the long days and warm close nights of that July. Here was the occasion for which so much of their lives had been but the large pretentious preparation, coming right into their hands to use or forgo, here was the opportunity that would put them into the very forefront of history for ever ; this journalist emperor with the paralysed arm, this common-fibred, sly, lascivious son. It is impossible that they did not dream of glory over all the world, of triumphant processions, of a world-throne that would outshine Cæsar's, of a god-like elevation, of acting Divus Cæsar while yet alive. And being what they were they must have imagined spectators, and the young man, who was after all a young man of particularly poor quality, imagined no doubt certain women onlookers, certain humiliated and astonished friends, and thought of the clothes he would wear and the gestures he would make. The nickname his English cousins had given this heir to all the glories was the " White Rabbit." He was the backbone of the war party at court. And presently he stole bric-à-brac. That will help posterity to the proper values of things in 1914. And the Teutonic generals and admirals and strategists with their patient and perfect plans, who were so confident of victory, each within a busy skull must have enacted anticipatory dreams of his personal success and marshalled his willing and unwilling admirers. Readers of histories and memoirs as most of this class of men are, they must have composed little eulogistic descriptions of the part themselves were to play in the opening drama, imagined pleasing vindications and interesting documents. Some of them perhaps saw difficulties, but few foresaw failure. For all this set of brains the thing came as a choice to take or reject ; they could make war or prevent it. And they chose war.

It is doubtful if any one outside the directing intelligence of Germany and Austria saw anything so plain. The initiative was with Germany. The Russian brains and the French brains and the British brains, the few that were really coming round to look at this problem squarely, had a far less simple set of problems and profounder uncertainties. To Mr. Britling's mind the Round Table Conference at Buckingham Palace was typical of the disunion and indecision that lasted up to the very outbreak of hostilities. The solemn violence of Sir Edward Carson was intensely antipathetic to Mr. Britling, and in his retrospective inquiries he pictured to himself that dark figure with its drooping underlip, seated, heavy and obstinate, at that discussion, still implacable though the King had but just departed after a little speech that was packed with veiled intimations of imminent danger. . . .

Mr. Britling had no mercy in his mind for the treason of obstinate egotism and for persistence in a mistaken course. His own temperamental weaknesses lay in such different directions. He was always ready to leave one trail for another ; he was always open to conviction, trusting to the essentials of his character for an ultimate consistency. He hated Carson in those days as a Scotch terrier might hate a bloodhound, as something at once more effective and impressive, and exasperatingly, infinitely, less intelligent.

§ 4

Thus—a vivid fact as yet only in a few hundred skulls or so—the vast catastrophe of the Great War gathered behind the idle, dispersed, and confused spectacle of an indifferent world, very much as the storms and rains of late September gather behind the glow and lassitudes of August, and with scarcely more of set human intention. For the greater part of mankind the European international situation was at most something in the papers, no more important than the political disturbances in South Africa, where the Herzogites were curiously uneasy, or the possible trouble between Turkey and Greece. The things that really interested people in England during the last months of peace were boxing and the summer sales. A brilliant young Frenchman, Carpentier, who had knocked out Bombardier Wells, came over again to defeat Gunboat Smith, and did so to the infinite delight of France and the whole Latin world, amidst the generous applause of Anglo-Saxondom. And there was also a British triumph over the Americans at polo, and a lively and cultured newspaper discussion about a proper motto for the arms of the London County Council. The trial of Madame Caillaux filled the papers with animated reports and vivid pictures ; Gregori Rasputin was stabbed and became the subject of much lively

gossip about the Russian Court; and Ulivi, the Italian im-
postor who claimed he could explode mines by means of an
" ultra-red " ray, was exposed and fled with a lady, very
amusingly. For a few days all the work at Woolwich Arsenal
was held up because a certain Mr. Entwhistle, having refused
to erect a machine on a concrete bed laid down by non-
unionists, was rather uncivilly dismissed, and the Irish trouble
pounded along its tiresome mischievous way. People gave a
divided attention to these various topics, and went about
their individual businesses.

And at Dower House they went about their businesses.
Mr. Direck's arm healed rapidly ; Cecily Corner and he talked
of their objects in life and Utopias and the books of Mr.
Britling, and he got down from a London bookseller Baedeker's
guides for Holland and Belgium, South Germany, and Italy ;
Herr Heinrich after some doubt sent in his application form
and his preliminary deposit for the Esperanto Conference
at Boulogne, and Billy consented to be stroked three times,
but continued to bite with great vigour and promptitude.
And the trouble about Hugh, Mr. Britling's eldest son, resolved
itself into nothing of any vital importance, and settled itself
very easily.

§ 5

After Hugh had cleared things up and gone back to London,
Mr. Britling was inclined to think that such a thing as apprehension was a sin against the general fairness and integrity of
life.

Of all things in the world Hugh was the one that could
most easily rouse Mr. Britling's unhappy aptitude for distressing imaginations. Hugh was nearer by far to his heart
and nerves than any other creature. In the last few years
Mr. Britling, by the light of a variety of emotional excursions
in other directions, had been discovering this. Whatever
Mr. Britling discovered he talked about ; he had evolved
from his realisation of this tenderness, which was without
an effort so much tenderer than all the subtle and tremendous
feelings he had attempted in his—excursions, the theory
that he had expounded to Mr. Direck that it is only through
our children that we are able to achieve disinterested love,
real love. But that left unexplained the far more intimate
emotional hold of Hugh than of his very jolly little step-
brothers. That was a fact into which Mr. Britling rather
sedulously wouldn't look. . . .

Mr. Britling was probably much franker and more open-
eyed with himself and the universe than a great number of
intelligent people, and yet there was quite a number of aspects
of his relations with his wife, with people about him, with
his country and God and the nature of things, upon which
he turned his back with an attentive persistence. But a back

too resolutely turned may be as indicative as a pointing finger, and in this retrogressive way, and tacitly even so far as his formal thoughts, his unspoken comments, went, Mr. Britling knew that he loved his son because he had lavished the most hope and the most imagination upon him, because he was the one living continuation of that dear life with Mary, so lovingly stormy at the time, so fine now in memory, that had really possessed the whole heart of Mr. Britling. The boy had been the joy and marvel of the young parents ; it was incredible to them that there had ever been a creature so delicate and sweet, and they brought considerable imagination and humour to the detailed study of his minute personality and to the forecasting of his future.   Mr. Britling's mind blossomed with wonderful schemes for his education.   All that mental growth no doubt contributed greatly to Mr. Britling's peculiar affection, and with it there interwove still tenderer and subtler elements, for the boy had a score of Mary's traits. But there were other things still more conspicuously ignored. One silent factor in the slow widening of the breach between Edith and Mr. Britling was her cool estimate of her stepson. She was steadfastly kind to this shock-headed, untidy little dreamer, he was extremely well cared for in her hands, she liked him and she was amused by him—it is difficult to imagine what more Mr. Britling could have expected—but it was as plain as daylight that she felt that this was not the child she would have cared to have borne. It was quite preposterous and perfectly natural that this should seem to Mr. Britling to be unfair to Hugh.

Edith's home was more prosperous than Mary's ; she brought her own money to it ; the bringing up of her children was a far more efficient business than Mary's instinctive proceedings.   Hugh had very nearly died in his first year of life ; some summer infection had snatched at him ; that had tied him to his father's heart by a knot of fear ; but no infection had ever come near Edith's own nursery.   And it was Hugh that Mr. Britling had seen, small and green-faced and pitiful under an anæsthetic for some necessary operation to his adenoids.   His younger children had never stabbed to Mr. Britling's heart with any such pitifulness ; they were not so thin-skinned as their elder brother, not so assailable by the little animosities of dust and germ.   And out of such things as this evolved a shapeless cloud of championship for Hugh. Jealousies and suspicions are latent in every human relationship.   We go about the affairs of life pretending magnificently that they are not so, pretending to the generosities we desire. And in all step-relationships jealousy and suspicion are not merely latent, they stir.

It was Mr. Britling's case for Hugh that he was something exceptional, something exceptionally good, and that the peculiar need there was to take care of him was due to a delicacy of nerve and fibre that was ultimately a virtue. The boy was quick, quick to hear, quick to move, very accurate in his swift way, he talked unusually soon, he began to sketch at an early age with an incurable roughness and a remarkable expressiveness. That he was sometimes ungainly, often untidy, that he would become so mentally preoccupied as to be uncivil to people about him, that he caught any malaise that was going, was all a part of that. The sense of Mrs. Britling's unexpressed criticism, the implied contrasts with the very jolly, very uninspired younger family, kept up a nervous desire in Mr. Britling for evidences and manifestations of Hugh's quality. Not always with happy results ; it caused much mutual irritation, but not enough to prevent the growth of a real response on Hugh's part to his father's solicitude. The youngster knew and felt that his father was his father just as certainly as he felt that Mrs. Britling was not his mother. To his father he brought his successes and to his father he appealed.

But he brought his successes more readily than he brought his troubles. So far as he himself was concerned he was disposed to take a humorous view of the things that went wrong and didn't come off with him, but as a " Tremendous Set-Down for the Proud Parent " they resisted humorous treatment. . . .

Now the trouble that he had been hesitating to bring before his father was concerned with that very grave interest of the young, his Object in Life. It had nothing to do with those erotic disturbances that distressed his father's imagination. Whatever was going on below the surface of Hugh's smiling or thoughtful presence in that respect had still to come to the surface and find expression. But he was bothered very much by divergent strands in his own intellectual composition. Two sets of interests pulled at him, one—it will seem a dry interest to many readers, but for Hugh it glittered and fascinated— was crystallography and molecular physics ; the other was caricature. Both aptitudes sprang no doubt from the same exceptional sensitiveness to form. As a schoolboy he exercised both very happily, but now he was getting to the age of specialisation, and he was fluctuating very much between science and art. After a spell of scientific study he would come upon a fatigue period and find nothing in life but absurdities and a lark that one could represent very amusingly ; after a bout of funny drawings his mind went back to his light and crystals and films like a Magdalen repenting in a church. After his public school he had refused Cambridge and gone to University College, London, to work under the great and inspiring Professor Cardinal ; simultaneously Cardinal had been arranging to go to Cambridge, and Hugh had scarcely embarked upon his London work when Cardinal was succeeded by the dull, conscientious and depressing Pelkingham, at whose touch crystals became as puddings, bubble films like cotton sheets, transparency vanished from the world, and X-rays dwarfed and died. And Hugh degenerated immediately into a scoffing trifler who wished to give up science for art.

He gave up science for art after grave consultation with his father, and the real trouble that had been fretting him, it seemed, was that now he repented and wanted to follow Cardinal to Cambridge, and—a year lost—go on with science again. He felt it was a discreditable fluctuation ; he knew it would be a considerable expense ; and so he took two weeks before he could screw himself up to broaching the matter.

" So *that* is all ! " said Mr. Britling, immensely relieved.

" My dear Parent, you didn't think I had backed a bill or forged a cheque ? "

" I thought you might have married a chorus girl or something of that sort," said Mr. Britling.

" Or bought a large cream-coloured motor-car for her on the instalment system, which she'd smashed up. No, that sort of thing comes later. . . . I'll just put myself down on the waiting-list of one of those bits of delight in the Cambridge tobacco-shops—and go on with my studies for a year or two. . . ."

§ 6

Though Mr. Britling's anxiety about his son was dispelled, his mind remained curiously apprehensive throughout July. He had a feeling that things were not going well with the world, a feeling he tried in vain to dispel by various distractions. Perhaps some subtler subconscious analysis of the situation was working out probabilities that his conscious self would not face. And when presently he bicycled off to Mrs. Harrowdean for flattery, amusement, and comfort generally, he found her by no means the exalting confirmation of everything he wished to believe about himself and the universe, that had been her delightful rôle in the early stages of their romantic friendship. She maintained her hostility to Edith ; she seemed bent on making things impossible. And yet there were one or two phases of the old sustaining intimacies.

On the afternoon of his arrival they walked across her absurd little park to the summer-house with the view, and they discussed the Irish pamphlet which was now nearly finished.

" Of course," she said, " it will be a wonderful pamphlet."

There was a reservation in her voice that made him wait.

" But I suppose all sorts of people could write an Irish pamphlet. Nobody but you could write ' The Silent Places.' Oh, *why* don't you finish that great beautiful thing, and leave all this world of reality and newspapers, all these Crude, Vulgar, Quarrelsome, Jarring things to other people ? You have the magic gift, you might be a poet, you can take us out of all these horrid things that are, away to Beautyland, and you are just content to be a critic and a disputer. It's your surroundings. It's your sordid realities. It's that Practicality at your elbow. You ought never to *see* a newspaper. You ought never to have an American come within ten miles of you. You ought to live on bowls of milk drunk in valleys of asphodel."

Mr. Britling, who liked this sort of thing in a way, and yet at the same time felt ridiculously distended and altogether preposterous while it was going on, answered feebly and self-consciously.

"There was your letter in *The Nation* the other day," she said. "Why do you get drawn into arguments? I wanted to rush into *The Nation* and pick you up and wipe the anger off you, and carry you out of it all—into some quiet beautiful place."

"But one *has* to answer these people," said Mr. Britling, rolling along by the side of her like the full moon beside Venus, and quite artlessly falling in with the tone of her.

She repeated lines from "The Silent Places" from memory. She threw quite wonderful emotion into her voice. She made the words glow. And he had only shown her the thing once. . . .

Was he indeed burying a marvellous gift under the dust of current affairs? When at last in the warm evening light they strolled back from the summer-house to dinner he had definitely promised her that he would take up and finish "The Silent Places." . . . And think over the Irish pamphlet again before he published it. . . .

Pyecrafts was like a crystal casket of finer soil withdrawn from the tarred highways of the earth. . . .

And yet the very next day this angel enemy of controversies broke out in the most abominable way about Edith, and he had to tell her more plainly than he had done hitherto that he could not tolerate that sort of thing. He wouldn't have Edith guyed. He wouldn't have Edith made to seem base. And at that there was much trouble between them, and tears and talk of Oliver. . . .

Mr. Britling found himself unable to get on either with "The Silent Places" or the pamphlet, and he was very unhappy. . . .

Afterwards she repented very touchingly, and said that if only he would love her she would swallow a thousand Ediths. He waived a certain disrespect in the idea of her swallowing Edith, and they had a beautiful reconciliation and talked of exalted things, and in the evening he worked quite well upon "The Silent Places" and thought of half-a-dozen quite wonderful lines, and in the course of the next day he returned to Dower House and Mr. Direck and considerable piles of correspondence and the completion of the Irish pamphlet.

But he was restless. He was more restless in his house than he had ever been. He could not understand it. Everything about him was just as it had always been, and yet it was unsatisfactory, and it seemed more unstable than anything had ever seemed before. He was bored by the solemn development of the Irish dispute ; he was irritated by the smouldering threat of the Balkans ; he was irritated by the suffragettes and by a string of irrational little strikes ; by the general absence of any main plot as it were to hold all these wranglings and trivialities together. . . . At the Dower House the most unpleasant thoughts would come to him. He even had doubts whether in " The Silent Places " he had been plagiarising, more or less unconsciously, from Henry James's " Great Good Place." . . .

On the 21st of July Gladys came back repaired and looking none the worse for her misadventure. Next day he drove her very carefully over to Pyecrafts, hoping to drug his uneasiness with the pretence of a grand passion and the praises of " The Silent Places," that beautiful work of art that was so free from any taint of application, and alas ! he found Mrs. Harrowdean in an evil mood. He had been away from her for ten days—ten whole days. No doubt Edith had manœuvred to keep him. She hadn't ! *Hadn't* she ? How was he, poor simple soul ! to tell that she hadn't ? That was the prelude to a stormy afternoon.

The burthen of Mrs. Harrowdean was that she was wasting her life, that she was wasting the poor, good, patient Oliver's life, that for the sake of friendship she was braving the worst imputations and that he treated her cavalierly, came when he wished to do so, stayed away heartlessly, never thought she needed *little* treats, *little* attentions, *little* presents. Did he think she could settle down to her poor work, such as it was, in neglect and loneliness ? He forgot women were dear little tender things, and had to be made happy and *kept* happy. Oliver might not be clever and attractive, but he did at least in his clumsy way understand and try to do his duty. . . .

Towards the end of the second hour of such complaints the spirit of Mr. Britling rose in revolt. He lifted up his voice against her, he charged his voice with indignant sorrow and declared that he had come over to Pyecrafts with no thought in his mind but sweet and loving thoughts, that he had but waited for Gladys to be ready before he came, that he had brought over the manuscript of " The Silent Places " with him to polish and finish up, that " for days and days " he had been longing to do this in the atmosphere of the dear old summer-house with its distant view of the dear old sea, and that now all that was impossible, that Mrs. Harrowdean had made it impossible, and that indeed she was rapidly making everything impossible. . . .

And having delivered himself of this judgment Mr. Britling,

a little surprised at the rapid vigour of his anger, once he had let it loose, came suddenly to an end of his words, made a renunciatory gesture with his arms, and as if struck with the idea, rushed out of her room and out of the house to where Gladys stood waiting.   He got into her and started her up, and after some trouble with the gear due to the violence of his emotion, he turned her round and departed with her— crushing the corner of a small bed of snapdragon as he turned —and drove her with a sulky sedulousness back to the Dower House and newspapers and correspondence and irritations, and that gnawing and irrational sense of a hollow and aimless quality in the world that he had hoped Mrs. Harrowdean would assuage.   And the farther he went from Mrs. Harrowdean the harsher and unjuster it seemed to him that he had been to her.

But he went on because he did not see how he could very well go back.

§ 7

Mr. Direck's damaged wrist healed sooner than he desired. From the first he had protested that it was the sort of thing that one can carry about in a sling, that he was quite capable of travelling about and taking care of himself in hotels, that he was only staying on at Matching's Easy because he just loved to stay on and wallow in Mrs. Britling's kindness and Mr. Britling's company.   While as a matter of fact he wallowed as much as he could in the freshness and friendliness of Miss Cecily Corner, and for more than a third of this period Mr. Britling was away from home altogether.

Mr. Direck, it should be clear by this time, was a man of more than European simplicity and directness, and his intentions towards the young lady were as simple and direct and altogether honest as such intentions can be.   It is the American conception of gallantry more than any other people's to let the lady call the tune in these affairs ; the man's place is to be protective, propitiatory, accommodating and clever, and the lady's to be difficult but delightful until he catches her and houses her splendidly and gives her a surprising lot of pocket-money, and goes about his business ; and upon these assumptions Mr. Direck went to work.   But quite early it was manifest to him that Cecily did not recognise his assumptions.   She was embarrassed when he got down one or two little presents of chocolates and flowers for her from London—the Britling boys were much more appreciative—she wouldn't let him contrive costly little expeditions for her, and she protested against compliments and declared she would stay away when he paid them.   And she was not contented by his general sentiments about life, but asked the most direct questions about his occupation and his activities.   His chief occupation was being the well-provided heir of a capable lawyer, and his

activities in the light of her inquiries struck him as being
light and a trifle amateurish, qualities he had never felt as
any drawback about them before.   So that he had to rely
rather upon aspirations and the possibility, under proper
inspiration, of a more actively serviceable life in future.

"There's a feeling in the States," he said, "that we've
had rather a tendency to overdo work, and that there is scope
for a leisure class to develop the refinement and the wider
meanings of life."

"But a leisure class doesn't mean a class that does nothing,"
said Cecily. "It only means a class that isn't busy in business."

"You're too hard on me," said Mr. Direck with that quiet
smile of his.

And then by way of putting her on the defensive he asked
her what she thought a man in his position ought to do.

"*Something*," she said, and in the expansion of this vague
demand they touched on a number of things. She said that
she was a Socialist, and there was still in Mr. Direck's composition a streak of the old-fashioned American prejudice
against the word.   He associated Socialists with Anarchists
and deported aliens.   It was manifest too that she was deeply
read in the essays and dissertations of Mr. Britling.   She
thought everybody, man or woman, ought to be chiefly engaged in doing something definite for the world at large.
("There's my secretaryship of the Massachusetts Modern
Thought Society, anyhow," said Mr. Direck.)   And she herself
wanted to be doing something—it was just because she did
not know what it was she ought to be doing that she was
reading so extensively and voraciously.   She wanted to lose
herself in something.   Deep in the being of Mr. Direck was
the conviction that what she ought to be doing was making
love in a rapturously egotistical manner, and enjoying every
scrap of her own delightful self and her own delightful vitality
—while she had it, but for the purposes of their conversation
he did not care to put it any more definitely than to say that
he thought we owed it to ourselves to develop our personalities.   Upon which she joined issue with great vigour.

"That is just what Mr. Britling says about you in his
'American Impressions,' " she said.   "He says that America
overdoes the development of personalities altogether, that,
whatever else is wrong about America, is most clearly wrong.
I read that this morning, and directly I read it I thought,
'Yes, that's exactly it! Mr. Direck is overdoing the development of personalities.' "

"Me!"

"Yes.   I like talking to you and I don't like talking to
you. And I see now it is because you keep on talking of my
Personality and your Personality. That makes me uncomfortable.   It's like having some one following me about with a
limelight.   And in a sort of way I do like it.   I like it and I'm

flattered by it, and then I go off and dislike it, dislike the effect of it. I find myself trying to be what you have told me I am—sort of acting myself. I want to glance at looking-glasses to see if I am keeping it up. It's just exactly what Mr. Britling says in his book about American women. They act themselves, he says ; they get a kind of story and explanation about themselves and they are always trying to make it perfectly plain and clear to every one. Well, when you do that you can't think nicely of other things."

" We like a clear light on people," said Mr. Direck.

" We don't. I suppose we're shadier," said Cecily.

" You're certainly much more in half-tones," said Mr. Direck. " And I confess it's the half-tones get hold of me. But still you haven't told me, Miss Cissie, what you think I ought to do with myself. Here I am, you see, very much at your disposal. What sort of business do you think it's my duty to go in for ? "

" That's for some one with more experience than I have, to tell you. You should ask Mr. Britling."

" I'd rather have it from you."

" I don't even know for myself," she said.

" So why shouldn't we start to find out together ? " he asked.

It was her tantalising habit to ignore all such tentatives.

" One can't help the feeling that one is in the world for something more than oneself," she said.

§ 8

Soon Mr. Direck could measure the time that was left to him at the Dower House no longer by days but by hours. His luggage was mostly packed, his tickets to Rotterdam, Cologne, Munich, Dresden, Vienna, were all in order. And things were still very indefinite between him and Cecily. But God has not made Americans clean-shaven and firm-featured for nothing, and he determined that matters must be brought to some sort of definition before he embarked upon travels that were rapidly losing their attractiveness in this concentration of his attention. . . .

A considerable nervousness betrayed itself in his voice and manner when at last he carried out his determination.

" There's just a lil' thing," he said to her, taking advantage of a moment when they were together after lunch, " that I'd value now more than anything else in the world."

She answered by a lifted eyebrow and a glance that had not so much inquiry in it as she intended.

" If we could just take a lil' walk together for a bit. Round by Claverings park and all that. See the deer again and the old trees. Sort of scenery I'd like to remember when I'm away from it."

He was a little short of breath, and there was a quite disproportionate gravity about her moment for consideration.

" Yes," she said with a cheerful acquiescence that came a couple of bars too late. " Let's. It will be jolly."

" These fine English afternoons are wonderful afternoons," he remarked after a moment or so of silence. " Not quite the splendid blaze we get in our summer, but—sort of glowing."

" It's been very fine all the time you've been here," she said. . . .

After which exchanges they went along the lane, into the road by the park fencing, and so to the little gate that lets one into the park, without another word.

The idea took hold of Mr. Direck's mind that until they got through the park gate it would be quite out of order to say anything. The lane and the road and the stile and the gate were all so much preliminary stuff to be got through before one could get to business. But after the little white gate the way was clear, the park opened out and one could get ahead without bothering about the steering. And Mr. Direck had, he felt, been diplomatically involved in lanes and byways long enough.

" Well," he said as he rejoined her after very carefully closing the gate. " What I really wanted was an opportunity of just mentioning something that happens to be of interest to you—if it does happen to interest you. . . . I suppose I'd better put the thing as simply as possible. . . . Practically. . . . I'm just right over the head and all in love with you. . . . I thought I'd like to tell you. . . ."

Immense silences.

" Of course I won't pretend there haven't been others," Mr. Direck suddenly resumed. " There have. One particularly. But I can assure you I've never felt the depth and height or anything like the sort of Quiet Clear Conviction. . . . And now I'm just telling you these things, Miss Corner, I don't know whether it will interest you if I tell you that you're really and truly the very first love I ever had as well as my last. I've had sent over—I got it only yesterday—this lil' photograph of a miniature portrait of one of my ancestor's relations —a Corner just as you are. It's here. . . ."

He had considerable difficulties with his pockets and papers. Cecily, mute and flushed and inconvenienced by a preposterous and unaccountable impulse to weep, took the picture he handed her.

" When I was a lil' fellow of fifteen," said Mr. Direck in the tone of one producing a melancholy but conclusive piece of evidence, " I *worshipped* that miniature. It seemed to me —the loveliest person. . . . And—it's just you. . . ."

He too was preposterously moved.

It seemed a long time before Cecily had anything to say, and then what she had to say she said in a softened indistinct voice. " You're very kind," she said, and kept hold of the little photograph.

They had halted for the photograph. Now they walked on again.

" I thought I'd like to tell you," said Mr. Direck and became tremendously silent.

Cecily found him incredibly difficult to answer. She tried to make herself light and offhand, and to be very frank with him.

" Of course," she said, " I knew—I felt somehow—you meant to say something of this sort to me—when you asked me to come with you——"

" Well ? " he said.

" And I've been trying to make my poor brain think of something to say to you."

She paused and contemplated her difficulties. . . .

" Couldn't you perhaps say something of the same kind—such as I've been trying to say ? " said Mr. Direck presently, with a note of earnest helpfulness. " I'd be very glad if you could."

" Not exactly," said Cecily, more careful than ever.

" Meaning ? "

" I think you know that you are the best of friends. I think you are, oh—a Perfect Dear."

" Well—that's all right—so far."

" That *is* as far."

" You don't know whether you love me ? That's what you mean to say."

" No. . . . I feel somehow it isn't that. . . . Yet. . ."

" There's nobody else by any chance ? "

" No." Cecily weighed things. " You needn't trouble about that."

" Only . . . only you don't know."

Cecily made a movement of assent.

" It's no good pretending I haven't thought about you," she said.

" Well, anyhow I've done my best to give you the idea," said Mr. Direck. " I seem now to have been doing that pretty nearly all the time."

" Only what should we do ? "

Mr. Direck felt this question was singularly artless. " Why ! —we'd marry," he said. " And all that sort of thing."

" Letty has married—and all that sort of thing," said Cecily, fixing her eye on him very firmly because she was colouring brightly. " And it doesn't leave Letty very much —forrader."

" Well now, they have a good time, don't they ? I'd have thought they have a lovely time ! "

" They've had a lovely time. And Teddy is the dearest husband. And they have a sweet little house and a most amusing baby. And they play hockey every Sunday. And Teddy does his work. And every week is like every other

week. It is just heavenly. Just always the same heavenly.
Every Sunday there is a fresh week of heavenly beginning.
And this, you see, isn't heaven; it is earth. And they don't
know it, but they are getting bored. I have been watching
them, and they are getting dreadfully bored. It's heart-
breaking to watch, because they are almost my dearest people.
Teddy used to be making perpetual jokes about the house and
the baby and his work and Letty, and now—he's made all the
possible jokes. It's only now and then he gets a fresh one. It's
like spring flowers and then—summer. And Letty sits about
and doesn't sing. They want something new to happen. . . .
And there's Mr. and Mrs. Britling. They love each other.
Much more than Mrs. Britling dreams, or Mr. Britling for the
matter of that. Once upon a time things were heavenly for
them too, I suppose. Until suddenly it began to happen to
them that nothing new ever happened. . . ."

"Well," said Mr. Direck, "people can travel."

"But that isn't *real* happening," said Cecily.

"It keeps one interested."

"But real happenings is doing something."

"You come back to that," said Mr. Direck. "I never met any
one before who'd quite got that spirit as you have it. I wouldn't
alter it. It's part of you. It's part of this place. It's what Mr.
Britling always seems to be saying and never quite knowing he's
said it. It's just as though all the things that are going on
weren't the things that ought to be going on—but something
else quite different. Somehow one falls into it. It's as if your
daily life didn't matter, as if politics didn't matter, as if the
King and the social round and business and all those things
weren't anything really, and as though you felt there was
something else—out of sight—round the corner—that you
ought to be getting at. Well, I admit that's got hold of me
too. And it's all mixed up with my idea of you. I don't see
that there's really a contradiction in it at all. I'm in love with
you, all my heart's in love with you, what's the good of being
shy about it? I'd just die for your littlest wish right here now,
it's just as though I'd got love in my veins instead of blood,
but that's not taking me away from that other thing. It's
bringing me round to that other thing. I feel as if without
you I wasn't up to anything at all, but *with* you—— We'd
not go settling down in a cottage or just touring about with
a Baedeker Guide or anything of that kind. Not for long anyhow. We'd naturally settle down side by side and *do* . . ."

"But what should we do?" asked Cecily.

There came a hiatus in their talk.

Mr. Direck took a deep breath.

"You see that old felled tree there. I was sitting on it the
day before yesterday and thinking of you. Will you come
there and sit with me on it? When you sit on it you get a
view, oh! a perfectly lovely English view, just a bit of the

house and those clumps of trees and the valley away there
with the lily-pond. I'd love to have you in my memory of
it. . . ."

They sat down, and Mr. Direck opened his case. He was
shy and clumsy about opening it, because he had been thinking
dreadfully hard about it, and he hated to seem heavy or profound or anything but artless and spontaneous to Cecily. And
he felt even when he did open his case that the effect of it was
platitudinous and disappointing. Yet when he had thought
it out it had seemed very profound and altogether living.

"You see one doesn't want to use terms that have been
used in a thousand different senses in any way that isn't a
perfectly unambiguous sense, and at the same time one doesn't
want to seem to be canting about things or pitching anything
a note or two higher than it ought legitimately to go, but it
seems to me that this sort of something that Mr. Britling is
always asking for in his essays and writings and things, and
what you are looking for just as much and which seems so
important to you that even love itself is a secondary kind of
thing until you can square the two together, is nothing more
nor less than Religion—I don't mean this Religion or that
Religion but just Religion itself, a Big, Solemn, Comprehensive
Idea that holds you and me and all the world together in one
great, grand universal scheme. And though it isn't quite the
sort of idea of love-making that's been popular—well, in places
like Carrierville—for some time, it's the right idea ; it's got
to be followed out if we don't want love-making to be a sort
of idle, troublesome game of treats and flatteries that is sure
as anything to lead right away to disappointments and foolishness and unfaithfulness, and—just Hell. What you are driving
at, according to my interpretation, is that marriage has got
to be a religious marriage or else you are splitting up life, that
religion and love are most of life and all the power there is in
it, and that they can't afford to be harnessed in two different
directions. . . . I never had these ideas until I came here and
met you, but they come up now in my mind as though they
had always been there. . . . And that's why you don't want
to marry in a hurry. And that's why I'm almost glad that you
don't want to marry in a hurry."

He considered. "That's why I'll have to go on to Germany,
and just let both of us turn things over in our minds."

"Yes," said Cecily weighing his speech. "I think that is
it. I think that I do want a religious marriage, and that what
is wrong with Teddy and Letty is that they aren't religious.
They pretend they are religious, somewhere out of sight and
round the corner. . . . Only——"

He considered her gravely.

"What *is* Religion ? " she asked.

Here again there was a considerable pause.

"Very nearly two-thirds of the papers read before our

Massachusetts society since my connection with it have dealt with that very question," Mr. Direck began. " And one of our most influential members was able to secure the services of a very able and highly trained young woman from Michigan University to make a digest of all these representative utterances. We are having it printed in a thoroughly artistic manner, as the club book for our autumn season. The drift of her results is that religion isn't the same thing as religions. That most religions are old and that religion is always new. . . . Well, putting it simply, religion is the perpetual rediscovery of that Great Thing Out There. . . . What the Great Thing is goes by all sorts of names, but if you know it's there and if you remember it's there, you've got religion. . . . That's about how she figured it out. . . . I shall send you the book as soon as a copy comes over to me. . . . I can't profess to put it as clearly as she puts it. She's got a real analytical mind. But it's one of the most suggestive lil' books I've ever seen. It just takes hold of you and *makes* you think."

He paused and regarded the ground before him—thoughtfully.

" Life," said Cecily, " has either got to be religious or else it goes to pieces. . . . Perhaps anyhow it goes to pieces. . . ."

Mr. Direck endorsed these observations by a slow nodding of the head.

He allowed a certain interval to elapse. Then a vaguely apprehended purpose that had been for a time forgotten in these higher interests came back to him. He took it up with a breathless sense of temerity.

" Well," he said, " then you don't hate me ? "

She smiled.

" You don't dislike me or despise me ? "

She was still reassuring.

" You don't think I'm just a slow American sort of portent ? "

" No."

" You think, on the whole, I might even—some day—— ? "

She tried to meet his eyes with a pleasant frankness, and perhaps she was franker than she meant to be.

" Look here," said Mr. Direck, with a little quiver of emotion softening his mouth. " I'll ask you something. We've got to wait. Until you feel clearer. Still . . . Could you bring yourself—— ?   If just once—I could kiss you. . . .

" I'm going away to Germany," he went on to her silence. " But I shan't be giving so much attention to Germany as I supposed I should when I planned it out. But somehow—if I felt—that I'd kissed you. . . ."

With a delusive effect of calmness the young lady looked first over her left shoulder and then over her right and surveyed the park about them. Then she stood up. " We can go that way home," she said with a movement of her head, " through the little covert."

Mr. Direck stood up too.

" If I was a poet or a bird," said Mr. Direck, " I should sing. But being just a plain American citizen all I can do is just to talk about all I'd do if I wasn't. . . ."

And when they had reached the little covert, with its pathway of soft moss and its sheltering screen of interlacing branches, he broke the silence by saying, " Well, what's wrong with right here and now ? " and Cecily stood up to him as straight as a spear, with gifts in her clear eyes. He took her soft cool face between his trembling hands and kissed her sweet half-parted lips. When he kissed her she shivered and he held her tighter and would have kissed her again. But she broke away from him, and he did not press her. And muter than ever, pondering deeply and secretly trembling in the queerest way, these two outwardly sedate young people returned to the Dower House. . . .

And after tea the taxicab from the junction came for him and he vanished, and was last seen as a waving hat receding along the top of the dog-rose hedge that ran beyond the hockey-field towards the village.

" He will see Germany long before I shall," said Herr Heinrich with a gust of nostalgia. " I wish almost I had not agreed to go to Boulogne."

And for some days Miss Cecily Corner was a very grave and dignified young woman indeed. Pondering. . . .

§ 9

After the departure of Mr. Direck things international began to move forward with great rapidity. It was exactly as if his American deliberation had hitherto kept things waiting. Before his postcard from Rotterdam reached the Dower House, Austria had sent an ultimatum to Serbia, and before Cecily had got the letter he wrote her from Cologne, a letter in that curiously unformed handwriting the stenographer and the typewriter are making an American characteristic, Russia was mobilising, and the vast prospect of a European war had opened like the rolling up of a curtain on which the interests of the former week had been but a trivial embroidery. So insistent was this reality that revealed itself that even the shooting of the Dublin people after the gun-running of Howth was dwarfed to unimportance. The mind of Mr. Britling came round from its restless wanderings to a more and more intent contemplation of the hurrying storm-clouds that swept out of nothingness to blacken all his sky. He watched it, he watched amazed and incredulous, he watched this contradiction of all his reiterated confessions of faith in German sanity and pacifism, he watched it with all that was impersonal in his being, and meanwhile his personal life ran in a continually deeper and narrower channel as his intelligence was withdrawn from it.

Never had the double refraction of his mind been more

clearly defined. On the one hand the Britling of the disinterested intelligence saw the habitual peace of the world vanish as the daylight vanishes when a shutter falls over the window of a cell ; and on the other the Britling of the private life saw all the pleasant comfort of his relations with Mrs. Harrowdean disappearing in a perplexing irrational quarrel. He did not want to lose Mrs. Harrowdean : he contemplated their breach with a profound and profoundly selfish dismay. It seemed the wanton termination of an arrangement of which he was only beginning to perceive the extreme and irreplaceable satisfactoriness.

It wasn't that he was in love with her. He knew, almost as clearly as though he had told himself as much, that he had not. But then, on the other hand, it was equally manifest in its subdued and ignored way that as a matter of fact she was hardly more in love with him. What constituted the satisfactoriness of the whole affair was its essential unlovingness and friendly want of emotion. It left their minds free to play with all the terms and methods of love without distress. She could summon tears and delights as one summons servants, and he could act his part as lover with no sense of lost control. They supplied in each other's lives a long-felt want—if only, that is, she could control her curious aptitude for jealousy and the sexual impulse to vex. There, he felt, she broke the convention of their relations and brought in serious realities, and this little rift it was that had widened to a now considerable breach. He knew that in every sane moment she dreaded and wished to heal that breach as much as he did. But the deep simplicities of the instincts they had tacitly agreed to bridge over washed the piers of their reconciliation away.

And unless they could restore the bridge things would end, and Mr. Britling felt that the ending of things would involve for him the most extraordinary exasperation. She would go to Oliver for comfort ; she would marry Oliver ; and he knew her well enough to be sure that she would thrust her matrimonial happiness with Oliver unsparingly upon his attention ; while he, on the other hand, being provided with no corresponding Olivette, would be left, a sort of emotional celibate, with his slack times and his afternoons and his general need for flattery and amusement dreadfully upon his own hands. He would be tormented by jealousy. In which case— and here he came to verities—his work would suffer. It wouldn't grip him while all these vague demands she satisfied fermented unassuaged.

And, after the fashion of our still too adolescent world, Mr. Britling and Mrs. Harrowdean proceeded to negotiate these extremely unromantic matters in the phrases of that simple, honest, and youthful passionateness which is still the only language available, and at times Mr. Britling came very near persuading himself that he had something of the passionate love for her that he had once had for his Mary, and that the possible loss of her had nothing to do with the convenience of Pyecrafts or any discretion in the world. Though indeed the only thing in the whole plexus of emotional possibility that still kept anything of its youthful freshness in his mind was the very strong objection indeed he felt to handing her over to anybody else in the world. And in addition he had just a touch of fatherly feeling that a younger man would not have had, and it made him very anxious to prevent her making a fool of herself by marrying a man out of spite. He felt that since an obstinate lover is apt to be an exacting husband, in the end the heavy predominance of Oliver might wring much sincerer tears from her than she had ever shed for himself. That generosity was but the bright edge to a jealousy mainly possessive.

It was Mr. Britling who reopened the correspondence by writing a little apology for the corner of the small snapdragon bed, and this evoked an admirably touching reply. He replied quite naturally with assurances and declarations. But before she got his second letter her mood had changed. She decided that if he had really and truly been lovingly sorry, instead of just writing her a note he would have rushed over to her in a wild, dramatic state of mind, and begged forgiveness on his knees. She wrote therefore a second letter to this effect, crossing his second one, and, her literary gift getting the better of her, she expanded her thesis into a general denunciation of his habitual offhandedness with her, to an abandonment of all hope of ever being happy with him, to a decision to end the matter once for all, and after a decent interval of dignified regrets to summon Oliver to the reward of his patience and goodness. The European situation was now at a pitch to get upon Mr. Britling's nerves, and he replied with a letter intended to be conciliatory, but which degenerated into earnest reproaches for her " unreasonableness." Meanwhile she had received his second and tenderly eloquent letter ; it moved her deeply, and having now cleared her mind of much that had kept it simmering uncomfortably, she replied with a sweetly loving epistle. From this point their correspondence had a kind of double quality, being intermittently angry and loving ; her third letter was tender, and it was tenderly answered in his fourth ; but in the interim she had received his third and answered it with considerable acerbity, to which his fifth was a retort, just missing her generous and conclusive fifth. She replied to his fifth on a Saturday evening—it was that eventful Saturday, Saturday the 1st of August, 1914—by a telegram. Oliver was abroad in Holland, engaged in a much-needed emotional rest, and she wired to Mr. Britling : " Have wired for Oliver, he will come to me, do not trouble to answer this."

She was astonished to get no reply for two days. She got no reply for two days because remarkable things were happening to the telegraph-wires of England just then, and her message, in the hands of a boy scout on a bicycle, reached Mr. Britling's house only on Monday afternoon. He was then at Claverings discussing the invasion of Belgium that made Britain's participation in the war inevitable, and he did not open the little red-brown envelope until about half-past six. He failed to mark the date and hours upon it, but he perceived that it was essentially a challenge. He was expected, he saw, to go over at once with his renovated Gladys and end this unfortunate clash for ever in one striking and passionate scene. His mind was now so full of the war that he found this the most colourless and unattractive of obligations. But he felt bound by the mysterious code of honour of the illicit love-affair to play his part. He postponed his departure until after supper—there was no reason why he should be afraid of motoring by moonlight if he went carefully—because Hugh came in with Cissie demanding a game of hockey. Hockey offered a nervous refreshment, a scampering forgetfulness of the tremendous disaster of this war he had always believed impossible, that nothing else could do, and he was very glad of the irruption. . . .

§ 10

For days the broader side of Mr. Britling's mind, as distinguished from its egotistical edge, had been reflecting more and more vividly and coherently the spectacle of civilisation casting aside the thousand dispersed activities of peace, clutching its weapons and setting its teeth, for a supreme struggle against militarist imperialism. From the point of view of Matching's Easy that colossal crystallising of accumulated antagonisms was for a time no more than a confusion of head-lines and a rearrangement of columns in the white windows of the newspapers through which those who lived in the securities of England looked out upon the world. It was a display in the sphere of thought and print immeasurably remote from the real green turf on which one walked, from the voice and the church-bells of Mr. Dimple that sounded their ample caresses in one's ears, from the clashing of the stags who were beginning to knock the velvet from their horns in the park, or the clatter of the butcher's cart and the respectful greeting of the butcher's boy down the lane. It was the spectacle of the world less real even to most imaginations than the world of novels or plays. People talked of these things always with an underlying feeling that they romanced and intellectualised.

On Thursday, July 23rd, the Austro-Hungarian minister at Belgrade presented his impossible ultimatum to the Serbian Government, and demanded a reply within forty-eight hours. With the wisdom of retrospect we know now clearly enough what that meant. The Sarajevo crime was to be resuscitated and made an excuse for war. But nine hundred and ninety-nine Europeans out of a thousand had still no suspicion of what was happening to them. The ultimatum figured prominently in the morning papers that came to Matching's Easy on Friday, but it by no means dominated the rest of the news ; Sir Edward Carson's rejection of the government proposals for Ulster was given the pride of place, and almost equally conspicuous with the Serbian news were the Caillaux trial and the storming of the St. Peterburg barricades by Cossacks. Herr Heinrich's questions at lunch-time received reassuring replies.

On Saturday Sir Edward Carson was still in the central limelight, Russia had intervened and demanded more time for Serbia, and *The Daily Chronicle* declared the day a critical one for Europe. Dublin with bayonet charges and bullets thrust Serbia into a corner on Monday. No shots had yet been fired in the East, and the mischief in Ireland that Germany had counted on was well ahead. Sir Edward Grey was said to be working hard for peace.

" It's the cry of wolf," said Mr. Britling to Herr Heinrich.

" But at last there did come a wolf," said Herr Heinrich. " I wish I had not sent my first moneys to that Conference upon Esperanto. I feel sure it will be put off."

" See ! " said Teddy very cheerfully to Herr Heinrich on Tuesday, and held up the paper, in which " The Bloodshed in Dublin " had squeezed the " War-Cloud Lifting " into a quite subordinate position.

" What did we tell you ? " said Mrs. Britling. " Nobody wants a European war."

But Wednesday's paper vindicated his fears. Germany had commanded Russia not to mobilise.

" Of course Russia will mobilise," said Herr Heinrich.

" Or else for ever after hold her peace," said Teddy.

" And then Germany will mobilise," said Herr Heinrich, " and all my holiday will vanish. I shall have to go and mobilise too. I shall have to fight. I have my papers."

" I never thought of you as a soldier before," said Teddy.

" I have deferred my service until I have done my thesis," said Herr Heinrich. " Now all that will be—Piff ! And my thesis three-quarters finished."

" That is serious," said Teddy.

" *Verdammte Dummheit !* " said Herr Heinrich. " Why do they do such things ? "

On Thursday, the 30th of July, Caillaux, Carson, strikes, and all the common topics of life had been swept out of the front page of the paper altogether ; the stock exchanges were in a state of wild perturbatiou, and food prices were leaping fantastically. Austria was bombarding Belgrade, contrary to the rules of war hitherto accepted ; Russia was mobilising ; Mr. Asquith was, he declared, not relaxing his efforts " to do everything possible to circumscribe the area of possible conflict," and the Vienna Conference of Peace Societies was postponed. " I do not see why a conflict between Russia and Austria should involve Western Europe," said Mr. Britling. " Our concern is only for Belgium and France."

But Herr Heinrich knew better. " No," he said. " It is the war. It has come. I have heard it talked about in Germany many times. But I have never believed that it was obliged to come. Ach ! It considers no one. So long as Esperanto is disregarded, all these things must be."

Friday brought photographs of the mobilisation in Vienna, and the news that Belgrade was burning. Young men in straw hats very like English or French or Belgian young men in straw hats were shown parading the streets of Vienna, carrying flags and banners portentously, blowing trumpets or waving hats and shouting. Saturday saw all Europe mobilising, and Herr Heinrich upon Teddy's bicycle in wild pursuit of evening papers at the junction. Mobilisation and the emotions of Herr Heinrich now became the central facts of the Dower House situation. The two younger Britlings mobilised with great vigour upon the play-room floor. The elder had one hundred and ninety toy soldiers with a considerable equipment of guns and wagons ; the younger had a force of a hundred and twenty-three, not counting three railway porters (with trucks complete), a policeman, five civilians and two ladies. Also they made a number of British and German flags out of paper. But as neither would allow his troops to be any existing foreign army, they agreed to be Redland and Blueland, according to the colour of their prevailing uniforms. Meanwhile Herr Heinrich confessed almost promiscuously the complication of his distresses by a hitherto unsuspected emotional interest in the daughter of the village publican. She was a placid receptive young woman named Maud Hickson on whom the young man had, it seemed, imposed the more poetical name of Marguerite.

" Often we have spoken together, oh yes, often," he assured Mrs. Britling. " And now it must all end. She loves flowers, she loves birds. She is most sweet and innocent. I have taught her many words in German and several times I have tried to draw her in pencil, and now I must go away and never see her any more."

His implicit appeal to the whole literature of Teutonic romanticism disarmed Mrs. Britling's objection that he had no business whatever to know the young woman at all.

" Also," cried Herr Heinrich, facing another aspect of his distresses, " how am I to pack my things ? Since I have been here I have bought many things, many books, and two pairs of white flannel trousers and some shirts and a tin instrument that I cannot work, for developing privately Kodak films.

All this must go into my little portmanteau. And it will not go into my little portmanteau !

" And there is Billy ! Who will now go on with the education of Billy ? "

The hands of fate paused not for Herr Heinrich's embarrassments and distresses. He fretted from his room downstairs and back to his room, he went out upon mysterious and futile errands towards the village inn, he prowled about the garden. His head and face grew pinker and pinker ; his eyes were flushed and distressed. Everybody sought to say and do kind and reassuring things to him.

" Ach ! " he said to Teddy ; " you are a civilian. You live in a free country. It is not your war. You can be amused at it. . . . "

But then Teddy was amused at everything.

Something but very dimly apprehended at Matching's Easy, something methodical and compelling away in London, seemed to be fumbling and feeling after Herr Heinrich, and Herr Heinrich it appeared was responding. Sunday's post brought the decision.

" I have to go," he said. " I must go right up to London to-day. To an address in Bloomsbury. Then they will tell me how to go to Germany. I must pack and I must get the taxicab from the junction and I must go. Why are there no trains on the branch line on Sundays for me to go by it ? "

At lunch he talked politics. " I am entirely opposed to the war," he said. " I am entirely opposed to any war."

" Then why go ? " asked Mr. Britling. " Stay here with us. We all like you. Stay here and do not answer your mobilisation summons."

" But then I shall lose all my country. I shall lose my papers. I shall be outcast. I must go."

" I suppose a man should go with his own country," Mr. Britling reflected.

" If there was only one language in all the world, none of such things would happen," Herr Heinrich declared. " There would be no English, no Germans, no Russians."

" Just Esperantists," said Teddy.

" Or Idoists," said Herr Heinrich. " I am not convinced of which. In some ways Ido is much better."

" Perhaps there would have to be a war between Ido and Esperanto to settle it," said Teddy.

" Who shall we play skat with when you have gone ? " asked Mrs. Britling.

" All this morning," said Herr Heinrich, expanding in the warmth of sympathy, " I have been trying to pack and I have been unable to pack. My mind is too greatly disordered. I have been told not to bring much luggage. Mrs. Britling, please."

Mrs. Britling became attentive.

" If I could leave much of my luggage, my clothes, some of them, and particularly my violin, it would be much more to my convenience. I do not care to be mobilised with my violin. There may be much crowding. Then I would but just take my rücksack. . . . "

" If you will leave your things packed up."

" And afterwards they could be sent."

But he did not leave them packed up. The taxi-cab to order which he had gone to the junction in the morning on Teddy's complaisant machine, came presently to carry him off, and the whole family and the first contingent of the usual hockey-players gathered about it to see him off. The elder boy of the two juniors put a distended rücksack upon the seat. Herr Heinrich then shook hands with every one.

" Write and tell us how you get on," cried Mrs. Britling.

" But if England also makes war ! "

" Write to Reynold's—let me give you his address ; he is my agent in New York," said Mr. Britling, and wrote it down.

" We'll come to the village corner with you, Herr Heinrich," cried the boys.

" No," said Herr Heinrich, sitting down in the automobile, " I will part with you altogether. It is too much. . . . "

" Auf wiedersehen ! " cried Mr. Britling. " Remember, whatever happens, there will be peace at last ! "

" Then why not at the beginning ? " Herr Heinrich demanded with a reasonable exasperation, and repeated his maturer verdict on the whole European situation : " Verdammte Bummelei ! "

" Go," said Mr. Britling to the taxi-driver.

" Auf wiedersehen, Herr Heinrich ! "

" Auf wiedersehen ! "

" Good-bye, Herr Heinrich ! "

" Good-luck, Herr Heinrich ! "

The taxi started with a whir, and Herr Heinrich passed out of the gates and along the same hungry road that has so recently consumed Mr. Direck. " Give him a last send-off," cried Teddy. " One, Two, Three ! Auf wiedersehen ! "

The voices, gruff and shrill, sounded raggedly together. The dog-rose hedge cut off the sight of the little face. Then the pink head bobbed up again. He was standing up and waving the panama hat. Careless of sunstroke. . . .

Then Herr Heinrich had gone altogether. . . .

" Well," said Mr. Britling, turning away.

" I do hope they won't hurt him," said a visitor.

" Oh, they won't put a youngster like that in the fighting line," said Mr. Britling. " He's had no training yet. And he has to wear glasses. How can he shoot ? They'll make a clerk of him."

" He hasn't packed at all," said Mrs. Britling to her husband.

" Just come up for an instant and peep at his room. It's—touching."

It was touching.

It was more than touching : in its minute absurd way it was symbolical and prophetic, it was the miniature of one small life uprooted.

The door stood wide open, as he had left it open, careless of all the little jealousies and privacies of occupation and ownership. Even the windows were wide open as though he had needed air ; he who had always so sedulously shut his windows since first he came to England. Across the empty fireplace stretched the great bough of oak he had brought in for Billy, but now its twigs and leaves had wilted, and many had broken off and fallen on the floor. Billy's cage stood empty upon a little table in the corner of the room. Instead of packing, the young man had evidently paced up and down in a state of emotional elaboration ; the bed was disordered as though he had several times flung himself upon it, and his books had been thrown about the room despairfully. He had made some commencements of packing in a borrowed cardboard box. The violin lay as if it lay in state upon the chest of drawers, the drawers were all partially open, and in the middle of the floor sprawled a pitiful shirt of blue, dropped there, the most flattened and broken-hearted of garments. The fireplace contained an unsuccessful pencil sketch of a girl's face, torn across. . . .

Husband and wife regarded the abandoned room in silence for a time, and when Mr. Britling spoke he lowered his voice.

" I don't see Billy," he said.

" Perhaps he has gone out of the window," said Mrs. Britling also in a hushed undertone. . . .

" Well," said Mr. Britling abruptly and loudly, turning away from this first intimation of coming desolations, " let us go down to our hockey ! He had to go, you know. And Billy will probably come back again when he begins to feel hungry. . . ."

§ 11

Monday was a public holiday, the First Monday in August, and the day consecrated by long-established custom to the Matching's Easy Flower-Show in Claverings Park. The day was to live in Mr. Britling's memory with a harsh brightness like the brightness of that sunshine one sees at times at the edge of a thunder-storm. There were tents with the exhibits, and a tent for " Popular Refreshments," there was a gorgeous gold and yellow steam roundabout with motor-cars and horses, and another in green and silver with wonderfully undulating ostriches and lions, and each had an organ that went by team ; there were cocoanut shies and many ingenious prize-giving shooting and dart-throwing and ring-throwing stalls, each displaying a marvellous array of crockery, clocks, metal ornaments, and suchlike rewards. There was a race of gas-balloons, each with a postcard attached to it begging the finder to say where it descended, and you could get a balloon for a shilling and have a chance of winning various impressive and embarrassing prizes if your balloon went far enough—fish-carvers, a silver-handled walking-stick, a bog-oak gramophone-record cabinet, and things like that. And by a special gate one could go for sixpence into the Claverings gardens, and the sixpence would be doubled by Lady Homartyn and devoted next winter to the Matching's Easy coal club. And Mr. Britling went through all the shows with his boys, and finally left them with a shilling each and his blessing, and paid his sixpence for the gardens and made his way, as he had promised, to have tea with Lady Homartyn.

The morning papers had arrived late, and he had been reading them and rereading them and musing over them intermittently until his family had insisted upon his coming out to the festivities. They said that if for no other reason he must come to witness Aunt Wilshire's extraordinary skill at the cocoanut shy. She could beat everybody. Well, one must not miss a thing like that. The headlines proclaimed, " The Great Powers at War ; France Invaded by Germany ; Germany Invaded by Russia ; 100,000 Germans March into Luxemburg ; Can England Abstain ? Fifty Million Loan to be Issued." And Germany had not only violated the Treaty of London but she had seized a British ship in the Kiel Canal. . . . The roundabouts were very busy and windily melodious, and the shooting-gallery kept popping and jingling as people shot and broke bottles, and the voices of the young men and women inviting the crowd to try their luck at this and that rang loud and clear. Teddy and Letty and Cissie and Hugh were developing a quite disconcerting skill at the dart-throwing, and were bent upon compiling a complete tea-set for the Teddy cottage out of their winnings. There were a score of automobiles and a number of traps and gigs about the entrance to the portion of the park that had been railed off for the festival, the small Britling boys had met some nursery visitors from Claverings House and were busy displaying skill and calm upon the roundabout ostriches, and less than four hundred miles away with a front that reached from Nancy to Liège more than a million and a quarter of grey-clad men, the greatest and best-equipped host the world had ever seen, were pouring westward to take Paris, grip and paralyse France, seize the Channel ports, invade England and make the German Empire the master-state of the earth. Their equipment was a marvel of foresight and scientific organisation, from the motor-kitchens that rumbled in their wake to the telescopic sights of the sharpshooters, the innumerable machine-guns of the infantry, the supply of entrenching material, the preparations already made in the invaded country. . . .

"Let's try at the other place for the sugar-basin!" said Teddy hurrying past. "Don't get *two* sugar-basins," said Cissie breathless in pursuit. "Hugh is trying for a sugar-basin at the other place."

Then Mr. Britling hears a bellicose note.

"Let's have a go at the bottles," said a cheerful young farmer. "Ought to keep up our shooting, these warlike times. . . ."

Mr. Britling ran against Hickson from the village inn, and learned that he was disturbed about his son being called up as a reservist. "Just when he was settling down here. It seems a pity they couldn't leave him for a bit.

" 'Tis a noosence," said Hickson, "but anyhow, they give first prize to his radishes. He'll be glad to hear they give first prize to his radishes. Do you think, sir, there's very much probability of this war ? It do seem to be beginning like."

"It looks more like beginning than it has ever done," said Mr. Britling. "It's a foolish business."

"I suppose if they start in on us we got to hit back at them," said Mr. Hickson. "Postman—he's got his papers too. . . ."

Mr. Britling made his way through the drifting throng towards the wicket that led into the gardens. . . .

He was swung round suddenly by a loud bang.

It was the gun proclaiming the start of the balloon-race.

He stood for some moments watching the scene. The balloon start had gathered a little crowd of people, village girls in white gloves and cheerful hats, young men in bright ties and ready-made Sunday suits, fathers and mothers, boy scouts, children, clerks in straw hats, bicyclists, and miscellaneous folk. Over their heads rose Mr. Chesthunt, the factotum of the estate. He was standing on a table and handing the balloons up into the air one by one. They floated up from his hand like many-coloured grapes, some rising and falling, some soaring steadily upward, some spinning and eddying, drifting eastward before the gentle breeze, a string of bubbles against the sky and the big trees that bounded the park. Farther away to the right were the striped canvas tents of the flower-show, still farther off the roundabouts churned out their music, the shooting-galleries popped, and the swing boats creaked through the air. Cut off from these things by a line of fencing lay the open park in which the deer grouped themselves under the great trees and regarded the festival mistrustfully. Teddy and Hugh appeared breaking away from the balloon-race cluster, and hurrying back to their dart-throwing. A man outside a little tent that stood apart was putting up a brave-looking notice, "Unstinted Teas One Shilling." The Teddy perambulator was moored against the cocoanut shy, and Aunt Wilshire was still displaying her terrible prowess at the cocoanuts. Already she had won twenty-seven. Strange children had been impressed by her to carry them, and formed her retinue. A wonderful old lady was Aunt Wilshire. . . .

Then across all the sunshine of this artless festival there appeared, as if it were writing showing through a picture, "France Invaded by Germany; Germany Invaded by Russia."

Mr. Britling turned again towards the wicket, with its collectors of tribute, that led into the gardens.

§ 12

The Claverings gardens, and particularly the great rockery, the lily-pond, and the herbaceous borders, were unusually populous with unaccustomed visitors and shy young couples. Mr. Britling had to go to the house for instructions, and guided by the under-butler found Lady Homartyn hiding in the walled Dutch garden behind the dairy. She had been giving away the prizes of the flower-show, and she was resting in a deck chair while a spinster relation presided over the tea. Mrs. Britling had fled the outer festival earlier, and was sitting by the tea-things. Lady Meade and two or three visitors had motored out from Hartleytree to assist, and Manning had come in with his tremendous confirmation of all that the morning papers had foreshadowed.

" Have you any news ? " asked Mr. Britling.

" It's *war !* " said Mrs. Britling.

" They are in Luxemburg," said Manning. " That can only mean that they are coming through Belgium."

" Then I was wrong," said Mr. Britling, " and the world is altogether mad. And so there is nothing else for us to do but win. . . . Why could they not leave Belgium alone ? "

" It's been in all their plans for the last twenty years," said Manning.

" But it brings us in for certain."

" I believe they have reckoned on that."

" Well ! " Mr. Britling took his tea and sat down, and for a time he said nothing.

" It is three against three," said one of the visitors, trying to count the Powers engaged.

" Italy," said Manning, " will almost certainly refuse to fight. In fact Italy is friendly to us. She is bound to be. This is, to begin with, an Austrian war. And Japan will fight for us. . . . "

" I think," said old Lady Meade, " that this is the suicide of Germany. They cannot possibly fight against Russia and France and ourselves. Why have they ever begun it ? "

" It may be a longer and more difficult war than people suppose," said Manning. " The Germans reckon they are going to win."

" Against us all ? "

" Against us all. They are tremendously prepared."

" It is impossible that Germany should win," said Mr. Britling breaking his silence.   " Against her Germany has something more than armies ; all reason, all instinct—the three greatest peoples in the world."

" At present very badly supplied with war material."

" That may delay things ; it may make the task harder ; but it will not alter the end. Of course we are going to win. Nothing else is thinkable. I have never believed they meant it. But I see now they meant it. This insolent arming and marching, this forty years of national blustering ; sooner or later it had to topple over into action. . . ."

He paused and found they were listening, and he was carried on by his own thoughts into further speech.

" This isn't the sort of war," he said, " that is settled by counting guns and rifles. Something that has oppressed us all has become intolerable and has to be ended. And it will be ended. I don't know what soldiers and politicians think of our prospects, but I do know what ordinary reasonable men think of the business. I know that all we millions of reasonable civilised onlookers are prepared to spend our last shillings and give all our lives now, rather than see Germany unbeaten. I know that the same thing is felt in America, and that given half a chance, given just one extra shake of that foolish mailed fist in the face of America, and America also will be in this war by our side. Italy will come in. She is bound to come in. France will fight like one man. I'm quite prepared to believe that the Germans have countless rifles and guns ; have got the most perfect maps, spies, plans you can imagine. I'm quite prepared to hear that they have got a thousand tremen- dous surprises in equipment up their sleeves. I'm quite pre- pared for sweeping victories for them and appalling disasters for us. Those are the first things. What I do know is that the Germans understand nothing of the spirit of man ; that they do not dream for a moment of the devil of resentment this war will arouse. Didn't we all trust them not to let off their guns ? Wasn't that the essence of our liberal and pacific faith ? And here they are in the heart of Europe letting off their guns ? "

" And such a lot of guns," said Manning.

" Then you think it will be a long war, Mr. Britling ? " said Lady Meade.

" Long or short, it will end in the downfall of Germany. But I do not believe it will be long. I do not agree with Mann- ing. Even now I cannot believe that a whole great people can be possessed by war madness. I think the war is the work of the German armaments party and of the Court party. They have forced this war on Germany. Well—they must win and go on winning. So long as they win, Germany will hold together, so long as their armies are not clearly defeated nor their navy destroyed. But once check them and stay them and beat them, then I believe that suddenly the spirit of Germany will change even as it changed after Jena. . . ."

"Willie Nixon," said one of the visitors, "who came back from Hamburg yesterday, says they are convinced they will have taken Paris and St. Petersburg and one or two other little places and practically settled everything for us by about Christmas."

"And London ? "

"I forgot if he said London. But I suppose a London more or less hardly matters. They don't think we shall dare come in, but if we do they will Zeppelin the fleet and walk through our army—if you can call it an army."

Manning nodded confirmation.

"They do not understand," said Mr. Britling.

"Sir George Padish told me the same sort of thing," said Lady Homartyn. "He was in Berlin in June."

"Of course the efficiency of their preparations is almost incredible," said another of Lady Meade's party. "They have thought out and got ready for everything—literally everything."

§ 13

Mr. Britling had been a little surprised by the speech he had made. He hadn't realised before he began to talk how angry and scornful he was at this final coming into action of the Teutonic militarism that had so long menaced his world. He had always said it would never really fight—and here it was fighting ! He was furious with the indignation of an apologist betrayed. He had only realised the strength and passion of his own belligerent opinions as he had heard them, and as he walked back with his wife through the village to the Dower House, he was still in the swirl of this self-discovery ; he was darkly silent, devising fiercely denunciatory phrases against Krupp and Kaiser. "Krupp and Kaiser," he grasped that obvious, convenient alliteration. "It is all that is bad in mediævalism allied to all that is bad in modernity," he told himself.

"The world," he said, startling Mrs. Britling with his sudden speech, "will be intolerable to live in, it will be unendurable for a decent human being, unless we win this war.

"We must smash or be smashed. . . ."

His brain was so busy with such stuff that for a time he stared at Mrs. Harrowdean's belated telegram without grasping the meaning of a word of it. He realised slowly that it was incumbent upon him to go over to her, but he postponed his departure very readily in order to play hockey. Besides which it would be a full moon, and he felt that summer moonlight was far better than sunset and dinner-time for the declarations he was expected to make. And then he went on phrase-making

again about Germany until he had actually bullied off at
hockey.

Suddenly in the midst of the game he had an amazing
thought. It came to him like a physical twinge.

" What the devil are we doing at this hockey ? " he asked
abruptly of Teddy, who was coming up to bully after a goal.
" We ought to be drilling or shooting against those infernal
Germans."

Teddy looked at him questioningly.

" Oh, come on ! " said Mr. Britling with a gust of impatience,
and snapped the sticks together.

§ 14

Mr. Britling started for his moonlight ride about half past
nine that night. He announced that he could neither rest nor
work, the war had thrown him into a fever ; the driving of
the automobile was just the distraction he needed ; he might
not, he added casually, return for a day or so. When he felt
he could work again he would come back. He filled up his
petrol tank by the light of an electric torch, and sat in his
car in the garage and studied his map of the district. His
thoughts wandered from the road to Pyecrafts to the coast,
and to the possible route of a raider. Suppose the enemy
anticipated a declaration of war ! Here he might come, and
here. . . . He roused himself from these speculations to the
business in hand.

The evening seemed as light as day, a cool moonshine filled
the world. The road was silver that flushed to pink at the
approach of Mr. Britling's headlight, the dark turf at the wayside and the bushes on the bank became for a moment an
acid green as the glare passed. The full moon was climbing
up the sky, and so bright that scarcely a star was visible in
the blue-grey of the heavens. Houses gleamed white a mile
away, and ever and again a moth would flutter and hang in
the light of the lamps, and then vanish again in the night.

Gladys was in excellent condition for a run, and so was Mr.
Britling. He went neither fast nor slow, and with a quite
unfamiliar confidence. Life, which had seemed all day a con-
gested confusion darkened by threats, became cool, mysterious
and aloof and with a quality of dignified reassurance.

He steered along the narrow road by the black dog-rose
hedge, and so into the highroad towards the village. The
village was alight at several windows but almost deserted.
Out beyond, a coruscation of lights burned like a group of
topaz and rubies set in the silver shield of the night. The
festivities of the flower-show were still in full progress, and
the reduction of the entrance fee after seven had drawn in
every lingering outsider. The roundabouts churned out their
relentless music, and the bottle-shooting galleries popped and
crashed. The well-patronised ostriches and motor-cars flickered

round in a pulsing rhythm; black, black, black, before the naphtha flares.

Mr. Britling pulled up at the side of the road, and sat for a little while watching the silhouettes move hither and thither from shadow to shadow across the bright spaces.

" On the very brink of war—on the brink of Armageddon," he whispered at last. " Do they understand ? Do any of us understand ? "

He slipped in his gear to starting, and was presently running quietly with his engine purring almost inaudibly along the level road to Hartleytree. The sounds behind him grew smaller and smaller, and died away leaving an immense unruffled quiet under the moon. There seemed no motion but his own, no sound but the neat, subdued, mechanical rhythm in front of his feet. Presently he ran out into the main road, and heedless of the lane that turned away towards Pyecrafts, drove on smoothly towards the east and the sea. Never before had he driven by night. He had expected a fumbling and tedious journey ; he found he had come into an undreamt-of silvery splendour of motion. For it seemed as though even the automobile was running on moonlight that night. . . . Pyecrafts could wait. Indeed the later he got to Pyecrafts the more moving and romantic the little comedy of reconciliation would be. And he was in no hurry for that comedy. He felt he wanted to apprehend this vast summer calm about him, that alone of all the things of the day seemed to convey anything whatever of the majestic tragedy that was happening to mankind. As one slipped through this still vigil one could imagine for the first time the millions away there marching, the wide river-valleys, the villages, cities, mountain ranges, ports and seas inaudibly busy.

" Even now," he said, " the battleships may be fighting."

He listened, but the sound was only the low intermittent drumming of his cylinders as he ran with his throttle nearly closed, down a stretch of gentle hill.

He felt that he must see the sea. He would follow the road beyond the Rodwell villages, and then turn up to the crest of Eastonbury Hill. And thither he went and saw in the gap of the low hills beyond a V-shaped level of moonlight water that glittered and yet lay still. He stopped his car by the roadside, and sat for a long time looking at this and musing. And once it seemed to him three little shapes like short black needles passed in line ahead across the molten silver.

But that may have been just the straining of the eyes. . . .

All sorts of talk had come to Mr. Britling's ears about the navies of England and France and Germany ; there had been public disputes of experts, much whispering and discussion in private. We had the heavier vessels, the bigger guns, but it was not certain that we had the pre-eminence in science and invention. Were they relying as we were relying on Dreadnoughts, or had they their secrets and surprises for us ? To-night, perhaps, the great ships were steaming to conflict. . .

To-night all over the world ships must be in flight and ships pursuing ; ten thousand towns must be ringing with the immediate excitement of war. . . .

Only a year ago Mr. Britling had been lunching on a battle-ship and looking over its intricate machinery. It had seemed to him then that there could be no better human stuff in the world than the quiet, sunburned, disciplined men and officers he had met. . . . And our little army, too, must be gathering to-night, the little army that had been chastened and reborn in South Africa, that he was convinced was individually more gallant and self-reliant and capable than any other army in the world. He would have sneered or protested if he had heard another Englishman say that, but in his heart he held the dear belief. . . .

And what other aviators in the world could fly as the Frenchmen and Englishmen he had met once or twice at Eastchurch and Salisbury could fly ? These are things of race and national quality. Let the German cling to his gas-bags. " We shall beat them in the air," he whispered. " We shall beat them on the seas. Surely we shall beat them on the seas. If we have men enough and guns enough we shall beat them on land. . . . Yet—— For years they have been preparing. . . . "

There was little room in the heart of Mr. Britling that night for any love but the love of England. He loved England now as a nation of men. There could be no easy victory. Good for us with our too easy natures that there could be no easy victory. But victory we must have now—or perish. . . .

He roused himself with a sigh, restarted his engine, and went on to find some turning-place. He still had a colourless impression that the journey's end was Pyecrafts.

" We must all do the thing we can," he thought, and for a time the course of his automobile along a winding down-hill road held his attention so that he could not get beyond it. He turned about and ran up over the hill again and down long slopes inland, running very softly and smoothly with his lights devouring the road ahead and sweeping the banks and hedges beside him, and as he came down a little hill through a village he heard a confused clatter and jingle of traffic ahead, and saw the danger triangle that warns of crossroads. He slowed down and then pulled up, abruptly.

Riding across the gap between the cottages was a string of horsemen, and then a grey cart, and then a team drawing a heavy object—a gun, and then more horsemen, and then a second gun. It was all a dim brown procession in the moonlight. A mounted officer came up beside him and looked at him and then went back to the crossroads, but as yet England was not troubling about spies. Four more guns passed, and then a string of carts and more mounted men, sitting stiffly. Nobody was singing or shouting; scarcely a word was audible, and through all the column there was an effect of quiet efficient haste. And so they passed, and rumbled and jingled and clattered out of the scene, leaving Mr. Britling in his car in the dreaming village. He restarted his engine once more, and went his way thoughtfully.

He went so thoughtfully that presently he missed the road to Pyecrafts—if ever he had been on the road to Pyecrafts at all—altogether. He found himself upon a highway running across a flattish plain, and presently discovered by the sight of the Great Bear, faint but traceable in the blue overhead, that he was going due north. Well, presently he would turn south and west; that in good time; now he wanted to feel; he wanted to think. How could he best help England in the vast struggle for which the empty silence and beauty of this night seemed to be waiting? But indeed he was not thinking at all, but feeling, feeling wonder, as he had never felt it since his youth had passed from him. This war might end nearly everything in the world as he had known the world; that idea struggled slowly through the moonlight into consciousness, and won its way to dominance in his mind.

The character of the road changed; the hedges fell away, and pine-trees and pine woods took the place of the black squat shapes of the hawthorn and oak and apple. The houses grew rarer and the world emptier and emptier, until he could have believed that he was the only man awake and out-of-doors in all the slumbering land. . . .

For a time a little thing caught hold of his dreaming mind. Continually as he ran on, black, silent birds rose startled out of the dust of the road before him, and fluttered noiselessly beyond his double wedge of light. What sort of bird could they be? Were they nightjars? Were they different kinds of birds snatching at the quiet of the night for a dustbath in the sand? This independent thread of inquiry ran through the texture of his mind and died away. . . .

And at one place there was a great bolting of rabbits across the road, almost under his wheels. . . .

The phrases he had used that afternoon at Claverings came back presently into his head. They were, he felt assured, the phrases that had to be said now. This war could be seen as the noblest of wars, as the crowning struggle of mankind against national dominance and national aggression; or else it was a mere struggle of nationalities and pure destruction and catastrophe. Its enormous significances, he felt, must not be lost in any petty bickering about the minor issues of the conflict. But were these enormous significances being stated clearly enough? Were they being understood by the mass of liberal and pacific thinkers? He drove more and more slowly as these questions crowded upon his attention until at last he came to a stop altogether. . . . " Certain things must be said clearly," he whispered. " Certain things—The meaning of England. . . . The deep and long-unspoken desire for kindliness and fairness. . . . Now is the time for speaking. It must be put as straight now as her gun-fire, as honestly as the steering of her ships."

Phrases and paragraphs began to shape themselves in his mind as he sat with one arm on his steering-wheel.

Suddenly he roused himself, turned over the map in the map-case beside him, and tried to find his position. . . .

So far as he could judge he had strayed right into Suffolk. . . .

About one o'clock in the morning he found himself in Newmarket. Newmarket too was a moonlit emptiness, but as he hesitated at the crossroads he became aware of a policeman standing quite stiff and still at the corner by the church.

" Matching's Easy ? " he cried.

" That road, sir, until you come to Market Saffron, and then to the left. . . . "

Mr. Britling had a definite purpose now in his mind, and he drove faster, but still very carefully and surely. He was already within a mile or so of Market Saffron before he remembered that he had made a kind of appointment with himself at Pyecrafts. He stared at two conflicting purposes. He turned over certain possibilities.

At the Market Saffron crossroads he slowed down, and for a moment he hung undecided.

" Oliver," he said, and as he spoke he threw over his steering-wheel towards the homeward way. . . . He finished his sentence when he had negotiated the corner safely. "Oliver must have her. . . . "

And then, perhaps fifty yards farther along and this time almost indignantly : " She ought to have married him long ago. . . . "

He put his automobile in the garage, and then went round under the black shadow of his cedars to the front door. He had no key, and for a long time he failed to rouse his wife by flinging pebbles and gravel at her half-open window. But at last he heard her stirring and called out to her.

He explained he had returned because he wanted to write. He wanted indeed to write quite urgently. He went straight up to his room, lit his reading-lamp, made himself some tea, and changed into his nocturnal suit.

Daylight found him still writing very earnestly at his pamphlet. The title he had chosen was : " And Now War Ends."

§ 15

In this fashion it was that the great war began in Europe and came to one man in Matching's Easy, as it came to countless intelligent men in countless pleasant homes that had scarcely heeded its coming through all the years of its relentless preparation. The familiar scenery of life was drawn aside, and War stood unveiled. " I am the Fact," said War, " and I stand astride the path of life. I am the threat of death and extinction that has always walked beside life, since life began. There can be nothing else and nothing more in human life until you have reckoned with me."

Book Two

Matching's Easy at War

CHAPTER ONE

ONLOOKERS

§ 1

ON that eventful night of the first shots and the first deaths Mr. Britling did not sleep until daylight had come. He sat writing at this pamphlet of his, which was to hail the last explosion and the ending of war. For a couple of hours he wrote with energy, and then his energy flagged. There came intervals when he sat still and did not write. He yawned and yawned again and rubbed his eyes. The day had come and the birds were noisy when he undressed slowly, dropping his clothes anyhow upon the floor, and got into bed. . . .

He woke to find his morning tea beside him and the housemaid going out of the room. He knew that something stupendous had happened to the world, but for a few moments he could not remember what it was. Then he remembered that France was invaded by Germany and Germany by Russia, and that almost certainly England was going to war. It seemed a harsh and terrible fact in the morning light, a demand for stresses, a certainty of destruction; it appeared now robbed of all the dark and dignified beauty of the night. He remembered just the same feeling of unpleasant, anxious expectation as he now felt when the Boer War had begun fifteen years ago, before the first news came. The first news of the Boer War had been the wrecking of a British armoured train near Kimberley. What similar story might not the overdue paper presently tell ?

Suppose, for instance, that some important division of our Fleet had been surprised and overwhelmed. . . .

Suppose the Germans were already crumpling up the French armies between Verdun and Belfort, very swiftly and dreadfully. . . .

Suppose after all that the Cabinet was hesitating, and that there would be no war for some weeks, but only a wrangle about Belgian neutrality. While the Germans smashed France. . . .

Or, on the other hand, there might be some amazing, prompt success on our part. Our army and navy people were narrow, but in their narrow way he believed they were extraordinarily good. . . .

What would the Irish do ? . . .

His thoughts were no more than a thorny jungle of unanswerable questions through which he struggled in unprogressive circles.

He got out of bed and dressed in a slow, distraught manner. When he reached his braces he discontinued dressing for a time; he opened the atlas at Northern France, and stood musing over the Belgian border. Then he turned to Whitaker's Almanack to browse upon the statistics of the great European armies. He was roused from this by the breakfast-gong.

At breakfast there was no talk of anything but war. Hugh was as excited as a cat in thundery weather, and the small boys wanted information about flags. The Russian and the Serbian flag were in dispute, and the flag page of Webster's Dictionary had to be consulted. Newspapers and letters were both abnormally late, and Mr. Britling, tiring of supplying trivial information to his offspring, smoked cigarettes in the garden. He had an idea of intercepting the postman. His eyes and ears informed him of the approach of Mrs. Faber's automobile. It was an old, resolute-looking machine painted red, and driven by a trusted gardener; there was no mistaking it.

Mrs. Faber was in it, and she stopped it outside the gate and made signals. Mrs. Britling, attracted by the catastrophic sounds of Mrs. Faber's vehicle, came out by the front door, and she and her husband both converged upon the caller.

§ 2

" I won't come in," cried Mrs. Faber, " but I thought I'd tell you. I've been getting food."

" Food ? "

" Provisions. There's going to be a run on provisions. Look at my flitch of bacon ! "

" But——"

" Faber says we have to lay in what we can. This war—it's going to stop everything. We can't tell what will happen. I've got the children to consider, so here I am. I was at Hickson's before nine. . . ."

The little lady was very flushed and bright-eyed. Her fair hair was disordered, her hat a trifle askew. She had an air of enjoying unwonted excitements. " All the gold's being hoarded too," she said, with a crow of delight in her voice. " Faber says that probably our cheques won't be worth *that* in a few days. He's rushed off to London to get gold at his clubs—while he can. I had to insist on Hickson taking a cheque. ' Never,' I said, ' will I deal with you again—never—unless you do. . . .'" Even then he looked at me almost as if he thought he wouldn't.

" It's Famine ! " she said, turning to Mr. Britling. " I've laid hands on all I can. I've got the children to consider."

" But why is it famine ? " asked Mr. Britling.

" Oh ! it *is* ! " she said.

" But why ? "

" Faber understands," she said. " Of course it's Famine. . . .

" And would you believe me," she went on, going back to Mrs. Britling, " that man Hickson stood behind his counter— where I've dealt with him for *years*, and refused absolutely to let me have more than a dozen tins of sardines. *Refused !* Point-blank !

" I was there before nine, and even then Hickson's shop was crowded—*crowded*, my dear ! "

" What have you got ? " said Mr. Britling with an inquiring movement towards the automobile.

She had got quite a lot. She had two sides of bacon, a case of sugar, bags of rice, eggs, a lot of flour.

" What are all these little packets ? " said Mr. Britling.

Mrs. Faber looked slightly abashed.

" Cerebos salt," she said. " One gets carried away a little. I just got hold of it and carried it out to the car. I thought we might have to salt things later."

" And the jars are pickles ? " said Mr. Britling.

" Yes. But look at all my flour ! That's what will go first. . . ."

The lady was a little flurried by Mr. Britling's too detailed examination of her haul. " What good is blacking ? " he asked. She would not hear him. She felt he was trying to spoil her morning. She declared she must get on back to her home. " Don't say I didn't warn you," she said. " I've got no end of things to do. There's peas ! I want to show cook how to bottle our peas. For this year—it's lucky, we've got no end of peas. I came by here just for the sake of telling you." And with that she presently departed—obviously ruffled by Mrs. Britling's lethargy and Mr. Britling's scepticism.

Mr. Britling watched her go off with a slowly rising indignation.

" And that," he said, " is how England is going to war ! Scrambling for food—at the very beginning."

" I suppose she is anxious for the children," said Mrs. Britling.

" Blacking ! "

" After all," said Mrs. Britling, " if other people are doing that sort of thing——"

" That's the idea of all panics. We've got not to do it. . . . The country hasn't even declared war yet ! Hallo, here we are ! Better late than never."

The head of the postman, bearing newspapers and letters, appeared gliding along the top of the hedge as he cycled down the road towards the Dower House corner.

§ 3

England was not yet at war, but all the stars were marching to that end. It was as if an event so vast must needs take its time to happen. No doubt was left upon Mr. Britling's mind, though a whole-page advertisement in *The Daily News*, in enormous type and of mysterious origin, implored Great

Britain not to play into the hands of Russia, Russia the Terrible,
that bugbear of the sentimental Radicals. The news was wide
and sweeping, and rather inaccurate. The Germans were said
to be in Belgium and Holland, and they had seized English
ships in the Kiel Canal. A moratorium had been proclaimed,
and the reports of a food panic showed Mrs. Faber to be merely
one example of a large class of excitable people.

Mr. Britling found the food panic disconcerting. It did not
harmonise with his leading *motif* of the free people of the world
rising against the intolerable burthen of militarism. It spoiled
his picture. . . .

Mrs. Britling shared the paper with Mr. Britling ; they stood
by the bed of begonias near the cedar-tree and read, and the
air was full of the cheerful activities of the lawn-mower that
was being drawn by a carefully booted horse across the hockey-
field

Presently Hugh came flitting out of the house to hear what
had happened. "One can't work, somehow, with all these
big things going on," he apologised. He secured *The Daily
News* while his father and mother read *The Times*. The voices
of the younger boys came from the shade of the trees ; they
had brought all their toy soldiers out-of-doors, and were making
entrenched camps in the garden.

" The financial situation is an extraordinary one," said Mr.
Britling, concentrating his attention. . . . "All sorts of
staggering things may happen. In a social and economic
system that has grown just anyhow. . . . Never been planned.
. . . In a world full of Mrs. Fabers. . . ."

" Moratorium ? " said Hugh over his *Daily News*. " In relation to debts and so on ? Modern side you sent me to, Daddy.
I live at hand to mouth in etymology. Morse and crematorium
—do we burn our bills instead of paying them ? "

" Moratorium," reflected Mr. Britling ; " moratorium.
What nonsense you talk ! It's something that delays, of course.
Nothing to do with death. Just a temporary stoppage of payments. . . . Of course there's bound to be a tremendous
change in values. . . ."

§ 4

" There's bound to be a tremendous change in values."

On that text Mr. Britling's mind enlarged very rapidly.
It produced a wonderful crop of possibilities before he got
back to his study. He sat down to his desk, but he did not
immediately take up his work. He had discovered something
so revolutionary in his personal affairs that even the war
issue remained for a time in suspense.

Tucked away at the back of Mr. Britling's consciousness
was something that had not always been there, something
warm and comforting that made life and his general thoughts
about life much easier and pleasanter than they would other-

wise have been, the sense of a neatly arranged investment list,
a shrewdly and geographically distributed system of holdings
in national loans, municipal investments, railway debentures,
that had amounted altogether to rather over five-and-twenty
thousand pounds ; his and Mrs. Britling's, a joint accumulation. It was, so to speak, his economic viscera. It sustained
him, and kept him going and comfortable.   When all
was well he did not feel its existence ; he had merely a
pleasant sense of general well-being.   When here or there a
security got a little disarranged he felt a vague discomfort.
Now he became aware of grave disorders. It was as if he discovered he had been accidentally eating toadstools, and didn't
quite know whether they weren't a highly poisonous sort.
But an analogy may be carried too far. . . .

At any rate, when Mr. Britling got back to his writing-desk
he was much too disturbed to resume " And Now War Ends."

" There's bound to be a tremendous change in values ! "

He had never felt quite so sure as most people about the
stability of the modern financial system. He did not, he felt,
understand the working of this moratorium, or the peculiar
advantage of prolonging the bank holidays.   It meant, he
supposed, a stoppage of payment all round, and a cutting off
of the supply of ready money. And Hickson the grocer, according to Mrs. Faber, was already looking askance at cheques.

Even if the bank did reopen, Mr. Britling was aware that
his current balance was low ; at the utmost it amounted to
twenty or thirty pounds. He had been expecting cheques
from his English and American publishers, and the usual
Times cheque. Suppose these payments were intercepted !

All these people might, so far as he could understand, stop
payment under this moratorium !   That hadn't at first
occurred to him. But, of course, quite probably they might
refuse to pay his account when it fell due.

And suppose *The Times* felt his peculiar vein of thoughtful-
ness unnecessary in these stirring days !

And then if the bank really did lock up his deposit account
and his securities became unsaleable !

Mr. Britling felt like an oyster that is invited to leave its
shell. . . .

He sat back from his desk contemplating these things. His
imagination made a weak attempt to picture a world in which
credit has vanished and money is of doubtful value. He supposed a large number of people would just go on buying and
selling at or near the old prices by force of habit.

His mind and conscience made a valiant attempt to pick
up " And Now War Ends " and go on with it, but before five
minutes were out he was back at the thoughts of food panic
and bankruptcy. . . .

§ 5

The conflict of interests at Mr. Britling's desk became unendurable. He felt he must settle the personal question first. He wandered out upon the lawn and smoked cigarettes.

His first conception of a great convergent movement of the nations to make a world peace and an end to militant Germany was being obscured by this second, entirely incompatible, vision of a world confused and disorganised. Mrs. Fabers in great multitudes hoarding provisions, riotous crowds attacking shops, moratorium, shut banks and waiting queues. Was it possible for the whole system to break down through a shock to its confidence ? Without any sense of incongruity the dignified pacification of the planet had given place in his mind to these more intimate possibilities. He heard a rustle behind him, and turned to face his wife.

" Do you think," she asked, " that there is any chance of a shortage of food ? "

" If all the Mrs. Fabers in the world run and grab——"

" Then every one must grab. I haven't much in the way of stores in the house."

" H'm," said Mr. Britling, and reflected. . . . " I don't think we must buy stores now."

" But if we are short."

" It's the chances of war," said Mr. Britling.

He reflected. " Those who join a panic make a panic. After all, there is just as much food in the world as there was last month. And short of burning it the only way of getting rid of it is to eat it. And the harvests are good. Why begin a scramble at a groaning board ? "

" But people *are* scrambling ! It would be awkward—with the children and everything—if we ran short."

" We shan't. And anyhow, you musn't begin hoarding even if it means hardship."

" Yes. But you won't like it if suddenly there's no sugar for your tea."

Mr. Britling ignored this personal application.

" What is far more serious than a food shortage is the possibility of a money panic."

He paced the lawn with her and talked. He said that even now very few people realised the flimsiness of the credit system by which the modern world was sustained. It was a huge growth of confidence, due very largely to the uninquiring indolence of—everybody. It was sound so long as mankind did, on the whole, believe in it ; give only a sufficient loss of faith and it might suffer any sort of collapse. It might vanish altogether—as the credit system vanished at the breaking up of Italy by the Goths—and leave us nothing but tangible things, real property, possession nine points of the law, and that sort of thing. Did she remember that last novel of Gissing's ?—' Veranilda,' it was called. It was a picture of the world when there was no wealth at all except what one could carry hidden or guarded about with one. That sort of thing came to the Roman Empire slowly, in the course of lifetimes, but nowadays we lived in a rapider world with flimsier institutions. Nobody knew the strength or the weakness of credit ; nobody knew whether even the present shock might not send it smashing down. . . . And then all the little life we had lived so far would roll away. . . .

Mrs. Britling, he noted, glanced ever and again at her sunlit house—there were new sun-blinds, and she had been happy in her choice of a colour—and listened with a sceptical expression to this disquisition.

" A few days ago," said Mr. Britling, trying to make things concrete for her, " you and I together were worth five-and-twenty thousand pounds. Now we don't know what we are worth : whether we have lost a thousand or ten thousand. . . ."

He examined his sovereign purse and announced he had six pounds. " What have you ? "

She had about eighteen pounds in the house.

" We may have to get along with that for an indefinite time."

" But the bank will open again presently," she said. " And people about here trust us."

" Suppose they don't ? "

She did not trouble about the hypothesis. " And our investments will recover. They always do recover."

" Everything may recover," he admitted. " But also nothing may recover. All this life of ours which has seemed so settled and secure—isn't secure. I have felt that we were fixed here and rooted—for all our lives. Suppose presently things sweep us out of it ? It's a possibility we may have to face. I feel this morning as if two enormous gates had opened in our lives, like the gates that give upon an arena, gates giving on a darkness—through which anything might come. Even death. Suppose suddenly we were to see one of those great Zeppelins in the air, or hear the thunder of guns away towards the coast. And if a messenger came upon a bicycle telling us to leave everything and go inland. . . ."

" I see no reason why one should go out to meet things like that."

" But there is no reason why one should not envisage them. . . .

" The curious thing," said Mr. Britling, pursuing his examination of the matter, " is that, looking at these things as one does now, as things quite possible, they are not nearly so terrifying and devastating to the mind as they would have seemed—last week. I believe I should load you all into Gladys and start off westward with a kind of exhilaration. . . ."

She looked at him as if she would speak, and said nothing. She suspected him of hating his home and affecting to care for it out of politeness to her. . . .

" Perhaps mankind tries too much to settle down. Perhaps these stirrings up have to occur to save us from our disposition to stuffy comfort. There's the magic call of the unknown experience, of dangers and hardships. One wants to go. But unless some push comes one does not go. There is a spell that keeps one to the lair and the old familiar ways. Now I am afraid—and at the same time I feel that the spell is broken. The magic prison is suddenly all doors. You may call this ruin, bankruptcy, invasion, flight ; they are doors out of habit and routine. . . . I have been doing nothing for so long, except idle things and discursive things."

" I thought that you managed to be happy here. You have done a lot of work."

" Writing is recording, not living. But now I feel suddenly that we are living intensely. It is as if the whole quality of life was changing. There are such times. There are times when the spirit of life changes altogether. The old world knew that better than we do. It made a distinction between week-days and Sabbaths, and between feasts and fasts and days of devotion. That is just what has happened now. Week-day rules must be put aside. Before—oh ! three days ago, competition was fair, it was fair and tolerable to get the best food one could and hold on to one's own. But that isn't right now. War makes a Sabbath, and we shut the shops. The banks are shut, and the world still feels as though Sunday was keeping on. . . ."

He saw his own way clear.

" The scale has altered. It does not matter now in the least if we are ruined. It does not matter in the least if we have to live upon potatoes and run into debt for our rent. These now are the most incidental of things. A week ago they would have been of the first importance. Here we are face to face with the greatest catastrophe and the greatest opportunity in history. We have to plunge through catastrophe to opportunity. There is nothing to be done now in the whole world except to get the best out of this tremendous fusing up of all the settled things of life."

He had got what he wanted. He left her standing upon the lawn and hurried back to his desk. . . .

§ 6

When Mr. Britling, after a strenuous morning among high ideals, descended for lunch, he found Mr. Lawrence Carmine had come over to join him at that meal. Mr. Carmine was standing in the hall with his legs very wide apart reading *The Times* for the fourth time. " I can do no work," he said, turning round. " I can't fix my mind. I suppose we are going

to war. I'd got so used to the war with Germany that I never
imagined it would happen. Gods ! what a bore it will be. . . .
And Maxse and all those scaremongers cock-a-hoop and ' I
told you so.' Damn these Germans ! "

He looked despondent and worried. He followed Mr. Britling
towards the dining-room with his hands deep in his pockets.

" It's going to be a tremendous thing," he said, after he
had greeted Mrs. Britling and Hugh and Aunt Wilshire and
Teddy, and seated himself at Mr. Britling's hospitable board.
" It's going to upset everything. We don't begin to imagine
all the mischief it is going to do."

Mr. Britling was full of the heady draught of liberal optimism he had been brewing upstairs. " I am not sorry I have
lived to see this war," he said. " It may be a tremendous
catastrophe in one sense, but in another it is a huge step
forward in human life. It is the end of forty years of evil
suspense. It is crisis and solution."

" I wish I could see it like that," said Mr. Carmine.

" It is like a thaw—everything has been in a frozen confusion since that Jew-German Treaty of Berlin. And since
1871."

" Why not since Schleswig-Holstein ? " said Mr. Carmine.

" Why not ? Or since the Treaty of Vienna ? "

" Or since—— One might go back."

" To the Roman Empire," said Hugh.

" To the first conquest of all," said Teddy. . . .

" I couldn't work this morning," said Hugh. " I have been
reading in the Encyclopædia about races and religions in the
Balkans. . . . It's very mixed."

" So long as it could only be dealt with piecemeal," said
Mr. Britling. " And that is just where the tremendous opportunity of this war comes in. Now everything becomes fluid.
We can redraw the map of the world. A week ago we were
all quarrelling bitterly about things too little for human
impatience. Now suddenly we face an epoch. This is an epoch.
The world is plastic for men to do what they will with it.
This is the end and the beginning of an age. This is something far greater than the French Revolution or the Refor-
mation. . . . And we live in it. . . . "

He paused impressively.

" I wonder what will happen to Albania ? " said Hugh,
but his comment was disregarded.

" War makes men bitter and narrow," said Mr. Carmine.

" War narrowly conceived," said Mr. Britling. " But this
is an indignant and generous war."

They speculated about the possible intervention of the
United States. Mr. Britling thought that the attack on Belgium demanded the intervention of every civilised power,
that all the best instincts of America would be for intervention.
" The more," he said, " the quicker."

" It would be strange if the last power left out to mediate
were to be China," said Mr. Carmine. " The one people in
the world who really believe in peace. . . . I wish I had your
confidence, Britling."

For a time they contemplated a sort of Grand Inquest on
Germany and militarism, presided over by the Wisdom of
the East. Militarism was, as it were, to be buried as a suicide
at four crossroads, with a stake through its body to prevent
any untimely resuscitation.

§ 7

Mr. Britling was in a phase of imaginative release. Such
a release was one of the first effects of the war upon many
educated minds. Things that had seemed solid for ever were
visibly in flux ; things that had seemed stone were alive. Every
boundary, every government, was seen for the provisional
thing it was. He talked of his World Congress meeting year
by year, until it ceased to be a speculation and became a mere
intelligent anticipation ; he talked of the " manifest necessity "
of a Supreme Court for the world. He beheld that vision at
The Hague, but Mr. Carmine preferred Delhi or Samarkand
or Alexandria or Nankin. " Let us get away from the delusion
of Europe anyhow," said Mr. Carmine. . . .

As Mr. Britling had sat at his desk that morning and surveyed the stupendous vistas of possibility that war was opening,
the catastrophe had taken on a more and more beneficial
quality. " I suppose that it is only through such crises as
these that the world can reconstruct itself," he said. And,
on the whole, that afternoon he was disposed to hope that the
great military machine would not smash itself too easily.
" We want the nations to feel the need of one another," he
said. " Too brief a campaign might lead to a squabble for
plunder. The Englishman has to learn his dependence on the
Irishman, the Russian has to be taught the value of education
and the friendship of the Pole. . . . Europe will now have to
look to Asia, and recognise that Indians and Chinamen are
also ' white.' . . . But these lessons require time and stresses
if they are to be learned properly. . . ."

They discussed the possible duration of the war.

Mr. Carmine thought it would be a long struggle ; Mr.
Britling thought that the Russians would be in Berlin by the
next May. He was afraid they might get there before the end
of the year. He thought that the Germans would beat out
their strength upon the French and Belgian lines, and never
be free to turn upon the Russian at all. He was sure they had
underrated the strength and energy of the French and of
ourselves. " The Russians meanwhile," he said, " will come
on, slowly, steadily, inevitably. . . ."

§ 8

That day of vast anticipations drew out into the afternoon. It was a day—obsessed. It was the precursor of a relentless series of doomed and fettered days. There was a sense of enormous occurrences going on just out of sound and sight— behind the mask of Essex peacefulness. From this there was no escape. It made all other interests fitful. Games of Bad- minton were begun and abruptly truncated by the arrival of the evening papers ; conversations started upon any topic whatever returned to the war by the third and fourth re- mark. . . .

After lunch Mr. Britling and Mr. Carmine went on talking. Nothing else was possible. They repeated things they had already said. They went into things more thoroughly. They sat still for a time, and then suddenly broke out with some new consideration. . . .

It had been their custom to play skat with Herr Heinrich, who had shown them the game very explicitly and thoroughly. But there was no longer any Herr Heinrich—and somehow German games were already out of fashion. The two philoso- phers admitted that they had already considered skat to be complicated without subtlety, and that its chief delight for them had been the pink earnestness of Herr Heinrich, his inability to grasp their complete but tacit comprehension of its innocent strategy, and his invariable ill success in bringing off the coups that flashed before his imagination.

He would survey the destructive counter-stroke with un- concealed surprise. He would verify his first impression by craning towards it and adjusting his glasses on his nose. He had a characteristic way of doing this with one stiff finger on either side of his sturdy nose.

" It is very fortunate for you that you have played that card," he would say, growing pinker and pinker with hasty cerebration. " Or else—yes "—a glance at his own cards— " it would have been altogether bad for you. I had taken only a very small risk. . . . Now I must—— "

He would reconsider his hand.

" Zo ! " he would say, dashing down a card. . . .

Well, he had gone and skat had gone. A countless multi- tude of such links were snapping that day between hundreds of thousands of English and German homes.

§ 9

The imminence of war produced a peculiar exaltation in Aunt Wilshire. She developed a point of view that was entirely her own.

It was Mr. Britling's habit, a habit he had set himself to acquire after much irritating experience, to disregard Aunt Wilshire. She was not, strictly speaking, his aunt ; she was one of those distant cousins we find already woven into our lives when we attain to years of responsibility. She had been a presence in his father's household when Mr. Britling was a boy. Then she had been called " Jane," or " Cousin Jane," or " Your cousin Wilshire." It had been a kindly freak of Mr. Britling's to promote her to Auntly rank.

She eked out a small inheritance by staying with relatives. Mr. Britling's earlier memories presented her as a slender young woman of thirty, with a nose upon which small boys were forbidden to comment. Yet she commented upon it herself, and called his attention to its marked resemblance to that of the great Duke of Wellington. " He was, I am told," said Cousin Wilshire to the attentive youth, " a great friend of your great-grandmother's. At any rate, they were contemporaries. Since then this nose has been in the family. He would have been the last to draw a veil over it, but other times, other manners. ' Publish,' he said, ' and be damned.' "

She had a knack of exasperating Mr. Britling's father, a knack which to a less marked degree she also possessed in relation to the son. But Mr. Britling senior never acquired the art of disregarding her. Her method—if one may call the natural expression of a personality a method—was an invincibly superior knowledge, a firm and ill-concealed belief that all statements made in her hearing were wrong and most of them absurd, and a manner calm, assured, restrained. She may have been born with it : it is on record that at the age of ten she was pronounced a singularly trying child. She may have been born with the air of thinking the doctor a muff and knowing how to manage all this business better. Mr. Britling had known her only in her ripeness. As a boy, he had enjoyed her confidences—about other people and the general neglect of her advice. He grew up rather to like her—most people rather liked her—and to attach a certain importance to her unattainable approval. She was sometimes kind, she was frequently absurd. . . .

With very little children she was quite wise and jolly. . . . So she circulated about a number of houses which at any rate always welcomed her coming. In the opening days of each visit she performed marvels of tact, and set a watch upon her lips. Then the demons of controversy and dignity would get the better of her. She would begin to correct, quietly but firmly, she would begin to disapprove of the tone and quality of her treatment. It was quite common for her visit to terminate in speechless rage both on the side of host and of visitor. The remarkable thing was that this speechless rage never endured. Though she could exasperate she could never offend. Always after an interval during which she was never mentioned, people began to wonder how Cousin Jane was getting on. . . . A tentative correspondence would begin, leading slowly up to a fresh invitation.

She spent more time in Mr. Britling's house than in any other. There was a legend that she had "drawn out" his mind, and that she had "stood up" for him against his father. She had certainly contradicted quite a number of those unfavourable comments that fathers are wont to make about their sons. Though certainly she contradicted everything. And Mr. Britling hated to think of her knocking about alone in boarding-houses and hydropathic establishments with only the most casual chances for contradiction.

Moreover, he liked to see her casting her eye over the morning paper. She did it with a manner as though she thought the terrestrial globe a great fool and quite beyond the reach of advice. And as though she understood and was rather amused at the way in which the newspaper people tried to keep back the real facts of the case from her.

And now she was scornfully entertained at the behaviour of everybody in the war crisis.

She confided various secrets of state to the elder of the younger Britlings—preferably when his father was within earshot.

"None of these things they are saying about the war," she said, "really matter in the slightest degree. It is all about a spoiled carpet and nothing else in the world—a madman and a spoiled carpet. If people had paid the slightest attention to common sense none of this war would have happened. The thing was perfectly well known. He was a delicate child, difficult to rear and given to screaming fits. Consequently he was never crossed, allowed to do everything. Nobody but his grandmother had the slightest influence with him. And she prevented him spoiling this carpet as completely as he wished to do. The story is perfectly well known. It was at Windsor—at the age of eight. After that he had but one thought : war with England. . . .

"Everybody seems surprised," she said suddenly at tea to Mr. Carmine. "I at least am not surprised. I am only surprised it did not come sooner. If any one had asked me I could have told them, three years, five years ago."

The day was one of flying rumours, Germany was said to have declared war on Italy, and to have invaded Holland as well as Belgium.

"They'll declare war against the moon next!" said Aunt Wilshire.

"And send a lot of Zeppelins," said the smallest boy. "Herr Heinrich told us they can fly thousands of miles."

"He will go on declaring war until there is nothing left to declare war against. That is exactly what he has always done. Once started he cannot desist. Often he has had to be removed from the dinner-table for fear of injury. *Now*, it is ultimatums."

She was much pleased by a headline in *The Daily Express*

that streamed right across the page : " The Mad Dog of Europe." Nothing else, she said, had come so near her feelings about the war.

" Mark my words," said Aunt Wilshire in her most impressive tones. " He is insane. It will be proved to be so. He will end his days in an asylum—as a lunatic. I have felt it myself for years and said so in private. . . . Knowing what I did. . . . To such friends as I could trust not to misunderstand me. . . . Now at least I can speak out.

" With his moustaches turned up ! " exclaimed Aunt Wilshire after an interval of accumulation. . . . They say he has completely lost the use of the joint in his left arm, he carries it stiff like a Punch and Judy—and he wants to conquer Europe. . . . While his grandmother lived there was some one to keep him in order. He stood in Awe of her. He hated her but he did not dare defy her. Even his uncle had some influence. Now, nothing restrains him.

" A double-headed mad dog," said Aunt Wilshire. " Him and his eagles ! . . . A man like that ought never to have been allowed to make a war. . . . Not even a little war. . . . If he had been put under restraint when I said so, none of these things would have happened. But, of course, I am nobody. . . . It was not considered worth attending to."

§ 10

One remarkable aspect of the English attitude towards the war was the disposition to treat it as a monstrous joke. It is a disposition traceable in a vast proportion of the British literature of the time. In spite of violence, cruelty, injustice, and the vast destruction and still vaster dangers of the struggle, that disposition held. The English mind refused flatly to see anything magnificent or terrible in the German attack, or to regard the German Emperor or the Crown Prince as anything more than figures of fun. From first to last their conception of the enemy was an overstrenuous, foolish man, red with effort, with protruding eyes and a forced frightfulness of demeanour. That he might be tremendously lethal did not in the least obscure the fact that he was essentially ridiculous. And if as the war went on the joke grew grimmer, still it remained a joke. The German might make a desert of the world ; that could not alter the British conviction that he was making a fool of himself.

And this disposition kept coming to the surface throughout the afternoon, now in a casual allusion, now in some deliberate jest. The small boys had discovered the goose-step, and it filled their little souls with amazement and delight. That human beings should consent to those ridiculous paces seemed to them almost incredibly funny. They tried it themselves, and then set out upon a goose-step propaganda. Letty and Cissie had come up to the Dower House for tea and news,

and they were enrolled with Teddy and Hugh. The six of
them, chuckling and swaying, marched in vast scissor strides
across the lawn. " Left," cried Hugh. " Left."

" Toes *out* more," said Mr. Lawrence Carmine.

" Keep stiffer," said the youngest Britling.

" Watch the Zeppelins and look proud," said Hugh. " With
chest out. *Zo !* "

Mrs. Britling was so much amused that she went in for her
camera, and took a snap-shot of the detachment. It was a
very successful snap-shot, and a year later Mr. Britling was to
find a print of it among his papers, and recall the sunshine and
the merriment. . . .

§ 11

That night brought the British declaration of war against
Germany. To nearly every Englishman that came as a matter
of course, and it is one of the most wonderful facts in history
that the Germans were surprised by it. When Mr. Britling,
as a sample Englishman, had said that there would never be
war between Germany and England, he had always meant
that it was inconceivable to him that Germany should ever
attack Belgium or France. If Germany had been content to
fight a merely defensive war upon her western frontier and
let Belgium alone, there would scarcely have been such a thing
as a war-party in Great Britain. But the attack upon Belgium,
the westward thrust, made the whole nation flame unani-
mously into war. It settled a question that was in open debate
up to the very outbreak of the conflict. Up to the last the
English had cherished the idea that in Germany, just as in
England, the mass of people were kindly, pacific, and detached.
That had been the English mistake. Germany was really and
truly what Germany had been professing to be for forty years,
a War State. With a sigh—and a long-forgotten thrill—England roused herself to fight. Even now she still roused herself
sluggishly. It was going to be an immense thing, but just
how immense it was going to be no one in England had yet
imagined.

Countless men that day whom Fate had marked for death
and wounds stared open-mouthed at the news, and smiled
with the excitement of the headlines, not dreaming that any
of these things would come within three hundred miles of
them. What was war to Matching's Easy—to all the Matching's
Easies great and small that make up England ? The last
home that was ever burned by an enemy within a hundred
miles of Matching's Easy was burned by the Danes rather
more than a thousand years ago. . . . And the last trace of those
particular Danes in England was certain horny scraps of
indurated skin under the heads of the nails in the door of St.
Clement Danes in London. . . .

Now again, England was to fight in a war which was to

light fires in England and bring death to English people on
English soil. These were inconceivable ideas in August, 1914.
Such things must happen before they can be comprehended as
possible.

§ 12

This story is essentially the history of the opening and
of the realisation of the Great War as it happened to one
small group of people in Essex, and more particularly as it
happened to one human brain.   It came at first to all these
people in a spectacular manner, as a thing happening dramatically and internationally, as a show, as something in the
newspapers, something in the character of an historical epoch
rather than a personal experience ;   only by slow degrees
did it and its consequences invade the common texture of
English life.   If this story could be represented by sketches
or pictures the central figure would be Mr. Britling, now
sitting at his desk by day or by night and writing first at
his tract " And Now War Ends " and then at other things,
now walking about his garden or in Claverings Park or going
to and fro in London, in his club reading the ticker or in his
hall reading the newspaper, with ideas and impressions continually clustering, expanding, developing more and more
abundantly in his mind, arranging themselves, reacting upon
one another, building themselves into generalisations and conclusions. . . .

All Mr. Britling's mental existence was soon threaded on
the war.   His more or less weekly *Times* leaders became dissertations upon the German point of view ;   his reviews of
books and Literary Supplement articles were all oriented
more and more exactly to that one supreme fact. . . .

It was rare that he really seemed to be seeing the war ;
few people saw it ;   for most of the world it came as an illi-
mitable multitude of incoherent, loud, and confusing impressions.   But all the time he was at least doing his utmost to
see the war, to simplify it and extract the essence of it until
it could be apprehended as something epic and explicable, as
a stateable issue. . . .

Most typical picture of all would be Mr. Britling writing
in a little circle of orange lamplight, with the blinds of his
room open for the sake of the moonlight but the window
shut to keep out the moths that beat against it.   Outside
would be the moon and the high summer sky and the old
church-tower dim above the black trees half a mile away,
with its clock—which Mr. Britling heard at night but never
noted by day—beating its way round the slow semicircle of
the nocturnal hours.   He had always hated conflict and destruction, and felt that war between civilised states was the
quintessential expression of human failure, it was a stupidity
that stopped progress and all the free variation of humanity,

a thousand times he had declared it impossible, but even now with his country fighting he was still far from realising that this was a thing that could possibly touch him more than intellectually. He did not really believe with his eyes and finger-tips and backbone that murder, destruction, and agony on a scale monstrous beyond precedent were going on in the same world as that which slumbered outside the black ivy and silver shining window-sill that framed his peaceful view.

War had not been a reality of the daily life of England for more than a thousand years. The mental habit of the nation for fifty generations was against its emotional recognition. The English were the spoiled children of peace. They had never been wholly at war for three hundred years, and for over eight hundred years they had not fought for life against a foreign power. Spain and France had threatened in turn, but never even crossed the seas. It is true that England had had her civil dissensions and had made wars and conquests in every part of the globe and established an immense empire, but that last, as Mr. Britling had told Mr. Direck, was " an excursion." She had just sent out younger sons and surplus people, emigrants and expeditionary forces. Her own soil had never seen any successful foreign invasion ; her homeland, the bulk of her households, her general life, had gone on untouched by these things. Nineteen people out of twenty, the middle class and most of the lower class, knew no more of the empire than they did of the Argentine Republic or the Italian Renaissance. It did not concern them. War that calls upon every man and threatens every life in the land, war of the whole national being, was a thing altogether outside English experience and the scope of the British imagination. It was still incredible, it was still outside the range of Mr. Britling's thoughts all through the tremendous onrush and check of the German attack in the west that opened the Great War. Through those two months he was, as it were, a more and more excited spectator at a show, a show like a baseball match, a spectator with money on the event, rather than a really participating citizen of a nation thoroughly at war. . . .

§ 13

After the jolt of the food panic and a brief financial scare, the vast inertia of everyday life in England asserted itself. When the public went to the banks for the new paper money, the banks tendered gold—apologetically. The supply of the new notes was very insufficient, and there was plenty of gold. After the first impression that a universal catastrophe had happened there was an effect as if nothing had happened.

Shops reopened after the Bank Holiday, in a tentative spirit that speedily became assurance ; people went about their business again, and the war, so far as the mass of British folk were concerned, was for some weeks a fever of the mind and intelligence rather than a physical and personal actuality. There was a keen demand for news, and for a time there was very little news. The press did its best to cope with this immense occasion. Led by *The Daily Express*, all the half-penny newspapers adopted a new and more resonant sort of headline, the streamer, a band of emphatic type that ran clean across the page and announced victories or disconcerting happenings. They did this every day, whether there was a great battle or the loss of a trawler to announce, and the public mind speedily adapted itself to the new pitch.

There was no invitation from the government and no organisation for any general participation in war. People talked unrestrictedly ; every one seemed to be talking ; they waved flags and displayed much vague willingness to do something. Any opportunity of service was taken very eagerly. Lord Kitchener was understood to have demanded five hundred thousand men ; the War Office arrangements for recruiting, arrangements conceived on a scale altogether too small, were speedily overwhelmed by a rush of willing young men. The flow had to be checked by raising the physical standard far above the national average, and recruiting died down to manageable proportions. There was a quite genuine belief that the war might easily be too exclusively considered ; that for the great mass of people it was a disturbing and distracting rather than a vital interest. The phrase " Business as Usual " ran about the world, and the papers abounded in articles in which going on as though there was no war at all was demonstrated to be the truest form of patriotism. " Leave things to Kitchener " was another watchword with a strong appeal to the national quality. " Business as usual during Alterations to the Map of Europe " was the advertisement of one cheerful barber, widely quoted. . . .

Hugh was at home all through August. He had thrown up his rooms in London with his artistic ambitions, and his father was making all the necessary arrangements for him to follow Cardinal to Cambridge. Meanwhile Hugh was taking up his scientific work where he had laid it down. He gave a reluctant couple of hours in the afternoon to the mysteries of Little-go Greek, and for the rest of his time he was either working at mathematics and mathematical physics or experimenting in a small upstairs room that had been carved out of the general space of the barn. It was only at the very end of August that it dawned upon him or Mr. Britling that the war might have more than a spectacular and sympathetic appeal for him. Hitherto contemporary history had happened without his personal intervention. He did not see why it should not continue to happen with the same detachment. The last elections—and a general election is really the only point at which the life of the reasonable Englishman becomes in any way public—had happened four years ago, when he was thirteen.

§ 14

For a time it was believed in Matching's Easy that the German armies had been defeated and very largely destroyed at Liège. It was a mistake not confined to Matching's Easy.

The first raiding attack was certainly repulsed with heavy losses, and so were the more systematic assaults on August the 6th and 7th. After that the news from Liège became uncertain, but it was believed in England that some or all of the forts were still holding out right up to the German entry into Brussels. Meanwhile the French were pushing into their lost provinces, occupying Altkirch, Malhausen and Saarburg ; the Russians were invading Bukovina and East Prussia ; the *Goeben,* the *Breslau* and the *Panther* had been sunk by the newspapers in an imaginary battle in the Mediterranean, and Togoland was captured by the French and British. Neither the force nor the magnitude of the German attack through Belgium was appreciated by the general mind, and it was possible for Mr. Britling to reiterate his fear that the war would be over too soon, long before the full measure of its possible benefits could be secured. But these apprehensions were unfounded ; the lessons the war had in store for Mr. Britling were far more drastic than anything he was yet able to imagine even in his most exalted moods.

He resisted the intimations of the fall of Brussels and the appearance of the Germans at Dinant. The first real check to his excessive anticipations of victory for the Allies came with the sudden reappearance of Mr. Direck in a state of astonishment and dismay at Matching's Easy. He wired from the Strand office, " Coming to tell you about things," and arrived on the heels of his telegram.

He professed to be calling upon Mr. and Mrs. Britling, and to a certain extent he was ; but he had a quick eye for the door or windows ; his glance roved irrelevantly as he talked. A faint expectation of Cissie came in with him and hovered about him, as the scent of violets follows the flower.

He was, however, able to say quite a number of things before Mr. Britling's natural tendency to do the telling asserted itself.

" My word," said Mr. Direck, " but this is *some* war. It is going on regardless of every decent consideration. As an American citizen I naturally expected to be treated with some respect, war or no war. That expectation has not yet been realised. . . . Europe is dislocated. . . . You have no idea here yet how completely Europe is dislocated. . . .

" I came to Europe in a perfectly friendly spirit—and I must say I am surprised. Practically I have been thrown out, neck and crop. All my luggage is lost. Away at some one-horse junction near the Dutch frontier that I can't even learn the name of. There's joy in some German home, I guess, over my shirts ; they were real good shirts. This tweed suit I have is all the wardrobe I've got in the world. All my money —good American notes—well, they laughed at them. And when I produced English gold they suspected me of being English and put me under arrest. . . . I can assure you that the English are most unpopular in Germany at the present time, thoroughly unpopular. . . . Considering that they are getting exactly what they were asking for, these Germans are really remarkably annoyed. . . . Well, I had to get the American consul to advance me money, and I've done more waiting about and irregular fasting and travelling on an empty stomach and viewing the world, so far as it was per-mitted, from railway sidings—for usually they made us pull the blinds down when anything important was on the track—than any cow that ever came to Chicago. . . . I was handled as freight—low-grade freight. . . . It doesn't bear recalling."

Mr. Direck assumed as grave and gloomy an expression as the facial habits of years would permit.

" I tell you I never knew there was such a thing as war until this happened to me. In America we don't know there is such a thing. It's like pestilence and famine ; something in the story-books. We've forgotten it for anything real. There's just a few grandfathers go around talking about it. Judge Holmes and sage old fellows like him. Otherwise it's just a game the kids play at. . . . And then suddenly here's everybody running about in the streets—hating and threaten-ing—and nice old gentlemen with white moustaches and fathers of families scheming and planning to burn houses and kill and hurt and terrify. And nice young women, too, looking for an Englishman to spit at ; I tell you I've been within range and very uncomfortable several times. . . . And what one can't believe is that they are really doing these things. There's a little village called Visé near the Dutch frontier ; some old chap got fooling there with a fowling-piece ; and they've wiped it out. Shot the people by the dozen, put them out in rows three deep and shot them, and burned the place. Short of scalping, Red Indians couldn't have done worse. Respectable German soldiers. . . .

" No one in England really seems to have any suspicion what is going on in Belgium. You hear stories——People tell them in Holland. It takes your breath away. They have set out just to cow those Belgians. They have started in to be deliberately frightful. You do not begin to understand. . . . Well. . . . Outrages. The sort of outrages Americans have never heard of. That one doesn't speak of. . . . Well. . . . Rape. . . . They have been raping women for disciplinary purposes on tables in the market-place of Liège. Yes, sir. It's a fact.

I was told it by a man who had just come out of Belgium. Knew the people, knew the place, knew everything. People over here do not seem to realise that those women are the same sort of women that you might find in Chester or Yarmouth, or in Matching's Easy for the matter of that. They still seem to think that Continental women are a different sort of women—more amenable to that sort of treatment. They seem to think there is some special Providential law against such things happening to English people. And it's within two hundred miles of you—even now. And as far as I can see there's precious little to prevent it coming nearer. . . . "

Mr. Britling thought there were a few little obstacles.

" I've seen the new British army drilling in London, Mr. Britling. I don't know if you have. I saw a whole battalion. And they hadn't got half-a-dozen uniforms, and not a single rifle to the whole battalion.

" You don't begin to realise in England what you are up against. You have no idea what it means to be in a country where everybody, the women, the elderly people, the steady middle-aged men, are taking war as seriously as business. They haven't the slightest compunction. I don't know what Germany was like before the war, I had hardly gotten out of my train before the war began ; but Germany to-day is one big armed camp. It's all crawling with soldiers. And every soldier has his uniform and his boots and his arms and his kit.

" And they're as sure of winning as if they had got London now. They mean to get London. They're cocksure they are going to walk through Belgium, cocksure they will get to Paris by Sedan day, and then they are going to destroy your fleet with Zeppelins and submarines and make a dash across the Channel. They say it's England they are after, in this invasion of Belgium. They'll just down France by the way. They say they've got guns to bombard Dover from Calais. They make a boast of it. They know for certain you can't arm your troops. They know you can't turn out ten thousand rifles a week. They come and talk to any one in the trains, and explain just how your defeat is going to be managed. It's just as though they were talking of rounding up cattle."

Mr. Britling said they would soon be disillusioned.

Mr. Direck, with the confidence of his authentic observations, remarked after a perceptible interval, " I wonder how."

He reverted to the fact that had most struck upon his imagination.

" Grown-up people, ordinary intelligent experienced people, taking war seriously, talking of punishing England ; it's a revelation. A sort of solemn enthusiasm. High and low. . . .

" And the train-loads of men and the train-loads of guns. . . . "

" Liége," said Mr. Britling.

" Liége was just a scratch on the paint," said Mr. Direck.

" A few thousand dead, a few score thousand dead, doesn't matter—not a red cent to them. There's a man arrived at the Cecil who saw them marching into Brussels. He sat at table with me at lunch yesterday. All day it went on, a vast unending river of men in grey. Endless wagons, endless guns, the whole manhood of a nation and all its stuff, marching. . . .

" I thought war," said Mr. Direck, " was a thing where most people stood about and did the shouting, and a sort of special team did the fighting. Well, Germany isn't fighting like that. . . . I confess it, I'm scared. . . . It's the very biggest thing on record ; it's the very limit in wars. . . . I dreamt last night of a grey flood washing everything in front of it. You and me—and Miss Corner—curious thing, isn't it ? that she came into it—were scrambling up a hill higher and higher, with that flood pouring after us. Sort of splashing into a foam of faces and helmets and bayonets—and clutching hands— and red stuff. . . . Well, Mr. Britling, I admit I'm a little bit over-wrought about it, but I can assure you you don't begin to realise in England what it is you've butted against. . . . "

§ 15

Cissie did not come up to the Dower House that afternoon, and so Mr. Direck, after some vague and transparent excuses, made his way to the cottage.

Here his report became even more impressive. Teddy sat on the writing-desk beside the typewriter and swung his legs slowly. Letty brooded in the arm-chair. Cissie presided over certain limited crawling operations of the young heir.

" They could have the equal of the whole British army killed three times over and scarcely know it had happened. They're *all* in it. It's a whole country in arms."

Teddy nodded thoughtfully.

" There's our fleet," said Letty.

" Well, *that* won't save Paris, will it ? "

Mr. Direck didn't, he declared, want to make disagreeable talk, but this was a thing people in England had to face. He felt like one of them himself—" naturally." He'd sort of hurried home to them—it was just like hurrying home— to tell them of the tremendous thing that was going to hit them. He felt like a man in front of a flood, a great grey flood. He couldn't hide what he had been thinking. " Where's our army ? " asked Letty suddenly.

" Lost somewhere in France," said Teddy. " Like a needle in a bottle of hay."

" What I keep on worrying at is this," Mr. Direck resumed. " Suppose they did come, suppose somehow they scrambled over, sixty or seventy thousand men perhaps."

" Every man would turn out and take a shot at them," said Letty.

" But there's no rifles ! "

" There's shotguns."

" That's exactly what I'm afraid of," said Mr. Direck. " They'd massacre. . . .

" You may be the bravest people on earth," said Mr. Direck, " but if you haven't got arms and the other chaps have—you're just as if you were sheep."

He became gloomily pensive.

He roused himself to describe his experiences at some length, and the extraordinary disturbance of his mind. He related more particularly his attempts to see the sights of Cologne during the stir of mobilisation. After a time his narrative flow lost force, and there was a general feeling that he ought to be left alone with Cissie. Teddy had a letter that must be posted ; Letty took the infant to crawl on the mossy stones under the pear-tree. Mr. Direck leaned against the window-sill and became silent for some moments after the door closed on Letty.

" As for you, Cissie," he began at last, " I'm anxious. I'm real anxious. I wish you'd let me throw the mantle of Old Glory over you."

He looked at her earnestly.

" Old Glory ? " asked Cissie.

" Well—the Stars and Stripes. I want you to be able to claim American citizenship—in certain eventualities. It wouldn't be so very difficult. All the world over, Cissie, Americans are respected. . . . Nobody dares touch an American citizen. We are—an inviolate people."

He paused. " But how ? " asked Cissie.

" It would be perfectly easy—perfectly."

" How ? "

" Just marry an American citizen," said Mr. Direck, with his face beaming with ingenuous self-approval. " Then you'd be safe, and I'd not have to worry."

" Because we're in for a stiff war ! " cried Cissie, and Direck perceived he had blundered.

" Because we may be invaded ! " she said, and Mr. Direck's sense of error deepened.

" I vow—— " she began.

" No ! " cried Mr. Direck, and held out a hand.

There was a moment of crisis.

" Never will I desert my country—while she is at war," said Cissie, reducing her first fierce intention, and adding as though she regretted her concession, " Anyhow."

" Then it's up to me to end the war, Cissie," said Mr. Direck, trying to get her back to a less spirited attitude.

But Cissie wasn't to be got back so easily. The war was already beckoning to them in the cottage, and drawing them down from the auditorium into the arena.

" This is the rightest war in history," she said. " If I was an American I should be sorry to be one now and to have to stand out of it. I wish I was a man now so that I could do something for all the decency and civilisation these Germans have outraged.   I can't understand how any man can be content to keep out of this, and watch Belgium being destroyed. It is like looking on at a murder. It is like watching a dog killing a kitten. . . . "

Mr. Direck's expression was that of a man who is suddenly shown strange lights upon the world.

§ 16

Mr. Britling found Mr. Direck's talk indigestible.

He was parting very reluctantly from his dream of a disastrous collapse of German imperialism, of a tremendous, decisive demonstration of the inherent unsoundness of militarist monarchy, to be followed by a world conference of chastened but hopeful nations, and—the Millennium.   He tried now to think that Mr. Direck had observed badly and misconceived what he saw.   An American, unused to any sort of military occurrences, might easily mistake tens of thousands for millions, and the excitement of a few commercial travellers for the enthusiasm of a united people.   But the newspapers now, with a kindred reluctance, were beginning to qualify, bit by bit, their first representation of the German attack through Belgium as a vast and already partly thwarted parade of incompetence.   The Germans, he gathered, were being continually beaten in Belgium ; but just as continually they advanced.   Each fresh newspaper name he looked up on the map marked an oncoming tide.   Alost—Charleroi. Farther east the French were retreating from the Saales Pass. Surely the British, who had now been in France for a fortnight, would presently be manifest, stemming the onrush ; somewhere, perhaps in Brabant or East Flanders.   It gave Mr. Britling an unpleasant night to hear at Claverings that the French were very ill equipped ; had no good modern guns either at Lille or Maubeuge, were short of boots and equipment generally, and rather depressed already at the trend of things.   Mr. Britling dismissed this as pessimistic talk, and built his hopes on the still invisible British army, hovering somewhere——

He would sit over the map of Belgium, choosing where he would prefer to have the British hover. . . .

Namur fell.   The place names continued to shift southward and westward.   The British army or a part of it came to light abruptly at Mons.   It had been fighting for thirty-eight hours and defeating enormously superior forces of the enemy.   That was reassuring until a day or so later " the Cambrai-Le Cateau line " made Mr. Britling realise that the victorious British had recoiled five-and-twenty-miles. . . .

And then came the Sunday of *The Times* telegram, which

spoke of a " retreating and a broken army." Mr. Britling did not see this, but Mr. Manning brought over the report of it in a state of profound consternation. Things, he said, seemed to be about as bad as they could be. The English were retreating towards the coast and in much disorder. They were " in the air " and already separated from the French. They had narrowly escaped " a Sedan " under the fortifications of Maubeuge. . . . Mr. Britling was stunned. He went to his study and stared helplessly at maps. It was as if David had flung his pebble—and missed !

But in the afternoon Mr. Manning telephoned to comfort his friend. A reassuring despatch from General French had been published and all was well—practically—and the British had been splendid. They had been fighting continuously for several days round and about Mons ; they had been attacked at odds of six to one, and they had repulsed and inflicted enormous losses on the enemy. They had established an incontestable personal superiority over the Germans. The Germans had been mown down in heaps ; the British had charged through their cavalry like charging through paper. So at last and very gloriously for the British, British and German had met in battle. After the hard fighting of the 26th about Landrecies, the British had been comparatively unmolested, reinforcements covering double the losses had joined them and the German advance was definitely checked. . . . Mr. Britling's mind swung back to elation. He took down the entire despatch from Mr. Manning's dictation, and ran out with it into the garden where Mrs. Britling, with an unwonted expression of anxiety, was presiding over the teas of the usual casual Sunday gathering. . . . The despatch was read aloud twice over. After that there was hockey and high spirits, and then Mr. Britling went up to his study to answer a letter from Mrs. Harrowdean, the first letter that had come from her since their breach at the outbreak of the war, and which he was now in a better mood to answer than he had been hitherto.

She had written ignoring his silence and absence, or rather treating it as if it were an incident of no particular importance. Apparently she had not called upon the patient and devoted Oliver as she had threatened ; at any rate there were no signs of Oliver in her communication. But she reproached Mr. Britling for deserting her, and she clamoured for his presence and for kind and strengthening words. She was, she said, scared by this war. She was only a little thing, and it was all too dreadful, and there was not a soul in the world to hold her hand, at least no one who understood in the slightest degree how she felt. (But why was not Oliver holding her hand ?) She was like a child left alone in the dark. It was perfectly horrible the way that people were being kept in the dark. The stories one heard, " *often from quite trust-*

worthy sources," were enough to depress and terrify any one. Battleship after battleship had been sunk by German torpedoes, a thing kept secret from us for no earthly reason, and Prince Louis of Battenberg had been discovered to be a spy and had been sent to the Tower. Haldane too was a spy. Our army in France had been " practically *sold* " by the French. Almost all the French generals were in German pay. The censorship and the press were keeping all this back, but what good was it to keep it back ? Such folly not to trust the people! But it was all too dreadful for a poor little soul whose only desire was to live happily. Why didn't he come along to her and make her feel she had protecting arms round her ? She couldn't think in the daytime ; she couldn't sleep at night. . . .

Then she broke away into the praises of serenity. Never had she thought so much of his beautiful " Silent Places " as she did now. How she longed to take refuge in some such dreamland from violence and treachery and foolish rumours ! She was weary of every reality. She wanted to fly away into some secret hiding-place and cultivate her simple garden there—as Voltaire had done. . . . Sometimes at night she was afraid to undress. She imagined the sound of guns, she imagined landings and frightful scouts " in masks " rushing inland on motor bicycles. . . .

It was an ill-timed letter. The nonsense about Prince Louis of Battenberg and Lord Haldane and the torpedoed battleships annoyed Mr. Britling extravagantly. He had just sufficient disposition to believe such tales to find their importunity exasperating. The idea of going over to Pyecrafts to spend his days in comforting a timid little dear obsessed by such fears attracted him not at all. He had already heard enough adverse rumours at Claverings to make him thoroughly uncomfortable. He had been doubting whether after all his " Examination of War " was really much less of a futility than " And Now War Ends " ; his mind was full of a sense of incomplete statement and unsubstantial arguments. He was indeed in a state of extreme intellectual worry. He was moreover extraordinarily out of love with Mrs. Harrowdean. Never had any affection in the whole history of Mr. Britling's heart collapsed so swiftly and completely. He was left incredulous of ever having cared for her at all. Probably he hadn't. Probably the whole business had been deliberate illusion from first to last. This " dear little thing " business, he felt, was all very well as a game of petting, but times were serious now, and a woman of her intelligence should do something better than wallow in fears and elaborate a winsome feebleness. A very unnecessary and tiresome feebleness. He came almost to the pitch of writing that to her.

The despatch from General French put him into a kindlier frame of mind. He wrote instead briefly but affectionately. As a gentleman should. " How could you doubt our fleet or our army ? " was the gist of his letter. He ignored completely every suggestion of a visit to Pyecrafts that her letter had conveyed. He pretended that it had contained nothing of the sort. . . . And that she passed out of his mind again under the stress of more commanding interests. . . .

Mr. Britling's mood of relief did not last through the week. The defeated Germans continued to advance. Through a week of deepening disillusionment the main tide of battle rolled back steadily towards Paris. Lille was lost without a struggle. It was lost with mysterious ease. . . . The next name to startle Mr. Britling as he sat with newspaper and atlas following these great events was Compiègne. " Here ! " Manifestly the British were still in retreat. Then the Germans were in possession of Laon and Rheims and still pressing south. Maubeuge, surrounded and cut off for some days, had apparently fallen. . . .

It was on Sunday, September the 6th, that the final capitulation of Mr. Britling's facile optimism occurred.

He stood in the sunshine reading *The Observer* which the gardener's boy had just brought from the May Tree. He had spread it open on a garden table under the blue cedar, and father and son were both reading it, each as much as the other would let him. There was fresh news from France, a story of further German advances, fighting at Senlis—" But that is quite close to Paris ! "—and the appearance of German forces at Nogent-sur-Seine. " Sur Seine ! " cried Mr. Britling. " But where can that be ? South of the Marne ? Or below Paris perhaps ? "

It was not marked upon *The Observer's* map, and Hugh ran into the house for the atlas.

When he returned Mr. Manning was with his father, and they both looked grave.

Hugh opened the map of northern France. " Here it is," he said.

Mr. Britling considered the position.

" Manning says they are at Rouen," he told Hugh. " Our base is to be moved round to La Rochelle. . . . "

He paused before the last distasteful conclusion.

" Practically," he admitted, taking his dose, " they have got Paris. It is almost surrounded now."

He sat down to the map. Mr. Manning and Hugh stood regarding him. He made a last effort to imagine some tremendous strategic reversal, some stone from an unexpected sling that should fell this Goliath in the midst of his triumph.

" Russia," he said, without any genuine hope. . . .

§ 17

And then it was that Mr. Britling accepted the truth.

" One talks," he said, " and then weeks and months later one learns the meaning of the things one has been saying. I was saying a month ago that this is the biggest thing that has happened in history. I said that this was the supreme call upon the will and resources of England. I said there was not a life in all our empire that would not be vitally changed by this war. I said all these things ; they came through my mouth ; I suppose there was a sort of thought behind them. . . . Only at this moment do I understand what it is that I said. Now—let me say it over as if I had never said it before ; this *is* the biggest thing in history, that we *are* all called upon to do our utmost to resist this tremendous attack upon the peace and freedom of the world. Well, doing our utmost does not mean standing about in pleasant gardens waiting for the newspaper. . . . It means the abandonment of ease and security. . . .

" How lazy we English are nowadays ! How readily we grasp the comforting delusion that excuses us from exertion. For the last three weeks I have been deliberately believing that a little British army—they say it is scarcely a hundred thousand men—would somehow break this rush of millions. But it has been driven back, as any one not in love with easy dreams might have known it would be driven back—here and then here and then here. It has been fighting night and day. It has made the most splendid fight—and the most ineffectual fight. . . . You see the vast swing of the German flail through Belgium. And meanwhile we have been standing about talking of the use we would make of our victory. . . .

" We have been asleep," he said. " This country has been asleep. . . .

" At the back of our minds," he went on bitterly, " I suppose we thought the French would do the heavy work on land—while we stood by at sea. So far as we thought at all. We're so temperate-minded ; we're so full of qualifications and discretions. . . . And so leisurely. . . . Well, France is down. We've got to fight for France now over the ruins of Paris. Because you and I, Manning, didn't grasp the scale of it, because we indulged in generalisations when we ought to have been drilling and working. Because we've been doing ' business as usual ' and all the rest of that sort of thing, while Western civilisation has been in its death-agony. If this is to be another '71, on a larger scale and against not merely France but all Europe, if Prussianism is to walk rough-shod over civilisation, if France is to be crushed and Belgium murdered, then life is not worth having. Compared with such an issue as that no other issue, no other interest matters. Yet what are we doing to decide it—you and I ? How can it end in anything but a German triumph if you and I, by the million, stand by ? . . . "

He paused despairfully and stared at the map.

" What ought we to be doing ? " asked Mr. Manning.

" Every man ought to be in training," said Mr. Britling.

" Every one ought to be participating. . . . In some way. . . .
At any rate we ought not to be taking our ease at Matching's
Easy any more. . . . "

§ 18

It interrupts everything," said Hugh suddenly. "These
Prussians are the biggest nuisance the world has ever seen."

He considered. " It's like every one having to run out
because the house catches fire. But of course we have to beat
them. It has to be done. And every one has to take a share.

" Then we can get on with our work again."

Mr. Britling turned his eyes to his eldest son with a startled
expression. He had been speaking—generally. For the moment
he had forgotten Hugh.

CHAPTER TWO

TAKING PART

§ 1

THERE were now two chief things in the mind of Mr.
Britling. One was a large and valiant thing, a thing of
heroic and processional quality, the idea of taking up
one's share in the great conflict, of leaving the Dower House
and its circle of habits and activities and going out——. From
that point he wasn't quite sure where he was to go, nor
exactly what he meant to do. His imagination inclined to
the figure of a volunteer in an improvised uniform inflicting
great damage upon a raiding invader from behind a hedge.
The uniform one presumes would have been something in
the vein of the costume in which he met Mr. Direck. With
a " brassard." Or he thought of himself as working at a
telephone or in an office engaged upon any useful quasi-
administrative work that called for intelligence rather than
training. Still, of course, with a " brassard." A month ago
he would have had doubts about the meaning of " brassard " ;
now it seemed to be the very key-word for national organisation. He had started for London by the early train on Monday
morning with the intention of immediate enrolment in any
such service that offered ; of getting, in fact, into his brassard
at once. The morning papers he bought at the station dashed
his conviction of the inevitable fall of Paris into hopeful
doubts, but did not shake his resolution. The effect of rout
and pursuit and retreat and retreat and retreat had disappeared from the news. The German right was being counter-
attacked, and seemed in danger of getting pinched between
Paris and Verdun with the British on its flank. This relieved

his mind, but it did nothing to modify his new realisation of the tremendous gravity of the war. Even if the enemy were held and repulsed a little there was still work for every man in the task of forcing them back upon their own country. This war was an immense thing, it would touch everybody. . . . . That meant that every man must give himself. That he had to give himself. He must let nothing stand between him and that clear understanding. It was utterly shameful now to hold back and not to do one's utmost for civilisation, for England, for all the ease and safety one had been given—against these drilled, commanded, obsessed millions.

Mr. Britling was a flame of exalted voluntaryism, of patriotic devotion that day.

But behind all this bravery was the other thing, the second thing in the mind of Mr. Britling, a fear. He was prepared now to spread himself like some valiant turkey gobbler, every feather at its utmost, against the aggressor. He was prepared to go out and flourish bayonets, march and dig to the limit of his power, shoot, die in a ditch if needful, rather than permit German militarism to dominate the world. He had no fear for himself. He was prepared to perish upon the battle-field or cut a valiant figure in the military hospital. But what he perceived very clearly and did his utmost not to perceive was this qualifying and discouraging fact, that the war monster was not nearly so disposed to meet him as he was to meet the war, and that its eyes were fixed on something beside and behind him, that it was already only too evidently stretching out a long and shadowy arm past him towards Teddy—and towards Hugh. . . .

The young are the food of war. . . .

Teddy wasn't Mr. Britling's business anyhow. Teddy must do as he thought proper. Mr. Britling would not even advise upon that. And as for Hugh——

Mr. Britling did his best to brazen it out.

" My eldest boy is barely seventeen," he said. " He's keen to go, and I'd be sorry if he wasn't. He'll get into some cadet corps, of course—he's already done something of that kind at school. Or they'll take him into the Territorials. But before he's nineteen everything will be over, one way or another. I'm afraid, poor chap, he'll feel sold. . . ."

And having thrust Hugh safely into the background of his mind as—juvenile, doing a juvenile share, no sort of man yet, Mr. Britling could give a free rein to his generous imaginations of a national uprising. From the idea of a universal participation in the struggle he passed by an easy transition to an anticipation of all Britain armed and gravely embattled. Across gulfs of obstinate reality. He himself was prepared to say, and accordingly he felt that the great mass of the British must be prepared to say to the government : " Here we are at your disposal. This is not a diplomatist's war nor a War

Office war ; this is a war of the whole people. We are all willing and ready to lay aside our usual occupations and offer our property and ourselves. Whim and individual action are for peace times. Take us and use us as you think fit. Take all we possess." When he thought of the government in this way, he forgot the governing class he knew. The slack-trousered Raeburn, the prim, attentive Philbert, Lady Frensham at the top of her voice, stern, preposterous Carson, boozy Bandershoot, and artful Taper, wily Asquith, the eloquent yet unsubstantial George, and the immobile Grey, vanished out of his mind ; all those representative exponents of the way things are done in Great Britain faded in the glow of his imaginative effort ; he forgot the dreary debates, the floundering newspapers, the " bluffs," the intrigues, the sly bargains of the week-end party, the " schoolboy honour " of grown men, the universal weak dishonesty in thinking ; he thought simply of a simplified and ideal government that governed. He thought vaguely of something behind and beyond them, England, the ruling genius of the land ; something with a dignified assurance and a stable will. He imagined this shadowy ruler miraculously provided with schemes and statistics against this supreme occasion which had for so many years been the most conspicuous probability before the country. His mind, leaping forward to the conception of a great nation reluctantly turning its vast resources to the prosecution of a righteous defensive war, filled in the obvious corollaries of plan and calculation. He thought that somewhere " up there " there must be people who could count and who had counted everything that we might need for such a struggle, and organisers who had schemed and estimated down to practicable and manageable details. . . .

Such lapses from knowledge to faith are perhaps necessary that human heroism may be possible. . . .

His conception of his own share in the great national uprising was a very modest one. He was a writer, a foot-note to reality ; he had no trick of command over men, his rôle was observation rather than organisation, and he saw himself only as an insignificant individual dropping from his individuality into his place in a great machine, taking a rifle in a trench, guarding a bridge, filling a cartridge—just with a brassard or something like that on—until the great task was done. Sunday night was full of imaginations of order, of the countryside standing up to its task, of roads cleared and resources marshalled, of the petty interests of the private life altogether set aside. And mingling with that it was still possible for Mr. Britling, he was still young enough, to produce such dreams of personal service, of sudden emergencies swiftly and bravely met, of conspicuous daring and exceptional rewards, such dreams as hover in the brains of every imaginative recruit. . . .

The detailed story of Mr. Britling's two days' search for some easy and convenient ladder into the service of his threatened country would be a voluminous one. It would begin with the figure of a neatly brushed patriot, with an intent expression upon his intelligent face, seated in the Londonward train, reading the war news—the first comforting war news for many days—and trying not to look as though his life was torn up by the roots and all his being aflame with devotion ; and it would conclude after forty-eight hours of fuss, inquiry, talk, waiting, telephoning, with the same gentleman, a little fagged and with a kind of weary apathy in his eyes, returning by the short cut from the station across Claverings Park to resume his connection with his abandoned roots. The essential process of the interval had been the correction of Mr. Britling's temporary delusion that the government of the British Empire is either intelligent, instructed, or wise.

The great " Business as Usual " phase was already passing away, and London was in the full tide of recruiting enthusiasm. That tide was breaking against the most miserable arrangements for enlistment it is possible to imagine. Overtaxed and not very competent officers, whose one idea of being efficient was to refuse civilian help and be very, very slow and circumspect and very dignified and overbearing, sat in dirty little rooms and snarled at this unheard-of England that pressed at door and window for enrolment. Outside every recruiting office crowds of men and youths waited, leaning against walls, sitting upon the pavements, waiting for long hours, waiting to the end of the day and returning next morning, without shelter, without food, many sick with hunger ; men who had hurried up from the country, men who had thrown up jobs of every kind, clerks, shopmen, anxious only to serve England and " teach those damned Germans a lesson." Between them and this object they had discovered a perplexing barrier ; an inattention. As Mr. Britling made his way by St. Martin's Church and across Trafalgar Square and marked the weary accumulation of this magnificently patriotic stuff, he had his first inkling of the imaginative insufficiency of the War Office that had been so suddenly called upon to organise victory. He was to be more fully informed when he reached his club.

His impression of the streets through which he passed was an impression of great unrest. There were noticeably fewer omnibuses and less road traffic generally, but there was a quite unusual number of drifting pedestrians. The current on the pavements was irritatingly sluggish. There were more people standing about, and fewer going upon their business. This was particularly the case with the women he saw. Many of them seemed to have drifted in from the suburbs and outskirts of London in a state of vague expectation, unable to stay in their homes.

Everywhere there were the flags of the Allies; in shop-windows, over doors, on the bonnets of automobiles, on people's breasts, and there was a great quantity of recruiting posters on the hoardings and in windows: " Your King and Country Need You " was the chief text, and they still called for " A Hundred Thousand Men " although the demand of Lord Kitchener had risen to half a million. There were also placards calling for men on nearly all the taxicabs. The big windows of the offices of the Norddeutscher Lloyd in Cockspur Street were boarded up, and plastered thickly with recruiting appeals.

At his club Mr. Britling found much talk and belligerent stir. In the hall Wilkins the author was displaying a dummy rifle of bent iron rod to several interested members. It was to be used for drilling until rifles could be got, and it could be made for eighteenpence. This was the first intimation Mr. Britling got that the want of foresight of the War Office only began with its unpreparedness for recruits. Men were talking very freely in the club; one of the temporary effects of the war in its earlier stages was to produce a partial thaw in the constitutional British shyness; and men who had glowered at Mr. Britling over their lunches and had been glowered at by Mr. Britling in silence for years now started conversations with him.

" What is a man of my sort to do ? " asked a clean-shaven barrister.

" Exactly what I have been asking," said Mr. Britling. " They are fixing the upward age for recruits at thirty; it's absurdly low. A man well over forty like myself is quite fit to line a trench or guard a bridge. I'm not so bad a shot. . . ."

" We've been discussing home defence volunteers," said the barrister. " Anyhow we ought to be drilling. But the War Office sets its face as sternly against our doing anything of the sort as though we were going to join the Germans. It's absurd. Even if we older men aren't fit to go abroad, we could at least release troops who could."

" If you had the rifles," said a sharp-featured man in grey to the right of Mr. Britling.

" I suppose they are to be got," said Mr. Britling. The sharp-featured man indicated by appropriate facial action and head-shaking that this was by no means the case.

" Every dead man, many wounded men, most prisoners," he said, " mean each one a rifle lost. We have lost five-and-twenty thousand rifles alone since the war began. Quite apart from arming new troops we have to replace those rifles with the drafts we send out. Do you know what is the maximum weekly output of rifles at the present time in this country ? "

Mr. Britling did not know.

" Nine thousand."

Mr. Britling suddenly understood the significance of Wilkins and his dummy gun.

The sharp-featured man added with an air of concluding the matter : " It's the barrels are the trouble. Complicated machinery. We haven't got it and we can't make it in a hurry. And there you are ! "

The sharp-featured man had a way of speaking almost as if he was throwing bombs. He threw one now. " Zinc," he said.

" We're not short of zinc ? " said the lawyer.

The sharp-featured man nodded, and then became explicit. Zinc was necessary for cartridges ; it had to be refined zinc and very pure, or the shooting went wrong. Well, we had let the refining business drift away from England to Belgium and Germany. There were just one or two British firms still left. . . . Unless we bucked up tremendously we should get caught short of cartridges. . . . At any rate of cartridges so made as to ensure good shooting. " And there you are ! " said the sharp-featured man.

But the sharp-featured man did not at that time represent any considerable section of public thought. " I suppose after all we can get rifles from America," said the lawyer. " And as for zinc, if the shortage is known the shortage will be provided for. . . ."

The prevailing topic in the smoking-room upstairs was the inability of the War Office to deal with the flood of recruits that was pouring in, and its hostility to any such volunteering as Mr. Britling had in mind. Quite a number of members wanted to volunteer ; there was much talk of their fitness ; " I'm fifty-four," said one, " and I could do my twenty-five miles in marching kit far better than half those boys of nineteen." Another was thirty-eight. " I must hold the business together," he said ; " but why anyhow shouldn't I learn to shoot and use a bayonet ? " The personal pique of the rejected lent force to their criticisms of the recruiting and general organisation. " The War Office has one incurable system," said a big mine-owner. " During peace-time it runs all its home administration with men who will certainly be wanted at the front directly there is a war. Directly war comes, therefore, there is a shift all round, and a new untried man—usually a dugout in an advanced state of decay—is stuck into the job. Chaos follows automatically. The War Office always has done this, and so far as one can see it always will. It seems incapable of realising that another man will be wanted until the first is taken away. Its imagination doesn't even run to that."

Mr. Britling found a kindred spirit in Wilkins.

Wilkins was expounding his tremendous scheme for universal volunteering. Everybody was to be accepted. Everybody was to be assigned and registered and—*badged*.

" A brassard," said Mr. Britling.

" It doesn't matter whether we really produce a fighting force or not," said Wilkins. " Everybody now is enthusiastic —and serious. Everybody is willing to put on some kind of uniform and submit to some sort of orders. And the thing to do is to catch them in the willing stage. Now is the time to get the country lined up and organised, ready to meet the internal stresses that are bound to come later. But there's no disposition whatever to welcome this universal offering. It's just as though this war was a treat to which only the very select friends of the War Office were to be admitted. And I don't admit that the national volunteers would be in-effective—even from a military point of view. There are plenty of fit men of our age, and men of proper age who are better employed at home—armament workers for example, and there are all the boys under the age. They may not be under the age before things are over. . . ."

He was even prepared to plan uniforms.

" A brassard," repeated Mr. Britling, " and perhaps coloured strips on the reverse of a coat."

" Colours for the counties," said Wilkins, " and if there isn't coloured cloth to be got there's—red flannel. Anything is better than leaving the mass of people to mob about. . . ."

A momentary vision danced before Mr. Britling's eyes of red flannel petticoats being torn up in a rapid improvisation of soldiers to resist a sudden invasion. Passing washerwomen suddenly requisitioned. But one must not let oneself be laughed out of good intentions because of ridiculous accessories. The idea at any rate was a sound one. . . .

The vision of what ought to be done shone brightly while Mr. Britling and Mr. Wilkins maintained it. But presently under discouraging reminders that there were no rifles, no instructors, and, above all, the open hostility of the established authorities, it faded again. . . .

Afterwards in other conversations Mr. Britling reverted to more modest ambitions.

" Is there no clerical work, no minor administrative work, a man might be used for ? " he asked.

" Any old dugout," said the man with the thin face, " any old doddering Colonel Newcome, is preferred to you in that matter. . . ."

Mr. Britling emerged from his club about half past three with his mind rather dishevelled and with his private de-termination to do something promptly for his country's needs blunted by a perplexing " How ? " His search for doors and ways where no doors and ways existed went on with a gathering sense of futility.

He had a ridiculous sense of pique at being left out, like a child shut out from a room in which a vitally interesting game is being played.

"After all, it is *our* war," he said.

He caught the phrase as it dropped from his lips with a feeling that it said more than he intended. He turned it over and examined it, and the more he did so the more he was convinced of its truth and soundness. . . .

§ 2

By night there was a new strangeness about London. The authorities were trying to suppress the more brilliant illumination of the chief thoroughfares, on account of the possibility of an air-raid. Shopkeepers were being compelled to pull down their blinds, and many of the big standard lights were unlit. Mr. Britling thought these precautions were very fussy and unnecessary, and likely to lead to accidents amidst the traffic. But it gave a Rembrantesque quality to the London scene, turned it into mysterious arrangements of brown shadows and cones and bars of light. At first many people were recalcitrant, and here and there a restaurant or a draper's window still blazed out and broke the gloom. There were also a number of insubordinate automobiles with big headlights. But the police were being unusually firm. . . .

"It will all glitter again in a little time," he told himself.

He heard an old lady who was projecting from an offending automobile at Piccadilly Circus in hot dispute with a police officer. "Zeppelins indeed!" she said. "What nonsense! As if they would *dare* to come here! Who would *let* them, I should like to know?"

Probably a friend of Lady Frensham's, he thought. Still—the idea of Zeppelins over London did seem rather ridiculous to Mr. Britling. He would not have liked to be caught talking of it himself. . . . There never had been Zeppelins over London. They were gas-bags. . . .

§ 3

On Wednesday morning Mr. Britling returned to the Dower House, and he was still a civilian unassigned.

In the hall he found a tall figure in khaki standing and reading *The Times* that usually lay upon the hall table. The figure turned at Mr. Britling's entry, and revealed the aquiline features of Mr. Lawrence Carmine.

It was as if his friend had stolen a march on him.

But Carmine's face showed nothing of the excitement and patriotic satisfaction that would have seemed natural to Mr. Britling. He was white and jaded, as if he had not slept for many nights. "You see," he explained almost apologetically of the three stars upon his sleeve, "I used to be a captain of volunteers." He had been put in charge of a volunteer force which had been re-embodied and entrusted with the care of the bridges, gas-works, factories and railway tunnels, and with a number of other minor but necessary duties round about

Easinghampton. " I've just got to shut up my house," said
Captain Carmine, " and go into lodgings. I confess I hate it.
. . . But anyhow it can't last six months. . . . But it's
beastly. . . . Ugh ! . . ."

He seemed disposed to expand that " Ugh," and then
thought better of it. And presently Mr. Britling took control
of the conversation.

His two days in London had filled him with matter, and
he was glad to have something more than Hugh and Teddy
and Mrs. Britling to talk it upon. What was happening now in
Great Britain, he declared, was *adjustment*. It was an attempt
on the part of a great unorganised nation, an attempt, instinctive at present rather than intelligent, to readjust its government and particularly its military organisation to the new scale
of warfare that Germany had imposed upon the world. For
two strenuous decades the British navy had been growing
enormously under the pressure of German naval preparations,
but the British military establishment had experienced no
corresponding expansion. It was true there had been a futile,
rather foolishly conducted agitation for universal military
service, but there had been no accumulation of material, no
preparation of armament-making machinery, no planning and
no foundations for any sort of organisation that would have
facilitated the rapid expansion of the fighting forces of the
country in a time of crisis. Such an idea was absolutely antagonistic to the mental habits of the British military caste. The
German method of incorporating all the strength and resources
of the country into one national fighting machine was quite
strange to the British military mind—still. Even after a
month of war. War had become the comprehensive business
of the German nation ; to the British it was an incidental
adventure. In Germany the nation was militarised, in England
the army was specialised. The nation for nearly every practical
purpose got along without it. Just as political life had also
become specialised. . . . Now suddenly we wanted a government to speak for every one, and an army of the whole people.
How were we to find them ?

Mr. Britling dwelt upon this idea of the specialised character
of the British army and navy and government. It seemed to
him to be the clue to everything that was jarring in the London
spectacle. The army had been a thing aloof, for a special end.
It had developed all the characteristics of a caste. It had very
high standards along the lines of its specialisation, but it was
inadaptable and conservative. Its exclusiveness was not so
much a deliberate culture as a consequence of its detached
function. It touched the ordinary social body chiefly through
three other specialised bodies, the court, the church, and the
stage. Apart from that it saw the great unofficial civilian world
as something vague, something unsympathetic, something
possibly antagonistic, which it comforted itself by snubbing

when it dared and tricking when it could, something that projected members of Parliament towards it and was stingy about money. Directly one grasped how apart the army lived from the ordinary life of the community, from industrialism, or from economic necessities, directly one understood that the great mass of Englishmen were simply " outsiders " to the War Office mind, just as they were " outsiders " to the political clique, one began to realise the complete unfitness of either government or War Office for the conduct of so great a national effort as was now needed. These people " up there " did not know anything of the broad mass of English life at all, they did not know how or where things were made ; when they wanted things they just went to a shop somewhere and got them. This was the necessary psychology of a small army under a clique government. Nothing else was to be expected. But now— somehow—the nation had to take hold of the government that it had neglected so long. . . .

" You see," said Mr. Britling, repeating a phrase that was becoming more and more essential to his thoughts, " this is *our* war. . . .

" Of course," said Mr. Britling, " these things are not going to be done without a conflict. We aren't going to take hold of our country which we have neglected so long without a lot of internal friction. But in England we can make these readjustments without revolution. It is our strength. . . .

" At present England is confused—but it's a healthy confusion. It's astir. We have more things to defeat than just Germany. . . .

" These hosts of recruits—weary, uncared for, besieging the recruiting-stations. It's symbolical. . . . Our tremendous reserves of will and manhood. Our almost incredible insufficiency of direction. . . .

" Those people up there have no idea of the Will that surges up in England. They are timid little manœuvring people, afraid of property, afraid of newspapers, afraid of trade unions. They aren't leading us against the Germans ; they are just being shoved against the Germans by necessity. . . .

From this Mr. Britling broke away into a fresh addition to his already large collection of contrasts between England and Germany. Germany was a nation which has been swallowed up and incorporated by an army and an administration ; the Prussian military system had assimilated to itself the whole German life. It was a State in a state of repletion, a State that had swallowed all its people. Britain was not a State. It was an unincorporated people. The British army, the British War Office, and the British administration has assimilated nothing ; they were little old partial things ; the British nation lay outside them, beyond their understanding and tradition ; a formless new thing, but a great thing ; and now this British nation, this real nation, the " outsiders," had to take up arms.

Suddenly all the underlying ideas of that outer, greater English
life beyond politics, beyond the services, were challenged, its
tolerant good humour, its freedom, and its irresponsibility.
It was not simply English life that was threatened ; it was all
the latitudes of democracy, it was every liberal idea and every
liberty. It was civilisation in danger. The unchartered liberal
system had been taken by the throat ; it had to " make good "
or perish. . . .

"I went up to London expecting to be told what to do.
There is no one to tell any one what to do. . . . Much less is
there any one to compel us what to do. . . .

"There's a War Office like a college during a riot, with its
doors and windows barred ; there's a government like a cockle-
boat in an Atlantic gale.   . . .

"One feels the thing ought to have come upon us like the
sound of a trumpet. Instead, until now, it has been like a great
noise, that we just listened to, in the next house. . . . And
now slowly the nation awakes. London is just like a dazed
sleeper waking up out of a deep sleep to fire and danger, tumult
and cries for help, near at hand. The streets give you exactly
that effect. People are looking about and listening. One feels
that at any moment, in a pause, in a silence, there may come,
from far away, over the houses, faint and little, the boom of
guns or the small outcries of little French or Belgian villages
in agony. . . ."

Such was the gist of Mr. Britling's discourse.

He did most of the table talk, and all that mattered. Teddy
was an assenting voice, Hugh was silent and apparently a
little inattentive, Mrs. Britling was thinking of the courses
and the servants and the boys, and giving her husband only
half an ear, Captain Carmine said little and seemed to be
troubled by some disagreeable preoccupation. Now and then
he would endorse or supplement the things Mr. Britling was
saying. Thrice he remarked : " People still do not begin to
understand." . . .

§ 4

It was only when they sat together in the barn court out of
the way of Mrs. Britling and the children that Captain Carmine
was able to explain his listless bearing and jaded appearance.
He was suffering from a bad nervous shock. He had hardly
taken over his command before one of his men had been killed—
and killed in a manner that had left a scar upon his mind.

The man had been guarding a tunnel, and he had been
knocked down by one train when crossing the line behind
another. So it was that the bomb of Sarajevo killed its first
victim in Essex. Captain Carmine had found the body. He
had found the body in a cloudy moonlight ; he had almost
fallen over it ; and his sensations and emotions had been
eminently disagreeable. He had had to drag the body—it was

very dreadfully mangled—off the permanent way, the damaged, almost severed head had twisted about very horribly in the uncertain light, and afterwards he had found his sleeves saturated with blood. He had not noted this at the time, and when he had discovered it he had been sick. He had thought the whole thing more horrible and hateful than any nightmare, but he had succeeded in behaving with a sufficient practicality to set an example to his men. Since this had happened he had not had an hour of dreamless sleep.

"One doesn't expect to be called upon like that," said Captain Carmine, "suddenly here in England. . . . When one is smoking after supper. . . ."

Mr. Britling listened to this experience with distressed brows. All his talking and thinking became to him like the open page of a monthly magazine. Across it this bloody smear, this thing of red and black, was dragged. . . .

§ 5

The smear was still bright red in Mr. Britling's thoughts when Teddy came to him.

"I must go," said Teddy, "I can't stop here any longer."

"Go where ? "

"Into khaki. I've been thinking of it ever since the war began. Do you remember what you said when we were bullying off at hockey on Bank Holiday—the day before war was declared ? "

Mr. Britling had forgotten completely ; he made an effort. "What did I say ? "

"You said : 'What the devil are we doing at this hockey ? We ought to be drilling or shooting against those confounded Germans ! ' . . . I've never forgotten it. . . . I ought to have done it before. I've been a scout-master. In a little while they will want officers. In London, I'm told, there are a lot of officers' training corps putting men through the work as quickly as possible. . . . If I could go. . . ."

"What does Letty think ? " said Mr. Britling after a pause. This was right, of course—the only right thing—and yet he was surprised.

"She says if you'd let her try to do my work for a time. . . ."

"She *wants* you to go ? "

"Of course she does," said Teddy. "She wouldn't like me to be a shirker. . . . But I can't unless you help."

"I'm quite ready to do that," said Mr. Britling. "But somehow I didn't think it of you. I hadn't somehow thought of *you*——"

"What *did* you think of me ? " asked Teddy.

"It's bringing the war home to us. . . . Of course you ought to go—if you want to go."

He reflected. It was odd to find Teddy in this mood, strung up and serious and businesslike. He felt that in the past he had done Teddy injustice ; this young man wasn't as trivial as he had thought him. . . . .

They fell to discussing ways and means ; there might have to be a loan for Teddy's outfit, if he did presently secure a commission. And there were one or two other little matters. . . . Mr. Britling dismissed a ridiculous fancy that he was paying to send Teddy away to something that neither that young man nor Letty understood properly. . . .

The next day Teddy vanished Londonward on his bicycle. He was going to lodge in London in order to be near his training. He was zealous. Never before had Teddy been zealous. Mrs. Teddy came to the Dower House for the correspondence, trying not to look self-conscious and important.

Two Mondays later a very bright-eyed, excited little boy came running to Mr. Britling, who was smoking after lunch in the rose-garden. " Daddy ! " squealed the small boy. " Teddy ! In khaki ! "

The other junior Britling danced in front of the hero, who was walking beside Mrs. Britling and trying not to be too aggressively a soldierly figure. He looked a very man in khaki and more of a boy than ever. Mrs. Teddy came behind, quietly elated.

Mr. Britling had a recurrence of that same disagreeable fancy that these young people didn't know exactly what they were going into. He wished he was in khaki himself ; then he fancied this compunction wouldn't trouble him quite so much.

The afternoon with them deepened his conviction that they really didn't in the slightest degree understand. Life had been so good to them hitherto, that even the idea of Teddy's going off to the war seemed a sort of fun to them. It was just a thing he was doing, a serious, seriously amusing, and very creditable thing. It involved his dressing up in these unusual clothes, and receiving salutes in the street. . . . They discussed every possible aspect of his military outlook with the zest of children who recount the merits of a new game. They were putting Teddy through his stages at a tremendous pace. In quite a little time he thought he would be given the chance of a commission.

" They want subalterns badly. Already they've taken nearly a third of our people," he said, and added with the wistfulness of one who glances at inaccessible delights : " one or two may get out to the front quite soon."

He spoke as a young actor might speak of a star part. And with a touch of the quality of one who longs to travel in strange lands. . . . One must be patient. Things come at last. . . .

" If I'm killed she gets eighty pounds a year," Teddy explained among many other particulars.

He smiled—the smile of a confident immortal at this amusing idea.

" He's my little annuity," said Letty, also smiling, " dead or alive."

" We'll miss Teddy in all sorts of ways," said Mr. Britling.

" It's only for the duration of the war," said Teddy. " And Letty's very intelligent. I've done my best to chasten the evil in her."

" If you think you're going to get back your job after the war," said Letty, " you're very much mistaken. I'm going to raise the standard."

" *You !* " said Teddy, regarding her coldly, and proceeded ostentatiously to talk of other things.

§ 6

" Hugh's going to be in khaki too," the elder junior told Teddy. " He's too young to go out in Kitchener's army, but he s joined the Territorials. He went off on Thursday. . . . I wish Gilbert and me was older. . . ."

Mr. Britling had known his son's purpose since the evening of Teddy's announcement.

Hugh had come to his father's study as he was sitting musing at his writing-desk over the important question whether he should continue his " Examination of War " uninterruptedly, or whether he should not put that on one side for a time and set himself to state as clearly as possible the not too generally recognised misfit between the will and strength of Britain on the one hand and her administrative and military organisation on the other. He felt that an enormous amount of human enthusiasm and energy was being refused and wasted ; that if things went on as they were going there would continue to be a quite disastrous shortage of gear, and that some broadening change was needed immediately if the swift exemplary victory over Germany that his soul demanded was to be ensured. Suppose he were to write some noisy articles at once, an article, for instance, to be called " The War of the Mechanics " or " The War of Gear," and another on " Without Civil Strength there is no Victory." If he wrote such things would they be noted or would they just vanish indistinguishably into the general mental tumult ? Would they be audible and helpful shouts, or just waste of shouting ? . . . That at least was what he supposed himself to be thinking ; it was, at any rate, the main current of his thinking ; but all the same, just outside the circle of his attention a number of other things were dimly apprehended, bobbing up and down in the flood and ready at the slightest chance to swirl into the centre of his thoughts. There was, for instance, Captain Carmine in the moonlight lugging up a railway embankment something horrible, something loose and wet and warm that had very recently been a man. There was Teddy, serious and patriotic—filling a futile penman with incredulous respect. There was the thin-faced man at the club, and a curious satisfaction he had betrayed in the public disarrangement. And there was Hugh.

Particularly there was Hugh, silent but watchful. The boy never babbled. He had his mother's gift of deep dark silences. Out of which she was wont to flash, a Black Princess waving a sword. He wandered for a little while among memories. . . . But Hugh didn't come out like that, though it always seemed possible he might—perhaps he didn't come out because he was a son. Revelation to his father wasn't his business. . . . What was he thinking of it all ? What was he going to do ? Mr. Britling was acutely anxious that his son should volunteer ; he was almost certain that he would volunteer, but there was just a little shadow of doubt whether some extraordinary subtlety of mind mightn't have carried the boy into a pacifist attitude. No ! that was impossible. In the face of Belgium. . . . But as greatly—and far more deeply in the warm-flesh of his being—did Mr. Britling desire that no harm, no evil should happen to Hugh. . . .

The door opened, and Hugh came in. . . .

Mr. Britling glanced over his shoulder with an affectation of indifference. " Hal-*lo* ! " he said. " What do *you* want ? "

Hugh walked awkwardly to the hearth-rug.

" Oh ! " he said in an offhand tone ; " I suppose I've got to go soldiering for a bit. I just thought—I'd rather like to go off with a man I know to-morrow. . . ."

Mr. Britling's manner remained casual.

" It's the only thing to do now, I'm afraid," he said.

He turned in his chair and regarded his son. " What do you mean to do ?   O.T.C. ? "

" I don't think I should make much of an officer. I hate giving orders to other people. We thought we'd just go together into the Essex Regiment as privates. . . ."

There was a little pause. Both father and son had rehearsed this scene in their minds several times, and now they found that they had no use for a number of sentences that had been most effective in these rehearsals. Mr. Britling scratched his cheek with the end of his pen. " I'm glad you want to go, Hugh," he said.

" I *don't* want to go," said Hugh with his hands deep in his pockets. " I want to go and work with Cardinal. But this job has to be done by every one. Haven't you been saying as much all day ? . . . It's like turning out to chase a burglar or suppress a mad dog. It's like necessary sanitation. . . ."

" You aren't attracted by soldiering ? "

" Not a bit. I won't pretend it, Daddy. I think the whole business is a bore. Germany seems to me now just like some heavy horrible dirty mass that has fallen across Belgium and France. We've got to shove the stuff back again. That's all. . . ."

He volunteered some further remarks to his father's silence.

" You know I can't get up a bit of tootle about this business," he said, " I think killing people or getting killed is a thoroughly nasty habit. . . . I expect my share will be just drilling and

fatigue duties and route marches, and loafing here in England. . . ."

"You can't possibly go out for two years," said Mr. Britling,
as if he regretted it.

A slight hesitation appeared in Hugh's eyes. "I suppose
not," he said.

"Things ought to be over by then—anyhow," Mr. Britling
added, betraying his real feelings.

"So it's really just helping at the farthest end of the shove,"
Hugh endorsed, but still with that touch of reservation in his
manner. . . .

The pause had the effect of closing the theoretical side of the
question. "Where do you propose to enlist?" said Mr.
Britling, coming down to practical details.

§ 7

The battle of the Marne passed into the battle of the Aisne,
and then the long lines of the struggle streamed north-westward
until the British were back in Belgium, failing to clutch Menin
and then defending Ypres. The elation of September followed
the bedazzlement and dismay of August into the chapter of
forgotten moods ; and Mr. Britling's sense of the magnitude,
the weight and duration of this war beyond all wars, increased
steadily. The feel of it was less and less a feeling of crisis and
more and more a feeling of new conditions. It wasn't as it had
seemed at first, the end of one human phase and the beginning
of another ; it was in itself a phase. It was a new way of living.
And still he could find for himself no real point of contact with
it all except the point of his pen. Only at his writing-desk, and
more particularly at night, were the great presences of the
conflict his. Yet he was always desiring some more personal and
physical participation.

Hugh came along one day in October in an ill-fitting uniform,
looking already coarser in fibre and with a nose scorched red
by the autumnal sun. He said the life was rough, but it made
him feel extraordinarily well ; perhaps man was made to toil
until he dropped asleep from exhaustion, to fast for ten or
twelve hours and then eat like a wolf. He was acquiring a taste
for Woodbine cigarettes, and a heady variety of mineral waters
called Monsters. He feared promotion ; he felt he could never
take the high line with other human beings demanded of a
corporal. He was still trying to read a little chemistry and
crystallography, but it didn't "go with the life." In the scanty
leisure of a recruit in training it was more agreeable to lie about
and write doggerel verses and draw caricatures of the men in
one's platoon. Invited to choose what he liked by his family,
he demanded a large tuck-box such as he used to have at school,
only "*much* larger," and a big tin of insect powder. It must be
able to kill ticks. . . .

When he had gone, the craving for a personal share in the

nation's physical exertions became overpowering in Mr. Britling. He wanted, he felt, to " get his skin into it." He had decided that the volunteer movement was a hopeless one. The War Office, after a stout resistance to any volunteer movement at all, decided to recognise it in such a manner as to make it ridiculous. The volunteers were to have no officers and no uniforms that could be remotely mistaken for those of the regulars, so that in the event of an invasion the Germans would be able to tell what they had to deal with miles away. Wilkins found his conception of a whole nation, all enrolled, all listed and badged according to capacity, his dream of every one falling into place in one great voluntary national effort, treated as the childish dreaming of that most ignorant of all human types, a " novelist." *Punch* was delicately funny about him ; he was represented as wearing a preposterous cocked hat of his own design, designing cocked hats for every one.

Wilkins was told to " shut up " in a multitude of anonymous letters, and publicly and privately to " leave things to Kitchener." To bellow in loud clear tones " leave things to Kitchener," and to depart for the theatre or the river or an automobile tour, was felt very generally at that time to be the proper conduct for a patriot. There was a very general persuasion that to become a volunteer when one ought to be just modestly doing nothing at all, was in some obscure way a form of disloyalty. . . .

So Mr. Britling was out of conceit with volunteering, and instead he went and was duly sworn, and entrusted with the badge of a special constable. The duties of a special constable were chiefly not to understand what was going on in the military sphere, and to do what he was told in the way of watching and warding conceivably vulnerable points. He had also to be available in the event of civil disorder. Mr. Britling was provided with a truncheon and sent out to guard various culverts, bridges, and fords in the hilly country to the north-westward of Matching's Easy. It was never very clear to him what he would do if he found a motor-car full of armed enemies engaged in undermining a culvert, or treacherously deepening some strategic ford. He supposed he would either engage them in conversation, or hit them with his truncheon, or perhaps do both things simultaneously. But as he really did not believe for a moment that any human being was likely to tamper with the telegraphs, telephones, ways and appliances committed to his care, his uncertainty did not trouble him very much. He prowled the lonely lanes and paths in the darkness, and became better acquainted with a multitude of intriguing little cries and noises that came from the hedges and coverts at night. One night he rescued a young leveret from a stoat, who seemed more than half inclined to give him battle for its prey until he cowed and defeated it with the glare of his electric torch. . . .

As he prowled the countryside under the great hemisphere

of Essex sky, or leaned against fences or sat drowsily upon
gates or sheltered from wind and rain under ricks or sheds, he
had much time for meditation, and his thoughts went down
and down below his first surface impressions of the war. He
thought no longer of the rights and wrongs of this particular
conflict but of the underlying forces in mankind that made war
possible ; he planned no more ingenious treaties and conventions between the nations, and instead he faced the deeper
riddles of essential evil and of conceivable changes in the
heart of man. And the rain assailed him and thorns tore him,
and the soaked soft meadows bogged and betrayed his wandering feet, and the little underworld of the hedges and ditches
hissed and squealed in the darkness and pursued and fled, and
devoured or were slain.

And one night in April he was perplexed by a commotion
among the pheasants and a barking of distant dogs, and then
to his great astonishment he heard noises like a distant firework
display and saw something like a phantom yellowish fountain-
pen in the sky far away to the east lit intermittently by a
quivering searchlight and going very swiftly. And after he had
rubbed his eyes and looked again, he realised that he was
looking at a Zeppelin—a Zeppelin flying Londonward over
Essex.

And all that night was wonder. . . .

§ 8

While Mr. Britling was trying to find his duty in the routine
of a special constable, Mrs. Britling set to work with great
energy to attend various classes and qualify herself for Red
Cross work. And early in October came the great drive of
the Germans towards Antwerp and the sea, the great drive
that was apparently designed to reach Calais, and which swept
before it multitudes of Flemish refugees. There was an exodus
of all classes from Antwerp into Holland and England, and
then a huge process of depopulation in Flanders and the Pas
de Calais. This flood came to the eastern and southern parts
of England and particularly to London, and there hastily
improvised organisations distributed it to a number of local
committees, each of which took a share of the refugees,
hired and furnished unoccupied houses for the use of the
penniless, and assisted those who had means into comfortable
quarters. The Matching's Easy committee found itself with
accommodation for sixty people, and with a miscellaneous
bag of thirty individuals entrusted to its care, who had been
part of the load of a little pirate steamboat from Ostend.
There were two Flemish peasant families, and the rest were
more or less middle-class refugees from Antwerp. They were
brought from the station to the Tithe barn at Claverings,
and there distributed, under the personal supervision of Lady

Homartyn and her agent, among those who were prepared for their entertainment. There was something like competition among the would-be hosts ; everybody was glad of the chance of " doing something," and anxious to show these Belgians what England thought of their plucky little country. Mr. Britling was proud to lead off a Mr. Van der Pant, a neat little bearded man in a black tail-coat, a black bowler hat, and a knitted muffler, with a large rucksack and a conspicuously foreign-looking bicycle, to the hospitalities of the Dower House. Mr. Van der Pant had escaped from Antwerp at the eleventh hour ; he had caught a severe cold and, it would seem, lost his wife and family in the process ; he had much to tell Mr. Britling, and in his zeal to tell it he did not at once discover that though Mr. Britling knew French quite well he did not know it very rapidly.

The dinner that night at the Dower House marked a distinct fresh step in the approach of the Great War to the old habits and securities of Matching's Easy. The war had indeed filled every one's mind to the exclusion of all other topics since its very beginning ; it had carried off Herr Heinrich to Germany, Teddy to London, and Hugh to Colchester, it had put a special brassard round Mr. Britling's arm and carried him out into the night, given Mrs. Britling several certificates, and interrupted the frequent visits and gossip of Mr. Lawrence Carmine ; but so far it had not established a direct contact between the life of Matching's Easy and the grim business of shot, shell, and bayonet at the front. But now here was the Dower House accomplishing wonderful idioms in Anglo-French, and an animated guest telling them—sometimes one understood clearly and sometimes the meaning was clouded —of men blown to pieces under his eyes, of fragments of human beings lying about in the streets ; there was trouble over the expression *omoplate d'une femme*, until one of the youngsters got the dictionary and found out it was the shoulder-blade of a woman ; of pools of blood—everywhere —and of flight in the darkness.

Mr. Van der Pant had been in charge of the dynamos at the Antwerp Power Station, he had been keeping the electrified wires in the entanglements " alive," and he had stuck to his post until the German high explosives had shattered his wires and rendered his dynamos useless. He gave vivid little pictures of the noises of the bombardment, of the dead lying casually in the open spaces, of the failure of the German guns to hit the bridge of boats across which the bulk of the defenders and refugees escaped. He produced a little tourist's map of the city of Antwerp, and dotted at it with a pencil-case. " The—what do you call ?—*obus*, ah, shells ! fell, so and so and so." Across here he had fled on his *bécane*, and along here and here. He had carried off his rifle, and hid it with the rifles of various other Belgians between floor and ceiling of a house in Zeebrugge. He had found the pirate steamer in the harbour, its captain resolved to extract the uttermost fare out of every refugee he took to London. When they were all aboard and started they found there was no food except the hard ration biscuits of some Belgian soldiers. They had portioned this out like shipwrecked people on a raft. . . . The *mer* had been *calme ;* thank Heaven! All night they had been pumping. He had helped with the pumps. But Mr. Van der Pant hoped still to get a reckoning with the captain of that ship.

Mr. Van der Pant had had shots at various Zeppelins. When the Zeppelins came to Antwerp everybody turned out on the roofs and shot at them. He was contemptuous of Zeppelins. He made derisive gestures to express his opinion of them. They could do nothing unless they came low, and if they came low you could hit them. One which ventured down had been riddled ; it had had to drop all its bombs —luckily they fell in an open field—in order to make its lame escape. It was all nonsense to say, as the English papers did, that they took part in the final bombardment. Not a Zeppelin. . . . So he talked, and the Britling family listened and understood as much as they could, and replied and questioned in Anglo-French. Here was a man who but a few days ago had been steering his bicycle in the streets of Antwerp to avoid shell craters, pools of blood, and the torn-off arms and shoulder-blades of women. He had seen houses flaring, set afire by incendiary bombs, and once at a corner he had been knocked off his bicycle by the pouff of a bursting shell. . . . Not only were these things in the same world with us, they were sitting at our table.

He told one grim story of an invalid woman unable to move, lying in bed in her *appartement,* and of how her husband went out on the balcony to look at the Zeppelin. There was a great noise of shooting. Ever and again he would put his head back into the room, and tell her things, and then after a time he was silent and looked in no more. She called to him and called again. Becoming frightened, she raised herself by a great effort and peered through the glass. At first she was too puzzled to understand what had happened. He was hanging over the front of the balcony, with his head twisted oddly. Twisted and shattered. He had been killed by shrapnel fired from the outer fortifications. . . .

These are the things that happen in histories and stories. They do not happen at Matching's Easy. . . .

Mr. Van der Pant did not seem to be angry with the Germans. But he manifestly regarded them as people to be killed. He denounced nothing that they had done ; he related. They were just an evil accident that had happened to Belgium and mankind. They had to be destroyed. He gave Mr. Britling an extraordinary persuasion that knives were being sharpened

in every cellar in Brussels and Antwerp against the day of
inevitable retreat, of a resolution to exterminate the invader
that was far too deep to be vindictive. . . . And the man
was most amazingly unconquered. Mr. Britling perceived the
label on his habitual dinner wine with a slight embarrassment.
"Do you care," he asked, "to drink a German wine ? This is
Berncasteler from the Moselle." Mr. Van der Pant reflected.
"But it is a good wine," he said. "After the peace it will
be Belgian. . . . Yes, if we are to be safe in the future from
such a war as this, we must have our boundaries right up to
the Rhine."

So he sat and talked, flushed, and as it were, elated by
the vividness of all that he had undergone. He had no trace
of tragic quality, no hint of subjugation. But for his costume
and his trimmed beard and his language he might have been
a Dubliner or a Cockney.

He was astonishingly cut off from all his belongings. His
house in Antwerp was abandoned to the invader ; valuables
and cherished objects very skilfully buried in the garden ;
he had no change of clothing except what the rucksack held.
His only footwear were the boots he came in. He could not
get on any of the slippers in the house, they were all too
small for him, until suddenly Mrs. Britling bethought herself
of Herr Heinrich's pair, still left unpacked upstairs. She
produced them, and they fitted exactly. It seemed only
poetical justice, a foretaste of national compensations, to
annex them to Belgium forthwith. . . .

Also it became manifest that Mr. Van der Pant was cut
off from all his family. And suddenly he became briskly critical
of the English way of doing things. His wife and child had
preceded him to England, crossing by Ostend and Folkestone
a fortnight ago ; her parents had come in August ; both
groups had been seized upon by improvised British organisations and very thoroughly and completely lost. He had
written to the Belgian Embassy and they had referred him
to a committee in London, and the committee had begun
its services by discovering a Madame Van der Pant hitherto
unknown to him at Camberwell, and displaying a certain
suspicion and hostility when he said she would not do. There
had been some futile telegrams. "What," asked Mr. Van
der Pant, "ought one to do ? "

Mr. Britling temporised by saying he would "make inquiries," and put Mr. Van der Pant off for two days. Then
he decided to go up to London with him and "make inquiries
on the spot." Mr. Van der Pant did not discover his family,
but Mr. Britling discovered the profound truth of a comment
of Herr Heinrich's which he had hitherto considered utterly
trivial, but which had nevertheless stuck in his memory.
"The English," Herr Heinrich had said, "do not understand
indexing. It is the root of all good organisation."

Finally, Mr. Van der Pant adopted the irregular course of asking every Belgian he met if they had seen any one from his district in Antwerp, if they had heard of the name of " Van der Pant," if they had encountered So-and-so or So-and-so. And by obstinacy and good fortune he really got on to the track of Madame Van der Pant ; she had been carried off into Kent, and a day later the Dower House was the scene of a happy reunion. Madame was a slender lady, dressed well and plainly, with a Belgian common sense and a Catholic reserve, and André was like a child of wax, delicate and charming and unsubstantial. It seemed incredible that he could ever grow into anything so buoyant and incessant as his father. The Britling boys had to be warned not to damage him. A sitting-room was handed over to the Belgians for their private use, and for a time the two families settled into the Dower House side by side. Anglo-French became the table language of the household. It hampered Mr. Britling very considerably. And both families set themselves to much unrecorded observation, much unspoken mutual criticism, and the exercise of great patience. It was tiresome for the English to be tied to a language that crippled all spontaneous talk ; these linguistic gymnastics were fun to begin with, but soon they became very troublesome ; and the Belgians suspected sensibilities in their hosts and a vast unwritten code of etiquette that did not exist ; at first they were always waiting, as it were, to be invited or told or included ; they seemed always deferentially backing out from intrusions. Moreover, they would not at first reveal what food they liked or what they didn't like, or whether they wanted more or less. . . . But these difficulties were soon smoothed away, they Anglicised quickly and cleverly. André grew bold and cheerful, and lost his first distrust of his rather older English playmates. Every day at lunch he produced a new carefully prepared piece of English, though for some time he retained a marked preference for " Good morning, saire," and " Thank you very mush," over all other locutions, and fell back upon them on all possible and many impossible occasions. And he could do some sleight-of-hand tricks with remarkable skill and humour, and fold paper with quite astonishing results. Meanwhile Mr. Van der Pant sought temporary employment in England, went for long rides upon his bicycle, exchanged views with Mr. Britling upon a variety of subjects, and became a wonderful player of hockey.

He played hockey with an extraordinary zest and nimbleness. Always he played in the tail-coat, and the knitted muffler was never relinquished ; he treated the game entirely as an occasion for quick tricks and personal agility ; he bounded about the field like a kitten, he pirouetted suddenly, he leaped into the air and came down in new directions ; his fresh-coloured face was alive with delight, the coat-tails

and the muffler trailed and swished about breathlessly behind
his agility. He never passed to other players; he never
realised his appointed place in the game; he sought simply
to make himself a leaping screen about the ball as he drove
it towards the goal. But André he would not permit to play
at all, and Madame played like a lady, like a Madonna, like
a saint carrying the instrument of her martyrdom. The
game and its enthusiasms flowed round her and receded
from her; she remained quite valiant but tolerant, restrained;
doing her best to do the extraordinary things required of her,
but essentially a being of passive dignities, living chiefly for
them; Letty careering by her, keen and swift, was like a
creature of a different species. . . .

Mr. Britling celebrated abundantly about these contrasts.

"What has been blown in among us by these German
shells," he said, "is essentially a Catholic family. Blown
clean out of its setting. . . . We who are really—Neo-Europeans. . . .

"At first you imagine there is nothing separating us but
language. Presently you find that language is the least of
our separations. These people are people living upon fundamentally different ideas from ours, ideas far more definite
and complete than ours. You imagine that home in Antwerp
as something much more rounded off, much more closed in,
a cell, a real social unit, a different thing altogether from
this place of meeting. Our boys play cheerfully with all
comers; little André hasn't learned to play with any outside
children at all. We must seem incredibly *open* to these Van
der Pants. A house without sides. . . . Last Sunday I could
not find out the names of the two girls who came on bicycles
and played so well. They came with Kitty Westropp. And Van
der Pant wanted to know how they were related to us. Or
how was it they came ? . . .

"Look at Madame. She's built on a fundamentally different
plan from any of our womenkind here. Tennis, the bicycle,
co-education, the two-step, the higher education of women.
. . . Say these things over to yourself, and think of her. It's
like talking of a nun in riding-breeches. She's a specialised
woman, specialising in womanhood, her sphere is the home.
Soft, trailing, draping skirts, slow movements, a veiled face ;
for no Oriental veil could be more effectual than her beautiful
Catholic quiet. Catholicism invented the invisible purdah.
She is far more akin to that sweet little Indian lady with
the wonderful robes whom Carmine brought over with her
tall husband last summer, than she is to Letty or Cissie. She,
too, undertook to play hockey. And played it very much
as Madame Van der Pant played it. . . .

"The more I see of our hockey," said Mr. Britling, "the
more wonderful it seems to me as a touchstone of character
and culture and breeding. . . ."

Mr. Manning, to whom he was delivering this discourse, switched him on to a new track by asking what he meant by " Neo-European."

" It's a bad phrase," said Mr. Britling.   " I'll withdraw it.   Let me try and state exactly what I have in mind.   I mean something that is coming up in America and here, and the Scandinavian countries and Russia, a new culture, an escape from the Levantine religion and the Catholic culture that came to us from the Mediterranean.   Let me drop Neo-European ; let me say Northern.   We are Northerners.   The key, the heart, the nucleus and essence of every culture is its conception of the relations of men and women ; and this new culture tends to diminish the specialisation of women as women, to let them out from the cell of the home into common citizenship with men.   It's a new culture, still in process of development, which will make men more social and co-operative and women bolder, swifter, more responsible and less cloistered.   It minimises instead of exaggerating the importance of sex. . . .

" And," said Mr. Britling, in very much the tones in which a preacher might say " Sixthly," " it is just all this Northern tendency that this world struggle is going to release.   This war is pounding through Europe, smashing up homes, dispersing and mixing homes, setting Madame Van der Pant playing hockey, and André climbing trees with my young ruffians ; it is killing young men by the million, altering the proportions of the sexes for a generation, bringing women into business and office and industry, destroying the accumulated wealth that kept so many of them in refined idleness, flooding the world with strange doubts and novel ideas. . . ."

§ 9

But the conflict of manners and customs that followed the invasion of the English villages by French and Belgian refugees did not always present the immigrants as Catholics and the hosts as " Neo-Europeans."   In the case of Mr. Dimple it was the other way round.   He met Mr. Britling in Claverings Park and told him his troubles. . . .

" Of course," he said, " we have to do our Utmost for Brave Little Belgium.   I would be the last to complain of any little inconvenience one may experience in doing that. Still, I must confess I think you and dear Mrs. Britling are fortunate, exceptionally fortunate, in the Belgians you have got.   My guests—it's unfortunate—the man is some sort of journalist and quite—oh ! much too much—an Atheist. An open positive one.   Not simply Honest Doubt.   I'm quite prepared for honest doubt nowadays.   You and I have no quarrel over that.   But he is aggressive.   He makes remarks about miracles, quite derogatory remarks. and not always

in French. Sometimes he almost speaks English. And in
front of my sister. And he goes out, he says, looking for a
Café. He never finds a Café, but he certainly finds every public
house within a radius of miles. And he comes back smelling
dreadfully of beer. When I drop a Little Hint, he blames
the beer. He says it is not good beer—our good Essex beer !
He doesn't understand any of our Simple Ways. He's
sophisticated. The girls about here wear Belgian flags—
and air their little bits of French. And he takes it as an
encouragement. Only yesterday there was a scene. It seems
he tried to kiss the Hickson girl at the inn—Maudie. . . .
And his wife ; a great big slow woman—in every way she
is—Ample ; it's dreadful even to seem to criticise, but I do
so *wish* she would not see fit to sit down and nourish her
baby in my poor old bachelor drawing-room—often at the
most *unseasonable* times. And—so lavishly. . . ."

Mr. Britling attempted consolations.

"But anyhow," said Mr. Dimple, "I'm better off than
poor dear Mrs. Bynne. She secured two milliners. She insisted
upon them. And their clothes were certainly beautifully
made—even my poor old unworldly eye could tell that.
And she thought two milliners would be so useful with a
large family like hers. They certainly *said* they were milliners.
But it seems—I don't know what we shall do about them.
. . . My dear Mr. Britling, those young women are anything
but milliners—anything but milliners. . . ."

A faint gleam of amusement was only too perceptible through
the good man's horror.

"Sirens, my dear Mr. Britling. Sirens. By profession. . . ."

§ 10

October passed into November, and day by day Mr. Britling
was forced to apprehend new aspects of the war, to think
and rethink the war, to have his first conclusions checked
and tested, twisted askew, replaced. His thoughts went far
and wide and deeper—until all his earlier writing seemed
painfully shallow to him, seemed a mere automatic response
of obvious comments to the stimulus of the war's surprise.
As his ideas became subtler and profounder, they became
more difficult to express ; he talked less ; he became abstracted
and irritable at table. To two people in particular Mr. Britling
found his real ideas inexpressible, to Mr. Direck and to Mr.
Van der Pant.

Each of these gentlemen brought with him the implication
or the intimation of a critical attitude towards England. It
was all very well for Mr. Britling himself to be critical of
England ; that is an Englishman's privilege. To hear Mr.
Van der Pant questioning British efficiency or to suspect
Mr. Direck of high, thin American superiorities to war, was

almost worse than to hear Mrs. Harrowdean saying hostile things about Edith. It roused an even acuter protective emotion.

In the case of Mr. Van der Pant matters were complicated by the difficulty of the language, which made anything but the crudest statements subject to incalculable misconception.

Mr. Van der Pant had not the extreme tactfulness of his so typically Catholic wife ; he made it only too plain that he thought the British postal and telegraph service slow and slack, and the management of the Great Eastern branch lines wasteful and inefficient. He said the workmen in the fields and the workmen he saw upon some cottages near the junction worked slowlier and with less interest than he had ever seen any workmen display in all his life before. He marvelled that Mr. Britling lit his house with acetylene and not electric light. He thought fresh eggs were insanely dear, and his opinion of Matching's Easy pig-keeping was uncomplimentary. The roads, he said, were not a means of getting from place to place, they were a *dédale ;* he drew derisive maps with his finger on the table-cloth of the lane system about the Dower House. He was astonished that there was no Café in Matching's Easy ; he declared that the "public house" to which he went with considerable expectation was no public house at all ; it was just a sly place for drinking beer. . . . All these were things Mr. Britling might have remarked himself ; from a Belgian refugee he found them intolerable.

He set himself to explain to Mr. Van der Pant firstly that these things did not matter in the slightest degree, the national attention, the national interest ran in other directions ; and secondly that they were, as a matter of fact and on the whole, merits slightly disguised. He produced a pleasant theory that England is really not the Englishman's field, it is his breeding-place, his resting-place, a place not for efficiency, but good humour. If Mr. Van der Pant were to make inquiries he would find there was scarcely a home in Matching's Easy that had not sent some energetic representative out of England to become one of the English of the world. England was the last place in which English energy was spent. These hedges, these dilatory roads were full of associations. There was a road that turned aside near Market Saffron to avoid Turk's wood ; it had been called Turk's wood first in the fourteenth century after a man of that name. He quoted Chesterton's happy verses to justify these winding lanes.

> " The road turned first towards the left,
>   Where Perkin's quarry made the cleft ;
>   The path turned next towards the right,
>   Because the mastiff used to bite. . . ."

And again :

> " And I should say they wound about
> To find the town of Roundabout,
> The merry town of Roundabout
> That makes the world go round."

If our easy-going ways hampered a hard efficiency, they did at least develop humour and humanity. Our diplomacy at any rate had not failed us. . . .

He did not believe a word of this stuff. His deep irrational love for England made him say these things. . . . For years he had been getting himself into hot water because he had been writing and hinting just such criticisms as Mr. Van der Pant expressed so bluntly. . . . But he wasn't going to accept foreign help in dissecting his mother. . . .

And another curious effect that Mr. Van der Pant had upon Mr. Britling was to produce an obstinate confidence about the war and the nearness of the German collapse. He would promise Mr. Van der Pant that he should be back in Antwerp before May ; that the Germans would be over the Rhine by July. He knew perfectly well that his ignorance of all the military conditions was unqualified, but still he could not restrain himself from this kind of thing so soon as he began to speak Entente Cordiale—Anglo-French, that is to say. Something in his relationship to Mr. Van der Pant obliged him to be acutely and absurdly the protecting Briton. . . . At times he felt like a conscious bankrupt talking off the hour of disclosure. But indeed all that Mr. Britling was trying to say against the difficulties of a strange language and an alien temperament was that the honour of England would never be cleared until Belgium was restored and avenged. . . .

While Mr. Britling was patrolling unimportant roads and entertaining Mr. Van der Pant with discourses upon the nearness of victory and the subtle estimableness of all that was indolent, wasteful and evasive in English life, the war was passing from its first swift phases into a slower, grimmer struggle. The German retreat ended at the Aisne, and the long outflanking manœuvres of both hosts towards the Channel began. The English attempts to assist Belgium in October came too late for the preservation of Antwerp, and after a long and complicated struggle in Flanders the British failed to outflank the German right, lost Ghent, Menin and the Belgian coast, but held Ypres and beat back every attempt of the enemy to reach Dunkirk and Calais. Meanwhile the smaller German colonies and islands were falling to the navy, the Australian battleship *Sydney* smashed the *Emden* at Cocos Island, and the British naval disaster of Coronel was wiped out by the battle of the Falklands. The Russians were victorious upon their left and took Lemberg, and after some vicissitudes of fortune advanced to Przemysl, occupying the larger part of Galicia ; but the disaster of Tannenberg had broken their progress in East Prussia, and the Germans were pressing towards Warsaw. Turkey had joined the war, and suffered enormous losses in the Caucasus. The Dardenelles had been shelled for the first time, and the British were at Basra on the Euphrates.

§ 11

The Christmas of 1914 found England, whose landscape had hitherto been almost as peaceful and soldierless as Massachusetts, already far gone along the path of transformation into a country full of soldiers and munition-makers and military supplies. The soldiers came first, on the well-known and greatly admired British principle of "first catch your hare" and then build your kitchen. Always before, Christmas had been a time of much gaiety and dressing-up and prancing and two-stepping at the Dower House, but this year everything was too uncertain to allow of any gathering of guests. Hugh got leave for the day after Christmas, but Teddy was tied ; and Cissie and Letty went off with the baby to take lodgings near him. The Van der Pants had hoped to see an English Christmas at Matching's Easy, but within three weeks of Christmas Day Mr. Van der Pant found a job that he could do in Nottingham, and carried off his family. The two small boys cheered their hearts with paper decorations, but the Christmas Tree was condemned as too German, and it was discovered that Santa Claus had suddenly become Old Father Christmas again. The small boys discovered that the price of lead soldiers had risen, and were unable to buy electric torches, on which they had set their hearts. There was to have been a Christmas party at Claverings, but at the last moment Lady Homartyn had to hurry off to an orphan nephew who had been seriously wounded near Ypres, and the light of Claverings was darkened.

Soon after Christmas there were rumours of an impending descent of the Headquarters staff of the South-Eastern army upon Claverings. Then Mr. Britling found Lady Homartyn back from France, and very indignant because after all the Headquarters were to go to Lady Wensleydale at Ladyholt. It was, she felt, a reflection upon Claverings. Lady Homartyn became still more indignant when presently the new armies, which were gathering now all over England like floods in a low-lying meadow, came pouring into the parishes about Claverings to the extent of a battalion and a Territorial battery. Mr. Britling heard of their advent only a day or two before they arrived ; there came a bright young officer with an orderly, billeting ; he was much exercised to get, as he expressed it several times. a quart into a pint bottle. He was

greatly pleased with the barn. He asked the size of it and
did calculations. He could "stick twenty-five men into it—
easy." It would go far to solve his problems. He could manage
without coming into the house at all. It was a ripping place.
"No end."

"But beds," said Mr. Britling.

"Lord ! they don't want *beds*," said the young officer. . . .

The whole Britling family, who were lamenting the loss of
their Belgians, welcomed the coming of the twenty-five with
great enthusiasm. It made them feel that they were doing
something useful once more. For three days Mrs. Britling had
to feed her new lodgers—the kitchen motors had as usual gone
astray—and she did so in a style that made their boastings
about their billet almost insufferable to the rest of their
battery. The billeting allowance at that time was ninepence a
head, and Mr. Britling, ashamed of making a profit out of his
country, supplied not only generous firing and lighting, but
unlimited cigarettes, cards and games, illustrated newspapers,
a cocoa supper with such little surprises as sprats and jam roly-
poly, and a number of more incidental comforts. The men
arrived fasting under the command of two very sage middle-
aged corporals, and responded to Mrs. Britling's hospitalities
by a number of good resolutions, many of which they kept.
They never made noises after half-past ten, or at least only
now and then when a singsong broke out with unusual violence ;
they got up and went out at five or six in the morning without
a sound ; they were almost inconveniently helpful with washing
up and tidying round.

In quite a little time Mrs. Britling's mind had adapted itself
to the spectacle of half-a-dozen young men in khaki breeches
and shirts performing their toilets in and about her scullery,
or improvising an unsanctioned game of football between the
hockey goals. These men were not the miscellaneous men of the
new armies ; they were the earlier Territorial type with no
heroics about them ; they came from the midlands ; and their
two middle-aged corporals kept them well in hand and ruled
them like a band of brothers. But they had a lawless side, that
developed in directions that set Mr. Britling theorising. They
seemed, for example, to poach by nature, as children play and
sing. They possessed a promiscuous white dog. They began
to add rabbits to their supper menu, unaccountable rabbits.
One night there was a mighty smell of frying fish from the
kitchen, and the cook reported trout. "Trout !" said Mr.
Britling to one of the corporals ; "now where did you chaps
get trout ? "

The "fisherman," they said, had got them with a hair
noose. They produced the fisherman, of whom they were
manifestly proud. It was, he explained, a method of fishing he
had learned when in New York Harbour. He had been a stoker.
He displayed a confidence in Mr. Britling that made that gentle-

man an accessory after his offence, his very serious offence against pre-war laws and customs. It was plain that the trout were the trout that Mr. Pumshock, the stock-broker and amateur gentleman, had preserved so carefully in the Easy. Hitherto the countryside had been forced to regard Mr. Pumshock's trout with an almost superstitious respect. A year ago young Snooker had done a month for one of those very trout. But now things were different.

" But I don't really fancy fresh-water fish," said the fisherman. " It's just the ketchin' of 'em I like. . . ."

And a few weeks later the trumpeter, an angel-faced freckled child with deep-blue eyes, brought in a dozen partridge eggs which he wanted Mary to cook for him. . . .

The domesticity of the sacred birds, it was clear, was no longer safe in England. . . .

Then again the big guns would go swinging down the road and into Claverings Park, and perform various exercises with commendable smartness and a profound disregard for Lady Homartyn's known objection to any departure from the public footpath. . . .

And one afternoon as Mr. Britling took his constitutional walk, a reverie was set going in his mind by the sight of a neglected-looking pheasant with a white collar. The world of Matching's Easy was getting full now of such elderly birds. Would *that* go on after the war ? He imagined his son Hugh as a grandfather, telling the little ones about parks and preserves and game-laws, and footmen and butlers and the marvellous game of golf, and how, suddenly, Mars came tramping through the land in khaki and all these things faded and vanished, so that presently it was discovered they were gone. . . .

CHAPTER THREE

MALIGNITY

§ I

AND while the countryside of England changed steadily from its lax pacific amenity to the likeness of a rather slovenly armed camp, while long-fixed boundaries shifted and dissolved and a great irreparable wasting of the world's resources gathered way, Mr. Britling did his duty as a special constable, gave his eldest son to the Territorials, entertained Belgians, petted his soldiers in the barn, helped Teddy to his commission, contributed to war charities, sold out securities at a loss and subscribed to the War Loan, and thought, thought endlessly about the war.

He could think continuously day by day of nothing else.

His mind was as caught as a galley-slave, as unable to escape
from tugging at this oar. All his universe was a magnetic
field which oriented everything, whether he would have it so
or not, to this one polar question.

His thoughts grew firmer and clearer ; they went deeper
and wider. His first superficial judgments were endorsed and
deepened or replaced by others. He thought along the lonely
lanes at night ; he thought at his desk ; he thought in bed ;
he thought in his bath ; he tried over his thoughts in essays
and leading articles and reviewed them and corrected them.
Now and then came relaxation and lassitude, but never release.
The war towered over him like a vigilant teacher, day after
day, week after week, regardless of fatigue and impatience,
holding a rod in its hand.

§ 2

Certain things had to be forced upon Mr. Britling, because
they jarred so greatly with his habits of mind that he would
never have accepted them if he could have avoided doing
so.

Notably he would not recognise at first the extreme bitterness of this war. He would not believe that the attack upon
Britain and Western Europe generally expressed the concentrated emotion of a whole nation. He thought that the
Allies were in conflict with a system and not with a national
will. He fought against the persuasion that the whole mass of a
great civilised nation could be inspired by a genuine and
sustained hatred. Hostility was an uncongenial thing to him ;
he would not recognise that the greater proportion of human
beings are more readily hostile than friendly. He did his best
to believe—in his " And Now War Ends " he did his best to
make other people believe—that this war was the perverse
exploit of a small group of people, of limited but powerful
influences, an outrage upon the general geniality of mankind.
The cruelty, mischief, and futility of war were so obvious to
him that he was almost apologetic in asserting them.   He
believed that war had but to begin and demonstrate its quality
among the Western nations in order to unify them all against
its repetition. They would exclaim : " But we can't do things
like this to one another ! " He saw the aggressive imperialism
of Germany called to account even by its own people ; a
struggle, a collapse, a liberal-minded conference of world
powers, and a universal resumption of amiability upon a more
assured basis of security. He believed—and many people in
England believed with him—that a great section of the Germans would welcome triumphant Allies as their liberators from
intolerable political obsessions.

The English because of their insularity had been political
amateurs for endless generations. It was their supreme vice,
it was their supreme virtue, to be easy-going. They had lived

in an atmosphere of comedy, and denied in the whole tenor of their lives that life is tragic. Not even the Americans had been more isolated. The Americans had had their Indians, their negroes, their War of Secession. Until the Great War the Channel was as broad as the Atlantic for holding off every vital challenge. Even Ireland was away—a four-hour crossing. And so the English had developed to the fullest extent the virtues and vices of safety and comfort ; they had a hatred of science and dramatic behaviour ; they could see no reason for exactness or intensity ; they disliked proceeding " to extremes." Ultimately everything would turn out all right. But they knew what it is to be carried into conflicts by energetic minorities and the trick of circumstances, and they were ready to understand the case of any other country which has suffered that fate. All their habits inclined them to fight good-temper-edly and comfortably, to quarrel with a government and not with a people. It took Mr. Britling at least a couple of months of warfare to understand that the Germans were fighting in an altogether different spirit.

The first intimations of this that struck upon his mind were the news of the behaviour of the Kaiser and the Berlin crowd upon the declaration of war, and the violent treatment of the British subjects seeking to return to their homes. Everywhere such people had been insulted and ill-treated. It was the spontaneous expression of a long-gathered bitterness. While the British ambassador was being howled out of Berlin, the German ambassador to England was taking a farewell stroll, quite unmolested, in St. James's Park. . . . One item that struck particularly upon Mr. Britling's imagination was the story of the chorus of young women who assembled on the rail-way platform of the station through which the British ambas-sador was passing to sing—to his drawn blinds—" Deutschland, Deutschland über Alles." Mr. Britling could imagine those young people, probably dressed more or less uniformly in white, with flushed faces and shining eyes, letting their voices go, full-throated, in the modern German way. . . .

And then came stories of atrocities, stories of the shooting of old men and the butchery of children by the wayside, stories of wounded men bayoneted or burned alive, of massacres of harmless citizens, of looting and filthy outrages. . . .

Mr. Britling did his utmost not to believe these things. They contradicted his habitual world. They produced horrible strains in his mind. They might, he hoped, be misreported so as to seem more violent or less justifiable than they were. They might be the acts of stray criminals, and quite dis-connected from the normal operations of the war. Here and there some weak-minded officer may have sought to make himself terrible. . . . And as for the bombardment of cathedrals and the crime of Louvain, well, Mr. Britling was prepared to argue that Gothic architecture is not sacrosanct if military necessity

cuts through it. . . . It was only after the war had been going
on some months that Mr. Britling's fluttering, unwilling mind
was pinned down by official reports and a cloud of witnesses
to a definite belief in the grim reality of systematic rape and
murder, destruction, dirtiness and abominable compulsions that
blackened the first rush of the Prussians into Belgium and
Champagne. . . .

They came hating and threatening the lands they outraged.
They sought occasion to do frightful deeds. . . . When they
could not be frightful in the houses they occupied, then to the
best of their ability they were destructive and filthy. The facts
took Mr. Britling by the throat. . . .

The first thing that really pierced him with the conviction
that there was something essentially different in the English
and the German attitude towards the war was the sight of a bale
of German comic papers in the study of a friend in London.
They were filled with caricatures of the Allies and more
particularly of the English, and they displayed a force and
quality of passion—an incredible force and quality of passion.
Their amazing hate and their amazing filthiness alike overwhelmed Mr. Britling. There was no appearance of national
pride or national dignity, but a bellowing patriotism and a
limitless desire to hurt and humiliate. They spat. They were
red in the face and they spat. He sat with these violent sheets
in his hands—*ashamed*.

" But I say ! " he said feebly. " It's the sort of thing that
might come out of a lunatic asylum. . . ."

One incredible craving was manifest in every one of them.
The German caricaturist seemed unable to represent his
enemies except in extremely tight trousers or in none ; he was
equally unable to represent them without thrusting a sword
or bayonet, spluttering blood, into the more indelicate parts
of their persons. This was the *leit-motif* of the war as the
German humorist presented it. " But," said Mr. Britling,
" these things can't represent anything like the general state
of mind in Germany."

" They do," said his friend.

" But it's blind fury—at the dirt-throwing stage."

" The whole of Germany is in that blind fury," said his
friend. " While we are going about astonished and rather
incredulous about this war, and still rather inclined to laugh,
that's the state of mind of Germany. . . . There's a sort of
deliberation in it. They think it gives them strength. They
want to foam at the mouth. They do their utmost to foam
more. They write themselves up. Have you heard of the
' Hymn of Hate ' ? "

Mr. Britling had not.

" There was a translation of it in last week's *Spectator*. . . .
This is the sort of thing we are trying to fight in good temper
and without extravagance. Listen, Britling !

" *You* will we hate with a lasting hate ;
We will never forgo our hate—
Hate by water and hate by land,
Hate of the head and hate of the hand,
Hate of the hammer and hate of the crown,
Hate of seventy millions, choking down ;
We love as one, we hate as one,
We have *one* foe, and one alone—
ENGLAND ! "

He read on to the end.

" Well," he said when he had finished reading, " what do you think of it ? "

" I want to feel his bumps," said Mr. Britling after a pause. " It's incomprehensible."

" They're singing that up and down Germany. Lissauer, I hear, has been decorated. . . ."

" It's—stark malignity," said Mr. Britling. " What have we done ? "

" It's colossal. What is to happen to the world if these people prevail ? "

" I can't believe it—even with this evidence before me. . . . No ! I want to feel their bumps. . . ."

§ 3

" You see," said Mr. Britling, trying to get it into focus, " I have known quite decent Germans. There must be some sort of misunderstanding. . . . I wonder what makes them hate us. There seems to me no reason in it."

" I think it is just thoroughness," said his friend. " They are at war. To be at war is to hate."

" That isn't at all my idea."

" We're not a thorough people. When we think of anything, we also think of its opposite. When we adopt an opinion we also take in a provisional idea that it is probably nearly as wrong as it is right. We are—atmospheric. They are concrete. . . . All this filthy, vile, unjust and cruel stuff is honest genuine war. We pretend war does not hurt. They know better. . . . The Germans are a simple honest people. It is their virtue. Possibly it is their only virtue. . . ."

§ 4

Mr. Britling was only one of a multitude who wanted to feel the bumps of Germany at that time. The effort to understand a people who had suddenly become incredible was indeed one of the most remarkable facts in English intellectual life during the opening phases of the war. The English state of mind was unlimited astonishment. There was an enormous sale of any German books that seemed likely to illuminate the mystery of his amazing concentration of hostility ; the works of Bernhardi, Treitschke, Nietzsche, Houston Stewart Chamberlain, became the material of countless articles and interminable discussions. One saw little clerks on the way to the office and workmen going home after their work earnestly reading these remarkable writers. They were asking, just as Mr. Britling was asking, what it was the British Empire had struck against. They were trying to account for this wild storm of hostility that was coming at them out of Central Europe.

It was a natural next stage to this, when after all it became manifest that instead of there being a liberal and reluctant Germany at the back of imperialism and Junkerdom, there was apparently one solid, enthusiastic people, to suppose that the Germans were in some distinctive way evil, that they were racially more envious, arrogant, and aggressive than the rest of mankind. Upon that supposition a great number of English people settled. They concluded that the Germans had a peculiar devil of their own—and had to be treated accordingly. That was the second stage in the process of national apprehension, and it was marked by the first beginnings of a spy hunt, by the first denunciation of naturalised aliens, and by some anti-German rioting among the mixed alien population in the East End. Most of the bakers in the East End of London were Germans, and for some months after the war began they went on with their trade unmolested. Now many of these shops were wrecked. . . . It was only in October that the British gave these first signs of a sense that they were fighting not merely political Germany but the Germans.

But the idea of a peculiar malignity in the German quality as a key to the broad issue of the war was even less satisfactory and less permanent in Mr Britling's mind than his first crude opposition of militarism and a peaceful humanity as embodied respectively in the Central Powers and the Russo-Western alliance. It led logically to the conclusion that the extermination of the German peoples was the only security for the general amiability of the world, a conclusion that appealed but weakly to his essential kindliness. After all, the Germans he had met and seen were neither cruel nor hate-inspired. He came back to that obstinately. From the harshness and vileness of the printed word and the unclean picture, he fell back upon the flesh and blood, the humanity and sterling worth, of—as a sample—young Heinrich.

Who was moreover a thoroughly German young German—a thoroughly Prussian young Prussian.

At times young Heinrich alone stood between Mr. Britling and the belief that Germany and the whole German race was essentially wicked, essentially a canting robber nation. Young Heinrich became a sort of advocate for his people before the tribunal of Mr. Britling's mind. (And on his shoulder sat an absurdly pampered squirrel.) Heinrich's fresh pink sedulous face, very earnest, adjusting his glasses, saying " Please," intervened and insisted upon an arrest of judgment. . . .

Since the young man's departure he had sent two postcards of greeting directly to the " Familie Britling," and one letter through the friendly intervention of Mr. Britling's American publisher. Once also he sent a message through a friend in Norway. The postcards simply recorded stages in the passage of a distraught pacifist across Holland to his enrolment. The letter by way of America came two months later. He had been converted into a combatant with extreme rapidity. He had been trained for three weeks, had spent a fortnight in hospital with a severe cold, and had then gone to Belgium as a transport driver—his father had been a horse-dealer and he was familiar with horses. " If anything happens to me," he wrote, " please send my violin at least very carefully to my mother." It was characteristic that he reported himself as very comfortably quartered in Courtrai with " very nice people." The niceness involved restraints. " Only never," he added, " do we talk about the war. It is better not to do so." He mentioned the violin also in the later communication through Norway. Therein he lamented the lost flesh-pots of Courtrai. He had been in Posen, and now he was in the Carpathians, up to his knees in snow and very " uncomfortable." . . .

And then abruptly all news from him ceased.

Month followed month, and no further letter came.

" Something has happened to him.   Perhaps he is a prisoner." . . .

" I hope our little Heinrich hasn't got seriously damaged. . . . He may be wounded. . . ."

" Or perhaps they stop his letters. . . . Very probably they stop his letters."

§ 5

Mr. Britling would sit in his arm-chair and stare at his fire, and recall conflicting memories of Germany—of a pleasant land, of friendly people. He had spent many a jolly holiday there. So recently as 1911 all the Britling family had gone up the Rhine from Rotterdam, had visited a string of great cities and stayed for a cheerful month of sunshine at Neun-kirchen in the Odenwald.

The little village perches high among the hills and woods, and at its very centre is the inn and the linden-tree and— Adam Meyer. Or at least Adam Meyer *was* there. Whether he is there now, only the spirit of change can tell ; if he live to be a hundred no friendly English will ever again come tramping along by the track of the Blaue Dreiecke or the Weisse Streiche to enjoy his hospitality ; there are rivers of blood between, and a thousand memories of hate. . . .

It was a village distended with hospitalities. Not only the inn but all the houses about the place of the linden-tree, the shoemaker's, the post-mistress's, the white house beyond,

every house indeed except the pastor's house, were full of
Adam Meyer's summer guests. And about it and over it
went and soared Adam Meyer, seeing they ate well, seeing
they rested well, seeing they had music and did not miss the
moonlight—a host who forgot profit in hospitality, an inn-
keeper with the passion of an artist for his inn.

Music, moonlight, the simple German sentiment, the hearty
German voices, the great picnic in a Stuhl Wagen, the orderly
round games the boys played with the German children, and
the tramps and confidences Hugh had with Kurt and Karl,
and at last a crowning jollification, a dance, with some gipsy
musicians discovered by Mr. Britling, when the Germans
taught the English various entertaining sports with baskets
and potatoes and forfeits and the English introduced the
Germans to the licence of the two-step. And everybody sang
" Britannia, Rule the Waves," and " Deutschland, Deutschland
über Alles," and Adam Meyer got on a chair and made a
tremendous speech more in dialect than ever, and there was
much drinking of beer and sirops in the moonlight under the
linden. . . .

Afterwards there had been a periodic sending of postcards
and greetings, which indeed only the war had ended.

Right pleasant people those Germans had been, sun and
green-leaf lovers, for whom " Frisch Auf " seemed the most
natural of national cries. Mr. Britling thought of the individual Germans who had made up the assembly, of the
men's amusingly fierce little hats of green and blue with the
inevitable feather thrust perkily into the hatband behind,
of the kindly plumpnesses behind their turned-up moustaches,
of the blonde, sedentary women, very wise about the comforts
of life and very kind to the children, of their earnest pleasure
in landscape and Art and Great Writers, of their general
frequent desire to sing, of their plasticity under the directing
hands of Adam Meyer. He thought of the mellow south
German landscape, rolling away broad and fair, of the little
clean red-roofed townships, the old castles, the big prosperous
farms, the neatly marked pedestrian routes, the hospitable
inns, and the artless abundant Aussichtthurms. . . .

He saw all those memories now through a veil of indescribable sadness—as of a world lost, gone down like the cities of
Lyonesse beneath deep seas. . . .

Right pleasant people in a sunny land ! Yet here pressing
relentlessly upon his mind were the murders of Visé, the
massacres of Dinant, the massacres of Louvain, murder red-
handed and horrible upon an inoffensive people, foully invaded,
foully treated ; murder done with a sickening cant of righteousness and racial pretension. . . .

The two pictures would not stay steadily in his mind together. When he thought of the broken faith that had poured
those slaughtering hosts into the decent peace of Belgium,

that had smashed her cities, burned her villages and filled
the pretty gorges of the Ardennes with blood and smoke and
terror, he was flooded with self-righteous indignation, a self-
righteous indignation that was indeed entirely Teutonic in
its quality, that for a time drowned out his former friendship
and every kindly disposition towards Germany, that inspired
him with destructive impulses, and obsessed him with a
desire to hear of death and more death and yet death in
every German town and home. . . .

§ 6

It will be an incredible thing to the happier reader of a
coming age—if ever this poor record of experience reaches
a reader in the days to come—to learn how much of the
mental life of Mr. Britling was occupied at this time with
the mere horror and atrocity of warfare. It is idle and hopeless
to speculate now how that future reader will envisage this war ;
it may take on broad dramatic outlines, it may seem a thing
just, logical, necessary, the burning of many barriers, the
destruction of many obstacles. Mr. Britling was too near to
the dirt and pain and heat for any such broad landscape consolations. Every day some new detail of evil beat into his
mind. Perhaps it would be the artless story of a refugee. There
was a girl from Alost in the village, for example, who had
heard the fusillade that meant the shooting of citizens, the
shooting of people she had known, she had seen the still
blood-stained wall against which two murdered cousins had
died, the streaked sand along which their bodies had been
dragged ; three German soldiers had been quartered in her
house with her and her invalid mother, and had talked freely
of the massacres in which they had been employed. One
of them was in civil life a young schoolmaster, and he had
had, he said, to kill a woman and a baby. The girl had been
incredulous. Yes, he had done so ! Of course he had done so !
His officer had made him do it, had stood over him. He could
do nothing but obey. But since then he had been unable
to sleep, unable to forget.
" We had to punish the people," he said. " They had
fired on us."
And besides, his officer had been drunk. It had been impossible to argue. His officer had an unrelenting character
at all times. . . .
Over and over again Mr. Britling would try to imagine that
young schoolmaster soldier at Alost. He imagined him with
a weak staring face and watery blue eyes behind his glasses,
and that memory of murder. . . .
Then again it would be some incident of death and mutilation in Antwerp, that Van der Pant described to him. The
Germans in Belgium were shooting women frequently, not
simply for grave spying but for trivial offences. . . . Then

came the battleship raid on Whitby and Scarborough, and
the killing among other victims of a number of children on
their way to school. This shocked Mr. Britling absurdly,
much more than the Belgian crimes had done. They were
English children. At home! . . . The drowning of a great
number of people on a torpedoed ship full of refugees from
Flanders filled his mind with pitiful imaginings for days.
The Zeppelin raids, with their slow crescendo of blood-stained
futility, began before the end of 1914. . . . It was small
consolation for Mr. Britling to reflect that English homes
and women and children were, after all, undergoing only
the same kind of experience that our ships have inflicted
scores of times in the past upon innocent people in the villages
of Africa and Polynesia. . . .

Each month the war grew bitter and more cruel. Early
in 1915 the Germans began their submarine war, and for a
time Mr. Britling's concern was chiefly for the sailors and
passengers of the ships destroyed. He noted with horror the
increasing indisposition of the German submarines to give
any notice to their victims ; he did not understand the grim
reasons that were turning every submarine attack into a
desperate challenge of death. For the Germans under the
seas had pitted themselves against a sea power far more
resourceful, more steadfast and skilful, sterner and more
silent, than their own. It was not for many months that
Mr. Britling learned the realities of the submarine blockade.
Submarine after submarine went out of the German harbours
into the North Sea, never to return. No prisoners were reported, no boasting was published by the British fishers of
men ; U-boat after U-boat vanished into a chilling mystery.
. . . Only later did Mr. Britling begin to hear whispers and
form ideas of the noiseless, suffocating grip that sought through
the waters for its prey.

The *Falaba* crime, in which the German sailors were reported to have jeered at the drowning victims in the water,
was followed by the sinking of the *Lusitania*. At that a wave
of real anger swept through the Empire. Hate was begetting
hate at last. There were violent riots in Great Britain and
in South Africa. Wretched little German hairdressers and
bakers and so forth fled for their lives, to pay for the momentary satisfaction of the Kaiser and Herr Ballin. Scores of
German homes in England were wrecked and looted ; hundreds
of Germans maltreated. War is war. Hard upon the *Lusitania*
storm came the publication of the Bryce Report, with its
relentless array of witnesses, its particulars of countless acts
of cruelty and arrogant unreason and uncleanness in Belgium
and the occupied territory of France. Came also the gasping
torture of " gas," the use of flame jets, and a new exacerbation
of the savagery of the actual fighting. For a time it seemed
as though the taking of prisoners along the western front

would cease. Tales of torture and mutilation, tales of the kind that arise nowhere and out of nothing, and poison men's minds to the most pitiless retaliations, drifted along the opposing fronts. . . .

The realities were evil enough without any rumours. Over various dinner-tables Mr. Britling heard this and that first-hand testimony of harshness and spite. One story that stuck in his memory was of British prisoners on the journey into Germany being put apart at a station from their French companions in misfortune, and forced to " run the gauntlet " back to their train between the fists and bayonets of files of German soldiers. And there were convincing stories of the same prisoners robbed of overcoats in bitter weather, baited with dogs, separated from their countrymen, and thrust among Russians and Poles with whom they could hold no speech. So Lissauer's Hate Song bore its fruit in a thousand cruelties to wounded and defenceless men. The English had cheated great Germany of another easy victory like that of '71. They had to be punished. That was all too plainly the psychological process. At one German station a woman had got out of a train and crossed a platform to spit on the face of a wounded Englishman. . . . And there was no monopoly of such things on either side. At some journalistic gathering Mr. Britling met a little white-faced, resolute lady who had recently been nursing in the north of France. She told of wounded men lying among the coal of coal-sheds, of a shortage of nurses and every sort of material, of an absolute refusal to permit any share in such things to reach the German " swine." . . . " Why have they come here ? Let our own boys have it first. Why couldn't they stay in their own country ? Let the filth die."

Two soldiers impressed to carry a wounded German officer on a stretcher had given him a " joy ride," pitching him up and down as one tosses a man in a blanket. " He was lucky to get off with that." . . .

" All *our* men aren't angels," said a cheerful young captain back from the front. " If you had heard a little group of our East London boys talking of what they meant to do when they got into Germany, you'd feel anxious. . . ."

" But that was just talk," said Mr. Britling weakly, after a pause. . . .

There were times when Mr. Britling's mind was imprisoned beyond any hope of escape amidst such monstrous realities. . . .

He was ashamed of his one secret consolation. For nearly two years yet Hugh could not go out to it. There would surely be peace before that. . . .

§ 7

Tormenting the thought of Mr. Britling almost more acutely than this growing tale of stupidly inflicted suffering and waste and sheer destruction was the collapse of the British mind from its first fine phase of braced-up effort into a state of bickering futility.

Too long had British life been corrupted by the fictions of loyalty to an uninspiring and alien Court, of national piety in an official Church, of freedom in a politician-rigged State, of justice in an economic system where the advertiser, the sweater and usurer had a hundred advantages over the producer and artisan, to maintain itself now steadily at any high pitch of heroic endeavour. It had bought its comfort with the demoralisation of its servants. It had no completely honest organs ; its spirit was clogged by its accumulated insincerities. Brought at last face to face with a bitter hostility and a powerful and unscrupulous enemy, an enemy socialistic, scientific and efficient to an unexampled degree, it seemed indeed to be inspired for a time by an unwonted energy and unanimity. Youth and the common people shone. The sons of every class went out to fight and die, full of a splendid dream of this war. Easy-going vanished from the foreground of the picture. But only to creep back again as the first inspiration passed. Presently the older men, the seasoned politicians, the owners and hucksters, the charming women and the habitual consumers, began to recover from this blaze of moral exaltation. Old habits of mind and procedure reasserted themselves. The war which had begun so dramatically missed its climax ; there was neither heroic swift defeat nor heroic swift victory. There was indecision ; the most trying test of all for an undisciplined people. There were great spaces of uneventful fatigue. Before the Battle of the Yser had fully developed the dramatic quality had gone out of the war. It had ceased to be either a tragedy or a triumph ; for both sides it became a monstrous strain and wasting. It had become a wearisome thrusting against a pressure of evils. . . .

Under that strain the dignity of England broke, and revealed a malignity less focused and intense than the German, but perhaps even more distressing. No paternal government had organised the British spirit for patriotic ends ; it became now peevish and impatient, like some ill-trained man who is sick, it directed itself no longer against the enemy alone but fitfully against imagined traitors and shirkers ; it wasted its energies in a deepening and spreading net of internal squabbles and accusations. Now it was the wily indolence of the Prime Minister, now it was the German culture of the Lord Chancellor, now the imaginative enterprise of the First Lord of the Admiralty that focused a vindictive campaign. There began a hunt for spies and for suspects of German origin in every quarter except the highest ; a denunciation now of " traitors," now of people with imaginations, now of scientific men, now of the personal friends of the Commander-in-Chief, now of this group and then of that group. . . . Every day Mr. Britling read his three or four newspapers with a deepening disappointment.

When he turned from the newspaper to his post, he would find the anonymous letter-writer had been busy. . . .

Perhaps Mr. Britling had remarked that Germans were after all human beings, or that if England had listened to Matthew Arnold in the eighties our officers by this time might have added efficiency to their courage and good temper. Perhaps he had himself put a touch of irritant acid into his comment. Back flared the hate. " Who are *you*, sir ? What are *you*, sir ? What right have *you*, sir ? What claim have *you*, sir ? " . . .

§ 8

" Life had a wrangling birth. On the head ot every one of us rests the ancestral curse of fifty million murders."

So Mr. Britling's thoughts shaped themselves in words as he prowled one night in March, chill and melancholy, across a rushy meadow under an overcast sky. The death squeal of some little beast caught suddenly in a distant copse had set loose this train of thought. " Life struggling under a birth curse ? " he thought. " How nearly I come back at times to the Christian theology ! . . . And then, Redemption by the shedding of blood."

" Life, like a rebellious child, struggling out of the control of the hate which made it what it is."

But that was Mr. Britling's idea of Gnosticism, not of orthodox Christianity. He went off for a time into faded reminiscences of theological reading. What had been the Gnostic idea ? That the God of the Old Testament was the Devil of the New ? But that had been the idea of the Manichæans ! . . .

Mr. Britling, between the black hedges, came back presently from his attempts to recall his youthful inquiries into man's ancient speculations, to the enduring riddles that have outlasted a thousand speculations. Has hate been necessary, and is it still necessary, and will it always be necessary ? Is all life a war for ever ? The rabbit is nimble, lives keenly, is prevented from degenerating into a diseased crawling eater of herbs by the incessant ferret. Without the ferret of war, what would life become ? . . . War is murder truly, but is not Peace decay ?

It was during these prowling nights in the first winter of the war that Mr. Britling planned a new writing that was to go whole abysses beneath the facile superficiality of " And Now War Ends." It was to be called the " Anatomy of Hate." It was to deal very faithfully with the function of hate, as a corrective to inefficiency. So long as men were slack, men must be fierce. This conviction pressed upon him. . . .

In spite of his detestation of war, Mr. Britling found it

impossible to maintain that any sort of peace state was better than a state of war. If wars produced destructions and cruelties, peace could produce indolence, perversity, greedy accumulation and selfish indulgences. War is discipline for evil, but peace may be relaxation from good. The poor man may be as wretched in peace-time as in war-time. The gathering forces of an evil peace, the malignity and waste of war, are but obverse and reverse of the medal of ill-adjusted human relationships. Was there no Greater Peace possible ; not a mere recuperative pause in killing and destruction, but a phase of noble and creative living, a phase of building, of discovery, of beauty and research ? He remembered, as one remembers the dead, dreams he had once dreamt of the great cities, the splendid freedoms, of a coming age, of marvellous enlargements of human faculty, of a coming science that would be light and of art that could be power. . . .

But would that former peace have ever risen to this ? . . .

After all, had such visions ever been more than idle dreams ? Had the war done more than unmask reality ? . . .

He came to a gate and leaned over it.

The darkness drizzled about him ; he turned up his collar and watched the dim shapes of trees and hedges gather out of the night to meet the dismal dawn. He was cold and hungry and weary.

He may have drowsed ; at least he had a vision, very real and plain, a vision very different from any dream of Utopia.

It seemed to him that suddenly a mine burst under a great ship at sea, that men shouted and women sobbed and cowered, and flares played upon the rain-pitted black waves ; and then the picture changed and showed a battle upon land, and searchlights were flickering through the rain and shells flashed luridly, and men darkly seen in silhouette against red flames ran with fixed bayonets and slipped and floundered over the mud, and at last, shouting thinly through the wind, leaped down into the enemy trenches. . . .

And then he was alone again staring over a wet black field towards a dim crest of shapeless trees.

§ 9

Abruptly and shockingly, this malignity of warfare, which had been so far only a festering cluster of reports and stories and rumours and suspicions, stretched out its arm into Essex and struck a barb of grotesque cruelty into the very heart of Mr. Britling. Late one afternoon came a telegram from Filmington-on-Sea, where Aunt Wilshire had been recovering her temper in a boarding-house after a round of visits in Yorkshire and the moorlands. And she had been " very seriously injured ' by an overnight German air-raid. It was a raid that had not been even mentioned in the morning's papers. She had asked to see him.

It was, ran the compressed telegraphic phrase, "advisable come at once."

Mrs. Britling helped him pack a bag, and came with him to the station in order to drive the car back to the Dower House; for the gardener's boy who had hitherto attended to these small duties had now gone off as an unskilled labourer to some munition works at Chelmsford. Mr. Britling sat in the slow train that carried him across country to the junction for Filmington, and failed altogether to realise what had happened to the old lady. He had an absurd feeling that it was characteristic of her to intervene in affairs in this manner. She had always been so tough and unbent an old lady that until he saw her he could not imagine her as being really seriously and pitifully hurt. . . .

But he found her in the hospital very much hurt indeed. She had been smashed in some complicated manner that left the upper part of her body intact, and lying slantingly upon pillows. Over the horror of bandaged broken limbs and tormented flesh below sheets and a counterpane were drawn. Morphia had been injected, he understood, to save her from pain, but presently it might be necessary for her to suffer. She lay up in her bed with an effect of being enthroned, very white and still, her strong profile with its big nose and her straggling hair and a certain dignity gave her the appearance of some very important, very old man, of an aged pope, for instance, rather than of an old woman. She had made no remark after they had set her and dressed her and put her to bed except "send for Hughie Britling, The Dower House, Matching's Easy. He is the best of the bunch." She had repeated the address and this commendation firmly over and over again, in large print as it were, even after they had assured her that a telegram had been despatched.

In the night, they said, she had talked of him.

He was not sure at first that she knew of his presence.

"Here I am, Aunt Wilshire," he said.

She gave no sign.

"Your nephew Hugh."

"Mean and preposterous," she said very distinctly.

But she was not thinking of Mr. Britling. She was talking of something else.

She was saying: "It should not have been known I was here. There are spies everywhere. Everywhere. There is a spy now —or a lump very like a spy. They pretend it is a hot-water bottle. Pretext. . . . Oh, yes! I admit—absurd. But I have been pursued by spies. Endless spies. Endless, endless spies. Their devices are almost incredible. . . . He has never forgiven me. . . .

"All this on account of a carpet. A palace carpet. Over

which I had no control. I spoke my mind. He knew I knew
of it. I never concealed it. So I was hunted. For years he
had meditated revenge. Now he has it. But at what a cost !
And they call him Emperor. Emperor !

"His arm is withered ; his son—imbecile. He will die—
without dignity. . . ."

Her voice weakened, but it was evident she wanted to say
something more.

"I'm here," said Mr. Britling. "Your nephew Hughie."

She listened.

"Can you understand me ? " he asked.

She became suddenly an earnest, tender human being.
"My dear ! " she said, and seemed to search for something
in her mind and fail to find it.

"You have always understood me," she said.

"You have always been a good boy to me, Hughie," she
said, rather vacantly, and added after some moments of still
reflection, " *au fond.*"

After that she was silent for some minutes, and took no
notice of his whispers.

Then she recollected what had been in her mind. She put
out a hand that sought for Mr. Britling's sleeve.

"Hughie ! "

"I'm here, Auntie," said Mr. Britling. "I'm here."

"Don't let him get at *your* Hughie. . . . Too good for it,
dear. Oh ! much—much too good. . . . People let these
wars and excitements run away with them. . . . They put
too much into them. . . . They aren't—they aren't worth
it. Don't let him get at your Hughie."

"No !"

"You understand me, Hughie ? "

"Perfectly, Auntie."

"Then don't forget it. Ever."

She had said what she wanted to say. She had made her
testament. She closed her eyes. He was amazed to find this
grotesque old creature had suddenly become beautiful, in
that silvery vein of beauty one sometimes finds in very old
men. She was exalted as great artists will sometimes exalt
the portraits of the aged. He was moved to kiss her forehead.

Then came a little tug at his sleeve.

"I think that is enough," said the nurse, who had stood
forgotten at his elbow.

"But I can come again ? "

"Perhaps."

She indicated departure by a movement of her hand.

§ 10

The next day Aunt Wilshire was unconscious of her visitor.
They had altered her position so that she lay now horizon-

tally, staring inflexibly at the ceiling and muttering queer old
disconnected things.

The Windsor Castle carpet story was still running through
her mind, but mixed up with it now were scraps of the current
newspaper controversies about the conduct of the war. And
she was still thinking of the dynastic aspects of the war. And
of spies. She had something upon her mind about the King's
more German aunts.

"As a precaution," she said, "as a precaution. Watch
them all. . . . The Princess Christian. . . . Laying foundation-stones. . . . Cement. . . . Guns. Or else why should
they always be laying foundation-stones ? . . . Always. . . .
Why ? . . . Hushed up. . . .

"None of these things," she said, "in the newspapers.
They ought to be."

And then after an interval, very distinctly, " The Duke of
Wellington. My ancestor—in reality. . . . Publish and be
damned."

After that she lay still. . . .

The doctors and nurses could hold out only very faint hopes
to Mr. Britling's inquiries ; they said indeed it was astonishing that she was still alive.

And about seven o'clock that evening she died. . . .

§ 11

Mr. Britling, after he had looked at his dead cousin for the
last time, wandered for an hour or so about the silent little
watering-place before he returned to his hotel. There was
no one to talk to and nothing else to do but to think of her
death.

The night was cold and bleak, but full of stars. He had
already mastered the local topography, and he knew now
exactly where all the bombs that had been showered upon
the place had fallen. Here was the corner of blackened walls
and roasted beams where three wounded horses had been
burned alive in a barn, here the row of houses, some smashed,
some almost intact, where a mutilated child had screamed for
two hours before she could be rescued from the débris that
had pinned her down, and taken to the hospital. Everywhere
by the dim light of the shaded street-lamps he could see the
black holes and gaps of broken windows ; sometimes abundant,
sometimes rare and exceptional, among otherwise uninjured
dwellings. Many of the victims he had visited in the little
cottage hospital where Aunt Wilshire had just died. She was
the eleventh dead. Altogether fifty-seven people had been
killed or injured in this brilliant German action. They were
all civilians, and only twelve were men.

Two Zeppelins had come in from over the sea, and had been
fired at by an anti-aircraft gun coming on an automobile from
Ipswich. The first intimation the people of the town had had

of the raid was the report of this gun. Many had run out to
see what was happening. It was doubtful if any one had really
seen the Zeppelins, though every one testified to the sound
of their engines. Then suddenly the bombs had come streaming
down. Only six had made hits upon houses or people ; the rest
had fallen ruinously and very close together on the local golf-
links, and at least half had not exploded at all and did not seem
to have been released to explode.

A third at least of the injured people had been in bed when
destruction came upon them.

The story was like a page from some fantastic romance of
Jules Verne's ; the peace of the little old town, the people going
to bed, the quiet streets, the quiet starry sky, and then for ten
minutes an uproar of guns and shells, a clatter of breaking
glass, and then a fire here, a fire there, a child's voice pitched
high by pain and terror, scared people going to and fro with
lanterns, and the sky empty again, the raiders gone. . . .

Five minutes before, Aunt Wilshire had been sitting in the
boarding-house drawing-room playing a great stern " Patience,"
the Emperor Patience (" Napoleon, my dear !—not that Pots-
dam creature ") that took hours to do. Five minutes later she
was a thing of elemental terror and agony, bleeding wounds
and shattered bones, plunging about in the darkness amidst
a heap of wreckage. And already the German airmen were
buzzing away to sea again, proud of themselves, pleased no
doubt—like boys who have thrown a stone through a window,
beating their way back to thanks and rewards, to iron crosses,
and the proud embraces of Fräus and Fräuleins. . . .

For the first time it seemed to Mr. Britling he really saw
the immediate horror of war, the dense cruel stupidity of the
business, plain and close. It was as if he had never perceived
anything of the sort before, as if he had been dealing with
stories, pictures, shows and representations that he knew to be
shams. But that this dear, absurd old creature, this thing of
home, this being of familiar humours and familiar irritations,
should be torn to pieces, left in torment like a smashed mouse
over which an automobile has passed, brought the whole
business to a raw and quivering focus. Not a soul among all
those who had been rent and torn and tortured in this agony
of millions, but was to any one who understood and had been
near to it, in some way lovable, in some way laughable, in some
way worthy of respect and care. Poor Aunt Wilshire was but
the sample thrust in his face of all this mangled multitude,
whose green-white lips had sweated in anguish, whose broken
bones had thrust raggedly through red, dripping flesh. . . .
The detested features of the German Crown Prince jerked into
the centre of Mr. Britling's picture. The young man stood
in his dapper uniform and grinned under his long nose, carrying
himself jauntily, proud of his extreme importance to so many
lives. . . .

And for a while Mr. Britling could do nothing but rage.

" Devils they are ! " he cried to the stars.

" Devils ! Devilish fools rather. Cruel blockheads. Apes with all science in their hands ! My God ! but *we will teach them a lesson yet !* " . . .

That was the key of his mood for an hour of aimless wandering, wandering that was only checked at last by a sentinel who turned him back towards the town. . . .

He wandered, muttering. He found great comfort in scheming vindictive destruction for countless Germans. He dreamt of swift armoured aeroplanes swooping down upon the flying airship, and sending it reeling earthward, the men screaming. He imagined a shattered Zeppelin staggering earthward in the fields behind the Dower House, and how he would himself run out with a spade and smite the Germans down. " Quarter indeed ! Kamerad ! Take *that*, you foul murderer ! "

In the dim light the sentinel saw the retreating figure of Mr. Britling make an extravagant gesture, and wondered what it might mean. Signalling ? What ought an intelligent sentry to do ? Let fly at him ? Arrest him ? . . . Take no notice ? . . .

Mr. Britling was at that moment killing Count Zeppelin and beating out his brains. Count Zeppelin was killed that night and the German Emperor was assassinated ; a score of lesser victims were offered up to the *manes* of Aunt Wilshire ; there were memorable cruelties before the wrath and bitterness of Mr. Britling was appeased. And then suddenly he had had enough of these thoughts ; they were thrust aside, they vanished out of his mind.

§ 12

All the while that Mr. Britling had been indulging in these imaginative slaughterings and spending the tears and hate that had gathered in his heart, his reason had been sitting apart and above the storm, like the sun waiting above thunder, like a wise nurse watching and patient above the wild passions of a child. And all the time his reason had been maintaining silently and firmly, without shouting, without speech, that the men who had made this hour were indeed not devils, were no more devils than Mr. Britling was a devil, but sinful men of like nature with himself, hard, stupid, caught in the same web of circumstance. " Kill them in your passion if you will," said reason, " but understand. This thing was done neither by devils nor fools, but by a conspiracy of foolish motives, by the weak acquiescences of the clever, by a crime that was no man's crime but the natural necessary outcome of the ineffectiveness, the blind motives and muddle-headedness of all mankind."

So reason maintained her thesis, like a light above the head of Mr. Britling at which he would not look, while he hewed airmen to quivering rags with a spade that he had sharpened, then stifled German princes with their own poison-gas, given slowly and as painfully as possible. " And what of the towns *our* ships have bombarded ? " asked reason unheeded. " What of those Tasmanians *our* people utterly swept away ?

" What of French machine-guns in the Atlas ? " reason pressed the case. " Of Himalayan villages burning ? Of the things we did in China ? Especially of the things we did in China. . . ."

Mr. Britling gave no need to that.

" The Germans in China were worse than we were," he threw out. . . .

He was maddened by the thought of the Zeppelin making off, high and far in the sky, a thing dwindling to nothing among the stars, and the thought of those murderers escaping him. Time after time he stood still and shook his fist at Boötes, slowly sweeping up the sky. . . .

And at last, sick and wretched, he sat down on a seat upon the deserted parade under the stars, close to the soughing of the invisible sea below. . . .

His mind drifted back once more to those ancient heresies of the Gnostics and the Manichæans which saw the God of the World as altogether evil, which sought only to escape by the utmost abstinences and evasions and perversions from the black wickedness of being. For a while his soul sank down into the uncongenial darknesses of these creeds of despair. " I who have loved life," he murmured, and could have believed for a time that he wished he had never had a son. . . .

Is the whole scheme of nature evil ? Is life in its essence cruel ? Is man stretched quivering upon the table of the eternal vivisector for no end—and without pity.

These were thoughts that Mr. Britling had never faced before the war. They came to him now, and they came only to be rejected by the inherent quality of his mind. For weeks, consciously and subconsciously, his mind had been grappling with this riddle. He had thought of it during his lonely prowlings as a special constable ; it had flung itself in monstrous symbols across the dark canvas of his dreams. " Is there indeed a devil of pure cruelty ? Does any creature, even the very cruelest of creatures, really apprehend the pain it causes, or inflict it for the sake of the infliction ? " He summoned a score of memories, a score of imaginations, to bear their witness before the tribunal of his mind. He forgot cold and loneliness in this speculation. He sat, trying all Being, on this score, under the cold indifferent stars.

He thought of certain instances of boyish cruelty that had horrified him in his own boyhood, and it was clear to him that indeed it was not cruelty, it was curiosity, dense-textured, thick-skinned, so that it could not feel even the anguish of a blinded cat. Those boys who had wrung his childish soul to nigh intolerable misery had not indeed been tormenting so much as observing torment, testing life as wantonly as one breaks thin ice in the early days of winter. In very much cruelty the real motive is surely no worse than that obtuse curiosity ; a mere step of understanding, a mere quickening of the nerves and mind, makes it impossible. But that is not true of all or most cruelty. Most cruelty has something else in it, something more than the clumsy plunging into experience of the hobbledehoy ; it is vindictive or indignant ; it is never tranquil and sensuous ; it draws its incentive, however crippled and monstrous the justification may be, from something punitive in man's instinct, something therefore that implies a sense, however misguided, of righteousness and vindication. That factor is present even in spite ; when some vile or atrocious thing is done out of envy or malice, that envy and malice has in it always—*always* ? Yes, always—a genuine condemnation of the hated thing as an unrighteous thing, as an unjust usurpation, as an inexcusable privilege, as a sinful overconfidence. Those men in the airship ?—he was coming to that. He found himself asking himself whether it was possible for a human being to do any cruel act without an excuse—or, at least, without the feeling of excusability. And in the case of these Germans and the outrages they had committed and the retaliations they had provoked, he perceived that always there was the element of a perceptible if inadequate justification. Just as there would be if presently he were to maltreat a fallen German airman. There was anger in their vileness. These Germans were an unsubtle people, a people in the worst and best sense of the words, plain and honest ; they were prone to moral indignation ; and moral indignation is the mother of most of the cruelty in the world. They perceived the indolence of the English and Russians, they perceived their disregard of science and system, they could not perceive the longer reach of these greater races, and it seemed to them that the mission of Germany was to chastise and correct this laxity. Surely, they had argued, God was not on the side of those who kept an untilled field. So they had butchered these old ladies and slaughtered these children just to show us the consequences :

" All along of dirtiness, all along of mess,
    All along of doing things rather more or less."

The very justification our English poet has found for a thousand overbearing actions in the East ! " Forget not order and the real," that was the underlying message of bomb and gas and submarine. After all, what right had we English *not* to have a gun or an aeroplane fit to bring down that Zeppelin ignominiously and conclusively ? Had we not undertaken Empire ? Were we not the leaders of great nations ? Had we indeed much right to complain if our imperial pose was flouted ? " There, at least," said Mr. Britling's reason, " is one of the lines of thought that brought that unseen cruelty out of the night high over the houses of Filmington-on-Sea. That, in a sense, is the cause of this killing. Cruel it is and abominable, yes, but is it altogether cruel ? Hasn't it, after all, a sort of stupid rightness ?—isn't it a stupid reaction to an indolence at least equally stupid ? "

What was this rightness that lurked below cruelty ? What was the inspiration of this pressure of spite, this anger that was aroused by ineffective gentleness and kindliness ? Was it indeed an altogether evil thing ; was it not rather an impulse, blind as yet, but in its ultimate quality *as good as mercy*, greater perhaps in its ultimate values than mercy ?

This idea had been gathering in Mr. Britling's mind for many weeks ; it had been growing and taking shape as he wrote, making experimental beginnings for his essay, " The Anatomy of Hate." Is there not, he now asked himself plainly, a creative and corrective impulse behind all hate ? Is not this malignity indeed only the ape-like precursor of the great disciplines of a creative state ?

The invincible hopefulness of his sanguine temperament had now got Mr. Britling well out of the pessimistic pit again. Already he had been on the verge of his phrase while wandering across the rushy fields towards Market Saffron ; now it came to him again like a legitimate monarch returning from exile.

" When hate shall have become creative energy. . . .

" Hate which passes into creative power ; gentleness which is indolence and the herald of euthanasia. . . .

" Pity is but a passing grace ; for mankind will not always be pitiful."

But meanwhile, meanwhile. . . . How long were men so to mingle wrong with right, to be energetic without mercy and kindly without energy ? . . .

For a time Mr. Britling sat on the lonely parade under the stars and in the sound of the sea, brooding upon these ideas.

His mind could make no further steps. It had worked for its spell. His rage had ebbed away now altogether. His despair was no longer infinite. But the world was dark and dreadful still. It seemed none the less dark because at the end there was a gleam of light. It was a gleam of light far beyond the limits of his own life, far beyond the life of his son. It had no balm for these sufferings. Between it and himself stretched the weary generations still to come, generations of bickering and accusation, greed and faint-heartedness, the half-truth and the hasty blow. And all those years would be full of pitiful things, such pitiful things as the blackened ruins in the town behind, the little grey-faced corpses, the lives torn and wasted, the hopes extinguished and the gladness gone. . . .

He was no longer thinking of the Germans as diabolical.

They were human ; they had a case. It was a stupid case, but our case, too, was a stupid case. How stupid were all our cases ! What was it we missed ? Something, he felt, very close to us, and very elusive. Something that would resolve a hundred tangled oppositions. . . .

His mind hung at that. Back upon his consciousness came crowding the horrors and desolations that had been his daily food now for three-quarters of a year. He groaned aloud. He struggled against that renewed envelopment of his spirit. " Oh, blood-stained fools ! " he cried, " oh, pitiful, tormented fools !

" Even that vile airship was a ship of fools !

" We are all fools still. Striving apes, irritated beyond measure by our own striving, easily moved to anger."

Some train of subconscious suggestion brought a long-forgotten speech back into Mr. Britling's mind, a speech that is full of that light which still seeks so mysteriously and indefatigably to break through the darkness and thickness of the human mind.

He whispered the words. No unfamiliar words could have had the same effect of comfort and conviction.

He whispered it of those men whom he still imagined flying far away there eastward, through the clear freezing air beneath the stars, those muffled sailors and engineers who had caused so much pain and agony in this little town.

" *Father, forgive them, for they know not what they do.*"

CHAPTER FOUR

IN THE WEB OF THE INEFFECTIVE

§ 1

HUGH'S letters were becoming a very important influence upon Mr. Britling's thought. Hugh had always been something of a letter-writer, and now what was perhaps an inherited desire to set things down was manifest. He had been accustomed to decorate his letters from school with absurb little sketches—sometimes his letters had been all sketches—and now he broke from drawing to writing and back to drawing in a way that pleased his father mightily. The father loved this queer trick of caricature ; he did not possess it himself, and so it seemed to him the most wonderful of all Hugh's little equipment of gifts. Mr. Britling used to carry these letters about until their edges got grimy ; he would show them to any one he felt capable of appreciating their youthful freshness ; he would quote them as final and conclusive evidence to establish this or that. He did not dream how many thousands of mothers and fathers were treasuring such documents. He thought other sons were dull young men by comparison with Hugh.

The earlier letters told much of the charms of discipline and the open air. "All the bother about what one has to do with oneself is over," wrote Hugh. "One has disposed of oneself. That has the effect of a great relief. Instead of telling oneself that one ought to get up in the morning, a bugle tells you that. . . . And there's no nonsense about it, no chance of lying and arguing about it with oneself. . . . I begin to see the sense of men going into monasteries and putting themselves under rules. One is carried along in a sort of moral automobile instead of trudging the road. . . . "

And he was also sounding new physical experiences.

"Never before," he declared, "have I known what fatigue is. It's a miraculous thing. One drops down in one's clothes on any hard old thing and sleeps. . . . "

And in his early letters he was greatly exercised by the elementary science of drill and discipline, and the discussion of whether these things were necessary. He began by assuming that their importance was overrated. He went on to discover that they constituted the very essentials of all good soldering. "In a crisis," he concluded, "there is no telling what will get hold of a man, his higher instincts or his lower. He may show courage of a very splendid sort—or a hasty discretion. A habit is much more trustworthy than an instinct. So discipline sets up a habit of steady and courageous bearing. If you keep your head you are at liberty to be splendid. If you lose it, the habit will carry you through."

The young man was also very profound upon the effects of the suggestion of various exercises upon the mind.

"It is surprising how bloodthirsty one feels in a bayonet charge. We have to shout ; we are encouraged to shout. The effect is to paralyse one's higher centres. One ceases to question—anything. One becomes a ' bayoneteer.' As I go bounding forward I imagine fat men, succulent men ahead, and I am filled with the desire to do them in neatly. This sort of thing——"

A sketch of slaughter followed, with a large and valiant Hugh leaving a train of fallen behind him.

"Not like this. This is how I used to draw it in my innocent childhood, but it is incorrect. More than one German on the bayonet at a time is an encumbrance. And it would be swank —a thing we detest in the army."

The second sketch showed the same brave hero with half-a-dozen of the enemy skewered like cat's meat.

"As for the widows and children, I disregard 'em."

§ 2

But presently Hugh began to be bored.

"Route marching again," he wrote. "For no earthly reason than that they can do nothing else with us. We are getting no decent musketry training because there are no rifles.

We are wasting half our time. If you multiply half a week by the number of men in the army you will see we waste centuries weekly. . . . If most of these men here had just been enrolled and left to go about their business while we trained officers and instructors and got equipment for them, and if they had then been put through their paces as rapidly as possible, it would have been infinitely better for the country. . . . In a sort of way we are keeping raw ; in a sort of way we are getting stale. . . . I get irritated by this. I feel we are not being properly done by.

" Half our men are educated men, reasonably educated, but we are always being treated as though we were too stupid for words. . . .

" No good grousing, I suppose, but after Statesminster and a glimpse of old Cardinal's way of doing things, one gets a kind of toothache in the mind at the sight of everything being done twice as slowly and half as well as it need be."

He went off at a tangent to describe the men in his platoon. " The best man in our lot is an ex-grocer's assistant, but in order to save us from vain generalisations it happens that the worst man—a moon-faced creature, almost incapable of lacing up his boots without help and objurgation—is also an ex-grocer's assistant. Our most offensive member is a little cad with a snub nose, who had read Kipling and imagines he is the nearest thing that ever has been to Private Ortheris. He goes about looking for the other two of the Soldiers Three ; it is rather like an unpopular politician trying to form a ministry. And he is conscientiously foul-mouthed. He feels losing a chance of saying ' bloody ' as acutely as a snob feels dropping an H. He goes back sometimes and says the sentence over again and puts the ' bloody ' in. I used to swear a little out of the range of your parental ear, but Ortheris has cured me. When he is about I am mincing in my speech. I perceive now that cursing is a way of chewing one's own dirt. In a platoon there is no elbow-room for indifference ; you must either love or hate. I have a feeling that my first taste of battle will not be with Germans, but with Private Ortheris. . . ."

And one letter was just a picture, a parody of the well-known picture of the bivouac below and the soldier's dream of return to his beloved above. But Master Hugh in the dream was embracing an enormous retort, while a convenient galvanometer registered his emotion and little tripods danced around him.

§ 3

Then came a letter which plunged abruptly into criticism. " My dear Parent, this is a swearing letter. I must let go to somebody. And somehow none of the other chaps are convenient. I don't know if I ought to be put against a wall and shot for it, but I hereby declare that all the officers of this battalion over and above the rank of captain are a constellation of incapables—and several of the captains are herewith included. Some of them are men of a pleasant disposition and carefully aborted mental powers, and some are men of an unpleasant disposition and no mental powers at all. And I believe—a little enlightenment by your recent letter to *The Times*—that they are a fair sample of the entire ' army ' class which has got to win this war. Usually they are indolent, but when they are thoroughly roused they are fussy. The time they should spend in enlarging their minds and increasing their military efficiency they devote to keeping fit. They are, roughly speaking, fit—for nothing. They cannot move us thirty miles without getting half of us left about, without losing touch with food and shelter and starving us for thirty-six hours or so in the process, and they cannot count beyond the fingers of one hand, not having learned to use the nose for arithmetical operations. . . . I conclude this war is going to be a sort of Battle of Inkerman on a large scale. We chaps in the ranks will have to do the job. Leading is ' off.' . . .

" All of this, my dear Parent, is just a blow off. I have been needlessly starved, and fagged to death and exasperated. We have moved five-and-twenty miles across country in fifty-seven hours. And without food for about eighteen hours. I have been with my Captain, who has been billeting us here in Cheasingholt. Oh, he is a MUFF ! Oh God ! oh God of Heaven ! what a MUFF ! He is afraid of printed matter, but he controls himself heroically. He prides himself upon having no ' sense of locality, confound it ! ' Prides himself ! He went about this village, which is a little dispersed, at a slight trot, and wouldn't avail himself of the one-inch map I happened to have. He judged the capacity of each room with his eye and wouldn't let me measure, even with God's own paces. Not with the legs I inherit. ' We'll put five fellahs hea ! ' he said. ' What d'you want to measure the room for ? We haven't come to lay down carpets.' Then, having assigned men by *coup d'œil*, so as to congest half the village miserably, he found the other half unoccupied and had to begin all over again. ' If you measured the floor space first, sir,' I said, ' and made a list of the houses—— ' ' That isn't the way I'm going to do it,' he said, fixing me with a pitiless eye. . . .

" That isn't the way they are going to do it, Daddy ! The sort of thing that is done over here in the green army will be done over there in the dry. They won't be in time ; they'll lose their guns where now they lose our kitchens. I'm a mute soldier ; I've got to do what I'm told ; still, I begin to understand the Battle of Neuve Chapelle.

" They say the relations of men and officers in the new army are beautiful. Some day I may learn to love my officer —but not just yet. Not till I've forgotten the operations leading up to the occupation of Cheasingholt. . . . He muffs his real job without a blush, and yet he would rather be shot than do his bootlaces up crisscross. What I say about officers applies only and solely to him really. . . . How well I understand now the shooting of officers by their men. . . . But indeed, fatigue and exasperation apart, this shift has been done atrociously. . . . ''

The young man returned to these criticisms in a later letter.

" You will think I am always carping, but it does seem to me that nearly everything is being done here in the most wasteful way possible. We waste time, we waste labour, we waste material, oh Lord ! how we waste our country's money. These aren't, I can assure you, the opinions of a conceited young man. It's nothing to be conceited about. . . . We're bored to death by standing about this infernal little village. There is nothing to do—except trail after a small number of slatternly young women we despise and hate. I *don't*, Daddy. And I don't drink. Why have I inherited no vices ? We had a fight here yesterday—sheer boredom. Ortheris has a swollen lip, and another private has a bad black eye. There is to be a return match. I perceive the chief horror of warfare is boredom. . . .

" Our feeding here is typical of the whole system. It is a system invented not with any idea of getting the best results —that does not enter into the War Office philosophy—but to have a rule for everything, and avoid arguments. There is rather too generous an allowance of bread and stuff per man, and there is a very fierce but not very efficient system of weighing and checking. A rather too generous allowance is, of course, a direct incentive to waste or stealing—as any one but our silly old duffer of a War Office would know. The checking is for quantity, which any fool can understand, rather than for quality. The test for the quality of army meat is the smell. If it doesn't smell bad, it is good. . . .

" Then the raw material is handed over to a cook. He is a common soldier who has been made into a cook by a simple ceremony. He is told, ' You are a cook.' He does his best to be. Usually he roasts or bakes to begin with, guessing when the joint is done, afterwards he hacks up what is left of his joints and makes a stew for next day. A stew is hacked meat boiled up in a big pot. It has much fat floating on the top. After you have eaten your fill you want to sit about quiet. The men are fed usually in a large tent or barn. We have a barn. It is not a clean barn, and just to make it more like a picnic there are insufficient plates, knives and forks. (I tell you, no army people can count beyond eight or ten.) The corporals after their morning's work have to carve. When they have done carving they tell me they feel they have had enough dinner. They sit about looking pale, and wander off afterwards to the village pub. (I shall probably become a corporal soon.) In these islands before the war began there was a sur-

plus of women over men of about a million. (See the publications of the Fabian Society, now so popular among the young.)
None of these women have been trusted by the government
with the difficult task of cooking and giving out food to our
soldiers. No man of the ordinary soldier class ever cooks
anything until he is a soldier. . . . All food left over after the
stew or otherwise rendered uneatable by the cook is thrown
away. We throw away pail-loads. *We bury meat.* . . .

"Also we get three pairs of socks. We work pretty hard.
We don't know how to darn socks. When the heels wear
through, come blisters. Bad blisters disable a man. Of the
million of surplus women (see above) the government has not
had the intelligence to get any to darn our socks. So a certain
percentage of us go lame. And so on. And so on.

"You will think all this is awful grousing, but the point
I want to make—I hereby to ease my feelings make it now in
a fair round hand—is that all this business could be done
far better and far cheaper if it wasn't left to these absolutely
inexperienced and extremely exclusive military gentlemen.
They think they are leading England and showing us all how ;
instead of which they are just keeping us back. Why in
thunder are they doing everything ? Not one of them, when
he is at home, is allowed to order the dinner or poke his nose
into his own kitchen or check the household books. . . . The
ordinary British colonel is a helpless old gentleman ; he
ought to have a nurse. . . . This is not merely the trivial
grievance of my insulted stomach, it is a serious matter for
the country. Sooner or later the country may want the food
that is being wasted in all these capers. In the aggregate it
must amount to a daily destruction of tons of stuff of all sorts.
Tons. . . . Suppose the war lasts longer than we reckon ! "

From this point Hugh's letter jumped to a general discussion of the military mind.

"Our officers are beastly good chaps, nearly all of them.
That's where the perplexity of the whole thing comes in.
If only they weren't such good chaps ! If only they were
like the Prussian officers to their men, then we'd just take
on a revolution as well as the war, and make everything
tidy at once. But they are decent, they are charming. . . .
Only they do not think hard, and they do not understand
that doing a job properly means doing it as directly and
thought-outly as you possibly can. They won't worry about
things. If their tempers were worse perhaps their work might
be better. They won't use maps or time-tables or books of
reference. When we move to a new place they pick up what
they can about it by hearsay ; not one of our lot has the
gumption to possess a contoured map, or a Michelin guide.
They have hearsay minds. They are fussy and petty and
wasteful—and, in the way of getting things done, pretentious.
By their code they're paragons of honour. Courage—they're

all right about that ; no end of it ; honesty, truthfulness, and so on—high. They have a kind of horsy standard of smartness and pluck, too, that isn't bad, and they have a fine horror of whiskers and being unbuttoned. But the mistake they make is to class thinking with whiskers, as a sort of fussy sidegrowth. Instead of classing it with buttoned-upness. They hate economy. And preparation. . . .

"They won't see that inefficiency is a sort of dishonesty. If a man doesn't steal sixpence, they think it a light matter if he wastes half a crown. Here follows wisdom ! *From the point of view of a nation at war, sixpence is just a fifth part of half a crown.* . . .

"When I began this letter I was boiling with indignation, complicated, I suspect, by this morning's ' stew ' ; now I have written thus far I feel I'm an ungenerous grumbler. . . . It is remarkable, my dear Parent, that I let off these things to you. I like writing to you. I couldn't possibly say the things I can write. Heinrich had a confidential friend at Breslau to whom he used to write about his Soul. I never had one of these Teutonic friendships. And I haven't got a Soul. But I have to write. One must write to some one— and in this place there is nothing else to do. And now the old lady downstairs is turning down the gas ; she always does at half past ten. She didn't ought. She gets—ninepence each. Excuse the pencil. . . ."

That letter ended abruptly. The next two were brief and cheerful. Then suddenly came a new note.

"We've got rifles ! We're real armed soldiers at last. Every blessed man has got a rifle. And they come from Japan ! They are of a sort of light wood that is like new oak and art furniture, and makes one feel that one belongs to the First Garden Suburb Regiment ; but I believe much can be done with linseed-oil. And they are real rifles, they go bang. We are a little light-headed about them. Only our training and discipline prevent our letting fly at incautious spectators on the sky-line. I saw a man yesterday about half a mile off. I was possessed by the idea that I could get him—right in the middle. . . . Ortheris, the little beast, has got a motor-bicycle, which he calls his ' b——y oto '—no one knows why —and only death or dishonourable conduct will save me, I gather, from becoming a corporal in the course of the next month. . . ."

§ 4

A subsequent letter threw fresh light on the career of the young man with the " oto." Before the rifle and the " oto," and in spite of his fights with some person or persons unknown, Ortheris found trouble. Hugh told the story with the unblushing *savoir-faire* of the very young.

"By-the-by, Ortheris, following the indications of his

creator and succumbing to the universal boredom before the rifles came, forgot Lord Kitchener's advice and attempted ' seduktion.' With painful results which he insists upon confiding to the entire platoon. He has been severely smacked and scratched by the proposed victim, and warned off the premises (licensed premises) by her father and mother—both formidable persons. They did more than warn him off the premises. They had displayed neither a proper horror of Don Juan nor a proper respect for the King's uniform. Mother, we realise, got hold of him, and cuffed him severely. ' What the 'ell's a chap to do ? ' cried Ortheris. ' You can't go 'itting a woman back.' Father had set a dog on him. A less ingenuous character would be silent about such passages—I should be too egotistical and humiliated altogether—but that is not his quality. He tells us in tones of naïve wonder. He talks about it and talks about it. ' I don't care what the old woman did,' he says, ' not—reely. What 'urts me about it is that I jest made a sort of mistake 'ow *she'd* tike it. You see, I sort of feel I've 'urt and insulted *'er*. And reely I didn't mean to. Swap me, I didn't mean to. Gawd 'elp me. I wouldn't 'ave 'ad it 'appen as it 'as 'appened, not for worlds. And now I can't get round to 'er, or anyfing, not to explain. . . . You chaps may laugh, but you don't know what there is *in* it. . . . I tell you it worries me something frightful. You think I'm just a little cad who took liberties he didn't ought to. (Note of anger drowning uncharitable grunts of assent.) 'Ow the 'ell is 'e to know *when* 'e didn't ought to ? . . . I *swear* she liked me. . . . "

" This sort of thing goes on for hours—in the darkness.

" ' I'd got regular sort of fond of 'er.'

" And the extraordinary thing is it makes me begin to get regular fond of Ortheris.

" I think it is because the affair has surprised him right out of acting Ortheris and Tommy Atkins for a bit, into his proper self. He's frightfully like some sort of mongrel with a lot of wire-haired terrier and a touch of Airedale in it. A mongrel you like in spite of the flavour of all the horrid things he's been nosing into. And he's as hard as nails and, my dear daddy ! he can't box for nuts."

§ 5

Mr. Britling, with an understanding much quickened by Hugh's letters, went about Essex in his automobile, and on one or two journeys into Berkshire and Buckinghamshire, and marked the steady conversion of the old pacific countryside into an armed camp. He was disposed to minimise Hugh's criticisms. He found in them something of the harshness of youth, which is far too keen-edged to be tolerant with half performance and our poor human evasion of perfection's overstrain. " Our poor human evasion of perfection's overstrain " ; this phrase was Mr. Britling's. To Mr. Britling, looking less closely and more broadly, the new army was a pride and a marvel.

He liked to come into some quiet village and note the clusters of sturdy khaki-clad youngsters going about their business, the tethered horses, the air of subdued bustle, the occasional glimpses of guns and ammunition trains. Wherever one went now there were soldiers and still more soldiers. There was a steady flow of men into Flanders, and presently to Gallipoli, but it seemed to have no effect upon the multitude in training at home. He was pleasantly excited by the evident increase in the proportion of military material upon the railways ; he liked the promise and mystery of the long lines of trucks bearing tarpaulin-covered wagons and carts and guns that he would pass on his way to Liverpool Street station. He could apprehend defeat in the silence of the night, but when he saw the men, when he went about the land, then it was impossible to believe in any end but victory. . . .

But through the spring and summer there was no victory. The " great offensive " of May was checked and abandoned after a series of ineffective and very costly attacks between Ypres and Soissons. The Germans had developed a highly scientific defensive in which machine-guns replaced rifles and a maximum of punishment was inflicted upon an assaulting force with a minimum of human loss. The War Office had never thought much of machine-guns before, but now it thought a good deal. Moreover, the energies of Britain were being turned more and more towards the Dardanelles.

The idea of an attack upon the Dardanelles had a traditional attractiveness for the British mind. Old men had been brought up from childhood with " forcing the Dardanelles " as a familiar phrase ; it had none of the flighty novelty and vulgarity about it that made an " aerial offensive " seem so unwarrantable a proceeding. Forcing the Dardanelles was historically British. It made no break with tradition. Soon after Turkey entered the war British submarines appeared in the Sea of Marmora, and in February a systematic bombardment of the Dardanelles began ; this was continued intermittently for a month, the defenders profiting by their experiences and by spells of bad weather to strengthen their works. This first phase of the attack culminated in the loss of the *Irresistible*, *Ocean*, and *Bouvet*, when on the 17th of March the attacking fleet closed in upon the Narrows. After an interlude of six weeks to allow of further preparations on the part of the defenders, who were now thoroughly alive to what was coming, the Allied armies gathered upon the scene, and a difficult and costly landing was achieved at two points upon the peninsula of Gallipoli. With that began a slow and bloody siege of the defences of the Dardanelles, clambering up to the surprise landing of a fresh British army

in Suvla Bay in August, and its failure in the battle of Anafarta, through incompetent commanders and a general slop-
piness of leading, to cut off and capture Maidos and the
Narrows defences. . . . Meanwhile the Russian hosts, which
had reached their high-water mark in the capture of Przemysl,
were being forced back first in the south and then in the north.
The Germans recaptured Lemberg, entered Warsaw, and
pressed on to take Brest Litowsk. The Russian lines rolled
back with an impressive effect of defeat, and the Germans
thrust towards Riga and Petrograd, reaching Vilna about the
middle of September. . . .

Day after day Mr. Britling traced the swaying fortunes of
the conflict, with impatience, with perplexity, but with no
loss of confidence in the ultimate success of Britain. The
country was still swarming with troops, and still under summer
sunshine. A second hay-harvest redeemed the scantiness of
the first, the wheat-crops were wonderful, and the great fig-
tree at the corner of the Dower House had never borne so
bountifully nor such excellent juicy figs. . . .

And one day in early June while those figs were still only
a hope, Teddy appeared at the Dower House with Letty, to
say good-bye before going to the front. He was going out
in a draft to fill up various gaps and losses ; he did not know
where. Essex was doing well but bloodily over there. Mrs.
Britling had tea set out upon the lawn under the blue cedar,
and Mr. Britling found himself at a loss for appropriate sayings,
and talked in his confusion almost as though Teddy's departure
was of no significance at all. He was still haunted by that
odd sense of responsibility for Teddy. Teddy was not nearly
so animated as he had been in his pre-khaki days ; there was
a quiet exultation in his manner rather than a lively excitement. He knew now what he was in for. He knew now that
war was not a lark, that for him it was to be the gravest
experience he had ever had or was likely to have. There
were no more jokes about Letty's pension, and a general
avoidance of the topics of high explosives and asphyxiating
gas. . . .

Mr. and Mrs. Britling took the young people to the gate.

" Good luck ! " cried Mr. Britling as they receded.

Teddy replied with a wave of the hand.

Mr. Britling stood watching them for some moments as
they walked towards the little cottage which was to be the
scene of their private parting.

" I don't like his going," he said. " I hope it will be all
right with him. . . . . Teddy's so grave nowadays. It's a mean
thing, I know, it has none of the Roman touch, but I am
glad that this can't happen with Hugh—— " He computed.
" Not for a year and three months, even if they march him
into it upon his very birthday. . . .

" It may all be over by then. . . . "

§ 6

In that computation he reckoned without Hugh.

Within a month Hugh was also saying " Good-bye."

" But how's this ? " protested Mr. Britling, who had already guessed the answer. " You're not nineteen."

" I'm nineteen enough for this job," said Hugh. " In fact, I enlisted as nineteen."

Mr. Britling said nothing for a little while. Then he spoke with a catch in his breath. " I don't blame you," he said. " It was—the right spirit."

Drill and responsibilities of non-commissioned rank had imposed a novel manliness upon the bearing of Corporal Britling. " I always classified a little above my age at States-minster," he said as though that cleared up everything.

He looked at a rosebud as though it interested him. Then he remarked rather casually :

" I thought," he said, " that if I was to go to war I'd better do the thing properly. It seemed—sort of half and half—not to be eligible for the trenches. . . . I ought to have told you. . . ."

" Yes," Mr. Britling decided.

" I was shy about it at first. . . . I thought perhaps the war would be over before it was necessary to discuss anything. . . . Didn't want to go into it."

" Exactly," said Mr. Britling as though that was a complete explanation.

" It's been   good year for your roses," said Hugh.

§ 7

Hugh was to stay the night. He spent what seemed to him and every one a long, shy, inexpressive evening. Only the small boys were really natural and animated. They were much impressed and excited by his departure, and wanted to ask a hundred questions about the life in the trenches. Many of them Hugh had to promise to answer when he got there. Then he would see just exactly how things were. Mrs. Britling was motherly and intelligent about his outfit. " Will you want winter things ? " she asked. . . .

But when he was alone with his father after every one had gone to bed they found themselves able to talk.

" This sort of thing seems more to us than it would be to a French family," Hugh remarked, standing on the hearth-rug.

" Yes," agreed Mr. Britling. " Their minds would be better prepared. . . . They'd have their appropriate things to say. They have been educated by the tradition of service—and '71."

Then he spoke—almost resentfully.

" The older men ought to go before you boys. Who is to carry on if a lot of you get killed ? "

Hugh reflected.   " In the stiffest battle that ever can be the odds are against getting killed," he said.

" I suppose they are."

" One in three or four in the very hottest corners."

Mr. Britling expressed no satisfaction.

" Every one is going through something of this sort."

" All the decent people, at any rate," said Mr. Britling. . . .

" It will be an extraordinary experience. Somehow it seems out of proportion—— "

" With what ? "

" With life generally. As one has known it."

" It isn't in proportion," Mr. Britling admitted.

" Incommensurables," said Hugh.

He considered his phrasing.   " It's not," he said, " as though one was going into another part of the same world, or turning up another side of the world one was used to. It is just as if one had been living in a room and one had been asked to step outside. . . . It makes me think of a queer little thing that happened when I was in London last winter. I got into Queer Company. I don't think I told you. I went to have supper with some students in Chelsea.   I hadn't been to the place before, but they seemed all right—just people like me—and everybody.   And after supper they took me on to some people *they* didn't know very well ; people who had to do with some School of Dramatic Art. There were two or three young actresses there and a singer and people of that sort, sitting about smoking cigarettes, and we began talking plays and books and picture-shows and all that stuff ; and suddenly there was a knocking at the door and some one went out and found a policeman with a warrant on the landing. They took off our host's son. . . . It had to do with a murder. . . . "

Hugh paused.   " It was the Bedford Mansions mystery. I don't suppose you remember about it or read about it at the time. He'd killed a man. . . . It doesn't matter about the particulars anyhow, but what I mean is the effect. The effect of a comfortable well-lit orderly room and the sense of harmless people—and then the door opening and the policeman and the cold draught flowing in. *Murder !* A girl who seemed to know the people well explained to me in whispers what was happening. It was like the opening of a trap-door going down into some pit you have always known was there, but never really believed in."

" I know," said Mr. Britling. " I know."

" That's just how I feel about this war business. There's no real death over here. It's laid out and boxed up. And accidents are all padded about. If one got a toss from a horse here, you'd be in bed and comfortable in no time. . . . And there ; It's like another planet. It's outside. . . . I'm going outside. . . . instead of there being no death anywhere, it is death everywhere, outside there. We shall be using our utmost wits to kill each other. A kind of reverse to this world."

Mr. Britling nodded.

" I've never seen a dead body yet. In Dower-Houseland there aren't dead bodies."

" We've kept things from you—horrid things of that sort."

" I'm not complaining," said Hugh. . . . " But—Master Hugh—the Master Hugh you kept things from—will never come back."

He went on quickly as his father raised distressed eyes to him. " I mean that anyhow *this* Hugh will never come back. Another one may. But I shall have been outside, and it will all be different. . . ."

He paused. Never had Mr. Britling been so little disposed to take up the discourse.

" Like a man," he said, seeking an image and doing no more than imitate his son's, " who goes out of a busy lighted room through a trap-door into a blizzard, to mend the roof. . . ."

For some moments neither father nor son said anything more. They had a queer sense of insurmountable insufficiency. Neither was saying what he had wanted to say to the other, but it was not clear to them now what they had to say to one another. . . .

" It's wonderful," said Mr. Britling.

Hugh could only manage : " The world has turned right over. . . ."

" The job has to be done," said Mr. Britling.

" The job has to be done," said Hugh.

The pause lengthened.

" You'll be getting up early to-morrow," said Mr. Britling. . . .

§ 8

When Mr. Britling was alone in his own room all the thoughts and feelings that had been held up downstairs began to run more and more rapidly and abundantly through his mind.

He had a feeling—every now and again in the last few years he had had the same feeling—as though he were only just beginning to discover Hugh. This perpetual rediscovery of one's children is the experience of every observant parent. He had always considered Hugh as a youth, and now a man stood over him and talked, as one man to another. And this man, this very new man, mint new and clean and clear, filled Mr. Britling with surprise and admiration.

It was as if he perceived the beauty of youth for the first time in Hugh's slender, well-balanced, khaki-clad body. There was infinite delicacy in his clear complexion, his clear eyes ; the delicately pencilled eyebrow that was so exactly like his mother's. And this thing of brightness and bravery talked as gravely and as wisely as any weather-worn, shop-soiled, old fellow. . . .

The boy was wise.

Hugh thought for himself ; he thought round and through his position, not egotistically but with a quality of responsibility. He wasn't just hero-worshipping and imitating, just spinning some self-centred romance. If he was a fair sample of his generation, then it was a better generation than Mr. Britling's had been. . . .

At that Mr. Britling's mind went off at a tangent to the grievance of the rejected volunteer. It was acutely shameful to him that all these fine lads should be going off to death and wounds while the men of forty and over lay snug at home. How stupid it was to fix things like that ! Here were the fathers, who had done their work, shot their bolts, returned some value for the costs of their education, unable to get training, unable to be of any service, shamefully safe, doing April fool work as special constables ; while their young innocents, untried, all their gathering possibilities of service unbroached, went down into the deadly trenches. . . . The war would leave the world a world of cripples and old men and children. . . .

He felt himself as a cowardly brute, fat, wheezy, out of training, sheltering behind this dear one branch of Mary's life.

He writhed with impotent humiliation. . . .

How stupidly the world is managed.

He began to fret and rage. He could not lie in peace in his bed ; he got up and prowled about his room, blundering against chairs and tables in the darkness. . . . We were too stupid to do the most obvious things ; we were sending all these boys into hardship and pitiless danger ; we were sending them ill equipped, insufficiently supported, we were sending our children through the fires to Moloch, because essentially we English were a world of indolent, pampered, sham good-humoured, old and middle-aged men. (So he distributed the intolerable load of self-accusation.) Why was he doing nothing to change things, to get them better ? What was the good of an assumed modesty, an effort at tolerance for and confidence in these boozy old lawyers, these ranting platform men, these stiff-witted officers and hide-bound officials ? They were butchering the youth of England. Old men sat out of danger contriving death for the lads in the trenches. That was the reality of the thing. " My son ! " he cried sharply in the darkness. His sense of our national deficiencies became torment-ingly, fantastically acute. It was as if all his cherished delusions had fallen from the scheme of things. . . . What was the good of making believe that up there they were planning some great counter-stroke that would end in victory ? It was as plain as daylight that they had neither the power of imagination nor the collective intelligence even to conceive of a counter-stroke. Any dull mass may resist, but only imagination can strike. Imagination ! To the end we should not strike. We might strike through the air. We might strike across the sea. We might strike hard at Gallipoli instead of dribbling inadequate armies thither as our fathers dribbled men at the Redan. . . . But the old men would sit at their tables, replete and sleepy, and shake their cunning old heads. The press would chatter and make odd ambiguous sounds like a ship-load of monkeys in a storm. The political harridans would get the wrong men appointed, would attack every possible leader with scandal and abuse and falsehood. . . .

The spirit and honour and drama had gone out of this war.

Our only hope now was exhaustion. Our only strategy was to barter blood for blood—trusting that our tank would prove the deeper. . . .

While into this tank stepped Hugh, young and smiling. . . .

The war became a nightmare vision.

§ 9

In the morning Mr. Britling's face was white from his overnight brainstorm, and Hugh's was fresh from wholesome sleep. They walked about the lawn, and Mr. Britling talked hopefully of the general outlook until it was time for them to start to the station. . . .

The little old station-master grasped the situation at once, and presided over their last hand-clasp.

" Good luck, Hugh ! " cried Mr. Britling.

" Good luck ! " cried the little old station-master.

" It's not easy aparting," he said to Mr. Britling as the train slipped down the line. " There's been many a parting hea' since this here old war began. Many. And some as won't come back again neether."

§ 10

For some days Mr. Britling could think of nothing but Hugh, and always with a dull pain at his heart. He felt as he had felt long ago while he had waited downstairs and Hugh upstairs had been under the knife of a surgeon. But this time the operation went on and still went on. At the worst his boy had but one chance in five of death or serious injury, but for a time he could think of nothing but that one chance. He felt it pressing upon his mind, pressing him down. . . .

Then instead of breaking under that pressure, he was released by the trick of the sanguine temperament. His mind turned over, abruptly, to the four chances out of five. It was like a dislocated joint slipping back into place. It was as sudden as that. He found he had adapted himself to the prospect of Hugh in mortal danger. It had become a fact established, a usual thing. He could bear with it and go about his affairs.

He went up to London, and met other men at the club in the same emotional predicament. He realised that it was neither very wonderful nor exceptionally tragic now to have a son at the front.

"My boy is in Gallipoli," said one. "It's tough work there."

"My lad's in Flanders," said Mr. Britling. "Nothing would satisfy him but the front. He's three months short of eighteen. He misstated his age."

And they went on to talk newspaper just as if the world was where it had always been.

But until a postcard came from Hugh Mr. Britling watched the postman like a love-sick girl.

Hugh wrote more frequently than his father had dared to hope, pencilled letters for the most part. It was as if he were beginning to feel an inherited need for talk, and was a little at a loss for a sympathetic ear. Park, his schoolmate, who had enlisted with him, wasn't, it seemed, a theoriser. "Park becomes a martinet," Hugh wrote. "Also he is a sergeant now, and this makes rather a gulf between us." Mr. Britling had the greatest difficulty in writing back. There were many grave deep things he wanted to say, and never did. Instead he gave elaborate details of the small affairs of the Dower House. Once or twice, with a half-unconscious imitation of his boy's style, he took a shot at the theological and philosophical hares that Hugh had started. But the exemplary letters that he composed of nights from a Father to a Son at War were never written down. It was just as well, for there are many things of that sort that are good to think and bad to say. . . .

Hugh was not very explicit about his position or daily duties. What he wrote now had to pass through the hands of a Censor, and any sort of definite information might cause the suppression of his letter. Mr. Britling conceived him for the most part as quartered some way behind the front, but in a flat, desolated country and within hearing of great guns. He assisted his imagination with the illustrated papers. Sometimes he put him farther back into pleasant old towns after the fashion of Beauvais, and imagined loitering groups in the front of cafés ; sometimes he filled in the obvious suggestions of the phrase that all the Pas de Calais was now one vast British camp. Then he crowded the picture with tethered horses and tents and grey-painted wagons, and Hugh in the foreground—bare-armed, with a bucket. . . .

Hugh's letters divided themselves pretty fairly between two main topics ; the first was the interest of the art of war, the second the reaction against warfare. "After one has got over the emotion of it," he wrote, "and when one's mind has just accepted and forgotten (as it does) the horrors and waste of it all, then I begin to perceive that war is absolutely the best game in the world. That is the real strength of war, I submit. Not as you put it in that early pamphlet of yours; ambition, cruelty, and all those things. Those things give an excuse for war, they rush timid and base people into war, but the essential matter is the hold of the thing itself upon an active imagination. It's such a big game. Instead of being fenced into a field and tied down to one set of tools as you are in almost every other game, you have all the world to play with, and you may use whatever you can use. You can use every scrap of imagination and invention that is in you. And it's wonderful. . . . But real soldiers aren't cruel. And war isn't cruel in its essence. Only in its consequences. Over here one gets hold of scraps of talk that light up things. Most of the barbarities were done—it is quite clear—by an excited civilian sort of men, men in a kind of inflamed state. The great part of the German army in the early stage of the war was really an army of demented civilians. Trained civilians no doubt, but civilians in soul. They were nice orderly clean law-abiding men suddenly torn up by the roots and flung into quite shocking conditions. They felt they were rushing at death, and that decency was at an end. They thought every Belgian had a gun behind the hedge and a knife in his trouser leg. They saw villages burning and dead people, and men smashed to bits. They lived in a kind of nightmare. They didn't know what they were doing. They did horrible things just as one does them sometimes in dreams. . . ."

He flung out his conclusion with just his mother's leaping consecutiveness. "Conscript soldiers are the ruin of war. . . . Half the Germans and a lot of the French ought never to have been brought within ten miles of a battle-field.

"What makes all this so plain are the diaries the French and English have been finding on the dead. You know at the early stage of the war every German soldier was expected to keep a diary. He was ordered to do it. The idea was to keep him interested in the war. Consequently, from the dead and wounded our people have got thousands. . . . It helps one to realise that the Germans aren't really soldiers at all. Not as our men are. They are obedient, law-abiding, intelligent people, who have been shoved into this. They have to see the war as something romantic and melodramatic, or as something moral, or as tragic fate. They have to bellow songs about 'Deutschland,' or drag in 'Gott.' They don't take to the game as our men take to the game. . . .

"I confess I'm taking to the game. I wish at times I had gone into the O.T.C. with Teddy, and got a better hold of it. I was too high-browed about this war business. I dream now of getting a commission. . . .

"That diary-hunting strategy is just the sort of thing that makes this war intellectually fascinating. Everything is being thought out and then tried over that can possibly make victory. The Germans go in for psychology much more than we do, just as they go in for war more than we do, but they don't seem to be really clever about it. So they set out to make all their men understand the war, while our chaps are singing ' Tipperary.' But what the men put down aren't the beautiful things they ought to put down ; most of them shove down lists of their meals, some of the diaries are all just lists of things eaten, and a lot of them have written the most damning stuff about outrages and looting. Which the French are translating and publishing. The Germans would give any-thing now to get back these silly diaries. And now they have made an order that no one shall go into battle with any written papers at all. . . . Our people got so keen on documenting and the value of chance writings, that one of the principal things to do after a German attack had failed had been to hook in the documentary dead, and find out what they had on them. . . . It's a curious sport, this body-fishing. You have a sort of triple hook on a rope, and you throw it and drag. They do the same. The other day one body near Hooghe was hooked by both sides, and they had a tug of war. With a sharpshooter or so cutting in whenever our men got too excited. Several men were hit. The Irish—it was an Irish regiment—got him—or at least they got the better part of him. . . .

" Now that I am a sergeant, Parks talks to me again about all these things, and we have a first lieutenant too keen to resist such technical details. They are purely technical details. You must take them as that. One does not think of the dead body as a man recently deceased, who had perhaps a wife and business connections and a weakness for oysters or pale brandy. Or as something that laughed and cried and didn't like getting hurt. That would spoil everything. One thinks of him merely as a uniform with marks upon it that will tell us what kind of stuff we have against us, and possibly with papers that will give us a hint of how far he and his lot are getting sick of the whole affair. . . .

" There's a kind of hardening not only of the body but of the mind through all this life out here. One is living on a different level. You know just before I came away — you talked of Dower-House-land—and outside. This is outside. It's different. Our men here are kind enough still to little things—kittens or birds or flowers. Behind the front, for example, everywhere there are Tommy gardens. Some are quite bright little patches. But it's just nonsense to suppose we are tender to the wounded up here—and, putting it plainly, there isn't a scrap of pity left for the enemy. Not a scrap. Not a trace of such feeling. They were tender about the wounded in the early days—men tell me—and reverent about the dead. It's all gone now. There have been atrocities, gas, unforgettable things. Everything is harder. Our people are inclined now to laugh at a man who gets hit, and to be annoyed at a man with a troublesome wound. The other day, they say, there was a big dead German outside the Essex trenches. He became a nuisance, and he was dragged in and taken behind the line and buried. After he was buried, a kindly soul was putting a board over him with ' Somebody's Fritz ' on it, when a shell burst close by. It blew the man with the board a dozen yards and wounded him, and it restored Fritz to the open air. He was lifted clean out. He flew head over heels like a wind-mill. This was regarded as a tremendous joke against the men who had been at the pains of burying him. For a time nobody else would touch Fritz, who was now some yards behind his original grave. Then as he got worse and worse he was buried again by some devoted sanitarians, and this time the inscription was ' Somebody's Fritz. R.I.P.' And as luck would have it, he was spun up again. In pieces. The trench howled with laughter and cries of ' Good old Fritz ! ' ' This isn't the Resurrection, Fritz.' . . .

" Another thing that appeals to the sunny humour of the trenches as a really delicious practical joke is the trick of the fuses. We have two kinds of fuse, a slow-burning fuse such as is used for hand-grenades and suchlike things, a sort of yard-a-minute fuse, and a rapid fuse that goes a hundred yards a second—for firing mines and so on. The latter is carefully distinguished from the former by a conspicuous red thread. Also, as you know, it is the habit of the enemy and ourselves when the trenches are near enough, to enliven each other by the casting of homely but effective hand-grenades made out of tins. When a grenade drops in a British trench somebody seizes it instantly and throws it back. To hoist the German with his own petard is particularly sweet to the British mind. When a grenade drops into a German trench everybody runs. (At least that is what I am told happens by the men from our trenches ; though possibly each side has its exceptions.) If the bomb explodes, it explodes. If it doesn't, Hans and Fritz presently come creeping back to see what has happened. Sometimes the fuse hasn't caught properly, it has been thrown by a nervous man ; or it hasn't burned properly. Then Hans or Fritz puts in a new fuse and sends it back with loving care. To hoist the Briton with his own petard is particularly sweet to the German mind. . . . But here it is that military genius comes in. Some gifted spirit in our side procured (probably by larceny) a length of mine fuse, the rapid sort, and spent a laborious day removing the red thread and making it into the likeness of its slow brother. Then bits of it were attached to tin-bombs and shied—unlit of course—into the German trenches. A long but happy pause followed. I can see the chaps holding themselves in. Hans and Fritz were understood to be creeping back, to be examining the unlit fuse, to be

applying a light thereunto, in order to restore it to its maker
after their custom. . . .

"A loud bang in the German trenches indicated the moment
of lighting, and the exit of Hans and Fritz to worlds less
humorous.

"The genius in the British trenches went on with the preparation of the next surprise bomb—against the arrival of
Kurt and Karl. . . .

"Hans, Fritz, Kurt, Karl, Michael and Wilhelm; it went
for quite a long time before they grew suspicious. . . .

"You once wrote that all fighting ought to be done nowadays by metal soldiers. I perceive, my dear Daddy, that all
real fighting is. . . ."

§ 11

Not all Hugh's letters were concerned with these grim
technicalities. It was not always that news and gossip came
along; it was rare that a young man with a commission would
condescend to talk shop to two young men without one; there
were few newspapers and fewer maps, and even in France and
within sound of guns, Hugh could presently find warfare
almost as much a bore as it had been at times in England.
But his criticism of military methods died away. "Things
are done better out here," he remarked, and "We're nearer
reality here. I begin to respect my Captain. Who is developing
a sense of locality. Happily for our prospects." And in another
place he speculated in an oddly characteristic manner whether
he was getting used to the army way, whether he was beginning to see the sense of the army way, or whether it really
was that that army way braced up nearer and nearer to
efficiency as it got nearer to the enemy. "And here one hasn't
the haunting feeling that war is after all an hallucination.
It's already common sense and the business of life. . . .

"In England I always had a sneaking idea that I had
'dressed up' in my uniform. . . .

"I never dreamt before I came here how much war is a
business of waiting about and going through duties and exercises that were only too obviously a means of preventing our
discovering just how much waiting about we were doing.
I suppose there is no great harm in describing the place I am
in here; it's a kind of scenery that is somehow all of a piece
with the life we lead day by day. It is a village that has been
only partly smashed up; it has never been fought through,
indeed the Germans were never within two miles of it, but it
was shelled intermittently for months before we made our
advance. Almost all the houses are still standing, but there is
not a window left with a square foot of glass in the place. One
or two houses have been burned out, and one or two are just
as though they had been kicked to pieces by a lunatic giant.
We sleep in batches of four or five on the floors of the rooms;

there are very few inhabitants about, but the village inn still goes on. It has one poor weary billiard-table, very small with very big balls, and the cues are without tops ; it is The Amusement of the place. Ortheris does miracles at it. When he leaves the army he says he's going to be a marker, ' a b———y marker.' The country about us is flat—featureless—desolate. How I long for hills, even for Essex mud hills. Then the road runs on towards the front, a brick road frightfully worn, lined with poplars. Just at the end of the village mechanical transport ends and there is a kind of depot from which all the stuff goes up by mules or men or bicycles to the trenches. It is the only movement in the place, and I have spent hours watching men shift grub or ammunition or lending them a hand. All day one hears guns, a kind of thud at the stomach, and now and then one sees an aeroplane, very high and small. Just beyond this point there is a group of poplars which have been punished by a German shell. They are broken off and splintered in the most astonishing way ; all split and ravelled out like the end of a cane that has been broken and twisted to get the ends apart. The choice of one's leisure is to watch the A.S.C. or play football, twenty a side, or sit about indoors, or stand in the doorway, or walk down to the Estaminet and wait five or six deep for the billiard-table. Ultimately one sits. And so you get these unconscionable letters."

" Unconscionable ! " said Mr. Britling.   " Of course—he will grow out of that sort of thing."

" And he'll write some day, sure enough. He'll write."

He went on reading the letter.

" We read, of course. But there never could be a library here big enough to keep us going. We can do with all sorts of books, but I don't think the ordinary sensational novel is quite the catch it was for a lot of them in peace-time. Some break towards serious reading in the oddest fashion. Old Park, for example, says he wants books you can chew ; he is reading a cheap edition of ' The Origin of Species.' He used to regard Florence Warden and William le Queux as the supreme delights of print. I wish you could send him Metchnikoff's ' Nature of Man ' or Pearson's ' Ethic of Freethought.' I feel I am building up his tender mind. Not for me though, Daddy. Nothing of that sort for me. These things take people differently. What I want here is literary opium. I want something about fauns and nymphs in broad low glades. I would like to read Spenser's ' Faerie Queen.' I don't think I have read it, and yet I have a very distinct impression of knights and dragons and sorcerers and wicked magic ladies moving through a sort of Pre-Raphaelite tapestry scenery—only with a light on them. I could do with some Hewlett of the ' Forest Lovers ' kind. Or with Joseph Conrad in his Kew Palm-house mood. And there is a book, I once looked into it at a man's rooms in London ; I don't know the title, but it was by Richard Garnett, and it was all about gods who were in reduced circumstances but amidst sunny picturesque scenery. Scenery without steel or poles or wire. A thing after the manner of Heine's ' Florentine Nights.' Any books about Greek gods would be welcome, anything about temples of ivory-coloured stone and purple seas, red caps, chests of jewels, and lizards in the sun. I wish there was another ' Thaïs.' The men here are getting a kind of newspaper sheet of literature scraps called *The Times* Broadsheets. Snippets, but mostly from good stuff. They're small enough to stir the appetite, but not to satisfy it. Rather an irritant—and one wants no irritant. . . . I used to imagine reading was meant to be a stimulant. Out here it has to be an anodyne. . . .

"Have you heard of a book called ' Tom Cringle's Log ' ?

"War is an exciting game—that I never wanted to play. It excites once in a couple of months. And the rest of it is dirt and muddle and boredom, and smashed houses and spoiled roads and muddy scenery and boredom, and the lumbering along of supplies and the lumbering back of the wounded and weary—and boredom, and continual vague guessing of how it will end and boredom and boredom and boredom, and thinking of the work you were going to do and the travel you were going to have, and the waste of life and the waste of days and boredom, and splintered poplars and stink, everywhere stink and dirt and boredom. . . . And all because these accursed Prussians were too stupid to understand what a boredom they were getting ready when they pranced and stuck their chests out and earned the praises of Mr. Thomas Carlyle. . . . *Gott strafe Deutschland.* . . . So send me some books, books of dreams, books about China and the willow-pattern plate and the golden age and fairyland. And send them soon and address them very carefully. . . ."

§ 12

Teddy's misadventure happened while figs were still ripening on Mr. Britling's big tree. It was Cissie brought the news to Mr. Britling. She came up to the Dower House with a white, scared face.

"I've come up for the letters," she said. "There's bad news of Teddy, and Letty's rather in a state."

"He's not—— ? " Mr. Britling left the word unsaid.

"He's wounded and missing," said Cissie.

"A prisoner ! " said Mr. Britling.

"And wounded. *How*, we don't know."

She added : " Letty has gone to telegraph."

"Telegraph to whom ? "

"To the War Office, to know what sort of wound he has. They tell nothing. It's disgraceful."

"It doesn't say *severely* ? "

" It says just nothing. Wounded and missing ! Surely they ought to give us particulars."

Mr. Britling thought. His first thought was that now news might come at any time that Hugh was wounded and missing. Then he set himself to persuade Cissie that the absence of " seriously " meant that Teddy was only quite bearably wounded, and that if he was also " missing " it might be difficult for the War Office to ascertain at once just exactly what she wanted to know. But Cissie said merely that " Letty was in an awful state," and after Mr. Britling had given her a few instructions for his typing, he went down to the cottage to repeat these mitigatory considerations to Letty. He found her much whiter than her sister, and in a state of cold indignation with the War Office. It was clear she thought that organization ought to have taken better care of Teddy. She had a curious effect of feeling that something was being kept back from her. It was manifest too that she was disposed to regard Mr. Britling as biased in favour of the authorities.

" At any rate," she said, " they could have answered my telegram promptly. I sent it at eight. Two hours of scornful silence."

This fierce, strained, unjust Letty was a new aspect to Mr. Britling. Her treatment of his proffered consolations made him feel slightly henpecked.

" And just fancy ! " she said. " They have no means of knowing if he has arrived safely on the German side. How can they know he is a prisoner without knowing that ? "

" But the word is ' missing.' "

" That *means* a prisoner," said Letty uncivilly. . . .

§ 13

Mr. Britling returned to the Dower House perplexed and profoundly disturbed. He had a distressful sense that things were far more serious with Teddy than he had tried to persuade Letty they were ; that " wounded and missing " meant indeed a man abandoned to very sinister probabilities. He was distressed for Teddy, and still more acutely distressed for Mrs. Teddy, whose every note and gesture betrayed suppositions even more sinister than his own. And that preposterous sense of liability, because he had helped Teddy to get his commission, was more distrustful than it had ever been. He was surprised that Letty had not assailed him with railing accusations.

And this event had wiped off at one sweep all the protective scab of habituation that had gathered over the wound of Hugh's departure. He was back face to face with the one evil chance in five. . . .

In the hall there was lying a letter from Hugh that had come by the second post. It was a relief even to see it. . . .

Hugh had had his first spell in the trenches.

Before his departure he had promised his half-brothers a long and circumstantial account of what the trenches were really like. Here he redeemed his promise. He had evidently written with the idea that the letter would be handed over to them.

"Tell the bruddykinses I'm glad they're going to Brinsmead school. Later on, I suppose, they will go on to Statesminster. I suppose that you don't care to send them so far in these troubled times. . . .

"And now about those trenches—as I promised. The great thing to grasp is that they are narrow. They are a sort of negative wall. They are more like giant cracks in the ground than anything else. . . . But perhaps I had better begin by telling how we got there. We started about one in the morning ladened up with everything you can possibly imagine on a soldier, and in addition I had a kettle—filled with water—most of the chaps had bundles of firewood, and some had extra bread. We marched out of our quarters along the road for a mile or more, and then we took the fields, and presently came to a crest and dropped into a sort of maze of zigzag trenches going up to the front trench. These trenches, you know, are much deeper than one's height; you don't see anything. It's like walking along a mud walled passage. You just trudge along them in single file. Every now and then some one stumbles into a soakaway for rain-water or swears at a soft place, or somebody blunders into the man in front of him. This seems to go on for hours and hours. It certainly went on for an hour; so I suppose we did two or three miles of it. At one place we crossed a dip in the ground and a ditch, and the trench was built up with sand-bags up to the ditch and there was a plank. Overhead there were stars, and now and then a sort of blaze thing they send up lit up the edge of the trench and gave one a glimpse of a tree-top or a factory roof far away. Then for a time it was more difficult to go on because you were blinded. Suddenly just when you were believing that this sort of trudge was going on for ever, we were in the support trenches behind the firing-line, and found the men we were relieving ready to come back.

"And the firing-line itself? Just the same sort of ditch with a parapet of sand-bags, but with dugouts, queer big holes helped out with sleepers from a nearby railway track, opening into it from behind. Dugouts vary a good deal. Many are rather like the cubby-house we made at the end of the orchard last summer; only the walls are thick enough to stand a high-explosive shell. The best dugout in our company's bit of front was quite a dressy affair with some wood-work and a door got from the ruins of a house twenty or thirty yards behind us. It had a stove in it too, and a chimbley, and pans to keep water in. It was the best dugout for

miles. This house had a well, and there was a special trench
ran back to that, and all day long there was a coming and
going for water. There had once been a pump over the well,
but a shell had smashed that. . . .

" And now you expect me to tell of Germans and the fight
and shelling and all sorts of things. *I haven't seen a live German* ; I haven't been within two hundred yards of a shell
burst, there has been no attack and I haven't got the V.C.
I have made myself muddy beyond describing ; I've been
working all the time, but I've not fired a shot or fought a
ha'porth. We were busy all the time—just at work, repairing
the parapet, which had to be done gingerly because of snipers,
bringing our food in from the rear in big carriers, getting
water, pushing our trench out from an angle slantingways
forward. Getting meals, clearing up and so on takes a lot of
time. We make tea in big kettles in the big dugout, which
two whole companies use for their cooking, and carry them
with a pole through the handles to our platoons. We wash
up and wash and shave. Dinner preparation (and consumption)
takes two or three hours. Tea too uses up time. It's like
camping out and picnicking in the park. This first time (and
next too) we have been mixed with some Sussex men who
have been here longer and know the business. . . . It works
out that we do most of the fatigue. Afterwards we shall go
up alone to a pitch of our own. . . .

" But all the time you want to know about the Germans.
They are a quarter of a mile away at this part, or nearly
a quarter of a mile. When you snatch a peep at them it is
like a low parti-coloured stone wall—only the stones are
sand-bags. The Germans have them black and white, so that
you cannot tell which are loopholes and which are black bags.
Our people haven't been so clever—and the War Office love
of uniformity has given us only white bags. No doubt it looks
neater. But it makes our loopholes plain. For a time black
sand-bags were refused. The Germans sniped at us, but not
very much. Only one of our lot was hit, by a chance shot
that came through the sand-bag at the top of the parapet.
He just had a cut in the neck which didn't prevent his walking
back. They shelled the trenches half a mile to the left of us
though, and it looked pretty hot. The sand-bags flew about.
But the men lie low, and it looks worse than it is. The weather
was fine and pleasant, as General French always says. And
after three days and nights of cramped existence and petty
chores, one in the foremost trench and two a little way back,
and then two days in support, we came back—and here we
are again waiting for our second Go.

" The night-time is perhaps a little more nervy than the
day. You get your head up and look about, and see the flat
dim country with its ruined houses and its lumps of stuff
that are dead bodies and its long vague lines of sand-bags,

and the search-lights going like white windmill arms and an occasional flare or star shell. And you have a nasty feeling of people creeping and creeping all night between the trenches. . . .

"Some of us went out to strengthen a place in the parapet that was only one sand-bag thick, where a man had been hit during the day. We made it four bags thick right up to the top. All the while you were doing it, you dreaded to find yourself in the white glare of a search-light, and you had a feeling that something would hit you suddenly from behind. I had to make up my mind not to look round, or I should have kept on looking round. . . . Also our chaps kept shooting over us, within a foot of one's head. Just to persuade the Germans that we were not out of the trench. . . .

"Nothing happened to us. We got back all right. It was silly to have left that parapet only one bag thick. There's the truth, and all of my first time in the trenches.

"And the Germans?

"I tell you there was no actual fighting at all. I never saw the head of one.

"But now see what a good bruddykins I am. I have seen a fight, a real exciting fight, and I have kept it to the last to tell you about. . . . It was a fight in the air. And the British won. It began with a German machine appearing, very minute and high, sailing towards our lines a long way to the left. We could tell it was a German because of the black cross; they decorate every aeroplane with a black Iron Cross on its wings and tail; that our officer could see with his glasses. (He let me look.) Suddenly whack, whack, whack came a line of little puffs of smoke behind it, and then one in front of it, which meant that our anti-aircraft guns were having a go at it. Then, as suddenly, Archibald stopped, and we could see the British machine buzzing across the path of the German. It was just like two birds circling in the air. Or wasps. They buzzed like wasps. There was a little crackling—like brushing your hair in frosty weather. They were shooting at each other. Then our lieutenant called out, 'Hit, by Jove!' and handed the glasses to Park and instantly wanted them back. He says he saw bits of the machine flying off.

"When he said that you could fancy you saw it too, up there in the blue.

"Anyhow the little machine cocked itself up on end. Rather slowly. . . . Then down it came like dropping a knife. . . .

"It made you say 'Ooooo!' to see that dive. It came down, seemed to get a little bit under control, and then dive down again. You could hear the engine roar louder and louder as it came down. I never saw anything fall so fast. We saw it hit the ground among a lot of smashed-up buildings on the crest behind us. It went right over and flew to pieces, all to smithereens. . . .

" It hurt your nose to see it hit the ground. . . .

" Somehow—I was sort of overcome by the thought of the men in that dive. I was trying to imagine how they felt it. From the moment when they realised they were going.

" What on earth must it have seemed like at last ?

" They fell seven thousand feet, the men say ; some say nine thousand feet. A mile and a half !

" But all the chaps were cheering. . . . And there was our machine hanging in the sky. You wanted to reach up and pat it on the back. It went up higher and away towards the German lines, as though it was looking for another German. It seemed to go now quite slowly. It was an English machine, though for a time we weren't sure ; our machines are done in tri-colour just as though they were French. But everybody says it was English. It was one of our crack fighting-machines, and from first to last it has put down seven Germans. . . . And that's really all the fighting there was. There has been fighting here ; a month ago. There are perhaps a dozen dead Germans lying out still in front of the lines. Little twisted figures, like overthrown scarecrows, about a hundred yards away. But that is all.

" No, the trenches have disappointed me. They are a scene of tiresome domesticity. They aren't a patch on our quarters in the rear. There isn't the traffic. I've not found a single excuse for firing my rifle. I don't believe I shall ever fire my rifle at an enemy—ever. . . .

" You've seen Rendezvous' fresh promotion, I suppose ? He's one of the men the young officers talk about. Everybody believes in him. Do you remember how Manning used to hide from him ? . . . "

§ 14

Mr. Britling read this through, and then his thoughts went back to Teddy's disappearance and then returned to Hugh. The youngster was right in the front now, and one had to steel oneself to the possibilities of the case. Somehow Mr. Britling had not expected to find Hugh so speedily in the firing-line, though he would have been puzzled to find a reason why this should not have happened. But he found he had to begin the lesson of stoicism all over again.

He read the letter twice, and then he searched for some indication of its date. He suspected that letters were sometimes held back. . . .

Four days later this suspicion was confirmed by the arrival of another letter from Hugh in which he told of his second spell in the trenches. This time things had been much more lively. They had been heavily shelled and there had been a German attack. And this time he was writing to his father, and wrote more freely. He had scribbled in pencil.

" Things are much livelier here than they were. Our guns

are getting to work. They are firing in spells of an hour or so, three or four times a day, and just when they seem to be leaving off they begin again. The Germans suddenly got the range of our trenches the day before yesterday, and began to pound us with high explosive. . . . Well, it's trying. You never seem quite to know when the next bang is coming, and that keeps your nerves hung up ; it seems to tighten your muscles and tire you. We've done nothing but lie low all day, and I feel as weary as if I had marched twenty miles. Then ' whop ' one's near you, and there is a flash and everything flies. It's a mad sort of smash-about. One came much too close to be pleasant ; as near as the old oil-jars are from the barn court door. It bowled me clean over and sent a lot of gravel over me. When I got up there was twenty yards of trench smashed into a mere hole, and men lying about, and some of them groaning and one three-quarters buried. We had to turn to and get them out as well as we could. . . .

" I felt stunned and insensitive ; it was well to have something to do. . . .

" Our guns behind felt for the German guns. It was the damnedest racket. Like giant lunatics smashing about amidst colossal pots and pans. They fired different sorts of shells ; stink shells as well as Jack Johnsons, and though we didn't get much of that at our corner there was a stink of chlorine in the air all through the afternoon. Most of the stink shells fell short. We hadn't masks, but we rigged up a sort of protection with our handkerchiefs. And it didn't amount to very much. It was rather like the chemistry room after Heinrich and the kids had been mixing things. Most of the time I was busy helping with the men who had got hurt. Suddenly there came a lull. Then some one said the Germans were coming, and I had a glimpse of them.

" You don't look at anything steadily while the guns are going. When a big gun goes off or a shell bursts anywhere near you, you seem neither to see nor hear for a moment. You keep on being intermittently stunned. One sees in a kind of flicker in between the impacts. . . .

" Well, there they were. This time I saw them. They were coming out and running a little way and dropping, and our shell was bursting among them and behind them. A lot of it was going too far. I watched what our men were doing, and poured out a lot of cartridges ready to my hand and began to blaze away. Half the German attack never came out of their trench. If they really intended business against us, which I doubt, they were half-hearted in carrying it out. They didn't show for five minutes, and they left two or three score men on the ground. Whenever we saw a man wriggle we were told to fire at him ; it might be an unwounded man trying to crawl back. For a time our guns gave them beans. Then it was practically over, but about sunset their guns got back at us again, and the artillery fight went on until it was moonlight. The chaps in our third company caught it rather badly, and then our guns seemed to find something and get the upper hand. . . .

" In the night some of our men went out to repair the wire entanglements, and one man crawled half-way to the enemy trenches to listen. But I had done my bit for the day, and I was supposed to sleep in the dugout. I was far too excited to sleep. All my nerves were jumping about, and my mind was like a lot of flying fragments flying about very fast. . . .

" They shelled us again next day and our tea dixy was hit ; so that we didn't get any tea. . . .

" I slept thirty hours after I got back here. And now I am slowly digesting these experiences. Most of our fellows are. My mind and nerves have been rather bumped and bruised by the shelling, but not so much as you might think. I feel as though I'd presently not think very much of it. Some of our men have got the stun of it a lot more than I have. It gets at the older men more. Everybody says that. The men of over thirty-five don't recover from a shelling for weeks. They go about—sort of hesitatingly. . . .

" Life is very primitive here—which doesn't mean that one is getting down to anything fundamental, but only going back to something immediate and simple. It's fetching and carrying and getting water and getting food and going up to the firing-line and coming back. One goes on for weeks, and then one day one finds oneself crying out, ' What is all this for ? When is it to end ? ' I seemed to have something ahead of me before this war began, education, science, work, discoveries ; all sorts of things ; but it is hard to feel that there is anything ahead of us here. . . .

" Somehow the last spell in the fire trench has shaken up my mind a lot. I was getting used to the war before, but now I've got back to my original amazement at the whole business. I find myself wondering what we are really up to, why the war began, why we were caught into this amazing routine. It looks, it feels orderly, methodical, purposeful. Our officers give us orders and get their orders, and the men back there get their orders. Everybody is getting orders. Back, I suppose, to Lord Kitchener. It goes on for weeks with the effect of being quite sane and intended and the right thing, and then, then suddenly it comes whacking into one's head, ' But this— this is utterly *mad !* ' This going to and fro and to and fro and to and fro ; this monotony which breaks ever and again into violence—violence that never gets anywhere—is exactly the life that a lunatic leads. Melancholia and mania. . . . It's just a collective obsession—by war. The world is really quite mad. I happen to be having just one gleam of sanity, that won't last after I have finished this letter. I suppose when an individual man goes mad and gets out of the window because he imagines the door is magically impossible, and dances about in the street without his trousers, jabbing at passers-by with a toasting fork, he has just the same sombre sense of unavoidable necessity that we have, all of us, when we go off with our packs into the trenches. . . .

" It's only by an effort that I can recall how life felt in the spring of 1914. Do you remember Heinrich and his attempt to make a table chart of the roses, so that we could sit outside the barn and read the names of all the roses in the barn court ? Like the mountain charts they have on tables in Switzerland. What an inconceivable thing that is now ! For all I know I shot Heinrich the other night. For all I know he is one of the lumps that we counted after the attack went back.

" It's a queer thing, Daddy, but I have a sort of *seditious* feeling in writing things like this. One gets to feel that it is wrong to think. It's the effect of discipline. Of being part of a machine. Still, I doubt if I ought to think. If one really looks into things in this spirit, where is it going to take us ? Ortheris—his real name by-the-by is Arthur Jewell—hasn't any of these troubles. ' The b——y Germans butted into Belgium,' he says. ' We've got to 'oof 'em out again. That's all abart it. Leastways it's all *I* know. . . . I don't know nothing about Serbia, I don't know nothing about anything, except that the Germans got to stop this sort of Gime for Everlasting, Amen.' . . .

" Sometimes I think he's righter than I am. Sometimes I think he is only madder."

§ 15

These letters weighed heavily upon Mr. Britling's mind. He perceived that this precociously wise, subtle youngster of his was now close up to the line of injury and death, going to and fro from it, in a perpetual fluctuating danger. At any time now in the day or night the evil thing might wing its way to him. If Mr. Britling could have prayed, he would have prayed for Hugh. He began and never finished some ineffectual prayers.

He tried to persuade himself of a Roman stoicism ; that he would be sternly proud, sternly satisfied, if this last sacrifice for his country was demanded from him. He perceived he was merely humbugging himself. . . .

This war had no longer the simple greatness that would make any such stern happiness possible. . . .

The disaster to Teddy and Mrs. Teddy hit him hard. He winced at the thought of Mrs. Teddy's white face ; the unspoken accusation in her eyes. He felt he could never bring himself to say his one excuse to her : " I did not keep Hugh back. If I had done that, then you might have the right to blame."

If he had overcome every other difficulty in the way to an heroic pose there was still Hugh's unconquerable lucidity of outlook. War *was* a madness. . . .

But what else was to be done ? What else could be done ? We could not give in to Germany. If a lunatic struggles, sane men must struggle too. . . .

Mr. Britling had ceased to write about the war at all. All his later writings about it had been abandoned unfinished. He could not imagine them counting, affecting any one, producing any effect. Indeed he was writing now very intermittently. His contributions to *The Times* had fallen away. He was perpetually thinking now about the war, about life and death, about the religious problems that had seemed so remote in the days of the peace ; but none of his thinking would become clear and definite enough for writing. All the clear stars of his mind were hidden by the stormy clouds of excitement that the daily newspaper perpetually renewed and by the daily developments of life. And just as his professional income shrank before his mental confusion and impotence, the private income that came from his and his wife's investments became uncertain. She had had two thousand pounds in the Constantinople loan, seven hundred in debentures of the Ottoman railway ; he had held similar sums in two Hungarian and one Bulgarian loan. There seemed no limit set to the possibilities of shrinkage of capital and income. Income tax had leaped to colossal dimensions, the cost of most things had risen, and the tangle of life was now increased by the need for retrenchments and economies. He decided that Gladys, his facetiously named automobile, was a luxury, and sold her for a couple of hundred pounds. He lost his gardener, who had gone to higher-priced work with a miller, and he had great trouble to replace him, so that the garden became disagreeably unkempt and unsatisfactory. He had to give up his frequent trips to London. He was obliged to defer Statesminster for the boys. For a time at any rate they must go as day boys to Brinsmead. At every point he met this uncongenial consideration of ways and means. For years now he had gone easy, lived with a certain self-indulgence. It was extraordinarily vexatious to have one's greater troubles for one's country and one's son and one's faith crossed and complicated by these little troubles of the extra sixpence and the untimely bill.

What worried his mind perhaps more than anything else was his gradual loss of touch with the essential issues of the war. At first the militarism, the aggression of Germany, had seemed so bad that he could not see the action of Britain and her allies as anything but entirely righteous. He had seen the war plainly and simply in the phrase. " Now this militarism must end." He had seen Germany as a system, as imperialism and junkerism, as a callous materialist aggression, as the spirit that makes war, and the Allies as the protest of humanity against all these evil things.

Insensibly, in spite of himself, this first version of the war was giving place to another. The tawdry, rhetorical German Emperor, who had been the great antagonist at the outset, the last upholder of Cæsarism, God's anointed with the withered arm and the mailed fist, had receded from the foreground of the picture ; that truer Germany which is thought and system, which is the will to do things thoroughly, the Germany of Ostwald and the once rejected Hindenburg, was coming to the fore. It made no apology for the errors and crimes that had been imposed upon it by its Hohenzollern leadership, but it fought now to save itself from the destruction and division that would be its inevitable lot if it accepted defeat too easily ; fought to hold out, fought for a second chance, with discipline, with skill and patience, with a steadfast will. It fought with science, it fought with economy, with machines and thought against all too human antagonists. It necessitated an implacable hostility, but also it commanded respect. Against it fought three great peoples with as fine a will ; but they had neither the unity, the habitual discipline, nor the science of Germany, and it was the latter defect that became more and more the distressful matter of Mr. Britling's thoughts. France after her initial experiences, after her first reeling month, had risen from the very verge of defeat to a steely splendour of resolution, but England and Russia, those twin slack giants, still wasted force, were careless, negligent, uncertain. Everywhere up and down the scale, from the stupidity of the uniform sand-bags and Hugh's young officer who would not use a map, to the general conception and direction of the war, Mr. Britling's inflamed and oversensitised intelligence perceived the same bad qualities for which he had so often railed upon his countrymen in the days of the peace, that impatience, that indolence, that wastefulness and inconclusiveness, that failure to grip issues and do obviously necessary things. The same lax qualities that had brought England so close to the supreme imbecility of a civil war in Ireland in July, 1914, were now muddling and prolonging the war, and postponing, it might be for ever, the victory that had seemed so certain only a year ago. The politician still intrigued, the ineffectives still directed. Against brains used to the utmost their fight was a stupid thrusting forth of men and men and yet more men, men badly trained, under-equipped, stupidly led. A press clamour for invention and scientific initiative was stifled under a committee of elderly celebrities and eminent dufferdom ; from the outset, the Ministry of Munitions seemed under the influence of the " business man." . . .

It is true that righteousness should triumph over the tyrant and the robber, but have carelessness and incapacity any right to triumph over capacity and foresight ? Men were

coming now to dark questionings between this intricate choice.
And, indeed, was our cause all righteousness ?

There surely is the worst doubt of all for a man whose son
is facing death.

Were we indeed standing against tyranny for freedom ?

There came drifting to Mr. Britling's ears a confusion of
voices, voices that told of reaction, of the schemes of employers
to best the trade-unions, of greedy shippers and greedy house-
landlords reaping their harvest, of waste and treason in the
very households of the Ministry, of religious cant and in-
tolerance at large, of self-advertisement written in letters of
blood, of forestalling and jobbery, of irrational and exasperating oppressions in India and Egypt. . . . It came with a shock
to him, too, that Hugh should see so little else than madness
in the war, and have so pitiless a realisation of its essential
futility. The boy forced his father to see—what indeed all
along he had been seeing more and more clearly. The war,
even by the standards of adventure and conquest, had long
since become a monstrous absurdity. Some way there must
be out of this bloody entanglement that was yielding victory
to neither side, that was yielding nothing but waste and death
beyond all precedent. The vast majority of people everywhere
must be desiring peace, willing to buy peace at any reasonable
price, and in all the world it seemed there was insufficient
capacity to end the daily butchery and achieve the peace that
was so universally desired, the peace that would be anything
better than a breathing space for further warfare. . . . Every
day came the papers with the balanced story of battles, losses,
destructions, ships sunk, towns smashed. And never a decision, never a sign of decision.

One Saturday afternoon Mr. Britling found himself with
Mrs. Britling at Claverings. Lady Homartyn was in mourning
for her two nephews, the Glassington boys, who had both
been killed, one in Flanders, the other in Gallipoli. Raeburn
was there too, despondent and tired-looking. There were three
young men in khaki, one with the red of a staff officer ; there
were two or three women whom Mr. Britling had not met
before, and Miss Sharsper, the novelist, fresh from nursing
experience among the convalescents in the south of France.
But he was disgusted to find that the gathering was dominated
by his old antagonist, Lady Frensham, unsubdued, unaltered,
rampant over them all, arrogant, impudent, insulting. She
was in mourning, she had the most splendid black furs Mr.
Britling had ever seen ; her large triumphant profile came
out of them like the head of a vulture out of its ruff ; her
elder brother was a wounded prisoner in Germany, her second
was dead ; it would seem that hers were the only sacrifices
the war had yet extorted from any one. She spoke as though
it gave her the sole right to criticise the war or claim compensation for the war.

Her incurable propensity to split the country, to make mischievous accusations against classes and districts and public servants, was having full play. She did her best to provoke Mr. Britling into a dispute, and throw some sort of imputation upon his patriotism as distinguished from her own noisy and intolerant conceptions of "loyalty."

She tried him first with conscription. She threw out insults at the shirkers and the "funk classes." All the middle-class people clung on to their wretched little businesses, made any sort of excuse. . . .

Mr. Britling was stung to defend them. "A business," he said acidly, "isn't like land, which waits and grows rich for its owner. And these people can't leave ferrety little agents behind them when they go off to serve. Tens of thousands of middle-class men have ruined themselves and flung away every prospect they had in the world to go to this war."

"And scores of thousands haven't!" said Lady Frensham. "They are the men I'm thinking of." . . .

Mr. Britling ran through a little list of aristocratic stay-at-homes that began with a duke.

"And not a soul speaks to him in consequence," she said.

She shifted her attack to the Labour people. They would rather see the country defeated than submit to a little discipline.

"Because they have no faith in the house of lawyers or the house of landlords," said Mr. Britling. "Who can blame them?"

She proceeded to tell everybody what she would do with strikers. She would give them "short shrift." She would give them a taste of the Prussian way—homœopathic treatment. "But of course old vote-catching Asquith daren't—he daren't!" Mr. Britling opened his mouth and said nothing; he was silenced. The men in khaki listened respectfully but ambiguously ; one of the younger ladies it seemed was entirely of Lady Frensham's way of thinking, and anxious to show it. The good lady having now got her hands upon the Cabinet proceeded to deal faithfully with its two-and-twenty members. Winston Churchill had overridden Lord Fisher upon the question of Gallipoli, and incurred terrible responsibilities. Lord Haldane—she called him "Tubby Haldane"— was a convicted traitor. "The man's a German out and out. Oh ! what if he hasn't a drop of German blood in his veins ? He's a German by choice—which is worse."

"I thought he had a certain capacity for organisation," said Mr. Britling.

"We don't want his organisation, and we don't want *him*," said Lady Frensham.

Mr. Britling pleaded for particulars of the late Lord Chancellor's treasons. There were no particulars. It was just an idea the good lady had got into her head, that had got into

a number of accessible heads. There was only one strong man
in all the country now, Lady Frensham insisted. That was Sir
Edward Carson.

Mr. Britling jumped in his chair.

" But has he ever done anything ? " he cried, " except
embitter Ireland ? "

Lady Frensham did not hear that question. She pursued
her glorious theme. Lloyd George, who had once been worthy
only of the gallows, was now the sole minister fit to put beside
her hero. He had won her heart by his condemnation of the
working man. He was the one man who was not afraid to
speak out, to tell them they drank, to tell them they shirked
and loafed, to tell them plainly that if defeat came to this
country the blame would fall upon *them !*

" *No !* " cried Mr. Britling.

" Yes," said Lady Frensham. " Upon them and those who
have flattered and misled them. . . . "

And so on. . . .

It presently became necessary for Lady Homartyn to
rescue Mr. Britling from the great lady's patriotic tramp-
lings. He found himself drifting into the autumnal garden
—the show of dahlias had never been so wonderful—in the
company of Raeburn and the staff-officer and a small woman
who was presently discovered to be remarkably well informed.
They were all despondent. " I think all this promiscuous
blaming of people is quite the worst—and most ominous—
thing about us just now," said Mr. Britling after the restful
pause that followed their departure from the presence of Lady
Frensham.

" It goes on everywhere," said the staff-officer.

" Is it really—honest ? " said Mr. Britling.

Raeburn, after reflection, decided to answer. " As far as
it is stupid, yes. There's a lot of blame coming ; there's
bound to be a day of reckoning, and I suppose we've all got
an instinctive disposition to find a scapegoat for our common
sins. The Tory press is pretty rotten, and there's a strong
element of mere personal spite—in the Churchill attacks for
example. Personal jealousy probably. Our ' old families '
seem to have got vulgar-spirited imperceptibly—in a generation or so. They quarrel and shirk and lay blame exactly
as bad servants do—and things are still far too much in their
hands. Things are getting muffed, there can be no doubt
about that—not fatally, but still rather seriously. And the
government—it was human before the war, and we've added
no archangels. There's muddle. There's mutual suspicion.
You never know what newspaper office Lloyd George won't
be in touch with next. He's honest and patriotic and energetic, but he's mortally afraid of old women and class intrigues.
He doesn't know where to get his backing. He's got all a
labour member's terror of the dagger at his back. There's

a lack of nerve, too, in getting rid of prominent officers—who have friends."

The staff-officer nodded.

" Northcliffe seems to me to have a case," said Mr. Britling. " Everyone abuses him."

" I'd stop his *Daily Mail*," said Raeburn, " I'd leave *The Times*, but I'd stop *The Daily Mail* on the score of its placards alone. It overdoes Northcliffe. It translates him into the shrieks and yells of underlings. The plain fact is that North-cliffe is scared out of his wits by German efficiency—and in war-time when a man is scared out of his wits, whether he is honest or not, you put his head in a bag or hold a pistol to it to calm him. . . . What is the good of all this clamouring for a change of government ? We haven't change of govern-ment. It's like telling a tramp to get a change of linen. Our men, all our public men, are second-rate men, with the habits of advocates. There is nothing masterful in their minds. How can you expect the system to produce anything else ? But they are doing as well as they can, and there is no way of putting in any one else now, and there you are."

" Meanwhile," said Mr. Britling, " our boys—get killed."

" They'd get killed all the more if you had—let us say—Carson and Lloyd George and Northcliffe and Lady Fren-sham, with, I suppose, Austin Harrison and Horatio Bot-tomley thrown in—as a Strong Silent Government. . . . I'd rather have Northcliffe as dictator than that. . . . We can't suddenly go back on the past and alter our type. We didn't listen to Matthew Arnold. We've never thoroughly turned out and cleaned up our higher schools. We've resisted instruction. We've preferred to maintain our national luxuries of a bench of bishops and party politics. And compulsory Greek and the university sneer. And Lady Frensham. And all that sort of thing. And here we are ! . . . Well, damn it, we're in for it now ; we've got to plough through with it—with what we have —as what we are."

The young staff-officer nodded. He thought that was " about it."

" You've got no sons," said Mr. Britling.

" I'm not even married," said Raeburn, as though he thanked God.

The little well-informed lady remarked abruptly that she had two sons ; one was just home wounded from Suvla Bay. What her son told her made her feel very grave. She said that the public was still quite in the dark about the battle of Anafarta. It had been a hideous muddle, and we had been badly beaten. The staff work had been awful. Nothing joined up, nothing was on the spot and in time. The water supply, for example, had gone wrong ; the men had been mad with thirst. One regiment which she named had not been supported by another ; when at last the first came back the two battalions fought in the trenches regardless of the enemy. There had been no leading, no correlation, no plan. Some of the guns, she declared, had been left behind in Egypt. Some of the train was untraceable to this day. It was mislaid somewhere in the Levant. At the beginning Sir Ian Hamilton had not even been present. He had failed to get there in time. It had been the reckless throwing away of an army. And so hopeful an army ! Her son declared it meant the complete failure of the Dardanelles project. . . .

" And when one hears how near we came to victory ! " she cried, and left it at that.

" Three times this year," said Raeburn, " we have missed victories because of the badness of our staff work. It's no good picking out scapegoats. It's a question of national habit. It's because the sort of man we turn out from our public schools has never learned how to catch trains, get to an office on the minute, pack a knapsack properly, or do anything smartly and quickly—anything whatever that he can possibly get done for him. You can't expect men who are habitually easy-going to keep bucked up to a high pitch of efficiency for any length of time. All their training is against it. All their tradition. They hate being prigs. An Englishman will be any sort of stupid failure rather than appear a prig. That's why we've lost three good fights that we ought to have won —and thousands and thousands of men—and material and time, precious beyond reckoning. We've lost a year. We've dashed the spirit of our people."

" My boy in Flanders," said Mr. Britling, " says about the same thing. He says our officers have never learned to count beyond ten, and that they are scared at the sight of a map. . . ."

" And the war goes on," said the little woman.

" How long, oh Lord ! how long ? " cried Mr. Britling.

" I'd give them another year," said the staff-officer. " Just going as we are going. Then something *must* give way. There will be no money anywhere. There'll be no more men. . . . I suppose they'll feel that shortage first anyhow. Russia alone has over twenty millions."

" That's about the size of it," said Raeburn. . . .

" Do you think, sir, there'll be civil war ? " asked the young staff-officer abruptly after a pause.

There was a little interval before any one answered this surprising question.

" After the peace, I mean," said the young officer.

" There'll be just the devil to pay," said Raeburn.

" One thing after another in the country is being pulled up by its roots," reflected Mr. Britling.

" We've never produced a plan for the war, and it isn't likely we shall have one for the peace," said Raeburn, and added : " and Lady Frensham's little lot will be doing their level best to sit on the safety-valve. . . . They'll rake up

Ireland and Ulster from the very start. But I doubt if Ulster will save 'em.''

" We shall squabble. What else do we ever do ? "

No one seemed able to see more than that. A silence fell on the little party.

" Well, thank heaven for these dahlias,'' said Raeburn, affecting the philosopher.

The young staff-officer regarded the dahlias without enthusiasm. . . .

§ 16

Mr. Britling sat one September afternoon with Captain Lawrence Carmine in the sunshine of the barn court, and smoked with him and sometimes talked and sometimes sat still.

" When it began I did not believe that this war could be like other wars,'' he said. " I did not dream it. I thought that we had grown wiser at last. It seemed to me like the dawn of a great clearing up. I thought the common sense of mankind would break out like a flame, an indignant flame, and consume all this obsolete foolery of empires and banners and militarism directly it made its attack upon human happiness. A score of things that I see now were preposterous, I thought must happen—naturally. I thought America would declare herself against the Belgian outrage ; that she would not tolerate the smashing of the great sister republic—if only for the memory of Lafayette. Well—I gather America is chiefly concerned about our making cotton contraband. I thought the Balkan States were capable of a reasonable give and take ; of a common care for their common freedom. I see now three German royalties trading in peasants, and no men in their lands to gainsay them. I saw this war, as so many Frenchmen have seen it, as something that might legitimately command a splendid enthusiasm of indignation. . . . It was all a dream, the dream of a prosperous comfortable man who had never come to the cutting edge of life. Everywhere cunning, everywhere small feuds and hatreds, distrusts, dishonesties, timidities, feebleness of purpose, dwarfish imaginations, swarm over the great and simple issues. . . . It is a war now like any other of the mobbing, many-aimed cataclysms that have shattered empires and devastated the world ; it is a war without point, a war that has lost its soul, it has become mere incoherent fighting and destruction, a demonstration in vast and tragic forms of the stupidity and ineffectiveness of our species. . . .''

He stopped, and there was a little interval of silence.

Captain Carmine tossed the fag end of his cigar very neatly into a tub of hydrangeas. " Three thousand years ago in China,'' he said, " there were men as sad as we are, for the same cause.''

" Three thousand years ahead perhaps," said Mr. Britling, " there will still be men with the same sadness. . . . And yet —and yet. . . . No. Just now I have no elasticity. It is not in my nature to despair, but things are pressing me down. I don't recover as I used to recover. I tell myself still that though the way is long and hard the spirit of hope, the spirit of creation, the generosities and gallantries in the heart of man, must end in victory. But I say that over as one repeats a worn-out prayer. The light is out of the sky for me. Sometimes I doubt if it will ever come back. Let younger men take heart and go on with the world. If I could die for the right thing now—instead of just having to live on in this world of ineffective struggle—I would be glad to die now, Carmine. . . ."

§ 17

In these days also Mr. Direck was very unhappy.

For Cissie, at any rate, had not lost touch with the essential issues of the war. She was as clear as ever that German militarism and the German attack on Belgium and France was the primary subject of the war. And she dismissed all secondary issues. She continued to demand why America did not fight. " We fight for Belgium. Won't you fight for the Dutch and Norwegian ships ? Won't you even fight for your own ships that the Germans are sinking ? "

Mr. Direck attempted explanations that were ill received.

" You were ready enough to fight the Spaniards when they blew up the *Maine*. But the Germans can sink the *Lusitania !* That's—as you say—a different proposition."

His mind was shot by an extraordinary suspicion that she thought the *Lusitania* an American vessel. But Mr. Direck was learning his Cissie, and he did not dare to challenge her on this score.

" You haven't got hold of the American proposition," he said. " We're thinking beyond wars."

" That's what we have been trying to do," said Cissie. " Do you think we came into it for the fun of the thing ? "

" Haven't I shown in a hundred ways that I sympathise ? "

" Oh—sympathy ! . . ."

He fared little better at Mr. Britling's hands. Mr. Britling talked darkly, but pointed all the time only too plainly at America. " There's two sorts of liberalism," said Mr. Britling, " that pretend to be the same thing ; there's the liberalism of great aims and the liberalism of defective moral energy. . . ."

§ 18

It was not until Teddy had been missing for three weeks that Hugh wrote about him. The two Essex battalions on the Flanders front were apparently wide apart, and it was only from home that Hugh learned what had happened.

" You can't imagine how things narrow down when one is

close up against them. One does not know what is happening even within a few miles of us, until we get the newspapers. Then, with a little reading between the lines and some bold guessing, we fit our little bit of experience with a general shape. Of course I've wondered at times about Teddy. But oddly enough I've never thought of him very much as being out here. It's queer, I know, but I haven't. I can't imagine why. . . .

" I don't know about ' missing.' We've had nothing going on here that has led to any missing. All our men have been accounted for. But every few miles along the front conditions alter. His lot may have been closer up to the enemy, and there may have been a rush and a fight for a bit of trench either way. In some parts the German trenches are not thirty yards away, and there is mining, bomb-throwing, and perpetual creeping up and give and take. Here we've been getting a bit forward. But I'll tell you about that presently. And, anyhow, I don't understand about ' missing.' There's very few prisoners taken now. But don't tell Letty that. I try to imagine old Teddy in it. . . .

" Missing's a queer thing. It isn't tragic—or pitiful. Or partly reassuring like ' prisoner.' It just sends one speculating and speculating. I can't find any one who knows where the 14th Essex are. Things move about here so mysteriously that for all I know we may find them in the next trench next time we go up. But there *is* a chance for Teddy. It's worth while bucking Letty all you can. And at the same time there's odds against him. There plainly and unfeelingly is how things stand in my mind. I think chiefly of Letty. I'm glad Cissie is with her, and I'm glad she's got the boy. Keep her busy. She was frightfully fond of him. I've seen all sorts of things between them, and I know that. . . . I'll try and write to her soon, and I'll find something hopeful to tell her.

" Meanwhile I've got something to tell you. I've been through a fight, a big fight, and I haven't got a scratch. I've taken two prisoners with my lily hand. Men were shot close to me. I didn't mind that a bit. It was as exciting as one of those bitter fights we used to have round the hockey-goal. I didn't mind anything till afterwards. Then when I was in the trench in the evening I trod on something slippery—pah ! And after it was all over one of my chums got it—sort of unfairly. And I kept on thinking of those two things so much that all the early part is just dreamlike. It's more like something I've read in a book, or seen in *The Illustrated London News* than actually been through. One had been thinking so often, how will it feel ? how shall I behave ? that when it came it had an effect of being flat and ordinary.

" They say we hadn't got enough guns in the spring or enough ammunition. That's all right now—anyhow. They started in plastering the Germans overnight, and right on until it was just daylight. I never heard such a row, and their trenches—we could stand up and look at them without getting a single shot at us—were flying about like the crater of a volcano. We were not in our firing trench. We had gone back into some new trenches at the rear—I think to get out of the way of the counter-fire. But this morning they weren't doing very much. For once our guns were on top. There was a feeling of anticipation—very like waiting for an examination paper to be given out ; then we were at it. Getting out of a trench to attack gives you an odd feeling of being just hatched. Suddenly the world is big. I don't remember our gun-fire stopping. And then you rush. ' Come on ! Come on ! ' say the officers. Everybody gives a sort of howl and rushes. When you see men dropping, you rush the faster. The only thing that checks you at all is the wire twisted about everywhere. You don't want to trip over that. The frightening thing is the exposure. After being in the trenches so long you feel naked. You run like a scared child for the German trench ahead. I can't understand the iron nerve of a man who can expose his back by turning to run away. And there's a thirsty feeling with one's bayonet. But they didn't wait. They dropped rifles and ran. But we ran so fast after them that we caught one or two in the second trench. I got down into that, heard a voice behind me, and found my two prisoners lying artful in a dugout. They held up their hands as I turned. If they hadn't I doubt if I should have done anything to them. I didn't feel like it. I felt *friendly*.

" Not all the Germans ran. Three or four stuck to their machine-guns until they got bayoneted. Both the trenches were frightfully smashed about, and in the first one there were little knots and groups of dead. We got to work at once shying the sand-bags over from the old front of the trench to the parados. Our guns had never stopped all the time ; they were now plastering the third-line trenches. And almost at once the German shells began dropping into us. Of course they had the range to an inch. One didn't have any time to feel and think ; one just set oneself with all one's energy to turn the trench over. . . .

" I don't remember that I helped or cared for a wounded man all the time, or felt anything about the dead except to step over them and not on them. I was just possessed by the idea that we had to get the trench into a sheltering state before they tried to come back. And then stick there. I just wanted to win, and there was nothing else in my mind. . . .

" They did try to come back, but not very much. . . .

" Then when I began to feel sure of having got hold of the trench for good, I began to realise just how tired I was and how high the sun had got. I began to look about me, and found most of the other men working just as hard as I had been doing. ' We've done it ! ' I said, and that was the first word I'd spoken since I told my two Germans to come out of it, and stuck a man with a wounded leg to watch them. ' It's a bit of All Right,' said Ortheris, knocking off also, and lighting a half-consumed cigarette. He had been wearing it behind his ear, I believe, ever since the charge. Against this occasion. He'd kept close up to me all the time, I realised. And then old Park turned up very cheerful with a weak bayonet jab in his forearm that he wanted me to rebandage. It was good to see him practically all right too.

" ' I took two prisoners,' I said, and everybody I spoke to I told that. I was fearfully proud of it.

" I thought that if I could take two prisoners in my first charge I was going to be some soldier.

" I had stood it all admirably. I didn't feel a bit shaken. I was as tough as anything. I'd seen death and killing, and it was all just hockey.

" And then that confounded Ortheris must needs go and get killed.

" The shell knocked me over, and didn't hurt me a bit. I was a little stunned, and some dirt was thrown over me, and when I got up on my knees I saw Jewell lying about six yards off—and his legs were all smashed about. Ugh ! Pulped !

" He looked amazed. ' Bloody,' he said, ' bloody.' He fixed his eyes on me, and suddenly grinned. You know we'd once had two fights about his saying ' bloody,' I think I told you at the time, a fight and a return match, he couldn't box for nuts, but he stood up like a Briton, and it appealed now to his sense of humour that I should be standing there too dazed to protest at the old offence. ' I thought *you* was done in,' he said. ' I'm in a mess—a bloody mess, ain't I ? Like a stuck pig. Bloody—right enough. Bloody ! I didn't know I 'ad it *in* me.'

" He looked at me and grinned with a sort of pale satisfaction in keeping up to the last—dying good Ortheris to the finish. I just stood up helpless in front of him, still rather dazed.

" He said something about having a thundering thirst on him.

" I really don't believe he felt any pain. He would have done if he had lived.

" And then while I was fumbling with my water-bottle, he collapsed. He forgot all about Ortheris. Suddenly he said something that cut me all to ribbons. His face puckered up just like the face of a fretful child which refuses to go to bed. ' I didn't want to be aut of it,' he said petulantly. ' And I'm done ! ' And then—then he just looked discontented and miserable and died—right off. Turned his head a little way over. As if he was impatient at everything. Fainted—and fluttered out.

" For a time I kept trying to get him to drink. . . .

" I couldn't believe he was dead. . . .

" And suddenly it was all different. I began to cry. Like
a baby. I kept on with the water-bottle at his teeth long after
I was convinced he was dead. I didn't want him to be *out* of
it ! God knows how I didn't. I wanted my dear little Cockney
cad back. Oh ! most frightfully I wanted him back.

" I shook him. I was like a scared child. I blubbered and
howled things. . . . . It's all different since he died.

" My dear, dear Father, I am grieving and grieving—and
it's altogether nonsense. And it's all mixed up in my mind
with the mess I trod on. And it gets worse and worse. So that
I don't seem to feel anything really, even for Teddy.

" It's been just the last straw of all this hellish foolery. . . .

" If ever there was a bigger lie, my dear Daddy, than any
other, it is that man is a reasonable creature. . . .

" War is just foolery—lunatic foolery—hell's foolery. . . .

" But, anyhow, your son is sound and well—if sorrowful and
angry. We were relieved that night. And there are rumours
that very soon we are to have a holiday and a refit. We lost
rather heavily. We have been praised. But all along, Essex
has done well. I can't reckon to get back yet, but there are
such things as leave for eight-and-forty hours or so in England. . . .

" I shall be glad of that sort of turning round. . . .

" I'm tired. Oh ! I'm tired. . . .

" I wanted to write all about Jewell to his mother or his
sweetheart or some one ; I wanted to wallow in his praises, to
say all the things I really find now that I thought about him,
but I haven't even had that satisfaction. He was a Poor Law
child ; he was raised in one of those awful places between
Sutton and Banstead in Surrey. I've told you of all the sweet-
hearting he had. ' Soldiers Three ' was his Bible ; he was
always singing ' Tipperary,' and he never got the tune right
nor learned more than three lines of it. He laced all his talk
with ' b——y ' ; it was his jewel, his ruby. But he had the
pluck of a robin or a squirrel ; I never knew him scared or
anything but cheerful. Misfortunes, humiliations, only made
him chatty. And he'd starve to have something to give away.

" Well, well, this is the way of war, Daddy. This is what
war is. Damn the Kaiser ! Damn all fools. . . . Give my love
to the Mother and the bruddykins and everyone. . . .''

§ 19

It was just a day or so over three weeks after this last letter
from Hugh that Mr. Direck reappeared at Matching's Easy.
He had had a trip to Holland—a trip that was as much a
flight from Cissie's reproaches as a mission of inquiry. He
had intended to go on into Belgium, where he had already
been doing useful relief work under Mr. Hoover, but the con-

fusion of his own feelings had checked him and brought him back.

Mr. Direck's mind was in a perplexity only too common during the stresses of that tragic year. He was entangled in a paradox; like a large majority of Americans at that time his feelings were quite definite pro-Ally, and like so many in that majority he had a very clear conviction that it would be wrong and impossible for the United States to take part in the war. His sympathies were intensely with the Dower House and its dependent cottage ; he would have wept with generous emotion to see the Stars and Stripes interwoven with the three other great banners of red white and blue that led the world against German imperialism and militarism, but for all that his mind would not march to that tune. Against all these impulses fought something very fundamental in Mr. Direck's composition, a preconception of America that had grown almost insensibly in his mind, the idea of America as a polity aloof from the Old World system, as a fresh start for humanity, as something altogether too fine and precious to be dragged into even the noblest of European conflicts. America was to be the beginning of the fusion of mankind, neither German nor British nor French nor in any way national. She was to be the great experiment in peace and reasonableness. She had to hold civilisation and social order out of this fray, to be a refuge for all those finer things that die under stress and turmoil ; it was her task to maintain the standards of life and the claims of humanitarianism in the conquered province and the prisoners' compound, she had to be the healer and arbitrator, the remonstrance and not the smiting hand. Surely there were enough smiting hands.

But this idea of an America judicial, remonstrating, and aloof, led him to a conclusion that scandalised him. If America will not, and should not use force in the ends of justice, he argued, then America has no right to make and export munitions of war. She must not trade in what she disavows. He had a quite exaggerated idea of the amount of munitions that America was sending to the Allies, he was inclined to believe that they were entirely dependent upon their transatlantic supplies, and so he found himself persuaded that the victory of the Allies and the honour of America were incompatible things. And—in spite of his ethical aloofness—he loved the Allies. He wanted them to win, and he wanted America to abandon a course that he believed was vitally necessary to their victory. It was an intellectual dilemma. He hid this self-contradiction from Matching's Easy with much the same feelings that a curate might hide a poisoned dagger at a tea-party.

It was entirely against his habits of mind to hide anything— more particularly an entanglement with a difficult proposition —but he perceived quite clearly that neither Cecily nor Mr.

Britling was really to be trusted to listen calmly to what, under happier circumstances, might be a profoundly interesting moral complication. Yet it was not in his nature to conceal ; it was in his nature to state.

And Cecily made things much more difficult. She was pitiless with him. She kept him aloof. " How can I let you make love to me," she said, " when our Englishmen are all going to the war, when Teddy is a prisoner and Hugh is in the trenches. If I were a man——! "

She couldn't be induced to see any case for America. England was fighting for freedom, and America ought to be beside her. " All the world ought to unite against this German wickedness," she said.

" I'm doing all I can to help in Belgium," he protested. " Aren't I working ? We've fed four million people."

He had backbone, and he would not let her, he was resolved, bully him into a falsehood about his country. America was aloof. She was right to be aloof. . . . At the same time, Cecily's reproaches were unendurable. And he could feel he was drifting apart from her. . . .

He couldn't make America go to war.

In the quiet of his London hotel he thought it all out. He sat at a writing-table making notes of a perfectly lucid statement of the reasonable, balanced liberal American opinion. An instinct of caution determined him to test it first on Mr. Britling.

But Mr. Britling realised his worst expectations. He was beyond listening.

" I've not heard from my boy for more than three weeks," said Mr. Britling in the place of any salutation. " This morning makes three-and-twenty days without a letter."

It seemed to Mr. Direck that Mr. Britling had suddenly grown ten years older. His face was more deeply lined ; the colour and texture of his complexion had gone grey. He moved restlessly and badly ; his nerves were manifestly unstrung.

" It's intolerable that one should be subjected to this ghastly suspense. The boy isn't three hundred miles away."

Mr. Direck made obvious inquiries.

" Always before he's written—generally once a fortnight."

They talked of Hugh for a time, but Mr. Britling was fitful and irritable and quite prepared to hold Mr. Direck accountable for the laxity of the War Office, the treachery of Bulgaria, the ambiguity of Roumania or any other barb that chanced to be sticking into his sensibilities. They lunched precariously. Then they went into the study to smoke.

There Mr. Direck was unfortunate enough to notice a copy of that innocent American publication *The New Republic*, lying close to two or three numbers of *The Fatherland*, a pro-German periodical which at that time inflicted itself upon

English writers with the utmost determination. Mr. Direck remarked that *The New Republic* was an interesting effort on the part of " *la Jeunesse Americaine.*" Mr. Britling regarded the interesting effort with a jaded, unloving eye.

" You Americans," he said, " are the most extraordinary people in the world."

" Our conditions are exceptional," said Mr. Direck.

" You think they are," said Mr. Britling, and paused, and then began to deliver his soul about America in a discourse of accumulating bitterness. At first he reasoned and explained, but as he went on he lost self-control ; he became dogmatic, he became denunciatory, he became abusive. He identified Mr. Direck more and more with his subject ; he thrust the uncivil " You " more and more directly at him. He let his cigar go out, and flung it impatiently into the fire. As though America was responsible for its going out. . . .

Like many Britons Mr. Britling had that touch of patriotic feeling towards America which takes the form of impatient criticism. No one in Britain ever calls an American a foreigner. To see faults in Germany or Spain is to tap boundless fountains of charity ; but the faults of America rankle in an English mind almost as much as the faults of England. Mr. Britling could explain away the faults of England readily enough ; our Hanoverian monarchy, our Established Church and its deadening effect on education, our imperial obligations and the strain they made upon our supplies of administrative talent were all very serviceable for that purpose. But there in America was the old race, without Crown or Church or international embarrassment, and it was still falling short of splendour. His speech to Mr. Direck had the rancour of a family quarrel. Let me only give a few sentences that were to stick in Mr. Direck's memory.

" You think you are out of it for good and all. So did we think. We were as smug as you are when France went down in '71. . . . Yours is only one further degree of insularity. You think this vacuous aloofness of yours is some sort of moral superiority. So did we, so did we. . . .

" It won't last you ten years if we go down. . . .

" Do you think that our disaster will leave the Atlantic for you ? Do you fancy there is any freedom of the Seas possible beyond such freedom as we maintain except the freedom to attack you ? For forty years the British fleet has guarded all America from European attack. Your Monroe Doctrine skulks behind it now. . . .

" I'm sick of this high thin talk of yours about the war. . . . You are a nation of ungenerous onlookers—watching us throttle or be throttled. You gamble on our winning. And we shall win ; we shall win. And you will profit. And when we have won a victory only one shade less terrible than defeat, then you think you will come in and tinker with our peace.

Blee⌐ us a little more to please your hyphenated patriots. . . ."

He came to his last shaft. " You talk of your New Ideals of Peace. You say that you are too proud to fight. But your business men in New York give the show away. There's a little printed card now in half the offices in New York that tells of the real pacificism of America. They're busy, you know. Trade's real good. And so as not to interrupt it they stick up this card : ' Nix on the war ! ' Think of it !—' Nix on the war ! ' Here is the whole fate of mankind at stake, and America's contribution is a little grumbling when the Germans sank the *Lusitania*, and no end of grumbling when we hold up a ship or two and some fool of a harbourmaster makes an overcharge. Otherwise—' Nix on the war ! ' . . .

" Well, let it be Nix on the war ! Don't come here and talk to me ! You who were searching registers a year ago to find your Essex kin. Let it be Nix ! Explanations ! What do I want with explanations ? And "—he mocked his guest's accent and his guest's mode of thought—" dif'cult prap'-sitions."

He got up and stood irresolute. He knew he was being preposterously unfair to America, and outrageously uncivil to a trusting guest ; he knew he had no business now to end the talk in this violent fashion. But it was an enormous relief. And to mend matters——

No ! He was glad he'd said these things. . . .

He swung a shoulder to Mr. Direck, and walked out of the room. . . .

Mr. Direck heard him cross the hall and slam the door of the little parlour. . . .

Mr. Direck had been stirred deeply by the tragic indignation of this explosion, and the ring of torment in Mr. Britling's voice. He had stood up also, but he did not follow his host.

" It's his boy," said Mr. Direck at last, confidentially to the writing-desk. " How can one argue with him ? It's just hell for him. . . ."

§ 20

Mr. Direck took his leave of Mrs. Britling, and went very slowly towards the little cottage. But he did not go to the cottage. He felt he would only find another soul in torment there.

" What's the good of hanging round talking ? " said Mr. Direck.

He stopped at the stile in the lane, and sat thinking deeply. " Only one thing will convince her," he said.

He held out his fingers. " First this," he whispered, " and then that. Yes."

He went on as far as the bend from which one sees the cottage, and stood for a little time regarding it.

He returned still more sorrowfully to the junction, and with every step he took it seemed to him that he would rather see Cicily angry and insulting than not see her at all.

At the post-office he stopped and wrote a letter-card.

" Dear Cissie," he wrote. " I came down to-day to see you —and thought better of it. I'm going right off to find out about Teddy. Somehow I'll get that settled. I'll fly around and do that somehow if I have to go up to the German front to do it. And when I've got that settled I've got something else in my mind—well, it will wipe out all this little trouble that's got so big between us about neutrality. And I love you dearly, Cissie."

That was all the card would hold.

§ 21

And then as if it were something that every one in the Dower House had been waiting for, came the message that Hugh had been killed.

The telegram was brought up by a girl in a pinafore instead of the boy of the old dispensation, for boys now were doing the work of youths, and youths the work of the men who had gone to the war.

Mr. Britling was standing at the front door ; he had been surveying the late October foliage, touched by the warm light of the afternoon, when the messenger appeared. He opened the telegram, hoping as he had hoped when he opened any telegram since Hugh had gone to the front that it would not contain the exact words he read ; that it would say wounded, that at the worst it would say " missing," that perhaps it might even tell of some pleasant surprise, a brief return to home such as the last letter had foreshadowed. He read the final, unqualified statement, the terse regrets. He stood quite still for a moment or so, staring at the words. . . .

It was a mile and a quarter from the post-office to the Dower House, and it was always his custom to give telegraph-messengers who came to his house twopence, and he wanted very much to get rid of the telegraph girl, who stood expec- tantly before him holding her red bicycle. He felt now very sick and strained ; he had a conviction that if he did not by an effort maintain his bearing cool and dry he would howl aloud. He felt in his pocket for money ; there were some coppers and a shilling. He pulled it all out together and stared at it.

He had an absurd conviction that this ought to be a six- penny telegram. The thing worried him. He wanted to give the brat sixpence, and he had only threepence and a shilling, and he didn't know what to do and his brain couldn't think. It would be a shocking thing to give her a shilling, and he couldn't somehow give just coppers for so important a thing as Hugh's death. Then all this problem vanished and he handed

the child the shilling. She stared at him, inquiring, incredulous.
" Is there a reply, sir, please ? "

" No," he said, " that's for you. All of it. . . . This is a
peculiar sort of telegram. . . . It's news of importance. . . ."

As he said this he met her eyes, and had a sudden persuasion that she knew exactly what it was the telegram had
told him, and that she was shocked at this gala-like treatment
of such terrible news. He hesitated, feeling that he had to say
something else, that he was socially inadequate, and then he
decided that at any cost he must get his face away from her
staring eyes. She made no movement to turn away. She
seemed to be talking him in, recording him, for repetition,
greedily, with every fibre of her being.

He stepped past her into the garden, and instantly forgot
about her existence. . . .

§ 22

He had been thinking of this possibility for the last few
weeks almost continuously, and yet now that it had come
to him he felt that he had never thought about it before, that
he must go off alone by himself to envisage this monstrous
and terrible fact, without distraction or interruption.

He saw his wife coming down the alley between the roses.

He was wrenched by emotions as odd and unaccountable
as the emotions of adolescence. He had exactly the same
feeling now that he had had when in his boyhood some unpleasant admission had to be made to his parents. He felt
he could not go through a scene with her yet, that he could
not endure the task of telling her, of being observed. He
turned abruptly to his left. He walked away as if he had not
seen her, across his lawn towards the little summer-house
upon a knoll that commanded the high-road. She called to
him, but he did not answer. . . .

He would not look towards her, but for a time all his senses
were alert to hear whether she followed him. Safe in the
summer-house he could glance back.

It was all right. She was going into the house.

He drew the telegram from his pocket again furtively,
almost guiltily, and reread it. He turned it over and read it
again. . . .

Killed.

Then his own voice, hoarse and strange to his ears, spoke
his thought.

" My God ! how unutterably silly. . . . Why did I let him
go ? Why did I let him go ? "

§ 23

Mrs. Britling did not learn of the blow that had struck
them until after dinner that night. She was so accustomed
to ignore his incomprehensible moods that she did not perceive

that there was anything tragic about him until they sat at table together. He seemed heavy and sulky and disposed to avoid her, but that sort of moodiness was nothing very strange to her. She knew that things that seemed to her utterly trivial, the reading of political speeches in *The Times*, little comments on life made in the most casual way, mere movements, could so avert him. She had cultivated a certain disregard of such fitful darknesses. But at the dinner-table she looked up, and was stabbed to the heart to see a haggard white face and eyes of deep despair regarding her ambiguously.

" Hugh ! " she said, and then with a chill intimation, " *What is it ?* "

They looked at each other. His face softened and winced.

" My Hugh," he whispered, and neither spoke for some seconds.

" *Killed*," he said, and suddenly stood up whimpering, and fumbled with his pocket.

It seemed he would never find what he sought. It came at last, a crumpled telegram. He threw it down before her, and then thrust his chair back clumsily and went hastily out of the room. She heard him sob. She had not dared to look at his face again.

" *Oh !* " she cried, realising that an impossible task had been thrust upon her.

" But what can I *say* to him ? " she said, with the telegram in her hand.

The parlour-maid came into the room.

" Clear the dinner away !" said Mrs. Britling, standing at her place. " Master Hugh is killed. . . ." And then wailing : " Oh ! what can I *say* ? " What can I *say* ? "

§ 24

That night Mrs. Britling made the supreme effort of her life to burst the prison of self-consciousness and inhibition in which she was confined. Never before in all her life had she so desired to be spontaneous and unrestrained ; never before had she so felt herself hampered by her timidity, her self-criticism, her deeply ingrained habit of never letting herself go. She was rent by reflected distress. It seemed to her that she would be ready to give her life and the whole world to be able to comfort her husband now. And she could conceive no gesture of comfort. She went out of the dining-room into the hall and listened. She went very softly upstairs until she came to the door of her husband's room. There she stood still. She could hear no sound from within. She put out her hand and turned the handle of the door a little way, and then she was startled by the loudness of the sound it made, and at her own boldness. She withdrew her hand, and then with a gesture of despair, with a face of white agony, she flitted along the corridor to her own room.

Her mind was beaten to the ground by this catastrophe, of which to this moment she had never allowed herself to think. She had never allowed herself to think of it. The figure of her husband, like some pitiful beast, wounded and bleeding, filled her mind. She gave scarcely a thought to Hugh. " Oh, what can I *do* for him ? " she asked herself, sitting down before her unlit bedroom fire. . . . " What can I say or do ? "

She brooded until she shivered, and then she lit her fire. . . .

It was late that night and after an eternity of resolutions and doubts and indecisions that Mrs. Britling went to her husband. He was sitting close up to the fire with his chin upon his hands, waiting for her ; he felt that she would come to him, and he was thinking meanwhile of Hugh with a slow unprogressive movement of the mind. He showed by a movement that he heard her enter the room, but he did not turn to look at her. He shrank a little from her approach.

She came and stood beside him. She ventured to touch him very softly, and to stroke his head. " My dear," she said. " My poor dear ! "

" It is so dreadful for you," she said, " it is so dreadful for you. I know how you loved him. . . ."

He spread his hands over his face and became very still.

" My poor dear ! " she said, still stroking his hair, " my poor dear ! "

And then she went on saying " poor dear," saying it presently because there was nothing more had come into her mind. She desired supremely to be his comfort and in a little while she was acting comfort so poorly that she perceived her own failure. And that increased her failure, and that increased her paralysing sense of failure. . . .

And suddenly her stroking hand ceased. Suddenly the real woman cried out from her.

" I can't *reach* you ! " she cried aloud. " I can't reach you. I would do anything. . . . You ! You with your heart half broken. . . ."

She turned towards the door. She moved clumsily, she was blinded by her tears.

Mr. Britling uncovered his face. He stood up astonished, and then pity and pitiful understanding came storming across his grief. He made a step and took her in his arms. " My dear," he said, " don't go from me. . . ."

She turned to him weeping, and put her arms about his neck, and he too was weeping.

" My poor wife ! " he said, " my dear wife. If it were not for you—I think I could kill myself to-night. Don't cry, my dear. Don't, don't cry. You do not know how you comfort me. You do not know how you help me."

He drew her to him ; he put her cheek against his own. . . .

His heart was so sore and wounded that he could not endure

that another human being should go wretched. He sat down
in his chair and drew her upon his knees, and said everything
he could think of to console her and reassure her and make
her feel that she was of value to him. He spoke of every pleasant
aspect of their lives, of every aspect, except that he never
named that dear pale youth who waited now. . . . He could
wait a little longer. . . .

At last she went from him.

" Good night," said Mr. Britling, and took her to the door.

" It was very dear of you to come and comfort me," he said. . . .

§ 25

He closed the door softly behind her.

The door had hardly shut upon her before he forgot her.
Instantly he was alone again, utterly alone. He was alone
in an empty world. . . .

Loneliness struck him like a blow. He had dependents,
he had cares. He had never a soul to whom he might weep. . . .

For a time he stood beside his open window. He looked at
the bed—but no sleep, he knew, would come that night—until
the sleep of exhaustion came. He looked at the bureau at
which he had so often written. But the writing there was a
shrivelled thing. . . .

This room was unendurable. He must go out. He turned
to the window, and outside was a troublesome noise of nightjars and a distant roaring of stags, black trees, blacknesses,
the sky clear and remote with a great company of stars. . . .
The stars seemed attentive. They stirred and yet were still.
It was as if they were the eyes of watchers. He would go out
to them. . . .

Very softly he went towards the passage door, and still
more softly felt his way across the landing and down the
staircase. Once or twice he paused to listen.

He let himself out with elaborate precautions. . . .

Across the dark he went, and suddenly his boy was all
about him, playing, climbing the cedars, twisting miraculously about the lawn on a bicycle, discoursing gravely upon
his future, lying on the grass, breathing very hard and drawing
preposterous caricatures. Once again they walked side by
side up and down—it was athwart this very spot—talking
gravely but rather shyly. . . .

And here they had stood a little awkwardly, before the
boy went in to say good-bye to his step-mother and go off
with his father to the station. . . .

" I will work to-morrow again," whispered Mr. Britling,
" but to-night—to-night. . . . To-night is yours. . . . Can you
hear me, can you hear ? Your father . . . who had counted
on you. . . ."

§ 26

He went into the far corner of the hockey paddock, and there he moved about for a while and then stood for a long time holding the fence with both hands and staring blankly into the darkness. At last he turned away, and went stumbling and blundering towards the rose-garden. A spray of creeper tore his face and distressed him. He thrust it aside fretfully, and it scratched his hand. He made his way to the seat in the arbour, and sat down and whispered a little to himself, and then became very still with his arm upon the back of the seat and his head upon his arm.

Book Three

The Testament of Matching's Easy

CHAPTER ONE

MRS. TEDDY GOES FOR A WALK

§ 1

ALL over England now, where the livery of mourning had been a rare thing to see, women and children went about in the October sunshine in new black clothes. Everywhere one met these fresh griefs, mothers who had lost their sons, women who had lost their men, lives shattered and hopes destroyed. The dyers had a great time turning coloured garments to black. And there was also a growing multitude of crippled and disabled men. It was so in England, much more was it so in France and Russia, in all the countries of the Allies, and in Germany and Austria; away into Asia Minor and Egypt, in India and Japan and Italy there was mourning, the world was filled with loss and mourning and impoverishment and distress.

And still the mysterious powers that required these things of mankind were unappeased and each day added its quota of heart-stabbing messages and called for new mourning, and sent home fresh consignments of broken and tormented men.

Some clung to hopes that became at last almost more terrible than black certainties. . . .

Mrs. Teddy went about the village in a coloured dress bearing herself confidently. Teddy had been listed now as " missing, since reported killed," and she had had two letters from his comrades. They said Teddy had been left behind in the ruins of a farm with one or two other wounded, and that when the Canadians retook the place these wounded had all been found butchered. None had been found alive. Afterwards the Canadians had had to fall back. Mr. Direck had been at great pains to hunt up wounded men from Teddy's company, and also any likely Canadians both at the base hospital in France and in London, and to get what he could from them. He had made it a service to Cissie. Only one of his witnesses was quite clear about Teddy, but he, alas! was dreadfully clear. There had been only one lieutenant among the men left behind, he said, and obviously that must have been Teddy. " He had been prodded in half-a-dozen places. His head was nearly severed from his body."

Direck came down and told the story to Cissie. " Shall I tell it to her ? " he asked.

Cissie thought. " Not yet," she said. . . .

Letty's face changed in those pitiful weeks when she was denying death. She lost her pretty colour, she became white ;

her mouth grew hard and her eyes had a hard brightness. She never wept, she never gave a sign of sorrow, and she insisted upon talking about Teddy, in a dry offhand voice. Constantly she referred to his final return. " Teddy," she said, " will be surprised at this," or " Teddy will feel sold when he sees how I have altered that."

" Presently we shall see his name in a list of prisoners," she said. " He is a wounded prisoner in Germany."

She adopted that story. She had no justification for it, but she would hear no doubts upon it. She presently began to prepare parcels to send him. " They want almost everything," she told people. " They are treated abominably. He has not been able to write to me yet, but I do not think I ought to wait until he asks me."

Cissie was afraid to interfere with this.

After a time Letty grew impatient at the delay in getting any address and took her first parcel to the post-office.

" Unless you know what prison he is at," said the postmistress.

" Pity ! " said Letty. " I don't know that. Must it wait for that ? I thought the Germans were so systematic that it didn't matter."

The postmistress made tedious explanations that Letty did not seem to hear. She stared straight in front of her at nothing. Then in a pause in the conversation she picked up her parcel.

" It's tiresome for him to have to wait," she said. " But it can't be long before I know."

She took the parcel back to the cottage.

" After all," she said, " it gives us time to get the better sort of throat lozenges for him—the sort the syndicate shop doesn't keep."

She put the parcel conspicuously upon the dresser in the kitchen where it was most in the way, and set herself to make a jersey for Teddy against the coming of the cold weather.

But one night the white mask fell for a moment from her face.

Cissie and she had been sitting in silence before the fire. She had been knitting—she knitted very badly—and Cissie had been pretending to read, and had been watching her furtively. Cissie eyed the slow, toilsome growth of the slack woolwork for a time, and the touch of angry effort in every stroke of the knitting-needles. Then she was stirred to remonstrance.

" Poor Letty ! " she said very softly. " Suppose, after all, he is dead ? "

Letty met her with a pitiless stare.

" He is a prisoner," she said. " Isn't that enough ? Why do you jab at me by saying that ? A wounded prisoner. Isn't

that enough despicable trickery for God even to play on
Teddy—our Teddy ? To the very last moment he shall not
be dead. Until the war is over. Until six months after the
war. . . .

" I will tell you why, Cissie. . . ."

She leaned across the table and pointed her remarks with
her knitting-needles, speaking in a tone of reasonable remonstrance. " You see," she said, " if people like Teddy are to be
killed, then all our ideas that life is meant for honesty and
sweetness and happiness are wrong, and this world is just a
place of devils ; just a dirty cruel hell. Getting born would be
getting damned. And so one must not give way to that idea,
however much it may seem likely that he is dead. . . .

" You see, if he *is* dead, then Cruelty is the Law, and some
one must pay me for his death. . . . Some one must pay
me. . . . I shall wait for six months after the war, dear, and
then I shall go off to Germany and learn my way about there.
And I will murder some German. Not just a common German,
but a German who belongs to the guilty kind. A sacrifice. It
ought, for instance, to be comparatively easy to kill some of
the children of the Crown Prince or some of the Bavarian
princes. I shall prefer German children. I shall sacrifice them
to Teddy. It ought not to be difficult to find people who can
be made directly responsible, the people who invented the
poison-gas, for instance, and kill them, or to kill people who
are dear to them. Or necessary to them. . . . Women can
do that so much more easily than men. . . .

" That perhaps is the only way in which wars of this kind
will ever be brought to an end. By women insisting on killing
the kind of people who make them. Rooting them out. By
a campaign of pursuit and assassination that will go on for
years and years after the war itself is over. . . . Murder is
such a little gentle punishment for the crime of war. . . . It
would be hardly more than a reproach for what has happened.
Falling like snow. Death after death. Flake by flake. This
prince. That statesman. The count who writes so fiercely for
war. . . . That is what I am going to do. If Teddy is really
dead. . . . We women were ready enough a year or so ago
to starve and die for the Vote, and that was quite a little
thing in comparison with this business. . . . Don't you see
what I mean ? It's so plain and sensible, Cissie. Whenever
a man sits and thinks whether he will make a war or not,
then he will think too of women, women with daggers, bombs ;
of a vengeance that will never tire nor rest ; of consecrated
patient women ready to start out upon a pilgrimage that will
only end with his death. . . . I wouldn't hurt these war-
makers. No. In spite of the poison-gas. In spite of trench
feet and the men who have been made blind and the wounded
who have lain for days, dying slowly in the wet. Women ought
not to hurt. But I would kill. Like killing dangerous vermin.

It would go on year by year. Balkan kings. German princes, chancellors, they would have schemed for so much—and come to just a rattle in the throat. . . . And if presently other kings and emperors began to prance about and review armies, they too would go. . . .

" Until all the world understood that women would not stand war any more for ever. . . .

" Of course I shall do something of the sort. What else is there to do now for me ? "

Letty's eyes were bright and intense, but her voice was soft and subdued. She went on after a pause in the same casual voice. " You see now, Cissie, why I cling to the idea that Teddy is alive. If Teddy is alive, then even if he is wounded he will get some happiness out of it—and all this won't be—just rot. If he is dead, then everything is so desperately silly and cruel from top to bottom——"

She smiled wanly to finish her sentence.

" But, Letty," said Cissie, " there is the boy ! "

" I shall leave the boy to you. Compared with Teddy I don't care *that* for the boy. I never did. What is the good of pretending ? Some women are made like that."

She surveyed her knitting. " Poor stitches," she said. . . .

" I'm hard stuff, Cissie. I take after mother more than father. Teddy is my darling. All the tenderness of my life is Teddy. If he goes, it goes. . . . I won't crawl about the world like all these other snivelling widows. If they've killed my man I shall kill. Blood for blood and loss for loss. I shall get just as close to the particular Germans who made this war as I can, and I shall kill them and theirs. . . .

" The Women's Association for the Extirpation of the whole breed of War Lords," she threw out. " If I do happen to hurt —does it matter ? "

She looked at her sister's shocked face and smiled again.

" You think I go about staring at nothing," she remarked. . . . " Not a bit of it ! I have been planning all sorts of things. . . . I have been thinking how I could get to Germany. . . . Or one might catch them in Switzerland. . . . I've had all sorts of plans. They can't go guarded for ever. . . .

" Oh, it makes me despise humanity to see how many soldiers and how few assassins there are in the world. . . . After the things we have seen. If people did their duty by the dagger there wouldn't be such a thing as a War Lord in the world. Not one. . . . The Kaiser and his son and his sons' sons would know nothing but fear now for all their lives. Fear would only cease to pursue as the coffin went down into the grave. Fear by sea, fear by land, for the vessel he sailed in, the train he travelled in, fear when he slept for the death in his dreams, fear when he waked for the death in every shadow ; fear in every crowd, fear whenever he was alone. Fear would stalk him through the trees, hide in the corner of the staircase ; make all his food taste perplexingly, so that he would want to spit it out. . . ."

She sat very still brooding on that idea for a time, and then stood up.

" What nonsense one talks ! " she cried, and yawned. " I wonder why poor Teddy doesn't send me a postcard or some-thing to tell me his address. I tell you what I *am* afraid of sometimes about him, Cissie."

" Yes ? " said Cissie.

" Loss of memory. Suppose a beastly lump of shell or something whacked him on the head. . . . I had a dream of him looking strange about the eyes and not knowing me. That, you know, really *may* have happened. . . . It would be beastly, of course. . . ."

Cissie's eyes were critical, but she had nothing ready to say.

There were some moments of silence.

" Oh ! bed," said Letty. " Though I shall just lie scheming."

§ 2

Cissie lay awake that night thinking about her sister as if she had never thought about her before.

She began to weigh the concentrated impressions of a thousand memories. She and her sister were near in age ; they knew each other with an extreme intimacy, and yet it seemed to Cissie that night as though she did not know Letty at all. A year ago she would have been certain she knew everything about her. But the old familiar Letty, with the bright complexion and the wicked eye, with her rebellious schoolgirl insistence upon the beautifulness of " Boof'l young men," and her frank and glowing passion for Teddy, with her delight in humorous mystifications and open-air exercise and all the sunshine and laughter of life, this sister Letty who had been so satisfactory and complete and final, had been thrust aside like a mask. Cissie no longer knew her sister's eyes. Letty's hands had become thin and unfamiliar and a little wrinkled ; she was sharp-featured and thin-lipped ; her acts, which had once been predictable, were incomprehensible, and Cissie was thrown back upon speculations. In their school-days Letty had had a streak of intense sensibility ; she had been easily moved to tears. But never once had she wept or given any sign of weeping since Teddy's name had appeared in the casualty list. . . . What was the strength of this tragic tension ? How far would it carry her ? Was Letty really capable of becoming a Charlotte Corday ? Of carrying out a scheme of far-seeing vengeance, of making her way through long months and years nearer and nearer to revenge ?

Were such revenges possible ?

Would people presently begin to murder the makers of the Great War ? What a strange thing it would be in history if so there came a punishment and end to the folly of kings !

Only a little while ago Cissie's imagination might have been captured by so romantic a dream. She was still but a year or so out of the stage of melodrama. But she was out of it. She was growing up now to a subtler wisdom. People, she was beginning to realise, do not do these simple things. They make vows of devotion and they are not real vows of devotion ; they love—quite honestly—and qualify. There are no great revenges but only little mean ones ; no lifelong vindications except the unrelenting vengeance of the law. There is no real concentration of people's lives anywhere such as romance demands. There is change, there is forgetfulness. Everywhere there is dispersal. Even to the tragic story of Teddy would come the modifications of time. Even to the wickedness of the German princes would presently be added some conflicting aspects. Could Letty keep things for years in her mind, hard and terrible, as they were now ? Surely they would soften ; other things would overlay them. . . .

There came a rush of memories of Letty in a dozen school-girl adventures, times when she had ventured, and times when she had failed ; Letty frightened, Letty vexed, Letty launching out to great enterprises, going high and hard and well for a time, and then failing. She had seen Letty snivelling and dirty; Letty ashamed and humiliated. She knew her Letty to the soul. Poor Letty ! Poor dear Letty ! With a sudden clearness of vision Cissie realised what was happening in her sister's mind. All this tense scheming of revenges was the imaginative play with which Letty warded off the black alternative to her hope ; it was not strength, it was weakness. It was a form of giving way. She could not face starkly the simple fact of Teddy's death. That was too much for her. So she was building up this dream of a mission of judgment against the day when she could resist the facts no longer. She was already persuaded, only she would not be persuaded until her dream was ready. If this state of suspense went on she might establish her dream so firmly that it would at last take complete possession of her mind. And by that time also she would have squared her existence at Matching's Easy with the elaboration of her reverie.

She would go about the place then, fancying herself preparing for this tremendous task she would never really do ; she would study German maps ; she would read the papers about German statesmen and rulers ; perhaps she would even make weak attempts to obtain a situation in Switzerland or in Germany. Perhaps she would buy a knife or a revolver. Perhaps presently she would begin to hover about Windsor or Sandringham when peace was made, and the German cousins came visiting again. . . .

Into Cissie's mind came the image of the thing that might be ; Letty, shabby, draggled, and her sharp bright prettiness become haggard, an assassin dreamer, still dependent on Mr. Britling, doing his work rather badly, in a distraught unpunctual fashion.

She must be told, she must be convinced soon, or assuredly she would become an eccentric, a strange character, a Matching's Easy Miss Flite. . . .

§ 3

Cissie could think more clearly of Letty's mind than of her own.

She herself was in a tangle. She had grown to be very fond of Mr. Direck and to have a profound trust and confidence in him, and her fondness seemed able to find no expression at all except a constant girding at his and America's avoidance of war. She had fallen in love with him when he was wearing fancy dress ; she was a young woman with a stronger taste for body and colour than she supposed ; what indeed she resented about him, though she did not know it, was that he seemed never disposed to carry the spirit of fancy dress into everyday life. To begin with he had touched both her imagination and senses, and she wanted him to go on doing that. Instead of which he seemed lapsing more and more into reiterated assurances of devotion and the flat competent discharge of humanitarian duties. Always nowadays he was trying to persuade her that what he was doing was the right and honourable thing for him to do ; what he did not realise, what indeed she did not realise, was the exasperation his rightness and reasonableness produced in her. When he saw he exasperated her he sought very earnestly to be righter and reasonabler and more plainly and demonstrably right and reasonable than ever.

Withal, as she felt and perceived, he was such a good thing, such a very good thing; so kind, so trustworthy with a sort of slow strength, with a careful honesty, a big good childishness, a passion for fairness. And so helpless in her hands. She could lash him and distress him. Yet she could not shake his slowly formed convictions.

When Cissie had dreamt of the lover that fate had in store for her in her old romantic days, he was to be *perfect* always, he and she were always to be absolutely in the right (and, if the story needed it, the world in the wrong). She had never expected to find herself tied by her affections to a man with whom she disagreed, and who went contrary to her standards, very much as if she was lashed on the back of a very nice elephant that would wince to but not obey the goad. . . .

So she nagged him and taunted him, and would hear no word of his case. And he wanted dreadfully to discuss his case. He felt that the point of conscience about the munitions was particularly fine and difficult. He wished she would listen and enter into it more. But she thought with that more rapid English flash which is not so much thinking as feeling. He loved that flash in her in spite of his persuasion of its injustice.

Her thought that he ought to go to the war made him feel like a renegade; her claim that he was somehow still English held him in spite of his reason. In the midst of such perplexities he was glad to find one neutral task wherein he could find himself wholeheartedly with and for Cissie.

He hunted up the evidence of Teddy's fate with a devoted pertinacity.

And in the meanwhile the other riddle resolved itself. He had had a certain idea in his mind for some time. He discovered one day that it was an inspiration. He could keep his conscientious objection about America, and still take a line that would satisfy Cissie. He took it.

When he came down to Matching's Easy at her summons to bear his convincing witness of Teddy's fate, he came in an unwonted costume. It was a costume so wonderful in his imagination that it seemed to cry aloud, to sound like a trumpet as he went through London to Liverpool Street Station; it was a costume like an international event; it was a costume that he felt would blare right away to Berlin. And yet it was a costume so commonplace, so much the usual wear now, that Cissie, meeting him at the station and full of the thought of Letty's trouble, did not remark it, felt indeed rather than observed that he was looking more strong and handsome than he had ever done since he struck upon her imagination in the fantastic wrap that Teddy had found for him in the merry days when there was no death in the world. And Letty too, resistant, incalculable, found no wonder in the wonderful suit.

He bore his testimony. It was the queer halting telling of a patched-together tale. . . .

"I suppose," said Letty, "if I tell you now that I don't believe that that officer was Teddy you will think I am cracked. . . . But I don't."

She sat staring straight before her for a time after saying this. Then suddenly she got up and began taking down her hat and coat from the peg behind the kitchen door. The hanging strap of the coat was twisted and she struggled with it petulantly until she tore it.

"Where are you going?" cried Cissie.

Letty's voice over her shoulder was the harsh voice of a scolding woman.

"I'm going out—anywhere." She turned, coat in hand. "Can't I go out if I like?" she asked. "It's a beautiful day. . . . Mustn't I go out? . . . I suppose you think I ought to take in what you have told me in a moment. Just smile and say ' Indeed !' . . . Abandoned !—while his men retreated ! How jolly ! And then not think of it any more. . . . Besides,

I must go out. You two want to be left together. You want to
canoodle. Do it while you can ! "

Then she put on coat and hat, jamming her hat down on her
head, and said something that Cissie did not immediately
understand.

" *He'll* have his turn in the trenches soon enough. Now
that he's made up his mind. . . . He might have done it
sooner. . . ."

She turned her back as though she had forgotten them.
She stood for a moment as though her feet were wooden, not
putting her feet as she usually put her feet. She took slow,
wide, unsure steps. She went out—like something that is
mortally injured and still walks—into the autumnal sunshine.
She left the door wide open behind her.

§ 4

And Cissie, with eyes full of distress for her sister, had still to
grasp the fact that Direck was wearing a Canadian uniform. . . .

He stood behind her, ashamed that in such a moment this
fact and its neglect by everyone could be so vivid in his mind.

§ 5

Cissie's estimate of her sister's psychology had been just.
The reverie of revenge had not yet taken a grip upon Letty's
mind sufficiently strong to meet the challenge of this conclusive evidence of Teddy's death. She walked out into a
world of sunshine now almost completely convinced that
Teddy was dead, and she knew quite well that her dream of
some dramatic and terrible vindication had gone from her
She knew that in truth she could do nothing of that sort. . . .

She walked out with a set face and eyes that seemed unseeing,
and yet it was as if some heavy weight had been lifted from her
shoulders. It was over ; there was not more to hope for and
there was nothing more to fear. She would have been shocked
to realise that her mind was relieved.

She wanted to be alone. She wanted to be away from every
eye. She was like some creature that after a long nightmare
incubation is at last born into a clear, bleak day. She had to
feel herself ; she had to stretch her mind in this cheerless
sunshine, this new world, where there was to be no more
Teddy and no real revenge nor compensation for Teddy.
Teddy was past. . . .

Hitherto she had had an angry sense of being deprived of
Teddy—almost as though he were keeping away from her.
Now, there was no more Teddy to be deprived of. . . .

She went through the straggling village and across the
fields to the hillside that looks away towards Mertonsome
and its steeple. And where the hill begins to fall away she
threw herself down under the hedge by the path, near by the

stile into the lane, and lay still. She did not so much think as remain blank, waiting for the beginning of impressions. . . .

It was as it were a blank stare at the world. . . .

She did not know if it was five minutes or half an hour later that she became aware that some one was looking at her. She turned with a start, and discovered the Reverend Dimple with one foot on the stile, and an expression of perplexity and consternation upon his chubby visage.

Instantly she understood. Already on four different occasions since Teddy's disappearance she had seen the good man coming towards her, always with a manifest decision, always with the same faltering doubt as now. Often in their happy days had she and Teddy discussed him and derided him and rejoiced over him. They had agreed he was as good as Jane Austen's Mr. Collins. He really was very like Mr. Collins, except that he was plumper. And now, it was as if he was transparent to her hard defensive scrutiny. She knew he was impelled by his tradition, by his sense of fitness, by his respect for his calling, to offer her his ministrations and consolations, to say his large flat amiabilities over her and pat her kindly with his hands. And she knew too that he dreaded her. She knew that the dear old humbug knew at the bottom of his heart quite certainly that he was a poor old humbug, and that she was in his secret. And at the bottom of his heart he found himself too honest to force his poor platitudes upon any who would not be glad of them. If she could have been glad of them he would have had no compunction. He was a man divided against himself ; failing to carry through his rich pretences, dismayed.

He had been taking his afternoon " constitutional." He had discovered her beyond the stile just in time to pull up. Then had came a fatal, a preposterous hesitation. She stared at him now, with hard, expressionless eyes.

He stared back at her, until his plump pink face was all consternation. He was extraordinarily distressed. It was as if a thousand unspoken things had been said between them.

" No wish," he said, " intrude."

If he had had the certain balm, how gladly would he have given it !

He broke the spell by stepping back into the lane. He made a gesture with his hands, as if he would have wrung them. And then he had fled down the lane—almost at a run.

" Po' girl," he cried. " Po' girl," and left her staring.

Staring—and then she laughed.

This was good. This was the sort of thing one could tell Teddy, when at last he came back and she could tell him anything. And then she realised again ; there was no more Teddy, there would be no telling. And suddenly she fell weeping.

" Oh, Teddy, Teddy," she cried through her streaming tears. " How could you leave me ? How can I bear it ? "

Never a tear had she shed since the news first came, and

now she could weep, she could weep her grief out. She abandoned herself unreservedly to this blessed relief. . . .

§ 6

There comes an end to weeping at last, and Letty lay still,
in the red light of the sinking sun.

She lay so still that presently a little foraging robin came
flirting down to the grass not ten yards away and stopped and
looked at her. And then it came a hop or so nearer.

She had been lying in a state of passive abandonment, her
swollen wet eyes open, regardless of everything. But those
quick movements caught her back to attention. She began to
watch the robin, and to note how it glanced sidelong at her
and appeared to meditate further approaches. She made an
almost imperceptible movement, and straightway the little
creature was in a projecting spray of berried hawthorn overhead.

Her tear-washed mind became vaguely friendly. With an
unconscious comfort it focused down to the robin. She rolled
over, sat up, and imitated his friendly " cheep."

§ 7

Presently she became aware of footsteps rustling through the
grass towards her.

She looked over her shoulder and discovered Mr. Britling
approaching by the field path. He looked white and tired and
listless, even his bristling hair and clipped moustache conveyed
his depression ; he was dressed in an old tweed knickerbocker
suit and carrying a big atlas and some papers. He had an
effect of hesitation in his approach. It was as if he wanted to
talk to her and doubted her reception for him.

He spoke without any preface. " Direck has told you ? "
he said, standing over her.

She answered with a sob.

" I was afraid it was so, and yet I did not believe it," said
Mr. Britling. " Until now."

He hesitated as if he would go on, and then he knelt down
on the grass a little way from her and seated himself. There
was an interval of silence.

" At first it hurts like the devil," he said at last, looking
away at Mertonsome spire and speaking as if he spoke to no
one in particular. " And then it hurts. It goes on hurting. . . .
And one can't say much to any one. . . ."

He said no more for a time. But the two of them comforted
one another, and knew that they comforted each other. They
had a common feeling of fellowship and ease. They had been
stricken by the same thing ; they understood how it was with
each other. It was not like the attempted comfort they got
from those who had not loved and dreaded. . . .

She took up a little broken twig and dug small holes in the ground with it.

" It's strange," she said, " but I'm glad I know for sure."

" I can understand that," said Mr. Britling.

" It stops the nightmares. . . . It isn't hopes I've had so much as fears. . . . I wouldn't admit he was dead or hurt. Because—— I couldn't think it without thinking it—horrible. *Now*——"

" It's final," said Mr. Britling.

" It's definite," she said after a pause. " It's like thinking he's asleep—for good."

But that did not satisfy her. There was more than this in her mind. " It does away with the half and half," she said. " He's dead or he is alive. . . ."

She looked up at Mr. Britling as if she measured his understanding.

" You don't still doubt ? " he said.

" I'm content now in my mind—in a way. He wasn't anyhow there—unless he was dead. But if I saw Teddy coming over the hedge there to me—— It would be just natural. . . . No, don't stare at me. I know really he is dead. And it is a comfort. It is peace. . . . All the thoughts of him being crushed dreadfully or being mutilated or lying and screaming—or things like that—they've gone. He's out of his spoiled body. He's my unbroken Teddy again. . . . Out of sight somewhere. . . . Unbroken. . . . Sleeping."

She resumed her excavation with the little stick, with the tears running down her face.

Mr. Britling presently went on with the talk. " For me it came all at once, without a doubt or a hope. I hoped until the last that nothing would touch Hugh. And then it was like a black shutter falling—in an instant. . . ."

He considered. " Hugh, too, seems just round the corner at times. But at times, it's a blank place. . . .

" At times," said Mr. Britling, " I feel nothing but astonishment. The whole thing becomes incredible. Just as for weeks after the war began I couldn't believe that a big modern nation could really go to war—seriously—with its whole heart. . . . And they have killed Teddy and Hugh. . . .

" They have killed millions. Millions—who had fathers and mothers and wives and sweethearts. . . ."

§ 8

" Somehow I can't talk about this to Edith. It is ridiculous, I know. But in some way, I can't. . . . It isn't fair to her. If I could, I would. . . . Quite soon after we were married I ceased to talk to her. I mean talking really and simply—as I do to you. And it's never come back. I don't know why. . . . And particularly I can't talk to her of Hugh. . . . Little things, little shadows of criticism, but enough to make it impossible. . . . And I go about thinking about Hugh, and what has happened to him, sometimes. . . as though I was stifling."

Letty compared her case.

" I don't want to talk about Teddy—not a word."

" That's queer. . . . But perhaps—a son is different. Now I come to think of it—I've never talked of Mary. . . . Not to any one ever. I've never thought of that before. But I haven't. I couldn't. No. Losing a lover, that's a thing for oneself. I've been through that, you see. But a son's more outside you. Altogether. And more your own making. It's not losing a thing *in* you ; it's losing a hope and a pride. . . . Once when I was a little boy I did a drawing very carefully. It took me a long time. . . . And a big boy tore it up. For no particular reason. Just out of cruelty. . . . That—that was exacty like losing Hugh. . . ."

Letty reflected.

" No," she confessed, " I'm more selfish than that."

" It isn't selfish," said Mr. Britling. " But it's a different thing. It's less intimate, and more personally important.

" I've just thought, ' He's gone. He's gone.' Sometimes, do you know, I have felt quite angry with him. Why need he have gone—so soon ? "

Mr. Britling nodded understandingly.

" I'm not angry. I'm not depressed. I'm just bitterly hurt by the ending of something I had hoped to watch—always— all my life," he said. " I don't know how it is between most fathers and sons, but I admired Hugh. I found exquisite things in him. I doubt if other people saw them. He was quiet. He seemed clumsy. But he had an extraordinary fineness. He was a creature of the most delicate and rapid responses. . . . These aren't my fond delusions. It was so. . . . You know, when he was only a few days old, he would start suddenly at any strange sound. He was alive like an Æolian harp from the very beginning. . . . And his hair when he was born—he had a lot of hair—was like the down on the breast of a bird. I remember that now very vividly—and how I used to like to pass my hand over it. It was silk, spun silk. Before he was two he could talk— whole sentences. He had the subtlest ear. He loved long words. . . . And then," he said with tears in his voice, " all this beautiful fine structure, this brain, this fresh life as nimble as water—as elastic as a steel spring, it is destroyed. . . .

" I don't make out he wasn't human. Often and often I have been angry with him, and disappointed in him. There were all sorts of weaknesses in him. We all knew them. And we didn't mind them. We loved him the better. And his odd queer cleverness. . . . And his profound wisdom. And then all this beautiful and delicate fabric, all those clear memories in his dear brain, all his whims, his sudden inventions. . . .

" You know, I have had a letter from his chum Park. He

was shot through a loophole. The bullet went through his eye
and brow. . . . Think of it !

" An amazement . . . a blow . . . a splattering of blood.
Rags of tormented skin and brain stuff. . . . In a moment.
What had taken eighteen years—love and care. . . ."

He sat thinking for an interval, and then went on, " The
reading and writing alone ! I taught him to read myself—
because his first governess, you see, wasn't very clever. She
was a very good methodical sort, but she had no inspiration.
So I got up all sorts of methods for teaching him to read.
But it wasn't necessary. He seemed to leap all sorts of
difficulties. He leaped to what one was trying to teach him.
It was as quick as the movement of some wild animal. . . .

" He came into life as bright and quick as this robin looking
for food. . . .

" And he's broken up and thrown away. . . . Like a
cartridge-case by the side of a covert. . . ."

He choked and stopped speaking. His elbows were on his
knees, and he put his face between his hands and shuddered
and became still. His hair was troubled. The end of his stumpy
moustache and a little roll of flesh stood out at the side of his
hand, and made him somehow twice as pitiful. His big atlas,
from which papers projected, seemed forgotten by his side.
So he sat for a long time, and neither he nor Letty moved or
spoke. But they were in the same shadow. They found great
comfort in one another. They had not been so comforted before
since their losses came upon them.

§ 9

It was Mr. Britling who broke silence. And when he drew
his hands down from his face and spoke, he said one of the most
amazing and unexpected things she had ever heard in her life.

" The only possible government in Albania," he said, looking
steadfastly before him down the hillside, " is a group of republican cantons after the Swiss pattern. I can see no other solution
that is not offensive to God. It does not matter in the least
what we owe to Serbia or what we owe to Italy. We have got
to set this world on a different footing. We have got to set up
the world at last—on justice and reason."

Then, after a pause, " The Treaty of Bucharest was an evil
treaty. It must be undone. Whatever this German King of
Bulgaria does, that treaty must be undone and the Bulgarians
united again into one people. They must have themselves,
whatever punishment they deserve, they must have nothing
more, whatever reward they win."

She could not believe her ears.

" After this precious blood, after this precious blood, if we
leave one plot of wickedness or cruelty in the world——"

And therewith he began to lecture Letty on the importance
of international politics—to every one. How he and she and

every one must understand, however hard it was to understand.

" No life is safe, no happiness is safe, there is no chance of bettering life until we have made an end to all that causes war. . . .

" We have to put an end to the folly and vanity of kings, and to any people ruling any people but themselves. There is no convenience, there is no justice in any people ruling any people but themselves ; the ruling of men by others, who have not their creeds and their languages and their ignorances and prejudices, that is the fundamental folly that has killed Teddy and Hugh—and these millions. To end that folly is as much our duty and business as telling the truth or earning a living. . . ."

" But how can you alter it ? "

He held out a finger at her. " Men may alter anything if they have motive enough and faith enough."

He indicated the atlas beside him.

" Here I am planning the real map of the world," he said. " Every sort of district that has a character of its own must have its own rule ; and the great republic of the United States of the World must keep the federal peace between them all. That's the plain sense of life ; the federal world-republic. Why do we bother ourselves with loyalties to any other government but that ? It needs only that sufficient men should say it, and that republic would be here now. Why have we loitered so long—until these tragic punishments come ? We have to map the world out into its states, and plan its government and the way of its tolerations."

" And you think it will come ? "

" It will come."

" And you believe that men will listen to such schemes ? " said Letty.

Mr. Britling, with his eyes far away over the hills, seemed to think. " Yes," he said. " Not perhaps to-day—not steadily. But kings and empires die ; great ideas, once they are born, can never die again. In the end this world-republic, this sane government of the world, is as certain as the sunset. Only. . . ."

He sighed, and turned over a page of his atlas blindly.

" Only we want it soon. The world is weary of this bloodshed, weary of all this weeping, of this wasting of substance, and this killing of sons and lovers. We want it soon, and to have it soon we must work to bring it about. We must give our lives. What is left of our lives. . . .

" That is what you and I must do, Letty. What else is there left for us to do ? . . . I will write of nothing else, I will think of nothing else now but of safety and order. So that all these dear dead—not one of them but will have brought the great days of peace and man's real beginning nearer, and these cruel things that make men whimper like children, that break down bright lives into despair and kill youth at the very moment when it puts out its clean hands to take hold of life—these cruelties, these abominations of confusion, shall cease from the earth for ever."

§ 10

Letty regarded him frowning, and with her chin between her fists. . . .

" But do you really believe," said Letty, " that things can be better than they are ? "

" But—*Yes !* " said Mr. Britling.

" I don't," said Letty. " The world is cruel. It is just cruel. So it will always be."

" It need not be cruel," said Mr. Britling.

" It is just a place of cruel things. It is all set with knives. It is full of diseases and accidents. As for God—either there is no God or he is an idiot. He is a slobbering idiot. He is like some idiot who pulls off the wings of flies."

" No," said Mr. Britling.

" There is no progress. Nothing gets better. How can *you* believe in God after Hugh ? *Do* you believe in God ? "

" Yes," said Mr. Britling after a long pause ; " I do believe in God."

" Who lets these things happen ! " She raised herself on her arm and thrust her argument at him with her hand. " Who kills my Teddy and your Hugh—and millions."

" No," said Mr. Britling.

" But he *must* let these things happen. Or why do they happen ? "

" No," said Mr. Britling. " It is the theologians who must answer that. They have been extravagant about God. They have had silly absolute ideas—that he is all-powerful. That he's omni-everything. But the common sense of men knows better. Every real religious thought denies it. After all, the real God of the Christians is Christ, not God Almighty ; a poor mocked and wounded God nailed on a cross of matter. . . . Some day he will triumph. . . . But it is not fair to say that he causes all things now. It is not fair to make out a case against him. You have been misled. It is a theologian's folly. God is not absolute ; God is finite. . . . A finite God who struggles in his great and comprehensive way as we struggle in our weak and silly way—who is *with* us—that is the essence of all real religion. . . . I agree with you so—— Why ! if I thought there was an omnipotent God who looked down on battles and deaths and all the waste and horror of this war—able to prevent these things—doing them to amuse himself—I would spit in his empty face. . . ."

" Any one would. . . ."

" But it's your teachers and catechisms have set you against God. . . . They want to make out he owns all Nature. And all sorts of silly claims. Like the heralds in the Middle Ages who insisted that Christ was certainly a great gentleman entitled to bear arms. But God is within Nature and necessity. Necessity is a thing beyond God—beyond good and ill, beyond space and time, a mystery everlastingly impenetrable. God is nearer than that. Necessity is the uttermost thing, but God is the innermost thing. Closer he is than breathing and nearer than hands and feet. He is the Other Thing than this world. Greater than Nature or Necessity, for he is a spirit and they are blind, but not controlling them. . . . Not yet. . . ."

" They always told me he was the maker of Heaven and Earth."

" That's the Jew God the Christians took over. It's a Quack God, a Panacea. It's not my God."

Letty considered these strange ideas.

" I never thought of him like that," she said at last. " It makes it all seem different."

" Nor did I. But I do now. . . . I have suddenly found it and seen it plain. I see it so plain that I am amazed that I have not always seen it. . . . It is, you see, so easy to understand that there is a God, and how complex and wonderful and brotherly he is, when one thinks of these dear boys who by the thousand, by the hundred thousand, have laid down their lives. . . . Aye, and there were German boys too who did the same. . . . The cruelties, the injustice, the brute aggression—they saw it differently. They laid down their lives—they laid down their lives. . . . Those dear lives, those lives of hope and sunshine. . . .

" Don't you see that it must be like that, Letty ? Don't you see that it must be like that ? "

" No," she said, " I've seen things differently from that."

" But it's so plain to me," said Mr. Britling. " If there was nothing else in all the world but our kindness for each other, or the love that made you weep in this kind October sunshine, or the love I bear Hugh—if there was nothing else at all—if everything else was cruelty and mockery and filthiness and bitterness, it would still be certain that there was a God of love and righteousness. If there were no signs of God in all the world but the godliness we have seen in those two boys of ours ; if we had no other light but the love we have between us. . . .

" You don't mind if I talk like this ? " said Mr. Britling. " It's all I can think of now—this God, this God who struggles, who was in Hugh and Teddy, clear and plain, and how he must become the ruler of the world. . . ."

" This God who struggles," she repeated. "I have never thought of him like that."

" Of course he must be like that," said Mr. Britling. " How can God be a Person ; how can he be anything that matters to man, unless he is limited and defined and—human like ourselves. . . . With things outside him and beyond him."

§ 11

Letty walked back slowly through the fields of stubble to her cottage.

She had been talking to Mr. Britling for an hour, and her mind was full of the thought of this changed and simplified man, who talked of God as he might have done of a bird he had seen or of a tree he had sheltered under. And all mixed up with this thought of Mr. Britling was this strange idea of God who was also a limited person, who could come as close as Teddy, whispering love in the darkness. She had a ridiculous feeling that God really struggled like Mr. Britling, and that with only some indefinable inferiority of outlook Mr. Britling loved like God. She loved him for his maps and his dreams and the bareness of his talk to her. It was strange how the straining thought of the dead Teddy had passed now out of her mind. She was possessed by a sense of ending and beginning, as though a page had turned over in her life and everything was new. She had never given religion any thought but contemptuous thought for some years, since indeed her growing intelligence had dismissed it as a scheme of inexcusable restraints and empty pretences, a thing of discords where there were no discords except of its making. She had been a happy Atheist. She had played in the sunshine, a natural creature with the completest confidence in the essential goodness of the world in which she found herself. She had refused all thought of painful and disagreeable things. Until the bloody paw of war had wiped out all her assurance. Teddy, the playmate, was over, the love-game was ended for ever ; the fresh happy acceptance of life as life ; and in the place of Teddy was the sorrow of life, the pity of life, and this coming of God out of utter remoteness into a conceivable relation to her own existence.

She had left Mr. Britling to his atlas. He lay prone under the hedge with it spread before him. His occupation would have seemed to her only a little while ago the absurdest imaginable. He was drawing boundaries on his maps very carefully in red ink, with a fountain pen. But now she understood.

She knew that those red-ink lines of Mr. Britling's might in the end prove wiser and stronger than the bargains of the diplomats. . . .

In the last hour he had come very near to her. She found herself full of an unwonted affection for him. She had never troubled her head about her relations with any one except Teddy before. Now suddenly she seemed to be opening out to all the world for kindness. This new idea of a friendly God, who had a struggle of his own, who could be thought of as kindred to Mr. Britling, as kindred to Teddy—had gripped her imagination. He was behind the autumnal sunshine ; he was in the little bird that had seemed so confident and friendly.

Whatever was kind, whatever was tender; there was God. And a thousand old phrases she had read and heard and given little heed to, that had lain like dry bones in her memory, suddenly were clothed in flesh and became alive. This God— if this was God—then indeed it was not nonsense to say that God was love, that he was a friend and companion. . . . With him it might be possible to face a world in which Teddy and she would never walk side by side again nor plan any more happiness for ever. After all she had been very happy; she had had wonderful happiness. She had had far more happiness, far more love, in her short year or so than most people had in their whole lives. And so in the reaction of her emotions, Letty who had gone out with her head full of murder and revenge, came back through the sunset thinking of pity, of the thousand kindnesses and tendernesses of Teddy that were after all, perhaps, only an intimation of the limitless kindnesses and tendernesses of God. . . . What right had she to a white and bitter grief, self-centred and vindictive, while old Britling could still plan an age of mercy in the earth and a red-gold sunlight that was warm as a smile from Teddy lay on all the world? . . .

She must go into the cottage and kiss Cissie, and put away that parcel out of sight until she could find some poor soldier to whom she could send it. She had been pitiless towards Cissie in her grief. She had, in the egotism of her sorrow, treated Cissie as she might have treated a chair or a table, with no thought that Cissie might weary, might dream of happiness still to come. Cissie had still to play the lover, and her man was already in khaki. There would be no such year as Letty had had in the days before the war darkened the world. Before Cissie's marrying the peace must come, and the peace was still far away. And Direck too would have to take his chances. . . .

Letty came through the little wood and over the stile that brought her into sight of the cottage. The windows of the cottage as she saw it under the bough of the big walnut-tree were afire from the sun. The crimson rambler over the porch that she and Teddy had planted was still bearing roses. The door was open and people were moving in the porch.

Some one was coming out of the cottage, a stranger, in an unfamiliar costume, and behind him was a man in khaki—but that was Mr. Direck! And behind him again was Cissie.

But the stranger!

He came out of the frame of the porch towards the garden-gate. . . .

Who—who was this stranger?

It was a man in queer-looking foreign clothes, baggy trousers of some soft-looking blue stuff and a blouse, and he had a white-bandaged left arm. He had a hat stuck at the back of his head, and a beard. . . .

He was entirely a stranger, a foreigner. Was she going insane? Of course he was a stranger!

And then he moved a step, he made a queer sideways pace, a caper, on the path, and instantly he ceased to be strange and foreign. He became amazingly, incredibly, familiar by virtue of that step. . . .

No !

Her breath stopped. All Letty's being seemed to stop. And this stranger who was also incredibly familiar, after he had stared at her motionless form for a moment, waved his hat with a gesture—a gesture that crowned and sealed the effect of familiarity. She gave no sign in reply.

No, that familiarity was just a mad freakishness in things. This strange man came from Belgium perhaps, to tell something about Teddy. . . .

And then she surprised herself by making a groaning noise, an absurd silly noise, just like the noise when one imitates a cow to a child. She said, " Mooo-oo."

And she began to run forward, with legs that seemed misfits, waving her hands about, and as she ran she saw more and more certainly that this wounded man in strange clothing was Teddy. She ran faster and still faster, stumbling and nearly falling. If she did not get to him speedily the world would burst.

To hold him, to hold close to him ! . . .

" Letty ! Letty ! Just one arm. . . ."

She was clinging to him and he was holding her. . . .

It was all right. She had always known it was all right. (Hold close to him.) Except just for a little while. But that had been foolishness. Hadn't she always known he was alive ? And here he was alive ! (Hold close to him.) Only it was so good to be sure—after all her torment ; to hold him, to hang about him, to feel the solid man, kissing her, weeping too, weeping together with her. " Teddy my love ! "

§ 12

Letty was in the cottage struggling to hear and understand things too complicated for her emotion-crowded mind. There was something that Mr. Direck was trying to explain about a delayed telegram that had come soon after she had gone out. There was much indeed that Mr. Direck was trying to explain. What did any explanation really matter when you had Teddy, with nothing but a strange beard and a bandaged arm between him and yourself ? She had an absurd persuasion at first that those two strangenesses would also presently be set aside, so that Teddy would become just exactly what Teddy had always been.

Teddy had been shot through the upper arm. . . .

" My hand has gone, dear little Letty. It's my left hand, luckily. I shall have to wear a hook like some old pirate. . . ."

There was something about his being taken prisoner. " That other officer "—that was Mr. Direck's officer—" had been

lying there for days." Teddy had been shot through the upper
arm, and stunned by a falling beam. When he came to he
was disarmed, with a German standing over him. . . .

Then afterwards he had escaped. In quite a little time he
had escaped. He had been in a railway station somewhere in
Belgium; locked in a waiting-room with three or four French
prisoners, and the junction had been bombed by French and
British-aeroplanes. Their guard and two of the prisoners had
been killed. In the confusion the others had got away into the
town. There were trucks of hay on fire, and a store of petrol
was in danger. " After that one was bound to escape. One
would have been shot if one had been found wandering about."

The bomb had driven some splinters of glass and corrugated
iron into Teddy's wrist; it seemed a small place at first; it
didn't trouble him for weeks. But then some dirt got into it.

In the narrow cobbled street beyond the station he had
happened upon a woman who knew no English, but who took
him to a priest, and the priest had hidden him.

Letty did not piece together the whole story at first. She
did not want the story very much; she wanted to know about
this hand and arm.

There would be queer things in the story when it came to be
told. There was an old peasant who had made Teddy work in
his fields in spite of his smashed and aching arm, and who had
pointed to a passing German when Teddy demurred; there
were the people called " they " who had at that time organised
the escape of stragglers into Holland. There was the night-
watch, those long nights in succession before the dash for
liberty. But Letty's concern was all with the hand. Inside the
sling there was something that hurt the imagination, something
bandaged, a stump. She could not think of it. She could not
get away from the thought of it.

" But why did you lose your hand ? "

It was only a little place at first, and then it got painful. . . .

" But I didn't go into a hospital, because I was afraid they
would intern me, and so I wouldn't be able to come home.
And I was dying to come home. I was—homesick. No one
was ever so homesick. I've thought of this place and the garden,
and how one looked out of the window at the passers-by, a
thousand times. I seemed always to be seeing them. Old
Dimple with his benevolent smile, and Mrs. Wolker at the end
cottage, and how she used to fetch her beer and wink when she
caught us looking at her, and little Charlie Slobberface sniffing
on his way to the pigs and all the rest of them. And you,
Letty. Particularly you. And how we used to lean on the
window-sill with our shoulders touching, and your cheek just
in front of my eyes. . . . And nothing aching at all in one. . . .

" How I thought of that and longed for that ! . . .

" And so, you see, I didn't go to the hospital. I kept hoping
to get to England first. And I left it too long. . . ."

" Life's come back to me with you ! " said Letty. " Until just to-day I've believed you'd come back. And to-day—I doubted. . . . I thought it was all over—all the real life, love, and the dear fun of things, and that there was nothing before me, nothing before me but just holding out—and keeping your memory. . . . Poor arm. Poor arm. And being kind to people. And pretending you were alive somewhere. . . . I'll not care about the arm. In a little while. . . . I'm glad you've gone, but I'm gladder you're back and can never go again. . . . And I will be your right hand, dear, and your left hand and all your hands. Both my hands for your dear lost left one. You shall have three hands instead of two. . . ."

§ 13

Letty stood by the window as close as she could to Teddy in a world that seemed wholly made up of unexpected things. She could not heed the others, it was only when Teddy spoke to the others, or when they spoke to Teddy, that they existed for her.

For instance, Teddy was presently talking to Mr. Direck.

They had spoken about the Canadians who had come up and relieved the Essex men after the fight in which Teddy had been captured. And then it was manifest that Mr. Direck was talking of his regiment. " I'm not the only American who has gone Canadian—for the duration of the war."

He had got to his explanation at last.

" I've told a lie," he said triumphantly. " I've shifted my birthplace six hundred miles.

" Mind you, I don't admit a thing that Cissie has ever said about America—not one thing. You don't understand the sort of proposition America is up against. America is the New World, where there are no races and nations any more ; she is the Melting-Pot, from which we will cast the better state. I've believed that always—in spite of a thousand little things I believe it now. I go back on nothing. I'm not fighting as an American either. I'm fighting simply as myself. . . . I'm not going fighting for England, mind you. Don't you fancy that. I don't know I'm so particularly in love with a lot of English ways as to do that. I don't see how any one can be very much in love with your Empire, with its dead-alive Court, its artful politicians, its lords and ladies and snobs, its way with the Irish and its way with India, and everybody shifting responsibility and telling lies about your common people. I'm not going fighting for England. I'm going fighting for Cissie—and justice and Belgium and all that—but more particularly for Cissie. And anyhow I can't look Pa Britling in the face any more. . . . And I want to see those trenches—close. I reckon they're a thing it will be interesting to talk about some day. . . . So I'm going," said Mr. Direck. " But chiefly—it's Cissie. See ?"

She looked from poor broken Teddy to him and back again.
" Up to now," she said, " I've wanted you to go. . . ."
Tears came into her eyes.
" I suppose I must let you go," she said. " Oh ! I'd hate you
not to go. . . ."

§ 14

" Good God ! how old the Master looks ! " cried Teddy
suddenly.
He was standing at the window, and as Mr. Direck came
forward inquiringly he pointed to the figure of Mr. Britling
passing along the road towards the Dower House.
" He does look old. I hadn't noticed," said Mr. Direck.
" Why, he's gone grey ! " cried Teddy, peering. " He wasn't
grey when I left."
They watched the knickerbockered figure of Mr. Britling
receding up the hill, atlas and papers in his hands behind his
back.
" I must go out to him," said Teddy, disengaging himself
from Letty.
" No," she said, arresting him with her hand.
" But he will be glad——"
She stood in her husband's way. She had a vision of Mr.
Britling suddenly called out of his dreams of God ruling the
United States of the World, to rejoice at Teddy's restoration. . . .
" No," she said ; " it will only make him think again of
Hugh—and how he died. Don't go out, Teddy. Not now.
What does he care for *you* ? . . . Let him rest from such
things. . . . Leave him to dream over his atlas. . . . He isn't
so desolate—if you knew. . . . I will tell you, Teddy—when
I can. . . .
" But just now—— No, he will think of Hugh again. . . .
Let him go. . . He has God and his atlas there. . . . They're
more than you think."

CHAPTER TWO

MR. BRITLING WRITES UNTIL SUNRISE

§ 1

IT was some weeks later. It was now the middle of November,
and Mr. Britling, very warmly wrapped in his thick dressing-
gown and his thick llama-wool pyjamas, was sitting at his
night desk, and working ever and again at an essay, an essay
of preposterous ambitions, for the title of it was " The Better
Government of the World."
Latterly he had had much sleepless misery. In the day life
was tolerable, but in the night—unless he defended himself
by working, the losses and cruelties of the war came and

grimaced at him, insufferably. Now he would be haunted by long processions of refugees, now he would think of the dead lying stiff and twisted in a thousand dreadful attitudes. Then again he would be overwhelmed with anticipations of the frightful economic and social dissolution that might lie ahead. . . . At other times he thought of wounds and the deformities of body and spirit produced by injuries. And sometimes he would think of the triumph of evil. Stupid and triumphant persons went about a world that stupidity had desolated with swaggering gestures, with a smiling consciousness of enhanced importance, with their scornful hatred of all measured and temperate and kindly things turned now to scornful contempt. And mingling with the soil they walked on lay the dead body of Hugh, face downward. At the back of the boy's head, rimmed by blood-stiffened hair—the hair that had once been " as soft as the down of a bird "—was a big red hole. That hole was always pitilessly distinct. They stepped on him heedlessly. They heeled the scattered stuff of his exquisite brain into the clay. . . .

From all such moods of horror Mr. Britling's circle of lamp-light was his sole refuge. His work could conjure up visions, like opium visions, of a world of order and justice. Amidst the gloom of world bankruptcy he stuck to the prospectus of a braver enterprise—reckless of his chances of subscribers. . . .

§ 2

But this night even this circle of lamplight would not hold his mind. Doubt had crept into this last fastness. He pulled the papers towards him, and turned over the portion he had planned.

His purpose in the book he was beginning to write was to reason out the possible methods of government that would give a stabler, saner control to the world. He believed still in democracy, but he was realising more and more that democracy had yet to discover its method. It had to take hold of the consciences of men, it had to equip itself with still unformed organisations. Endless years of patient thinking, of experimenting, of discussion lay before mankind ere this great idea could become reality, and right, the proven right thing, could rule the earth.

Meanwhile the world must still remain a scene of blood-stained melodrama, of deafening noise, contagious follies, vast irrational destructions. One fine life after another went down from study and university and laboratory to be slain and silenced. . . .

Was it conceivable that this mad monster of mankind would ever be caught and held in the thin-spun webs of thought ?

Was it, after all, anything but pretension and folly for a man to work out plans for the better government of the world ?—was it any better than the ambitious scheming of some fly upon the wheel of the romantic gods ?

Man has come, floundering and wounding and suffering, out of the breeding darknesses of Time, that will presently crush and consume him again. Why not flounder with the rest, why not eat, drink, fight, scream, weep and pray, forget Hugh, stop brooding upon Hugh, banish all these priggish dreams of " The Better Government of the World," and turn to the brighter aspects, the funny and adventurous aspects of the war, the Chestertonian jolliness, the *Punch* side of things. Think you because your sons are dead that there will be no more cakes and ale ? Let mankind blunder out of the mud and blood as mankind has blundered in. . . .

Let us at any rate keep our precious Sense of Humour. . . .

He pulled his manuscript towards him. For a time he sat decorating the lettering of his title, " The Better Government of the World," with little grinning gnomes' heads and waggish tails. . . .

§ 3

On the top of Mr. Britling's desk, beside the clock, lay a letter, written in clumsy English and with its envelope resealed by a label which testified that it had been " OPENED BY CENSOR."

The friendly go-between in Norway had written to tell Mr. Britling that Herr Heinrich also was dead ; he had died a wounded prisoner in Russia some months ago. He had been wounded and captured, after undergoing great hardships, during the great Russian attack upon the passes of the Carpathians in the early spring, and his wound had mortified. He had recovered partially for a time, and then he had been beaten and injured again in some struggle between German and Croatian prisoners, and he had sickened and died. Before he died he had written to his parents, and once again he had asked that the fiddle he had left in Mr. Britling's care should if possible be returned to them. It was manifest that both for him and them now it had become a symbol with many associations.

The substance of this letter invaded the orange circle of the lamp ; it would have to be answered, and the potentialities of the answer were running through Mr. Britling's brain to the exclusion of any impersonal composition. He thought of the old parents away there in Pomerania—he believed but he was not quite sure, that Heinrich had been an only son—and of the pleasant spectacled figure that had now become a broken and decaying thing in a prisoner's shallow grave. . . .

Another son had gone—all the world was losing its sons. . . .

He found himself thinking of young Heinrich in the very manner, if with a lesser intensity, in which he thought about his own son, as of hopes senselessly destroyed. His mind took no note of the fact that Heinrich was an enemy, that by the reckoning of a " war of attrition " his death was balance and compensation for the death of Hugh. He went straight to the root fact that they had been gallant and kindly beings, and that the same thing had killed them both. . . .

By no conceivable mental gymnastics could he think of the two as antagonists. Between them there was no imaginable issue. They had both very much the same scientific disposition ; with perhaps more dash and inspiration in the quality of Hugh ; more docility and method in the case of Karl. Until war had smashed them one against the other.

He recalled his first sight of Heinrich at the junction, and how he had laughed at the sight of his excessive Teutonism. The close-cropped shining fair head surmounted by a yellowish-white corps cap had appeared dodging about among the people upon the platform, and manifestly asking questions. The face had been very pink with the effort of an unaccustomed tongue. The young man had been clad in a suit of white flannel refined by a purple line ; his boots were of that greenish-yellow leather that only a German student could esteem " chic "; his rucksack was upon his back, and the precious fiddle in its case was carried very carefully in one hand ; this same dead fiddle. The other hand held a stick with a carved knob and a pointed end. He had been too German for belief. " Herr Heinrich ! " Mr. Britling had said, and straightway the heels had closed together for a bow, a bow from the waist, a bow that a heedless old lady much burthened with garden produce had greatly disarranged. From first to last amidst our offhand English ways Herr Heinrich had kept his bow—and always it had been getting disarranged.

That had been his constant effect ; a little stiff, a little absurd, and always clean and pink and methodical. The boys had liked him without reserve, Mrs. Britling had liked him ; everybody had found him a likeable creature. He never complained of anything except picnics. But he did object to picnics; to the sudden departure of the family to wild surroundings for the consumption of cold, knifeless and forkless meals in the serious middle hours of the day. He protested to Mr. Britling, respectfully but very firmly. It was, he held, implicit in their understanding that he should have a cooked meal in the middle of the day. Otherwise his Magen was perplexed and disordered. In the evening he could not eat with any gravity or profit. . . .

Their disposition towards underfeeding and a certain lack of fine sentiment were the only flaws in the English scheme that Herr Heinrich admitted. He certainly found the English unfeeling. His heart went even less satisfied than his Magen. He was a being of expressive affections ; he wanted great friendships, mysterious relationships, love. He tried very bravely to revere and to understand and be occultly understood

by Mr. Britling ; he sought long walks and deep talks with
Hugh and the small boys ; he tried to fill his heart with Cissie ;
he found at last marvels of innocence and sweetness in the
Hickson girl. She wore her hair in a pigtail when first he met
her, and it made her almost Marguerite. This young man had
cried aloud for love, warm and filling, like the Mittagsessen
that was implicit in their understanding. And all these Essex
people failed to satisfy him ; they were silent, they were subtle,
they slipped through the fat yet eager fingers of his heart, so
that he fell back at last upon himself and his German corre-
spondents and the idealisation of Maud Hickson and the moral
education of Billy. Billy. Mr. Britling's memories came back
at last to the figure of young Heinrich with the squirrel on his
shoulder, that had so often stood in the way of the utter condemnation of Germany. That, seen closely, was the stuff of one
brutal Prussian. What quarrel had we with him ? . . .
    Other memories of Heinrich flitted across Mr. Britling's
reverie. Heinrich at hockey, running with extreme swiftness
and little skill, tricked and baffled by Letty, dodged by Hugh,
going headlong forward and headlong back, and then with a
cry flinging himself flat on the ground exhausted. . . . Or
again Heinrich very grave and very pink, peering through his
glasses at his cards at Skat. . . . Or Heinrich in the boats
upon the great pond, or Heinrich swimming, or Heinrich hiding
very, very artfully from the boys about the garden on a theory
of his own, or Heinrich in strange postures, stalking the deer
in Claverings Park. For a time he had had a great ambition
to creep quite close to a deer and *touch* it. . . . Or Heinrich
indexing. He had a passion for listing and indexing books,
music, any loose classifiable thing. His favourite amusement
was devising schemes for the indentation of dictionary leaves,
so that one could turn instantly to the needed word. He had
bought and cut the edges of three dictionaries ; each in
succession improved upon the other ; he had had great hopes
of patents and wealth arising therefrom. . . . And his room
had been a source of strange sounds ; his search for music upon
the violin. He had hoped when he came to Matching's Easy
to join " some string quartet." But Matching's Easy produced
no string quartet. He had to fall back upon the pianola, and
try to play duets with that. Only the pianola did all the duet
itself, and in the hands of a small Britling was apt to betray a
facetious moodiness ; sudden alterations between extreme
haste and extreme lassitude. . . .
    Then there came a memory of Heinrich talking very seriously;
his glasses magnifying his round blue eyes, talking of his ideas
about life, of his beliefs and disbeliefs, of his ambitions and
prospects in life.
    He confessed two principal ambitions. They varied perhaps
in their absolute dimensions, but they were of equal importance
in his mind. The first of these was, so soon as he had taken his

doctorate in philology, to give himself to the perfecting of an International Language ; it was to combine all the virtues of Esperanto and Ido. "And then," said Herr Heinrich, " I do not think there will be any more wars—ever." The second ambition, which was important first because Herr Heinrich found much delight in working at it, and secondly because he thought it would give him great wealth and opportunity for propagating the perfect speech, was the elaboration of his system of marginal indentations for dictionaries and alphabetical books of reference of all sorts. It was to be so complete that one would just stand over the book to be consulted, run hand and eye over its edges and open the book—" at the very exact spot." He proposed to follow this business up with a quite Germanic thoroughness. " Presently," he said, " I must study the machinery by which the edges of books are cut. It is possible I may have to invent these also." This was the double-barrelled scheme of Herr Heinrich's career. And along it he was to go, and incidentally develop his large vague heart that was at present so manifestly unsatisfied. . . .

Such was the brief story of Herr Heinrich.

That story was over—just as Hugh's story was over. That first volume would never now have a second and a third. It ended in some hasty grave in Russia. The great scheme for marginal indices would never be patented, the duets with the pianola would never be played again.

Imagination glimpsed a little figure toiling manfully through the slush and snow of the Carpathians ; saw it staggering under its first experience of shell-fire ; set it amidst attacks and flights and fatigue and hunger and a rush perhaps in the darkness ; guessed at the wounding blow. Then came the pitiful pilgrimage of the prisoners into captivity, captivity in a land desolated, impoverished and embittered. Came wounds wrapped in filthy rags, pain and want of occupation, and a poor little bent and broken Heinrich sitting aloof in a crowded compound nursing a mortifying wound. . . .

He used always to sit in a peculiar attitude with his arms crossed on his crossed legs, looking slantingly through his glasses. . . .

So he must have sat, and presently he lay on some rough bedding and suffered, untended, in infinite discomfort ; lay motionless and thought at times, it may be, of Matching's Easy and wondered what Hugh and Teddy were doing. Then he became fevered, and the world grew bright-coloured and fantastic and ugly for him. Until one day an infinite weakness laid hold of him, and his pain grew faint and all his thoughts and memories grew faint—and still fainter. . . .

The violin had been brought into Mr. Britling's study that afternoon, and lay upon the farther window-seat. Poor little broken shred, poor little fragment of a shattered life ! It looked in its case like a baby in a coffin.

" I must write a letter to the old father and mother," Mr.
Britling thought. " I can't just send the poor little fiddle—
without a word. In all this pitiful storm of witless hate—surely
there may be one greeting—not hateful.

" From my blackness to yours," said Mr. Britling aloud.

He would have to write it in English. But even if they knew
no English some one would be found to translate it to them.
He would have to write very plainly.

§ 4

He pushed aside the manuscript of " The Better Government of the World," and began to write rather slowly, shaping
his letters roundly and distinctly :

Dear Sir,
*I am writing this letter to you to tell you I am sending back
the few little things I had kept for your son at his request when
the war broke out. I am sending them——*

Mr. Britling left that blank for the time until he could
arrange the method of sending to the Norwegian intermediary.

*Especially I am sending his violin, which he had asked me
thrice to convey to you. Either it is a gift from you or it symbolised
many things for him that he connected with home and you. I
will have it packed with particular care, and I will do all in my
power to ensure its safe arrival.*

*I want to tell you that all the stress and passion of this war has
not made us here in Matching's Easy forget our friend your son.
He was one of us, he had our affection, he had friends here who
are still his friends. We found him honourable and companionable,
and we share something of your loss. I have got together for you
a few snap-shots I chance to possess in which you will see him
in the sunshine, and which will enable you perhaps to picture a
little more definitely than you would otherwise do the life he led
here. There is one particularly that I have marked. Our family
is lunching out-of-doors, and you will see that next to your son is a
youngster, a year or so his junior, who is touching glasses with
him. I have put a cross over his head. He is my eldest son, he was
very dear to me, and he too has been killed in this war. They are,
you see, smiling very pleasantly at each other.*

While writing this Mr. Britling had been struck by the
thought of the photographs, and he had taken them out of the
little drawer into which he was accustomed to thrust them.
He picked out the ones that showed the young German, but
there were others, bright with sunshine, that were now charged
with acquired significances ; there were two showing the
children and Teddy and Hugh and Cissie and Letty doing the
goose-step, and there was one of Mr. Van der Pant, smiling at
the front door, in Heinrich's abandoned slippers. There were
endless pictures of Teddy also. It is the happy instinct of the
Kodak to refuse those days that are overcast, and the photo-

graphic record of a life is a chain of all its kindlier aspects. In the drawer above these snap-shots there were Hugh's letters and a miscellany of trivial documents touching on his life.

Mr. Britling discontinued writing and turned these papers over and mused. Heinrich's letters and postcards had got in among them, and so had a letter of Teddy's. . . .

The letters reinforced the photographs in their reminder how kind and pleasant a race mankind can be. Until the wild asses of nationalism came kicking and slaying amidst them, until suspicion and jostling greed and malignity poison their minds, until the fools with the high explosives blow that elemental goodness into shrieks of hate and splashes of blood. How kindly men are—up to the very instant of their cruelties ! His mind teemed suddenly with little anecdotes and histories of the good-will of men breaking through the ill-will of war, of the mutual help of sorely wounded Germans and English lying together in the mud and darkness between the trenches, of the fellowship of captors and prisoners, of the Saxons at Christmas fraternising with the English. . . . Of that he had seen photographs in one of the daily papers. . . .

His mind came back presently from these wanderings, to the task before him.

He tried to picture these Heinrich parents. He supposed they were kindly, civilised people. It was manifest the youngster had come to him from a well-ordered and gentle-spirited home. But he imagined them—he could not tell why—as people much older than himself. Perhaps young Heinrich had on some occasion said they were old people—he could not remember. And he had a curious impulse too to write to them in phrases of consolation ; as if their loss was more pitiable than his own. He doubted whether they had the consolation of his sanguine temperament, whether they could resort as readily as he could to his faith, whether in Pomerania there was the same consoling possibility of an essay on the Better Government of the World. He did not think this very clearly, but that was what was at the back of his mind. He went on writing.

If you think that these two boys have both perished, not in some noble common cause but one against the other in a struggle of dynasties and boundaries and trade routes and tyrannous ascendancies, then it seems to me that you must feel as I feel that this war is the most tragic and dreadful thing that has ever happened to mankind.

He sat thinking for some minutes after he had written that, and when presently he resumed his writing, a fresh strain of thought was traceable even in his opening sentence.

If you count dead and wounded this is the most dreadful war in history ; for you as for me, it has been almost the extremity of personal tragedy. . . . Black sorrow. . . .

But is it the most dreadful war ?

Cissie had come and stood by the side of him.

I do not think it is. I can write to you and tell you that I do indeed believe that our two sons have died not altogether in vain. Our pain and anguish may not be wasted—may be necessary. Indeed they may be necessary. Here am I bereaved and wretched— and I hope. Never was the fabric of war so black ; that I admit. But never was the black fabric of war so threadbare. At a thousand points the light is shining through.

Mr. Britling's pen stopped.

There was perfect stillness in the study bedroom.

" The tinpot style," said Mr. Britling at last in a voice of extreme bitterness.

He fell into an extraordinary quarrel with his style. He forgot about those Pomeranian parents altogether in his exasperation at his own inexpressiveness, at his incomplete control of these rebel words and phrases that came trailing each its own associations and suggestions to hamper his purpose with it. He read over the offending sentence.

" The point is that it is true," he whispered. " It is exactly what I want to say." . . .

Exactly ? . . .

His mind stuck on that " exactly." . . . When one has much to say style is troublesome. It is as if one fussed with one's uniform before a battle. . . . But that is just what one ought to do before a battle. . . . One ought to have everything in order. . . .

He took a fresh sheet and made three trial beginnings.

" *War is like a black fabric.*" . . .

" *War is a curtain of black fabric across the pathway.*"

" *War is a curtain of dense black fabric across all the hopes and kindliness of mankind. Yet always it has let through some gleams of light, and now—I am not dreaming—it grows threadbare, and here and there and at a thousand points the light is breaking through. We owe it to all these dear youths——*"

His pen stopped again.

" I must work on a rough draft," said Mr. Britling.

§ 5

Three hours later Mr. Britling was working by daylight, though his study lamp was still burning, and his letter to old Heinrich was still no better than a collection of material for a letter. But the material was falling roughly into shape, and Mr. Britling's intentions were finding themselves. It was clear to him now that he was no longer writing as his limited personal self to those two personal selves grieving, in the old large high-walled steep-roofed household amidst pinewoods, of which Heinrich had once shown him a picture. He knew them too little for any such personal address. He was writing, he perceived, not as Mr. Britling but as an Englishman—that was all he could be to them—and he was writing to them as Germans ; he could apprehend them as nothing more. He was just England bereaved to Germany bereaved. . . .

He was no longer writing to the particular parents of one particular boy, but to all that mass of suffering, regret, bitterness and fatigue that lay behind the veil of the " front." Slowly, steadily, the manhood of Germany was being wiped out. As he sat there in the stillness he could think that at least two million men of the Central Powers were dead, and an equal number maimed and disabled. Compared with that our British losses, immense and universal as they were by the standard of any previous experience, were still slight ; our larger armies had still to suffer, and we had lost irrevocably not very much more than a quarter of a million. But the tragedy gathered against us. We knew enough already to know what must be the reality of the German homes to which those dead men would nevermore return. . . .

If England had still the longer account to pay, the French had paid already nearly to the limits of endurance. They must have lost well over a million of their mankind, and still they bled and bled. Russia too in the East had paid far more than man for man in this vast swapping off of lives. In a little while no Censorship would hold the voice of the peoples. There would be no more talk of honour and annexations, hegemonies and trade routes, but only Europe lamenting for her dead. . . .

The Germany to which he wrote would be a nation of widows and children, rather pinched boys and girls, crippled men, old men, deprived men, men who had lost brothers and cousins and friends and ambitions. No triumph now on land or sea could save Germany from becoming that. France too would be that, Russia, and lastly Britain, each in their degree. Before the war there had been no Germany to which an Englishman could appeal ; Germany had been a threat, a menace, a terrible trampling of armed men. It was as little possible then to think of talking to Germany as it would have been to stop the Kaiser in mid-career in his hooting car down the Unter den Linden and demand a quiet talk with him. But the Germany that had watched those rushes with a slightly doubting pride had her eyes now full of tears and blood. She had believed, she had obeyed, and no real victory had come. Still she fought on, bleeding, agonising, wasting her substance and the substance of the whole world, to no conceivable end but exhaustion, so capable she was, so devoted, so proud and utterly foolish. And the mind of Germany, whatever it was before the war, would now be something residual, something left over and sitting beside a reading-lamp as he was sitting beside a reading-lamp, thinking, sorrowing, counting the cost, looking into the dark future. . . .

And to that he wrote, to that dimly apprehended figure outside a circle of the light like his own circle of light—which was the father of Heinrich, which was great Germany, Germany which lived before and which will yet outlive the flapping of the eagles. . . .

Our boys, he wrote, *have died, fighting one against the other. They have been fighting upon an issue so obscure that your German press is still busy discussing what it was. For us it was that Belgium was invaded and France in danger of destruction. Nothing else could have brought the English into the field against you. But why you invaded Belgium and France and whether that might have been averted we do not know to this day. And still this war goes on and still more boys die, and these men who do not fight, these men in the newspaper offices and in the ministries, plan campaigns and strokes and counter-strokes that belong to no conceivable plan at all. Except that now for them there is something more terrible than war. And that is the day of reckoning with their own people.*

What have we been fighting for ? What are we fighting for ? Do you know ? Does any one know ? Why am I spending what is left of my substance and you what is left of yours to keep on this war against each other ? What have we to gain from hurting one another still further ? Why should we be puppets any longer in the hands of crowned fools and witless diplomatists ? Even if we were dumb and acquiescent before, does not the blood of our sons now cry out to us that this foolery should cease ? We have let these people send our sons to death.

It is you and I who must stop these wars, these massacres of boys.

Massacres of boys ! That indeed is the essence of modern war. The killing off of the young. It is the destruction of the human inheritance, it is the spending of all the life and material of the future upon present-day hate and greed. Fools and knaves, politicians, tricksters, and those who trade on the suspicions and thoughtless, generous angers of men, make wars ; the indolence and modesty of the mass of men permit them. Are you and I to suffer such things until the whole fabric of our civilisation, that has been so slowly and so laboriously built up, is altogether destroyed ?

When I sat down to write to you I had meant only to write to you of your son and mine. But I feel that what can be said in particular of our loss, need not be said : it can be understood without saying. What needs to be said and written about is this, that war must be put an end to and that nobody else but you and me and all of us can do it. We have to do that for the love of our sons and our race and all that is human. War is no longer human ; the chemist and the metallurgist have changed all that. My boy was shot through the eye ; his brain was blown to pieces by some man who never knew what he had done. Think what that means ! . . . It is plain to me, surely it is plain to you and all the world, that war is now a mere putting of the torch to explosives that flare out to universal ruin. There is nothing for one sane man to write to another about in these days but the salvation of mankind from war.

Now I want you to be patient with me and hear me out. There was a time in the earlier part of this war when it was hard to be patient because there hung over us the dread of losses and disaster. Now we need dread no longer. The dreaded thing has happened. Sitting together as we do in spirit beside the mangled bodies of our dead, surely we can be as patient as the hills.

I want to tell you quite plainly and simply that I think that Germany, which is chief and central in this war, is most to blame for this war. Writing to you as an Englishman to a German, and with war still being waged, there must be no mistake between us upon this point. I am persuaded that in the decade that ended with your overthrow of France in 1871, Germany turned her face towards evil, and that her refusal to treat France generously and to make friends with any other great power in the world, is the essential cause of this war. Germany triumphed—and she trampled on the loser. She inflicted intolerable indignities. She set herself to prepare for further aggressions ; long before this killing began she was making war upon land and sea, launching war-ships, building strategic railways, setting up a vast establishment of war material, threatening, straining all the world to keep pace with her threats. . . . At last there was no choice before any European nation but submission to the German will, or war. And it was no will to which righteous men could possibly submit. It came as an illiberal and ungracious will. It was the will of Zabern. It is not as if you had set yourselves to be an imperial people and embrace and unify the world. You did not want to unify the world. You wanted to set the foot of an intensely national Germany, a sentimental and illiberal Germany, a Germany that treasured the portraits of your ridiculous Kaiser and his litter of sons, a Germany wearing uniform, reading black letter, and despising every kultur but her own, upon the neck of a divided and humiliated mankind. It was an intolerable prospect. I had rather the whole world died.

Forgive me for writing " you." You are as little responsible for that Germany as I am for—Sir Edward Grey. But this happened over you ; you did not do your utmost to prevent it— even as England has happened, and I have let it happen over me. . . .

" It is so dry ; so general," whispered Mr. Britling. " And yet—it is this that has killed our sons."

He sat still for a time, and then went on reading a fresh sheet of his manuscript.

When I bring these charges against Germany I have little disposition to claim any righteousness for Britain. There has been small splendour in this war for either Germany or Britain or Russia ; we three have chanced to be the biggest of the combatants, but the glory lies with invincible France. It is France and Belgium and Serbia who shine as the heroic lands. They have fought defensively and beyond all expectation, for dear land and freedom. This war for them has been a war of simple, definite issues, to which they have risen with an entire nobility. Englishman and German alike may well envy them that simplicity. I look to you, as an honest man schooled by the fierce lessons of this war, to meet me in my passionate desire to see France, Belgium and Serbia emerge restored from all this blood and struggle, enlarged to the limits of their nationality, vindicated and secure. Russia I will not write about here ; let me go on at once to tell you about my own country ; remarking only that between England and Russia there are endless parallelisms. We have similar complexities, kindred difficulties. We have for instance an imported dynasty, we have a soul-destroying State Church which cramps and poisons the education of our ruling class, we have a people out of touch with a secretive government, and the same traditional contempt for science. We have our Irelands and Polands. Even our kings bear a curious likeness. . . .

At this point there was a break in the writing, and Mr. Britling made, as it were, a fresh beginning.

Politically the British Empire is a clumsy collection of strange accidents. It is a thing as little to be proud of as the outline of a flint or the shape of a potato. For the mass of English people India and Egypt and all that side of our system mean less than nothing ; our trade is something they do not understand, our imperial wealth something they do not share. Britain has been a group of four democracies caught in the net of a vast yet casual imperialism ; the common man here is in a state of political perplexity from the cradle to the grave. None the less there is a great people here even as there is a great people in Russia, a people with a soul and character of its own, a people of unconquerable kindliness and with a peculiar genius, which still struggle towards will and expression. We have been beginning that same great experiment that France and America and Switzerland and China are making, the experiment of democracy. It is the newest form of human association, and we are still but half awake to its needs and necessary conditions. For it is idle to pretend that the little city democracies of ancient times were comparable to the great essays in practical republicanism that mankind is making to-day. This age of the democratic republics that dawns is a new age. It has not yet lasted for a century, not for a paltry hundred years. . . . All new things are weak things ; a rat can kill a man child with ease ; the greater the destiny, the weaker the immediate self-protection may be. And to me it seems that your complete and perfect imperialism, ruled by Germans for Germans, is in its scope and outlook a more antiquated and smaller and less noble thing than these sprawling emergent giant democracies of the West that struggle so confusedly against it. . . .

But we do not struggle confusedly, with pitiful leaders and infinite waste and endless delay ; that it is to our indisciplines and to the dishonesties and tricks our incompleteness provokes, that the prolongation of this war is to be ascribed, I readily admit. At the outbreak of this war I had hoped to see militarism felled within a year. . . .

§ 6

From this point onward Mr. Britling's notes became more fragmentary. They had a consecutiveness, but they were discontinuous. His thought had leaped across gaps that his pen had had no time to fill. And he had begun to realise that his letter to the old people in Pomerania was becoming impossible. It had broken away into dissertation.

" Yet there must be dissertations," he said. " Unless such men as we are take these things in hand, always we shall be misgoverned, always the sons will die. . . . "

§ 7

I do not think you Germans realise how steadily you were conquering the world before this war began. Had you given half the energy and intelligence you have spent upon this war to the peaceful conquest of men's minds and spirits, I believe that you would have taken the leadership of the world tranquilly—no man disputing. Your science was five years, your social and economic organisation was a quarter of a century, in front of ours. . . . Never has it so lain in the power of a great people to lead and direct mankind towards the world republic and universal peace. It needed but a certain generosity of the imagination. . . .

But your Junkers, your Imperial court, your foolish vicious Princes ; what were such dreams to them ?. . . With an envious satisfaction they hurled all the accomplishment of Germany into the fires of war. . . .

§ 8

Your boy, as no doubt you know, dreamt constantly of such a world peace as this that I have foreshadowed ; he was more generous than his country. He could envisage war and hostility only as misunderstanding. He thought that a world that could explain itself clearly would surely be at peace. He was scheming always therefore for the perfection and propagation of Esperanto or Ido, or some such universal link. My youngster too was full of a kindred and yet larger dream, the dream of human science, which knows neither king nor country nor race. . . .

These boys, these hopes, this war has killed. . . .

That fragment ended so. Mr. Britling ceased to read for a time. " But has it killed them ? " he whispered. . . .

" If you had lived, my dear, you and your England would have talked with a younger Germany—better than I can ever do. . . . "

He turned the pages back, and read here and there with an accumulating discontent.

§ 9

" Dissertations," said Mr. Britling.

Never had it been so plain to him that he was a weak, silly, ill-informed, and hasty-minded writer, and never had he felt so invincible a conviction that the Spirit of God was in him, and that it fell to him to take some part in the establishment of a new order of living upon the earth ; it might be the most trivial part by the scale of the task, but for him it was to be now his supreme concern. And it was an almost intolerable grief to him that his services should be, for all his desire, so poor in quality, so weak in conception. Always he seemed to be on the verge of some illuminating and beautiful statement of his cause ; always he was finding his writing inadequate, a thin treachery to the impulse of his heart, always he was finding his effort weak and ineffective. In this instance, at the outset he seemed to see with a golden clearness the message of brotherhood, of forgiveness, of a common call. To whom could such a message be better addressed than to those sorrowing parents ; from whom could it come with a better effect than from himself ? And now he read what he had made of this message. It seemed to his jaded mind a pitifully jaded effort. It had no light, it had no depth. It was like the disquisition of a debating society.

He was distressed by a fancy of an old German couple, spectacled and peering, puzzled by his letter. Perhaps they would be obscurely hurt by his perplexing generalisations. Why, they would ask, should this Englishman preach to them ?

He sat back in his chair wearily, with his chin sunk upon his chest. For a time he did not think, and then he read again the sentence in front of his eyes.

" *These boys, these hopes, this war has killed.*"

The words hung for a time in his mind.

" No ! " said Mr. Britling stoutly. " They live ! "

And suddenly it was borne in upon his mind that he was not alone. There were thousands and tens of thousands of men and women like himself, desiring with all their hearts to say, as he desired to say, the reconciling word. It was not only his hand that thrust against the obstacles. . . . Frenchmen and Russians sat in the same stillness, facing the same perplexities ; there were Germans seeking a way through to him. Even as he sat and wrote. And for the first time clearly he felt a Presence of which he had thought very many times in the last few weeks, a Presence so close to him that it was behind his eyes and in his brain and hands. It was no trick of his vision : it was a feeling of immediate reality. And it was Hugh, Hugh that he had thought was dead, it was young Heinrich living also, it was himself, it was those others that sought, it was all these and it was more, it was the Master the Captain of Mankind, it was God, there present with him, and he knew that it was God. It was as if he had been groping all this time in the darkness, thinking himself alone amidst rocks and pitfalls and pitiless things, and suddenly a hand, a firm strong hand, had touched his own. And a voice within him bade him be of good courage. There was no magic trickery in that moment ; he was still weak and weary ; a discouraged rhetorician, a good intention ill equipped ; but he was no longer lonely and wretched, no longer in the same world with despair. God was beside him and within him and about him. . . . It was the crucial moment of Mr. Britling's life. It was a thing as light as the passing of a cloud on an April morning ; it was a thing as great as the first day of creation. For some moments he still sat back with his chin upon his chest and his hands dropping from the arms of his chair. Then he sat up and drew a deep breath. . . .

This had come almost as a matter of course.

For weeks his mind had been playing about this idea. He had talked to Letty of this Finite God, who is the king of man's adventure in space and time. But hitherto God had been for him a thing of the intelligence, a theory, a report, something told about but not realised. . . . Mr. Britling's thinking about God hitherto had been like some one who has found an empty house, very beautiful and pleasant, full of the promise of a fine personality. And then as the discoverer makes his lonely, curious explorations, he hears downstairs, dear and friendly, the voice of the Master coming in. . . .

There was no need to despair because he himself was one of the feeble folk. God was with him indeed, and he was with God. The King was coming to his own. Amidst the darknesses and confusions, the nightmare cruelties and the hideous stupidities of the great war, God, the Captain of the World Republic, fought his way to empire. So long as one did one's best and utmost in a cause so mighty, did it matter though the thing one did was little and poor ?

" I have thought too much of myself," said Mr. Britling, " and of what I would do by myself. I have forgotten *that which was with me.* . . . "

§ 10

He turned over the rest of the night's writing presently, and read it now as though it was the work of another man.

These later notes were fragmentary, and written in a sprawling hand.

" *Let us make ourselves watchers and guardians of the order of the world.* . . .

" *If only for love of our dead.* . . .

" *Let us pledge ourselves to service. Let us set ourselves with all our minds and with all our hearts to the perfecting and working out of the methods of democracy and the ending for ever of the*

*kings and emperors and priestcrafts and the bands of adventurers,
the traders and owners and forestallers who have betrayed mankind into this morass of hate and blood—in which our sons are
lost—in which we flounder still. . . ."*

How feeble was this squeak of exhortation ! It broke into
a scolding note.

" Who have betrayed," read Mr. Britling, and judged the
phrase.

" Who have fallen with us," he emended. . . .

" One gets so angry and bitter—because one feels alone,
I suppose. Because one feels that for them one's reason is
no reason. One is enraged by the sense of their silent and
regardless contradiction, and one forgets the Power of which
one is a part. . . ."

The sheet that bore the sentence he criticised was otherwise blank except that written across it obliquely in a very
careful hand were the words " Hugh " and " Hugh Philip
Britling." . . .

On the next sheet he had written : " Let us set up the
peace of the World Republic amidst these ruins. Let it be
our religion, our calling."

There he had stopped.

The last sheet of Mr. Britling's manuscript may be more
conveniently given in facsimile than described. (See next page.)

§ 11

He sighed.

He looked at the scattered papers, and thought of the letter
they were to have made.

His fatigue spoke first.

" Perhaps after all I'd better just send the fiddle. . . ."

He rested his cheeks between his hands, and remained so
for a long time. His eyes stared unseeingly. His thoughts
wandered and spread and faded. At length he recalled his
mind to that last idea. " Just send the fiddle without a word."

" No. I must write to them plainly.

" About God as I have found Him.

" As He has found me. . . ."

He forgot the Pomeranians for a time. He murmured to
himself. He turned over the conviction that had suddenly
become clear and absolute in his mind.

" Religion is the first thing and the last thing, and until
a man has found God and been found by God, he begins at
no beginning, he works to no end. He may have his friendships, his partial loyalties, his scraps of honour. But all these
things fall into place and life falls into place only with God.
Only with God. God, who fights through men against Blind
Force and Night and Non-Existence ; who is the end, who is
the meaning. He is the only King. . . . Of course I must write
about Him. I must tell all my world of Him. And before th

coming of the true King, the inevitable King, the King who is present whenever just men foregather, this blood-stained rubbish of the ancient world, these puny kings and tawdry emperors, these wily politicians and artful lawyers, these men who claim and grab and trick and compel, these war-makers and oppressors, will presently shrivel and pass—like paper thrust into a flame. . . ."

Then after a time he said :

" Our sons who have shown us God. . . . "

§ 12

He rubbed his open hands over his eyes and forehead.

The night of effort had tired his brain, and he was no longer thinking actively. He had a little interval of blankness, sitting at his desk with his hands pressed over his eyes. . . .

He got up presently, and stood quite motionless at the window, looking out.

His lamp was still burning, but for some time he had not been writing by the light of his lamp. Insensibly the day had come and abolished his need for that individual circle of yellow light. Colour had returned to the world, clean pearly colour, clear and definite like the glance of a child or the voice of a girl, and a golden wisp of cloud hung in the sky over the tower of the church. There was a mist upon the pond, a soft grey mist not a yard high. A covey of partridges ran and halted and ran again in the dewy grass outside his garden railings. The partridges were very numerous this year because there had been so little shooting. Beyond in the meadow a hare sat up as still as a stone. A horse neighed. . . . Wave after wave of warmth and light came sweeping before the sunrise across the world of Matching's Easy. It was as if there was nothing but morning and sunrise in the world.

From away towards the church came the sound of some early worker whetting a scythe.

IN THE DAYS
OF THE COMET

" The World's Great Age begins anew,
    The Golden Years return,
The Earth doth like a Snake renew
    Her Winter Skin outworn :
Heaven smiles, and Faiths and Empires gleam
Like Wrecks of a Dissolving Dream."

CONTENTS

Prologue

Book the First
The Comet

Book the Second
The Green Vapours

Book the Third
The New World

The Epilogue

CONTENTS

The Man who Wrote in the Tower

PROLOGUE

THE MAN WHO WROTE IN THE TOWER

I saw a grey-haired man, a figure of hale age, sitting at a desk and writing.

He seemed to be in a room in a tower, very high, so that through the tall window on his left one perceived only distances, a remote horizon of sea, a headland, and that vague haze and glitter in the sunset that many miles away marks a city. All the appointments of this room were orderly and beautiful, and in some subtle quality, in this small difference and that, new to me and strange. They were in no fashion I could name, and the simple costume the man wore suggested neither period nor country. It might, I thought, be the Happy Future, or Utopia ; an errant mote of memory, Henry James's phrase and story of " The Great Good Place," twinkled across my mind, and passed and left no light.

The man I saw wrote with a thing like a fountain pen, a modern touch that prohibited any historical reference, and as he finished each sheet, writing in an easy flowing hand, he added it to a growing pile upon a graceful little table under the window. His last done sheets lay loose, partly covering others that were clipped together into fascicles.

Clearly he was unaware of my presence, and I stood waiting until his pen should come to a pause. Old as he certainly was he wrote with a steady hand. . . .

I discovered that a concave speculum hung slantingly high over his head ; a movement in this caught my attention sharply, and I looked up to see, distorted and made fantastic but bright and beautifully coloured, the magnified, reflected, evasive rendering of a palace, of a terrace, of the vista of a great roadway with many people, people exaggerated, impossible-looking because of the curvature of the mirror, going to and fro. I turned my head quickly that I might see more clearly through the window behind me, but it was too high for me to survey this nearer scene directly, and after a momentary pause I came back to that distorting mirror again.

But now the writer was leaning back in his chair. He put down his pen and sighed the half resentful sigh—" ah ! you work, you ! how you gratify and tire me ! "—of a man who has been writing to his satisfaction.

" What is this place," I asked, " and who are you ? "

He looked around with the quick movement of surprise.

" What is this place ? " I repeated, " and where am I ? "

He regarded me steadfastly for a moment under his wrinkled brows, and then his expression softened to a smile. He pointed to a chair beside the table. " I am writing," he said.

" About this ? "

" About the Change."

321

I sat down. It was a very comfortable chair, and well placed under the light.

" If you would like to read——— " he said.

I indicated the manuscript. " This explains ? " I asked.

" That explains," he answered.

He drew a fresh sheet of paper towards him as he looked at me.

I glanced from him about his apartment and back to the little table. A fascicle marked very distinctly " 1 " caught my attention, and I took it up. I smiled in his friendly eyes. " Very well," said I, suddenly at my ease, and he nodded and went on writing. And in a mood between confidence and curiosity, I began to read.

This is the story that happy, active-looking old man in that pleasant place had written.

Book One

The Comet

CHAPTER ONE

DUST IN THE SHADOWS

§ I

I HAVE set myself to write the story of the Great Change, so far as it has affected my own life and the lives of one or two people closely connected with me, primarily to please myself. Long ago, in my crude unhappy youth, I conceived a desire to write a book. To scribble secretly and dream of authorship was one of my chief alleviations, and I read with a sympathetic envy every scrap I could get about the world of literature and the lives of literary people. It is something, even amidst this present happiness, to find leisure and opportunity to take up and partially realise these old and hopeless dreams. But that alone, in a world where so much of vivid and increasing interest presents itself to be done, even by an old man, would not, I think, suffice to set me at this desk. I find some such recapitulation of my past as this will involve, is becoming necessary to my own secure mental continuity. The passage of years brings a man at last to retrospection ; at seventy-two one's youth is far more important than it was at forty. And I am out of touch with my youth. The old life seems so cut off from the new, so alien and so unreasonable, that at times I find it bordering upon the incredible. The data have gone, the buildings and places. I stopped dead the other afternoon in my walk across the moor, where once the dismal outskirts of Swathinglea straggled towards Leet, and asked, " Was it here indeed that I crouched among the weeds and refuse and broken crockery and loaded my revolver ready for murder ? Did ever such a thing happen in my life ? Was such a mood and thought and intention ever possible to me ? Rather, has not some queer nightmare spirit out of dreamland slipped a pseudo-memory into the records of my vanished life ? " There must be many alive still who have the same perplexities. And I think too that those who are now growing up to take our places in the great enterprise of mankind, will need many such narratives as mine for even the most partial conception of the old world of shadows that came before our day. It chances too that my case is fairly typical of the Change ; I was caught midway in a gust of passion ; and a curious accident put me for a time in the very nucleus of the new order. . . .

My memory takes me back across the interval of fifty years to a little ill-lit room with a sash window open to a starry sky, and instantly there returns to me the characteristic smell of that room, the penetrating odour of an ill-trimmed lamp, burning cheap paraffin. Lighting by electricity had then been perfected for fifteen years, but still the larger portion of the world used these lamps. All this first scene will go, in my mind at least, to that olfactory accompaniment. That was the evening smell of the room. By day it had a more subtle aroma, a closeness, a peculiar sort of faint pungency that I associate—I know not why—with dust.

Let me describe this room to you in detail. It was perhaps eight feet by seven in area and rather higher than either of these dimensions ; the ceiling was of plaster, cracked and bulging in places, grey with the soot of the lamp,. and in one place discoloured by a system of yellow and olive-green stains caused by the percolation of damp from above. The walls were covered with dun-coloured paper, upon which had been printed in oblique reiteration a crimson shape, something of the nature of a curly ostrich feather, or an acanthus flower, that had in its less faded moments a sort of dingy gaiety. There were several big plaster-rimmed wounds in this, caused by Parload's ineffectual attempts to get nails into the wall, whereby there might hang pictures. One nail had hit between two bricks and got home, and from this depended, sustained a little insecurely by frayed and knotted blind-cord, Parload's hanging bookshelves, planks painted over with a treacly blue enamel and further decorated by a fringe of pinked American cloth insecurely fixed by tacks. Below this was a little table that behaved with a mulish vindictiveness to any knee that was thrust beneath it suddenly ; it was covered with a cloth whose pattern of red and black had been rendered less monotonous by the accidents of Parload's versatile ink bottle, and on it, *leit motif* of the whole, stood and stank the lamp. This lamp, you must understand, was of some whitish translucent substance that was neither china nor glass, it had a shade of the same substance, a shade that did not protect the eyes of a reader in any measure, and it seemed admirably adapted to bring into pitiless prominence the fact that, after the lamp's trimming, dust and paraffin had been smeared over its exterior with a reckless generosity.

The uneven floor boards of this apartment were covered with scratched enamel of chocolate hue, on which a small island of frayed carpet dimly blossomed in the dust and shadows.

There was a very small grate, made of cast-iron in one piece and painted buff, and a still smaller misfit of a cast-iron fender that confessed the grey stone of the hearth. No fire was laid, only a few scraps of torn paper and the bowl of a broken corn-cob pipe were visible behind the bars, and in the corner and rather thrust away was an angular japanned coalbox with a damaged hinge. It was the custom in those days to warm every room separately from a separate fireplace, more prolific of dirt than heat, and the rickety sash window, the small chimney, and the loose-fitting door were expected to organize the ventilation of the room among themselves without any further direction.

Parload's truckle bed hid its grey sheets beneath an old patchwork counterpane on one side of the room, and veiled his boxes and such-like oddments, and invading the two corners of the window were an old whatnot and the washhandstand, on which were distributed the simple appliances of his toilet.

This washhandstand had been made of deal by someone with an excess of turnery appliances in a hurry, who had tried to distract attention from the rough economies of his workmanship by an arresting ornamentation of blobs and bulbs upon the joints and legs. Apparently the piece had then been placed in the hands of some person of infinite leisure equipped with a pot of ocherous paint, varnish, and a set of flexible combs. This person had first painted the article, then, I fancy, smeared it with varnish, and then sat down to work with the combs to streak and comb the varnish into a weird imitation of the grain of some nightmare timber. The washhandstand so made had evidently had a prolonged career of violent use, had been chipped, kicked, splintered, punched, stained, scorched, hammered, dessicated, damped, and defiled, had met indeed with almost every possible adventure except a conflagration or a scrubbing, until at last it had come to this high refuge of Parload's attic to sustain the simple requirements of Parload's personal cleanliness. There were, in chief, a basin and a jug of water and a slop-pail of tin, and, further, a piece of yellow soap in a tray, a tooth-brush, a rat-tailed shaving brush, one huckaback towel, and one or two other minor articles. In those days only very prosperous people had more than such an equipage, and it is to be remarked that every drop of water Parload used had to be carried by an unfortunate servant girl,—the " slavey," Parload called her—up from the basement to the top of the house and subsequently down again. Already we begin to forget how modern an invention is personal cleanliness. It is a fact that Parload had never stripped for a swim in his life ; never had a simultaneous bath all over his body since his childhood. Not one in fifty of us did in the days of which I am telling you.

A chest, also singularly grained and streaked, of two large and two small drawers, held Parload's reserve of garments, and pegs on the door carried his two hats and completed this inventory of a " bed-sitting-room " as I knew it before the Change. But I had forgotten—there was also a chair with a " squab " that apologised inadequately for the defects of its cane seat. I forgot that for the moment because I was sitting on the chair on the occasion that best begins this story.

I have described Parload's room with such particularity because it will help you to understand the key in which my earlier chapters are written, but you must not imagine that this singular equipment or the smell of the lamp engaged my attention at that time to the slightest degree. I took all this grimy unpleasantness as if it were the most natural and proper setting for existence imaginable. It was the world as I knew it. My mind was entirely occupied then by graver and intenser matters, and it is only now in the distant retrospect that I see these details of environment as being remarkable, as significant, as indeed obviously the outward visible manifestations of the old world disorder in our hearts.

§ 2

Parload stood at the open window, opera-glass in hand, and sought and found and was uncertain about and lost again, the new comet.

I thought the comet no more than a nuisance then because I wanted to talk of other matters. But Parload was full of it. My head was hot, I was feverish with interlacing annoyances and bitterness, I wanted to open my heart to him—at least I wanted to relieve my heart by some romantic rendering of my troubles—and I gave but little heed to the things he told me. It was the first time I had heard of this new speck among the countless specks of heaven, and I did not care if I never heard of the thing again.

We were two youths much of an age together; Parload was two and twenty, and eight months older than I. He was —I think his proper definition was " engrossing clerk " to a little solicitor in Overcastle, while I was third in the office staff of Rawdon's pot-bank in Clayton. We had met first in the " Parliament " of the Young Men's Christian Association of Swathinglea; we had found we attended simultaneous classes in Overcastle, he in science and I in shorthand, and had started a practice of walking home together, and so our friendship came into being. (Swathinglea, Clayton, and Overcastle were contiguous towns, I should mention, in the great industrial area of the Midlands.) We had shared each other's secret of religious doubt, we had confided to one another a common interest in Socialism, he had come twice to supper at my mother's on a Sunday night, and I was free of his apartment. He was then a tall, flaxen-haired, gawky youth, with a disproportionate development of neck and wrist, and capable of vast enthusiasm; he gave two evenings a week to the evening classes of the organised science school in Overcastle, physiography was his favourite " subject," and through this insidious opening of his mind the wonder of outer space had come to take possession of his soul. He had commandeered an old opera-glass from his uncle who farmed at Leet over the moors, he had bought a cheap paper planisphere and *Whitaker's Almanac*, and for a time day and moonlight were mere blank interruptions to the one satisfactory reality in his life—s tar gazing. It was the deeps that had seized him, the immensities, and the mysterious possibilities that might float unlit in that unplumbed abyss. With infinite labour and the help of a very precise article in *The Heavens*, a little monthly magazine that catered for those who were under this obsession, he had at last got his opera-glass upon the new visitor to our system from the outer space. He gazed in a sort of rapture upon that quivering little smudge of light among the shining pin-points—and gazed. My troubles had to wait for him.

" Wonderful," he sighed, and then as though his first emphasis did not satisfy him, " wonderful ! "

He turned to me. " Wouldn't you like to see ? "

I had to look, and then I had to listen, how that this scarce-visible intruder was to be, was presently to be, one of the largest comets this world has ever seen, how that its course must bring it within at most—so many score of millions of miles from the earth, a mere step, Parload seemed to think that ; how that the spectroscope was already sounding its chemical secrets, perplexed by the unprecedented band in the green, how it was even now being photographed in the very act of unwinding—in an unusual direction—a sunward tail (which presently it wound up again), and all the while in a sort of undertow I was thinking first of Nettie Stuart and the letter she had just written me, and then of old Rawdon's detestable face as I had seen it that afternoon. Now I planned answers to Nettie and now belated repartees to my employer, and then again " Nettie " was blazing all across the back-ground of my thoughts. . . .

Nettie Stuart was daughter of the head gardener of the rich Mr. Verrall's widow, and she and I had kissed and become sweethearts before we were eighteen years old. My mother and hers were second cousins and old schoolfellows, and though my mother had been widowed untimely by a train accident, and had been reduced to letting lodgings (she was the Clayton curate's landlady), a position esteemed much lower than that of Mrs. Stuart, a kindly custom of occasional visits to the gardener's cottage at Checkshill Towers still kept the friends in touch. Commonly I went with her. And I remember it was in the dusk of one bright evening in July, one of those long golden evenings that do not so much give way to night as admit at last, upon courtesy, the moon and a choice retinue of stars, that Nettie and I, at the pond of goldfish where the yew-bordered walks converged, made our shy beginners' vow. I remember still—something will always stir in me at that memory—the tremulous emotion of that adventure. Nettie was dressed in white, her hair went off in waves of soft dark-ness from above her dark shining eyes ; there was a little necklace of pearls about her sweetly modelled neck, and a little coin of gold that nestled in her throat. I kissed her half-reluctant lips, and for three years of my life thereafter—nay !

I almost think for all the rest of her life and mine—I could have died for her sake.

You must understand—and every year it becomes increasingly difficult to understand—how entirely different the world was then from what it is now. It was a dark world ; it was full of preventable disorder, preventable diseases, and preventable pain, of harshness and stupid unpremeditated cruelties ; but yet, it may be even by virtue of the general darkness, there were moments of a rare and evanescent beauty that seems no longer possible in my experience. The great Change has come for ever more, happiness and beauty are our atmosphere, there is peace on earth and good will to all men. None would dare to dream of returning to the sorrows of the former time, and yet that misery was pierced, ever and again its grey curtain was stabbed through and through by joys of an intensity, by perceptions of a keenness that it seems to me are now altogether gone out of life. Is it the Change, I wonder, that has robbed life of its extremes, or is it perhaps only this, that youth has left me—even the strength of middle years leaves me now—and taken its despairs and raptures, leaving me judgment perhaps, sympathy, memories ?

I cannot tell. One would need to be young now and to have been young then as well, to decide that impossible problem.

Perhaps a cool observer even in the old days would have found little beauty in our grouping. I have our two photographs at hand in this bureau as I write, and they show me a gawky youth in ill-fitting ready-made clothing, and Nettie—indeed Nettie is badly dressed, and her attitude is more than a little stiff ; but I can see her through the picture, and her living brightness and something of that mystery of charm she had for me, comes back again to my mind. Her face had triumphed over the photographer—or I would long ago have cast this picture away.

The reality of beauty yields itself to no words. I wish that I had the sister art and could draw in my margin something that escapes description. There was a sort of gravity in her eyes. There was something, a matter of the minutest difference, about her upper lip so that her mouth closed sweetly and broke very sweetly to a smile. That grave, sweet smile !

After we had kissed and decided not to tell our parents for awhile of the irrevocable choice we had made, the time came for us to part, shyly and before others, and I and my mother went off back across the moonlit park—the bracken thickets rustling with startled deer—to the railway station at Checkshill and so to our dingy basement in Clayton, and I saw no more of Nettie—except that I saw her in my thoughts—for nearly a year. But at our next meeting it was decided that we must correspond, and this we did with much elaboration of secrecy, for Nettie would have no one at home, not even her only sister, know of her attachment. So I had to send my

precious documents sealed and under cover by way of a con
fidential schoolfellow of hers who lived near London. . . . I
could write that address down now, though house and street
and suburb have gone beyond any man's tracing.

Our correspondence began our estrangement, because for
the first time we came into more than sensuous contact and
our minds sought expression.

Now you must understand that the world of thought in
those days was in the strangest condition, it was choked with
obsolete inadequate formulæ, it·was tortuous to a maze-like
degree with secondary contrivances and adaptations, sup-
pressions, conventions, and subterfuges. Base immediacies
fouled the truth on every man's lips. I was brought up by
my mother in a quaint old-fashioned narrow faith in certain
religious formulæ, certain rules of conduct, certain conceptions of social and political order, that has no more relevance
to the realities and needs of everyday contemporary life than
if they were clean linen that had been put away with lavender
in a drawer. Indeed, her religion did actually smell of lavender;
on Sundays she put away all the things of reality, the garments
and even the furnishings of everyday, hid her hands, that
were gnarled and sometimes chapped with scrubbing, in black,
carefully mended gloves, assumed her old black silk dress and
bonnet and took me, unnaturally clean and sweet also, to
church. There we sang and bowed and heard sonorous prayers
and joined in sonorous responses, and rose with a congre-
gational sigh refreshed and relieved when the doxology, with
its opening " Now to God the Father, God the Son," bowed
out the tame, brief sermon. There was a hell in that religion
of my mother's, a red-haired hell of curly flames that had once
been very terrible ; there was a devil, who was also *ex officio*
the British King's enemy, and much denunciation of the
wicked lusts of the flesh ; we were expected to believe that
most of our poor unhappy world was to atone for its muddle
and trouble here by suffering exquisite torments for ever after,
world without end, Amen. But indeed those curly flames
looked rather jolly. The whole thing had been mellowed and
faded into a gentle unreality long before my time ; if it had
much terror even in my childhood I have forgotten it, it was
not so terrible as the giant who was killed by the Beanstalk,
and I see it all now as a setting for my poor old mother's worn
and grimy face, and almost lovingly as a part of her. And
Mr. Gabbitas, our plump little lodger, strangely transformed
in his vestments and lifting his voice manfully to the quality
of those Elizabethan prayers, seemed, I think, to give her a
special and peculiar interest with God. She radiated her own
tremulous gentleness upon Him, and redeemed Him from all
the implications of vindictive theologians ; she was in truth,
had I but perceived it, the effectual answer to all she would
have taught me.

So I see it now, but there is something harsh in the earnest intensity of youth ; and having at first taken all these things quite seriously, the fiery hell and God's vindictiveness at any neglect, as though they were as much a matter of fact as Bladden's iron-works and Rawdon's pot-bank, I presently with an equal seriousness flung them out of my mind again.

Mr. Gabbitas, you see, did sometimes, as the phrase went, " take notice " of me, he had induced me to go on reading after I left school, and with the best intentions in the world and to anticipate the poison of the times, he had lent me Burble's " Scepticism Answered," and drawn my attention to the library of the Institute in Clayton.

The excellent Burble was a great shock to me. It seemed clear from his answers to the sceptic that the case for doctrinal orthodoxy and all that faded and by no means awful hereafter, which I had hitherto accepted as I accepted the sun, was an extremely poor one, and to hammer home that idea the first book I got from the Institute happened to be an American edition of the collected works of Shelley, his gassy prose as well as his atmospheric verse. I was soon ripe for blatant unbelief. And at the Young Men's Christian Association I presently made the acquaintance of Parload, who told me, under promises of the most sinister secrecy, that he was " a Socialist out and out." He lent me several copies of a periodical with the clamant title of *The Clarion*, which was just taking up a crusade against the accepted religion. The adolescent years of any fairly intelligent youth lie open, and will always lie healthily open, to the contagion of philosophical doubts, of scorns and new ideas, and I will confess I had the fever of that phase badly. Doubt, I say, but it was not so much doubt—which is a complex thing—as startled emphatic denial. " Have I believed *this* !" And I was also, you must remember, just beginning love-letters to Nettie.

We live now in these days, when the Great Change has been in most things accomplished, in a time when everyone is being educated to a sort of intellectual gentleness, a gentleness that abates nothing from our vigour, and it is hard to understand the stifled and struggling manner in which my generation of common young men did its thinking. To think at all about certain questions was an act of rebellion that set one oscillating between the furtive and the defiant. People begin to find Shelley—for all his melody—noisy and ill-conditioned now because his Anarchs have vanished, yet there was a time when novel thought *had* to go to that tune of breaking glass. It becomes a little difficult to imagine the yeasty state of mind, the disposition to shout and say, " Yah!" at constituted authority, to sustain a persistent note of provocation such as we raw youngsters displayed. I began to read with avidity such writing as Carlyle, Browning, and Heine have left for the perplexity of posterity, and not only to read and admire but to imitate. My letters to Nettie, after one or two genuinely intended displays of perfervid tenderness, broke out towards theology, sociology, and the cosmos in turgid and startling expressions. No doubt they puzzled her extremely.

I retain the keenest sympathy and something inexplicably near to envy for my own departed youth, but I should find it difficult to maintain my case against anyone who would condemn me altogether as having been a very silly, posturing, emotional hobbledehoy indeed and quite like my faded photograph. And when I try to recall what exactly must have been the quality and tenor of my more sustained efforts to write memorably to my sweetheart, I confess I shiver. . . . Yet I wish they were not all destroyed.

Her letters to me were simple enough, written in a roundish, unformed hand and badly phrased. Her first two or three showed a shy pleasure in the use of the word " dear," and I remember being first puzzled and then, when I understood, delighted, because she had written " Willie *asthore* " under my name. " Asthore," I gathered, meant " darling." But when the evidences of my fermentation began, her answers were less happy.

I will not weary you with the story of how we quarrelled in our silly youthful way, and how I went the next Sunday, all uninvited, to Checkshill, and made it worse, and how afterwards I wrote a letter that she thought was " lovely," and mended the matter. Nor will I tell of all our subsequent fluctuations of misunderstanding. Always I was the offender and the final penitent until this last trouble that was now beginning; and in between we had some tender near moments, and I loved her very greatly. There was this misfortune in the business, that in the darkness, and alone, I thought with great intensity of her, of her eyes, of her touch, of her sweet and delightful presence, but when I sat down to write I thought of Shelley and Burns and myself, and other such irrelevant matters. When one is in love in this fermenting way, it is harder to make love than it is when one does not love at all. And as for Nettie, she loved, I know, not me but those gentle mysteries. It was not my voice should rouse her dreams to passion. . . . So our letters continued to jar. Then suddenly she wrote me one doubting whether she could ever care for anyone who was a Socialist and did not believe in Church, and then hard upon it came another note with unexpected novelties of phrasing. She thought we were not suited to each other, we differed so in tastes and ideas, she had long thought of releasing me from our engagement. In fact, though I really did not apprehend it fully at the first shock, I was dismissed. Her letter had reached me when I came home after old Rawdon's none too civil refusal to raise my wages. On this particular evening of which I write, therefore, I was in a state

of feverish adjustment to two new and amazing, two nearly
overwhelming facts, that I was neither indispensable to Nettie
nor at Rawdon's. And to talk of comets !

Where did I stand ?

I had grown so accustomed to think of Nettie as inseparably
mine—the whole tradition of " true love " pointed me to that
—that for her to face about with these precise small phrases
towards abandonment, after we had kissed and whispered
and come so close in the little adventurous familiarities of
the young, shocked me profoundly. I ! I ! And Rawdon
didn't find me indispensable either. I felt I was suddenly
repudiated by the universe and threatened with effacement,
that in some positive and emphatic way I must at once assert
myself. There was no balm in the religion I had learned, or
in the irreligion I had adopted, for wounded self-love.

Should I fling up Rawdon's place at once and then in some
extraordinary, swift manner make the fortune of Frobisher's
adjacent and closely competitive pot-bank ?

The first part of that programme at any rate would be
easy of accomplishment, to go to Rawdon and say, " You
will hear from me again," but for the rest, Frobisher might
fail me. That, however, was a secondary issue. The predominant affair was with Nettie. I found my mind thick-shot
with flying fragments of rhetoric that might be of service in
the letter I would write her. Scorn, irony, tenderness—what
was it to be ? . . .

" Bother ! " said Parload suddenly.

" What ? " said I.

" They're firing up at Bladden's iron-works, and the smoke
comes right across my bit of sky."

The interruption came just as I was ripe to discharge my
thoughts upon him.

" Parload," said I, " very likely I shall have to leave all
this. Old Rawdon won't give me a rise in my wages, and after
having asked I don't think I can stand going on upon the old
terms any more. See ? So I may have to clear out of Clayton
for good and all."

§ 3

That made Parload put down the opera-glass and look at
me.

" It's a bad time to change just now," he said after a little
pause.

Rawdon had said as much, in a less agreeable tone.

But with Parload I felt always a disposition to the heroic
note. " I'm tired," I said, " of humdrum drudgery for other
men. One may as well starve one's body out of a place as
starve one's soul in one."

" I don't know about that altogether," began Parload,
slowly. . . .

And with that we began one of our interminable conversations, one of those long, wandering, intensely generalising, diffusely personal talks that will be dear to the hearts of intelligent youths until the world comes to an end. The Change has not abolished that, anyhow.

It would be an incredible feat of memory for me now to recall all that meandering haze of words, indeed I recall scarcely any of it, though its circumstances and atmosphere stand out, a sharp, clear picture in my mind. I posed after my manner and behaved very foolishly no doubt, a wounded, smarting egotist, and Parload played his part of the philosopher preoccupied with the deeps.

We were presently abroad, walking through the warm summer's night and talking all the more freely for that. But one thing that I said I can remember. " I wish at times," said I, with a gesture at the heavens, " that comet of yours or some such thing would indeed strike this world—and wipe us all away, strikes, wars, tumults, loves, jealousies, and all the wretchedness of life ! "

" Ah ! " said Parload, and the thought seemed to hang about him.

" It could only add to the miseries of life," he said irrelevantly, when presently I was discoursing of other things.

" What would ? "

" Collision with a comet. It would only throw things back. It would only make what was left of life more savage than it is at present."

" But why should *anything* be left of life ? " said I. . . .

That was our style, you know, and meanwhile we walked together up the narrow street outside his lodging, up the stepway and the lanes towards Clayton Crest and the high road.

But my memories carry me back so effectually to those days before the Change that I forget that now all these places have been altered beyond recognition, that the narrow street and the stepway and the view from Clayton Crest, and indeed all the world in which I was born and bred and made, has vanished clean away, out of space and out of time, and wellnigh out of the imagination of all those who are younger by a generation than I. You cannot see, as I can see, the dark empty way between the mean houses, the dark empty way lit by a bleary gas-lamp at the corner, you cannot feel the hard checkered pavement under your boots, you cannot mark the dimly lit windows here and there, and the shadows upon the ugly and often patched and crooked blinds of the people cooped within. Nor can you presently pass the beerhouse with its brighter gas and its queer screening windows, not get a whiff of foul air and foul language from its door, nor see the crumpled furtive figure—some rascal child—that slinks past us down the steps.

We crossed the longer street, up which a clumsy steam tram, vomiting smoke and sparks, made its clangorous way, and adown which one saw the greasy brilliance of shop fronts and the naphtha flares of hawkers' barrows dripping fire into the night. A hazy movement of people swayed along that road, and we heard the voice of an itinerant preacher from a waste place between the houses. You cannot see these things as I can see them, nor can you figure—unless you know the pictures that great artist Hyde has left the world—the effect of the hoarding by which we passed, lit below by a gas-lamp and towering up to a sudden sharp black edge against the pallid sky.

Those hoardings ! They were the brightest coloured things in all that vanished world. Upon them, in successive layers of paste and paper, all the rough enterprises of that time joined in chromatic discord ; pill venders and preachers, theatres and charities, marvellous soaps and astonishing pickles, typewriting machines and sewing machines, mingled in a sort of visualised clamour. And passing that there was a muddy lane of cinders, a lane without a light, that used its many puddles to borrow a star or so from the sky. We splashed along unheeding as we talked.

Then across the allotments, a wilderness of cabbages and evil-looking sheds, past a gaunt abandoned factory, and so to the high road. The high road ascended in a curve past a few houses and a beerhouse or so, and round until all the valley in which four industrial towns lay crowded and confluent was overlooked.

I will admit that with the twilight there came a spell of weird magnificence over all that land and brooded on it until dawn. The horrible meanness of its details was veiled, the hutches that were homes, the bristling multitudes of chimneys, the ugly patches of unwilling vegetation amidst the makeshift fences of barrel-stave and wire. The rusty scars that framed the opposite ridges where the iron ore was taken and the barren mountains of slag from the blast furnaces were veiled ; the reek and boiling smoke and dust from foundry, pot-bank, and furnace, transfigured and assimilated by the night. The dust-laden atmosphere that was grey oppression through the day became at sundown a mystery of deep translucent colours, of blues and purples, of sombre and vivid reds, of strange bright clearness of green and yellow athwart the darkling sky. Each upstart furnace, when its monarch sun had gone, crowned itself with flames, the dark cinder heaps began to glow with quivering fires, and each pot-bank squatted rebellious in a volcanic coronet of light. The empire of the day broke into a thousand feudal baronies of burning coal. The minor streets across the valley picked themselves out with gas-lamps of faint yellow, that brightened and mingled at all the principal squares and crossings with the greenish pallor of incandescent mantles and the high cold glare of the electric arc. The interlacing railways lifted bright signal-boxes over their intersections, and signal stars of red and green in rectangular constellations. The trains became articulated black serpents breathing fire. . . .

Moreover, high overhead, like a thing put out of reach and near forgotten, Parload had rediscovered a realm that was ruled by neither sun nor furnace, the universe of stars.

This was the scene of many a talk we two had held together. And if in the daytime we went right over the crest and looked westward there was farmland, there were parks and great mansions, the spire of a distant cathedral, and sometimes when the weather was near raining, the crests of remote mountains hung clearly in the sky. Beyond the range of sight indeed, out beyond, there was Checkshill ; I felt it there always, and in the darkness more than I did by day. Checkshill, and Nettie !

And to us two youngsters, as we walked along the cinder path beside the rutted road and argued out our perplexities, it seemed that this ridge gave us compendiously a view of our whole world.

There on the one hand in a crowded darkness, about the ugly factories and work-places, the workers herded together, ill clothed, ill nourished, ill taught, badly and expensively served at every occasion in life, uncertain even of their insufficient livelihood from day to day, the chapels and churches and public-houses swelling up amidst their wretched homes like saprophytes amidst a general corruption, and on the other, in space, freedom, and dignity, scarce heeding the few cottages, as overcrowded as they were picturesque, in which the labourers festered, lived the landlords and masters who owned pot-banks and forge and farm and mine. Far away, distant, beautiful, irrelevant, from out of a little cluster of second-hand bookshops, ecclesiastical residences, and the inns and incidentals of a decaying market town, the cathedral of Lowchester pointed a beautiful, unemphatic spire to vague incredible skies. So it seemed to us that the whole world was planned in those youthful first impressions.

We saw everything simple, as young men will. We had our angry, confident solutions, and whosoever would criticise them was a friend of the robbers. It was a clear case of robbery, we held, visibly so ; there in those great houses lurked the Landlord and the Capitalist, with his scoundrel the Lawyer, with his cheat the Priest, and we others were all the victims of their deliberate villainies. No doubt they winked and chuckled over their rare wines, amidst their dazzling, wickedly dressed women, and plotted further grinding for the faces of the poor. And amidst all the squalor on the other hand, amidst brutalities, ignorance, and drunkenness, suffered multitudinously their blameless victim, the Working Man. And we, almost at the first glance, had found all this out, it had merely to be asserted now with sufficient rhetoric and vehemence to change the face of the whole world. The Working Man would arise—in the form of a Labour Party, and with young men like Parload and myself to represent him—and come to his own, and then—— ?

Then the robbers would get it hot, and everything would be extremely satisfactory.

Unless my memory plays me strange tricks, that does no injustice to the creed of thought and action that Parload and I held as the final result of human wisdom. We believed it with heat, and rejected with heat the most obvious qualification of its harshness. At times in our great talks we were full of heady hopes for the near triumph of our doctrine, more often our mood was hot resentment at the wickedness and stupidity that delayed so plain and simple a reconstruction of the order of the world. Then we grew malignant, and thought of barricades and significant violence. I was very bitter, I know, upon this night of which I am now particularly telling ; and the only face upon the hydra of Capitalism and Monopoly that I could see at all clearly, smiled exactly as old Rawdon had smiled when he refused to give me more than a paltry twenty shillings a week.

I wanted intensely to salve my self-respect by some revenge upon him, and I felt that if that could be done by slaying the hydra, I might drag its carcass to the feet of Nettie, and settle my other trouble as well. " What do you think of me *now*, Nettie ? "

That at any rate comes near enough to the quality of my thinking then, for you to imagine how I gesticulated and spouted to Parload that night. You see us as little black figures, unprepossessing in outline, set in the midst of that desolating night of flaming industrialism, and my little voice with a rhetorical twang protesting, denouncing. . . .

You will consider those notions of my youth poor silly violent stuff ; particularly if you are of the younger generation born since the Change you will be of that opinion. Nowadays the whole world thinks clearly, thinks with deliberation, pellucid certainties ; you find it impossible to imagine how any other thinking could have been possible. Let me tell you then how you can bring yourself to something like the condition of our former state. In the first place you must get yourself out of health by unwise drinking and eating, and out of condition by neglecting your exercise ; then you must contrive to be worried very much and made very anxious and uncomfortable, and then you must work very hard for four or five days and for long hours every day at something too petty to be interesting, too complex to be mechanical, and without any personal significance to you whatever. This done, get straightway into a room that is not ventilated at all, and that is already full of

foul air, and there set yourself to think out some very complicated problem. In a little while you will find yourself in a state
of intellectual muddle, annoyed, impatient, snatching at the
obvious, presently choosing and rejecting conclusions haphazard. Try to play chess under such conditions and you will
play stupidly and lose your temper. Try to do anything that
taxes the brain or temper and you will fail.

Now the whole world before the Change was as sick and
feverish as that; it was worried and over-worked and perplexed by problems that would not get stated simply, that
changed and evaded solution, it was in an atmosphere that
had corrupted and thickened past breathing; there was no
thorough cool thinking in the world at all. There was nothing
in the mind of the world anywhere but half-truths, hasty
assumptions, hallucinations, and emotions. Nothing. . . .

I know it seems incredible, that already some of the younger
men are beginning to doubt the greatness of the Change our
world has undergone, but read—read the newspapers of that
time. Every age becomes mitigated and a little ennobled in
our minds as it recedes into the past. It is the part of those
who like myself have stories of that time to tell, to supply,
by a scrupulous spiritual realism, some antidote to that
glamour.

§ 4

Always with Parload I was chief talker.

I can look back upon myself with, I believe, an almost
perfect detachment, things have so changed that indeed now
I am another being, with scarce anything in common with that
boastful foolish youngster whose troubles I recall. I see him
vulgarly theatrical, egotistical, insincere; indeed I do not
like him save with that instinctive material sympathy that
is the fruit of incessant intimacy. Because he was myself
I may be able to feel and write understandingly about motives
that will put him out of sympathy with nearly every reader,
but why should I palliate or defend his quality?

Always, I say, I did the talking, and it would have amazed
me beyond measure if any one had told me that mine was not
the greater intelligence in these wordy encounters. Parload
was a quiet youth, and stiff and restrained in all things, while
I had that supreme gift for young men and democracies, the
gift of copious expression. Parload I diagnosed in my secret
heart as a trifle dull; he posed as pregnant quiet, I thought,
and was obsessed by the congenial notion of "scientific
caution." I did not remark that while my hands were chiefly
useful for gesticulation or holding a pen, Parload's hands
could do all sorts of things; and I did not think therefore that
fibres must run from those fingers to something in his brain.
Nor, though I bragged perpetually of my shorthand, of my
literature, of my indispensable share in Rawdon's business,

did Parload lay stress on the conics and calculus he "mugged" in the organised science school. Parload is a famous man now, a great figure in a great time; his work upon intersecting radiations has broadened the intellectual horizon of mankind for ever; and I, who am at best a hewer of intellectual wood, a drawer of living water, can smile, and he can smile, to think how I patronised and posed and jabbered over him in the darkness of those early days.

That night I was shrill and eloquent beyond measure. Rawdon was, of course, the hub upon which I went round—Rawdon and the Rawdonesque employer and the injustice of "wages slavery" and all the immediate conditions of that industrial blind alley up which it seemed our lives were thrust. But ever and again I glanced at other things. Nettie was always there in the background of my mind, regarding me enigmatically. It was part of my pose to Parload that I had a romantic love-affair somewhere away beyond the sphere of our intercourse, and that note gave a Byronic resonance to many of the nonsensical things I produced for his astonishment.

I will not weary you with too detailed an account of the talk of a foolish youth who was also distressed and unhappy, and whose voice was balm for the humiliations that smarted in his eyes. Indeed now in many particulars I cannot disentangle this harangue of which I tell from many of the things I may have said in other talks to Parload. For example I forget if it was then or before or afterwards that, as it were by accident, I let out what might be taken as an admission that I was addicted to drugs.

"You shouldn't do that," said Parload, suddenly. "It won't do to poison your brains with that."

My brains, my eloquence, were to be very important assets to our party in the coming revolution. . . .

But one thing does clearly belong to this particular conversation I am recalling. When I started out it was quite settled in the back of my mind that I must not leave Rawdon's. I simply wanted to abuse my employer to Parload. But I talked myself quite out of touch with all the cogent reasons there were for sticking to my place, and I got home that night irrevocably committed to a spirited—not to say a defiant—policy with my employer.

"I can't stand Rawdon's much longer," I said to Parload by way of a flourish.

"There's hard times coming," said Parload.

"Next winter."

"Sooner. The Americans have been overproducing, and they mean to dump. The iron trade is going to have convulsions."

"I don't care. Pot-banks are steady."

"With a corner in borax? No. I've heard——"

" What have you heard ? "

" Office secrets. But it's no secret there's trouble coming to potters. There's been borrowing and speculation. The masters don't stick to one business as they used to do. I can tell that much. Half the valley may be ' playing ' before two months are out." Parload delivered himself of this unusually long speech in his most pithy and weighty manner.

" Playing " was our local euphemism for a time when there was no work and no money for a man, a time of stagnation and dreary hungry loafing day after day. Such interludes seemed in those days a necessary consequence of industrial organisation.

" You'd better stick to Rawdon's," said Parload.

" Ugh," said I, affecting a noble disgust.

" There'll be trouble," said Parload.

" Who cares ? " said I. " Let there be trouble—the more the better. This system has got to end, sooner or later. These capitalists with their speculation and corners and trusts make things go from bad to worse. Why should I cower in Rawdon's office, like a frightened dog, while hunger walks the streets ? Hunger is the master revolutionary. When he comes we ought to turn out and salute him. Anyway, *I'm* going to do so now."

" That's all very well," began Parload.

" I'm tired of it," I said. " I want to come to grips with all these Rawdons. I think perhaps if I was hungry and savage I could talk to hungry men——"

" There's your mother," said Parload, in his slow judicial way.

That *was* a difficulty.

I got over it by a rhetorical turn. " Why should one sacrifice the future of the world—why should one even sacrifice one's own future—because one's mother is totally destitute of imagination ? "

§ 5

It was late when I parted from Parload and came back to my own home.

Our house stood in a highly respectable little square near the Clayton parish church. Mr. Gabbitas, the curate of all work, lodged on our ground floor, and upstairs there was an old lady, Miss Holroyd, who painted flowers on china and maintained her blind sister in an adjacent room ; my mother and I lived in the basement and slept in the attics. The front of the house was veiled by a Virginian creeper that defied the Clayton air and clustered in untidy dependent masses over the wooden porch.

As I came up the steps I had a glimpse of Mr. Gabbitas printing photographs by candle light in his room. It was the chief delight of his little life to spend his holiday abroad in the company of a queer little snap-shot camera, and to return with a great multitude of foggy and sinister negatives that he had made in beautiful and interesting places. These the camera company would develop for him on advantageous terms, and he would spend his evenings the year through in printing from them in order to inflict copies upon his undeserving friends. There was a long frameful of his work in the Clayton National School, for example, inscribed in old English lettering, " Italian Travel Pictures, by the Rev. E. B. Gabbitas." For this it seemed he lived and travelled and had his being. It was his only real joy. By his shaded light I could see his sharp little nose, his little pale eyes behind his glasses, his mouth pursed up with the endeavour of his employment. . . .

" Hireling Liar," I muttered, for was not he also part of the system, part of the scheme of robbery that made wages serfs of Parload and me ?—though his share in the proceedings was certainly small.

" Hireling Liar," said I, standing in the darkness, outside even his faint glow of travelled culture. . . .

My mother let me in.

She looked at me, mutely, because she knew there was something wrong and that it was no use for her to ask what.

" Good night, mummy," said I, and kissed her a little roughly, and lit and took my candle and went off at once up the staircase to bed, not looking back at her.

" I've kept some supper for you, dear."

" Don't want any supper."

" But, dearie——"

" Good night, mother," and I went up and slammed my door upon her, blew out my candle, and lay down at once upon my bed, lay there a long time before I got up to undress.

There were times when that dumb beseeching of my mother's face irritated me unspeakably. It did so that night. I felt I had to struggle against it, that I could not exist if I gave way to its pleadings, and it hurt me and divided me to resist it, almost beyond endurance. It was clear to me that I had to think out for myself religious problems, social problems, questions of conduct, questions of expediency, that her poor dear simple beliefs could not help me at all—and she did not understand ! Hers was the accepted religion, her only social ideas were blind submissions to the accepted order—to laws, to doctors, to clergymen, lawyers, masters, and all respectable persons in authority over us, and with her to believe was to fear. She knew from a thousand little signs—though still at times I went to church with her—that I was passing out of touch of all these things that ruled her life, into some terrible unknown. From things I said she could infer such clumsy concealments as I made. She felt my socialism, felt my spirit in revolt against the accepted order, felt the impotent resent-

ments that filled me with bitterness against all she held sacred.
Yet, you know, it was not her dear gods she sought to defend
so much as me! She seemed always to be wanting to say
to me, " Dear, I know it's hard—but revolt is harder. Don't
make war on it, dear—don't! Don't do anything to offend it.
I'm sure it will hurt you if you do—it will hurt you if you do."

She had been cowed into submission, as so many women of
that time had been, by the sheer brutality of the accepted
thing. The existing order dominated her into a worship of
abject observances. It had bent her, aged her, robbed her of
eyesight so that at fifty-five she peered through cheap spectacles at my face and saw it only dimly, filled her with a
habit of anxiety, made her hands— Her poor dear hands!
Not in the whole world now could you find a woman with
hands so grimy, so needle-worn, so misshapen by toil, so
chapped and coarsened, so evilly entreated. . . . At any
rate, there is this I can say for myself, that my bitterness
against the world and fortune was for her sake as well as for
my own.

Yet that night I pushed by her harshly. I answered her
curtly, left her concerned and perplexed in the passage, and
slammed my door upon her.

And for a long time I lay raging at the hardship and evil of
life, at the contempt of Rawdon and the loveless coolness of
Nettie's letter, at my weakness and insignificance, at the
things I found intolerable, and the things I could not mend.
Over and over went my poor little brain, tired out and
unable to stop on my treadmill of troubles. Nettie. Rawdon.
My mother. Gabbitas. Nettie. . . .

Suddenly I came upon emotional exhaustion. Some clock
was striking midnight. After all, I was young; I had these
quick transitions. I remember quite distinctly, I stood up
abruptly, undressed very quickly in the dark, and had hardly
touched my pillow again before I was asleep.

But how my mother slept that night I do not know.

Oddly enough, I do not blame myself for behaving like this
to my mother, though my conscience blames me acutely for
my arrogance to Parload. I regret my behaviour to my mother
before the days of the Change, it is a scar among my memories
that will always be a little painful to the end of my days,
but I do not see how something of the sort was to be escaped
under those former conditions. In that time of muddle and
obscurity people were overtaken by needs and toil and hot
passions before they had the chance of even a year or so of
clear thinking ; they settled down to an intense and strenuous
application to some partial but immediate duty, and the
growth of thought ceased in them. They set and hardened
into narrow ways. Few women remained capable of a new
idea after five and twenty, few men after thirty-one or two.
Discontent with the thing that existed was regarded as im-

moral, it was certainly an annoyance, and the only protest against it, the only effort against that universal tendency in all human institutions to thicken and clog, to work loosely and badly, to rust and weaken towards catastrophes, came from the young—the crude unmerciful young. It seemed in those days to thoughtful men the harsh law of being—that either we must submit to our elders and be stifled, or disregard them, disobey them, thrust them aside, and make our little step of progress before we too ossified and became obstructive in our turn.

My pushing past my mother, my irresponsive departure to my own silent meditations, was, I now perceive, a figure of the whole hard relationship between parents and son in those days. There appeared no other way ; that perpetually recurring tragedy was, it seemed, part of the very nature of the progress of the world. We did not think then that minds might grow ripe without growing rigid, or children honour their parents and still think for themselves. We were angry and hasty because we stifled in the darkness, in a poisoned and vitiated air. That deliberate animation of the intelligence which is now the universal quality, that vigour with consideration, that judgment with confident enterprise which shine through all our world, were things disintegrated and unknown in the corrupting atmosphere of our former state.

(*So the first fascicle ended. I put it aside and looked for the second.*

"*Well ?*" *said the man who wrote.*

"*This is fiction ?*"

"*It's my story.*"

"*But you— Amidst this beauty— You are not this illconditioned, squalidly bred lad of whom I have been reading ?*"

He smiled. "*There intervenes a certain Change,*" *he said.* "*Have I not hinted at that ?*"

I hesitated upon a question, then saw the second fascicle at hand, and picked it up.)

CHAPTER TWO

NETTIE

§ 1

I CANNOT now remember (*the story resumed*) what interval separated that evening on which Parload first showed me the comet—I think I only pretended to see it then—and the Sunday afternoon I spent at Checkshill.

Between the two there was time enough for me to give notice and leave Rawdon's, to seek for some other situation very strenuously in vain, to think and say many hard and violent things to my mother and to Parload, and to pass through some phases of very profound wretchedness. There must have been a passionate correspondence with Nettie, but all the froth and fury of that has faded now out of my memory. All I have clear now is that I wrote one magnificent farewell to her, casting her off for ever, and that I got in reply a prim little note to say that even if there was to be an end to everything, that was no excuse for writing such things as I had done, and then I think I wrote again in a vein I considered satirical. To that she did not reply. That interval was at least three weeks, and probably four, because the comet which had been on the first occasion only a dubious speck in the sky, certainly visible only when it was magnified, was now a great white presence, brighter than Jupiter, and casting a shadow on its own account. It was now actively present in the world of human thought, every one was talking about it, every one was looking for its waxing splendour as the sun went down—the papers, the music-halls, the hoardings, echoed it.

Yes ; the comet was already dominant before I went over to make everything clear to Nettie. And Parload had spent two hoarded pounds in buying himself a spectroscope, so that he could see for himself, night after night, that mysterious, that stimulating line—the unknown line in the green. How many times I wonder did I look at the smudgy quivering symbol of the unknown things that were rushing upon us out of the inhuman void, before I rebelled ? But at last I could stand it no longer, and I reproached Parload very bitterly for wasting his time in " astronomical dilettantism."

" Here," said I, " we're on the verge of the biggest lockout in the history of this countryside ; here's distress and hunger coming, here's all the capitalistic competitive system like a wound inflamed, and you spend your time gaping at the damned silly streak of nothing in the sky ! "

Parload stared at me. " Yes, I do," he said slowly, as though it was a new idea. " Don't I ? . . . I wonder why."

" *I* want to start meetings of an evening on Howden's Waste."

" You think they'd listen ? "

" They'd listen fast enough now."

" They didn't before," said Parload, looking at his pet instrument.

" There was a demonstration of unemployed at Swathinglea on Sunday. They got to stone throwing."

Parload said nothing for a little while and I said several things. He seemed to be considering something.

" But, after all," he said at last, with an awkward movement towards his spectroscope, " that does signify something."

" The comet ? "

" Yes."

" What can it signify ? You don't want me to believe in astrology. What does it matter what flames in the heavens— when men are starving on earth ? "

" It's—it's science."

" Science ! What we want now is socialism—not science."

He still seemed reluctant to give up his comet.

" Socialism's all right," he said, " but if that thing up there *was* to hit the earth it might matter."

" Nothing matters but human beings."

" Suppose it killed them all."

" Oh," said I, " that's Rot."

" I wonder," said Parload, dreadfully divided in his allegiance. He looked at the comet. He seemed on the verge of repeating his growing information about the nearness of the paths of the earth and comet, and all that might ensue from that. So I cut in with something I had got out of a now forgotten writer called Ruskin, a volcano of beautiful language and nonsensical suggestions, who prevailed very greatly with eloquent excitable young men in those days. Something it was about the insignificance of science and the supreme importance of Life. Parload stood listening, half turned towards the sky with the tips of his fingers on his spectroscope. He seemed to come to a sudden decision.

" No. I don't agree with you, Leadford," he said. " You don't understand about science."

Parload rarely argued with that bluntness of opposition. I was so used to entire possession of our talk that his brief contradiction struck me like a blow. " Don't agree with me ! " I repeated.

" No," said Parload.

" But how ? "

" I believe science is of more importance than socialism," he said. " Socialism's a theory. Science—science is something more."

And that was really all he seemed to be able to say.

We embarked upon one of those queer arguments illiterate young men used always to find so heating. Science or Socialism? It was, of course, like arguing which is right, left-handedness or a taste for onions, it was altogether impossible opposition. But the range of my rhetoric enabled me at last to exasperate Parload, and his mere repudiation of my conclusions sufficed to exasperate me, and we ended in the key of a positive quarrel. " Oh, very well ! " said I. " So long as I know where we are ! '

I slammed his door as though I dynamited his house, and went raging down the street but I felt that he was already back at the window worshipping his blessed line in the green, before I got round the corner.

I had to walk for an hour or so, before I was cool enough to go home.

And it was Parload who had first introduced me to socialism ! Recreant !

The most extraordinary things used to run through my head in those days. I will confess that my mind ran persistently that evening upon revolutions after the best French pattern, and I sat on a Committee of Safety and tried backsliders. Parload was there, among the prisoners, backsliderissimus, aware too late of the error of his ways. His hands were tied behind his back ready for the shambles ; through the open door one heard the voice of justice, the rude justice of the people. I was sorry, but I had to do my duty.

" If we punish those who would betray us to Kings," said I, with a sorrowful deliberation, " how much the more must we punish those who would give over the State to the pursuit of useless knowledge " ; and so with a gloomy satisfaction sent him off to the guillotine.

" Ah, Parload ! Parload ! If only you'd listened to me earlier, Parload ! " . . .

None the less that quarrel made me extremely unhappy. Parload was my only gossip, and it cost me much to keep away from him and think evil of him with no one to listen to me, evening after evening.

That was a very miserable time for me, even before my last visit to Checkshill. My long unemployed hours hung heavily on my hands. I kept away from home all day, partly to support a fiction that I was sedulously seeking another situation, and partly to escape the persistent question in my mother's eyes. " Why did you quarrel with Mr. Rawdon ? Why did you ? Why do you keep on going about with a sullen face and risk offending it more ? " I spent most of the morning in the newspaper-room of the public library, writing impossible applications for impossible posts—I remember that among other things of the sort I offered my services to a firm of private detectives, a sinister breed of traders upon base jealousies now happily vanished from the world, and wrote apropos of an advertisement for " stevedores " that I did not know what the duties of a stevedore might be, but that I was apt and willing to learn—and in the afternoons and evenings I wandered through the strange lights and shadows of my native valley and hated all created things. Until my wanderings were checked by the discovery that I was wearing out my boots.

The stagnant inconclusive malaria of that time !

I perceive that I was an evil-tempered, ill-disposed youth with a great capacity for hatred, *but*——

There was an excuse for hate.

It was wrong of me to hate individuals, to be rude, harsh, and vindictive to this person or that, but indeed it would have been equally wrong to have taken the manifest offer life

made me, without resentment. I see now clearly and calmly,
what I then felt obscurely and with an unbalanced intensity,
that my conditions were intolerable. My work was tedious
and laborious and it took up an unreasonable proportion of
my time; I was ill clothed, ill fed, ill housed, ill educated,
and ill trained; my will was suppressed and cramped to the
pitch of torture; I had no reasonable pride in myself and no
reasonable chance of putting anything right. It was a life
hardly worth living. That a large proportion of the people
about me had no better a lot, that many had a worse, does
not affect these facts. It was a life in which contentment
would have been disgraceful. If some of them were contented
or resigned, so much the worse for every one. No doubt it
was hasty and foolish of me to throw up my situation, but
everything was so obviously aimless and foolish in our social
organisation that I do not feel disposed to blame myself even
for that, except in so far as it pained my mother and caused
her anxiety.

Think of the one comprehensive fact of the lock-out !

That year was a bad year, a year of world-wide economic
disorganisation. Through their want of intelligent direction
the great " Trust " of American ironmasters, a gang of energetic, narrow-minded furnace owners, had smelted far more
iron than the whole world had any demand for. (In those
days there existed no means of estimating any need of that
sort beforehand.) They had done this without even consulting
the ironmasters of any other country. During their period
of activity they had drawn into their employment a great
number of workers, and had erected a huge productive plant.
It is manifestly just that people who do headlong stupid
things of this sort should suffer, but in the old days it was
quite possible, it was customary, for the real blunderers in
such disasters to shift nearly all the consequences of their
incapacity. No one thought it wrong for a light-witted "captain
of industry " who had led his work-people into overproduction,
into the disproportionate manufacture, that is to say, of some
particular article, to abandon and dismiss them, nor was there
anything to prevent the sudden frantic underselling of some
trade rival in order to surprise and destroy his trade, secure
his customers for one's own destined needs, and shift a portion
of one's punishment upon him. This operation of spasmodic
underselling was known as " dumping." The American ironmasters were now dumping on the British market. The British
employers were, of course, taking their loss out of their work-
people as much as possible, but in addition they were agitating
for some legislation that would prevent—not stupid relative
excess in production, but " dumping "—not the disease, but
the consequences of the disease. The necessary knowledge to
prevent either dumping or its cause, the uncorrelated production of commodities, did not exist, but this hardly weighed

with them at all ; and in answer to their demands there had
arisen a curious party of retaliatory-protectionists who com-
bined vague proposals for spasmodic responses to these convulsive attacks from foreign manufacturers, with the very
evident intention of achieving financial adventures. The
dishonest and reckless elements were indeed so evident in this
movement as to add very greatly to the general atmosphere
of distrust and insecurity, and in the recoil from the prospect
of fiscal power in the hands of the class of men known as the
" New Financiers," one heard frightened old-fashioned statesmen asserting with passion that " dumping " didn't occur,
or that it was a very charming sort of thing to happen. Nobody
would face and handle the rather intricate truth of the business.
The whole effect upon the mind of a cool observer was a covey
of unsubstantial jabbering minds drifting over a series of
irrational economic cataclysms, prices and employment
tumbled about like towers in an earthquake, and amidst the
shifting masses were the common work-people going on with
their lives as well as they could, suffering, perplexed, unorganised, and for anything but violent, fruitless protests,
impotent. You cannot hope now to understand the infinite
want of adjustment in the old order of things. At one time
there were people dying of actual starvation in India, while
men were burning unsalable wheat in America. It sounds
like the account of a particularly mad dream, does it not ?
It was a dream, a dream from which no one on earth expected
an awakening.

To us youngsters with the positiveness, the rationalism of
youth, it seemed that the strikes and lockouts, the overproduction and misery could not possibly result simply from
ignorance and want of thought and feeling. We needed more
dramatic factors than these mental fogs, these mere atmospheric devils. We fled therefore to that common refuge of
the unhappy ignorant, a belief in callous insensate plots—we
called them " plots "—against the poor.

You can still see how we figured it in any museum by looking up the caricatures of capital and labour that adorned the
German and American socialistic papers of the old time.

§ 2

I had cast Nettie off in an eloquent epistle, had really
imagined the affair was over for ever—" I've done with .
women," I said to Parload—and then there was silence for
more than a week.

Before that week was over I was wondering with a growing
emotion what next would happen between us.

I found myself thinking constantly of Nettie, picturing
her—sometimes with stern satisfaction, sometimes with
sympathetic remorse—mourning, regretting, realising the

absolute end that had come between us. At the bottom of my heart I no more believed that there was an end between us, than that an end would come to the world. Had we not kissed one another, had we not achieved an atmosphere of whispering nearness, breached our virgin shyness with one another ? Of course she was mine, of course I was hers, and separations and final quarrels and harshness and distance were no more than flourishes upon that eternal fact. So at least I felt the thing, however I shaped my thoughts.

Whenever my imagination got to work as that week drew to its close, she came in as a matter of course, I thought of her recurrently all day and dreamt of her at night. On Saturday night I dreamt of her very vividly. Her face was flushed and wet with tears, her hair a little disordered, and when I spoke to her she turned away. In some manner this dream left in my mind a feeling of distress and anxiety. In the morning I had a raging thirst to see her.

That Sunday my mother wanted me to go to church very particularly. She had a double reason for that ; she thought that it would certainly exercise a favourable influence upon my search for a situation throughout the next week, and in addition Mr. Gabbitas, with a certain mystery behind his glasses, had promised to see what he could do for me, and she wanted to keep him up to that promise. I half consented, and then my desire for Nettie took hold of me. I told my mother I wasn't going to church, and set off about eleven to walk the seventeen miles to Checkshill.

It greatly intensified the fatigue of that long tramp that the sole of my boot presently split at the toe, and after I had cut the flapping portion off, a nail worked through and began to torment me. However, the boot looked all right after that operation and gave no audible hint of my discomfort. I got some bread and cheese at a little inn on the way, and was in Checkshill park about four. I did not go by the road past the house and so round to the gardens, but cut over the crest beyond the second keeper's cottage, along a path Nettie used to call her own. It was a mere deer track. It led up a miniature valley and through a pretty dell in which we had been accustomed to meet, and so through the hollies and along a narrow path close by the wall of the shrubbery to the gardens.

In my memory that walk through the park before I came upon Nettie stands out very vividly. The long tramp before it is foreshortened to a mere effect of dusty road and painful boot, but the bracken valley and sudden tumult of doubts and unwonted expectations that came to me, stands out now as something significant, as something unforgettable, something essential to the meaning of all that followed. Where should I meet her ? What would she say ? I had asked these questions before and found an answer. Now they came again with a trail of fresh implications and I had no answer for them at all. As I approached Nettie she ceased to be the mere butt of my egotistical self-projection, the custodian of my sexual pride, and drew together and became over and above this a personality of her own, a personality and a mystery, a sphinx I had evaded only to meet again.

I find a little difficulty in describing the quality of the old-world love-making so that it may be understandable now.

We young people had practically no preparation at all for the stir and emotions of adolescence. Toward the young the world maintained a conspiracy of stimulating silences. There came no initiation. There were books, stories of a curiously conventional kind that insisted on certain qualities in every love-affair and greatly intensified one's natural desire for them, perfect trust, perfect loyalty, life-long devotion. Much of the complex essentials of love were altogether hidden. One read these things, got accidental glimpses of this and that, wondered and forgot, and so one grew. Then strange emotions, novel alarming desires, dreams strangely charged with feeling ; an inexplicable impulse of self-abandonment began to trickle queerly amongst the familiar purely egotistical and materialistic things of boyhood and girlhood. We were like misguided travellers who had camped in the dry bed of a tropical river. Presently we were knee deep and neck deep in the flood. Our beings were suddenly going out from ourselves seeking other beings—we knew not why. This novel craving for abandonment to some one of the other sex, bore us away. We were ashamed and full of desire. We kept the thing a guilty secret, and were resolved to satisfy it against all the world. In this state it was we drifted in the most accidental way against some other blindly seeking creature, and linked like nascent atoms.

We were obsessed by the books we read, by all the talk about us that once we had linked ourselves we were linked for life. Then afterwards we discovered that other was also an egotism, a thing of ideas and impulses, that failed to correspond with ours.

So it was, I say, with the young of my class and most of the young people in our world. So it came about that I sought Nettie on the Sunday afternoon and suddenly came upon her, light bodied, slenderly feminine, hazel eyed, with her soft sweet young face under the shady brim of her hat of straw, the pretty Venus I had resolved should be wholly and exclusively mine.

There, all unaware of me still, she stood, my essential feminine, the embodiment of the inner thing in life forme— and moreover an unknown other, a person like myself.

She held a little book in her hand, open as if she were walking along and reading it. That chanced to be her pose, but indeed she was standing quite still, looking away towards the grey and lichenous shrubbery wall and, as I think now, listening. Her lips were a little apart, curved to that faint, sweet shadow of a smile.

§ 3

I recall with a vivid precision her queer start when she heard the rustle of my approaching feet, her surprise, her eyes almost of dismay for me. I could recollect, I believe, every significant word she spoke during our meeting, and most of what I said to her. At least, it seems I could, though indeed I may deceive myself. But I will not make the attempt. We were both too ill educated to speak our full meanings, we stamped out our feelings with clumsy stereotyped phrases ; you who are better taught would fail to catch our intention. The effect would be inanity. But our first words I may give you, because though they conveyed nothing to me at the time, afterwards they meant much.

" *You*, Willie ! " she said.

" I have come," I said—forgetting in the instant all the elaborate things I had intended to say. " I thought I would surprise you—— "

" Surprise me ? "

" Yes."

She stared at me for a moment. I can see her pretty face now as it looked at me—her impenetrable dear face. She laughed a queer little laugh and her colour went for a moment, and then so soon as she had spoken, came back again.

" Surprise me at what ? " she said with a rising note.

I was too intent to explain myself to think of what might lie in that.

" I wanted to tell you," I said, " that I didn't mean quite . . . the things I put in my letter."

§ 4

When I and Nettie had been sixteen we had been just of an age and contemporaries altogether. Now we were a year and three-quarters older, and she—her metamorphosis was almost complete, and I was still only at the beginning of a man's long adolescence.

In an instant she grasped the situation. The hidden motives of her quick-ripened little mind flashed out their intuitive scheme of action. She treated me with that neat perfection of understanding a young woman has for a boy.

" But how did you come ? " she asked.

I told her I had walked.

" Walked ! " In an instant she was leading me towards the gardens. I *must* be tired. I must come home with her at once and sit down. Indeed it was near tea-time (the Stuarts had tea at the old-fashioned hour of five). Every one would be *so* surprised to see me. Fancy walking ! Fancy ! But she supposed a man thought nothing of seventeen miles. When *could* I have started !

All the while, keeping me at a distance, without even the touch of her hand.

" But, Nettie ! I came over to talk to you ! "

" My dear boy ! Tea first, if you please ! And besides—aren't we talking ? "

The " dear boy " was a new note, that sounded oddly to me.

She quickened her pace a little.

" I wanted to explain—— " I began.

Whatever I wanted to explain I had no chance to do so. I said a few discrepant things that she answered rather by her intonation than her words.

When we were well past the shrubbery, she slackened a little in her urgency, and so we came along the slope under the beeches to the garden. She kept her bright, straight-forward-looking girlish eyes on me as we went; it seemed she did so all the time, but now I know, better than I did then, that every now and then she glanced over me and behind me towards the shrubbery. And all the while, behind her quick breathless inconsecutive talk, she was thinking.

Her dress marked the end of her transition.

Can I recall it ?

Not, I am afraid, in the terms a woman would use. But her bright brown hair, which had once flowed down her back in a jolly pig-tail tied with a bit of scarlet ribbon, was now caught up into an intricacy of pretty curves above her little ear and cheek, and the soft long lines of her neck ; her white dress had descended to her feet ; her slender waist, which had once been a mere geographical expression, an imaginary line like the equator, was now a thing of flexible beauty. A year ago she had been a pretty girl's face sticking out from a little unimportant frock that was carried upon an extremely active and efficient pair of brown-stockinged legs. Now there was coming a strange new body that flowed beneath her clothes with a sinuous insistence. Every movement, and particularly the novel droop of her hand and arm to the unaccustomed skirts she gathered about her, and a graceful forward inclination that had come to her, called softly to my eyes. A very fine scarf—I suppose you would call it a scarf—of green gossamer, that some new-wakened instinct had told her to fling about her shoulders, clung now closely to the young undulations of her body, and now streamed fluttering out for a moment in a breath of wind, and like some shy independent tentacle with a secret to impart, came into momentary contact with my arm.

She caught it back and reproved it.

We went through the green gate in the high garden wall. I held it open for her to pass through, for this was one of my restricted stock of stiff politenesses, and then for a second she was near touching me. So we came to the trim array of flower-beds near the head gardener's cottage and the vistas of " glass " on our left. We walked between the box edgings and beds of begonias, and into the shadow of a yew hedge within twenty yards of that very pond with the gold-fish at whose brim we had plighted our vows, and so we came to the wistaria-smothered porch.

The door was wide open, and she walked in before me. " Guess who has come to see us ! " she cried.

Her father answered indistinctly from the parlour, and a chair creaked. I judged he was disturbed in his nap.

" Mother ! " she called in her clear young voice. " Puss ! " Puss was her sister.

She told them in a marvelling key that I had walked all the way from Clayton, and they gathered about me and echoed her notes of surprise.

" You'd better sit down, Willie," said her father, " now you have got here. How's your mother ? "

He looked at me curiously as he spoke.

He was dressed in his Sunday clothes, a sort of brownish tweeds, but the waistcoat was unbuttoned for greater comfort in his slumbers. He was a brown-eyed ruddy man, and I still have now in my mind the bright effect of the red-golden hairs that started out from his cheek to flow down into his beard. He was short but strongly built, and his beard and moustache were the biggest things about him. She had taken all the possibility of beauty he possessed, his clear skin, his bright, hazel-brown eyes, and wedded them to a certain quickness she got from her mother. Her mother I remember as a sharp-eyed woman of great activity ; she seems to me now to have been perpetually bringing in or taking out meals or doing some such service, and to me—for my mother's sake and my own—she was always welcoming and kind. Puss was a youngster of fourteen perhaps, of whom a hard bright stare, and a pale skin like her mother's, are the chief traces on my memory. All these people were very kind to me, and among them there was a common recognition, sometimes very agreeably finding expression, that I was—" clever." They all stood about me as if they were a little at a loss.

" Sit down ! " said her father. " Give him a chair, Puss."

We talked a little stiffly—they were evidently surprised by my sudden apparition, dusty, fatigued, and white-faced ; but Nettie did not remain to keep the conversation going.

" There ! " she cried suddenly, as if she were vexed. " I declare ! " and she darted out of the room.

" Lord ! what a girl it is ! " said Mrs. Stuart. " I don't know what's come to her."

It was half an hour before Nettie came back. It seemed a long time to me, and yet she had been running, for when

she came in again she was out of breath. In the meantime, I
had thrown out casually that I had given up my place at
Rawdon's. " I can do better than that," I said.

" I left my book in the dell," she said, panting. " Is tea
ready ? " and that was her apology. . . .

We didn't shake down into comfort even with the coming
of the tea-things. Tea at the gardener's cottage was a serious
meal, with a big cake and little cakes, and preserves and fruit,
a fine spread upon a table. You must imagine me, sullen,
awkward, and preoccupied, perplexed by the something that
was inexplicably unexpected in Nettie, saying little, and
glowering across the cake at her, and all the eloquence I had
been concentrating for the previous twenty-four hours, miserably lost somewhere in the back of my mind. Nettie's father
tried to set me talking ; he had a liking for my gift of ready
speech, for his own ideas came with difficulty, and it pleased
and astonished him to hear me pouring out my views. Indeed,
over there I was, I think, even more talkative than with
Parload, though to the world at large I was a shy young
lout. " You ought to write it out for the newspapers," he
used to say. " That's what you ought to do. I never heard
such nonsense."

Or, " You've got the gift of the gab, young man. We ought
to have made a lawyer of you."

But that afternoon, even in his eyes, I didn't shine. Failing
any other stimulus, he reverted to my search for a situation,
but even that did not engage me.

§ 5

For a long time I feared I should have to go back to Clayton
without another word to Nettie, she seemed insensible to the
need I felt for a talk with her, and I was thinking even of a
sudden demand for that before them all. It was a transparent
manœuvre of her mother's, who had been watching my face,
that sent us out at last together to do something—I forget
now what—in one of the greenhouses. Whatever that little
mission may have been it was the merest, most barefaced
excuse, a door to shut, or a window to close, and I don't think
it got done.

Nettie hesitated and obeyed. She led the way through one
of the hot-houses. It was a low, steamy, brick-floored alley
between staging that bore a close crowd of pots and ferns, and
behind big branching plants that were spread and nailed overhead so as to make an impervious cover of leaves, and in that
close green privacy she stopped and turned on me suddenly
like a creature at bay.

" Isn't the maidenhair fern lovely ? " she said, and looked
at me with eyes that said, " Now."

" Nettie," I began, " I was a fool to write to you as I did."

She startled me by the assent that flashed out upon her face. But she said nothing, and stood waiting.

"Nettie," I plunged, "I can't do without you. I—love you."

"If you loved me," she said trimly, watching the white fingers she plunged among the green branches of a selaginella, "could you write the things you do to me?"

"I don't mean them," I said. "At least not always."

I thought really they were very good letters, and that Nettie was stupid to think otherwise, but I was for the moment clearly aware of the impossibility of conveying that to her.

"You wrote them."

"But then I tramp seventeen miles to say I don't mean them."

"Yes. But perhaps you do."

I think I was at a loss; then I said, not very clearly, "I don't."

"You think you—you love me, Willie. But you don't."

"I do. Nettie! You know I do."

For answer she shook her head.

I made what I thought was a most heroic plunge. "Nettie," I said, "I'd rather have you than—than my own opinions."

The selaginella still engaged her. "You think so now," she said.

I broke out into protestations.

"No," she said shortly. "It's different now."

"But why should two letters make so much difference?" I said.

"It isn't only the letters. But it is different. It's different for good."

She halted a little with that sentence, seeking expression. She looked up abruptly into my eyes and moved, indeed slightly, but with the intimation that she thought our talk might end.

But I did not mean it to end like that.

"For good?" said I. "No! . . . Nettie! Nettie! You don't mean that!"

"I do," she said deliberately, still looking at me, and with all her pose conveying her finality. She seemed to brace herself for the outbreak that must follow.

Of course I became wordy. But I did not submerge her. She stood intrenched, firing her contradictions like guns into my scattered discussive attack. I remember that our talk took the absurd form of disputing whether I could be in love with her or not. And there was I, present in evidence, in a deepening and widening distress of soul because she could stand there, defensive, brighter and prettier than ever, and in some inexplicable way cut off from me and inaccessible.

You know, we had never been together before without little enterprises of endearment, without a faintly guilty, quite delightful excitement.

I pleaded, I argued. I tried to show that even my harsh and difficult letters came from my desire to come wholly into contact with her. I made exaggerated fine statements of the longing I felt for her when I was away, of the shock and misery of finding her estranged and cool. She looked at me feeling the emotion of my speech and impervious to its ideas. I had no doubt—whatever poverty in my words, coolly written down now, might convey—that I was eloquent then. I meant most intensely what I said, indeed I was wholly concentrated upon it. I was set upon conveying to her with absolute sincerity my sense of distance, and the greatness of my desire. I toiled towards her painfully and obstinately through a jungle of words.

Her face changed very slowly—by such imperceptible degrees as when at dawn light comes into a clear sky. I could feel that I touched her, that her hardness was in some manner melting, her determination softening towards hesitations. The habit of an old familiarity lurked somewhere within her. But she would not let me reach her.

" No," she cried abruptly, starting into motion.

She laid a hand on my arm. A wonderful new friendliness came into her voice. " It's impossible, Willie. Everything is different now—everything. We made a mistake. We two young sillies made a mistake and everything is different for ever. Yes, yes."

She turned about.

" Nettie ! " cried I, and, still protesting, pursued her along the narrow alley between the staging toward the hot-house door. I pursued her like an accusation, and she went before me like one who is guilty and ashamed. So I recall it now.

She would not let me talk to her again.

Yet I could see that my talk to her had altogether abolished the clear-cut distance of our meeting in the park. Ever and again I found her hazel eyes upon me. They expressed something novel—a surprise, as though she realised an unwonted relationship, and a sympathetic pity. And still—something defensive.

When we got back to the cottage, I fell talking rather more freely with her father about the nationalisation of railways, and my spirits and temper had so far mended at the realisation that I could still produce an effect upon Nettie, that I was even playful with Puss. Mrs. Stuart judged from that that things were better with me than they were, and began to beam mightily.

But Nettie remained thoughtful and said very little. She was lost in perplexities I could not fathom, and presently she slipped away from us and went upstairs.

§ 6

I was, of course, too footsore to walk back to Clayton, but I had a shilling and a penny in my pocket for the train between Checkshill and Two-Mile Stone, and that much of the distance I proposed to do in the train. And when I got ready to go, Nettie amazed me by waking up to the most remarkable solicitude for me. I must, she said, go by the road. It was altogether too dark for the short way to the lodge gates.

I pointed out that it was moonlight. " With the comet thrown in," said old Stuart.

" No," she insisted, " you *must* go by the road."

I still disputed.

She was standing near me. " To please *me*," she urged, in a quick undertone, and with a persuasive look that puzzled me. Even in the moment I asked myself why should this please her.

I might have agreed had she not followed that up with, " The hollies by the shrubbery are as dark as pitch. And there's the deer-hounds."

" I'm not afraid of the dark," said I. " Nor of the deer-hounds, either."

" But those dogs ! Supposing one was loose ! "

That was a girl's argument, a girl who still had to understand that fear is an overt argument only for her own sex. I thought too of those grisly lank brutes straining at their chains and the chorus they could make of a night when they heard belated footsteps along the edge of the Killing Wood, and the thought banished my wish to please her. Like most imaginative natures I was acutely capable of dreads and retreats, and constantly occupied with their suppression and concealment, and to refuse the short cut when it might appear that I did it on account of half a dozen almost certainly chained dogs was impossible.

So I set off in spite of her, feeling valiant and glad to be so easily brave, but a little sorry that she should think herself crossed by me.

A thin cloud veiled the moon, and the way under the beeches was dark and indistinct. I was not so preoccupied with my love-affairs as to neglect what I will confess was always my custom at night across that wild and lonely park. I made myself a club by fastening a big flint to one end of my twisted handkerchief and tying the other about my wrist, and with this in my pocket, went on comforted.

And it chanced that as I emerged from the hollies by the corner of the shrubbery I was startled to come unexpectedly upon a young man in evening dress smoking a cigar.

I was walking on turf, so that the sound I made was slight. He stood clear in the moonlight, his cigar glowed like a blood-red star, and it did not occur to me at the time that I advanced towards him almost invisibly in an impenetrable shadow.

"Hullo," he cried, with a sort of amiable challenge. "I'm here first!"

I came out into the light. "Who cares if you are?" said I.

I had jumped at once to an interpretation of his words. I knew that there was an intermittent dispute between the House people and the villager public about the use of this track, and it is needless to say where my sympathies fell in that dispute.

"Eh!" he cried in surprise.

"Thought I would run away, I suppose," said I, and came close up to him.

All my enormous hatred of his class had flared up at the sight of his costume, at the fancied challenge of his words. I knew him. He was Edward Verrall, son of the man who owned not only this great estate but more than half of Rawdon's pot-bank, and who had interests and possessions, collieries and rents, all over the district of the Four Towns. He was a gallant youngster, people said, and very clever. Young as he was there was talk of parliament for him; he had been a great success at the university, and he was being sedulously popularised among us. He took with a light confidence, as a matter of course, advantages that I would have faced the rack to get, and I firmly believed myself a better man than he. He was, as he stood there, a concentrated figure of all that filled me with bitterness. One day he had stopped in a motor outside our house, and I remember the thrill of rage with which I had noted the dutiful admiration in my mother's eyes as she peered through her blind at him. "That's young Mr. Verrall," she said. "They say he's very clever."

"They would," I answered. "Damn them and him!"

But that is by the way.

He was clearly astonished to find himself face to face with a man. His note changed.

"Who the devil are *you*?" he asked.

My retort was the cheap expedient of re-echoing, "Who the devil are you?"

"*Well*," he said.

"I'm coming along this path if I like," I said. "See? It's a public path—just as this used to be public land. You've stolen the land—you and yours, and now you want to steal the right of way. You'll ask us to get off the face of the earth next. I shan't oblige. See?"

I was shorter and I suppose a couple of years younger than he, but I had the improvised club in my pocket gripped ready, and I would have fought with him very cheerfully. But he fell a step backward as I came towards him.

"Socialist, I presume?" he said, alert and quiet and with the faintest note of badinage.

" One of many."

" We're all socialists nowadays," he remarked philosophically, " and I haven't the faintest intention of disputing your right of way."

" You'd better not," I said.

" No ! "

" No."

He replaced his cigar, and there was a brief pause. " Catching a train ? " he threw out.

It seemed absurd not to answer. " Yes," I said shortly.

He said it was a pleasant evening for a walk.

I hovered for a moment and there was my path before me, and he stood aside. There seemed nothing to do but go on. " Good night," said he, as that intention took effect.

I growled a surly good night.

I felt like a bombshell of swearing that must presently burst with some violence as I went on my silent way. He had so completely got the best in our encounter.

§ 7

There comes a memory, an odd intermixture of two entirely divergent things, that stands out with the intensest vividness.

As I went across the last open meadow, following the short cut to Checkshill station, I perceived I had two shadows.

The thing jumped into my mind and stopped its tumid flow for a moment. I remember the intelligent detachment of my sudden interest. I turned sharply, and stood looking at the moon and the great white comet, that the drift of the clouds had now rather suddenly unveiled.

The comet was perhaps twenty degrees from the moon. What a wonderful thing it looked floating there, a greenish-white apparition in the dark blue deeps ! It looked ,brighter than the moon because it was smaller, but the shadow it cast, though clearer cut, was much fainter than the moon's shadow. . . . I went on noting these facts, watching my two shadows precede me.

I am totally unable to account for the sequence of my thoughts on this occasion. But suddenly, as if I had come on this new fact round a corner, the comet was out of my mind again, and I was face to face with an absolutely new idea. I wonder sometimes if the two shadows I cast, one with a sort of feminine faintness with regard to the other and not quite so tall, may not have suggested the word or the thought of an assignation to my mind. All that I have clear is that with the certitude of intuition I knew what it was that had brought the youth in evening dress outside the shrubbery. Of course ! He had come to meet Nettie !

Once the mental process was started it took no time at all. The day which had been full of perplexities for me, the mysterious invisible thing that had held Nettie and myself

apart, the unaccountable strange something in her manner,
was revealed and explained.

I knew now why she had looked guilty at my appearance,
what had brought her out that afternoon, why she had hurried
me in, the nature of the " book " she had run back to fetch,
the reason why she had wanted me to go back by the highroad, and why she had pitied me. It was all in the instant
clear to me.

You must imagine me a black little creature, suddenly
stricken still—for a moment standing rigid—and then again
suddenly becoming active with an impotent gesture, becoming
audible with an inarticulate cry, with two little shadows
mocking my dismay, and about this figure you must conceive
a great wide space of moonlit grass, rimmed by the looming
suggestion of distant trees—trees very low and faint and dim,
and over it all the domed serenity of that wonderful luminous
night.

For a little while this realisation stunned my mind. My
thoughts came to a pause, staring at my discovery. Meanwhile my feet and my previous direction carried me through
the warm darkness to Checkshill station with its little lights,
to the ticket-office window, and so to the train.

I remember myself as it were waking up to the thing—I
was alone in one of the dingy " third-class " compartments
of that time—and the sudden nearly frantic insurgence of my
rage. I stood up with the cry of an angry animal, and smote
my fist with all my strength against the panel of wood before
me. . . .

Curiously enough I have completely forgotten my mood
after that for a little while, but I know that later, for a minute
perhaps, I hung for a time out of the carriage with the door
open, contemplating a leap from the train. It was to be a
dramatic leap, and then I would go storming back to her,
denounce her, overwhelm her ; and I hung, urging myself to
do it. I don't remember how it was I decided not to do this,
at last, but in the end I didn't.

When the train stopped at the next station I had given up
all thoughts of going back. I was sitting in the corner of the
carriage with my bruised and wounded hand pressed under
my arm, and still insensible to its pain, trying to think out
clearly a scheme of action—action that should express the
monstrous indignation that possessed me.

CHAPTER THREE

THE REVOLVER

§ 1

"THAT comet is going to hit the earth ! "

So said one of the two men who got into the train and settled down.

" Ah ! " said the other man.

" They do say that it is made of gas, that comet. We shan't blow up, shall us ? " . . .

What did it matter to me ?

I was thinking of revenge—revenge against the primary conditions of my being. I was thinking of Nettie and her lover. I was firmly resolved he should not have her—though I had to kill them both to prevent it. I did not care what else might happen, if only that end was insured. All my thwarted passions had turned to rage. I would have accepted eternal torment that night without a second thought, to be certain of revenge. A hundred possibilities of action, a hundred stormy situations, a whirl of violent schemes, chased one another through my shamed exasperated mind. The sole prospect I could endure was of some gigantic, inexorably cruel vindication of my humiliated self.

And Nettie ? I loved Nettie still, but now with the intensest jealousy, with the keen, unmeasuring hatred of wounded pride, and baffled, passionate desire.

§ 2

As I came down the hill from Clayton Crest—for my shilling and a penny only permitted my travelling by train as far as Two-Mile Stone, and thence I had to walk over the hill—I remember very vividly a little man with a shrill voice who was preaching under a gas-lamp against a hoarding to a thin crowd of Sunday evening loafers. He was a short man, bald, with a little fair curly beard and hair, and watery blue eyes, and he was preaching that the end of the world drew near.

I think that is the first time I heard any one link the comet with the end of the world. He had got that jumbled up with international politics and prophecies from the Book of Daniel.

I stopped to hear him only for a moment or so, I do not think I should have halted at all but his crowd blocked my path, and the sight of his queer wild expression, the gesture of his upward-pointing finger, held me.

" There is the end of all your Sins and Follies," he bawled. " There ! There is the Star of Judgments, the Judgments of the most High God ! It is appointed unto all men to die—

unto all men to die "—his voice changed to a curious flat chant—" and after death, the Judgment ! The Judgment ! "

I pushed and threaded my way through the bystanders and went on, and his curious harsh flat voice pursued me. I went on with the thoughts that had occupied me before—where I could buy a revolver, and how I might master its use—and probably I should have forgotten all about him had he not taken a part in the hideous dream that ended the little sleep I had that night. For the most part I lay awake thinking of Nettie and her lover.

Then came three strange days—three days that seem now to have been wholly concentrated upon one business.

This dominant business was the purchase of my revolver. I held myself resolutely to the idea that I must either restore myself by some extraordinary act of vigour and violence in Nettie's eyes or I must kill her. I would not let myself fall away from that. I felt that if I let this matter pass, my last shred of pride and honour would pass with it, that for the rest of my life I should never deserve the slighest respect or any woman's love. Pride kept me to my purpose between my gusts of passion.

Yet it was not easy to buy that revolver.

I had a kind of shyness of the moment when I should have to face the shopman, and I was particularly anxious to have a story ready if he should see fit to ask questions why I bought such a thing. I determined to say I was going to Texas, and I thought it might prove useful there. Texas in those days had the reputation of a wild lawless land. As I knew nothing of caliber or impact, I wanted also to be able to ask with a steady face at what distance a man or woman could be killed by the weapon that might be offered me. I was pretty cool-headed in relation to such practical aspects of my affair. I had some little difficulty in finding a gunsmith. In Clayton there were some rook-rifles and so forth in a cycle shop, but the only revolvers these people had impressed me as being too small and toylike for my purpose. It was in a pawnshop window in the narrow High Street of Swathinglea that I found my choice, a reasonably clumsy and serious-looking imple-ment ticketed " As used in the American army."

I had drawn out my balance from the savings bank, a matter of two pounds and more, to make this purchase, and I found it at last a very easy transaction. The pawnbroker told me where I could get ammunition, and I went home that night with bulging pockets, an armed man.

The purchase of my revolver was, I say, the chief business of those days, but you must not think I was so intent upon it as to be insensible to the stirring things that were happening in the streets through which I went seeking the means to effect my purpose. They were full of murmurings : the whole region of the Four Towns scowled lowering from its narrow doors. The ordinary healthy flow of people going to work, people going about their business, was chilled and checked. Numbers of men stood about the streets in knots and groups, as corpuscles gather and catch in the blood-vessels in the opening stages of inflammation. The women looked haggard and worried. The ironworkers had refused the proposed reduction of their wages, and the lock-out had begun. They were already at "play." The Conciliation Board was doing its best to keep the coal-miners and masters from a breach, but young Lord Redcar, the greatest of our coal-owners and landlord of all Swathinglea and half Clayton, was taking a fine upstanding attitude that made the breach inevitable. He was a handsome young man, a gallant young man ; his pride revolted at the idea of being dictated to by a "lot of bally miners," and he meant, he said, to make a fight for it. The world had treated him sumptuously from his earliest years ; the shares in common stock of five thousand people had gone to pay for his handsome upbringing, and large, romantic, expensive ambitions filled his generously nurtured mind. He had early distinguished himself at Oxford by his scornful attitude towards democracy. There was something that appealed to the imagination in his fine antagonism to the crowd—on the one hand, was the brilliant young nobleman, picturesquely alone ; on the other, the ugly, inexpressive multitude, dressed inelegantly in shop-clothes, under-educated, under-fed, envious, base, and with a wicked disinclination for work and a wicked appetite for the good things it could so rarely get. For common imaginative purposes one left out the policeman from the design, the stalwart policeman protecting his lordship, and ignored the fact that while Lord Redcar had his hands immediately and legally on the workman's shelter and bread, they could touch him to the skin only by some violent breach of the law.

He lived at Lowchester House, five miles or so beyond Checkshill ; but partly to show how little he cared for his antagonists, and partly no doubt to keep himself in touch with the negotiations that were still going on, he was visible almost every day in and about the Four Towns, driving that big motor-car of his that could take him sixty miles an hour. The English passion for fair play one might have thought sufficient to rob this bold procedure of any dangerous possibilities, but he did not go altogether free from insult, and on one occasion at least an intoxicated Irish woman shook her fist at him. . . .

A dark, quiet crowd, that was greater each day, a crowd more than half women, brooded as a cloud will sometimes brood permanently upon a mountain crest, in the market-place outside the Clayton Town Hall, where the conference was held. . . .

I considered myself justified in regarding Lord Redcar's

passing automobile with a special animosity because of the
leaks in our roof.

We held our little house on lease ; the owner was a mean,
saving old man named Pettigrew, who lived in a villa adorned
with plaster images of dogs and goats, at Overcastle, and in
spite of our specific agreement, he would do no repairs for us
at all. He rested secure in my mother's timidity. Once, long
ago, she had been behind-hand with her rent, with half of her
quarter's rent, and he had extended the days of grace a month ;
her sense that some day she might need the same mercy again
made her his abject slave. She was afraid even to ask that he
should cause the roof to be mended for fear he might take
offence. But one night the rain poured in on her bed and gave
her a cold, and stained and soaked her poor old patchwork
counterpane.   Then she got me to compose an excessively
polite letter to old Pettigrew, begging him as a favour to perform his legal obligations. It is part of the general imbecility
of those days that such one-sided law as existed was a profound mystery to the common people, its provisions impossible
to ascertain, its machinery impossible to set in motion. Instead
of the clearly written code, the lucid statements of rules and
principles that are now at the service of every one, the law
was the muddled secret of the legal profession. Poor people,
overworked people, had constantly to submit to petty wrongs
because of the intolerable uncertainty not only of law but of
cost, and of the demands upon time and energy proceedings
might make. There was indeed no justice for any one too poor
to command a good solicitor's deference and loyalty ; there
was nothing but rough police protection and the magistrate's
grudging or eccentric advice for the mass of the population.
The civil law, in particular, was a mysterious upper-class
weapon, and I can imagine no injustice that would have been
sufficient to induce my poor old mother to appeal to it.

All this begins to sound incredible. I can only assure you
that it was so.

But I, when I learned that old Pettigrew had been down
to tell my mother all about his rheumatism, to inspect the
roof, and to allege that nothing was needed, gave way to my
most frequent emotion in those days, a burning indignation,
and took the matter into my own hands. I wrote and asked
him, with a withering air of technicality, to have the roof
repaired " as per agreement," and added, " if not done in one
week from now we shall be obliged to take proceedings." I
had not mentioned this high line of conduct to my mother
at first, and so when old Pettigrew came down in a state of
great agitation with my letter in his hand, she was almost
equally agitated.

" How could you write to old Mr. Pettigrew like that ? "
she asked me.

I said that old Pettigrew was a shameful old rascal, or

words to that effect, and I am afraid I behaved in a very undutiful way to her when she said that she had settled everything with him—she wouldn't say how, but I could guess well enough—and that I was to promise her, promise her faithfully, to do nothing more in the matter. I wouldn't promise her.

And—having nothing better to employ me then—I presently went raging to old Pettigrew in order to put the whole thing before him in what I considered the proper light. Old Pettigrew evaded my illumination ; he saw me coming up his front steps—I can still see his queer old nose and the crinkled brow over his eye and the little wisp of grey hair that showed over the corner of his window-blind—and he instructed his servant to put up the chain when she answered the door, and to tell me that he would not see me. So I had to fall back upon my pen.

Then it was, as I had no idea what were the proper " proceedings " to take, the brilliant idea occurred to me of appealing to Lord Redcar as the ground landlord, and, as it were, our feudal chief, and pointing out to him that his security for his rent was depreciating in old Pettigrew's hands. I added some general observations on leaseholds, the taxation of ground rents, and the private ownership of the soil. And Lord Redcar, whose spirit revolted at democracy, and who cultivated a pert humiliating manner with his inferiors to show as much, earned my distinguished hatred for ever by causing his secretary to present his compliments to me, and his request that I would mind my own business and leave him to manage his. At which I was so greatly enraged that I first tore this note into minute innumerable pieces, and then dashed it dramatically all over the floor of my room—from which to keep my mother from the job, I afterwards had to pick it up laboriously on all-fours.

I was still meditating a tremendous retort, an indictment of all Lord Redcar's class, their manners, morals, economic and political crimes, when my trouble with Nettie arose to swamp all minor troubles. Yet not so completely but that I snarled aloud when his lordship's motor-car whizzed by me, as I went about upon my long meandering quest for a weapon. And I discovered after a time that my mother had bruised her knee and was lame. Fearing to irritate me by bringing the thing before me again, she had set herself to move her bed out of the way of the drip without my help, and she had knocked her knee. All her poor furnishings, I discovered, were cowering now close to the peeling bedroom walls ; there had come a vast discoloration of the ceiling, and a washing-tub was in occupation of the middle of her chamber. . . .

It is necessary that I should set these things before you, should give the key of inconvenience and uneasiness in which all things were arranged, should suggest the breath of trouble that stirred along the hot summer streets, the anxiety about the strike, the rumours and indignations, the gatherings and meetings, the increasing gravity of the policemen's faces, the combative headlines of the local papers, the knots of picketers who scrutinised any one who passed near the silent, smokeless forges, but in my mind, you must understand, such impressions came and went irregularly ; they made a moving background, changing undertones, to my preoccupation by that darkly shaping purpose to which a revolver was so imperative an essential.

Along the darkling streets, amidst the sullen crowds, the thought of Nettie, my Nettie, and her gentleman lover made ever a vivid inflammatory spot of purpose in my brain.

§ 3

It was three days after this—on Wednesday, that is to say—that the first of those sinister outbreaks occurred that ended in the bloody affair of Peacock Grove and the flooding out of the entire line of the Swathinglea collieries. It was the only one of these disturbances I was destined to see, and at most a mere trivial preliminary of that struggle.

The accounts that have been written of this affair vary very widely. To read them is to realise the extraordinary carelessness of truth that dishonoured the press of those latter days. In my bureau I have several files of the daily papers of the old time—I collected them, as a matter of fact—and three or four of about that date I have just this moment taken out and looked through to refresh my impression of what I saw. They lie before me—queer, shrivelled, incredible things ; the cheap paper has already become brittle and brown and split along the creases, the ink faded or smeared, and I have to handle them with the utmost care when I glance among their raging headlines. As I sit here in this serene place, their quality throughout, their arrangement, their tone, their arguments and exhortations, read as though they came from drugged and drunken men. They give one the effect of faded bawling, of screams and shouts heard faintly in a little gramophone. . . . It is only on Monday I find, and buried deep below the war news, that these publications contain any intimation that unusual happenings were forward in Clayton and Swathinglea.

What I saw was towards evening. I had been learning to shoot with my new possession. I had walked out with it four or five miles across a patch of moorland and down to a secluded little coppice full of blue-bells, half-way along the high-road between Leet and Stafford. Here I had spent the afternoon, experimenting and practising with careful deliberation and grim persistence. I had brought an old kite-frame of cane with me, that folded and unfolded, and each shot-hole I made I marked and numbered to compare with my other endeavours. At last I was satisfied that I could hit a playing-card at thirty paces nine times out of ten ; the light was getting too bad for me to see my pencilled bull's-eye, and in that state of quiet moodiness that sometimes comes with hunger to passionate men, I returned by the way of Swathinglea towards my home.

The road I followed came down between banks of wretched-looking working-men's houses, in close-packed rows on either side, and took upon itself the *rôle* of Swathinglea High Street where, at a lamp and a pillar-box, the steam-trams began. So far that dirty hot way had been unusually quiet and empty, but beyond the corner, where the first group of beershops clustered, it became populous. It was very quiet still, even the children were a little inactive, but there were a lot of people standing dispersedly in little groups, and with a general direction towards the gates of the Bantock Burden coal-pit.

The place was being picketed, although at that time the miners were still nominally at work and the conferences between masters and men still in session at Clayton Town Hall. But one of the men employed at the Bantock Burden pit, Jack Briscoe, was a socialist, and he had distinguished himself by a violent letter upon the crisis to the leading socialist paper in England, *The Clarion*, in which he had adventured among the motives of Lord Redcar. The publication of this had been followed by instant dismissal. As Lord Redcar wrote a day or so later to the *Times*—I have that *Times*, I have all the London papers of the last month before the Change——

" The man was paid off and kicked out. Any self-respecting employer would do the same." The thing had happened over-night, and the men did not at once take a clear line upon what was, after all, a very intricate and debatable occasion. But they came out in a sort of semi-official strike from all Lord Redcar's collieries beyond the canal that besets Swathinglea. They did so without formal notice, committing a breach of contract by this sudden cessation. But in the long labour struggles of the old days the workers were constantly putting themselves in the wrong and committing illegalities through that overpowering craving for dramatic promptness natural to uneducated minds.

All the men had not come out of the Bantock Burden pit. Something was wrong there, an indecision if nothing else ; the mine was still working, and there was a rumour that men from Durham had been held in readiness by Lord Redcar, and were already in the mine. Now it is absolutely impossible to ascertain certainly how things stood at that time. The news-papers say this and that, but nothing trustworthy remains.

I believe I should have gone striding athwart the dark stage of that stagnant Industrial drama without asking a question, if Lord Redcar had not chanced to come upon the scene about the same time as myself and incontinently ended its stagnation.

He had promised that if the men wanted a struggle he would

put up the best fight they had ever had, and he had been active all that afternoon in meeting the quarrel half-way, and preparing as conspicuously as possible for the scratch force of " blacklegs "—as we called them—who were, he said and we believed, to replace the strikers in his pits.

I was an eye-witness of the whole of the affair outside the Bantock Burden pit, and—I do not know what happened.

Picture to yourself how the thing came to me.

I was descending a steep, cobbled, excavated road between banked-up footways, perhaps six feet high, upon which, in a monotonous series, opened the living-room doors of rows of dark, low cottages. The perspective of squat blue slate roofs and clustering chimneys drifted downward towards the irregular open space before the colliery—a space covered with coaly, wheel-scarred mud, with a patch of weedy dump to the left and the colliery gates to the right. Beyond, the High Street with shops resumed again in good earnest and went on, and the lines of the steam-tramway that started out from before my feet, and were here shining and acutely visible with reflected skylight and here lost in a shadow, took up for one acute moment the greasy yellow irradiation of a newly lit gas-lamp as they vanished round the bend. To the left spread a darkling marsh of homes, an infinitude of little smoking hovels, meagre churches, public-houses, board schools, and other buildings out of which the prevailing chimneys of Swathinglea rose detachedly. To the right, very clear and relatively high, the Bantock Burden pit-mouth was marked by a gaunt lattice bearing a great black wheel, sharp and distinct in the twilight, and beyond, in an irregular perspective, were others following the lie of the seams. The general effect, as one came down the hill, was of a dark compressed life beneath a very high and wide and luminous evening sky, against which these pit-wheels rose. And ruling the calm spaciousness of that heaven was the great comet, now green-white, and wonderful for all who had eyes to see.

The fading afterglow of the sunset threw up all the contours and skyline to the west, and the comet rose eastward out of the pouring tumult of smoke from Bladden's forges. The moon had still to rise.

By this time the comet had begun to assume the cloudlike form still familiar through the medium of a thousand photographs and sketches. At first it had been an almost telescopic speck : it had brightened to the dimensions of the greatest star in the heavens ; it had still grown, hour by hour, in its incredibly swift, noiseless and inevitable rush upon our earth, until it had equalled and surpassed the moon. Now it was the most splendid thing this sky of earth has ever held. I have never seen a photograph that gave a proper idea of it. Never at any time did it assume the conventional tailed outline comets are supposed to have. Astronomers talked of its double tail, one preceding it and one trailing behind it, but these were foreshortened to nothing, so that it had rather the form of a bellying puff of luminous smoke with an intenser, brighter heart. It rose a hot yellow colour, and only began to show its distinctive greenness when it was clear of the mists of the evening.

It compelled attention for a space. For all my earthly concentration of mind, I could but stare at it for a moment with a vague anticipation that, after all, in some way so strange and glorious an object must have significance, could not possibly be a matter of absolute indifference to the scheme and values of my life.

But how ?

I thought of Parload. I thought of the panic and uneasiness that was spreading in this very matter, and the assurances of scientific men that the thing weighed so little—at the utmost a few hundred tons of thinly diffused gas and dust—that even were it to smite this earth fully, nothing could possibly ensue. And after all, said I, what earthly significance has any one found in the stars ?

Then, as one still descended, the houses and buildings rose up, the presence of those watching groups of people, the tension of the situation ; and one forgot the sky.

Preoccupied with myself and with my dark dream about Nettie and my honour, I threaded my course through the stagnating threat of this gathering, and was caught unawares when suddenly the whole scene flashed into drama. . . .

The attention of every one swung round with an irresistible magnetism towards the High Street, and caught me as a rush of waters might catch a wisp of hay. Abruptly the whole crowd was sounding one note. It was not a word, it was a sound that mingled threat and protest, something between a prolonged " Ah ! " and " Ugh !" Then with a hoarse intensity of anger came a low heavy booing, " Boo ! boo—oo ! " a note stupidly expressive of animal savagery. " Toot, toot ! " said Lord Redcar's automobile in ridiculous repartee. " Toot, toot ! " One heard it whizzing and throbbing as the crowd obliged it to slow down.

Everybody seemed in motion towards the colliery gates ; I, too, with others.

I heard a shout. Through the dark figures about me I saw the motor-car stop and move forward again, and had a glimpse of something writhing on the ground. . . .

It was alleged afterwards that Lord Redcar was driving, and that he quite deliberately knocked down a little boy who would not get out of his way. It is asserted with equal confidence that the boy was a man who tried to pass across the front of the motor-car as it came slowly through the crowd, who escaped by a hair's breadth, and then slipped on the tram-rail and fell down. I have both accounts set forth, under screaming headlines, in two of these sere newspapers upon my desk. No one could ever ascertain the truth. Indeed, in such a blind tumult of passion, could there be any truth ?

There was a rush forward, the horn of the car sounded, everything swayed violently to the right for perhaps ten yards or so, and there was a report like a pistol-shot.

For a moment every one seemed running away. A woman, carrying a shawl-wrapped child, blundered into me, and sent me reeling back. Everyone thought of firearms, but as a matter of fact something had gone wrong with the motor, what in those old-fashioned contrivances was called a backfire. A thin puff of bluish smoke hung in the air behind the thing. The majority of the people scattered back in a disorderly fashion, and left a clear space about the struggle that centred upon the motor-car.

The man or boy who had fallen was lying on the ground with no one near him, a black lump, an extended arm and two sprawling feet. The motor-car had stopped, and its three occupants were standing up. Six or seven black figures surrounded the car, and appeared to be holding on to it as if to prevent it from starting again ; one—it was Mitchell, a well-known labour leader—argued in fierce low tones with Lord Redcar. I could not hear anything they said, I was not near enough. Behind me the colliery gates were open, and there was a sense of help coming to the motor-car from that direction. There was an unoccupied muddy space for fifty yards, perhaps, between car and gate, and then the wheels and head of the pit rose black against the sky. I was one of a rude semicircle of people that hung as yet indeterminate in action about this dispute.

It was natural, I suppose, that my fingers should close upon the revolver in my pocket.

I advanced with the vaguest intentions in the world, and not so quickly but that several men hurried past me to join the little knot holding up the car.

Lord Redcar, in his big furry overcoat, towered up over the group about him ; his gestures were free and threatening, and his voice loud. He made a fine figure there, I must admit ; he was a big, fair, handsome young man with a fine tenor voice and an instinct for gallant effect. My eyes were drawn to him at first wholly. He seemed a symbol, a triumphant symbol, of all that the theory of aristocracy claims, of all that filled my soul with resentment. His chauffeur sat crouched together, peering at the crowd under his lordship's arm. But Mitchell showed as a sturdy figure also, and his voice was firm and loud.

" You've hurt that lad," said Mitchell, over and over again. " You'll wait here till you see if he's hurt."

" I'll wait here or not as I please," said Redcar ; and to the chauffeur, " Here ! get down and look at it ! "

" You'd better not get down," said Mitchell; and the chauffeur stood bent and hesitating on the step.

The man on the back seat stood up, leant forward, and spoke to Lord Redcar, and for the first time my attention was drawn to him. It was young Verrall ! His handsome face shone clear and fine in the green pallor of the comet.

I ceased to hear the quarrel that was raising the voice of Mitchell and Lord Redcar. This new fact sent them spinning into the background. Young Verrall !

It was my own purpose coming to meet me half way.

There was to be a fight here, it seemed certain to come to a scuffle, and here we were——

What was I to do ? I thought very swiftly. Unless my memory cheats me, I acted with prompt decision. My hand tightened on my revolver, and then I remembered it was unloaded. I had thought my course out in an instant. I turned round and pushed my way out of the angry crowd that was now surging back towards the motor-car.

It would be quiet and out of sight, I thought, among the dump heaps across the road, and there I might load unobserved. . . .

A big young man striding forward with his fists clenched, halted for one second at the sight of me.

" What ! " said he. " Ain't afraid of them, are you ? "

I glanced over my shoulder and back at him, was near showing him my pistol, and the expression changed in his eyes. He hung perplexed at me. Then with a grunt he went on.

I heard the voices growing loud and sharp behind me.

I hesitated, half turned towards the dispute, then set off running towards the heaps. Some instinct told me not to be detected loading. I was cool enough therefore to think of the aftermath of the thing I meant to do.

I looked back once again towards the swaying discussion—or was it a fight now ? and then I dropped into the hollow, knelt among the weeds, and loaded with eager trembling fingers. I loaded one chamber, got up and went back a dozen paces, thought of possibilities, vacillated, returned and loaded all the others. I did it slowly because I felt a little clumsy, and at the end came a moment of inspection—had I forgotten anything ? And then for a few seconds I crouched before I rose, resisting the first gust of reaction against my impulse. I took thought, and for a moment that great green-white meteor overhead swam back into my conscious mind. For the first time then I linked it clearly with all the fierce violence that had crept into human life. I joined up that with what I meant to do. I was going to shoot young Verrall under the benediction of that green glare.

But about Nettie ?

I found it impossible to think out that obvious complication.

I came up over the heap again, and walked slowly back
towards the wrangle.

Of course I had to kill him. . . .

Now I would have you believe I did not want to murder
young Verrall at all at that particular time. I had not pictured
such circumstances as these, I had never thought of him in
connection with Lord Redcar and our black industrial world.
He was in that distant other world of Checkshill, the world
of parks and gardens, the world of sunlit emotions and Nettie.
His appearance here was disconcerting. I was taken by surprise.
I was too tired and hungry to think clearly, and the hard implication of our antagonism prevailed with me. In the tumult
of my past emotions I had thought constantly of conflicts,
confrontations, deeds of violence ; and now the memory of
these things took possession of me as though they were irrevocable resolutions.

There was a sharp exclamation, the shriek of a woman,
and the crowd came surging back. The fight had begun.

Lord Redcar, I believe, had jumped down from his car and
felled Mitchell, and men were already running out to his
assistance from the colliery gates.

I had some difficulty in shoving through the crowd ; I can
still remember very vividly being jammed at one time between
two big men so that my arms were pinned to my sides, but
all the other details are gone out of my mind until I found
myself almost violently projected forward into the " scrap."

I blundered against the corner of the motor-car, and came
round it face to face with young Verrall, who was descending
from the back compartment. His face was touched with
orange from the automobile's big lamps, which conflicted with
the shadows of the comet light, and distorted him oddly. That
effect lasted but an instant, but it put me out. Then he came
a step forward, and the ruddy lights and queerness vanished.

I don't think he recognised me, but he perceived immediately
I meant attacking. He struck out at once at me a haphazard
blow, and touched me on the cheek.

Instinctively I let go of the pistol, snatched my right hand
out of my pocket and brought it up in a belated parry, and
then let out with my left full in his chest.

It sent him staggering, and as he went back I saw recognition mingle with astonishment in his face.

" You know me, you swine," I cried, and hit again.

Then I was spinning sideways, half-stunned, with a huge
lump of a fist under my jaw. I had an impression of Lord
Redcar as a great furry bulk, towering like some Homeric
hero above the fray. I went down before him—it made him
seem to rush up—and he ignored me further. His big flat
voice counselled young Verrall ;

" Cut, Teddy ! It won't do. The picketa's got i'on bahs. . . ."

Feet swayed about me, and some hobnailed miner kicked

my ankle and went stumbling. There were shouts and curses,
and then everything had swept past me. I rolled over on my
face and beheld the chauffeur, young Verrall, and Lord Redcar
—the latter holding up his long skirts of fur, and making a
grotesque figure—one behind the other, in full bolt across a
coldly comet-lit interval, towards the open gates of the colliery.

I raised myself up on my hands.

Young Verrall!

I had not even drawn my revolver—I had forgotten it. I
was covered with coaly mud—knees, elbows, shoulders, back.
I had not even drawn my revolver ! . . .

A feeling of ridiculous impotence overwhelmed me. I
struggled painfully to my feet.

I hesitated for a moment towards the gates of the colliery,
and then went limping homeward, thwarted, painful, confused, and ashamed. I had not the heart nor desire to help
in the wrecking and burning of Lord Redcar's motor.

§ 4

In the night, fever, pain, fatigue—it may be the indigestion
of my supper of bread and cheese—roused me at last out of
a hag-rid sleep to face despair. I was a soul lost amidst desolations and shame, dishonoured, evilly treated, hopeless. I
raged against the God I denied, and cursed him as I lay.

And it was in the nature of my fever, which was indeed
only half fatigue and illness, and the rest the disorder of
passionate youth, that Nettie, a strangely distorted Nettie,
should come through the brief dreams that marked the ex-
haustions of that vigil, to dominate my misery. I was sensible,
with an exaggerated distinctness, of the intensity of her
physical charm for me, of her every grace and beauty ; she
took to herself the whole gamut of desire in me and the whole
gamut of pride. She, bodily, was my lost honour. It was not
only loss but disgrace to lose her. She stood for life and all
that was denied ; she mocked me as a creature of failure and
defeat. My spirit raised itself towards her, and then the bruise
upon my jaw glowed with a dull heat, and I rolled in the mud
again before my rivals.

There were times when something near madness took me,
and I gnashed my teeth and dug my nails into my hands
and ceased to curse and cry out only by reason of the insufficiency of words. And once towards dawn I got out of
bed, and sat by my looking-glass with my revolver loaded in
my hand. I stood up at last and put it carefully in my drawer
and locked it—out of reach of any gusty impulse. After that
I slept for a little while.

Such nights were nothing rare and strange in that old order
of the world. Never a city, never a night the whole year
round, but amidst those who slept were those who waked,
plumbing the deeps of wrath and misery. Countless thousands

there were so ill, so troubled, they agonise near to the very border-line of madness, each one the centre of a universe darkened and lost. . . .

The next day I spent in gloomy lethargy.

I had intended to go to Checkshill that day, but my bruised ankle was too swollen for that to be possible. I sat indoors in the ill-lit downstairs kitchen, with my foot bandaged, and mused darkly and read. My dear old mother waited on me, and her brown eyes watched me and wondered at my black silences, my frowning preoccupations. I had not told her how it was my ankle came to be bruised and my clothes muddy. She had brushed my clothes in the morning before I got up.

Ah well! Mothers are not treated in that way now. That I suppose must console me. I wonder how far you will be able to picture that dark, grimy, untidy room, with its bare deal table, its tattered wall paper, the saucepans and the kettle on the narrow, cheap, but by no means economical range, the ashes under the fireplace, the rust-spotted steel fender on which my bandaged feet rested; I wonder how near you can come to seeing the scowling pale-faced hobbledehoy I was, unshaven and collarless, in the Windsor chair, and the little timid, dirty, devoted old woman who hovered about me with love peering out from her puckered eyelids. . . .

When she went out to buy some vegetables in the middle of the morning she got me a half-penny journal. It was just such a one as these upon my desk, only that the copy I read was damp from the press, and these are so dry and brittle they crack if I touch them. I have a copy of the actual issue I read that morning ; it was a paper called emphatically the *New Paper*, but everybody bought it and everybody called it the " yell." It was full that morning of stupendous news and still more stupendous headlines, so stupendous that for a little while I was roused from my egotistical broodings to wider interests. For it seemed that Germany and England were on the brink of war.

Of all the monstrous irrational phenomena of the former time, war was certainly the most strikingly insane. In reality it was probably far less mischievous than such quieter evils as, for example, the general acquiescence in the private owner-ship of land, but its evil consequences showed so plainly that even in those days of stifling confusion one marvelled at it. On no conceivable grounds was there any sense in modern war. Save for the slaughter and mangling of a multitude of people, the destruction of vast quantities of material, and the waste of innumerable units of energy, it effected nothing. The old war of savage and barbaric nations did at least change humanity, you assumed yourselves to be a superior tribe in physique and discipline, you demonstrated this upon your neighbours, and if successful you took their land and their women and perpetuated and enlarged your superiority. The new war changed nothing but the colour of maps, the design of postage stamps, and the relationship of a few accidentally conspicuous individuals. In one of the last of these international epileptic fits, for example, the English, with much dysentery and bad poetry and a few hundred deaths in battle, conquered the South African Boers at a gross cost of about three thousand pounds per head—they could have bought the whole of that preposterous imitation of a nation for a tenth of that sum—and except for a few substitutions of personalities, this group of partially corrupt officials in the place of that, and so forth, the permanent change was altogether insignificant. (But an excitable young man in Austria committed suicide when at length the Transvaal ceased to be a " nation.") Men went through the seat of that war after it was all over, and found humanity unchanged except for a general impoverishment and the convenience of an unlimited supply of empty ration tins and barbed wire and cartridge cases—unchanged and resuming with a slight perplexity all its old habits and misunderstandings, the nigger still in his slum-like kraal, the white in his ugly ill-managed shanty. . . .

But we in England saw all these things, or did not see them, through the mirage of the *New Paper*, in a light of mania. All my adolescence from fourteen to seventeen went to the music of that monstrous resonating futility, the cheering, the anxieties, the songs and the waving of flags, the wrongs of generous Buller and the glorious heroism of De Wet—who *always* got away ; that was the great point about the heroic De Wet—and it never occurred to us that the total population we fought against was less than half the number of those who lived cramped ignoble lives within the compass of the Four Towns.

But before and after that stupid conflict of stupidities, a greater antagonism was coming into being, was slowly and quietly defining itself as a thing inevitable, sinking now a little out of attention only to resume more emphatically, now flashing into some acute definitive expression and now percolating and pervading some new region of thought, and that was the antagonism of Germany and Great Britain.

When I think of that growing proportion of readers who belong entirely to the new order, who are growing up with only the vaguest early memories of the old world, I find the greatest difficulty in writing down the unintelligible confusions that were matter of fact to their fathers.

Here were we British, forty-one millions of people, in a state of almost indescribably aimless economic and moral muddle that we had neither the courage, the energy, nor the intelligence to improve, that most of us had hardly the courage to think about, and with our affairs hopelessly entangled with the entirely different confusions of three hundred and fifty million other persons scattered about the globe, and here were the Germans over against us, fifty-six millions, in a state of confusion no whit better than our own ; and the noisy little creatures who directed papers and wrote books and gave lectures, and generally in that time of world-dementia pretended to be the national mind, were busy in both countries, with a sort of infernal unanimity, exhorting—and not only exhorting but successfully persuading—the two peoples to divert such small common store of material, moral and intellectual energy as either possessed, into the purely destructive and wasteful business of war. And—I have to tell you these things even if you do not believe them, because they are vital to my story—there was not a man alive who could have told you of any real permanent benefit of anything whatever to counterbalance the obvious waste and evil, that would result from a war between England and Germany, whether England shattered Germany or was smashed and overwhelmed, or whatever the end might be.

The thing was, in fact, an enormous irrational obsession ; it was, in the microcosm of our nation, curiously parallel to the egotistical wrath and jealousy that swayed my individual microcosm. It measured the excess of common emotion over the common intelligence, the legacy of inordinate passion we have received from the brute from which we came. Just as I had become the slave of my own surprise and anger and went hither and thither with a loaded revolver, seeking and intending vague fluctuating crimes, so these two nations went about the earth, hot eared and muddle headed, with loaded navies and armies terribly ready at hand. Only there was not even a Nettie to justify their stupidity. There was nothing but quite imaginary thwarting on either side.

And the press was the chief instrument that kept these two huge multitudes of people directed against one another.

The press—those newspapers that are now so strange to us—like the " Empires," the " Nations," the Trusts, and all the other great monstrous shapes of that extraordinary time—was in the nature of an unanticipated accident. It had happened, as weeds happen in abandoned gardens, just as all our world has happened,—because there was no clear Will in the world to bring about anything better. Towards the end this " press " was almost entirely under the direction of youngish men of that eager, rather unintelligent type that is never able to detect itself aimless, that pursues nothing with incredible pride and zeal ; and if you would really understand this mad era the comet brought to an end, you must keep in mind that every phase in the production of these queer old things was pervaded by a strong aimless energy and happened in a concentrated rush.

Let me describe to you, very briefly, a newspaper day.

Figure first, then, a hastily erected and still more hastily designed building in a dirty, paper-littered back street of old

London, and a number of shabbily dressed men coming and going in this with projectile swiftness, and within this factory companies of printers, tensely active with nimble fingers—they were always speeding up the printers—ply their type-setting machines, and cast and arrange masses of metal in a sort of kitchen inferno, above which, in a beehive of little brightly lit rooms, dishevelled men sit and scribble. There is a throbbing of telephones and a clicking of telegraph needles, a rushing of messengers, a running to and fro of heated men, clutching proofs and copy. Then begins a clatter roar of machinery catching the infection, going faster and faster, and whizzing and banging—engineers, who have never had time to wash since their birth, flying about with oil-cans, while paper runs off its rolls with a shudder of haste. The proprietor you must suppose arriving explosively on a swift motor-car, leaping out before the thing is at a standstill, with letters and documents clutched in his hand, rushing in, resolute to " hustle," getting wonderfully in everybody's way. At the sight of him even the messenger boys who are waiting, get up and scamper to and fro. Sprinkle your vision with collisions, curses, incoherencies. You imagine all the parts of this complex lunatic machine working hysterically towards a crescendo of haste and excitement as the night wears on. At last the only things that seem to travel deliberately in all those tearing vibrating premises are the hands of the clock.

Slowly things draw on towards publication, the consummation of all those stresses. Then in the small hours, into the now dark and deserted streets comes a wild whirl of carts and men, the place spurts papers at every door, bales, heaps, torrents of papers, that are snatched and flung about in what looks like a free fight, and off with a rush and clatter east, west, north, and south. The interest passes outwardly ; the men from the little rooms are going homeward, the printers disperse yawning, the roaring presses slacken. The paper exists. Distribution follows manufacture, and we follow the bundles.

Our vision becomes a vision of dispersal. You see those bundles hurling into stations, catching trains by a hair's breadth, speeding on their way, breaking up, smaller bundles of them hurled with a fierce accuracy out upon the platforms that rush by, and then everywhere a division of these smaller bundles into still smaller bundles, into dispersing parcels, into separate papers, and the dawn happens unnoticed amidst a great running and shouting of boys, a shoving through letter slots, openings of windows, spreading out upon book-stalls. For the space of a few hours you must figure the whole country dotted white with rustling papers—placards everywhere vociferating the hurried lie for the day ; men and women in trains, men and women eating and reading, men by study-fenders, people sitting up in bed, mothers and sons and daughters waiting for father to finish—a million scattered people reading—reading headlong—or feverishly ready to read. It is just as if some vehement jet had sprayed that white foam of papers over the surface of the land. . . .

And then you know, wonderfully gone—gone utterly, vanished as foam might vanish upon the sand.

Nonsense! The whole affair a noisy paroxysm of nonsense, unreasonable excitement, witless mischief and waste of strength —signifying nothing. . . .

And one of those white particles was the paper I held in my hands as I sat with a bandaged foot on the steel fender in that dark underground kitchen of my mother's, clean roused from my personal troubles by the yelp of the headlines. She sat, sleeves tucked up from her ropy arms, peeling potatoes as I read.

It was like one of a flood of disease germs that have invaded a body, that paper. There I was, one corpuscle in the big amorphous body of the English community, one of forty-one million such corpuscles; and, for all my preoccupations, these potent headlines, this paper ferment, caught me and swung me about. And all over the country that day, millions read as I read, and came round into line with me, under the same magnetic spell, came round—how did we say it?—Ah!— "to face the foe."

The comet had been driven into obscurity overleaf. The column headed "Distinguished Scientist says Comet will Strike our Earth. Does it Matter?" went unread. "Germany" —I usually figured this mythical malignant creature as a corseted stiff-moustached Emperor enhanced by heraldic black wings and a large sword—had insulted our flag. That was the message of the *New Paper*, and the monster towered over me, threatening fresh outrages, visibly spitting upon my faultless country's colours. Somebody had hoisted a British flag on the right bank of some tropical river I had never heard of before, and a drunken German officer under ambiguous instructions had torn it down. Then one of the convenient abundant natives of the country, a British subject indisputably, had been shot in the leg. But the facts were by no means clear. Nothing was clear except that we were not going to stand any nonsense from Germany. Whatever had or had not happened we meant to have an apology for, and apparently they did not mean apologising.

"HAS WAR COME AT LAST?"

That was the headline. One's heart leaped to assent. . . .

There were hours that day when I clean forgot Nettie, in dreaming of battles and victories by land and sea, of shell fire, and entrenchments, and the heaped slaughter of many thousands of men.

But the next morning I started for Checkshill, started, I remember, in a curiously hopeful state of mind, oblivious of comets, strikes, and wars.

§ 5

You must understand that I had no set plan of murder when I walked over to Checkshill. I had no set plan of any sort. There was a great confusion of dramatically conceived intentions in my head, scenes of threatening and denunciation and terror, but I did not mean to kill. The revolver was to turn upon my rival my disadvantage in age and physique. . . . But that was not it really ! The revolver !—I took the revolver because I had the revolver and was a foolish young lout. It was a dramatic sort of thing to take. I had, I say, no plan at all.

Ever and again during that second trudge to Checkshill I was irradiated with a novel unreasonable hope. I had awakened in the morning with the hope, it may have been the last unfaded trail of some obliterated dream, that after all Nettie might relent towards me, that her heart was kind towards me in spite of all that I imagined had happened. I even thought it possible that I might have misinterpreted what I had seen. Perhaps she would explain everything. My revolver was in my pocket for all that.

I limped at the outset, but after the second mile my ankle warmed to forgetfulness, and the rest of the way I walked well. Suppose, after all, I was wrong ?

I was still debating that as I came through the park. By the corner of the paddock near the keeper's cottage, I was reminded by some belated blue hyacinths of a time when I and Nettie had gathered them together. It seemed impossible that we could really have parted for good and all. A wave of tenderness flowed over me, and still flooded me as I came through the little dell and drew towards the hollies. But there the sweet Nettie of my boy's love faded, and I thought of the new Nettie of desire and the man I had come upon in the moonlight, I thought of the narrow, hot purpose that had grown so strongly out of my springtime freshness, and my mood darkened to night.

I crossed the beech wood and came towards the gardens with a resolute and sorrowful heart. When I reached the green door in the garden wall I was seized for a space with so violent a trembling that I could not grip the latch to lift it, for I no longer had any doubt how this would end. That trembling was succeeded by a feeling of cold and whiteness and self-pity. I was astonished to find myself grimacing, to feel my cheeks wet, and thereupon I gave way completely to a wild passion of weeping. I must take just a little time before the thing was done. . . . I turned away from the door and stumbled for a short distance, sobbing loudly, and lay down out of sight among the bracken, and so presently became calm again. I lay there some time. I had half a mind to desist, and then my emotion passed like the shadow of a cloud, and I walked very coolly into the gardens.

Through the open door of one of the glass houses I saw old Stuart. He was leaning against the staging, his hands in his pockets, and so deep in thought he gave no heed to me. . . . I hesitated and went on towards the cottage, slowly.

Something struck me as unusual about the place, but I could not tell at first what it was. One of the bedroom windows was open, and the customary short blind, with its brass upper rail partly unfastened, drooped obliquely across the vacant space. It looked negligent and odd, for usually everything about the cottage was conspicuously trim.

The door was standing wide open, and everything was still. But giving that usually orderly hall an odd look—it was about half-past two in the afternoon—was a pile of three dirty plates, with used knives and forks upon them, on one of the hall chairs.

I went into the hall, looked into either room, and hesitated. Then I fell to upon the door-knocker and gave a loud rat-tat-too, and followed this up with an amiable " Hel-lo ! "

For a time no one answered me, and I stood listening and expectant, with my fingers about my weapon. Some one moved about upstairs presently, and was still again. The tension of waiting seemed to brace my nerves.

I had my hand on the knocker for the second time, when Puss appeared in the doorway.

For a moment we remained staring at one another without speaking. Her hair was dishevelled, her face dirty, tear-stained, and irregularly red. Her expression at the sight of me was pure astonishment. I thought she was about to say something, and then she had darted away out of the house again.

" I say, Puss ! " I said. " Puss ! "

I followed her out of the door. " Puss ! What's the matter ? Where's Nettie ? "

She vanished round the corner of the house.

I hesitated, perplexed whether I should pursue her. What did it all mean ? Then I heard some one upstairs.

" Willie ! " cried the voice of Mrs. Stuart. " Is that you ? "

" Yes," I answered. " Where's every one ? Where's Nettie ? I want to have a talk with her."

She did not answer, but I heard her dress rustle as she moved. I judged she was upon the landing overhead.

I paused at the foot of the stairs, expecting her to appear and come down.

Suddenly came a strange sound, a rush of sounds, words jumbled and hurrying, confused and shapeless, borne along upon a note of throaty distress that at last submerged the words altogether and ended in a wail. Except that it came from a woman's throat it was exactly the babbling sound of a

weeping child with a grievance. " I can't," she said, " I can't,"
and that was all I could distinguish. It was to my young ears
the strangest sound conceivable from a kindly motherly little
woman, whom I had always thought of chiefly as an unparalleled maker of cakes. It frightened me. I went upstairs
at once in a state of infinite alarm, and there she was upon the
landing, leaning forward over the top of the chest of drawers
beside her open bedroom door, and weeping. I never saw such
weeping. One thick strand of black hair had escaped, and hung
with a spiral twist down her back ; never before had I noticed
that she had grey hairs.

As I came up upon the landing her voice rose again. " Oh
that I should have to tell you, Willie ! Oh that I should have
to tell you ! " She dropped her head again, and a fresh gust of
tears swept all further words away.

I said nothing, I was too astonished ; but I drew nearer to
her, and waited. . . .

I never saw such weeping ; the extraordinary wetness of her
dripping handkerchief abides with me to this day.

" That I should have lived to see this day ! " she wailed.
" I had rather a thousand times she was struck dead at my
feet."

I began to understand.

" Mrs. Stuart," I said, clearing my throat ; "what has
become of Nettie ? "

" That I should have lived to see this day ! " she said by way
of reply.

I waited till her passion abated.

There came a lull. I forgot the weapon in my pocket. I
said nothing, and suddenly she stood erect before me, wiping
her swollen eyes. " Willie," she gulped, " she's gone ! "

" Nettie ? "

" Gone ! . . . Run away. . . . Run away from her home.
Oh, Willie, Willie ! The shame of it ! The sin and shame of
it ! "

She flung herself upon my shoulder, and clung to me, and
began again to wish her daughter lying dead at our feet.

" There, there," said I, and all my being was a-tremble.
" Where has she gone ? " I said as softly as I could.

But for the time she was preoccupied with her own sorrow,
and I had to hold her there and comfort her with the blackness
of finality spreading over my soul.

" Where has she gone ? " I asked for the fourth time.

" I don't know—we don't know. And oh, Willie, she went
out yesterday morning ! I said to her, ' Nettie,' I said to her,
' you're mighty fine for a morning call.' ' Fine clo's for a fine
day,' she said, and that was her last words to me !—Willie !—
the child I suckled at my breast ! "

" Yes, yes. But where has she gone ? " I said.

She went on with sobs, and now telling her story with a

THE REVOLVER 383

sort of fragmentary hurry : " She went out bright and shining, out of this house for ever. She was smiling, Willie—as if she was glad to be going. (" Glad to be going," I echoed with soundless lips.) ' You're mighty fine for the morning,' I says ; ' mighty fine.' ' Let the girl be pretty,' says her father, ' while she's young ! ' And somewhere she'd got a parcel of her things hidden to pick up, and she was going off—out of this house for ever ! "

She became quiet.

" Let the girl be pretty," she repeated ; " let the girl be pretty while she's young. . . . Oh ! how can we go on *living*, Willie ? . . . He doesn't show it, but he's like a stricken beast. He's wounded to the heart. She was always his favourite. He never seemed to care for Puss like he did for her. And she's wounded him——"

" Where has she gone ? " I reverted at last to that.

" We don't know. She leaves her own blood, she trusts herself—Oh, Willie, it'll kill me ! I wish she and me together were lying in our graves."

" But "—I moistened my lips and spoke slowly—" she may have gone to marry."

" If that was so ! I've prayed to God it might be so, Willie. I've prayed that he'd take pity on her—him, I mean, she's with."

I jerked out : " Who's that ? "

" In her letter, she said he was a gentleman. She did say he was a gentleman."

" In her letter. Has she written ? Can I see her letter ? "

" Her father took it."

" But if she writes—— When did she write ? "

" It came this morning."

" But where did it come from ? You can tell——"

" She didn't say. She said she was happy. She said love took one like a storm——"

" Curse that ! Where is her letter ? Let me see it. And as for this gentleman——"

She stared at me.

" You know who it is."

" Willie ! " she protested.

" You know who it is, whether she said or not ? " Her eyes made a mute unconfident denial.

" Young Verrall ? "

She made no answer. " All I could do for you, Willie," she began presently.

" Was it young Verrall ? " I insisted.

For a second, perhaps, we faced one another in stark understanding. . . . Then she plumped back to the chest of drawers, and her wet pocket-handkerchief, and I knew she sought refuge from my relentless eyes.

My pity for her vanished. She knew it was her mistress's

son as well as I ! And for some time she had known, she had felt.

I hovered over her for a moment, sick with amazed disgust. I suddenly bethought me of old Stuart, out in the greenhouse, and turned and went downstairs. As I did so, I looked up to see Mrs. Stuart moving droopingly and lamely back into her own room.

§ 6

Old Stuart was pitiful.

I found him still inert in the greenhouse where I had first seen him. He did not move as I drew near him ; he glanced at me, and then stared hard again at the flowerpots before him.

" Eh, Willie," he said, " this is a black day for all of us."

" What are you going to do ? " I asked.

" The missus takes on so," he said. " I came out here."

" What do you mean to do ? "

" What *is* a man to do in such a case ? "

" Do ! " I cried, " why—— Do ! "

" He ought to marry her," he said.

" By God, yes ! " I cried. " He must do that anyhow."

" He ought to.   It's—it's cruel.   But what am *I* to do ? Suppose he won't ? Likely he won't. What then ? "

He drooped with an intensified despair.

" Here's this cottage," he said, pursuing some contracted argument. " We've lived here all our lives, you might say. . . . Clear out. At my age. . . . One can't die in a slum."

I stood before him for a space, speculating what thoughts might fill the gaps between these broken words. I found his lethargy, and the dimly shaped mental attitudes his words indicated, abominable. I said abruptly, " You have her letter ? "

He dived into his breast-pocket, became motionless for for ten seconds, then woke up again and produced her letter. He drew it clumsily from its envelope, and handed it to me silently.

" Why ! " he cried, looking at me for the first time, " What's come to your chin, Willie ? "

" It's nothing," I said. " It's a bruise ; " and I opened the letter.

It was written on greenish-tinted fancy note-paper, and with all and more than Nettie's usual triteness and inadequacy of expression. Her handwriting bore no traces of emotion ; it was round and upright and clear as though it had been done in a writing lesson. Always her letters were like masks upon her image ; they fell like curtains before the changing charm of her face ; one altogether forgot the sound of her light clear voice, confronted by a perplexing stereotyped thing that had mysteriously got a hold upon one's heart and pride. How did that letter run ?—

" My Dear Mother,

" Do not be distressed at my going away. I have gone some-where safe, and with some one who cares for me very much. I am sorry for your sakes, but it seems that it had to be. Love is a very difficult thing, and takes hold of one in ways one does not expect. Do not think I am ashamed about this, I glory in my love, and you must not trouble too much about me. I am very, very happy (deeply underlined).

" Fondest love to Father and Puss.

" Your loving
" Nettie."

That queer little document ! I can see it now for the childish simple thing it was, but at the time I read it in a suppressed anguish of rage. It plunged me into a pit of hopeless shame ; there seemed to remain no pride for me in life until I had revenge. I stood staring at those rounded upstanding letters, not trusting myself to speak or move. At last I stole a glance at Stuart.

He held the envelope in his hand, and stared down at the postmark between his horny thumbnails.

" You can't even tell where she is," he said, turning the thing round in a hopeless manner, and then desisting. " It's hard on us, Willie. Here she is ; she hadn't anything to com-plain of ; a sort of pet for all of us. Not even made to do her share of the 'ousework. And she goes off and leaves us like a bird that's learnt to fly. Can't *trust* us, that's what takes me. Puts 'erself—— But there ! What's to happen to her ? "

" What's to happen to him ? "

He shook his head to show that problem was beyond him.

" You'll go after her," I said in an even voice ; " you'll make him marry her ? "

" Where am I to go ? " he asked helplessly, and held out the envelope with a gesture ; " and what could I do ? Even if I knew—— How could I leave the gardens ? "

" Great God ! " I cried, " not leave these gardens ! It's your Honour, man ! If she was my daughter—if she was my daughter—I'd tear the world to pieces ! " . . . I choked. " You mean to stand it ? "

" What can I do ? "

" Make him marry her ! Horsewhip him ! Horsewhip him, I say !—I'd strangle him ! "

He scratched slowly at his hairy cheek, opened his mouth, and shook his head. Then, with an intolerable note of sluggish gentle wisdom, he said, " People of our sort, Willie, can't do things like that."

I came near to raving. I had a wild impulse to strike him in the face. Once in my boyhood I happened upon a bird terribly mangled by some cat, and killed it in a frenzy of horror and pity. I had a gust of that same emotion now, as this shameful mutilated soul fluttered in the dust before me. Then, you know, I dismissed him from the case.

" May I look ? " I asked.

He held out the envelope reluctantly.

" There it is," he said, and pointing with his garden-rough forefinger. " I.A.P.A.M.P. What can you make of that ? "

I took the thing in my hands. The adhesive stamp customary in those days was defaced by a circular postmark, which bore the name of the office of departure and the date. The impact in this particular case had been light or made without sufficient ink, and half the letters of the name had left no impression. I could distinguish—

I A P   A M P

and very faintly below D.S.O.

I guessed the name in an instant flash of intuition. It was Shaphambury. The very gaps shaped that to my mind. Perhaps in a sort of semi-visibility other letters were there, at least hinting themselves. It was a place somewhere on the east coast, I knew, either in Norfolk or Suffolk.

" Why ! " cried I—and stopped.

What was the good of telling him ?

Old Stuart had glanced up sharply, I am inclined to think almost fearfully, into my face. " You—you haven't got it ? " he said.

Shaphambury—I should remember that.

" You don't think you got it ? " he said.

I handed the envelope back to him.

" For a moment I thought it might be Hampton," I said.

" Hampton," he repeated. " Hampton. How could you make Hampton ? " He turned the envelope about. " H.A.M.— why, Willie, you're a worse hand at the job than me ! "

He replaced the letter in the envelope and stood erect to put it back in his breast pocket.

I did not mean to take any risks in this affair. I drew a stump of pencil from my waistcoat pocket, turned a little away from him and wrote " Shaphambury " very quickly on my frayed and rather grimy shirt cuff.

" Well," said I, with an air of having done nothing remarkable.

I turned to him with some unimportant observation—I have forgotten what.

I never finished whatever vague remark I commenced.

I looked up to see a third person waiting at the greenhouse door.

§ 7

It was old Mrs. Verrall.

I wonder if I can convey the effect of her to you. She was a little old lady with extraordinarily flaxen hair, her weak aquiline features were pursed up into an assumption of dignity, and she was richly dressed. I would like to underline that " richly dressed," or have the words printed in florid old English or Gothic lettering. No one on earth is now quite so richly dressed as she was, no one old or young indulges in so quiet and yet so profound a sumptuosity. But you must not imagine any extravagance of outline or any beauty or richness of colour. The predominant colours were black and fur browns, and the effect of richness was due entirely to the extreme costliness of the materials employed. She affected silk brocades with rich and elaborate patterns, priceless black lace over creamy or purple satin, intricate trimmings through which threads and bands of velvet wriggled, and in the winter rare furs. Her gloves fitted exquisitely, and ostentatiously simple chains of fine gold and pearls and a great number of bracelets laced about her little person. One was forced to feel that the slightest article she wore cost more than all the wardrobe of a dozen girls like Nettie ; her bonnet affected the simplicity that is beyond rubies. Richness, that is the first quality about this old lady that I would like to convey to you, and the second was cleanliness. You felt that old Mrs. Verrall was exquisitely clean. If you had boiled my poor dear old mother in soda for a month you couldn't have got her so clean as Mrs. Verrall constantly and manifestly was. And pervading all her presence shone her third great quality, her manifest confidence in the respectful subordination of the world.

She was pale and a little out of breath that day, but without any loss of her ultimate confidence ; and it was clear to me that she had come to interview Stuart upon the outbreak of passion that had bridged the gulf between their families.

And here again I find myself writing in an unknown language, so far as my younger readers are concerned. You who know only the world that followed the Great Change will find much that I am telling inconceivable. Upon these points I cannot appeal, as I have appealed for other confirmations, to the old newspapers ; these were the things that no one wrote about because every one understood and every one had taken up an attitude. There were in England and America, and indeed throughout the world, two great informal divisions of human beings—the Secure and the Insecure. There was not and never had been in either country a nobility—it was and remains a common error that the British peers were noble—neither in law nor custom were there noble families, and we altogether lacked the edification one found in Russia, for example, of a poor nobility. A peerage was an hereditary possession that, like the family land, concerned only the eldest sons of the house ; it radiated no lustre of *noblesse oblige*. The rest of the world was in law and practice common—and all America was common. But through the private ownership of land that had resulted from the neglect of feudal obligations in Britain and the utter want of political foresight in the Americas, large masses of property had become artifically stable in the hands of a small minority, to whom it was necessary to mortgage all new public and private enterprises, and who were held together not by any tradition of service and nobility but by the natural sympathy of common interests and a common large scale of living. It was a class without any very definite boundaries ; vigorous individualities, by methods for the most part violent and questionable, were constantly thrusting themselves from insecurity to security, and the sons and daughters of secure people, by marrying insecurity or by wild extravagance or flagrant vice, would sink into the life of anxiety and insufficiency which was the ordinary life of man. The rest of the population was landless and, except by working directly or indirectly for the Secure, had no legal right to exist. And such was the shallowness and insufficiency of our thought, such the stifled egotism of all our feelings before the Last Days, that very few indeed of the Secure could be found to doubt that this was the natural and only conceivable order of the world.

It is the life of the Insecure under the old order that I am displaying, and I hope that I am conveying something of its hopeless bitterness to you ; but you must not imagine that the Secure lived lives of paradisiacal happiness. The pit of insecurity below them made itself felt, even though it was not comprehended. Life about them was ugly ; the sight of ugly and mean houses, of ill-dressed people, the vulgar appeals of the dealers in popular commodities, were not to be escaped. There was below the threshold of their minds an uneasiness ; they not only did not think clearly about social economy but they displayed an instinctive disinclination to think. Their security was not so perfect that they had not a dread of falling towards the pit, they were always lashing themselves by new ropes, their cultivation of " connections," of interests, their desire to confirm and improve their positions, was a constant ignoble preoccupation. You must read Thackeray to get the full flavour of their lives. Then the bacterium was apt to disregard class distinctions, and they were never really happy in their servants. Read their surviving books. Each generation bewails the decay of that " fidelity " of servants no generation ever saw. A world that is squalid in one corner is squalid altogether, but that they never understood. They believed there was not enough of anything to go round, they believed that this was the intention of God and an incurable condition of life, and they held passionately and with a sense of right to their disproportionate share. They maintained a common intercourse as " Society " of all who were practically secure, and their choice of that word is exhaustively eloquent of the quality of their philosophy. But, if you can master these alien ideas upon which the old system rested, just in the same measure will you understand the horror these people had for marriages with the Insecure. In the case of their girls and women it was extraordinarily rare, and in the case of either sex it was regarded as a disastrous social crime. Anything was better than that.

You are probably aware of the hideous fate that was only too probably the lot, during those last dark days, of every girl of the insecure classes who loved and gave way to the impulse of self-abandonment without marriage, and so you will understand the peculiar situation of Nettie with young Verrall. One or other had to suffer. And as they were both in a state of great emotional exaltation and capable of strange generosities towards each other, it was an open question and naturally a source of great anxiety to a mother in Mrs. Verrall's position, whether the sufferer might not be her son—whether, as the outcome of that glowing irresponsible commerce, Nettie might not return prospective mistress of Checkshill Towers. The chances were greatly against that conclusion, but such things did occur.

These laws and customs sound, I know, like a record of some nasty-minded lunatic's inventions. They were invincible facts in that vanished world into which by some accident I had been born, and it was the dream of any better state of things that was scouted as lunacy. Just think of it! This girl I loved with all my soul, for whom I was ready to sacrifice my life, was not good enough to marry young Verrall. And I had only to look at his even, handsome, characterless face to perceive a creature weaker and no better than myself. She was to be his pleasure until he chose to cast her aside, and the poison of our social system had so saturated her nature—his evening dress, his freedom and his money had seemed so fine to her and I so clothed in squalor—that to this prospect she had consented. And to resent the social conventions that created their situation, was called "class envy;" and gently born preachers reproached us for the mildest resentment against an injustice no living man would now either endure or consent to profit by.

What was the sense of saying " peace " when there was no peace ? If there was one hope in the disorders of that old world it lay in revolt and conflict to the death.

But if you can really grasp the shameful grotesqueness of the old life, you will begin to appreciate the interpretation of old Mrs. Verrall's appearance that leaped up at once in my mind.

She had come to compromise the disaster !

And the Stuarts *would* compromise ! I saw that only too well.

An enormous disgust at the prospect of the imminent encounter between Stuart and his mistress made me behave in a violent and irrational way. I wanted to escape seeing that, seeing even Stuart's first gesture in that, at any cost.

"I'm off," said I, and turned my back on him without any further farewell.

My line of retreat lay by the old lady, and so I advanced towards her.

I saw her expression change, her mouth fell a little way open, her forehead wrinkled, and her eyes grew round. She found me a queer customer even at the first sight, and there was something in the manner of my advance that took away her breath.

She stood at the top of the three or four steps that descended to the level of the hothouse floor. She receded a pace or two, with a certain offended dignity at the determination of my rush.

I gave her no sort of salutation.

Well, as a matter of fact, I did give her a sort of salutation. There is no occasion for me to begin apologising now for the thing I said to her—I strip these things before you—if only I can get them stark enough you will understand and forgive. I was filled with a brutal and overpowering desire to insult her.

And so I addressed this poor little expensive old woman in the following terms, converting her by a violent metonymy into a comprehensive plural. "You infernal land thieves!" I said point-blank into her face. "*Have you come to offer them money?*"

And without waiting to test her powers of repartee, passed rudely beyond her and vanished, striding, with my fists clenched out of her world again. . . .

I have tried since to imagine how the thing must have looked to her. So far as her particular universe went I had not existed at all, or I had existed only as a dim black thing, an insignificant speck, far away across her park in irrelevant, unimportant transit, until this moment when she came, sedately troubled, into her own secure gardens and sought for Stuart among the greenhouses. Then abruptly I flashed into being down that green-walled, brickfloored vista as a black-avised, ill-clad young man, who first stared and then advanced scowling towards her. Once in existence I developed rapidly. I grew larger in perspective and became more and more important and sinister every moment. I came up the steps with inconceivable hostility and disrespect in my bearing, towered over her, becoming for an instant at least a sort of second French Revolution, and delivered myself with the intensest concentration of those wicked and incomprehensible words. Just for a second I threatened annihilation. Happily that was my climax.

And then I had gone by, and the Universe was very much as it had always been except for the wild swirl in it, and the faint sense of insecurity my episode left in its wake.

The thing that never entered my head in those days was that a large proportion of the rich were rich in absolute good faith.

I thought they saw things exactly as I saw them, and wickedly denied. But indeed old Mrs. Verrall was no more capable of doubting the perfection of her family's right to dominate a wide country side, than she was of examining the Thirty-nine Articles or dealing with any other of the adamantine pillars upon which her universe rested in security.

No doubt I startled and frightened her tremendously. But she could not understand.

None of her sort of people ever did seem to understand such livid flashes of hate, as ever and again lit the crowded darkness below their feet. The thing leaped out of the black for a moment and vanished, like a threatening figure by a desolate roadside lit for a moment by one's belated carriage-lamp and then swallowed up by the night. They counted it with night-mares, and did their best to forget what was evidently as insignificant as it was disturbing.

CHAPTER FOUR

WAR

§ 1

FROM that moment when I insulted old Mrs. Verrall I became representative, I was a man who stood for all the disinherited of the world. I had no hope of pride or pleasure left in me, I was raging rebellion against God and mankind. There were no more vague intentions swaying me this way and that ; I was perfectly clear now upon what I meant to do. I would make my protest and die.

I would make my protest and die. I was going to kill Nettie—Nettie, who had smiled and promised and given herself to another, and who stood now for all the conceivable delightfulnesses, the lost imaginations of the youthful heart, the unattainable joys in life ; and Verrall, who stood for all who profited by the incurable injustice of our social order. I would kill them both. And that being done I would blow my brains out and see what vengeance followed my blank refusal to live.

So indeed I was resolved. I raged monstrously. And above me, abolishing the stars, triumphant over the yellow waning moon that followed it below, the giant meteor towered up towards the zenith.

" Let me only kill ! " I cried. " Let me only kill ! "

So I shouted in my frenzy. I was in a fever that defied hunger and fatigue ; for a long time I had prowled over the heath towards Lowchester talking to myself, and now that night had fully come I was tramping homeward, walking the long seventeen miles without a thought of rest. And I had eaten nothing since the morning.

I suppose I must count myself mad, but I can recall my ravings.

There were times when I walked weeping through that brightness that was neither night nor day. There were times when I reasoned in a topsy-turvy fashion with what I called the Spirit of All Things. But always I spoke to that white glory in the sky.

" Why am I here only to suffer ignominies ? " I asked. " Why have you made me with pride that cannot be satisfied, with desires that turn and rend me ? Is it a jest, this world—a joke you play on your guests ? I—even I—have a better humour than that !

" Why not learn from me a certain decency of mercy ? Why not undo ? Have I ever tormented—day by day, some wretched worm—making filth for it to trail through, filth that disgusts it, starving it, bruising it, mocking it ? Why should you ? Your jokes are clumsy. Try—try some milder fun up there ; do you hear ? Something that doesn't hurt so infernally.

" You say this is your purpose—your purpose with me. You are making something with me—birth pangs of a soul. Ah! How can I believe you ? You forget I have eyes for other things. Let my own case go, but what of that frog beneath the cart-wheel, God ?—and the bird the cat had torn ? "

After such blasphemies I would fling out a ridiculous little debating society hand. " Answer me that ! "

A week ago it had been moonlight, white and black and hard across the spaces of the park, but now the light was livid and full of the quality of haze. An extraordinarily low white mist, not three feet above the ground, drifted broodingly across the grass, and the trees rose ghostly out of that phantom sea. Great and shadowy and strange was the world that night, no one seemed abroad ; I and my little cracked voice drifted solitary through the silent mysteries. Sometimes I argued as I have told, sometimes I stumbled along in moody vacuity, sometimes my torment was vivid and acute.

Abruptly out of apathy would come a boiling paroxysm of fury, when I thought of Nettie mocking me and laughing, and of her and Verrall clasped in one another's arms.

" I will not have it so ! " I screamed. " I will not have it so ! "

And in one of these raving fits I drew my revolver from my pocket and fired into the quiet night. Three times I fired it.

The bullets tore through the air, the startled trees told one another in diminishing echoes the thing I had done, and then, with a slow finality, the vast and patient night healed again to calm. My shots, my curses and blasphemies, my prayers—for anon I prayed—that Silence took them all.

It was—how can I express it ?—a stifled outcry tranquillised, lost, amid the serene assumptions, the overwhelming empire of that brightness. The noise of my shots, the impact upon things, had for the instant been enormous ; then it had passed away. I found myself standing with the revolver held up, astonished, my emotions penetrated by something I could not understand. Then I looked up over my shoulder at the great star, and remained staring at it.

" Who are *you* ? " I said at last.

I was like a man in a solitary desert who has suddenly heard a voice. . . .

That, too, passed.

As I came over Clayton Crest I recalled that I missed the multitude that now night after night walked out to stare at the comet ; and the little preacher in the waste beyond the hoardings, who warned sinners to repent before the Judgment, was not in his usual place.

It was long past midnight, and every one had gone home. But I did not think of this at first, and the solitude perplexed me and left a memory behind. The gas-lamps were all extinguished because of the brightness of the comet, and that too was unfamiliar. The little news-agent in the still High Street had shut up and gone to bed, but one belated board had been put out late and forgotten, and it still bore its placard.

The word upon it—there was but one word upon it in staring letters—was : " WAR."

You figure that empty mean street, emptily echoing to my footsteps—no soul awake and audible but me. Then my halt at the placard. And amidst that sleeping stillness, smeared hastily upon the board, a little askew and crumpled but quite distinct beneath that cool meteoric glare, preposterous and appalling, the measureless evil of that word—

" WAR ! "

§ 2

I awoke in that state of equanimity that so often follows an emotional drenching.

It was late, and my mother was beside my bed. She had some breakfast for me on a battered tray.

" Don't get up yet, dear," she said. " You've been sleeping. It was three o'clock when you got home last night. You must have been tired out.

" Your poor face," she went on, " was as white as a sheet and your eyes shining. . . . It frightened me to let you in. And you stumbled on the stairs."

My eyes went quietly to my coat pocket, where something still bulged. She probably had not noticed. " I went to Checkshill," I said. " You know—perhaps——? "

" I got a letter last evening, dear," and as she bent near me to put the tray upon my knees, she kissed my hair softly. For a moment we both remained still, resting on that, her cheek just touching my head.

I took the tray from her to end the pause.

" Don't touch my clothes, mummy," I said sharply, as she moved towards them. " I'm still equal to a clothes-brush."

And then, as she turned away, I astonished her by saying, " You dear mother, you ! A little—I understand. Only—now—dear mother, oh ! let me be ! Let me be ! "

And with the docility of a good servant, she went from me. Dear heart of submission that the world and I had used so ill !

It seemed to me that morning that I could never give way to a gust of passion again.   A sorrowful firmness of the mind possessed me. My purpose seemed now as inflexible as iron ; there was neither love nor hate nor fear left in me—only I pitied my mother greatly for all that was still to come. I ate my breakfast slowly, and thought where I could find out about Shaphambury, and how I might hope to get there. I had not five shillings in the world.

I dressed methodically, choosing the least frayed of my collars, and shaving much more carefully than was my wont ; then I went down to the Public Library to consult a map.

Shaphambury was on the coast of Essex, a long and complicated journey from Clayton. I went to the railway-station and made some memoranda from the time-tables. The porters I asked were not very clear about Shaphambury, but the booking-office clerk was helpful, and we puzzled out all I wanted to know. Then I came out into the coaly street again. At the least I ought to have two pounds.

I went back to the Public Library and into the newspaper room to think over this problem.

A fact intruded itself upon me.   People seemed in an altogether exceptional stir about the morning journals, there was something unusual in the air of the room, more people and more talking than usual, and for a moment I was puzzled. Then I bethought me : " This war with Germany, of course ! " A naval battle was supposed to be in progress in the North Sea. Let them ! I returned to the consideration of my own affairs.

Parload ?

Could I go and make it up with him, and then borrow ? I weighed the chances of that.   Then I thought of selling or pawning something, but that seemed difficult.   My winter overcoat had not cost a pound when it was new, my watch was not likely to fetch many shillings. Still, both these things might be factors. I thought with a certain repugnance of the little store my mother was probably making for the rent. She was very secretive about that, and it was locked in an old tea-caddy in her bedroom. I knew it would be almost impossible to get any of that money from her willingly, and though I told myself that in this issue of passion and death no detail mattered, I could not get rid of tormenting scruples whenever I thought of that tea-caddy. Was there no other course ? Perhaps after every other source had been tapped I might supplement with a few shillings frankly begged from her. "These others," I said to myself, thinking without passion for once of the sons of the Secure, "would find it difficult to run their romances on a pawnshop basis. However, we must manage it."

I felt the day was passing on, but I did not get excited about that. "Slow is swiftest," Parload used to say, and I meant to get everything thought out completely, to take a long aim and then to act as a bullet flies.

I hesitated at a pawnshop on my way home to my midday meal, but I determined not to pledge my watch until I could bring my overcoat also.

I ate silently, revolving plans.

§ 3

After our midday dinner—it was a potato-pie, mostly potato with some scraps of cabbage and bacon—I put on my overcoat and got it out of the house while my mother was in the scullery at the back.

A scullery in the old world was, in the case of such houses as ours, a damp, unsavoury, mainly subterranean region behind the dark living-room kitchen, that was rendered more than typically dirty in our case by the fact that into it the coal-cellar, a yawning pit of black uncleanness, opened, and diffused small crunchable particles about the uneven brick floor. It was the region of "washing-up," that greasy, damp function that followed every meal; its atmosphere had ever a cooling steaminess and the memory of boiled cabbage, and the sooty black stains where saucepan or kettle had been put down for a minute, scraps of potato-peel caught by the strainer of the escape-pipe, and rags of a quite indescribable horribleness of acquisition, called "dish-clouts," rise in my memory at the name. The altar of this place was the "sink," a tank of stone, revolting to a refined touch, grease-filmed and unpleasant to see, and above this was a tap for cold water, so arranged that when the water descended it splashed and wetted whoever had turned it on. This tap was our water supply. And in such a place you must fancy a little old woman, rather incompetent and very gentle, a soul of unselfishness and sacrifice, in dirty clothes, all come from their original colours to a common dusty dark grey, in worn, ill-fitting boots, with hands distorted by ill-use, and untidy greying hair—my mother. In the winter her hands would be "chapped," and she would have a cough. And while she washes up I go out, to sell my overcoat and watch in order that I may desert her.

I gave way to queer hesitations in pawning my two negotiable articles. A weakly indisposition to pawn in Clayton, where the pawnbroker knew me, carried me to the door of the place in Lynch Street, Swathinglea, where I had bought my revolver. Then came an idea that I was giving too many facts about

myself to one man, and I came back to Clayton after all. I
forget how much money I got, but I remember that it was
rather less than the sum I had made out to be the single fare
to Shaphambury. Still deliberate, I went back to the Public
Library to find out whether it was possible, by walking for
ten or twelve miles anywhere, to shorten the journey. My
boots were in a dreadful state, the sole of the left one also was
now peeling off, and I could not help perceiving that all my
plans might be wrecked if at this crisis I went on shoe leather
in which I could only shuffle. So long as I went softly they
would serve, but not for hard walking. I went to the shoemaker
in Hacker Street, but he would not promise any repairs for me
under forty-eight hours.

I got back home about five minutes to three, resolved to
start by the five train for Birmingham in any case, but still
dissatisfied about my money. I thought of pawning a book or
something of that sort, but I could think of nothing of obvious
value in the house. My mother's silver—two gravy-spoons and
a salt-cellar—had been pawned for some weeks, since, in fact,
the June quarter day. But my mind was full of hypothetical
opportunities.

As I came up the steps to our door, I remarked that Mr.
Gabbitas looked at me suddenly round his dull red curtains
with a sort of alarmed resolution in his eye and vanished, and
as I walked along the passage he opened his door upon me and
intercepted me.

You are figuring me, I hope, as a dark and sullen lout in
shabby, cheap, old-world clothes that are shiny at all the wearing surfaces, and with a discoloured red tie and frayed linen.
My left hand keeps in my pocket as though there is something it
prefers to keep a grip upon there. Mr. Gabbitas was shorter
than I, and the first note he struck in the impression he made
upon any one was of something bright and birdlike. I think he
wanted to be birdlike, he possessed the possibility of an avian
charm, but, as a matter of fact, there was nothing of the glowing
vitality of the bird in his being. And a bird is never out of
breath and with an open mouth. He was in the clerical dress
of that time, that costume that seems now almost the strangest
of all our old-world clothing, and he presented it in its cheapest
form—black of a poor texture, ill-fitting, strangely cut. Its
long skirts accentuated the tubbiness of his body, the shortness
of his legs. The white tie below his all-round collar, beneath his
innocent large-spectacled face, was a little grubby, and between
his not very clean teeth he held a briar pipe. His complexion
was whitish, and although he was only thirty-three or four
perhaps, his sandy hair was already thinning from the top of
his head.

To your eye, now, he would seem the strangest figure, in
the utter disregard of all physical beauty or dignity about him.
You would find him extraordinarily odd, but in the old days

he met not only with acceptance but respect. He was alive
until within a year or so ago, but his later appearance changed.
As I saw him that afternoon he was a very slovenly, ungainly
little human being indeed ; not only was his clothing altogether
ugly and queer, but had you stripped the man stark, you would
certainly have seen in the bulging paunch that comes from
flabby muscles and flabbily controlled appetites, and in the
rounded shoulders and flawed and yellowish skin, the same
failure of any effort towards clean beauty. You had an instinctive sense that so he had been from the beginning. You
felt he was not only drifting through life, eating what came in
his way, believing what came in his way, doing without any
vigour what came in his way, but that *into* life also he had
drifted. You could not believe him the child of pride and
high resolve, or of any splendid passion of love. He had just
happened. . . . But we all happened then. Why am I taking
this tone over this poor little curate in particular ?

"Hello ! " he said, with an assumption of friendly ease.
" Haven't seen you for weeks ! Come in and have a gossip."

An invitation from the drawing-room lodger was in the
nature of a command. I would have liked very greatly to have
refused it, never was invitation more inopportune, but I had
not the wit to think of an excuse. " All right," I said awkwardly, and he held the door open for me.

" I'd be very glad if you would," he amplified. " One doesn't
get much opportunity of intelligent talk in this parish."

What the devil was he up to, was my secret preoccupation.
He fussed about me with a nervous hospitality, talking in
jumpy fragments, rubbing his hands together, and taking peeps
at me over and round his glasses. As I sat down in his leather-
covered arm-chair, I had an odd memory of the one in the
Clayton dentist's operating-room—I know not why.

" They're going to give us trouble in the North Sea, it seems,"
he remarked with a sort of innocent zest. " I'm glad they mean
fighting."

There was an air of culture about his room that always
cowed me, and that made me constrained even on this occasion.
The table under the window was littered with photographic
material and the later albums of his continental souvenirs,
and on the American cloth trimmed shelves that filled the
recesses on either side of the fireplace were what I used to think
in those days a quite incredible number of books—perhaps
eight hundred altogether, including the reverend gentleman's
photograph albums and college and school text-books. This
suggestion of learning was enforced by the little wooden shield
bearing a college coat-of-arms that hung over the looking-glass,
and by a photograph of Mr. Gabbitas in cap and gown in an
Oxford frame that adorned the opposite wall. And in the middle
of that wall stood his writing-desk, which I knew to have pigeon-
holes when it was open, and which made him seem not merely

cultured but literary. At that he wrote sermons, composing them himself !

" Yes," he said, taking possession of the hearthrug, " the war had to come sooner or later. If we smash their fleet for them now—well, there's an end to the matter! "

He stood on his toes and then bumped down on his heels, and looked blandly through his spectacles at a water-colour by his sister—the subject was a bunch of violets—above the sideboard which was his pantry and tea-chest and cellar. " Yes," he said as he did so.

I coughed, and wondered how I might presently get away.

He invited me to smoke—that queer old practice !—and then when I declined, began talking in a confidential tone of this " dreadful business " of the strikes. " The war won't improve *that* outlook," he said, and was very grave for a moment.

He spoke of the want of thought for their wives and children shown by the colliers in striking merely for the sake of the union, and this stirred me to controversy, and distracted me a little from my resolution to escape.

" I don't quite agree with that," I said, clearing my throat. " If the men didn't strike for the union now, if they let that be broken up, where would they be when the pinch of reductions did come ? "

To which he replied that they couldn't expect to get top-price wages when the masters were selling bottom-price coal. I replied, " That isn't it. The masters don't treat them fairly. They have to protect themselves."

To which Mr. Gabbitas answered, " Well, I don't know. I've been in the Four Towns some time, and I must say I don't think the balance of injustice falls on the masters' side."

" It falls on the men," I agreed, wilfully misunderstanding him.

And so we worked our way towards an argument. " Confound this argument ! " I thought ; but I had no skill in self-extraction, and my irritation crept into my voice. Three little spots of colour came into the cheeks and nose of Mr. Gabbitas, but his voice showed nothing of his ruffled temper.

" You see," I said, " I'm a socialist. I don't think this world was made for a small minority to dance on the faces of every one else."

" My dear fellow," said the Rev. Gabbitas, " *I'm* a socialist too. Who isn't ? But that doesn't lead me to class hatred."

" You haven't felt the heel of this confounded system. *I* have."

" Ah ! " said he ; and catching him on that note came a rap at the front door, and, as he hung suspended, the sound of my mother letting some one in and a timid rap.

" *Now*," thought I, and stood up resolutely, but he would not let me. " No, no, no ! " said he. " It's only for the Dorcas money."

He put his hand against my chest with an effect of physical compulsion, and cried, " Come in ! "

" Our talk's just getting interesting," he protested ; and there entered Miss Ramell, an elderly little young lady who was mighty in Church help in Clayton.

He greeted her—she took no notice of me—and went to his bureau, and I remained standing by my chair but unable to get out of the room. " I'm not interrupting ? " asked Miss Ramell.

" Not in the least," he said ; drew out the carriers and opened his desk. I could not help seeing what he did.

I was so fretted by my impotence to leave him that at the moment it did not connect at all with the research of the morning that he was taking out money. I listened sullenly to his talk with Miss Ramell, and saw only, as they say in Wales, with the front of my eyes, the small flat drawer that had, it seemed, quite a number of sovereigns, scattered over its floor. " They're so unreasonable," complained Miss Ramell. Who could be otherwise in a social organisation that bordered on insanity ?

I turned away from them, put my foot on the fender, stuck my elbow on the plush-fringed mantel-board, and studied the photographs, pipes, and ashtrays that adorned it. What was it I had to think out before I went to the station ?

Of course ! My mind made a queer little reluctant leap—it felt like being forced to leap over a bottomless chasm—and alighted upon the sovereigns that were just disappearing again as Mr. Gabbitas shut his drawer.

" I won't interrupt your talk further," said Miss Ramell, receding doorward.

Mr. Gabbitas played round her politely, and opened the door for her and conducted her into the passage, and for a moment or so I had the fullest sense of proximity to those— it seemed to me there must be ten or twelve—sovereigns. . . .

The front door closed and he returned. My chance of escape had gone.

§ 4

" *I must* be going," I said, with a curiously reinforced desire to get away out of that room.

" My dear chap ! " he insisted, " I can't think of it. Surely— there's nothing to call you away." Then with an evident desire to shift the venue of our talk, he asked. " You never told me what you thought of Burble's little book."

I was now, beneath my dull display of submission, furiously angry with him. It occurred to me to ask myself why I should defer and qualify my opinions to him. Why should I pretend a feeling of intellectual and social inferiority towards him. He asked what I thought of Burble. I resolved to tell him—if necessary with arrogance. Then perhaps he would release me. I did not sit down again, but stood by the corner of the fireplace.

" That was the little book you lent me last summer ? " I said.

" He reasons closely, eh ? " he said, and indicated the arm chair with a flat hand, and beamed persuasively.

I remained standing. " I didn't think much of his reasoning powers," I said.

" He was one of the cleverest bishops London ever had."

" That may be. But he was dodging about in a jolly feeble case," said I.

" You mean ? "

" That he's wrong. I don't think he proves his case. I don't think Christianity is true. He knows himself for the pretender he is. His reasoning's—Rot."

Mr. Gabbitas went, I think, a shade paler than his wont, and propitiation vanished from his manner. His eyes and mouth were round, his face seemed to get round, his eyebrows curved at my remarks.

" I'm sorry you think that," he said at last, with a catch in his breath.

He did not repeat his suggestion that I should sit. He made a step or two towards the window and turned. " I suppose you will admit——" he began, with a faintly irritating note of intellectual condescension. . . .

I will not tell you of his arguments or mine. You will find if you care to look for them, in out-of-the-way corners of our book museums, the shrivelled cheap publications—the publications of the Rationalist Press Association, for example—on which my arguments were based. Lying in that curious limbo with them, mixed up with them and indistinguishable, are the endless " Replies " of orthodoxy, like the mixed dead in some hard-fought trench. All those disputes of our fathers, and they were sometimes furious disputes, have gone now beyond the range of comprehension. You younger people, I know, read them with impatient perplexity. You cannot understand how sane creatures could imagine they had joined issue at all in most of these controversies. All the old methods of systematic thinking, the queer absurdities of the Aristotelian logic, have followed magic numbers and mystical numbers, and the Rumpelstiltskin magic names now in the blackness of the unthinkable. You can no more understand our theological passions than you can understand the fancies that made all ancient peoples speak of their gods only by circumlocutions, that made savages pine away and die because they had been photographed, or an Elisabethan farmer turn back from a day's expedition because he had met three crows. Even I, who have been through it all, recall our controversies now with something near incredulity.

Faith we can understand to-day, all men live by faith ; but in the old time every one confused quite hopelessly Faith and a forced, incredible Belief in certain pseudo-concrete statements. I am inclined to say that neither believers nor

unbelievers had faith as we understand it—they had insufficient
intellectual power. They could not trust unless they had something to see and touch and say, like their barbarous ancestors
who could not make a bargain without exchange of tokens.
If they no longer worshipped stocks and stones, or eked out
their needs with pilgrimages and images, they still held fiercely
to audible images, to printed words and formulæ.

But why revive the echoes of the ancient logomachies ?

Suffice it that we lost our tempers very readily in pursuit
of God and Truth, and said exquisitely foolish things on either
side. And on the whole—from the impartial perspective of
my three and seventy years—I adjudicate that if my dialectic
was bad, that of the Rev. Gabbitas was altogether worse.

Little pink spots came into his cheeks, a squealing note into
his voice. We interrupted each other more and more rudely.
We invented facts and appealed to authorities whose names I
mispronounced ; and, finding Gabbitas shy of the higher
criticism and the Germans, I used the names of Karl Marx
and Engels as Bible exegetes with no little effect. A silly
wrangle ! a preposterous wrangle !—you must imagine our
talk becoming louder, with a developing quarrelsome note—
my mother no doubt hovering on the staircase and listening in
alarm as who should say, " My dear, don't offend it ! Oh, don't
offend it ! Mr. Gabbitas enjoys its friendship. Try to think
whatever Mr. Gabbitas says "—though we still kept in touch
with a pretence of mutual deference. The ethical superiority
of Christianity to all other religions came to the fore—I know
not how. We dealt with the matter in bold, imaginative
generalisations, because of the insufficiency of our historical
knowledge. I was moved to denounce Christianity as the ethic
of slaves, and declare myself a disciple of a German writer of
no little vogue in those days, named Nietzsche.

For a disciple I must confess I was particularly ill acquainted
with the works of the master. Indeed, all I knew of him had
come to me through a two-column article in *The Clarion* for
the previous week. . . . But the Rev. Gabbitas did not read
The Clarion.

I am, I know, putting a strain upon your credulity when I
tell you that I now have little doubt that the Rev. Gabbitas
was absolutely ignorant even of the name of Nietzsche, although
that writer presented a separate and distinct attitude of attack
upon the faith that was in the reverend gentleman's keeping.

" I'm a disciple of Nietzsche," said I, with an air of extensive
explanation.

He shied away so awkwardly at the name that I repeated it
at once.

" But do you know what Nietzsche says ? " I pressed him
viciously.

" He has certainly been adequately answered," said he, still
trying to carry it off.

" Who by ? " I rapped out hotly. " Tell me that ! " and became mercilessly expectant.

§ 5

A happy accident relieved Mr. Gabbitas from the embarrassment of that challenge, and carried me another step along my course of personal disaster.

It came on the heels of my question in the form of a clatter of horses without, and the gride and cessation of wheels. I glimpsed a straw-hatted coachman and a pair of greys. It seemed an incredibly magnificent carriage for Clayton.

" Eh ! " said the Rev. Gabbitas, going to the window. " Why, it's old Mrs. Verrall ! It's old Mrs. Verrall. Really ! What *can* she want with me ? "

He turned to me, and the flush of controversy had passed and his face shone like the sun. It was not every day, I perceived, that Mrs. Verrall came to see him.

" I get so many interruptions," he said, almost grinning. " You must excuse me a minute ! Then——then I'll tell you about that fellow. But don't go. I pray you don't go. I can assure you . . . *most* interesting."

He went out of the room waving vague prohibitory gestures.

" I *must* go," I cried after him.

" No, no, no ! " in the passage. " I've got your answer," I think it was he added, and " quite mistaken " ; and I saw him running down the steps to talk to the old lady.

I swore. I made three steps to the window, and this brought me within a yard of that accursed drawer.

I glanced at it, and then at that old woman who was so absolutely powerful, and instantly her son and Nettie's face were flaming in my brain. The Stuarts had, no doubt, already accepted accomplished facts. And I too——

What was I doing here ?

What was I doing here while judgment escaped me ?

I woke up. I was injected with energy. I took one reassuring look at the curate's obsequious back, at the old lady's projected nose and quivering hand, and then with swift, clean movements I had the little drawer open, four sovereigns in my pocket, and the drawer shut again. Then again at the window— they were still talking.

That was all right. He might not look in that drawer for hours. I glanced at his clock. Twenty minutes still before the Birmingham train. Time to buy a pair of boots and get away. But how was I to get to the station ?

I went out boldly into the passage, and took my hat and stick. . . . Walk past him ?

Yes. That was all right ! He could not argue with me while so important a person engaged him. . . . I came boldly down the steps.

" I want a list made, Mr. Gabbitas, of all the really *deserving* cases," old Mrs. Verrall was saying.

It is curious, but it did not occur to me that here was a mother whose son I was going to kill. I did not see her in that aspect at all. Instead, I was possessed by a realisation of the blazing imbecility of a social system that gave this palsied old woman the power to give or withhold the urgent necessities of life from hundreds of her fellow-creatures just according to her poor, foolish old fancies of desert.

" We could make a *provisional* list of that sort," he was saying, and glanced round with a preoccupied expression at me.

" I *must* go," I said at his flash of inquiry, and added, " I'll be back in twenty minutes," and went on my way. He turned again to his patroness as though he forgot me on the instant. Perhaps after all he was not sorry.

I felt extraordinarily cool and capable, exhilarated, if anything, by this prompt, effectual theft. After all, my great determination would achieve itself. I was no longer oppressed by a sense of obstacles, I felt I could grasp accidents and turn them to my advantage. I would go now down Hacker Street to the little shoemaker's—get a sound, good pair of boots—ten minutes—and then to the railway-station—five minutes more—and off ! I felt as efficient and non-moral as if I was Nietzsche's Over-man already come. It did not occur to me that the curate's clock might have a considerable margin of error.

§ 6

I missed the train.

Partly that was because the curate's clock was slow, and partly it was due to the commercial obstinacy of the shoemaker, who would try on another pair after I had declared my time was up. I bought the final pair however, gave him a wrong address for the return of the old ones, and only ceased to feel like the Nietzschean Over-man when I saw the train running out of the station.

Even then I did not lose my head. It occurred to me almost at once that in the event of a prompt pursuit there would be a great advantage in not taking a train from Clayton ; that, indeed, to have done so would have been an error from which only luck had saved me. As it was, I had already been very indiscreet in my inquiries about Shaphambury, for once on the scent the clerk could not fail to remember me. Now the chances were against his coming into the case. I did not go into the station therefore at all, I made no demonstration of having missed the train, but walked quietly past, down the road, crossed the iron footbridge, and took the way back circuitously by White's brickfields and the allotments to the way over Clayton Crest to Two-Mile Stone, where I calculated I should have an ample margin for the 6.13 train.

I was not very greatly excited or alarmed then. Suppose, I reasoned, that by some accident the curate goes to that drawer at once : will he be certain to miss four out of ten or eleven sovereigns ? If he does, will he at once think I have taken them ? If he does, will he act at once or wait for my return ? If he acts at once, will he talk to my mother or call in the police ? Then there are a dozen roads and even railways out of the Clayton region ; how is he to know which I have taken ? Suppose he goes straight at once to the right station, they will not remember my departure for the single reason that I didn't depart. But they may remember about Shaphambury ? It was unlikely.

I resolved not to go directly to Shaphambury from Birmingham, but to go thence to Monkshampton, thence to Wyvern, and then come down on Shaphambury from the north. That might involve a night at some intermediate stopping-place, but it would effectually conceal me from any but the most persistent pursuit. And this was not a case of murder yet, but only the theft of four sovereigns.

I had argued away all anxiety before I reached Clayton Crest.

At the Crest I looked back. What a world it was ! And suddenly it came to me that I was looking at it for the last time. If I overtook the fugitives and succeeded, I should die with them—or hang. I stopped and looked back more attentively at that wide ugly valley.

It was my native valley, and I was going out of it, I thought, never to return ; and yet in that last prospect the group of towns that had borne me and dwarfed and crippled and made me, seemed in some indefinable manner strange. I was, perhaps, more used to seeing it from this comprehensive viewpoint when it was veiled and softened by night ; now it came out in all its weekday reek, under a clear afternoon sun. That may account a little for its unfamiliarity. And perhaps, too, there was something in the emotions through which I had been passing for a week and more, to intensify my insight, to enable me to pierce the unusual, to question the accepted. But it came to me then, I am sure for the first time, how promiscuous, how higgledy-piggledy was the whole of that jumble of mines and homes, collieries and pot-banks, railway yards, canals, schools, forges and blast furnaces, churches, chapels, allotment hovels, a vast irregular agglomeration of ugly smoking accidents in which men lived as happy as frogs in a dustbin. Each thing jostled and damaged the other things about it, each thing ignored the other things about it ; the smoke of the furnace defiled the pot-bank clay, the clatter of the railway deafened the worshippers in church, the public-house thrust corruption at the school doors, the dismal homes squeezed miserably amidst the monstrosities of industrialism, with an effect of groping imbecility. Humanity choked amidst its products, and all its energy went in increasing its disorder, like a blind stricken thing that struggles and sinks in a morass.

I did not think these things clearly that afternoon. Much less did I ask how I, with my murderous purpose, stood to them all. I write down that realisation of disorder and suffocation here and now as though I had thought it, but indeed then I only felt it, felt it transitorily as I looked back, and then stood with the thing escaping from my mind.

I should never see that countryside again.

I came back to that. At any rate I wasn't sorry. The chances were I should die in sweet air, under a clean sky.

From distant Swathinglea came a little sound, the minute ululation of a remote crowd, and then rapidly three shots.

That held me perplexed for a space. . . . Well, anyhow I was leaving it all! Thank God I was leaving it all! Then, as I turned to go on, I thought of my mother.

It seemed an evil world in which to leave one's mother. My thoughts focused upon her very vividly for a moment. Down there, under that afternoon light, she was going to and fro, unaware as yet that she had lost me, bent and poking about in the darkling underground kitchen, perhaps carrying a lamp into the scullery to trim, or sitting patiently, staring into the fire, waiting tea for me. A great pity for her, a great remorse at the blacker troubles that lowered over her innocent head, came to me. Why, after all, was I doing this thing?

Why?

I stopped again dead, with the hill crest rising between me and home. I had more than half a mind to return to her.

Then I thought of the curate's sovereigns. If he had missed them already, what should I return to? And even if I returned, how could I put them back?

And what of the night after I renounced my revenge? What of the time when young Verrall came back? And Nettie?

No! The thing had to be done.

But at least I might have kissed my mother before I came away, left her some message, reassured her at least for a little while. All night she would listen and wait for me. . . .

Should I send her a telegram from Two-Mile Stone?

It was no good now; too late, too late. To do that would be to tell the course I had taken, to bring pursuit upon me, swift and sure, if pursuit there was to be. No. My mother must suffer!

I went on grimly towards Two-Mile Stone, but now as if some greater will than mine directed my footsteps thither.

I reached Birmingham before darkness came, and just caught the last train for Monkshampton, where I had planned to pass the night.

CHAPTER FIVE

THE PURSUIT OF THE TWO LOVERS

§ 1

As the train carried me on from Birmingham to Monks-hampton, it carried me not only into a country where I had never been before, but out of the commonplace daylight and the touch and quality of ordinary things, into the strange unprecedented night that was ruled by the giant meteor of the last days.

There was at that time a curious accentuation of the common alternation of night and day. They became separated with a widening difference of value in regard to all mundane affairs. During the day, the comet was an item in the newspapers, it was jostled by a thousand more living interests, it was as nothing in the skirts of the war storm that was now upon us. It was an astronomical phenomenon somewhere away over China, millions of miles away in the deeps. We forgot it. But directly the sun sank one turned ever and again towards the east, and the meteor resumed its sway over us.

One waited for its rising, and yet each night it came as a surprise. Always it rose brighter than one had dared to think, always larger and with some wonderful change in its outline, and now with a strange, less luminous, greener disc upon it that grew with its growth, the umbra of the earth. It shone also with its own light, so that this shadow was not hard or black but it shone phosphorescently and with a diminishing intensity where the stimulus of the sun's rays was withdrawn. As it ascended towards the zenith, as the last trailing daylight went after the abdicating sun, its greenish white illumination banished the realities of day, diffused a bright ghostliness over all things. It changed the starless sky about it to an extraordinary deep blue, the profoundest colour in the world, such as I have never seen before or since. I remember, too, that as I peered from the train that was rattling me along to Monkshampton, I perceived and was puzzled by a coppery red light that mingled with all the shadows that were cast by it.

It turned our ugly English industrial towns to phantom cities. Everywhere the local authorities discontinued street lighting—one could read small print in the glare,—and so at Monkshampton I went about through pale, white, unfamiliar streets, whose electric globes had shadows on the path. Lit windows here and there burnt ruddy orange, like holes cut in some dream curtain that hung before a furnace. A police-man with noiseless feet showed me an inn woven of moonshine, a green-faced man opened to us, and there I abode the night. And the next morning it opened with a mighty clatter, and was a dirty little beerhouse that stank of beer, and there was a fat and grimy landlord with red spots upon his neck, and much noisy traffic going by on the cobbles outside.

I came out, after I had paid my bill, into a street that echoed to the bawlings of two news-vendors and to the noisy yappings of a dog they had raised to emulation. They were shouting : " Great British disaster in the North Sea. A battleship lost with all hands ! "

I bought a paper, went on to the railway station reading such details as were given of this triumph of the old civilisation, of the blowing up of this great iron ship, full of guns and explosives and the most costly and beautiful machinery of which that time was capable, together with nine hundred able-bodied men, all of them above the average, by a contact mine towed by a German submarine. I read myself into a fever of warlike emotion. Not only did I forget the meteor, but for a time I forgot even the purpose that took me on to the railway station, bought my ticket, and was now carrying me onward to Shaphambury.

So the hot day came to its own again, and people forgot the night.

Each night there shone upon us more and more insistently, beauty, wonder, the promise of the deeps ; and we were hushed, and marvelled for a space. And at the first grey sounds of dawn again, at the shooting of bolts and the noise of milk-carts, we forgot, and the dusty habitual day came yawning and stretching back again. The stains of coal smoke crept across the heavens, and we rose to the soiled disorderly routine of life.

" Thus life has always been," we said ; " thus it will always be."

The glory of those nights was almost universally regarded as spectacular merely. It signified nothing to us. So far as western Europe went, it was only a small and ignorant section of the lower classes who regarded the comet as a portent of the end of the world. Abroad, where there were peasantries, it was different, but in England the peasantry had already disappeared. Every one read. The newspaper, in the quiet days before our swift quarrel with Germany rushed to its climax, had absolutely dispelled all possibilities of a panic in this matter. The very tramps upon the high-roads, the children in the nursery had learned that at the utmost the whole of that shining cloud could weigh but a few score tons. This fact had been shown quite conclusively by the enormous deflections that had at last swung it round squarely at our world. It had passed near three of the smallest asteroids without producing the minutest perceptible deflection in their course ; while, on its own part, it had described a course through nearly three degrees. When it struck our earth there was to be a magnificent spectacle, no doubt, for those who were on the right side of our planet to see ; but beyond that nothing. It was doubtful whether we were on the right side. The meteor would loom larger and larger in the sky, but with the umbra of our earth eating its heart of brightness out, and at last it would be the whole sky, a sky of luminous green clouds, with a white brightness about the horizon west and east. Then a pause—a pause of not very exactly definite duration—and then, no doubt, a great blaze of shooting stars. They might be of some unwonted colour because of the unknown element that line in the green revealed. For a little while the zenith would spout shooting stars. Some, it was hoped, would reach the earth and be available for analysis.

That, science said, would be all. The green clouds would whirl and vanish, and there might be thunder-storms. But through the attenuated wisps of comet shine, the old sky, the old stars, would reappear, and all would be as it had been before. And since this was to happen between one and eleven in the morning of the approaching Tuesday—I slept at Monkshampton on Saturday night,—it would be only partially visible, if visible at all, on our side of the earth. Perhaps, if it came late, one would see no more than a shooting star low down in the sky. All this we had with the utmost assurances of science. Still it did not prevent the last nights being the most beautiful and memorable of human experiences.

The nights had become very warm, and when next day I had ranged Shaphambury in vain, I was greatly tormented, as that unparalleled glory of the night returned, to think that under its splendid benediction young Verrall and Nettie made love to one another.

I walked backward and forward, backward and forward, along the sea front, peering into the faces of the young couples who promenaded, with my hand in my pocket ready and a curious ache in my heart that had no kindred with rage. Until at last all the promenaders had gone home to bed, and I was alone with the star.

My train from Wyvern to Shaphambury that morning was a whole hour late ; they said it was on account of the movement of troops to meet a possible raid from the Elbe.

§ 2

Shaphambury seemed an odd place to me even then. But something was quickening in me at that time to feel the oddness of many accepted things. Now in the retrospect I see it as intensely queer. The whole place was strange to my untravelled eyes ; the sea even was strange. Only twice in my life had I been at the seaside before, and then I had gone by excursion to places on the Welsh coast, whose great cliffs of rock and mountain backgrounds made the effect of the horizon very different from what it is upon the East Anglian seaboard. Here what they call a cliff was a crumbling bank of whitey-brown earth not fifty feet high.

So soon as I arrived I made a systematic exploration of Shaphambury. To this day I retain the clearest memories of the plan I shaped out then, and how my inquiries were incommoded by the overpowering desire of every one to talk of the chances of a German raid before the Channel Fleet got round to us. I slept at a small public-house in a Shaphambury back street on Sunday night. I did not get on to Shaphambury from Wyvern until two in the afternoon, because of the infrequency of Sunday trains, and I got no clue whatever until late in the afternoon of Monday. As the little local train bumped into sight of the place round the curve of a swelling hill, one saw a series of undulating grassy spaces, amidst which a number of conspicuous notice-boards appealed to the eye and cut up the distant sea horizon. Most of these referred to comestibles or to remedies to follow the comestibles ; and they were coloured with a view to be memorable rather than beautiful, to " stand out " amidst the gentle greyish tones of the east-coast scenery. The greater number, I may remark, of the advertisements that were so conspicuous a factor in the life of those days, and which rendered our vast tree-pulp news-papers possible, referred to foods, drinks, tobacco, and the drugs that promised a restoration of the equanimity these other articles had destroyed. Wherever one went one was reminded in glaring letters that, after all, man was little better than a worm, that eyeless, earless thing that burrows and lives uncomplainingly amidst nutritious dirt, " an alimentary canal with the subservient appendages thereto." But in addition to such boards there were also the big black-and-white boards of various grandiloquently named " estates." The individualistic enterprise of that time had led to the plotting out of nearly all the country round the seaside towns into roads and building-plots—all but a small portion of the south and east coast was in this condition, and had the promises of those schemes been realised the entire population of the island might have been accommodated upon the sea frontiers. Nothing of the sort happened, of course ; the whole of this uglification of the coast-line was done to stimulate a little foolish gambling in plots, and one saw everywhere agents' boards in every state of freshness and decay, ill-made exploitation roads overgrown with grass, and here and there at a corner, a label, " Trafalgar Avenue," or " Sea View Road." Here and there, too, some small investor, some shop-man with " savings," had delivered his soul to the local builders and built himself a house ; and there it stood, ill-designed, mean-looking, isolated, ill-placed on a cheaply fenced plot, athwart which his domestic washing fluttered in the breeze amidst a bleak desolation of enterprise. Then presently our railway crossed a high road, and a row of mean yellow-brick houses—workmen's cottages, and the filthy black sheds that made the "allotments" of that time a universal eyesore, marked our approach to the more central areas of—I quote the local guide-book—"one of the most delightful resorts in the East Anglian poppy-land." Then more mean houses, the gaunt ungainliness of the electric force station—it had a huge chimney, because no one understood how to make combustion of coal complete—and then we were in the railway station, and barely three-quarters of a mile from the centre of this haunt of health and pleasure.

I inspected the town thoroughly before I made my inquiries. The road began badly with a row of cheap, pretentious, insolvent-looking shops, and a public-house, and a cab-stand, but, after an interval of little red villas that were partly hidden amidst shrubbery gardens, broke into a confusedly bright but not unpleasing High Street, shuttered that afternoon and sabbatically still. Somewhere in the background a church bell jangled, and children in bright, new-looking clothes were going to Sunday-school. Thence through a square of stuccoed lodging-houses that seemed a finer and cleaner version of my native square, I came to a garden of asphalt and euonymus—the Sea Front. I sat down on a cast-iron seat, and surveyed first of all the broad stretches of muddy, sandy beach, with its queer wheeled bathing machines painted with the advertisements of somebody's pills, and then at the house fronts that stared out upon these visceral counsels. Boarding-houses, private hotels, and lodging-houses in terraces clustered right and left of me, and then came to an end ; in one direction scaffolding marked a building enterprise in progress, in the other, after a waste interval, rose a monstrous bulging red shape, a huge hotel, that dwarfed all other things. Northward were low pale cliffs with white denticulations of tents, where the local volunteers, all under arms, lay encamped ; and southward, a spreading waste of sandy dunes, with occasional bushes and clumps of stunted pine and an advertisement board or so. A hard blue sky hung over all this prospect, the sunshine cast inky shadows, and eastward was a whitish sea. It was Sunday, and the midday meal still held people indoors. . . .

A queer world ! thought I even then—to you now it must seem impossibly queer,—and after an interval I forced myself back to my own affair.

How was I to ask ? What was I to ask for ?

I puzzled for a long time over that—at first I was a little tired and indolent—and then presently I had a flow of ideas.

My solution was fairly ingenious. I invented the following story. I happened to be taking a holiday in Shaphambury, and I was making use of the opportunity to seek the owner of a valuable feather boa, which had been left behind in the hotel of my uncle at Wyvern by a young lady, travelling with

a young gentleman—no doubt a youthful married couple.
They had reached Shaphambury somewhen on Thursday.
I went over the story many times, and gave my imaginary
uncle and his hotel plausible names. At any rate this yarn
would serve as a complete justification for all the questions
I might wish to ask.

I settled that, but I still sat for a time, wanting the energy
to begin. Then I turned towards the big hotel. Its gorgeous
magnificence seemed to my inexpert judgment to indicate the
very place a rich young man of good family would select.

Huge draught-proof doors were swung round for me by an
ironically polite under-porter in a magnificent green uniform,
who looked at my clothes as he listened to my question and
then with a German accent referred me to a gorgeous head-
porter, who directed me to a princely young man behind a
counter of brass and polish, like a bank—like several banks.
This young man, while he answered me, kept his eye on my
collar and tie—and I knew that they were abominable.

" I want to find a lady and gentleman who came to Shaphambury on Tuesday," I said.

" Friends of yours ? " he asked with a terrible fineness of
irony.

I made out at last that here at any rate the young people
had not been. They might have lunched there, but they had
had no room. But I went out—door opened again for me
obsequiously—in a state of social discomfiture, and did not
attack any other establishment that afternoon.

My resolution had come to a sort of ebb. More people were
promenading, and their Sunday smartness abashed me. I
forgot my purpose in an acute sense of myself. I felt that the
bulge of my pocket caused by the revolver was conspicuous,
and I was ashamed. I went along the sea front away from the
town, and presently lay down among pebbles and sea poppies.
This mood of reaction prevailed with me all that afternoon.
In the evening, about sundown, I went to the station and
asked questions of the outporters there. But outporters,
I found, were a class of men who remembered luggage rather
than people, and I had no sort of idea what luggage young
Verrall and Nettie were likely to have with them.

Then I fell into conversation with a salacious wooden-legged
old man with a silver ring, who swept the steps that went
down to the beach from the parade. He knew much about
young couples, but only in general terms, and nothing of the
particular young couple I sought. He reminded me in the
most disagreeable way of the sensuous aspects of life, and I
was not sorry when presently a gunboat appeared in the
offing signalling the coastguard and the camp, and cut short
his observations upon holidays, beaches, and morals.

I went—and now I was past my ebb—and sat in a seat
upon the parade, and watched the brightening of those rising

clouds of chilly fire that made the ruddy west seem tame. My midday lassitude was going, my blood was running warmer again. And as the twilight and the filmy brightness replaced the dusty sunlight and robbed this unfamiliar place of all its matter-of-fact queerness, its sense of aimless materialism, romance returned to me, and passion, and my thoughts of honour and revenge. I remember that change of mood as occurring very vividly on this occasion, but I fancy that less distinctly I had felt this before many times. In the old times, night and the starlight had an effect of intimate reality the daytime did not possess. The daytime—as one saw it in towns and populous places—had hold of one, no doubt, but only as an uproar might, it was distracting, conflicting, insistent. Darkness veiled the more salient aspects of those agglomerations of human absurdity, and one could exist—one could imagine.

I had a queer illusion that night, that Nettie and her lover were close at hand, that suddenly I should come on them. I have already told how I went through the dusk seeking them in every couple that drew near. And I dropped asleep at last in an unfamiliar bedroom hung with gaudily decorated texts, cursing myself for having wasted a day.

§ 3

I sought them in vain the next morning, but after midday I came in quick succession on a perplexing multitude of clues. After failing to find any young couple that corresponded to young Verrall and Nettie, I presently discovered an unsatisfactory quartette of couples.

Any of these four couples might have been the one I sought ; with regard to none of them was there conviction. They had all arrived either on Wednesday or Thursday. Two couples were still in occupation of their rooms, but neither of these were at home. Late in the afternoon I reduced my list by eliminating a young man in drab, with side whiskers and long cuffs, accompanied by a lady of thirty or more, of consciously ladylike type. I was disgusted at the sight of them ; the other two young people had gone for a long walk, and though I watched their boarding-house until the fiery cloud shone out above, sharing and mingling in an unusually splendid sunset, I missed them. Then I discovered them dining at a separate table in the bow window, with red-shaded candles between them, peering out ever and again at this splendour that was neither night nor day. The girl in her pink evening dress looked very light and pretty to me—pretty enough to enrage me,—she had well-shaped arms and white, well-modelled shoulders, and the turn of her cheek and the fair hair about her ears was full of subtle delights ; but she was not Nettie, and the happy man with her was that degenerate type our old aristocracy produced with such odd frequency, chinless, large bony nose, small fair head, languid expression, and a neck that had demanded and received a veritable sleeve of collar. I stood outside in the meteor's livid light, hating them and cursing them for having delayed me so long. I stood until it was evident they remarked me, a black shape of envy, silhouetted against the glare.

That finished Shaphambury. The question I now had to debate was which of the remaining couples I had to pursue.

I walked back to the parade trying to reason my next step out, and muttering to myself, because there was something in that luminous wonderfulness that touched one's brain and made one feel a little light-headed.

One couple had gone to London ; the other had gone to the Bungalow village at Bone Cliff. Where, I wondered, was Bone Cliff ?

I came upon my wooden-legged man at the top of his steps.

" Hullo," said I.

He pointed seaward with his pipe, his silver ring shone in the sky light.

" Rum," he said.

" What is ? " I asked.

" Search-lights ! Smoke ! Ships going north ! If it wasn't for this blasted Milky Way gone green up there, we might see."

He was too intent to heed my questions for a time. Then he vouchsafed over his shoulder——

" Know Bungalow village ?—rather. Artis' and such. Nice goings on ! Mixed bathing—something scandalous. Yes."

" But where is it ? " I said, suddenly exasperated.

" There ! " he said. " What's that flicker ? A gun-flash— or I'm a lost soul ! "

" You'd hear," I said, " long before it was near enough to see a flash."

He didn't answer. Only by making it clear I would distract him until he told me what I wanted to know could I get him to turn from his absorbed contemplation of that phantom dance between the sea rim and the shine. Indeed I gripped his arm and shook him. Then he turned upon me cursing.

" Seven miles," he said, " along this road. And now go to 'ell with yer ! "

I answered with some foul insult by way of thanks, and so we parted ; and I set off towards the bungalow village.

I found a policeman, standing star-gazing, a little way beyond the end of the parade, and verified the wooden-legged man's directions.

" It's a lonely road, you know," he called after me. . . .

I had an odd intuition that now at last I was on the right track. I left the dark masses of Shaphambury behind me, and pushed out into the dim pallor of that night with the quiet assurance of a traveller who nears his end.

The incidents of that long tramp I do not recall in any orderly succession, the one progressive thing is my memory of a growing fatigue. The sea was for the most part smooth and shining like a mirror, a great expanse of reflecting silver barred by slow broad undulations, but at one time a little breeze breathed like a faint sigh and ruffled their long bodies into faint scaly ripples that never completely died out again. The way was sometimes sandy, thick with silvery colourless sand, and sometimes chalky and lumpy, with lumps that had shining facets ; a black scrub was scattered, sometimes in thickets, sometimes in single bunches, among the somnolent hummocks of sand. At one place came grass, and ghostly great sheep looming up among the grey. After a time black pinewoods intervened, and made sustained darknesses along the road, woods that frayed out at the edges to weirdly warped and stunted trees. Then isolated pine witches would appear, and make their rigid gestures at me as I passed. Grotesquely incongruous amidst these forms, I presently came on estate boards, appealing, " Houses can be built to suit purchaser," to the silence, to the shadows, and the glare.

Once I remember the persistent barking of a dog from somewhere inland of me, and several times I took out and examined my revolver very carefully. I must, of course, have been full of my intention when I did that, I must have been thinking of Nettie and revenge, but I cannot now recall those emotions at all. Only I see again very distinctly the greenish gleams that ran over lock and barrel as I turned the weapon in my hand.

Then there was the sky, the wonderful, luminous, starless, moonless sky, and the empty blue deeps of the edge of it, between the meteor and the sea. And once—strange phantoms !—I saw far out upon the shine, and very small and distant, three long black warships, without masts, or sails, or smoke, or any lights, dark, deadly, furtive things, travelling very swiftly and keeping an equal distance. And when I looked again they were very small, and then the shine had swallowed them up.

Then once a flash and what I thought was a gun, until I looked up and saw a fading trail of greenish light still hanging in the sky. And after that there was a shiver and whispering in the air, a stronger throbbing in one's arteries, a sense of refreshment, a renewal of purpose. . . .

Somewhere upon my way the road forked, but I do not remember whether that was near Shaphambury or near the end of my walk. The hesitation between two rutted unmade roads alone remains clear in my mind.

At last I grew weary. I came to piled heaps of decaying seaweed and cart tracks running this way and that, and then

I missed the road and was stumbling among sand hummocks quite close to the sea. I came out on the edge of the dimly glittering sandy beach, and something phosphorescent drew me to the water's edge. I bent down and peered at the little luminous specks that floated in the ripples.

Presently with a sigh I stood erect, and contemplated the lonely peace of that last wonderful night. The meteor had now trailed its shining nets across the whole space of the sky and was beginning to set; in the east the blue was coming to its own again; the sea was an intense edge of blackness, and now, escaped from that great shine, and faint and still tremulously valiant, one weak elusive star could just be seen hovering on the verge of the invisible.

How beautiful it was! how still and beautiful! Peace! peace!—the peace that passeth understanding, robed in light descending! . . . .

My heart swelled, and suddenly I was weeping.

There was something new and strange in my blood. It came to me that indeed I did not want to kill.

I did not want to kill. I did not want to be the servant of my passions any more. A great desire had come to me to escape from life, from the daylight which is heat and conflict and desire, into that cool night of eternity—and rest. I had played —I had done.

I stood upon the edge of the great ocean, and I was filled with an inarticulate spirit of prayer, and I desired greatly— peace from myself.

And presently, there in the east, would come again the red discolouring curtain over these mysteries, the finite world again, the grey and growing harsh certainties of dawn. My resolve I knew would take up with me again. This was a rest for me, an interlude; but to-morrow I should be William Leadford once more, ill-nourished, ill-dressed, ill-equipped and clumsy, a thief and shamed, a wound upon the face of life, a source of trouble and sorrow even to the mother I loved; no hope in life left for me now but revenge before my death.

Why this paltry thing, revenge? It entered into my thoughts that I might end the matter now and let these others go.

To wade out into the sea, into this warm lapping that mingled the natures of water and light, to stand there breast-high, to thrust my revolver barrel into my mouth——?

Why not?

I swung about with an effort. I walked slowly up the beach thinking. . . .

I turned and looked back at the sea. No! Something within me said, " No ! "

I must think.

It was troublesome to go farther because the hummocks and the tangled bushes began. I sat down amidst a black cluster of shrubs, and rested, chin on hand. I drew my revolver

from my pocket and looked at it, and held it in my hand.
Life ? Or Death ? . . .

I seemed to be probing the very deeps of being, but indeed
imperceptibly I fell asleep, and sat dreaming.

§ 4

Two people were bathing in the sea.

I had awakened.   It was still that white and wonderful
night, and the blue band of clear sky was no wider than before.
These people must have come into sight as I fell asleep, and
awakened me almost at once.   They waded breast-deep in the
water, emerging, coming shoreward, a woman, with her hair
coiled about her head, and in pursuit of her a man, graceful
figures of black and silver, with a bright green surge flowing
off from them, a pattering of flashing wavelets about them.
He smote the water and splashed it towards her, she retaliated,
and then they were knee-deep, and then for an instant their
feet broke the long silver margin of the sea.

Each wore a tightly fitting bathing dress that hid nothing
of the shining, dripping beauty of their youthful forms.

She glanced over her shoulder and found him nearer than
she thought, started, gesticulated, gave a little cry that pierced
me to the heart, and fled up the beach obliquely towards me,
running like the wind, and passed me, vanished amidst the
black distorted bushes, and was gone—she and her pursuer,
in a moment, over the ridge of sand.

I heard him shout between exhaustion and laughter. . . .

And suddenly I was a thing of bestial fury, standing with
hands held up and clenched, rigid in gesture of impotent
threatening, against the sky. . . .

For this striving, swift thing of light and beauty was Nettie
—and this was the man for whom I had been betrayed !

And, it blazed upon me, I might have died there by the
sheer ebbing of my will—unavenged !

In another moment I was running and stumbling, revolver
in hand, in quiet unsuspected pursuit of them, through the
soft and noiseless sand.

§ 5

I came up over the little ridge and discovered the bungalow
village I had been seeking, nestling in a crescent lap of dunes.
A door slammed, the two runners had vanished, and I halted
staring.

There was a group of three bungalows nearer to me than
the others.   Into one of these three they had gone, and I was
too late to see which.   All had doors and windows carelessly
open, and none showed a light.

This place, upon which I had at last happened, was a fruit
of the reaction of artistic-minded and carelessly living people
against the costly uncomfortable social stiffness of the more

formal seaside resorts of that time. It was, you must understand, the custom of the steam-railway companies to sell their
carriages after they had been obsolete for a sufficient length
of years, and some genius had hit upon the possibility of turning these into habitable cabins for the summer holiday. The
thing had become a fashion with a certain Bohemian-spirited
class ; they added cabin to cabin, and these little improvised
homes, gaily painted and with broad verandahs and supple-
mentary leanto's added to their accomodation, made the
brightest contrast conceivable to the dull rigidities of the
decorous resorts. Of course there were many discomforts in
such camping that had to be faced cheerfully, and so this
broad sandy beach was sacred to high spirits and the young.
Art muslin and banjoes, Chinese lanterns and frying, are
leading " notes," I find, in the impression of those who once
knew such places well. But so far as I was concerned this odd
settlement of pleasure-squatters was a mystery as well as a
surprise, enhanced rather than mitigated by an imaginative
suggestion or so I had received from the wooden-legged man
at Shaphambury. I saw the thing as no gathering of light
hearts and gay idleness, but grimly—after the manner of poor
men poisoned by the suppression of all their cravings after
joy. To the poor man, to the grimy workers, beauty and
cleanness were absolutely denied ; out of a life of greasy dirt,
of muddied desires, they watched their happier fellows with
a bitter envy and foul, tormenting suspicions. Fancy a world
in which the common people held love to be a sort of beastli-
ness, own sister to being drunk ! . . .

There was in the old time always something cruel at the
bottom of this business of sexual love. At least that is the
impression I have brought with me across the gulf of the
great Change. To succeed in love seemed such triumph as no
other success could give, but to fail was as if one was tainted. . . .

I felt no sense of singularity that this thread of savagery
should run through these emotions of mine and become now
the whole strand of these emotions. I believed, and I think
I was right in believing, that the love of all true lovers was a
sort of defiance then, that they closed a system in each other's
arms and mocked the world without. You loved against the
world, and these two loved *at* me. They had their business
with one another, under the threat of a watchful fierceness.
A sword, a sharp sword, the keenest edge in life, lay among
their roses.

Whatever may be true of this for others, for me and my
imagination, at any rate, it was altogether true. I was never
for dalliance, I was never a jesting lover. I wanted fiercely ;
I made love impatiently. Perhaps I had written irrelevant
love-letters for that very reason ; because with this stark
theme I could not play. . . .

The thought of Nettie's shining form, of her shrinking bold

abandon to her easy conqueror, gave me now a body of rage that was nearly too strong for my heart and nerves and the tense powers of my merely physical being. I came down among the pale sand-heaps slowly towards that queer village of careless sensuality, and now within my puny body I was coldly sharpset for pain and death, a darkly gleaming hate, a sword of evil, drawn.

§ 6

I halted, and stood planning what I had to do.

Should I go to bungalow after bungalow until one of the two I sought answered to my rap ? But suppose some servant intervened !

Should I wait where I was—perhaps until morning—watching ? And meanwhile——

All the nearer bungalows were very still now. If I walked softly to them, from open windows, from something seen or overheard, I might get a clue to guide me. Should I advance circuitously, creeping upon them, or should I walk straight to the door ? It was bright enough for her to recognise me clearly at a distance of many paces.

The difficulty to my mind lay in this, that if I involved other people by questions, I might at last confront my betrayers with these others close about me, ready to snatch my weapon and seize my hands. Besides, what names might they bear here ?

" Boom ! " the sound crept upon my senses, and then again it came.

I turned impatiently as one turns upon an impertinence, and beheld a great ironclad not four miles out, steaming fast across the dappled silver, and from its funnels sparks, intensely red, poured out into the night. As I turned, came the hot flash of its guns, firing seaward, and answering this, red flashes and a streaming smoke in the line between sea and sky. So I remembered it, and I remember myself staring at it—in a state of stupid arrest. It was an irrelevance. What had these things to do with me ?

With a shuddering hiss, a rocket from a headland beyond the village leaped up and burst hot gold against the glare, and the sound of the third and fourth guns reached me.

The windows of the dark bungalows, one after another, leaped out, squares of ruddy brightness that flared and flickered and became steadily bright. Dark heads appeared looking seaward, a door opened, and sent out a brief lane of yellow to mingle and be lost in the comet's brightness. That brought me back to the business in hand.

" Boom ! boom ! " and when I looked again at the great ironclad, a little torchlike spurt of flame wavered behind her funnels. I could hear the throb and clangour of her straining engines. . . .

I became aware of the voices of people calling to one another in the village. A white-robed, hooded figure, some man in a bathing wrap, absurdly suggestive of an Arab in his burnous, came out from one of the nearer bungalows, and stood clear and still and shadowless in the glare.

He put his hands to shade his seaward eyes, and shouted to people within.

The people within—*my* people! My fingers tightened on my revolver. What was this war nonsense to me? I would go round among the hummocks with the idea of approaching the three bungalows inconspicuously from the flank. This fight at sea might serve my purpose—except for that, it had no interest for me at all. Boom! boom! The huge voluminous concussions rushed past me, beat at my heart and passed. In a moment Nettie would come out to see.

First one and then two other wrapped figures came out of the bungalows to join the first. His arm pointed seaward, and his voice, a full tenor, rose in explanation. I could hear some of the words. "It's a German!" he said. "She's caught."

Some one disputed that, and there followed a little indistinct babble of argument. I went on slowly in the circuit I had marked out, watching these people as I went.

They shouted together with such a common intensity of direction that I halted and looked seaward. I saw the tall fountain flung by a shot that had just missed the great war-ship. A second rose still nearer us, a third, and a fourth, and then a great uprush of dust, a whirling cloud, leaped out of the headland whence the rocket had come, and spread with a slow deliberation right and left. Hard on that an enormous crash, and the man with the full voice leaped and cried, "Hit!"

Let me see! Of course, I had to go round beyond the bungalows, and then come up towards the group from behind.

A high-pitched woman's voice called, "Honeymooners! honeymooners! Come out and see!"

Something gleamed in the shadow of the nearer bungalow, and a man's voice answered from within. What he said I did not catch, but suddenly I heard Nettie calling very distinctly "We've been bathing."

The man who had first come out shouted, "Don't you hear the guns? They're fighting—not five miles from shore."

"Eh?" answered the bungalow, and a window opened.

"Out there!"

I did not hear the reply, because of the faint rustle of my own movements. Clearly these people were all too much occupied by the battle to look in my direction, and so I walked now straight towards the darkness that held Nettie and the black desire of my heart.

"Look!" cried some one, and pointed skyward.

I glanced up, and behold ! The sky was streaked with bright green trails. They radiated from a point halfway between the western horizon and the zenith, and within the shining clouds of the meteor a streaming movement had begun, so that it seemed to be pouring both westwardly and back towards the east, with a crackling sound, as though the whole heaven was stippled over with phantom pistol-shots. It seemed to me then as if the meteor was coming to help me, descending with those thousand pistols like a curtain to fend off this unmeaning foolishness of the sea.

" Boom ! " went a gun on the big ironclad, and " boom ! " and the guns of the pursuing cruisers flashed in reply.

To glance up at that streaky, stirring light scum of the sky made one's head swim. I stood for a moment dazed, and more than a little giddy. I had a curious instant of purely speculative thought. Suppose, after all, the fanatics were right, and the world *was* coming to an end ! What a score that would be for Parload !

Then it came into my head that all these things were happening to consecrate my revenge ! The war below, the heavens above, were the thunderous garment of my deed. I heard Nettie's voice cry out not fifty yards away, and my passion surged again. I was to return to her amid these terrors bearing unanticipated death. I was to possess her, with a bullet, amidst thunderings and fear. At the thought I lifted up my voice to a shout that went unheard, and advanced now recklessly, revolver displayed in my hand.

It was fifty yards, forty yards, thirty yards—the little group of people, still heedless of me, was larger and more important now, the green-shot sky and the fighting ships remoter. Some one darted out from the bungalow, with an interrupted question, and stopped, suddenly aware of me. It was Nettie, with some coquettish dark wrap about her, and the green glare shining on her sweet face and white throat. I could see her expression, stricken with dismay and terror at my advance, as though something had seized her by the heart and held her still—a target for my shots.

" Boom ! " came the ironclad's gunshot like a command. " Bang ! " the bullet leaped from my hand. Do you know, I did not want to shoot her then ! Indeed I did not want to shoot her then ! Bang ! and I had fired again, still striding on, and—each time it seemed I had missed.

She moved a step or so towards me, still staring, and then some one intervened, and near beside her I saw young Verrall.

A heavy stranger, the man in the hooded bathgown, a fat, foreign-looking man, came out of nowhere like a shield before them. He seemed a preposterous interruption. His face was full of astonishment and terror. He rushed across my path with arms extended and open hands, as one might try to stop a runaway horse. He shouted some nonsense. He seemed to want.to dissuade me, as though dissuasion had anything to do with it now.

"Not you, you fool!" I said hoarsely. "Not you!" But he hid Nettie nevertheless.

By an enormous effort I resisted a mechanical impulse to shoot through his fat body. Anyhow, I knew I mustn't shoot him. For a moment I was in doubt, then I became very active, turned aside abruptly and dodged his pawing arm to the left, and so found two others irresolutely in my way. I fired a third shot in the air, just over their heads, and ran at them. They hastened left and right; I pulled up and faced about within a yard of a foxy-faced young man coming sideways, who seemed about to grapple me. At my resolute halt he fell back a pace, ducked, and threw up a defensive arm, and then I perceived the course was clear, and ahead of me, young Verrall and Nettie—he was holding her arm to help her—running away. "Of course!" said I.

I fired a fourth ineffectual shot, and then in an access of fury at my misses, started to run them down and shoot them barrel to backbone. "These people!" I said, dismissing all these interferences. . . . "A yard," I panted, speaking aloud to myself, "a yard! Till then, take care, you mustn't—mustn't shoot again."

Some one pursued me, perhaps several people—I do not know, we left them all behind. . . .

We ran. For a space I was altogether intent upon the swift monotony of flight and pursuit. The sands were changed to a whirl of green moonshine, the air was thunder. A luminous green haze rolled about us. What did such things matter? We ran. Did I gain or lose? that was the question. They ran through a gap in a broken fence that sprang up abruptly out of the nothingness, and turned to the right. I noted we were on a road. But this green mist! One seemed to plough through it. They were fading into it, and at that thought I made a spurt that won a dozen feet or more.

She staggered. He gripped her arm, and dragged her forward. They doubled to the left. We were off the road again and on turf. It felt like turf. I tripped and fell at a ditch that was somehow full of smoke, and was up again, but now they were phantoms half gone into the livid swirls about me. . . .

Still I ran.

On, on! I groaned with the violence of my effort. I staggered again and swore. I felt the concussions of great guns tear past me through the murk.

They were gone! Everything was going, but I kept on running. Once more I stumbled. There was something about my feet that impeded me, tall grass or heather, but I could not see what it was, only this smoke that eddied about my knees. There was a noise and spinning in my brain, a vain resistance to a dark green curtain that was falling, falling,

falling, fold upon fold. Everything grew darker and darker.

I made one last frantic effort, and raised my revolver, fired my penultimate shot at a venture, and fell headlong to the ground. And behold! the green curtain was a black one, and the earth and I and all things ceased to be.

Book Two
The Green Vapours

CHAPTER ONE

THE CHANGE

§ 1

I SEEMED to awaken out of a refreshing sleep.

I did not awaken with a start, but opened my eyes, and lay very comfortably looking at a line of extraordinarily scarlet poppies that glowed against a glowing sky. It was the sky of a magnificent sunrise, and an archipelago of gold-beached purple islands floated in a sea of golden green. The poppies too, swan-necked buds, blazing corollas, translucent stout seed-vessels, stoutly upheld, had a luminous quality, seemed wrought only from some more solid kind of light.

I stared wonderingly at these things for a time, and then there rose upon my consciousness, intermingling with these, the bristling golden green heads of growing barley.

A remote faint question, where I might be, drifted and vanished again in my mind. Everything was very still.

Everything was as still as death.

I felt very light, full of the sense of physical well-being. I perceived I was lying on my side in a little trampled space in a weedy, flowering barley field, that was in some inexplicable way saturated with light and beauty. I sat up and remained for a long time filled with the delight and charm of the delicate little convolvulus that twined among the barley stems, the pimpernel that laced the ground below.

Then that question returned. What was this place ? How had I come to be sleeping here ?

I could not remember.

It perplexed me that somehow my body felt strange to me. It was unfamiliar—I could not tell how—and the barley, and the beautiful weeds, and the slowly developing glory of the dawn behind ; all those things partook of the same unfamiliarity. I felt as though I was a thing in some very luminous painted window, as though this dawn broke through me. I felt I was part of some exquisite picture painted in light and joy.

A faint breeze bent and rustled the barley-heads and jogged my mind forward.

Who was I ? That was a good way of beginning.

I held up my left hand and arm before me, a grubby hand, a frayed cuff ; but with a quality of painted unreality, transfigured as a beggar might have been by Botticelli. I looked for a time steadfastly at a beautiful pearl sleeve-link.

I remembered Willie Leadford, who had owned that arm and hand, as though he had been some one else.

Of course ! My history—its rough outline rather than the

immediate past—began to shape itself in my memory, very small, very bright and inaccessible, like a thing watched through a microscope. Clayton and Swathinglea returned to my mind ; the slums and darkness, Düreresque, minute and in their rich dark colours pleasing, and through them I went towards my destiny. I sat hands on knees recalling that queer passionate career that had ended with my futile shot into the growing darkness of the End. The thought of that shot awoke my emotions again.

There was something in it now, something absurd, that made me smile pityingly.

Poor little angry, miserable creature ! Poor little angry, miserable world !

I sighed for pity, not only pity for myself, but for all the hot hearts, the tormented brains, the straining, striving things of hope and pain, who had found their peace at last beneath the pouring mist and suffocation of the comet. Because certainly that world was over and done. They were all so weak and unhappy, and I was now so strong and so serene. For I felt sure I was dead ; no one living could have this perfect assurance of good, this strong and confident peace. I had made an end of the fever called living. I was dead, and it was all right, and these—— ?

I felt an inconsistency.

These, then, must be the barley fields of God !—the still and silent barley fields of God, full of unfading poppy flowers whose seeds bear peace.

§ 2

It was queer to find barley fields in heaven, but no doubt there were many surprises in store for me.

How still everything was ! Peace ! The peace that passeth understanding. After all it had come to me ! But, indeed, everything was very still ! No birds sang. Surely I was alone in the world ! No birds sang. Yes, and all the distant sounds of life had ceased, the lowing of cattle, the barking of dogs. . . .

Something that was like fear beatified came into my heart. It was all right, I knew ; but to be alone ! I stood up and met the hot summons of the rising sun, hurrying towards me, as it were, with glad tidings, over the spikes of the barley. . . .

Blinded, I made a step. My foot struck something hard, and I looked down to discover my revolver, a blue-black thing, like a dead snake at my feet.

For a moment that puzzled me.

Then I clean forgot about it. The wonder of the quiet took possession of my soul. Dawn, and no birds singing !

How beautiful was the world ! How beautiful, but how still ! I walked slowly through the barley towards a line of elder bushes, wayfaring tree and bramble that made the hedge of the field. I noted as I passed along a dead shrew mouse, as it seemed to me, among the halms ; then a still toad. I was surprised that this did not leap aside from my footfalls, and I stooped and picked it up. Its body was limp like life, but it made no struggle, the brightness of its eye was veiled, it did not move in my hand.

It seems to me now that I stood holding that lifeless little creature for some time. Then very softly I stooped down and replaced it. I was trembling—trembling with a nameless emotion. I looked with quickened eyes closely among the barley stems, and behold, now everywhere I saw beetles, flies, and little creatures that did not move, lying as they fell when the vapours overcame them ; they seemed no more than painted things. Some were novel creatures to me. I was very unfamiliar with natural things. " My God ! " I cried ; " but is it only I——— ? "

And then at my next movement something squealed sharply. I turned about, but I could not see it, only I saw a little stir in a rut and heard the diminishing rustle of the unseen creature's flight. And at that I turned to my toad again, and its eye moved and it stirred. And presently, with infirm and hesitating gestures, it stretched its limbs and began to crawl away from me.

But wonder, that gentle sister of fear, had me now. I saw a little way ahead a brown and crimson butterfly perched upon a cornflower. I thought at first it was the breeze that stirred it, and then I saw its wings were quivering. And even as I watched it, it started into life, and spread itself, and fluttered into the air.

I watched it fly, a turn this way, a turn that, until suddenly it seemed to vanish. And now, life was returning to this thing and that on every side of me, with slow stretchings and bendings, with twitterings, with a little start and stir. . . .

I came slowly, stepping very carefully because of these drugged, feebly awakening things, through the barley to the hedge. It was a very glorious hedge, so that it held my eyes. It flowed along and interlaced like splendid music. It was rich with lupin, honeysuckle, campions, and ragged-robin ; bed straw, hops, and wild clematis twined and hung among its branches, and all along its ditch border the starry stitch-wort lifted its childish faces, and chorused in lines and masses. Never had I seen such a symphony of note-like flowers and tendrils and leaves. And suddenly in its depths, I heard a chirrup and the whirr of startled wings.

Nothing was dead, but everything had changed to beauty ! And I stood for a time with clean and happy eyes looking at the intricate delicacy before me and marvelling how richly God has made his worlds. . . .

" Tweedle-Tweezle," a lark had shot the stillness with his shining thread of song ; one lark, and then presently another, invisibly in the air, making out of that blue quiet a woven cloth of gold. . . .

The earth recreated—only by the reiteration of such phrases may I hope to give the intense freshness of that dawn. For a time I was altogether taken up with the beautiful details of being, as regardless of my old life of jealous passion and impatient sorrow as though I was Adam new made. I could tell you now with infinite particularity of the shut flowers that opened as I looked, of tendrils and grass blades, of a bluetit I picked up very tenderly—never before had I remarked the great delicacy of feathers—that presently disclosed its bright black eye and judged me, and perched, swaying fearlessly, upon my finger, and spread unhurried wings and flew away, and of a great ebullition of tadpoles in the ditch ; like all the things that lived beneath the water, they had passed unaltered through the Change. Amid such incidents, I lived those first great moments, losing for a time in the wonder of each little part the mighty wonder of the whole.

A path ran between hedge and barley, and along this, leisurely and content and glad, looking at this beautiful thing and that, moving a step and stopping, then moving on again, I came presently to a stile ; and deep below it, and overgrown, was a lane.

And on the worn oak of the stile was a round label, and on the label these words, " Swindells' G 90 Pills."

I sat myself astraddle on the stile, not fully grasping all the implications of these words. But they perplexed me even more than the revolver and my dirty cuff.

About me now the birds lifted up their little hearts and sang, ever more birds and more.

I read the label over and over again, and joined it to the fact that I still wore my former clothes, and that my revolver had been lying at my feet. One conclusion stared out at me. This was no new planet, no glorious hereafter such as I had supposed.   This beautiful wonderland was the world, the same old world of my rage and death ! But at least it was like meeting a familiar house-slut, washed and dignified, dressed in a queen's robes, worshipful and fine. . . .

It might be the old world indeed, but something new lay upon all things, a glowing certitude of health and happiness. It might be the old world, but the dust and fury of the old life was certainly done. At least I had no doubt of that.

I recalled the last phases of my former life, that darkling climax of pursuit and anger and universal darkness and the whirling green vapours of extinction. The comet had struck the earth and made an end to all things ; of that too I was assured.

But afterwards ? . . .

And now ?

The imaginations of my boyhood came back as speculative possibilities. In those days I had believed firmly in the necessary advent of a last day, a great coming out of the sky, trumpetings and fear, the Resurrection, and the Judgment. My roving fancy now suggested to me that this Judgment must have come and passed. That it had passed and in some manner missed me. I was left alone here, in a swept and garnished world (except, of course, for this label of Swindells') to begin again perhaps. . . .

No doubt Swindells had got his deserts.

My mind ran for a time on Swindells, on the imbecile push-fulness of that extinct creature, dealing in rubbish, covering the country-side with lies in order to get—what had he sought? —a silly, ugly, great house, a temper-destroying motor-car, a number of disrespectful, abject servants ; thwarted intrigues for a party-fund baronetcy as the crest of his life, perhaps. You cannot imagine the littleness of those former times ; their naïve, queer absurdities ! And for the first time in my existence I thought of these things without bitterness. In former days I had seen wickedness, I had seen tragedy, but now I saw only the extraordinary foolishness of the old life. The ludicrous side of human wealth and importance turned itself upon me, a shining novelty, poured down upon me like the sunrise, and engulfed me in laughter. Swindells ! Swindells, damned ! My vision of Judgment became a delightful bur-lesque. I saw the chuckling Angel sayer with his face veiled, and the corporeal presence of Swindells upheld amidst the laughter of the spheres. " Here's a thing, and a very pretty thing, and what's to be done with this very pretty thing ?" I saw a soul being drawn from a rotund, substantial-looking body like a whelk from its shell. . . .

I laughed loudly and long. And behold ! even as I laughed the keen point of things accomplished stabbed my mirth, and I was weeping, weeping aloud, convulsed with weeping, and the tears were pouring down my face.

§ 3

Everywhere the awakening came with the sunrise. We awakened to the gladness of the morning ; we walked dazzled in a light that was joy. Everywhere that was so. It was always morning. It was morning because, until the direct rays of the sun touched it, the changing nitrogen of our atmo-sphere did not pass into its permanent phase, and the sleepers lay as they had fallen. In its intermediate state the air hung inert, incapable of producing either revival or stupefaction, no longer green, but not yet changed to the gas that now lives in us. . . .

To every one, I think, came some parallel to the mental states I have already sought to describe—a wonder, an im-pression of joyful novelty. There was also very commonly a certain confusion of the intelligence, a difficulty in self-recognition. I remember clearly as I sat on my stile that presently I had the clearest doubts of my own identity and fell into the oddest metaphysical questionings. " If this be I," I said, " then how is it I am no longer madly seeking Nettie ? Nettie is now the remotest thing—and all my wrongs. Why have I suddenly passed out of all that passion ? Why does not the thought of Verrall quicken my pulses ? " . . .

I was only one of many millions who that morning had the same doubts. I suppose one knows one's self for one's self when one returns from sleep or insensibility by the familiarity of one's bodily sensations, and that morning all our most intimate bodily sensations were changed. The intimate chemical processes of life were changed, its nervous metaboly. For the fluctuating, uncertain, passion-darkened thought and feeling of the old time came steady, full-bodied, wholesome processes. Touch was different, sight was different, sound and all the senses were subtler ; had it not been that our thought was steadier and fuller, I believe great multitudes of men would have gone mad. But, as it was, we understood. The dominant impression I would convey in this account of the Change is one of enormous release, of a vast substantial exaltation. There was an effect, as it were, of light-headedness that was also clear-headedness, and the alteration in one's bodily sensations, instead of producing the mental obfuscation, the loss of identity that was a common mental trouble under former conditions, gave simply a new detachment from the tumid passions and entanglements of the personal life.

In this story of my bitter, restricted youth that I have been telling you, I have sought constantly to convey the narrowness, the intensity, the confusion, muddle, and dusty heat of the old world. It was quite clear to me, within an hour of my awakening, that all that was, in some mysterious way, over and done. That, too, was the common experience. Men stood up ; they took the new air into their lungs—a deep long breath, and the past fell from them ; they could forgive, they could disregard, they could attempt. . . . And it was no new thing, no miracle that sets aside the former order of the world. It was a change in material conditions, a change in the atmosphere, that at one bound had released them. Some of them it had released to death. . . . Indeed, man himself had changed not at all. We knew before the Change, the meanest knew, by glowing moments in ourselves and others, by histories and music and beautiful things, by heroic instances and splendid stories, how fine mankind could be, how fine almost any human being could upon occasion be ; but the poison in the air, its poverty in all the nobler elements which made such moments rare and remarkable—all that has changed. The air was changed, and the Spirit of Man that had drowsed and slumbered and dreamt dull and evil things, awakened, and stood with wonder-clean eyes, refreshed, looking again on life.

§ 4

The miracle of the awakening came to me in solitude, the laughter, and then the tears. Only after some time did I come upon another man. Until I heard his voice calling I did not seem to feel there were any other people in the world. All that seemed past, with all the stresses that were past. I had come out of the individual pit in which my shy egotism had lurked, I had overflowed to all humanity, I had seemed to be all humanity ; I had laughed at Swindells as I could have laughed at myself, and this shout that came to me seemed like the coming of an unexpected thought in my own mind. But when it was repeated I answered.

" I am hurt," said the voice, and I descended into the lane forthwith, and so came upon Melmount sitting near the ditch with his back to me.

Some of the incidental sensory impressions of that morning bit so deeply into my mind that I verily believe, when at last I face the greater mysteries that lie beyond this life, when the things of this life fade from me as the mists of the morning fade before the sun, these irrelevant petty details will be the last to leave me, will be the last wisps visible of that attenuating veil. I believe, for instance, I could match the fur upon the collar of his great motoring coat now, could paint the dull red tinge of his big cheek with his fair eye-lashes just catching the light and showing beyond. His hat was off, his dome-shaped head, with its smooth hair between red and extreme fairness, was bent forward in scrutiny of his twisted foot. His back seemed enormous. And there was something about the mere massive sight of him that filled me with liking.

" What's wrong ? " said I.

" I say," he said, in his full deliberate tones, straining round to see me and showing a profile, a well-modelled nose, a sensitive, clumsy, big lip, known to every caricaturist in the world. " I'm in a fix. I fell and wrenched my ankle. Where are you ? "

I walked round him and stood looking at his face. I perceived he had his gaiter and sock and boot off, the motor gauntlets had been cast aside, and he was kneading the injured part in an exploratory manner with his thick thumbs.

" By Jove ! " I said, " you're Melmount ! "

" Melmount ! " He thought. " That's my name," he said, without looking up. . . . " But it doesn't affect my ankle."

We remained silent for a few moments except for a grunt of pain from him.

" Do you know ? " I asked, " what has happened to things ?"

He seemed to complete his diagnosis. " It's not broken," he said.

" Do you know," I repeated, " what has happened to everything ? "

" No," he said, looking up at me incuriously for the first time.

" There's some difference—— "

" There's a difference." He smiled, a smile of unexpected pleasantness, and an interest was coming into his eyes. " I've been a little preoccupied with my own internal sensations. I remark an extraordinary brightness about things. Is that it ? "

" That's part of it. And a queer feeling, a clear-headed-ness—— "

He surveyed me and meditated gravely. " I woke up," he said, feeling his way in his memory.

" And I."

" I lost my way—I forgot quite how. There was a curious green fog." He stared at his foot, remembering. " Something to do with a comet. I was by a hedge in the darkness. Tried to run. . . . Then I must have pitched into this lane. Look ! " He pointed with his head. " There's a wooden rail new broken there. I must have stumbled over that out of the field above." He scrutinised this and concluded : " Yes. . . . "

" It was dark," I said, " and a sort of green gas came out of nothing everywhere. That is the last *I* remember."

" And then you woke up ? So did I. . . . In a state of great bewilderment. Certainly there's something odd in the air. I was—I was rushing along a road in a motor-car, very much excited and preoccupied. I got down—" He held out a triumphant finger. " Ironclads !

" *Now* I've got it ! We'd strung our fleet from here to Texel. We'd got right across them, and the Elbe mined. We'd lost the *Lord Warden*. By Jove, yes. The *Lord Warden* ! A battleship that cost two million pounds—and that fool Rigby said it didn't matter ! Eleven hundred men went down. . . . I remember now. We were sweeping up the North Sea like a net, with the North Atlantic fleet waiting at the Faroes for 'em—and not one of 'em had three days' coal ! Now, was that a dream ? No ! I told a lot of people as much—a meeting was it ?—to reassure them. They were warlike but extremely frightened. Queer people—paunchy and bald like gnomes, most of them. Where ? Of course ! We had it all over—a big dinner—oysters !—Colchester. I'd been there, just to show all this raid scare was nonsense. And I was coming back here. . . . But it doesn't seem as though that was—recent. I suppose it was. Yes, of course !—it was. I got out of my car at the bottom of the rise with the idea of walking along the cliff path, because every one said one of their battleships was being chased along the shore. That's clear ! I heard their guns—— "

He reflected. " Queer I should have forgotten ! Did *you* hear any guns ? "

I said I had heard them.

" Was it last night ? "

" Late last night. One or two in the morning."

He leaned back on his hand and looked at me, smiling frankly. " Even now," he said, " it's odd, but the whole of that seems like a silly dream. Do you think there *was* a *Lord Warden ?* Do you really believe we sank all that machinery —for fun ? It was a dream. And yet—it happened."

By all the standards of the former time it would have been remarkable that I talked quite easily and freely with so great a man. " Yes," I said ; " that's it. One feels one has awakened —from something more than that green gas. As though the other things also—weren't quite real."

He knitted his brows and felt the calf of his leg thoughtfully. " I made a speech at Colchester," he said.

I thought he was going to add something more about that, but there lingered a habit of reticence in the man that held him for the moment. " It is a very curious thing," he broke away, " that this pain should be, on the whole, more interesting than disagreeable."

" You are in pain ? "

" My ankle is ! It's either broken or badly sprained—I think sprained ; it's very painful to move, but personally I'm not in pain. That sort of general sickness that comes with local injury—not a trace of it ! . . . " He mused and remarked, " I was speaking at Colchester, and saying things about the war. I begin to see it better. The reporters—scribble, scribble. Max Sutaine, 1885. Hubbub. Compliments about the oysters. Mm—mm. . . . What was it ? About the war ? A war that must needs be long and bloody, taking toll from castle and cottage, taking toll ! . . . Rhetorical gusto ! Was I drunk last night ? "

His eyebrows puckered. He had drawn up his right knee, his elbow rested thereon and his chin on his fist. The deepset grey eyes beneath his thatch of eyebrow stared at unknown things. " My God ! " he murmured, " My God ! " with a note of disgust. He made a big brooding figure in the sunlight, he had an effect of more than physical largeness ; he made me feel that it became me to wait upon his thinking. I had never met a man of this sort before ; I did not know such men existed. . . .

It is a curious thing, that I cannot now recall any ideas whatever that I had before the Change about the personalities of statesmen, but I doubt if ever in those days I thought of them at all as tangible individual human beings, conceivably of some intellectual complexity. I believe that my impression was a straightforward blend of caricature and newspaper leader. I certainly had no respect for them. And now without servility or any insincerity whatever, as if it were a first-fruit of the Change, I found myself in the presence of a human being towards whom I perceived myself inferior and subordinate, before whom I stood without servility or any insincerity whatever, in an attitude of respect and attention. My inflamed, my rancid egotism—or was it after all only the chances of life ?—had never once permitted that before the Change.

He emerged from his thoughts, still with a faint perplexity in his manner. " That speech I made last night," he said, " was damned mischievous nonsense, you know. Nothing can alter that. Nothing. . . . No ! . . . Little fat gnomes in evening dress—gobbling oysters. Gulp ! "

It was a most natural part of the wonder of that morning that he should adopt this incredible note of frankness, and that it should abate nothing from my respect for him.

" Yes," he said, " you are right. It's all indisputable fact, and I can't believe it was anything but a dream."

§ 5

That memory stands out against the dark past of the world with extraordinary clearness and brightness. The air, I remember, was full of the calling and piping and singing of birds. I have a curious persuasion too that there was a distant happy clamour of pealing bells, but that I am half convinced is a mistake. Nevertheless, there was something in the fresh bite of things, in the dewy newness of sensation that set bells rejoicing in one's brain. And that big, fair, pensive man sitting on the ground had beauty even in his clumsy pose, as though indeed some Great Master of strength and humour had made him.

And—it is so hard now to convey these things—he spoke to me, a stranger, without reservations, carelessly, as men now speak to men. Before those days, not only did we think badly, but what we thought, a thousand short-sighted considerations, dignity, objective discipline, discretion, a hundred kindred aspects of shabbiness of soul, made us muffle before we told it to our fellow-men.

" It's all returning now," he said, and told me half soliloquisingly what was in his mind.

I wish I could give every word he said to me ; he struck out image after image to my nascent intelligence, with swift broken fragments of speech. If I had a precise full memory of that morning I should give it you, verbatim, minutely. But here, save for the little sharp things that stand out, I find only blurred general impressions. Throughout I have to make up again his half-forgotten sentences and speeches, and be content with giving you the general effect. But I can see and hear him now as he said, " The dream got worst at the end. The war—a perfectly horrible business ! Horrible ! And it was just like a nightmare, you couldn't do anything to escape from it—every one was driven ! "

His sense of indiscretion was gone.

He opened the war out to me—as every one sees it now. Only that morning it was astonishing. He sat there on the ground, absurdly forgetful of his bare and swollen foot, treating me as the humblest accessory and as altogether an equal, talking out to himself the great obsessions of his mind. " We could have prevented it ! Any of us who chose to speak out could have prevented it. A little decent frankness. What was there to prevent us being frank with one another ? Their emperor—his position was a pile of ridiculous assumptions, no doubt, but at bottom—he was a sane man." He touched off the emperor in a few pithy words, the German press, the German people, and our own. He put it as we should put it all now, but with a certain heat as of a man half guilty and wholly resentful. " Their damned little buttoned-up professors ! " he cried, incidentally. " Were there ever such men ? And ours ! Some of us might have taken a firmer line. . . . If a lot of us had taken a firmer line and squashed that nonsense early. . . . "

He lapsed into inaudible whisperings, into silence. . . .

I stood regarding him, understanding him, learning marvellously from him. It is a fact that for the best part of the morning of the Change I forgot Nettie and Verrall as completely as though they were no more than characters in some novel that I had put aside to finish at my leisure, in order that I might talk to this man.

" Eh, well," he said, waking startlingly from his thoughts. " Here we are awakened ! The thing can't go on now ; all this must end. How it ever began— ! My dear boy, how did all those things ever begin ? I feel like a new Adam. . . . Do you think this has happened—generally ? Or shall we find all these gnomes and things ? . . . Who cares ? "

He made as if to rise, and remembered his ankle. He suggested I should help him as far as his bungalow. There seemed nothing strange to either of us that he should requisition my services or that I should cheerfully obey. I helped him bandage his ankle, and we set out, I his crutch, the two of us making up a sort of limping quadruped, along the winding lane towards the cliffs and the sea.

§ 6

His bungalow beyond the golf links was, perhaps, a mile and a quarter from the lane. We went down to the beach margin and along the pallid wave-smoothed sands, and we got along by making a swaying, hopping, tripod dance forward until I began to give under him, and then, as soon as we could, sitting down. His ankle was, in fact, broken, and he could not put it to the ground without exquisite pain. So that it took us nearly two hours to get to the house, and it would have taken longer if his butler-valet had not come out to assist me. They had found motor-car and chauffeur smashed and still at the bend of the road near the house, and had been on that side looking for Melmount, or they would have seen us before.

For most of that time we were sitting now on turf, now on a chalk boulder, now on a timber groin, and talking one to the other with the frankness proper to the intercourse of men of good intent, without reservations or aggressions, in the common, open fashion of contemporary intercourse to-day, but which then, nevertheless, was the rarest and strangest thing in the world. He for the most part talked, but at some shape of a question I told him—as plainly as I could tell of passions that had for a time become incomprehensible to me—of my murderous pursuit of Nettie and her lover, and how the green vapours overcame me. He watched me with grave eyes and nodded understandingly, and afterwards he asked me brief penetrating questions about my education, my upbringing, my work. There was a deliberation in his manner, brief full pauses, that had in them no element ot delay.

" Yes," he said, " yes—of course. What a fool I have been ! " and said no more until we had made another of our tripod struggles along the beach. At first I did not see the connection of my story with that self-accusation.

" Suppose," he said, panting on the groin, " there had been such a thing as a statesman ! . . ."

He turned to me. " If one had decided all this muddle shall end ! If one had taken it, as an artist takes his clay, as a man who builds takes site and stone, and made—" He flung out his big broad hand at the glories of sky and sea, and drew a deep breath, " something to fit that setting."

He added in explanation, " Then there wouldn't have been such stories as yours at all, you know. . . .

" Tell me more about it," he said, " tell me all about yourself. I feel all these things have passed away, all these things are to be changed for ever. . . . You won't be what you have been from this time forth. All the things you have done—don't matter now. To us, at any rate, they don't matter at all. We have met, who were separated in that darkness behind us. Tell me.

" Yes," he said ; and I told my story straight and as frankly as I have told it to you. " And there, where those little skerries of weed rock run out to the ebb, beyond the headland, is Bungalow village. What did you do with your pistol ? "

" I left it lying there—among the barley."

He glanced at me from under his light eyelashes. " If others feel as you and I do," he said, " there'll be a lot of pistols left among the barley to-day. . . . "

So we talked, I and that great, strong man, with the love of brothers so plain between us it needed not a word. Our souls went out to one another in stark good faith ; never before had I had anything but a guarded watchfulness for any fellow-man. Still I see him upon that wild desolate beach of the ebb tide. I see him leaning against the shelly buttress of a groin, looking down at the poor drowned sailor whose body we presently found. For we found a newly drowned man who had just chanced to miss this great dawn in which we rejoiced. We found him lying in a pool of water, among brown weeds in the dark shadow of the timberings. You must not overrate the horrors of the former days ; in those days it was scarcely more common to see death in England than it would be to-day. This dead man was a sailor from the *Rother Adler*, the great German battleship that—had we but known it—lay not four miles away along the coast amidst ploughed-up mountains of chalk ooze, a torn and battered mass of machinery, wholly submerged at high water, and holding in its interstices nine hundred drowned brave men, all strong and skilful, all once capable of doing fine things. . . .

I remember that poor boy very vividly. He had been drowned during the anæsthesia of the green gas, his fair young face was quiet and calm, but the skin of his chest had been crinkled by scalding water and his right arm was bent queerly back. Even to this needless death and all its tale of cruelty, beauty and dignity had come. Everything flowed together to significance as we stood there. I, the ill-clad, cheaply equipped proletarian, and Melmount in his great fur-trimmed coat—he was hot with walking but he had not thought to remove it—leaning upon the clumsy groins and pitying this poor victim of the war he had helped to make. " Poor lad ! " he said, " poor lad ! A child we blunderers sent to death ! Do look at the quiet beauty of that face, that body—to be flung aside like this ! "

(I remember that near this dead man's hand a stranded star-fish writhed its slowly feeling limbs, struggling back toward the sea. It left grooved traces in the sand.)

" There must be no more of this," panted Melmount, leaning on my shoulder, " no more of this. . . . "

But most I recall Melmount as he talked a little later, sitting upon a great chalk boulder with the sunlight on his big, perspiration-dewed face. He made his resolves. " We must end war," he said, in that full whisper of his ; " it is stupidity. With so many people able to read and think—even as it is—there is no need of anything of the sort. Gods ! What have we rulers been at ? . . . Drowsing like people in a stifling room, too dull and sleepy and too base towards each other for any one to get up and open the window. What haven't we been at ? "

A great powerful figure he sits there still in my memory, perplexed and astonished at himself and all things. " We must change all this," he repeated, and threw out his broad hands in a comprehensive gesture. " We have done so weakly

—Heaven alone knows why ! " I can see him now, queer giant that he looked on that dawnlit beach of splendour, the sea birds flying about us and that crumpled death hard by, no bad symbol in his clumsiness and needless heat of the unawakened powers of the former time. I remember it as an integral part of that picture that far away across the sandy stretches one of those white estate boards I have described, stuck up a little askew amidst the yellow-green turf upon the crest of the low cliffs.

He talked with a sort of wonder of the former things. " Has it ever dawned upon you to imagine the pettiness—the pettiness !—of every soul concerned in a declaration of war ? " he asked. He went on, as though speech was necessary to make it credible, to describe Laycock, who first gave the horror words at the cabinet council, " an undersized Oxford prig with a tenoring voice and a garbage of Greek—the sort of fool who is brought up on the admiration of his elder sisters. . . .

" All the time almost," he said, " I was watching him—thinking what an ass he was to be trusted with men's lives. . . . I might have done better to have thought that of myself. I was doing nothing to prevent it all ! The damned imbecile was up to his neck in the drama of the thing, he liked to trumpet it out, he goggled round at us. ' Then it is war ! ' he said. Rich-over shrugged his shoulders. I made some slight protest and gave ·in. . . . Afterwards I dreamt of him.

" What a lot we were ! All a little scared at ourselves—all, as it were, instrumental. . . .

" And it's fools like that lead to things like this ! " He jerked his head at that dead man near by us.

" It will be interesting to know what has happened to the world. . . . This green vapour—queer stuff. But I know what has happened to me. It's Conversion. I've always known. . . . But this is being a fool. Talk ! I'm going to stop it."

He motioned to rise with his clumsy outstretched hands.

" Stop what ? " said I, stepping forward instinctively to help him.

" War," he said in his great whisper, putting his big hand on my shoulder but making no further attempt to rise, " I'm going to put an end to war—to any sort of war ! And all these things that must end. The world is beautiful, life is great and splendid, we had only to lift up our eyes and see. Think of the glories through which we have been driving, like a herd of swine in a garden place. The colour in life—the sounds—the shapes ! We have had our jealousies, our quarrels, our ticklish rights, our invincible prejudices, our vulgar enterprise and sluggish timidities, we have chattered and pecked one another and fouled the world—like daws in the temple, like unclean birds in the holy place of God. All my life has been foolishness and pettiness, gross pleasures and mean discretions

—all. I am a meagre dark thing in this morning's glow, a penitence, a shame! And, but for God's mercy, I might have died this 'night—like that poor lad there—amidst the squalor of my sins! No more of this! No more of this!—whether the whole world has changed or no, matters nothing. *We two have seen this dawn! . . .*"

He paused.

" I will arise and go unto my Father," he began presently, " and will say unto Him——"

His voice died away in an inaudible whisper. His hand tightened painfully on my shoulder and he rose. . . .

CHAPTER TWO

THE AWAKENING

§ 1

So the great Day came to me.

And even as I had awakened so in that same dawn the whole world awoke.

For the whole world of living things had been overtaken by the same tide of insensibility ; in an hour, at the touch of this new gas in the comet, the shiver of catalytic change had passed about the globe. They say it was the nitrogen of the air, the old *azote*, that in the twinkling of an eye was changed out of itself, and in an hour or so became a respirable gas, differing indeed from oxygen, but helping and sustaining its action, a bath of strength and healing for nerve and brain. I do not know the precise changes that occurred, nor the names our chemists gave them ; my work has carried me away from such things ; only this I know—I and all men were renewed.

I picture to myself this thing happening in space, a planetary moment, the faint smudge, the slender whirl of meteor, drawing nearer to this planet,—this planet like a ball, like a shaded rounded ball, floating in the void, with its little, nearly impalpable coat of cloud and air, with its dark pools of ocean, its gleaming ridges of land. And as that midge from the void touches it, the transparent gaseous outer shell clouds in an instant green and then slowly clears again. . . .

Thereafter, for three hours or more,—we know the minimum time for the Change was almost exactly three hours because all the clocks and watches kept going—everywhere, no man nor beast nor bird nor any living thing that breathes the air stirred at all but lay still. . . .

Everywhere on earth that day, in the ears of every one who breathed, there had been the same humming in the air, the same rush of green vapours, the crepitation, the streaming down of shooting stars. The Hindoo had stayed his mornings work in the fields to stare and marvel and fall, the blue-clothed Chinaman fell head foremost athwart his midday bowl of rice, the Japanese merchant came out from some chaffering in his office amazed and presently lay there before his door, the evengazers by the Golden Gates were overtaken as they waited for the rising of the great star. This had happened in every city of the world, in every lonely valley, in every home and house and shelter and every open place. On the high seas, the crowding steamship passengers, eager for any wonder, gaped and marvelled, and were suddenly terror-stricken, and struggled for the gangways and were overcome ; the captain staggered on the bridge and fell, the stoker fell headlong among his coals, the engines throbbed upon their way untended, the fishing craft drove by without a hail, with swaying rudder, heeling and dipping. . . .

The great voice of material Fate cried Halt ! And in the midst of the play the actors staggered, dropped, and were still. The figure runs from my pen. In New York that very thing occurred. Most of the theatrical audiences dispersed, but in two crowded houses the company, fearing a panic, went on playing amidst the gloom, and the people, trained by many a previous disaster, stuck to their seats. There they sat, the back rows only moving a little, and there, in disciplined lines, they drooped and failed, nodded, and fell forward or slid down upon the floor. I am told by Parload—though indeed I know nothing of the reasoning on which his inference rests —that within an hour of the great moment of impact the first green modification of nitrogen had dissolved and passed away, leaving the air as translucent as ever. The rest of that wonderful interlude was clear, had any had eyes to see its clearness. In London it was night ; but in New York, for example, people were in the full bustle of the evening's enjoyment, in Chicago they were sitting down to dinner, the whole world was abroad. The moonlight must have illuminated streets and squares littered with crumpled figures, through which such electric cars as had no automatic brakes had ploughed on their way until they were stopped by the fallen bodies. People lay in their dress clothes, in dining-rooms, restaurants, on staircases, in halls, everywhere just as they had been overcome. Men gambling, men drinking, thieves lurking in hidden places, sinful couples, were caught, to arise with awakened mind and conscience amidst the disorder of their sin. America the comet reached in the full tide of evening life, but Britain lay asleep. But as I have told, Britain did not slumber so deeply but that she was in the full tide of what may have been battle and a great victory. Up and down the North Sea her warships swept together like a net about their foes. On land, too, that night was to have decided great issues. The German camps were under arms from Redingen to Markirch, their infantry columns were lying in swathes like mown hay, in arrested

night march on every track between Longnyon and Thian-
court, and between Avricourt and Donen. The hills beyond
Spincourt were dusted thick with hidden French riflemen ;
the thin lash of the French skirmishers sprawled out amidst
spades and unfinished rifle-pits in coils that wrapped about
the heads of the German columns, thence along the Vosges
watershed and out across the frontier near Belfort nearly to
the Rhine. . . .

The Hungarian, the Italian peasant, yawned and thought
the morning dark, and turned over to fall into a dreamless
sleep ; the Mahometan world spread its carpet and was taken
in prayer. And in Sydney, in Melbourne, in New Zealand,
the thing was a fog in the afternoon, that scattered the crowd
on racecourses and cricket-fields, and stopped the unloading
of shipping and brought men out from their afternoon rest
to stagger and litter the streets. . . .

§ 2

My thoughts go into the woods and wildernesses and jungles
of the world, to the wild life that shared man's suspension,
and I think of a thousand feral acts interrupted and truncated
—as it were frozen, like the frozen words Pantagruel met at
sea. Not only men it was that were quieted, all living creatures
that breathe the air became insensible, impassive things.
Motionless brutes and birds lay amidst the drooping trees and
herbage in the universal twilight, the tiger sprawled beside
his fresh-struck victim, who bled to death in a dreamless
sleep. The very flies came sailing down the air with wings
outspread ; the spider hung crumpled in his loaded net ; like
some gaily painted snowflake the butterfly drifted to earth
and grounded, and was still. And as a queer contrast one
gathers that the fishes in the sea suffered not at all. . . .

Speaking of the fishes reminds me of a queer little inset
upon that great world-dreaming. The odd fate of the crew of
the submarine vessel B 94 has always seemed memorable to
me. So far as I know, they were the only men alive who
never saw that veil of green drawn across the world. All the
while that the stillness held above, they were working into
the mouth of the Elbe, past the booms and the mines, very
slowly and carefully, a sinister crustacean of steel, explosive
crammed, along the muddy bottom. They trailed a long clue
that was to guide their fellows from the mother ship floating
awash outside. Then in the long channel beyond the forts
they came up at last to mark down their victims and get air.
That must have been before the twilight of dawn, for they
tell of the brightness of the stars. They were amazed to find
themselves not three hundred yards from an ironclad that
had run ashore in the mud, and heeled over with the falling
tide. It was afire amidships, but no one heeded that—no one

in all that strange clear silence heeded that—and not only
this wrecked vessel, but all the dark ships lying about them,
it seemed to their perplexed and startled minds, must be full
of dead men !

Theirs I think must have been one of the strangest of all
experiences ; they were never insensible ; at once, and, I am
told, with a sudden catch of laughter, they began to breathe
the new air. None of them has proved a writer ; we have no
picture of their wonder, no description of what was said. But
we know these men were active and awake for an hour and a
half at least before the general awakening came, and when at
last the Germans stirred and sat up they found these strangers
in possession of their battleship, the submarine carelessly
adrift, and the Englishmen, begrimed and weary, but with a
sort of furious exultation, still busy in the bright dawn, rescuing
insensible enemies from the sinking conflagration. . . .

But the thought of certain stokers the sailors of the submarine failed altogether to save brings me back to the thread
of grotesque horror that runs through all this event, the
thread I cannot overlook for all the splendours of human
well-being that have come from it. I cannot forget the un-
guided ships that drove ashore, that went down in disaster
with all their sleeping hands, nor how, inland, motor-cars
rushed to destruction upon the roads, and trains upon the
railways kept on in spite of signals, to be found at last by
their amazed, reviving drivers standing on unfamiliar lines,
their fires exhausted, or, less lucky, to be discovered by astonished peasants or awakening porters smashed and crumpled
up into heaps of smoking, crackling ruin. The foundry fires
of the Four Towns still blazed, the smoke of our burning still
defiled the sky. Fires burned indeed the brighter for the
Change—and spread. . . .

§ 3

Picture to yourself what happened between the printing
and composing of the copy of the *New Paper* that lies before
me now. It was the first newspaper that was printed upon
earth after the Great Change. It is pocket-worn and browned,
made of a paper no man ever intended for preservation. I
found it on the arbour table in the inn garden while I was
waiting for Nettie and Verrall, before that last conversation
of which I have presently to tell. As I look at it all that scene
comes back to me, and Nettie stands in her white raiment
against a blue-green background of sunlit garden, scrutinising
my face as I read. . . .

It is so frayed that the sheet cracks along the folds and
comes to pieces in my hands. It lies upon my desk, a dead
souvenir of the dead ages of the world, of the ancient passions
of my heart. I know we discussed its news, but for the life of

me I cannot recall what we said, only I remember that Nettie said very little, and that Verrall for a time read it over my shoulder. And I did not like him to read over my shoulder. . . .

The document before me must have helped us through the first awkwardness of that meeting.

But of all that we said and did then I must tell in a later chapter. . . .

It is easy to see the *New Paper* had been set up overnight, and then large pieces of the stereo plates replaced subsequently. I do not know enough of the old methods of printing to know precisely what happened. The thing gives one an impression of large pieces of type having been cut away and replaced by fresh blocks. There is something very rough and ready about it all, and the new portions print darker and more smudgily than the old, except towards the left, where they have missed ink and indented. A friend of mine, who knows something of the old typography, has suggested to me that the machinery actually in use for the *New Paper* was damaged that night, and that on the morning of the Change Banghurst borrowed a neighbouring office—perhaps in financial dependence upon him—to print in.

The outer pages belong entirely to the old period, the only parts of the paper that had undergone alteration are the two middle leaves. Here we found set forth in a curious little four-column oblong of print, WHAT HAS HAPPENED. This cut across a column with scare headings beginning, " Great Naval Battle Now in Progress. The Fate of Two Empires in the Balance. Reported Loss of Two More——"

These things, one gathered, were beneath notice now. Probably it was guesswork, and fabricated news in the first instance.

It is curious to piece together the worn and frayed fragments, and reread this discoloured first intelligence of the new epoch.

The simple clear statements in the replaced portion of the paper impressed me at the time, I remember, as bald and strange, in that framework of shouting bad English. Now they seem like the voice of a sane man amidst a vast faded violence. But they witness to the prompt recovery of London from the gas ; the new, swift energy of rebound in that huge population. I am surprised now, as I reread, to note how much research, experiment, and induction must have been accomplished in the day that elapsed before the paper was printed. . . . But that is by the way. As I sit and muse over this partly carbonised sheet, that same curious remote vision comes again to me that quickened in my mind that morning, a vision of those newspaper offices I have already described to you going through the crisis.

The catalytic wave must have caught the place in full swing, in its nocturnal high fever ; indeed in a quite exceptional state of fever, what with the comet and the war, and more particularly with the war. Very probably the Change crept into the office imperceptibly, amidst the noise and shouting, and the glare of electric light that made the night atmosphere in that place ; even the green flashes may have passed unobserved there, the preliminary descending trails of green vapour seemed no more than unseasonable drifting wisps of London fog. (In those days London even in summer was not safe against dark fogs.) And then at the last the Change poured in and overtook them.

If there was any warning at all for them, it must have been a sudden universal tumult in the street, and then a much more universal quiet. They could have had no other intimation.

There was no time to stop the presses before the main development of green vapour had overwhelmed every one. It must have folded about them, tumbled them to the earth, masked and stilled them. My imagination is always curiously stirred by the thought of that, because I suppose it is the first picture I succeeded in making for myself of what had happened in the towns. It has never quite lost its strangeness for me that when the Change came, machinery went on working. I don't precisely know why that should have seemed so strange to me, but it did, and still to a certain extent does. One is so accustomed, I suppose, to regard machinery as an extension of human personality that the extent of its autonomy the Change displayed came as a shock to me. The electric lights, for example, hazy green-haloed nebulæ, must have gone on burning at least for a time ; amidst the thickening darkness the huge presses must have roared on, printing, folding, throwing aside copy after copy of that fabricated battle report with its quarter column of scare headlines, and all the place must have still quivered and throbbed with the familiar roar of the engines. And this though no men ruled there at all any more ! Here and there beneath that thickening fog the crumpled or outstretched forms of men lay still.

A wonderful thing that would have seemed, had any man been able to resist the vapour, and could he have walked amidst it.

And soon the machines must have exhausted their feed of ink and paper, and thumped and banged and rattled emptily amidst the general quiet. Then, I suppose, the furnaces failed for want of stoking, the steam pressure fell in the pistons, the machinery slackened, the lights burned dim, and came and went with the ebb of energy from the power-station. Who can tell precisely the sequence of these things now ?

And then, you know, amidst the weakening and terminating noises of men, the green vapour cleared and vanished, in an hour indeed it had gone, and it may be a breeze stirred and blew and went about the earth.

The noises of life were all dying away, but some there were that abated nothing, that sounded triumphantly amidst the universal ebb. To a heedless world the church towers tolled out two and then three. Clocks ticked and chimed everywhere about the earth to deafened ears. . . .

And then came the first flush of morning, the first rustlings of the revival. Perhaps in that office the filaments of the lamps were still glowing, the machinery was still pulsing weakly, when the crumpled, booted heaps of cloth became men again and began to stir and stare. The chapel of the printers was, no doubt, shocked to find itself asleep. Amidst that dazzling dawn the *New Paper* woke to wonder, stood up and blinked at its amazing self. . . .

The clocks of the city churches, one pursuing another, struck four. The staffs, crumpled and dishevelled, but with a strange refreshment in their veins, stood about the damaged machinery, marvelling and questioning ; the editor read his overnight headlines with incredulous laughter. There was much involuntary laughter that morning. Outside, the mail men patted the necks and rubbed the knees of their awakening horses. . . .

Then, you know, slowly and with much conversation and doubt, they set about to produce the paper.

Imagine those bemused, perplexed people, carried on by the inertia of their old occupations and doing their best with an enterprise that had suddenly become altogether extraordinary and irrational. They worked amidst questionings, and yet light-heartedly. At every stage there must have been interruptions for discussion. The paper only got down to Menton five days late.

§ 4

Then let me give you a vivid little impression I received of a certain prosaic person, a grocer named Wiggins, and how he passed through the Change. I heard this man's story in the post-office at Menton, when, in the afternoon of the First Day, I bethought me to telegraph to my mother. The place was also a grocer's shop, and I found him and the proprietor talking as I went in. They were trade competitors, and Wiggins had just come across the street to break the hostile silence of a score of years. The sparkle of the Change was in their eyes, their slightly flushed cheeks, their more elastic gestures, spoke of new physical influences that had invaded their beings.

" It did us no good, all our hatred," Mr. Wiggins said to me, explaining the emotion of their encounter ; " it did our customers no good. I've come to tell him that. You bear that in mind, young man, if ever you come to have a shop of your own. It was a sort of stupid bitterness possessed us, and I can't make out we didn't see it before in that light. Not so much downright wickedness it wasn't as stupidity. A stupid jealousy! Think of it!—two human beings within a stone's throw, who have not spoken for twenty years, hardening our hearts against each other!"

" I can't think how we came to such a state, Mr. Wiggins," said the other, packing tea into pound packets out of mere habit as he spoke. " It was wicked pride and obstinacy. We *knew* it was foolish all the time."

I stood affixing the adhesive stamp to my telegram.

" Only the other morning," he went on to me, " I was cutting French eggs. Selling at a loss to do it. He'd marked down with a great staring ticket to ninepence a dozen—I saw it as I went past. Here's my answer!" He indicated a ticket. " ' Eightpence a dozen—same as sold elsewhere for ninepence. A whole penny down, bang off! Just a touch above cost—if that—and even then— " He leaned over the counter to say impressively, " *Not the same eggs!* "

" Now, what people in their senses would do things like that? " said Mr. Wiggins.

I sent my telegram; the proprietor despatched it for me, and while he did so I fell exchanging experiences with Mr. Wiggins. He knew no more than I did then the nature of the Change that had come over things. He had been alarmed by the green flashes, he said, so much so that after watching for a time from behind his bedroom window blind, he had got up and hastily dressed and made his family get up also, so that they might be ready for the end. He made them put on their Sunday clothes. They all went out into the garden together, their minds divided between admiration at the gloriousness of the spectacle and a great and growing awe. They were Dissenters, and very religious people out of business hours, and it seemed to them in those last magnificent moments that, after all, science must be wrong and the fanatics right. With the green vapours came conviction, and they prepared to meet their God. . . .

This man, you must understand, was a common-looking man, in his shirt-sleeves and with an apron about his paunch, and he told his story in an Anglian accent that sounded mean and clipped to my Staffordshire ears : he told his story without a thought of pride, and as it were incidentally, and yet he gave me a vision of something heroic.

These people did not run hither and thither as many others did. The four of them stood beyond their back door in their garden pathway between the gooseberry bushes, with the terrors of their God and His Judgments closing in upon them, swiftly and wonderfully—and there they began to sing. There they stood, father and mother and two daughters, chanting out stoutly, but no doubt a little flatly after the manner of their kind—

" In Zion's Hope abiding,
My soul in Triumph sings——— "

until one by one they fell, and lay still.

The postmaster had heard them in the gathering darkness,
" In Zion's Hope abiding." . . .

It was the most extraordinary thing in the world to hear
this flushed and happy-eyed man telling that story of his
recent death. It was like a scene shown to me, very small
and very distinctly painted, in a locket.

But that effect was not confined to this particular incident.
A vast number of things that had happened before the coming
of the comet had undergone the same transfiguring reduction.
Other people, too, I have learned since, had the same illusion,
a sense of enlargement. It seems to me even now that the
little dark creature who had stormed across England in pursuit
of Nettie and her lover must have been about an inch high,
that all that previous life of ours had been an ill-lit marionette
show, acted in the twilight. . . .

§ 5

The figure of my mother comes always into my conception
of the Change.

I remember how one day she confessed herself.

She had been very sleepless that night, she said, and took
the reports of the falling stars for shooting ; there had been
rioting in Clayton and through Swathinglea all day, and so
she got out of bed to look. She had a dim sense that I must
certainly be mixed up in that trouble.

But she was not looking when the Change came.

" When I saw the stars a-raining down, dear," she said,
" and thought of you out in it, I thought there'd be no harm
in saying a prayer for you, dear ? I thought you wouldn't
mind that."

And so I got another of my pictures—the green vapours
come and go, and there by her patched coverlet that dear
old woman kneels and droops, still clasping her poor gnarled
hands in the attitude of prayer—prayer to IT—for me !

Through the meagre curtains and blinds of the flawed refracting window I see the stars above the chimneys fade, the
pale light of dawn creeps into the sky, and her candle flares
and dies. . . .

That also went with me through the stillness—that silent
kneeling figure, that frozen prayer to God to shield me, silent
in a silent world, rushing through the emptiness of space. . . .

§ 6

With the dawn that awakening went about the earth. I
have told how it came to me, and how I walked in wonder

through the transfigured cornfields of Shaphambury. It came to every one. Near me, and for the time clean forgotten by me, Verrall and Nettie woke—woke near one another; each heard before all other sounds the other's voice amidst the stillness and the light. And the scattered people who had run to and fro, and fallen on the beach of Bungalow village, awoke; the sleeping villagers of Menton started, and sat up in that unwonted freshness and newness; the contorted figures in the garden, with the hymn still upon their lips, stirred amidst the flowers, and touched each other timidly, and thought of Paradise. My mother found herself crouched against the bed, and rose—rose with a glad invincible conviction of accepted prayer. . . .

Already, when it came to us, the soldiers, crowded between the lines of dusty poplars along the road to Allarmont, were chatting and sharing coffee with the French riflemen, who had hailed them from their carefully hidden pits among the vineyards up the slopes of Beauville. A certain perplexity had come to these marksmen, who had dropped asleep tensely ready for the rocket that should wake the whir and rattle of their magazines. At the sight and sound of the stir and human confusion in the roadway below, it had come to each man individually that he could not shoot. One conscript, at least, has told his story of his awakening, and how curious he thought the rifle there beside him in his pit, how he took it on his knees to examine. Then, as his memory of its purpose grew clearer, he dropped the thing, and stood up with a kind of joyful horror at the crime escaped, to look more closely at the men he was to have assassinated. " *Brave types*," he thought, they looked for such a fate. The summoning rocket never flew. Below, the men did not fall into ranks again, but sat by the roadside, or stood in groups talking, discussing with a novel incredulity the ostensible causes of the war. " The Emperor ! " said they; and " Oh, nonsense ! We're civilised men. Get some one else for this job ! . . . Where's the coffee ? "

The officers held their own horses, and talked to the men frankly, regardless of discipline. Some Frenchmen out of the rifle-pits came sauntering down the hill. Others stood doubtfully, rifles still in hand. Curious faces scanned these latter. Little arguments sprang as : " Shoot at us ! Nonsense ! They're respectable French citizens." There is a picture of it all, very bright and detailed in the morning light, in the battle gallery amidst the ruins at old Nancy, and one sees the old-world uniform of the " soldier," the odd caps and belts and boots, the ammunition-belt, the water-bottle, the sort of tourist's pack the men carried, a queer elaborate equipment. The soldiers had awakened one by one, first one and then another. I wonder sometimes whether, perhaps, if the two armies had come awake in an instant, the battle, by mere habit and inertia, might not have begun. But the men who

waked first, sat up, looked about them in astonishment, had
time to think a little. . . .

§ 7

Everywhere there was laughter, everywhere tears.

Men and women in the common life, finding themselves
suddenly lit and exalted, capable of doing what had hitherto
been impossible, incapable of doing what had hitherto been
irresistible, happy, hopeful, unselfishly energetic, rejected
altogether the supposition that this was merely a change in
the blood and material texture of life. They denied the bodies
God had given them, as once the Upper Nile savages struck
out their canine teeth because these made them like the beasts.
They declared that this was the coming of a spirit, and nothing
else would satisfy their need for explanations. And in a sense
the Spirit came. The Great Revival sprang directly from the
Change—the last, the deepest, widest, and most enduring of
all the vast inundations of religious emotion that go by that
name.

But indeed it differed essentially from its innumerable
predecessors. The former revivals were a phase of fever,
this was the first movement of health, it was altogether quieter,
more intellectual, more private, more religious than any of
those others. In the old time, and more especially in the
Protestant countries where the things of religion were out-
spoken, and the absence of confession and well-trained priests
made religious states of emotion explosive and contagious,
revivalism upon various scales was a normal phase in the
religious life, revivals were always going on—now a little
disturbance of consciences in a village, now an evening of
emotion in a Mission Room, now a great storm that swept a
continent, and now an organised effort that came to town
with bands and banners and handbills and motor-cars for the
saving of souls. Never at any time did I take part in nor was
I attracted by any of these movements. My nature, although
passionate, was too critical (or sceptical if you like, for it
amounts to the same thing) and shy to be drawn into these
whirls ; but on several occasions Parload and I sat, scoffing
but nevertheless disturbed, in the back seats of revivalist
meetings.

I saw enough of them to understand their nature, and I
am not surprised to learn now that before the comet came,
all about the world, even among savages, even among can-
nibals, these same, or at any rate closely similar, periodic
upheavals went on. The world was stifling ; it was in a fever,
and these phenomena were neither more nor less than the
instinctive struggle of the organism against the ebb of its
powers, the clogging of its veins, the limitation of its life.
Invariably these revivals followed periods of sordid and
restricted living. Men obeyed their base immediate motives

until the world grew unendurably bitter. Some disappointment, some thwarting, lit up for them—darkly indeed, but
yet enough for indistinct vision—the crowded squalor, the
dark enclosure of life. A sudden disgust with the insensate
smallness of the old-world way of living, a realisation of sin,
a sense of the unworthiness of all individual things, a desire
for something comprehensive, sustaining, something greater,
for wider communions and less habitual things, filled them.
Their souls, which were shaped for wider issues, cried out
suddenly amidst the petty interests, the narrow prohibitions,
of life, " Not this ! not this ! " A great passion to escape
from the jealous prison of themselves, an inarticulate, stammering, weeping passion shook them. . . .

I have seen—— I remember how once in Clayton Calvinistic
Methodist chapel I saw—his spotty fat face strangely distorted under the flickering gas-flares—old Pallet the iron-
monger repent. He went to the form of repentance, a bench
reserved for such exhibitions, and slobbered out his sorrow
and disgust for some sexual indelicacy—he was a widower—
and I can see now how his loose fat body quivered and swayed
with his grief. He poured it out to five hundred people, from
whom in common times he hid his every thought and purpose.
And it is a fact, it shows where reality lay, that we two youngsters laughed not at all at that blubbering grotesque, we did
not even think the distant shadow of a smile. We two sat
grave and intent—perhaps wondering.

Only afterwards with an effort did we scoff. . . .

Those old-time revivals were, I say, the convulsive movements of a body that suffocates. They are the clearest manifestations from before the Change of a sense in all men that
things were not right. But they were too often but momentary
illuminations. Their force spent itself in inco-ordinated shouting, gesticulations, tears. They were but flashes of outlook.
Disgust of the narrow life, of all baseness, took shape in narrowness and baseness. The quickened soul ended the night a
hypocrite ; prophets disputed for precedence ; seductions,
it is altogether indisputable, were frequent among penitents !
and Ananias went home converted and returned with a falsified
gift. And it was almost universal that the converted should
be impatient and immoderate, scornful of reason and any
choice of expedients, opposed to balance, skill, and knowledge.
Incontinently full of grace, like thin old wine-skins over-
filled, they felt they must burst if once they came into contact
with hard fact and sane direction.

So the former revivals spent themselves ; but the Great
Revival did not spend itself, but grew to be, for the majority
of Christendom at least, the permanent expression of the
Change. For many it has taken the shape of an outright
declaration that this was the Second Advent—it is not for
me to discuss the validity of that suggestion, for nearly all it

has amounted to an enduring broadening of the issues of life. . . .

§ 8

One irrelevant memory comes back to me, irrelevant, and yet by some subtle trick of quality it summarises the Change for me. It is the memory of a woman's very beautiful face, a woman with a flushed face and tear-bright eyes who went by me without speaking, rapt in some secret purpose. I passed her when in the afternoon of the first day, struck by a sudden remorse, I went down to Menton to send a telegram to my mother telling her all was well with me. Whither this woman went I do not know, nor whence she came ; I never saw her again, and only her face, glowing with that new and luminous resolve, stands out for me. . . .

But that expression was the world's.

CHAPTER THREE

THE CABINET COUNCIL

§ 1

A ND what a strange unprecedented thing was that cabinet council at which I was present, the council that was held two days later in Melmount's bungalow, and which convened the conference to frame the constitution of the World State. I was there because it was convenient for me to stay with Melmount. I had nowhere to go particularly, and there was no one at his bungalow, to which his broken ankle confined him, but a secretary and a valet to help him to begin his share of the enormous labours that evidently lay before the rulers of the world. I wrote shorthand, and as there was not even a phonograph available, I went in so soon as his ankle had been dressed, and sat at his desk to write at his dictation. It is characteristic of the odd slackness that went with the spasmodic violence of the old epoch, that the secretary could not use shorthand and that there was no telephone whatever in the place. Every message had to be taken to the village post-office in that grocer's shop at Menton, half a mile away. . . . So I sat in the back of Melmount's room, his desk had been thrust aside, and made such memoranda as were needed. At that time his room seemed to me the most beautifully furnished in the world, and I could identify now the vivid cheerfulness of the chintz of the sofa on which the great statesman lay just in front of me, the fine rich paper, the red sealing-wax, the silver equipage of the desk I used. I know now that my presence in that room was a strange and remarkable thing, the open door, even the coming and going of

Parker the secretary, innovations. In the old days a cabinet council was a secret conclave, secrecy and furtiveness were in the texture of all public life. In the old days everybody was always keeping something back from somebody, being wary and cunning, prevaricating, misleading—for the most part for no reason at all. Almost unnoticed, that secrecy had dropped out of life.

I close my eyes and see those men again, hear their deliberating voices. First I see them a little diffusely in the cold explicitness of daylight, and then concentrated and drawn together amidst the shadow and mystery about shaded lamps. Integral to this and very clear is the memory of biscuit crumbs and a drop of spilt water, that at first stood shining upon and then sank into the green table-cloth. . . .

I remember particularly the figure of Lord Adisham. He came to the bungalow a day before the others, because he was Melmount's personal friend. Let me describe this statesman to you, this one of the fifteen men who made the last war. He was the youngest member of the Government, and an altogether pleasant and sunny man of forty. He had a clear profile to his clean grey face, a smiling eye, a friendly, careful voice upon his thin, clean-shaven lips, an easy disabusing manner. He had the perfect quality of a man who had fallen easily into a place prepared for him. He had the temperament of what we used to call a philosopher—an indifferent, that is to say. The Change had caught him at his week-end recreation, fly-fishing ; and, indeed, he said, I remember, that he recovered to find himself with his head within a yard of the water's brim. In times of crisis Lord Adisham invariably went fly-fishing at the week-end to keep his mind in tone, and when there was no crisis then there was nothing he liked so much to do as fly-fishing, and so, of course, as there was nothing to prevent it, he fished. He arrived resolved, among other things, to give up fly-fishing altogether. I was present when he came to Melmount, and heard him say as much ; and by a more naïve route it was evident that he had arrived at the same scheme of intention as my master. I left them to talk, but afterwards I came back to take down their long telegrams to their coming colleagues. He was, no doubt, as profoundly affected as Melmount by the Change, but his tricks of civility and irony and acceptable humour had survived the Change, and he expressed his altered attitude, his expanded emotions, in a quaint modification of the old-time man-of-the-world style, with excessive moderation, with a trained horror of the enthusiasm that swayed him.

These fifteen men who ruled the British Empire were curiously unlike anything I had expected, and I watched them intently whenever my services were not in request. They made a peculiar class at that time, these English politicians and statesmen, a class that has now completely passed away.

In some respects they were unlike the statesmen of any other region of the world, and I do not find that any really adequate account remains of them. . . . Perhaps you are a reader of the old books. If so, you will find them rendered with a note of hostile exaggeration by Dickens in " Bleak House," with a mingling of gross flattery and keen ridicule by Disraeli, who ruled among them accidentally by misunderstanding them and pleasing the court ; and all their assumptions are set forth, portentously perhaps, but truthfully so far as people of the " permanent official " class saw them, in novels of Mrs. Humphry Ward. All these books are still in this world and at the disposal of the curious, and in addition the philosopher Bagehot and the picturesque historian Macaulay give something of their method of thinking, the novelist Thackeray skirts the seamy side of their social life, and there are some good passages of irony, personal descriptions, and reminiscence to be found in the " Twentieth Century Garner " from the pens of such writers, for example, as Sidney Low. But a picture of them as a whole is wanting. Then they were too near and too great ; now, very rapidly, they have become incomprehensible.

We common people of the old time based our conception of our statesmen almost entirely on the caricatures that formed the most powerful weapon in political controversy. Like almost every main feature of the old condition of things these caricatures were an unanticipated development, they were a sort of parasitic outgrowth from, which had finally altogether replaced, the thin and vague aspirations of the original democratic ideals. They presented not only the personalities who led our public life, but the most sacred structural conceptions of that life, in ludicrous, vulgar, and dishonourable aspects that in the end came near to destroying entirely all grave and honourable emotion or motive toward the State. The state of Britain was represented nearly always by a red-faced, purse-proud farmer with an enormous belly ; that fine dream of freedom, the United States, by a cunning, lean-faced rascal in striped trousers and a blue coat. The chief ministers of state were pick-pockets, washerwomen, clowns, whales, asses, elephants, and what not ; and issues that affected the welfare of millions of men were dressed and judged like a rally in some idiotic pantomime. A tragic war in South Africa, that wrecked many thousand homes, impoverished two whole lands, and brought death and disablement to fifty thousand men, was presented as a quite comical quarrel between a violent queer being named Chamberlain, with an eyeglass, an orchid, and a short temper, and " old Kroojer," an obstinate and very cunning old man in a shocking bad hat. The conflict was carried through in a mood sometimes of brutish irritability and sometimes of lax slovenliness, the merry peculator plied his trade congenially in that asinine squabble, and behind these fooleries and masked by them, marched Fate—until at last behind the clowning, the curtains of the booth opened and revealed—hunger and suffering, brands burning and swords and shame. . . . These men had come to fame and power in that atmosphere, and to me that day there was the oddest suggestion in them of actors who have suddenly laid aside grotesque and foolish parts ; the paint was washed from their faces, the posing put aside.

Even when the presentation was not frankly grotesque and degrading it was entirely misleading. When I read of Laycock, for example, there arises a picture of a large, active, if a little wrong-headed, intelligence in a compact heroic body, emitting that " Goliath " speech of his that did so much to precipitate hostilities ; it tallies not at all with the stammering, high-pitched, slightly bald, and very conscience-stricken personage I saw, nor with Melmount's contemptuous first description of him. I doubt if the world at large will ever get a proper vision of those men as they were before the Change. Each year they pass more and more incredibly beyond our intellectual sympathy. Our estrangement cannot, indeed, rob them of their portion in the past, but it will rob them of any effect of reality. The whole of their history becomes more and more foreign, more and more like some queer barbaric drama played in a forgotten tongue. There they strut through their weird meta-morphoses of caricature, those premiers and presidents, their height preposterously exaggerated by political buskins, their faces covered by great resonant inhuman masks, their voices couched in the foolish idiom of public utterance, disguised beyond any semblance to sane humanity, roaring and squeak-ing through the public press. There it stands, this incompre-hensible faded show, a thing left on one side, and now still and deserted by any interest, its many emptinesses as inexplicable now as the cruelties of mediæval Venice, the theology of old Bysantium. And they ruled and influenced the lives of nearly a quarter of mankind, these politicians, their clownish con-flicts swayed the world, made mirth perhaps, made excitement, and permitted—infinite misery.

I saw these men quickened indeed by the Change, but still wearing the queer clothing of the old time, the manners and conventions of the old time ; if they had disengaged themselves from the outlook of the old time they still had to refer back to it constantly as a common starting-point. My refreshed intelligence was equal to that, so that I think I did indeed see them. There was Gorrell-Browning, the Chancellor of the Duchy ; I remember him as a big round-faced man, the essential vanity and foolishness of whose expression, whose habit of voluminous platitudinous speech, triumphed absurdly once or twice over the roused spirit within. He struggled with it, he burlesqued himself, and laughed. Suddenly he said simply, intensely—it was a moment for every one of clean,

clear pain, " I have been a vain and self-indulgent and pre-
sumptuous old man. I am of little use here. I have given myself to politics and intrigues, and life is gone from me." Then
for a long time he sat still. There was Carton, the Lord Chancellor, a white-faced man with understanding ; he had a
heavy, shaven face that might have stood among the busts
of the Cæsars, a slow, elaborating voice, with self-indulgent,
slightly oblique, and triumphant lips, and a momentary,
voluntary, humorous twinkle. " We have to forgive," he said.
" We have to forgive—even ourselves."

These two were at the top corner of the table, so that I saw
their faces well. Madgett, the Home Secretary, a smaller man
with wrinkled eyebrows and a frozen smile on his thin wry
mouth, came next to Carton ; he contributed little to the
discussion save intelligent comments, and when the electric
lights above glowed out, the shadows deepened queerly in his
eye-sockets and gave him the quizzical expression of an
ironical goblin. Next him was that great peer, the Earl of
Richover, whose self-indulgent indolence had accepted the
rôle of a twentieth-century British-Roman patrician of culture,
who had divided his time almost equally between his jockeys,
politics, and the composition of literary studies in the key of
his rôle. " We have done nothing worth doing," he said. " As
for me, I have cut a figure ! " He reflected—no doubt on his
ample patrician years, on the fine great houses that had been
his setting, the teeming racecourses that had roared his name,
the enthusiastic meetings he had fed with fine hopes, the futile
Olympian beginnings. . . . " I have been a fool," he said
compactly. They heard him in a sympathetic and respectful
silence.

Gurker, the Chancellor of the Exchequer, was partially
occulted, so far as I was concerned, by the back of Lord
Adisham. Ever and again Gurker protruded into the discussion,
swaying forward, a deep throaty voice, a big nose, a coarse
mouth with a drooping everted lower lip, eyes peering amidst
folds and wrinkles. He made his confession for his race. " We
Jews," he said, " have gone through the system of this world,
creating nothing, consolidating many things, destroying much.
Our racial self-conceit has been monstrous. We seem to have
used our ample coarse intellectuality for no other purpose than
to develop and master and maintain the convention of property, to turn life into a sort of mercantile chess and spend our
winnings grossly. . . . We have had no sense of service to
mankind. Beauty which is godhead—we made it a possession."

These men and these sayings particularly remain in my
memory. Perhaps, indeed, I wrote them down at the time, but
that I do now remember. How Sir Digby Privet, Revel, Mark-
heimer, and the others sat I do not now recall ; they came in
as voices, interruptions, imperfectly assigned comments. . . .

One got a queer impression that except perhaps for Gurker

or Revel these men had not particularly wanted the power they held ; had desired to do nothing very much in the positions they had secured. They had found themselves in the cabinet, and until this moment of illumination they had not been ashamed ; but they had made no ungentlemanly fuss about the matter. Eight of that fifteen came from the same school, had gone through an entirely parallel education ; some Greek linguistics, some elementary mathematics, some emasculated " science," a little history, a little reading in the silent or timidly orthodox English literature of the seventeenth, eigh- teenth, and nineteenth centuries, all eight had imbibed the same dull gentlemanly tradition of behaviour ; essentially boyish, unimaginative—with neither keen swords nor art in it, a tradition apt to slobber into sentiment at a crisis and make a great virtue of a simple duty rather clumsily done. None of these eight had made any real experiments with life, they had lived in blinkers, they had been passed from nurse to governess, from governess to preparatory school, from Eton to Oxford, from Oxford to the politico-social routine. Even their vices and lapses had been according to certain conceptions of good form. They had all gone to the races surreptitiously from Eton, had all cut up to town from Oxford to see life—music- hall life—had all come to heel again. Now suddenly they discovered their limitations. . . .

"What are we to do ? " asked Melmount. " We have awakened ; this empire in our hands." . . . I know this will seem the most fabulous of all the things I have to tell of the old order, but, indeed, I saw it with my eyes, I heard it with my ears. It is a fact that this group of men who constituted the Government of one-fifth of the habitable land of the earth, who ruled over a million of armed men, who had such navies as mankind had never seen before, whose empire of nations, tongues, peoples, still dazzles in these greater days, had no common idea whatever of what they meant to do with the world. They had been a Government for three long years, and before the Change came to them it had never even occurred to them that it was necessary to have a common idea. There was no common idea at all. That great empire was no more than a thing adrift, an aimless thing that ate and drank and slept and bore arms, and was inordinately proud of itself because it had chanced to happen. It had no plan, no intention ; it meant nothing at all. And the other great empires adrift, perilously adrift like marine mines, were in the self-same case. Absurd as a British cabinet council must seem to you now, it was no whit more absurd than the controlling ganglion, autocratic council, president's committee, or what not, of each of its blind rivals. . . .

§ 2

I remember as one thing that struck me very forcibly at the time, the absence of any discussion, any difference of opinion, about the broad principles of our present state. These men had lived hitherto in a system of conventions and acquired motives, loyalty to a party, loyalty to various secret agreements and understandings, loyalty to the Crown ; they had all been capable of the keenest attention to precedence, all capable of the most complete suppression of subversive doubts and inquiries, all had their religious emotions under perfect control. They had seemed protected by invisible but impenetrable barriers from all the heady and destructive speculations, the socialistic, republican, and communistic theories that one may still trace through the literature of the last days of the comet. But now it was as if at the very moment of the awakening those barriers and defences had vanished, as if the green vapours had washed through their minds and dissolved and swept away a hundred once rigid boundaries and obstacles. They had admitted and assimilated at once all that was good in the ill-dressed propagandas that had clamoured so vehemently and vainly at the doors of their minds in the former days. It was exactly like the awakening from an absurd and limiting dream. They had come out together naturally and inevitably upon the broad daylight platform of obvious and reasonable agreement upon which we and all the order of our world now stand.

Let me try to give the chief things that had vanished from their minds. There was, first, the ancient system of " ownership " that made such an extraordinary tangle of our administration of the land upon which we lived. In the old time no one believed in that as either just or ideally convenient, but every one accepted it. The community which lived upon the land was supposed to have waived its necessary connection with the land, except in certain limited instances of highway and common. All the rest of the land was cut up in the maddest way into patches and oblongs and triangles of various sizes between a hundred square miles and a few acres, and placed under the nearly absolute government of a series of administrators called landowners. They owned the land almost as a man now owns his hat ; they bought it and sold it, and cut it up like cheese or ham ; they were free to ruin it, or leave it waste, or erect upon it horrible and devastating eyesores. If the community needed a road or a tramway, if it wanted a town or a village in any position, nay, even if it wanted to go to and fro, it had to do so by exorbitant treaties with each of the monarchs whose territory was involved. No man could find foothold on the face of the earth until he had paid toll and homage to one of them. They had practically no relations and no duties to the nominal, municipal, or national Government

amidst whose larger areas their own dominions lay. . . .
This sounds, I know, like a lunatic's dream, but mankind was
that lunatic ; and not only in the old countries of Europe and
Asia, where this system had arisen out of the delegation of local
control to territorial magnates, did it obtain, but the " new
countries," as we called them then—the United States of
America, Cape Colony, Australia, and New Zealand—spent
much of the nineteenth century in the frantic giving away
of land for ever to any casual person who would take it. Was
there coal, was there petroleum or gold, was there rich soil or
harbourage, or the site for a fine city, these obsessed and
witless Governments cried out for scramblers, and a stream of
shabby, tricky, and violent adventurers set out to found a new
section of the landed aristocracy of the world. After a brief
century of hope and pride, the great republic of the United
States of America, the hope as it was deemed of mankind,
became for the most part a drifting crowd of landless men ;
landlords and railway lords, food lords (for the land is food
and mineral lords ruled its life, gave it Universities as one gave
coins to a mendicant, and spent its resources upon such vain,
tawdry, and foolish luxuries as the world had never seen before.
Here was a thing none of these statesmen before the Change
would have regarded as anything but the natural order of the
world, which not one of them now regarded as anything but
the mad and vanished illusion of a period of dementia.

And as it was with the question of the land, so was it also
with a hundred other systems and institutions and complicated and disingenuous factors in the life of man.   They
spoke of trade, and I realised for the first time there could be
buying and selling that was no loss to any man ; they spoke
of industrial organisation, and one saw it under captains who
sought no base advantages.   The haze of old associations, of
personal entanglements and habitual recognitions had been
dispelled from every stage and process of the social training of
men.   Things long hidden appeared discovered with an amazing
clearness and nakedness.   These men who had awakened,
laughed dissolvent laughs, and the old muddle of schools and
colleges, books and traditions, the old fumbling, half-figurative,
half-formal teaching of the Churches, the complex of weakening
and confusing suggestions and hints, midst which the pride
and honour of adolescence doubted and stumbled and fell,
became nothing but a curious and pleasantly faded memory.
" There must be a common training of the young," said
Richover ; " a frank initiation. We have not so much educated
them as hidden things from them, and set traps. And it might
have been so easy—it can all be done so easily."

That hangs in my memory as the refrain of that council,
" It can all be done so easily," but when they said it then, it
came to my ears with a quality of enormous refreshment and
power.   It can all be done so easily, given frankness, given

courage. Time was when these platitudes had the freshness
and wonder of a gospel.

In this enlarged outlook the war with the Germans—that
mythical, heroic, armed female, Germany, had vanished from
men's imaginations—was a mere exhausted episode. A truce
had already been arranged by Melmount, and these ministers,
after some marvelling reminiscences, set aside the matter of
peace as a mere question of particular arrangements. . . .
The whole scheme of the world's government had become
fluid and provisional in their minds, in small details as in great,
the unanalysable tangle of wards and vestries, districts and
municipalities, counties, states, boards, and nations, the
interlacing, overlapping, and conflicting authorities, the felt
of little interests and claims, in which an innumerable and
insatiable multitude of lawyers, agents, managers, bosses,
organisers lived like fleas in a dirty old coat, the web of the
conflicts, jealousies, heated patchings up and jobbings apart,
of the old order—they flung it all on one side.

"What are the new needs ? " said Melmount. " This muddle
is too rotten to handle. We're beginning again. Well, let us
begin afresh."

§ 3

"Let us begin afresh ! " This piece of obvious common
sense seemed then to me instinct with courage, the noblest of
words. My heart went out to him as he spoke. It was, indeed,
that day as vague as it was valiant ; we did not at all see the
forms of what we were thus beginning. All that we saw was the
clear inevitableness that the old order should end. . . .

And then in a little space of time mankind in halting but
effectual brotherhood was moving out to make its world anew.
Those early years, those first and second decades of the new
epoch, were in their daily detail a time of rejoicing toil; one
saw chiefly one's own share in that, and little of the whole.
It is only now that I look back at it all from these ripe years,
from this high tower, that I see the dramatic sequence of its
changes, see the cruel old confusions of the ancient time become
clarified, simplified, and dissolve and vanish away. Where is
that old world now ? Where is London, that sombre city of
smoke and drifting darkness, full of the deep roar and haunting
music of disorder, with its oily, shining, mud-rimmed, barge-
crowded river, its black pinnacles and blackened dome, its
sad wildernesses of smut-greyed houses, its myriads of draggled
prostitutes, its millions of hurrying clerks ? The very leaves
upon its trees were foul with greasy black defilements. Where
is lime-white Paris, with its green and disciplined foliage, its
hard unflinching tastefulness, its smartly organised viciousness,
and the myriads of workers, noisily shod, streaming over the
bridges in the grey cold light of dawn ? Where is New York,
the high city of clangour and infuriated energy, wind swept

and competition swept, its huge buildings jostling one another and straining ever upward for a place in the sky, the fallen pitilessly overshadowed ? Where are its lurking corners of heavy and costly luxury, the shameful bludgeoning bribing vice of its ill-ruled underways, and all the gaunt extravagant ugliness of its strenuous life ? And where now is Philadelphia, with its innumerable small and isolated homes, and Chicago with its interminable blood-stained stock-yards, its polyglot underworld of furious discontent ?

All these vast cities have given way and gone, even as my native Potteries and the Black Country have gone, and the lives that were caught, crippled, starved, and maimed amidst their labyrinths, their forgotten and neglected maladjustments, and then vast, inhuman, ill-conceived industrial machinery have escaped—to life. Those cities of growth and accident are altogether gone, never a chimney smokes about our world to-day, and the sound of the weeping of children who toiled and hungered, the dull despair of overburdened women, the noise of brute quarrels in alleys, all shameful pleasures and all the ugly grossness of wealthy pride have gone with them, with the utter change in our lives. As I look back into the past I see a vast exultant dust of house-breaking and removal rise up into the clear air that followed the hour of the green vapours, I live again the Year of Tents, the Year of Scaffolding, and like the triumph of a new theme in a piece of music—the great cities of our new days arise. Come Caerlyon and Armedon, the twin cities of lower England, with the winding summer city of the Thames between, and I see the gaunt dirt of old Edinburgh die to rise again white and tall beneath the shadow of her ancient hill ; and Dublin too, reshaped, returning enriched, fair, spacious, the city of rich laughter and warm hearts, gleaming gaily in a shaft of sunlight through the soft warm rain. I see the great cities America has planned and made ; the Golden City, with ever-ripening fruit along its broad warm ways, and the bell-glad City of a Thousand Spires. I see again as I have seen, the city of theatres and meeting-places, the City of the Sunlight Bight, and the new city that is still called Utah ; and dominated by its observatory dome and the plain and dignified lines of the university façade upon the cliff, Martenābar the great white winter city of the upland snows. And the lesser places, too, the townships, the quiet resting-places, villages half forest with a brawl of streams down their streets, villages laced with avenues of cedar, villages of garden, of roses and wonderful flowers and the perpetual humming of bees. And through all the world go our children, our sons the old world would have made into servile clerks and shopmen, plough drudges and servants ; our daughters who were erst anæmic drudges, prostitutes, sluts, anxiety-racked mothers or sere, repining failures ; they go about this world glad and brave, learning, living, doing, happy and rejoicing, brave and free. I think of them wandering in the clear quiet of the ruins of Rome, among the tombs of Egypt or the temples of Athens, of their coming to Mainington and its strange happiness, to Orba and the wonder of its white and slender tower. . . . But who can tell of the fulness and pleasure of life, who can number all our new cities in the world ?—cities made by the loving hands of men for living men, cities men weep to enter, so fair they are, so gracious and so kind. . . .

Some vision surely of these things must have been vouch-safed me as I sat there behind Melmount's couch, but now my knowledge of accomplished things has mingled with and effaced my expectations. Something indeed I must have foreseen—or else why was my heart so glad ?

Book Three
The New World

CHAPTER ONE

LOVE AFTER THE CHANGE

§ 1

So far I have said nothing of Nettie. I have departed widely from my individual story. I have tried to give you the effect of the change in relation to the general framework of human life, its effect of swift, magnificent dawn, of an overpowering letting in and inundation of light, and the spirit of living. In my memory all my life before the change has the quality of a dark passage, with the dimmest side gleams of beauty that come and go. The rest is dull pain and darkness. Then suddenly the walls, the bitter confines, are smitten and vanish, and I walk, blinded, perplexed, and yet rejoicing, in this sweet, beautiful world, in its fair incessant variety, its satisfaction, its opportunities, exultant in this glorious gift of life. Had I the power of music I would make a world-wide *motif* swell and amplify, gather to itself this theme and that, and rise at last to sheer ecstasy of triumph and rejoicing. It should be all sound, all pride, all the hope of outsetting in the morning brightness, all the glee of unexpected happenings, all the gladness of painful effort suddenly come to its reward ; it should be like blossoms new opened and the happy play of children, like tearful, happy mothers holding their first-born, like cities building to the sound of music, and great ships, all hung with flags and wine-bespattered, gliding down through cheering multitudes to their first meeting with the sea. Through it all should march Hope, confident Hope, radiant and invincible, until at last it would be the triumph march of Hope the conqueror, coming with trumpetings and banners through the wide-flung gates of the world.

And then out of that luminous haze of gladness comes Nettie, transfigured.

So she came again to me—amazing, a thing incredibly forgotten.

She comes back, and Verrall is in her company. She comes back into my memories now, just as she came back then, rather quaintly at first—at first not seen very clearly, a little distorted by intervening things, seen with a doubt, as I saw her through the slightly discoloured panes of crinkled glass in the window of the Menton post-office and grocer's shop. It was on the second day after the Change, and I had been sending telegrams for Melmount, who was making arrangements for his departure for Downing Street. I saw the two of them at first as small, flawed figures. The glass made them seem curved, and it enhanced and altered their gestures and paces. I felt it became me to say " Peace " to them, and I went out, to the jangling of the door-bell. At the sight of me they stopped short, and Verrall cried with the note of one who has sought, " Here he is ! " And Nettie cried, " Willie ! "

I went towards them, and all the perspectives of my reconstructed universe altered as I did so.

I seemed to see these two for the first time ; how fine they were, how graceful and human. It was as though I had never really looked at them before, and, indeed, always before I had beheld them through a mist of selfish passion. They had shared the universal darkness and dwarfing of the former time ; they shared the universal exaltation of the new. Now suddenly Nettie, and the love of Nettie, a great passion for Nettie, lived again in me. This change which had enlarged men's hearts had made no end to love. Indeed, it had enormously enlarged and glorified love. She stepped into the centre of that dream of world reconstruction that filled my mind and took possession of it all. A little wisp of hair had blown across her cheek, her lips fell apart in that sweet smile of hers ; her eyes were full of wonder, of a welcoming scrutiny, of an infinitely courageous friendliness.

I took her outstretched hand, and wonder overwhelmed me. " I wanted to kill you," I said simply, trying to grasp that idea. It seemed now like stabbing the stars, or murdering the sunlight.

" Afterwards we looked for you," said Verrall ; " and we could not find you. . . . We heard another shot."

I turned my eyes to him, and Nettie's hand fell from me. It was then I thought of how they had fallen together, and what it must have been to have awakened in that dawn with Nettie by one's side. I had a vision of them as I had glimpsed them last amidst the thickening vapours, close together, hand in hand. The green hawks of the Change spread their darkling wings above their last stumbling paces. So they fell. And awoke—lovers together in a morning of Paradise. Who can tell how bright the sunshine was to them, how fair the flowers, how sweet the singing of the birds ? . . .

This was the thought of my heart. But my lips were saying, " When I awoke I threw my pistol away." Sheer blankness kept my thoughts silent for a little while ; I said empty things. " I am very glad I did not kill you—that you are here, so fair and well. . . .

" I am going back to Clayton on the day after to-morrow," I said, breaking away to explanations. " I have been writing shorthand here for Melmount, but that is almost over now. . . ."

Neither of them said a word, and though all facts had suddenly ceased to matter anything, I went on informatively, " He is to be taken to Downing Street where there is a proper staff, so that there will be no need of me. . . . Of course, you're a little perplexed at my being with Melmount. You see

I met him—by accident—directly I recovered. I found him
with a broken ankle—in that lane. . . . I am to go now to the
Four Towns to help prepare a report. So that I am glad to see
you both again "—I found a catch in my voice—" to say good-
bye to you, and wish you well."

This was after the quality of what had come into my mind
when first I saw them through the grocer's window, but it
was not what I felt and thought as I said it. I went on saying
it because otherwise there would have been a gap. It had come
to me that it was going to be hard to part from Nettie. My
words sounded with an effect of unreality. I stopped, and we
stood for a moment in silence looking at one another.

It was I, I think, who was discovering most. I was realising
for the first time how little the Change had altered in my
essential nature. I had forgotten this business of love for a
time in a world of wonder. That was all. Nothing was lost from
my nature, nothing had gone, only the power of thought and
restraint had been wonderfully increased, and new interests
had been forced upon me. The Green Vapours had passed, our
minds were swept and garnished, but we were ourselves still,
though living in a new and finer air. My affinities were unchanged ; Nettie's personal charm for me was only quickened
by the enhancement of my perceptions. In her presence,
meeting her eyes, instantly my desire, no longer frantic but
sane, was awake again.

It was just like going to Checkshill in the old time, after
writing about socialism. . . .

I relinquished her hand. It was absurd to part in these terms.

So we all felt it. We hung awkwardly over our sense of that.
It was Verrall, I think, who shaped the thought for me, and
said that to-morrow then we must meet and say good-bye,
and so turned our encounter into a transitory making of
arrangements. We settled we would come to the inn at Menton,
all three of us, and take our midday meal together. . .

Yes, it was clear that was all we had to say . . . now.

We parted a little awkwardly. I went on down the village
street, not looking back, surprised at myself, and infinitely
perplexed. It was as if I had discovered something overlooked
that disarranged all my plans, something entirely disconcerting.
For the first time I went back preoccupied and without eager-
ness to Melmount's work. I wanted to go on thinking about
Nettie ; my mind had suddenly become voluminously productive concerning her and Verrall.

§ 2

The talk we three had together in the dawn of the new time
is very strongly impressed upon my memory. There was
something fresh and simple about it, something young and
flushed and exalted. We took up, we handled with a certain naïve
timidity, the most difficult questions the Change had raised

for men to answer. I recall we made little of them. All the old scheme of human life had dissolved and passed away, the narrow competitiveness, the greed and base aggression, the jealous aloofness of soul from soul. Where had it left us ? That was what we and a thousand million others were discussing. . . .

It chances that this last meeting with Nettie is inseparably associated—I don't know why—with the landlady of the Menton inn.

The Menton inn was one of the rare pleasant corners of the old order ; it was an inn of an unusual prosperity, much frequented by visitors from Shaphambury, and given to the serving of lunches and teas. It had a broad mossy bowling-green, and round about it were creeper-covered arbours amidst beds of snap-dragon, and hollyhock, and blue delphinium, and many such tall familiar summer flowers. These stood out against a background of laurels and holly, and above these again rose the gables of the inn and its signpost—a white-horsed George slaying the dragon—against copper beeches under the sky.

While I waited for Nettie and Verrall in this agreeable trysting place, I talked to the landlady—a broad-shouldered, smiling, freckled woman—about the morning of the Change. That motherly, abundant, red-haired figure of health was buoyantly sure that everything in the world was now to be changed for the better. That confidence, and something in her voice, made me love her as I talked to her. " Now we're awake," she said, " all sorts of things will be put right that hadn't any sense in them. Why ? Oh ! I'm sure of it."

Her kind blue eyes met mine in an infinitude of friendliness. Her lips in her pauses shaped in a pretty faint smile.

Old tradition was strong in us ; all English inns in those days charged the unexpected, and I asked what our lunch was to cost.

" Pay or not," she said, " and what you like. It's holiday these days. I suppose we'll still have paying and charging, however we manage it, but it won't be the worry it has been— that I feel sure. It's the part I never had no fancy for. Many a time I peeped through the bushes worrying to think what was just and right to me and mine, and what would send 'em away satisfied. It isn't the money I care for. There'll be mighty changes, be sure of that ; but here I'll stay, and make people happy—them that go by on the roads. It's a pleasant place here when people are merry ; it's only when they're jealous, or mean, or tired, or eat up beyond any stomach's digesting, or when they got the drink in 'em that Satan comes into this garden. Many's the happy face I've seen here, and many that come again like friends, but nothing to equal what's going to be, now things are being set right."

She smiled, that bounteous woman, with the joy of life and

hope. " You shall have an omelette," she said, " you and your friends ; such an omelette—like they'll have 'em in heaven ! I feel there's cooking in me these days like I've never cooked before. I'm rejoiced to have it to do. . . ."

It was just then that Nettie and Verrall appeared under a rustic archway of crimson roses that led out from the inn. Nettie wore white and a sun-hat, and Verrall was a figure of grey. " Here are my friends," I said ; but for all the magic of the Change, something passed athwart the sunlight in my soul like the passing of the shadow of a cloud. " A pretty couple," said the landlady, as they crossed the velvet green towards us. . . .

They were indeed a pretty couple, but that did not greatly gladden me. No—I winced a little at that.

§ 3

This old newspaper, this first reissue of the *New Paper*, desiccated last relic of a vanished age, is like the little piece of identification the superstitious of the old days—those queer religionists who brought a certain black-clad Mrs. Piper to the help of Christ—used to put into the hand of a clairvoyant. At the crisp touch of it I look across a gulf of fifty years and see again the three of us sitting about that table in the arbour, and I smell again the smell of the sweet-brier that filled the air about us, and hear in our long pauses the abundant murmuring of bees among the heliotrope of the borders.

It is the dawn of the new time, but we still bear the marks and liveries of the old.

I see myself, a dark, ill-dressed youth, with the bruise Lord Redcar gave me still blue and yellow beneath my jaw ; and young Verrall sits cornerwise to me, better grown, better dressed, fair and quiet, two years my senior indeed, but looking no older than I because of his light complexion ; and opposite me is Nettie, with dark eyes upon my face, graver and more beautiful than I had ever seen her in the former time. Her dress is still that white one she had worn when I came upon her in the park, and still about her dainty neck she wears her string of pearls and that little coin of gold. She is so much the same, she is so changed ; a girl then and now a woman—and all my agony and all the marvel of the Change between ! Over the end of the green table about which we sit, a spotless cloth is spread, it bears a pleasant lunch spread out with a simple equipage. Behind me is the liberal sunshine of the green and various garden. I see it all. Again I sit there, eating awkwardly, this paper lies upon the table and Verrall talks of the Change.

" You can't imagine," he says in his sure, fine accents, " how much the Change has destroyed of me. I still don't feel awake. Men of my sort are so tremendously *made* ; I never suspected it before."

He leans over the table towards me with an evident desire to make himself perfectly understood. " I find myself like some creature that is taken out of its shell—soft and new. I was trained to dress in a certain way, to behave in a certain way, to think in a certain way ; I see now it's all wrong and narrow—most of it anyhow—a system of class shibboleths. We were decent to each other in order to be a gang to the rest of the world. Gentlemen indeed ! But it's perplexing——"

I can hear his voice saying that now, and see the lift of his eyebrows and his pleasant smile.

He paused. He had wanted to say that, but it was not the thing we had to say.

I leaned forward a little and took hold of my glass very tightly. " You two," I said, " will marry ? "

They looked at one another.

Nettie spoke very softly. " I did not mean to marry when I came away," she said.

" I know," I answered. I looked up with a sense of effort and met Verrall's eyes.

He answered me. " I think we two have joined our lives. . . . But the thing that took us was a sort of madness."

I nodded. " All passion," I said, " is madness."

Then I fell into a doubting of those words.

" Why did we do these things ? " he said, turning to her suddenly.

Her hands were clasped under her chin, her eyes downcast.

" We *had* to," she said, with her old trick of inadequate expression.

Then she seemed to open out suddenly.

" Willie," she cried with a sudden directness, with her eyes appealing to me, " I didn't mean to treat you badly—indeed I didn't. I kept thinking of you—and of father and mother, all the time. Only it didn't seem to move me. It didn't move me not one bit from the way I had chosen."

" Chosen ! " I said.

" Something seemed to have hold of me," she admitted. " It's all so unaccountable. . . ."

She gave a little gesture of despair.

Verrall's fingers played on the cloth for a space. Then he turned his face to me again.

" Something said ' Take her.' Everything. It was a raging desire—for her. I don't know. Everything contributed to that —or counted for nothing. You——"

" Go on," said I.

" When I knew of you——"

I looked at Nettie. " You never told him about me ? " I said, feeling, as it were, a sting out of the old time.

Verrall answered for her. " No. But things dropped ; I saw you that night, my instincts were all awake. I knew it was you."

" You triumphed over me ? . . . If I could I would have triumphed over you," I said. " But go on ! "

" Everything conspired to make it the finest thing in life. It had an air of generous recklessness. It meant mischief, it might mean failure in that life of politics and affairs for which I was trained, which it was my honour to follow. That made it all the finer. It meant ruin or misery for Nettie. That made it all the finer. No sane or decent man would have approved of what we did. That made it more splendid than ever. I had all the advantages of position and used them basely. That mattered not at all."

" Yes," I said ; " it is true. And the same dark wave that lifted you, swept me on to follow. With that revolver—and blubbering with hate. And the word to you, Nettie, what was it ? ' Give ? ' Hurl yourself down the steep ? "

Nettie's hands fell upon the table. " I can't tell what it was," she said, speaking barehearted straight to me. " Girls aren't trained as men are trained to look into their minds. I can't see it yet. All sorts of mean little motives were there—over and above the ' must.' Mean motives. I kept thinking of his clothes." She smiled—a flash of brightness at Verrall. " I kept thinking of being like a lady and sitting in an hotel— with men like butlers waiting. It's the dreadful truth, Willie. Things as mean as that ! Things meaner than that ! "

I can see her now pleading with me, speaking with a frankness as bright and amazing as the dawn of the first great morning.

" It wasn't all mean," I said slowly, after a pause.

" No ! " They spoke together.

" But a woman chooses more than a man does," Nettie added. " I saw it all in little bright pictures. Do you know— that jacket—there's something—— You won't mind my telling you ? But you won't now ! "

I nodded, " No."

She spoke as if she spoke to my soul, very quietly and very earnestly, seeking to give the truth. " Something cottony in that cloth of yours," she said. " I know there's something horrible in being swung round by things like that, but they did swing me round. In the old time—to have confessed that ! And I hated Clayton—and the grime of it. That kitchen ! Your mother's dreadful kitchen ! And besides, Willie, I was afraid of you. I didn't understand you and I did him. It's different now—but then I knew what he meant. And there was his voice."

" Yes," I said to Verrall, making these discoveries quietly, " yes, Verrall, you have a good voice. Queer I never thought of that before ! "

We sat silently for a time before our vivisected passions.

" Gods ! " I cried, " and there was our poor little top-hamper of intelligence on all these waves of instinct and wordless desire, these foaming things of touch and sight and feeling, like—like a coop of hens washed overboard and clucking amidst the seas."

Verrall laughed approval of the image I had struck out. " A week ago," he said, trying it further, " we were clinging to our chicken coops and going with the heave and pour. That was true enough a week ago. But to-day—— ? "

" To-day," I said, " the wind has fallen. The world storm is over. And each chicken coop has changed by a miracle to a vessel that makes head against the sea."

§ 4

" What are we to do ? " asked Verrall.

Nettie drew a deep crimson carnation from the bowl before us, and began very neatly and deliberately to turn down the sepals of its calyx and remove, one by one, its petals. I remember that went on through all our talk. She put those ragged crimson shreds in a long row and adjusted them and readjusted them. When at last I was alone with these vestiges the pattern was still incomplete.

" Well," said I, " the matter seems fairly simple. You two " —I swallowed it—" love one another."

I paused. They answered me by silence, by a thoughtful silence.

" You belong to each other. I have thought it over and looked at it from many points of view. I happened to want— impossible things. . . . I behaved badly. I had no right to pursue you." I turned to Verrall. " You hold yourself bound to her ? "

He nodded assent.

" No social influence, no fading out of all this generous clearness in the air—for that might happen—will change you back . . . ?"

He answered me with honest eyes meeting mine, " No, Leadford, no ! "

" I did not know you," I said. " I thought of you as something very different from this."

" I was," he interpolated.

" Now," I said, " it is all changed."

Then I halted—for my thread had slipped away from me.

" As for me," I went on, and glanced at Nettie's downcast face, and then sat forward with my eyes upon the flowers between us, " since I am swayed and shall be swayed by an affection for Nettie, since that affection is rich with the seeds of desire, since to see her yours and wholly yours is not to be endured by me—I must turn about and go from you ; you must avoid me and I you. . . . We must divide the world like Jacob and Esau. . . . I must direct myself with all the will I have to other things. After all—this passion is not life ! It is perhaps for brutes and savages, but for men—no ! We must part and I must forget. What else is there but that ? "

I did not look up, I sat very tense with the red petals printing an indelible memory in my brain, but I felt the assent of Verrall's pose. There were some moments of silence. Then Nettie spoke. " But——" she said, and ceased.

I waited for a little while. I sighed and leaned back in my chair. " It is perfectly simple," I smiled, " now that we have cool heads."

" But *is* it simple ? " asked Nettie, and slashed my discourse out of being.

I looked up and found her with her eyes on Verrall. " You see," she said, " I like Willie. It's hard to say what one feels—but I don't want him to go away like that."

" But then," objected Verrall, " how——? "

" No," said Nettie, and swept her half-arranged carnation petals back into a heap of confusion. She began to arrange them very quickly into one long straight line.

" It's so difficult—I've never before in all my life tried to get to the bottom of my mind. For one thing, I've not treated Willie properly. He—he counted on me. I know he did. I was his hope. I was a promised delight—something, something to crown life—better than anything he had ever had. And a secret pride. . . . He lived upon me. I knew—when we two began to meet together, you and I—it was a sort of treachery to him——"

" Treachery ! " I said. " You were only feeling your way through all these perplexities."

" You thought it treachery."

" I don't now."

" I did. In a sense I think so still. For you had need of me."

I made a slight protest at this doctrine and fell thinking.

" And even when he was trying to kill us," she said to her lover, " I felt for him down in the bottom of my mind. I can understand all the horrible things, the humiliation—the humiliation ! he went through."

" Yes," I said, " but I don't see——"

" *I* don't see. I'm only trying to see. But you know, Willie, you are a part of my life, I have known you longer than I have known Edward. I know you better. Indeed I know you with all my heart. You think all your talk was thrown away upon me, that I never understood that side of you, or your ambitions or anything. I did. More than I thought at the time. Now—now it is all clear to me. What I had to understand in you was something deeper than Edward brought me. I have it now. . . . You are a part of my life, and I don't want to cut all that off from me now I have comprehended it, and thrown it away."

" But you love Verrall."

" Love is such a queer thing ! . . . Is there one love ? I mean, only one love ? " She turned to Verrall. " I know I

love you. I can speak out about that now. Before this morning
I couldn't have done. It's just as though my mind had got out
of a scented prison. But what is it, this love for you ? It's a
mass of fancies—things about you—ways you look, ways you
have.   It's the senses—and the senses of certain beauties.
Flattery too, things you said, hopes and deceptions for myself.
And all that had rolled up together and taken to itself the wild
help of those deep emotions that slumbered in my body ; it
seemed everything. But it wasn't. How can I describe it ?
It was like having a very bright lamp with a thick shade—
everything else in the room was hidden. But you take the
shade off and there they are—it is the same light—still there !
Only it lights every one ! "

Her voice ceased. For awhile no one spoke, and Nettie, with
a quick movement, swept the petals into the shape of a
pyramid.

Figures of speech always distract me, and it ran through
my mind like some puzzling refrain, " It is still the same
light. . . ."

" No woman believes these things," she asserted abruptly.

" What things ? "

" No woman ever has believed them."

" You have to choose a man," said Verrall, apprehending
her before I did.

" We're brought up to that. We're told—it's in books, in
stories, in the way people look, in the way they behave—one
day there will come a man. He will be everything, no one else
will be anything. Leave everything else ; live in him."

" And a man, too, is taught that of some woman," said
Verrall.

" Only men don't believe it !   They have more obstinate
minds. . . . Men have never behaved as though they believed
it. One need not be old to know that. By nature they don't
believe it. But a woman believes nothing by nature. She goes
into a mould hiding her secret thoughts almost from herself."

" She used to," I said.

" You haven't," said Verrall, " anyhow."

" I've come out. It's this comet. And Willie. And because
I never really believed in the mould at all—even if I thought I
did. It's stupid to send Willie off—shamed, cast out, never to
see him again—when I like him as much as I do. It is cruel, it is
wicked and ugly, to prance over him as if he was a defeated
enemy, and pretend I'm going to be happy just the same.
There's no sense in a rule of life that prescribes that. It's
selfish. It's brutish. It's like something that has no sense.
I——" there was a sob in her voice. " Willie ! I *won't*."

I sat lowering, I mused with my eyes upon her quick fingers.

" It *is* brutish," I said at last, with a careful unemotional
deliberation. " Nevertheless—it is in the nature of things. . . .
No ! . . . You see, after all, we are still half brutes, Nettie.

And men, as you say, are more obstinate than women. The
comet hasn't altered that ; it's only made it clearer. We have
come into being through a tumult of blind forces. . . . I come
back to what I said just now ; we have found our poor reasonable minds, our wills to live well, ourselves, adrift on a wash of
instincts, passions, instinctive prejudices, half animal stupidities.
. . . . Here we are like people clinging to something—like
people awakening—upon a raft."

"We come back at last to my question," said Verrall, softly ;
" what are we to do ? "

"Part," I said. "You see, Nettie, these bodies of ours are
not the bodies of angels. They are the same bodies—— I have
read somewhere that in our bodies you can find evidence of
the lowliest ancestry ; that about our inward ears—I think it
is—and about our teeth, there remains still something of the
fish, that there are bones that recall little—what is it ?
marsupial forebears—and a hundred traces of the ape. Even
your beautiful body, Nettie, carries this taint. No ! Hear me
out." I leaned forward earnestly. "Our emotions, our passions,
our desires, the substance of them, like the substance of our
bodies, is an animal, a competing thing, as well as a desiring
thing. You speak to us now a mind to minds—one can do that
when one has had exercise and when one has eaten, when one
is not doing anything—but when one turns to live, one turns
again to matter."

"Yes," said Nettie, slowly following me, "but you control
it."

"Only through a measure of obedience. There is no magic
in the business—to conquer matter, we must divide the enemy,
and take the matter as an ally. Nowadays it is indeed true, by
faith a man can remove mountains ; he can say to a mountain,
' Be thou removed and be thou cast into the sea ' ; but he does
it because he helps and trusts his brother men, because he has
the wit and patience and courage to win over to his side iron,
steel, obedience, dynamite, cranes, trucks, the money of other
people. . . . To conquer my desire for you, I must not perpetually thwart it by your presence ; I must go away so that
I may not see you, I must take up other interests, thrust
myself into struggles and discussions——"

"And forget ? " said Nettie.

"Not forget," I said ; "but anyhow—cease to brood upon
you."

She hung on that for some moments.

"No," she said, demolished her last pattern and looked up
at Verrall as he stirred.

Verrall leaned forward on the table, elbows upon it, and the
fingers of his two hands intertwined.

"You know," he said, "I haven't thought much of these
things. At school and the University, one doesn't. . . . It was
part of the system to prevent it. They'll alter all that, no doubt.

We seem "—he thought—" to be skating about over questions that one came to at last in Greek—with variorum readings—in Plato, but which it never occurred to any one to translate out of a dead language into living realities. . . ." He halted and answered some unspoken question from his own mind with, " No. I think with Leadford, Nettie, that, as he put it, it is in the nature of things for men to be exclusive. . . . Minds are free things and go about the world, but only one man can possess a woman. You must dismiss rivals. We are made for the struggle for existence—we *are* the struggle for existence ; the things that live are the struggle for existence incarnate—and that works out that the men struggle for their mates ; for each woman one prevails. The others go away."

" Like animals," said Nettie.

" Yes. . . ."

" There are many things in life," I said, " but that is the rough universal truth."

" But," said Nettie, " you don't struggle. That has been altered because men have minds."

" You choose," I said.

" If I don't choose to choose ? "

" You have chosen."

She gave a little impatient " Oh ! Why are women always the slaves of sex ? Is this great age of Reason and Light that has come to alter nothing of that ? And men too ! I think it is all—stupid ! I do not believe this the right solution of the thing, or anything but the bad habits of the time that was. . . . Instinct ! You don't let your instincts rule you in a lot of other things. Here am I between you. Here is Edward. I—love him because he is gay and pleasant, and because—because I *like* him ! Here is Willie—a part of me—my first secret, my oldest friend ! Why must I not have both ? Am I not a mind that you must think of me as nothing but a woman ? Imagine me always as a thing to struggle for ? " She paused ; then she made her distressful proposition to me. " Let us three keep together," she said. " Let us not part. To part is hate, Willie. Why should we not anyhow keep friends ? Meet and talk ? "

" Talk ? " I said. " About this sort of thing ? "

I looked across at Verrall and met his eyes, and we studied one another. It was the clean, straight scrutiny of honest antagonism. " No," I decided. " Between us, nothing of that sort can be."

" Ever ? " said Nettie.

" Never," I said, convinced.

I made an effort within myself. " We cannot tamper with the law and customs of these things," I said ; " these passions are too close to one's essential self. Better surgery than a lingering disease ! From Nettie my love—asks all. A man's love is not devotion—it is a demand, a challenge. And besides "—and here I forced my theme—" I have given myself now to a new mistress—and it is I, Nettie, who am unfaithful. Behind you and above you rises the coming City of the World, and I am in that building. Dear heart! you are only happiness— and that—— Indeed that calls! If it is only that my life blood shall christen the foundation stones—I could almost hope that should be my part, Nettie. I will join myself in that." I threw all the conviction I could into these words. . . . " No conflict of passion," I added a little lamely, " must distract me."

There was a pause.

" Then we must part," said Nettie, with the eyes of a woman one strikes in the face.

I nodded assent. . . .

There was a little pause, and then I stood up. We stood up, all three. We parted almost sullenly, with no more memorable words, and I was left presently in the arbour alone.

I do not think I watched them go. I only remember myself left there somehow—horribly empty and alone. I sat down again and fell into a deep shapeless musing.

§ 5

Suddenly I looked up. Nettie had come back and stood looking down at me.

" Since we talked I have been thinking," she said. " Edward has let me come to you alone. And I feel perhaps I can talk better to you alone."

I said nothing and that embarrassed her.

" I don't think we ought to part," she said.

" No—I don't think we ought to part," she repeated.

" One lives," she said, " in different ways. I wonder if you will understand what I am saying, Willie. It is hard to say what I feel. But I want it said. If we are to part for ever I want it said—very plainly. Always before I have had the woman's instinct and the woman's training which makes one hide. But—Edward is not all of me. Think of what I am saying —Edward is not all of me. . . . I wish I could tell you better how I see it. I am not all of myself. You, at any rate, are a part of me and I cannot bear to leave you. And I cannot see why I should leave you. There is a sort of blood link between us, Willie. We grew together. We are in one another's bones. I understand you. Now indeed I understand. In some way I have come to an understanding at a stride. Indeed, I understand you and your dream. I want to help you. Edward— Edward has no dreams. . . . It is dreadful to me, Willie, to think we two are to part."

" But we have settled that—part we must."

" But *why* ? "

" I love you."

" Well, and why should I hide it, Willie ?—I love you. . . ."

Our eyes met. She flushed, she went on resolutely : " You

are stupid. The whole thing is stupid. I love you both."

I said, " You do not understand what you say. No ! "

" You mean that I must go."

" Yes, yes. Go ! "

For a moment we looked at one another, mute, as though deep down in the unfathomable darkness below the surface and present reality of things dumb meanings strove to be. She made to speak and desisted.

" But *must* I go ? " she said at last, with quivering lips, and the tears in her eyes were stars. Then she began, " Willie———"

" Go ! " I interrupted her. . . . " Yes."

Then again we were still.

She stood there, a tearful figure of pity, longing for me, pitying me. Something of that wider love, that will carry our descendants at last out of all the limits, the hard, clear obligations of our personal life, moved us, like the first breath of a coming wind out of heaven that stirs and passes away. I had an impulse to take her hand and kiss it, and then a trembling came to me, and I knew that if I touched her, my strength would all pass from me. . . .

And so, standing at a distance one from the other, we parted, and Nettie went, reluctant and looking back, with the man she had chosen, to the lot she had chosen, out of my life—like the sunlight out of my life. . . .

Then, you know, I suppose I folded up this newspaper and put it in my pocket. But my memory of that meeting ends with the face of Nettie turning to go.

§ 6

I remember all that very distinctly to this day. I could almost vouch for the words I have put into our several mouths. Then comes a blank. I have a dim memory of being back in the house near the Links and the bustle of Melmount's departure, of finding Parker's energy distasteful, and of going away down the road with a strong desire to say good-bye to Melmount alone.

Perhaps I was already doubting my decision to part for ever from Nettie, for I think I had it in mind to tell him all that had been said and done. . . .

I don't think I had a word with him or anything but a hurried hand clasp. I am not sure. It has gone out of my mind. But I have a very clear and certain memory of my phase of bleak desolation as I watched his car recede and climb and vanish over Mapleborough Hill, and that I got there my first full and definite intimation that, after all, this great Change and my new wide aims in life were not to mean indiscriminate happiness for me. I had a sense of protest, as against extreme unfairness, as I saw him go. " It is too soon," I said to myself, " to leave me alone."

I felt I had sacrificed too much, that after I had said good-bye to the hot immediate life of passion, to Nettie and desire, to physical and personal rivalry, to all that was most intensely myself, it was wrong to leave me alone and sore-hearted, to go on at once with these steely cold duties of the wider life. I felt new-born, and naked, and at a loss.

"Work!" I said with an effort at the heroic, and turned about with a sigh, and I was glad that the way I had to go would at least take me to my mother. . . .

But, curiously enough, I remember myself as being fairly cheerful in the town of Birmingham that night; I recall an active and interested mood. I spent the night in Birmingham because the train service was disarranged, and I could not go farther. I went to listen to a band that was playing its brassy old-world music in the public park, and I fell into conversation with a man who said he had been a reporter upon one of their minor local papers. He was full and keen upon all the plans of reconstruction that were now shaping over the lives of humanity, and I know that something of that noble dream came back to me with his words and phrases. We walked up to a place called Bourneville by moonlight, and talked of the new social groupings that must replace the old isolated homes, and how the people would be housed.

This Bourneville was germane to that matter. It had been an attempt on the part of a private firm of manufacturers to improve the housing of their workers. To our ideas to-day it would seem the feeblest of benevolent efforts, but at the time it was extraordinary and famous, and people came long journeys to see its trim cottages with baths sunk under the kitchen floors (of all conceivable places), and other brilliant inventions. No one seemed to see the danger to liberty in that aggressive age, that might arise through making workpeople tenants and debtors of their employer, though an Act called the Truck Act had long ago intervened to prevent minor developments in the same direction. . . . But I and my chance acquaintance seemed that night always to have been aware of that possibility, and we had no doubt in our minds of the public nature of the housing duty. Our interest lay rather in the possibility of common nurseries and kitchens and public rooms that should economise toil and give people space and freedom.

It was very interesting, but still a little cheerless ; and when I lay in bed that night I thought of Nettie and the queer modifications of preference she had made, and among other things and in a way, I prayed. I prayed that night, let me confess it, to an image I had set up in my heart, an image that still serves with me as a symbol for things inconceivable, to a Master Artificer, the unseen captain of all who go about the building of the world, the making of mankind.

But before and ofter I prayed I imagined I was talking and reasoning and meeting again with Nettie. . . . She never came into the temple of that worshipping with me.

CHAPTER TWO

MY MOTHER'S LAST DAYS

§ 1

NEXT day I came home to Clayton.

The new strange brightness of the world was all the brighter there, for the host of dark distressful memories, of darkened childhood, toilsome youth, embittered adolescence that wove about the place for me. It seemed to me that I saw morning there for the first time. No chimneys smoked that day, no furnaces were burning, the people were busy with other things. The clear strong sun, the sparkle in the dustless air, made a strange gaiety in the narrow streets. I passed a number of smiling people coming home from the public breakfasts that were given in the Town Hall until better things could be arranged, and happened on Parload among them. " You were right about that comet," I sang out at the sight of him ; and he came towards me and clasped my hand.

" What are people doing here ? " said I.

" They're sending us food from outside," he said, " and we're going to level all these slums—and shift into tents on to the moors ; " and he began to tell me of many things that were being arranged ; the Midland land committees had got to work with remarkable celerity and directness of purpose, and the redistribution of population was already in its broad outlines planned. He was working at an improvised college of engineering. Until schemes of work were made out, almost every one was going to school again to get as much technical training as possible against the demands of the huge enterprise of reconstruction that was now beginning.

He walked with me to my door, and there I met old Pettigrew coming down the steps. He looked dusty and tired, but his eye was brighter than it used to be, and he carried in a rather unaccustomed manner a workman's tool basket.

" How's the rheumatism, Mr. Pettigrew ? " I asked.

" Dietary," said old Pettigrew, " can work wonders. . . ." He looked me in the eye. " These houses," he said, " will have to come down, I suppose, and our notions of property must undergo very considerable revision—in the light of reason ; but meanwhile I've been doing something to patch that disgraceful roof of mine ! To think that I could have dodged and evaded——"

He raised a deprecatory hand, drew down the loose corners of his ample mouth, and shook his old head.

" The past is past, Mr. Pettigrew."

" Your poor dear mother ! So good and honest a woman !

So simple and kind and forgiving! To think of it! My dear young man!"—he said it manfully—" I'm ashamed."

"The whole world blushed at dawn the other day, Mr. Pettigrew," I said, "and did it very prettily. That's over now. God knows, who is *not* ashamed of all that came before last Tuesday."

I held out a forgiving hand, naïvely forgetful that in this place I was a thief, and he took it and went his way, shaking his head and repeating he was ashamed, but I think a little comforted.

The door opened and my poor old mother's face, marvellously cleaned, appeared. "Ah, Willie, boy! *You.* You!"

I ran up the steps to her, for I feared she might fall.

How she clung to me in the passage, the dear woman! . . .

But first she shut the front door. The old habit of respect for my unaccountable temper still swayed her. "Ah, deary!" she said, "ah, deary! But you were sorely tried," and kept her face close to my shoulder, lest she should offend me by the sight of the tears that welled within her.

She made a sort of gulping noise and was quiet for a while, holding me very tightly to her heart with her worn, long hands. . . .

She thanked me presently for my telegram, and I put my arm about her and drew her into the living room.

"It's all well with me, mother dear," I said, "and the dark times are over—are done with for ever, mother."

Whereupon she had courage and gave way and sobbed aloud, none chiding her.

She had not let me know she could still weep for five grimy years. . . .

§ 2

Dear heart! There remained for her but a very brief while in this world that had been renewed. I did not know how short that time would be, but the little I could do—perhaps after all it was not little to her—to atone for the harshness of my days of wrath and rebellion, I did. I took care to be constantly with her, for I perceived now her curious need of me. It was not that we had ideas to exchange or pleasures to share, but she liked to see me at table, to watch me working, to have me go to and fro. There was no toil for her any more in the world, but only such light services as are easy and pleasant for a worn and weary old woman to do, and I think she was happy even at her end.

She kept to her queer old eighteenth-century version of religion, too, without a change. She had worn this particular amulet so long it was a part of her. Yet the Change was evident even in that persistence. I said to her one day, "But do you still believe in that hell of flame, dear mother? You—with your tender heart!"

She vowed she did.

Some theological intricacy made it necessary to her, but still——

She looked thoughtfully at a bank of primulas before her for a time, and then laid her tremulous hand impressively on my arm. " You know, Willie, dear," she said, as though she was clearing up a childish misunderstanding of mine, " I don't think any one will *go* there. I never *did* think that. . . ."

§ 3

That talk stands out in my memory because of that agreeable theological decision of hers, but it was only one of a great number of talks. It used to be pleasant in the afternoon, after the day's work was done and before one went on with the evening's study—how odd it would have seemed in the old time for a young man of the industrial class to be doing post-graduate work in sociology, and how much a matter of course it seems now !—to walk out into the gardens of Lowchester House and smoke a cigarette or so and let her talk rambingly of the things that interested her. . . . Physically the Great Change did not do so very much to reinvigorate her—she had lived in that dismal underground kitchen in Clayton too long for any material rejuvenescence—she glowed out indeed as a dying spark among the ashes might glow under a draught of fresh air —and assuredly it hastened her end. But those closing days were very tranquil, full of an effortless contentment. With her, life was like a rainy, windy day that clears only to show the sunset afterglow. The light has passed. She acquired no new habits amid the comforts of the new life, did no new things, but only found a happier light upon the old.

She lived with a number of other old ladies belonging to our commune in the upper rooms of Lowchester House. Those upper apartments were simple and ample, fine and well done in the Georgian style, and they had been organised to give the maximum of comfort and convenience and to economise the need of skilled attendance. We had taken over the various " great houses," as they used to be called, to make communal dining-rooms and so forth—their kitchens were conveniently large—and pleasant places for the old people of over sixty whose time of ease had come, and for suchlike public uses. We had done this not only with Lord Redcar's house, but also with Checkshill House—where old Mrs. Verrall made a dignified and capable hostess—and indeed with most of the fine residences in the beautiful wide country between the Four Towns district and the Welsh mountains. About these great houses there had usually been good outbuildings, laundries, married servants' quarters, stabling, dairies, and the like, suitably masked by trees ; we turned these into homes, and to them we added first tents and wood chalets and afterwards quadrangular residential buildings. In order to be near my mother I had two small rooms in the new collegiate buildings which our commune was almost the first to possess, and they were very convenient for the station of the high-speed electric railway that took me down to our daily conferences and my secretarial and statistical work in Clayton.

Ours had been one of the first modern communes to get in order ; we were greatly helped by the energy of Lord Redcar, who had a fine feeling for the picturesque associations of his ancestral home—the detour that took our line through the beeches and bracken and bluebells of the West Wood and saved the open wildness of the park was one of his suggestions ; and we had many reasons to be proud of our surroundings. Nearly all the other communes that sprang up all over the pleasant parkland round the industrial valley of the Four Towns, as the workers moved out, came to us to study the architecture of the residential squares and quadrangles with which we had replaced the back streets between the great houses and the ecclesiastical residences about the cathedral, and the way in which we had adapted all those buildings to our new social needs. Some claimed to have improved on us. But they could not emulate the rhododendron garden out beyond our shrubberies ; that was a thing altogether our own in our part of England, because of its ripeness and of the rarity of good peat free from lime.

These gardens had been planned under the third Lord Redcar, fifty years ago and more ; they abounded in rhododendra and azaleas, and were in places so well sheltered and sunny that great magnolias flourished and flowered. There were tall trees smothered in crimson and yellow climbing roses, and an endless variety of flowering shrubs and fine conifers, and such pampas grass as no other garden can show. And barred by the broad shadows of these, were glades and broad spaces of emerald turf, and here and there banks of pegged roses and flower-beds, and banks given over some to spring bulbs and some to primroses and primulas and polyanthuses. My mother loved these latter banks and the little round staring eyes of their innumerable yellow, ruddy brown, and purple corollas, more than anything else the gardens could show ; and in the spring of the Year of Scaffolding she would go with me day after day to the seat that showed them in the greatest multitude.

It gave her, I think, among other agreeable impressions, a sense of gentle opulence. In the old time she had never known what it was to have more than enough of anything agreeable in the world at all.

We would sit and think, or talk—there was a curious effect of complete understanding between us whether we talked or were still.

" Heaven," she said to me one day, " Heaven is a garden."

I was moved to tease her a little. " There's jewels, you know, walls and gates of jewels—and singing."

" For such as like them," said my mother firmly, and thought for a while. " There'll be things for all of us, o' course. But for me it couldn't be Heaven, dear, unless it was a garden— a nice sunny garden. . . . And feeling such as we're fond of are close and handy by."

You of your happier generation cannot realise the wonderfulness of those early days in the new epoch, the sense of security, the extraordinary effects of contrast. In the morning, except in high summer, I was up before dawn, and breakfasted upon the swift, smooth train, and perhaps saw the sunrise as I rushed out of the little tunnel that pierced Clayton Crest, and so to work like a man. Now that we had got all the homes and schools and all the softness of life away from our coal and iron ore and clay, now that a thousand obstructive " rights " and timidities had been swept aside, we could let ourselves go, we merged this enterprise with that, cut across this or that anciently obstructive piece of private land, joined and separated, effected gigantic consolidations and gigantic economies, and the valley, no longer a pit of squalid human tragedies and meanly conflicting industries, grew into a sort of beauty of its own, a savage inhuman beauty of force and machinery and flames. One was a Titan in that Etna. Then back one came at midday to bathe and change in the train, and so to the leisurely gossiping lunch in the club dining-room in Lowchester House, and the refreshment of these green and sunlit afternoon tranquillities.

Sometimes in her profounder moments my mother doubted whether all this last phase of her life was not a dream.

" A dream," I used to say, " a dream indeed—but a dream that is one step nearer awakening than that nightmare of the former days."

She found great comfort and assurance in my altered clothes —she liked the new fashions of dress, she alleged. It was not simply altered clothes. I did grow two inches, broaden some inches round my chest, and increase in weight three stones before I was twenty-three. I wore a soft brown cloth and she would caress my sleeve and admire it greatly—she had the woman's sense of texture very strong in her.

Sometimes she would muse upon the past, rubbing together her poor rough hands—they never got softened—one over the other. She told me much I had not heard before about my father, and her own early life. It was like finding flat and faded flowers in a book still faintly sweet, to realise that once my mother had been loved with passion ; that my remote father had once shed hot tears of tenderness in her arms. And she would sometimes even speak tentatively in those narrow, old-world phrases that her lips could rob of all their bitter narrowness, of Nettie.

" She wasn't worthy of you, dear," she would say abruptly, leaving me to guess the person she intended.

"No man is worthy of a woman's love," I answered. "No woman is worthy of a man's. I love her, dear mother, and that you cannot alter."

"There's others," she would muse.

"Not for me," I said. "No! I didn't fire a shot that time; I burnt my magazine. I can't begin again, mother, not from the beginning."

She sighed and said no more then.

At another time she said—I think her words were: "You'll be lonely when I'm gone, dear."

"You'll not think of going, then," I said.

"Eh, dear! But man and maid should come together."

I said nothing to that.

"You brood overmuch on Nettie, dear. If I could see you married to some sweet girl of a woman, some good, *kind* girl——"

"Dear mother, I'm married enough. Perhaps some day—— Who knows? I can wait."

"But to have nothing to do with women!"

"I have my friends. Don't you trouble, mother. There's plentiful work for a man in this world though the heart of love is cast out from him. Nettie was life and beauty for me— is—will be. Don't think I've lost too much, mother."

(Because in my heart I told myself the end had still to come.)

And once she sprang a question on me suddenly that surprised me.

"Where are they now?" she asked.

"Who?"

"Nettie and—him."

She had pierced to the marrow of my thoughts. "I don't know," I said shortly.

Her shrivelled hand just fluttered into touch of mine.

"It's better so," she said, as if pleading. "Indeed . . . it is better so."

There was something in her quivering old voice that for a moment took me back across an epoch, to the protests of the former time, to those counsels of submission, those appeals not to offend It, that had always stirred an angry spirit of rebellion within me.

"That is the thing I doubt," I said, and abruptly I felt I could talk no more to her of Nettie. I got up and walked away from her, and came back after a while, to speak of other things, with a bunch of daffodils for her in my hand.

But I did not always spend my afternoons with her. There were days when my crushed hunger for Nettie rose again, and then I had to be alone; I walked or bicycled, and presently I found a new interest and relief in learning to ride. For the horse was already very swiftly reaping the benefit of the Change. Hardly anywhere was the inhumanity of horse traction to be found after the first year of the new epoch, everywhere lugging and dragging and straining was done by machines, and the horse had become a beautiful instrument for the pleasure and carriage of youth. I rode both in the saddle and, what is finer, naked and barebacked. I found violent exercises were good for the states of enormous melancholy that came upon me, and when at last horse riding palled, I went and joined the aviators who practised soaring upon aeroplanes beyond Horsemarden Hill. . . . But at least every alternate day I spent with my mother, and altogether I think I gave her two-thirds of my afternoons.

§ 4

When presently that illness, that fading weakness that made an euthanasia for so many of the older people in the beginning of the new time, took hold upon my mother, there came Anna Reeves to daughter her—after our new custom. She chose to come. She was already known to us a little from chance meetings and chance services she had done my mother in the garden ; she sought to give her help. She seemed then just one of those plainly good girls the world at its worst has never failed to produce, who were indeed in the dark old times the hidden antiseptic of all our hustling, hating, faithless lives. They made their secret voiceless worship, they did their steadfast, uninspired, unthanked, unselfish work as helpful daughters, as nurses, as faithful servants, as the humble providences of homes. She was almost exactly three years older than I. At first I found no beauty in her, she was short but rather sturdy and ruddy, with red-tinged hair, and fair hairy brows and red-brown eyes. But her freckled hands, I found, were full of apt help, her voice carried good cheer. . . .

At first she was no more than a blue-clad, white-aproned benevolence, that moved in the shadows behind the bed on which my old mother lay and sank restfully to death. She would come forward to anticipate some need, to proffer some simple comfort, and always then my mother smiled on her. In a little while I discovered the beauty of that helpful poise of her woman's body, I discovered the grace of untiring goodness, the sweetness of a tender pity, and the great riches of her voice, of her few reassuring words and phrases. I noted and remembered very clearly how once my mother's lean old hand patted the firm gold-flecked strength of hers, as it went by upon its duties with the coverlet.

" She is a good girl to me," said my mother one day. " A good girl. Like a daughter should be. . . . I never had a daughter really." She mused peacefully for a space. " Your little sister died," she said.

I had never heard of that little sister.

" November the tenth," said my mother. " Twenty-nine months and three days. . . . I cried. I cried. That was before you came, dear. So long ago—and I can see it now. I was a young wife then, and your father was very kind. But I can see its hands, its dear little quiet hands. . . . Dear, they say that now—now they will not let the little children die."

" No, dear mother," I said. " We shall do better now."

" The club doctor could not come. Your father went twice. There was some one else, some one who paid. So your father went on into Swathinglea, and that man wouldn't come unless he had his fee. And your father had changed his clothes to look more respectful and he hadn't any money, not even his tram fare home. It seemed cruel to be waiting there with my baby thing in pain. . . . And I can't help thinking perhaps we might have saved her. . . . But it was like that with the poor always in the bad old times—always. When the doctor came at last he was angry. ' Why wasn't I called before ? ' he said, and he took no pains. He was angry because some one hadn't explained. I begged him—but it was too late."

She said these things very quietly with drooping eyelids, like one who describes a dream. " We are going to manage all these things better now," I said, feeling a strange resentment at this pitiful story her faded, matter-of-fact voice was telling me.

" She talked," my mother went on. " She talked for her age wonderfully. . . . Hippopotamus."

" Eh ? " I said.

" Hippopotamus, dear—quite plainly one day, when her father was showing her pictures. . . . And her little prayers. ' Now I lay me . . . down to sleep.' . . . I made her little socks. Knitted they was, dear, and the heel most difficult."

Her eyes were closed now. She spoke no longer to me but to herself. She whispered other vague things, ghosts of long-dead moments. . . . Her words grew less distinct.

Soon she was asleep and I got up and went out of the room, but my mind was queerly obsessed by the thought of that small life that had been glad and hopeful only to pass so inexplicably out of hope again into nonentity, this sister of whom I had never heard before. . . .

And presently I was in a black rage at all the irrecoverable sorrows of the past, of that great ocean of avoidable suffering of which this was but one luminous and quivering red drop ; I walked in the garden and the garden was too small for me ; I went out to wander on the moors. " The past is past," I cried, and all the while across the gulf of five and twenty years I could hear my poor mother's heart-wrung weeping for that daughter baby who had suffered and died. Indeed that old spirit of rebellion has not altogether died in me, for all the transformation of the new time. . . . I quieted down at last to a thin and austere comfort in thinking that the whole is not told to us, that it cannot perhaps be told to such minds as ours ; and anyhow, and what was far more sustaining, that now we have strength and courage and this new gift of wise love, whatever cruel and sad things marred the past, none of these sorrowful things that made the very warp and woof of the old life need now go on happening. We could foresee, we could prevent and save. " The past is past," I said, between sighing and resolve, as I came into view again on my homeward way of the hundred sunset-lit windows of old Lowchester House. " Those sorrows are sorrows no more."

But I could not altogether cheat that common sadness of the new time, that memory and insoluble riddle of the countless lives that had stumbled and failed in pain and darkness before our air grew clear. . . .

CHAPTER THREE

BELTANE AND NEW YEAR'S EVE

§ 1

IN the end my mother died rather suddenly, and her death came as a shock to me. Diagnosis was still very inadequate at that time. The doctors were, of course, fully alive to the incredible defects of their common training and were doing all they could to supply its deficiencies, but they were still extraordinarily ignorant. Some unintelligently observed factor of her illness came into play with her, and she became feverish and sank and died very quickly. I do not know what remedial measures were attempted. I hardly knew what was happening until the whole thing was over.

At that time my attention was much engaged by the stir of the great Beltane festival that was held on May-day in the Year of Scaffolding. It was the first of the ten great rubbish burnings that opened the new age. Young people nowadays can scarcely hope to imagine the enormous quantities of pure litter and useless accumulation with which we had to deal ; had we not set aside a special day and season, the whole world would have been in incessant reek of small fires ; and it was, I think, a happy idea to revive this ancient festival of the May and November burnings. It was inevitable that the old idea of purification should revive with the name, it was felt to be a burning of other than material encumbrances, innumerable quasi-spiritual things, deeds, documents, debts, vindictive records, went up on those great flares. People passed praying between the fires, and it was a fine symbol of the new and wiser tolerance that had come to men, that those who still found their comfort in the orthodox faiths came hither unpersuaded, to pray that all hate might be burned out of their professions. For even in the fires of Baal, now that men have done with base hatred, one may find the living God.

Endless were the things we had to destroy in those great
purgings. First, there were nearly all the houses and buildings
of the old time. In the end we did not save in England one
building in five thousand that were standing when the comet
came. Year by year, as we made our homes afresh in accordance with the saner needs of our new social families, we
swept away more and more of those horrible structures, the
ancient residential houses, hastily built, without imagination,
without beauty, without common honesty, without even comfort or convenience, in which the early twentieth century had
sheltered until scarcely one remained ; we saved nothing but
what was beautiful or interesting out of all their gaunt and
melancholy abundance. The actual houses, of course, we could
not drag to our fires, but we brought all their ill-fitting deal
doors, their dreadful window sashes, their servant-tormenting
staircases, their dank, dark cupboards, the verminous papers
from their scaly walls, their dust and dirt-sodden carpets, their
ill-designed and yet pretentious tables and chairs, sideboards
and chests of drawers, the old dirt-saturated books, their
ornaments—their dirty, decayed, and altogether painful
ornaments—amidst which I remember there were sometimes
even *stuffed dead birds !*—we burned them all. The paint-
plastered woodwork, with coat above coat of nasty paint,
that in particular blazed finely. I have already tried to give
you an impression of old-world furniture, of Parload's bedroom, my mother's room, Mr. Gabbitas's sitting-room ; but,
thank Heaven ! there is nothing in life now to convey the
peculiar dinginess of it all. For one thing, there is no more
imperfect combustion of coal going on everywhere, and no
roadways like grassless open scars along the earth from which
dust pours out perpetually. We burned and destroyed most
of our private buildings and all the woodwork, all our furniture, except a few score thousand pieces of distinct and in-
tentional beauty from which our present forms have developed,
nearly all our hangings and carpets, and also we destroyed
almost every scrap of old-world clothing. Only a few carefully
disinfected types and vestiges of that remain now in our
museums.

One writes now with a peculiar horror of the dress of the
old world. The men's clothes were worn without any cleansing
process at all, except an occasional superficial brushing, for
periods of a year or so ; they were made of dark obscurely
mixed patterns to conceal the stage of defilement they had
reached, and they were of a felted and porous texture admirably
calculated to accumulate drifting matter. Many women wore
skirts of similar substances, and of so long and inconvenient
a form that they inevitably trailed among all the abomination
of our horse-frequented roads. It was our boast in England
that the whole of our population was booted—their feet were
for the most part ugly enough to need it,—but it becomes

now inconceivable how they could have imprisoned their feet in the amazing cases of leather and imitations of leather they used. I have heard it said that a large part of the physical decline that was apparent in our people during the closing years of the nineteenth century, though no doubt due in part to the miscellaneous badness of the food they ate, was in the main attributable to the vileness of the common footwear. They shirked open-air exercise altogether because their boots wore out ruinously and pinched and hurt them if they took it. I have mentioned, I think, the part my own boots played in the squalid drama of my adolescence. I had a sense of unholy triumph over a fallen enemy when at last I found myself steering truck after truck of cheap boots and shoes (unsold stock from Swathinglea) to the run-off by the top of the Glanville blast furnaces.

"Plup!" they would drop into the cone when Beltane came, and with the roar of their burning would fill the air. Never a cold would come from the saturation of their brown-paper soles, never a corn from their foolish shapes, never a nail in them get home at last in suffering flesh. . . .

Most of our public buildings we destroyed and burned as we reshaped our plan of habitation, our theatre sheds, our banks, and inconvenient business warrens, our factories, and all the unmeaning repetition of silly little sham Gothic churches and meeting-houses, mean looking shells of stone and mortar without love, invention, or any beauty at all in them, that men had thrust into the face of their sweated God even as they thrust cheap food into the mouths of their sweated workers ; all these we also swept away in the course of that first decade. Then we had the whole of the superseded steam-railway system to scrap and get rid of, stations, signals, fences, rolling-stock ; a plant of ill-planned, smoke-distributing nuisance apparatus, that would, under former conditions, have maintained an offensive dwindling obstructive life for perhaps half a century. Then also there was a great harvest of fences, notice boards, hoardings, ugly sheds, all the corrugated iron in the world, and everything that was smeared with tar, all our gas works and petroleum stores, all our horse vehicles and vans and lorries had to be erased. . . . But I have said enough now perhaps to give some idea of the bulk and quality of our great bonfires, our burnings up, our meltings down, our toil of sheer wreckage, over and above the constructive effort, in those early years.

But these were the coarse material bases of the Phœnix fires of the world. These were but the outward and visible signs of the innumerable claims, rights, adhesions, debts, bills, deeds, and charters that were cast upon the fires ; a vast accumulation of insignia and uniforms neither curious enough nor beautiful enough to preserve, went to swell the blaze, and all (saving a few truly glorious trophies and memories)

of our symbols, our apparatus and material of war.   Then
innumerable triumphs of our old, bastard, half-commercial
fine-art were presently condemned, great oil paintings, done
to please the half-educated middle-class, glared for a moment
and were gone.   Academy marbles crumbled to useful lime,
a gross multitude of silly statuettes and decorative crockery,
and hangings, and embroideries, and bad music, and musical
instruments shared this fate.   And books, countless books,
too, and bales of newspapers went also to these pyres.   From
the private houses in Swathinglea alone—which I had deemed,
perhaps not unjustly, altogether illiterate—we gathered a
whole dust-cart full of cheap ill-printed editions of the minor
English classics—for the most part very dull stuff indeed and
still clean—and about a truckload of thumbed and dog-eared
penny fiction, watery base stuff, the dropsy of our nation's
mind. . . . And it seemed to me that when we gathered those
books and papers together, we gathered together something
more than print and paper, we gathered warped and crippled
ideas and contagious base suggestions, the formulæ of dull
tolerances and stupid impatiences, the mean defensive ingenu-
ities of sluggish habits of thinking and timid and indolent
evasions.   There was more than a touch of malignant satisfaction for me in helping gather it all together.

I was so busy, I say, with my share in this dustman's work
that I did not notice, as I should otherwise have done, the
little indications of change in my mother's state.   Indeed,
I thought her stronger ; she was slightly flushed, slightly
more talkative. . . .

On Beltane Eve, and our Lowchester rummage being
finished, I went along the valley to the far end of Swathinglea
to help sort the stock of the detached group of pot-banks there
—their chief output had been mantel ornaments in imitation
of marble, and there was very little sorting, I found, to be
done—and there it was nurse Anna found me at last by tele
phone, and told me my mother had died in the morning
suddenly and very shortly after my departure.

For a while I did not seem to believe it ; this obviously
imminent event stunned me when it came, as though I had
never had an anticipatory moment.   For a while I went on
working, and then almost apathetically, in a mood of half-
reluctant curiosity, I started for Lowchester.

When I got there the last offices were over, and I was shown
my old mother's peaceful white face, very still, but a little
cold and stern to me, a little unfamiliar, lying among white
flowers.

I went in alone to her, into that quiet room, and stood for
a long time by her bedside.   I sat down then and thought.

Then at last, strangely hushed, and with the deeps of my
loneliness opening beneath me, I came out of that room and
down into the world again, a bright-eyed, active world, very

noisy, happy, and busy with its last preparations for the mighty cremation of past and superseded things.

§ 2

I remember that first Beltane festival as the most terribly lonely night in my life. It stands in my mind in fragments, fragments of intense feeling with forgotten gaps between.

I recall very distinctly being upon the great staircase of Lowchester House (though I don't remember getting there from the room in which my mother lay), and how upon the landing I met Anna ascending as I came down. She had but just heard of my return, and she was hurrying upstairs to me. She stopped and so did I, and we stood and clasped hands, and she scrutinised my face in the way women sometimes do. So we remained for a second or so. I could say nothing to her at all, but I could feel the wave of her emotion. I halted, answered the earnest pressure of her hand, relinquished it, and after a queer second of hesitation went on down, returning to my own preoccupations. It did not occur to me at all then to ask myself what she might be thinking or feeling.

I remember the corridor full of mellow evening light, and how I went mechanically some paces towards the dining-room. Then at the sight of the little tables, and a gusty outburst of talking voices as some one in front of me swung the door open and to, I remembered that I did not want to eat. . . . After that comes an impression of myself walking across the open grass in front of the house, and the purpose I had of getting alone upon the moors, and how somebody passing me said something about a hat. I had come out without my hat.

A fragment of thought has linked itself with an effect of long shadows upon turf golden with the light of the sinking sun. The world was singularly empty, I thought, without either Nettie or my mother. There wasn't any sense in it any more. Nettie was already back in my mind then. . . .

Then I was out on the moors. I avoided the crests where the bonfires were being piled, and sought the lonely places. . . .

I remember very clearly sitting on a gate beyond the park, in a fold just below the crest that hid the Beacon Hill bonfire and its crowd, and I was looking at and admiring the sunset. The golden earth and sky seemed like a bubble that floated in the globe of human futility. . . . Then in the twilight I walked along an unknown, bat-haunted road between high hedges.

I did not sleep under a roof that night. But I hungered and ate. I ate near midnight at an inn over towards Birmingham, and miles away from my home. Instinctively I had avoided the crests where the bonfire crowds gathered, but here there were many people, and I had to share a table with a man who had some useless mortgage deeds to burn. I talked to him about them—but my soul stood at a great distance behind my lips.

Soon each hilltop bore a tulip-shaped flame flower. Little black figures clustered round and dotted the base of its petals, and as for the rest of the multitude abroad, the kindly night swallowed them up. By leaving the roads and clear paths and wandering in the fields I contrived to keep alone, though the confused noise of voices and the roaring and crackling of great fires was always near me.

I wandered into a lonely meadow, and presently in a hollow of deep shadows I lay down to stare at the stars. I lay hidden in the darkness, and ever and again the sough and uproar of the Beltane fires that were burning up the sere follies of a vanished age, and the shouting of the people passing through the fires and praying to be delivered from the prison of themselves, reached my ears. . . .

And I thought of my mother, and then of my new loneliness and the hunger of my heart for Nettie.

I thought of many things that night, but chiefly of the overflowing personal love and tenderness that had come to me in the wake of the Change, of the greater need, the unsatisfied need in which I stood, for this one person who could fulfil all my desires. So long as my mother had lived, she had in a measure held my heart, given me a food these emotions could live upon, and mitigated that emptiness of spirit ; but now suddenly that one possible comfort had left me. There had been many at the season of the Change who had thought this great enlargement of mankind would abolish personal love ; but indeed it had only made it finer, fuller, more vitally necessary. They had thought that, seeing men now were all full of the joyful passion to make and do, and glad and loving and of willing service to all their fellows, there would be no need of the one intimate trusting communion that had been the finest thing of the former life. And indeed, so far as this was a matter of advantage and the struggle for existence, they were right. But so far as it was a matter of the spirit and the fine perceptions of life, it was altogether wrong.

We had indeed not eliminated personal love, we had but stripped it of its base wrappings, of its pride, its suspicions, its mercenary and competitive elements, until at last it stood up in our minds stark, shining and invincible. Through all the fine, divaricating ways of the new life, it grew ever more evident, there were for every one certain persons, mysteriously and indescribably in the key of one's self, whose mere presence gave pleasure, whose mere existence was interest, whose idiosyncrasy blended with accident to make a completing and predominant harmony for their predestined lovers. They were the essential thing in life. Without them the fine brave show of the rejuvenated world was a caparisoned steed without a rider, a bowl without a flower, a theatre without a play.

. . . And to me that night of Beltane, it was as clear as white flames that Nettie, and Nettie alone, roused those harmonies in me. And she had gone ! I had sent her from me ; I knew not whither she had gone. I had in my first virtuous foolishness cut her out of my life for ever !

So I saw it then, and I lay unseen in the darkness and called upon Nettie and wept for her, lay upon my face and wept for her, while the glad people went to and fro and the smoke streamed thick across the distant stars, and the red reflections, the shadows and the fluctuating glares, danced over the face of the world.

No ! the Change had freed us from our baser passions indeed, from habitual and mechanical concupiscence and mean issues and coarse imaginings, but from the passions of love it had not freed us. It had but brought the lord of life, Eros, to his own. All through the long sorrow of that night I, who had rejected him, confessed his sway with tears and inappeasable regrets. . . .

I cannot give the remotest guess of when I rose up, nor of my tortuous wanderings in the valleys between the midnight fires, nor how I evaded the laughing and rejoicing multitudes who went streaming home between three and four to resume their lives, swept and garnished, stripped and clean. But at dawn, when the ashes of the world's gladness were ceasing to glow it was a bleak dawn that made me shiver in my thin summer clothes—I came across a field to a little copse full of dim blue hyacinths. A queer sense of familiarity arrested my steps, and I stood puzzled. Then I was moved to go a dozen paces from the path, and at once a singularly misshapen tree hitched itself into a notch in my memory. This was the place ! Here I had stood, there I had placed my old kite, and shot with my revolver, learning to use it, against the day when I should encounter Verrall.

Kite and revolver had gone now, and all my hot and narrow past ; its last vestiges had shrivelled and vanished in the whirling gusts of the Beltane fires. So I walked through a world of grey ashes at last, back to the great house in which the dead, deserted image of my dear lost mother lay.

§ 3

I came back to Lowchester House very tired, very wretched ; exhausted by my fruitless longing for Nettie. I had no thought of what lay before me.

A miserable attraction drew me into the great house to look again on the stillness that had been my mother's face, and as I came into that room, Anna, who had been sitting by the open window, rose to meet me. She had the air of one who waits. She, too, was pale with watching ; all night she had watched between the dead within and the Beltane fires abroad, and longed for my coming. I stood mute between her and the bedside. . . .

" Willie," she whispered, and eyes and body seemed incarnate pity.

An unseen presence drew us together. My mother's face became resolute, commanding. I turned to Anna as a child may turn to its nurse. I put my hands about her strong shoulders, she folded me to her, and my heart gave way. I buried my face in her breast and clung to her weakly, and burst into a passion of weeping. . . .

She held me with hungry arms. She whispered to me, " There, there ! " as one whispers comfort to a child. . . . Suddenly she was kissing me. She kissed me with a hungry intensity of passion, on my cheeks, on my lips. She kissed me on my lips with lips that were salt with tears. And I returned her kisses. . . .

Then abruptly we desisted and stood apart—looking at one another.

§ 4

It seems to me as if the intense memory of Nettie vanished utterly out of my mind at the touch of Anna's lips. I loved Anna.

We went to the council of our group—commune it was then called—and she was given me in marriage, and within a year she had borne me a son. We saw much of one another, and talked ourselves very close together. My faithful friend she became and has been always, and for a time we were passionate lovers. Always she has loved me and kept my soul full of tender gratitude and love for her ; always when we met our hands and eyes clasped in friendly greeting, all through our lives from that hour we have been each other's secure help and refuge, each other's ungrudging fastness of help and sweetly frank and open speech. . . . And after a little while my love and desire for Nettie returned as though it had never faded away.

No one will have a difficulty now in understanding how that could be, but in the evil days of the world malaria, that would have been held to be the most impossible thing. I should have had to crush that second love out of my thoughts, to have kept it secret from Anna, to have lied about it to all the world. The old-world theory was there was only one love—we who float upon a sea of love find that hard to understand. The whole nature of a man was supposed to go out to the one girl or woman who possessed him, her whole nature to go out to him. Nothing was left over—it was a discreditable thing to have any overplus at all. They formed a secret secluded system of two, two and such children as she bore him. All other women he was held bound to find no beauty in, no sweetness, no interest ; and she likewise, in no other man. The old-time men and women went apart in couples, into defensive little houses, like beasts into little pits, and in these " homes " they sat down purposing to love, but really coming very soon to jealous watching of this extravagant mutual proprietorship. All freshness passed very speedily out of their love, out of their conversation, all pride out of their common life. To permit each other freedom was blank dishonour. That I and Anna should love, and after our love-journey together, go about our separate lives and dine at the public tables, until the advent of her motherhood, would have seemed a terrible strain upon our unmitigable loyalty. And that I should have it in me to go on loving Nettie—who loved in different manner both Verrall and me—would have outraged the very quintessence of the old convention.

In the old days love was a cruel proprietary thing. But now Anna could let Nettie live in the world of my mind, as freely as a rose will suffer the presence of white lilies. If I could hear notes that were not in her compass, she was glad, because she loved me, that I should listen to other music than hers. And she, too, could see the beauty of Nettie. Life is so rich and generous now, giving friendship, and a thousand tender interests and helps and comforts, that no one stints another of the full realisation of all possibilities of beauty. For me from the beginning Nettie was the figure of beauty, the shape and colour of the divine principle that lights the world. For every one there are certain types, certain faces and forms, gestures, voices and intonations that have that inexplicable unanalysable quality. These come through the crowd of kindly friendly fellow-men and women—one's own. These touch one mysteriously, stir deeps that must otherwise slumber, pierce and interpret the world. To refuse this interpretation is to refuse the sun, to darken and deaden all life. . . . I loved Nettie, I loved all who were like her, in the measure that they were like her, in voice, or eyes, or form, or smile. And between my wife and me there was no bitterness that the great goddess, the life-giver, Aphrodite, Queen of the living Seas, came to my imagination so. It qualified our mutual love not at all, since now in our changed world love is unstinted ; it is a golden net about our globe that nets all humanity together.

I thought of Nettie much, and always movingly beautiful things restored me to her ; all fine music, all pure deep colour, all tender and solemn things. The stars were hers, and the mystery of moonlight ; the sun she wore in her hair, powdered finely, beaten into gleams and threads of sunlight in the wisps and strands of her hair. . . . Then suddenly one day a letter came to me from her, in her unaltered clear handwriting, but in a new language of expression, telling me many things. She had learned of my mother's death, and the thought of me had grown so strong as to pierce the silence I had imposed

on her. We wrote to one another—like ordinary friends with
a certain restraint between us at first, and with a great longing
to see her once more arising in my heart. For a time I left
that hunger unexpressed, and then I was moved to tell it to
her. And so on New Year's Day in the Year Four, she came
to Lowchester and me. How I remember that coming, across
the gulf of fifty years ! I went out across the park to meet
her, so that we might meet alone. The windless morning
was clear and cold, the ground new carpeted with snow, and
all the trees motionless lace and glitter of frosty crystals. The
rising sun had touched the white with a spirit of gold, and
my heart beat and sang within me. I remember now the
snowy shoulder of the down, sunlit against the bright blue
sky. And presently I saw the woman I loved coming through
the white still trees. . . .

I had made a goddess of Nettie, and behold she was a
fellow-creature ! She came, warm-wrapped and tremulous,
to me, with the tender promise of tears in her eyes, with her
hands outstretched and that dear smile quivering upon her
lips. She stepped out of the dream I had made of her, a thing
of needs and regrets and human kindliness. Her hands as I
took them were a little cold. The goddess shone through her
indeed, glowed on all her body, she was a worshipful temple
of love for me—yes. But I could feel, like a thing new discovered, the texture and sinews of her living, her dear personal
and mortal hands. . . .

The Epilogue
The Window of the Tower

THE EPILOGUE

THIS was as much as this pleasant-looking grey-haired man had written. I had been lost in his story throughout the earlier portions of it, forgetful of the writer and his gracious room, and the high tower in which he was sitting. But gradually, as I drew near the end, the sense of strangeness returned to me. It was more and more evident to me that this was a different humanity from any I had known, unreal, having different customs, different beliefs, different interpretations, different emotions. It was no mere change in conditions and institutions the comet had wrought. It had made a change of heart and mind. In a manner it had dehumanised the world, robbed it of its spites, its intense jealousies, its inconsistencies, its humour. At the end, and particularly after the death of his mother, I felt his story had slipped away from my sympathies altogether. Those Beltane fires had burned something in him that worked living still and unsubdued in me, that rebelled in particular at that return of Nettie. I became inattentive. I no longer felt with him, nor gathered a sense of complete understanding from his phrases. His Lord Eros indeed! He and these transfigured people—they were beautiful and noble people, like the people one sees in great pictures, like the gods of noble sculpture, but they had no nearer fellowship than these to competitive men. As the Change was realised, with every stage of realisation the gulf widened and it was harder to follow his words.

I put down the last fascicle of all, and met his friendly eyes. It was hard to dislike him.

I felt a subtle embarrassment in putting the question that perplexed me. And yet it seemed so material to me I had to put it. "And did you——?" I asked. "Were you—lovers?"

His eyebrows rose. "Of course."

"But your wife——?"

It was manifest he did not understand me.

I hesitated still more. I was perplexed by a conviction of baseness. "But——" I began. "You remained lovers?"

"Yes." I had grave doubts if I understood him. Or he me.

I made a still more courageous attempt. "And had Nettie no other lovers?"

"A beautiful woman like that! I know not how many loved beauty in her, nor what she found in others. But we four from that time were very close, you understand, we were friends, helpers, personal lovers in a world of lovers."

"Four?"

"There was Verrall."

501

Then suddenly it came to me that the thoughts that stirred in my mind were sinister and base, that the queer suspicions, the coarseness and coarse jealousies of my old world were over and done for these more finely living souls. " You made," I said, trying to be liberal minded, " a home together."

" A home ! " He looked at me, and, I know not why, I glanced down at my feet. What a clumsy, ill-made thing a boot is, and how hard and colourless seemed my clothing ! How harshly I stood out amidst these perfected things. I had a moment of re-bellious detestation. I wanted to get out of all this. After all, it wasn't my style. I wanted intensely to say something that would bring him down a peg, make sure, as it were, of my suspicions by launching an offensive accusation. I looked up and he was standing.

" I forgot," he said. " You are pretending the old world is still going on. A home ! "

He put out his hand, and quite noiselessly the great window widened down to us, and the splendid nearer prospect of that dreamland city was before me. There for one clear moment I saw it ; its galleries and open spaces, its trees of golden fruit and crystal waters, its music and rejoicing, love and beauty without ceasing flowing through its varied and intricate streets. And the nearer people I saw now directly and plainly, and no longer in the distorted mirror that hung overhead. They really did not justify my suspicions, and yet——! They were such people as one sees on earth—save that they were changed. How can I express that change ? As a woman is changed in the eyes of her lover, as a woman is changed by the love of a lover. They were exalted. . . .

I stood up beside him and looked out. I was a little flushed, my ears a little reddened, by the inconvenience of my curiosities, and by my uneasy sense of profound moral differences. He was taller than I. . . .

" This is our home," he said smiling, and with thoughtful eyes on me.

Printed by H. Henderson at the Villafield Press, Bishopbrigg